EXILE

THE PRICE OF TALENT: BOOK FIVE

SPICY DYSTOPIAN ROMANCE

AK NEVERMORE

Cover design by Beholden Books

Photo by Julie Holden, The Dark Pen

Hardcover ISBN: 978-1-964466-46-0

Paperback ISBN: 978-1-964466-45-3

Digital ISBN: 978-1-964466-17-0

DEDICATION

To everyone who has suffered a loss
and wanted to UnMake it.

CONTENTS

A HEADS UP ON CONTENT

This book explores themes which some readers may find uncomfortable or offensive. If violence, smut, various kinks, salty language, references to alcoholism, drug use, abuse, self-harm, problematic pregnancies, non-con/dub-con, and generally unsavory behavior are triggers for you, please put this novel down and back away slowly.

There is also a lot that deals with mental health and loss that's pretty heavy. This book is all about the dark night of the soul, but I promise there's light at the end of the tunnel.

Still here? Awesome. Just remember, it's a fantasy, people. Don't try this stuff at home.

TERMS

*Talent [***tal****-uhnt] noun*

1. *An individual denoted by halos surrounding their irises with the ability to manipulate reality, i.e. Breakers, molecular destruction; Binders, molecular cohesion; Shifters, translocation; Fixers, transfixation; Finders, spatial orientation.*

– Excerpt from
A Treatise on Talents,
Third Edition

"If the lion knew his own strength, hard were it for any man to rule him."

– Sir Thomas More

Two Hours before the Plateau was Sundered

SERRA STOOD in the gallery above the Assembly, tapping her long, curved nails against the top of the marble balustrade ringing the room as Lord Crandall placated the members below. Unbelievable. She shook her head at the esteemed body lapping up his drivel.

By the smirk on the slimy little Intelligencer's face, their kowtowing pleased him to no end. He stood at the rail of his box, hands clasped behind his back, receiving their approbation as if it were his due. Such an odious little man, very obviously in his authoritarian glory without the Overlord in the room. Her lips pruned at Crandall's patronizing drawl, not nearly as eager to kiss his scrawny backside as the rest of them.

"...set your minds at ease," he was saying. "With the majority of the Source's army mitigated by Lord Scot's earlier use of talent, we expect a speedy resolution—"

"If by 'use of talent,' you're referring to the wholesale slaughter outside our gates, I'll beg your pardon, but that most certainly does not set my mind at ease!" a slight woman shrilled from the middle of the Fixers' section. "That a single man could do—do *that*—"

"He's not a man, he's a goddamned twist, and completely devoid of compunction!" blustered a short, rotund lord from the Shades' section. He stood, stabbing his finger into the air. "All that stolen power in the hands of a mongrel! I've said it before, and I'll say it again: he and that entire rotten House of his are a blight on Glynfyls—"

"I don't disagree with you, Madame Wence," Lord Crandall said sharply, ignoring the lord's diatribe. "However, until this unpleasantness with the Source is concluded, I'm afraid we must persevere…" His eyes flicked back to the portly man sputtering at the interruption. "And use a threat to quell a threat. After which, Lord Morris, who's to say what might happen?"

The lord swallowed his protest and grunted as he sat, apparently satisfied. The rest of the room broke into a low murmur of discussion, heads alternately bobbing and shaking. Serra snorted, noting there were far more of the former than the latter. Idiots. So willing to throw the man saving their worthless asses under the bus. As if Titus and his horde of Breakers were a minor inconvenience. Glory, there were so many small minds in this room, just begging for a firm hand.

The speaker banged his gavel and the Assembly reluctantly quieted. "Yes, well, I'm sure all our prayers are with Lord Scot and the others manning the wall." Lord Riggs doddered, squaring a stack of papers against the podium. "Now, where were…ah, here we are. Next on the docket is the status of the infirmaries, the hill's in particular—" He squinted at the top sheet and adjusted his glasses. "No. Is this right?" Riggs asked, incredulous as he pulled back, his watery gaze landing on the Binders' section. "The hill's infirmary has been abandoned?"

"Ah…abandoned is a strong word," Lord Ketsing prevaricated, running a finger under his cravat. Serra wasn't sure whether to frown at the man's lack of backbone or to congratulate his wife, Janice, for so thoroughly destroying it. Bit of both, she supposed.

"But unfortunately, the description is entirely accurate."

The small hairs on Serra's nape rose with the jump in her blood pressure as every eye snapped to Nora bloody Jester making her grand entrance into the chamber, an hour and a half late. Dressed in one of those idiotic Grecian gowns, she looked like she'd stepped right out of the marble frieze running the circumference of the room.

Serra gritted her teeth, eyes narrowing in perverse pleasure as she cataloged every fine line wrinkling the insufferable bitch's frigid demeanor. Something wasn't going well. Serra could only hope Nora's angst meant Kara had taken a turn for the worse. It would serve the little bitch right for being pregnant with a litter while her own daughter, Tamara—

No. Serra forced herself to breathe, refocusing on the interplay below. It wasn't the time nor the place to fixate on that old injustice.

"Unfortunately," Nora said, stepping into the First Binder's box, "the funds that should've been slated for maintaining the facility's generators were reallocated to its serenity glade and, without power, the building is uninhabitable."

Gasps of horrified delight peppered the room, along with incensed demands to know where loved ones had landed. Behind Nora, Lord Ketsing paled as he shrank against his seat. Serra bit back a cackle. She certainly wouldn't have to worry about him or his shrew wife leading the Binder line after this. They'd just guaranteed themselves pariahs with their misappropriation of funds.

No. As usual, there was only one person standing between Serra and her rightful position as First, but with this kind of fervor, who knew how long Nora would be an obstacle?

Hmm. Serra frowned. The Prydees had assured her of House Hess's inclusion in the voting roles as soon as the Assembly was back in regular session, but that wouldn't come fast enough. And without a vote, the delay left the floor, and the possibility of taking First, off-limits to a Talent from the Source. She bit back a curse, irked to no end that she had to wait upon the sufferance of others before she could exert her influence in an official capacity.

What a pity waiting wasn't something she excelled at.

Her gaze slid back to Lord Morris, and she wet her lips. No, there was plenty she could do to grease the wheels of her ascension in the meantime, and that nasty little man reeked of opportunity. She shifted her bosom, the corset of her gown digging into her ribs as she glared down at her rival.

Careful, Nono. Best not get too comfortable in that box.

As if she'd heard the warning, Nora's gaze rose to meet Serra's. *That's right…*she smirked. The frigid bitch didn't even blink as she turned away. Serra's blood pressure spiked, pounding through her temples at being so summarily dismissed. Glory, she hated her.

"Missives with the updated locations of patients have been sent out to anyone listed as an emergency contact," Nora said smoothly, not missing a damned beat. "For those without—"

"Fie!" a slovenly man in the Fixers' section cried, shooting to his feet. "Enough of this farce. None of this has to do with the Christ-begotten generators! It's all a distraction from the real issue—last night Julia Cree was murdered whilst under Lady Jester's care!"

The room went silent, and Nora's alabaster brow wrinkled for a split second. Serra swallowed a smile. What a lovely time for that bit of leaked information to hit.

Crandall cleared his throat. "Lord Ines. I can assure you that neither Lady Jester's stewardship of the hill's infirmary, nor its lack of habitability, have any bearing on Mistress Cree's death…but as it is an open investigation, I'm unable to comment further at this time. Rest assured that my Intelligencers are on the case."

Ines opened his mouth, but his retort was lost beneath the tide of outrage and conjecture rising from the room.

"Another murder?"

"Is it true her throat was slashed ear to ear?" a man called out.

"Oh, God, just like those poor men on the plateau—"

"Like the woman in the alley!"

"And the commons, all that Flat's trash, they're up here—"

"Jesus, Lady Scot let them into the tubes…"

"They're on the upper rungs!" a woman screamed as another fainted dead away.

"Shame on you!" a dowager in the Fetches' section shook her cane at the Crandall. "You never caught that murderous beast, and now he's struck again! The Glynfyls Gorer is still at large!"

The room descended into chaos.

Well, now. Serra watched the furor and licked her lips. Wasn't this an exquisite morsel of mayhem? Bit more of a beehive than she'd anticipated, but it was glaringly obvious how Laughlin Scot had ascended to Overlord so quickly. Save for the few wolves in the room, the rest were absolute sheep. Bully them enough and they'd bleat, but bare your teeth, and they ran.

And Laughlin Scot's teeth were sharper than most.

Serra sniffed as a lady seated below glanced up, then blatantly refused to meet her eye by snapping open one of those stupid fans. Yes, they certainly ran, which put whatever they were pointed at in danger of being trampled by the flock. Serra shivered and smoothed her gown over her hips, remembering just how thoroughly Scot had dressed her down at the infirmary. The amount of sway he held over the city, how everyone jumped to do his bidding—Glory, the ways she could use a man like that.

And there wasn't a chance in hell it was ever going to happen.

She bit her lip as the frenzy below intensified, Riggs's gavel punctuating the chaos. She was positive leading Scot around by the dick was no small feat. How Kara had him wrapped around her little finger… Serra was almost tempted to believe those mind control rumors she'd started. Though patently false, there was no way a mouse like Kara Jester had enough fire to interest Laughlin Scot.

Of course, back at the Source, Serra had thought the same about Veronica and then Nora, yet both Jester women had been able to consecutively secure the position of First Binder by doing the same to their former patron, Albanach.

Hmm. Serra drummed her fingers. Maybe she was on to something with the mind control thing, though she didn't recall Otto sharing genetics with their House. What Albanach had ever seen in that insipid bunch of sanctimonious cunts was beyond her, but she'd be damned if the Jesters fucked their way to the top in Glynfyls like they had down south.

Her gaze met Nora's again; the paragon an island of calm within the calamity Serra had instigated. Serra batted her lashes and blew her a kiss on the off chance there was any doubt as to who had put her there, then turned on her heel and left.

She'd learned what she needed to. Now she had work to do. The position of First Binder was House Hess's by right—Nora's damnable Gordian knot of talent notwithstanding—and Serra *would* have it. Her heels clicked across the marble floor, lips pruning as she drew in one last clean lungful of air before stepping through the opalescent mists of the gate at the end of the hall and out, into the city somewhere below the fifth rung.

Her nose wrinkled as the noxious combination of the unwashed masses, low tide, and diesel hit the back of her throat. Gagging, she waved ash from her face, her breath streaming behind her in a cloud as she trudged through the frigid morass coating the street.

Temporary. This was only temporary.

Serra grimaced. It would've been more so if she could've solved that damnable knot. Not for the first time, she cursed Bernice for offering to "have a look." It'd become so unwieldy after her poking at it that Serra couldn't put her arms around the bloody thing. As with everything else, Nora had somehow stacked the odds and turned the ludicrous Northern test to her advantage. Perhaps obstruction was House Jester's extra. They were excessively skilled at that.

Serra lingered at a local tea house over a pale cup of dishwater until what had spilled at Assembly reached her ears. She added a comment or two to ensure its run continued, then bustled through the neighborhood, collecting her washing along with the gossip before stopping to do some shopping.

She scowled. Shopping. More like scrounging. A loaf of bread, a bottle of wine versus the round of cheese...she seethed as she put the bottle back. The scant allowance of units she'd been allotted was barely enough to cover the basics after her one proper dinner of steak and caviar last night.

Vagrants gave her a wide berth as she stomped toward the tenement she was currently forced to inhabit. Ahead, a newsboy hawked papers at the corner. Her footsteps slowed. Hmm. An early edition of *The Post*. A smile tipped up her lips at the crowd surrounding him, engrossed with his wares.

How wonderful. Was this what'd just been leaked, or could it be attributed to her earlier visit to the paper's headquarters? Word of Julia's death had chummed the waters, but the information Serra had provided insinuating that the Jesters could coerce thoughts...? She chuckled. As soon as people read that, every interaction with their blighted House—past or present—would be questioned, guaranteeing their ostracization from society.

A smile slid across Serra's face. None of the rags up here would be able to resist printing such a juicy story.

The semi-literate crowd caught sight of Serra and scattered, their faces far too smug. Disgusting louts. Like any of their opinions mattered. Now, to make sure all the salient points had been included in the exposé. She thrust the stammering newsboy a unit and snatched a paper from him. He took off running and her smirk evaporated at the image on the front page.

A shot of Serra rising from her knees, wiping a hand across her mouth was not expected. She sniffed. Nor did it capture her best side. The lighting in the inset panel of Lord Crown zipping up was rather more favorable.

Damn it. So much for spinning it as alleged oral sex. The lady's censure at Assembly abruptly made sense. Serra's brow creased. Now she'd be forced to go the non-consensual route. After all, she was a single woman in a big city, and it was so very easy to be taken advantage of.

She rolled her eyes, but if they believed the drivel Crandall had been spewing, they'd gobble up a helping of hers while they were at it. Serra snapped the paper closed and tucked it under her arm, ignoring the snickers behind her as she continued down the grimy street to her unfortunate lodgings.

Damn Laughlin Scot for calling her out! Who would've thought there would be such a fuss over a blowjob? Perhaps if the puritanical ninnies up here made a practice of putting out, their husbands wouldn't be so eager to dally elsewhere. Glory, the women in this city were insane to leave that kind of power on the table.

She climbed the ash-encrusted steps and pushed through the tenement's graffitied double doors, slanted gaps at their edges thick with an accumulation of dirty ice. It shattered as the hinges bent back, cracking and popping, skidding across the threadbare carpet of the dismal hallway as she entered. She resisted the urge to trail a hand along the filthy wall to keep her balance, the pitch of the floor at least fifteen degrees higher on the left. Nothing in this damned city was level, and it got worse the farther you were from the crown of the hill.

The sad excuse for a clinic she'd been exiled to on Barris Street had slats of wood fixed to the edges of the work tables, for Glory's sake. Serra scowled at a flickering bulb as she passed, rummaging for her key. Her mouth soured further at the stupid piece of metal, knuckles whitening as she palmed it. She swallowed the growing lump in her throat, the longing for flat surfaces and a decent portlock, fierce.

Temporary. This was only temporary.

The door swung open, and she sighed as she stepped into the narrow room. A sad pallet she shared with Tamara lay at its far end, and a trio of boards hung from the ceiling at the other. Intended to serve as a table and chairs, they were the only things remotely close to flat and made the rest of the place seem even more off-kilter. She dropped her sundries and the paper onto the widest scarred slab, sending the plank swinging. Serra scowled, steadying it as she clicked on the thermocoil beneath the waiting kettle.

Her back to the slanted counter, she pursed her lips as she waited for the antiquated contraption to heat. Power. She needed power to change her circumstances, and if she played it right, the North's stigma against sex could be an asset. After all, the men up here were definitely in a drought, and wasn't scarcity the fuel by which economies were driven?

She was more than happy to exchange some taboo caresses for what they brought in return. The trick would be using them to get her into the upper echelon of society as opposed to being ostracized from it, but discretion wasn't anything she couldn't handle now that she knew the rules of engagement.

Her lips tipped up at the challenge as she retrieved a chipped mug from the sink and set it on the still-swaying plank. What was the saying? A lady in the streets and a whore between the sheets? Starting with Lord Morris, manipulating the sheep on the hill would be child's play. If the Overlord thought he'd seen the last of Serra Hess by shuffling her off to that filthy clinic of miscreants and whores on Barris Street, then he was going to be sadly—

The building shook and a cry escaped her lips. She went to steady herself on the table, and it swung forward. Serra grabbed onto a rope as she lost her footing, the coarse hemp ripping across her skin. Glass broke in the room beside hers and something above crashed to the floor. People screamed and more things fell, the violent shaking heaving the cabinets from the wall. Plates shattered, and she screamed as the edifice listed toward her—

The tremors stopped as abruptly as they'd started.

Serra threw out a weave, binding the cabinets back into place. She took a deep breath, surrounded by broken crockery, and slowly got to her feet, a quick pull of talent healing the lacerations on her palms. She wiped them against her skirts and cracked the door to the hallway. Wide-eyed people teemed from their rooms to whisper together in fearful clumps.

"You have earthquakes up here?" Serra asked the grubby whore who lived across the hall.

"Nah, dunno what's a do—"

She crouched in her doorway as another tremor gained in intensity, rocking the building. People scattered back into their rooms. Concrete groaned, and the window above the listing front doors imploded, atomizing dingy glass shards across the hall.

Serra threw an arm over her face and clung to her doorjamb with the other, fighting to remain upright as the building lurched. What was left of the window crashed to the floor, and the whore yelped. Sirens blared outside.

A pre-pube ran past them, as nimble as a goat through the destruction. "S'Lord Scot! He went scrambled ham!" the boy cried, gone before Serra could ask any questions.

"Laud, somewhat must've happened t'the lady," the whore gasped. "S'romance right out of them fae tales, way he loves her."

Serra's urge to vomit was cut off by a massive boom in the distance.

Her feet shot from under her as the tenement canted sharply. Stone grated against stone and dust filled the air. The whore screamed as she toppled forward, flying across the hall. She hit the wall beside Serra's door and groaned, struggling to right herself as the world trembled, the building settling at a different angle.

Serra panted, spread eagle on the floor, waiting for the aftershocks to subside. She licked her lips, tasting opportunity along with the grit. The whore was right. Something must've happened to Kara, but what?

"Sweet baby Jesus, I hope she ain't dead," the whore moaned.

Serra's brow rose. After that display, it was a distinct possibility. She turned to look up at the whore, and the woman blinked back at her, actual tears welling in her eyes—

Serra started. "What happened to your halos?"

"Me halos?"

"They're gone."

The whore rummaged through her skirts and pulled out a compact. She snapped it open and gasped. Thin green rings popped into existence around her irises. They shimmered, and she disappeared. Serra blinked, and the whore popped back into view, her face pale.

"Somewhat must've happened to the Overlord." She stared at the crusted over slice across her shaking palm, then met Serra's gaze again, rubbing her thumb over the poorly healed wound. "Me oath-bond... it's gone."

Serra's gaze snapped to her own palm. The whore was right. That faint tingle that'd resulted from pledging her fealty to Lord Scot had fuzzed out.

The doors to the outside slammed open, and Serra turned away, blinking from the influx of radiant sunshine. Glory, where the hell had that come from? She held up a hand, shading her eyes. One of the Binders from the hill infirmary peered in at them, pinch-faced. Behind him, a cacophony of blaring sirens, screams, and odd crashes drowned out the thudding of Serra's heart in her ears. The building across the street was rubble—

"Oh, Lady Hess!" he panted, running a sleeve over his forehead. "Thank God I've found you! Lady Jester just collapsed, people are pouring into the clinics. Half the city's been destroyed, and with the recent mandates, we're at a loss. We need you to take control of the line."

"Is that right?" Serra didn't bother to temper her smile as she clawed up the door frame and smoothed a hand over her hair, positively salivating at the man's nod.

Well. Fancy that. It didn't look like she'd have to begin consolidating power from her knees after all.

CHAPTER ONE

"Something's happened. A and Ro left to get supplies and only Ro returned. He won't say why A isn't with him, but his eyes are hard when he looks at El. I fear A's finally discovered how unfaithful she's been. Does he know she's pregnant? The timing is terrible. En is in a rage over it, and El has no idea who the father is. I'm praying it's A, otherwise, she'll have no one at her side. Lord, she may not even if he is. The names they've been calling her behind her back…

Does A know about the pregnancy? That he could be a father? I can't believe he would shun her—the baby—if he did.

The guilt I'm feeling…it's a stone around my neck. I'm so ashamed that I never said anything—none of us did—though we knew full well what she was doing. The way she begged me not to tell… Ugh. She's always been able to find the words to get what she wants, but I should've known better. Now I fear I've done more damage staying silent than speaking. I need to talk to Ro. I have to make this right…"

– Undated journal entry

A SHARP INHALE and breath filled Flynn's lungs.

He blinked. Muted colors sharpened, rendering shades and tones into angles and planes, gaining dimension they stretched outward. Sky met land and sea. The hazy line in the distance pulled him.

Called.

He ran a hand over his bare chest, brows furrowed as he chewed his lip. Whole, but something…something was missing.

Was gone.

Static. Sound like angry bees. Bells.

… A man glares down from the pulpit, frothing as he spews brimstone and damnation. "Your fate, to writhe within the inferno! Your torment, everlasting hell! Repent, ye sinners…"

Flames leapt at the edge of Flynn's vision, and he blinked them away.

… Flesh blackens, crackles and breaks. He screams and fire sears into his lungs, burning him from the inside out…

No. That was…wasn't right. Was it? He had repented. In the alley. She'd been there. His mom…she'd saved him. Made him promise. Had it been a dream? He'd kept them. Well, mostly. Until…

He closed his eyes. Exhaled.

Kara.

CAL GRIMACED and climbed to his feet as Glynfyls stopped shaking. He clutched his breast, groping for the ward Miriam had set some thirty-odd years ago that tied Flynn back to him. *Please, God…* Cal exhaled, his knees buckling in relief. Still there. Felt different, but the boy wasn't dead.

Not yet at least.

His gaze slid from the calamity outside the window to the blood spattered across the wall and the gore-soaked carpet. In the unlikely event House Scot survived the next seventy-two hours, the whole damned room would have to be gutted. He dropped the last of his cigarette and ground it out beside Cordelia Kerns's corpse.

And if they didn't survive, screw the resale value. What a goddamned mess.

"Here's a spot, there's a spot…" he muttered to himself, bastardizing lines from his brief stint in community theater. Seemed appropriate. He couldn't clearly remember his last wife's smile or the faces of any of the children he'd buried, but every goddamned line from that play, every goddamned moment he'd spent with *her*, was seared into his memory in high goddamned definition.

Her. Elize. Lizzy. His Lilith.

Cal ran a shaking hand down his face. Squatted. Knees cracking, he leaned forward to lower Kerns's lids and cover the look of surprise in her grayed-over baby blues, his gaze locking on the imprint of a bloody crescent between her brows—

A flash of memory—the same mark on his second wife—hit him hard.

He stumbled into a chair and pulled out his pouch of tobacco, cursing the tremor in his hands. Fingers fumbling, he threw aside the botched attempt. Deep breath. Rolled another. It was passible, barely. He lit it. Blew out a frenetic puff of smoke and spat tobacco from his lip.

His gaze drifted back to Kerns's corpse. Another woman with her throat slit. Wasn't related to Julia's earlier demise, but that wouldn't stop Crandall and the city's rumor mill from having a goddamned field day with it.

Christ. Between that and Flynn's tantrum destroying everything as far as the eye could see, House Scot was on borrowed time.

And when the press caught wind of Kara's abduction, it would be worse.

What a clusterfuck. If there'd been any place to go, Cal would've started packing his bags, but this time, there wasn't. Jane—Mother— had made sure of that.

He blew out a ragged stream of smoke and glanced at the couch as he brought the sad excuse for a cigarette to his lips again. Kara's cat glared back. Miserable animal was wrapped around Fitz's throat with its green eyes narrowed. Cal frowned at the rise and fall of the boy's chest. Looked like taking pity on fuck ups was still part of Elize's MO.

Not that the boy was losing any sleep over his brush with death. He was sawing wood like he didn't have a care in the world thanks to Nora's induced coma. Must be nice.

Cal took another drag, cursing himself and the lingering scent of Elize's perfume, the barest hint of bergamot dragging his mind back to that first summer they'd met. To the stolen kisses during rehearsals. To the way the lighting had hit the curve of her cheek and the look she'd throw over her shoulder as she sauntered into the wings. Christ, that still got his dick hard.

Too bad her seduction had been as much of a role as the one she'd played on stage.

He'd hauled sets around the whole damned summer for that shit, podunk production to be close to her. Senator Dashell's daughter. What she'd seen in the son of a pig farmer—Christ. In retrospect, he knew exactly what she'd seen. Or rather, what her father had. Man hadn't blinked twice at pimping her out for twelve hundred acres just outside of town where the Corporation could build their research facility.

And damn them, but they'd gotten it.

Why her and her brother had stuck around after, slumming with the five of them—

Cal shook his head, staring at the blood pooling beneath Kerns. What was done was done, and his hands had never been clean. No. He'd been up to his goddamned elbows in this shit from the get-go, but this right here? This was gonna sink him and everything he'd worked for since.

As intended.

He fished the slip of paper Elize had left on Kara's pillow from his breast pocket, his fingers shying from the braid coiled beside it. Entwined "E's" on the letterhead and beneath the monogram, a set of coordinates with four damning words.

40°49'26.99" N-73°55'20.99" W
QUEEN TAKES PAWN.
CHECK.

Elize...Enoch...the twins were just pieces, not who he'd been playing against. Cal stroked a heavy hand over his mustache, knowing the message for the invitation it was.

Jane had made her move, and now it was his. For better or worse, the endgame had begun.

MARCOS STEPPED BACK from the circle of melted earth, the soles of his boots uncomfortably warm. The stench of burnt stone hung heavy in the shimmering, superheated air, what was left of the plateau uncomfortably silent, even the wind gone still.

Behind them, Glynfyls shrilled—a cacophony of sirens, shouts, and the clamoring of bells. The city coming to arms after the fact, like an ant hill kicked. Seemed on par, and their scurrying was just as effective. Marcos frowned, ignoring the noise as he searched the horizon for any hint of movement. Had any of the Source's troops survived?

"Gimme your jacket," Rogan murmured, breaking Marcos from his thoughts.

"Pardon?" He turned to the other two men, the rest of their party still up on the barbican.

"Not you, him—Kyle. Give me your jacket."

"My…" Markham stared slack-jawed at Scot, then swallowed. "Oh. Yes. Yes, of course." The First Fetch paused for moment more before shaking his head then scrambling to take the garment off. He handed it over, and Rogan knelt, draping it like a bathrobe over Laughlin's bare shoulders.

"Flynn." Rogan lightly slapped the boy's cheek, then gripped his jaw, turning his face to him. "Hey, kid…" he coaxed, trying to catch Laughlin's gaze. His focus slowly drifted from the eastern horizon to stare at Rogan with the wide-eyed innocence of a child and zero recognition.

Marcos wiped the sweat from his brow and glanced up, searching the barbican for Nora. If anyone could put this into perspective… He knew what he'd seen—the city crumbling, land splintering into bits, the sea rushing in—but as far as what had happened to Laughlin Scot…Glory. If Marcos didn't know better, he'd swear the boy had reanimated from dust, but—No. It wasn't possible.

Was it?

Something far too close to awe rose in Marcos's chest. Laughlin blinked and turned away, his brows bunching as he refocused on the eastern horizon.

Rogan stood, by his swearing far more irritated than awed, and hefted Flynn up by the arm. The boy followed his lead without protest. Acid built in Marcos's gut at the show of compliance. He hadn't thought that was possible either. Rogan's frown deepened like he was thinking the same thing. He scowled, pinching his nose, and Marcos was abruptly struck by the lack of the boy's 'lust in the air. After being bathed in it for the past few days, his sense of dread grew. Had Laughlin burned out his talent?

Rogan's hand tightened around the boy's arm as he nodded to Markham. The Fetch fumbled with his handkerchief before he stepped close. Marcos joined them.

"Come on, kid, let's get you home—"

"She's not there," Flynn murmured in a hollow monotone.

Marcos, Rogan, and Markham exchanged glances.

"Pardon?" Markham asked, blotting his face. "Eh, she's not where? What do you mean?"

"Kara. She's gone." Laughlin's brow furrowed again, still looking east.

Markham's eyes darted between the two other men, his expression a fervent prayer that wasn't a euphemism. "I-I'm afraid I don't understand—"

"No, but we're gonna," Rogan growled, cutting him off. "Shift us to the flat, now."

Markham nodded, his jowls quivering. He pulled talent and colors ran.

They appeared back at the Scot's flat in the room with the poorly patched hole in the wall. Marcos stepped to the side as Rogan backed Flynn up to one of the grubby couches.

"Sit."

The boy's knees folded and his rear landed on the cushions. A puff of dust headed skyward, his blank gaze drifting up with it to stare at the ceiling.

"Am I the only one that makes ill?" Markham asked, his handkerchief at his lips.

"No," the two Breakers answered. Rogan opened his mouth like he was about to say something else, but swallowed whatever it was at the lift pinging in the hall.

A cloud of smoke proceeded Caliban Scot into the room. His feet rooted, eyes snapping to Laughlin, then to Rogan and the rest of them. "Shit. How bad is he?"

"Bad," the Alpha growled. "Where is she?"

Cal didn't blink. "Gone."

"So I heard. Any idea what happened?"

"Nope." The barest tremor shook his hand as he raised the nub of his cigarette to his lips.

"Huh." Rogan pulled an empty chain from under his shirt, and Cal's throat bobbed. "And here I would've put money on my gating stone disintegrating having something to do with her disappearance."

A muscle in Cal's jaw tensed as he finished his cigarette. Their gazes locked—

He made a break for it, and Rogan lunged.

"You motherfucker!" He grasped the gangly man around the waist for a half second before Cal phased, and the Breaker barreled through him, into the wall. Plaster crumbled. He cursed, scrambling to his feet and pulling talent, bathing the room in scarlet light. Static crackled and zagged between surfaces, sparks flying.

"Good lord!" Markham cried, stumbling against a couch.

Marcos fell back with him, all the small hairs on his body standing rigid. A crack of force shot through the air, outlining the invisible man hightailing it from the room. Cal bellowed, his back arching as he popped back into view. Rogan bared this teeth and rushed him.

"Cheat!" Cal threw a sloppy punch, and Rogan took it on the chin, landing his own jab and snapping Cal's head back.

Rogan grabbed him by the throat, shaking him. "It was her again, wasn't it? Wasn't it?!"

"Yes!" Cal choked out, gripping Rogan's wrists and struggling against him. "Yes, it was her. Who the hell else would it be?!" Cal spat and pulled talent, phasing through the Breaker.

"That's two, asshole!" Rogan growled, his halos flaring. Sheets of flames exploded across the room's exits. "We both know you don't got enough juice to phase again, so fucking spill. What does she want this time?"

Cal popped back into view, and the two of them glowered across the room at each other. Behind them, the hallways blackened and charred, smoke billowing—

"What the fuck does who want?" Laughlin growled. The flames snuffed out, and Rogan did a double take at where they'd been and then at Laughlin. The blank innocence of his gaze had been replaced by a hard emptiness that made Marcos's mouth go dry.

Rogan crossed his arms over his chest and glared at Cal. "You wanna clue him in, or shall I?"

Cal shot him the bird, his eye already swelling. "Have at it, if you're so hot to blab. I'll be waiting with bated breath and my bottle for the CliffsNotes," he muttered, probing the bruise as he slunk through the charred hallway to his office.

Markham hefted himself up from the couch and cleared his throat, eyeing the smoldering drywall. "Ah...while you attend to that, I believe I'll retrieve the rest of our party—"

"I'll go with you," Marcos quickly volunteered. Whatever the hell this was, he didn't want any part of it, and he needed to make sure Nora was all right. What he wasn't feeling from her through their bond was of concern.

"Good idea. Bring the rest of the cohort back here," Rogan said, leaking 'lust.

Marcos's hackles rose at the reminder of the Alpha's dominance. Laughlin didn't even blink, back to staring at the ceiling. Whatever had just surfaced hadn't stuck around for long. Marcos wasn't sure if that was a good thing or a bad thing.

Rogan was studying the boy like he was questioning the abrupt change as well, then shook his head. "Christ. The cohort needs to earn its keep and do damage control, and they need to do it now."

"Agreed," Marcos said, meeting Rogan's eye, "and I can do my part by dealing with any troops Titus left behind. Without Beritram influencing them, they'll need to be brought in." He'd be damned before he left any more good men die.

The Alpha Prime grunted. "You think they'll integrate like the ones that surrendered?"

Marcos did, if they were in any kind of condition to do so. "Only one way to find out."

"If they don't, you know what's gonna happen, right?"

He tensed. "I do."

"Make sure they do, too. Find Stonefist, and brief him before you head out."

"Ah, small point…" Markham blotted his brow. "With the plateau sundered, getting out there will require line-of-sight jumps, and there's not enough daylight left to do so safely, especially if you're planning on shifting a group. I'm afraid it will have to wait until morning."

Rogan nodded. "Good. Integration should be brought up at Conclave before you show up with a contingent at your back. You can start the process, and I'll get there when I can."

Damn it. Marcos scowled, but the two of them knew their business, for all he wanted to buck protocol and rush out there.

"Well, then we best be on our way," Markham said briskly. He put a hand on Marcos's shoulder—

"Going forward, a single hierarchy prevails, Commandant," Rogan said, forestalling the Fetch. "I'm making it your responsibility to ensure they walk the Way—otherwise they don't walk at all."

The Alpha Prime's gaze bored into Marcos's until he bent his head, acknowledging the order. Markham pulled talent in the uncomfortable silence that followed and shifted.

Colors ran.

Damn it. Marcos sighed as they appeared on the barbican, and the shattered landscape came into view. He understood the necessity of waiting, and the logic behind Rogan's kill order, but that didn't mean he liked either.

ROGAN PUSHED past the door to Cal's office with Flynn trailing close behind. Thankfully, French had shown up with a t-shirt and a pair of sweats for the kid to cover his bare ass, but the way he'd silently put them on and followed in Rogan's wake was making his skin crawl.

Yeah. That was it. Had nothing to do with the kid's fucking ashes binding back together from wherever the hell he'd blown them to, then reanimating like it was no big.

Rogan scrubbed a hand over his face. What the hell was Laughlin Scot? Shit. Better question was what the hell had Kara done to him? Rogan glanced over his shoulder, trying to take the whole resurrection thing in stride. Christ, just when you think you've seen everything…

He snorted and bellied up to the sideboard to peruse the lackluster selection of booze. Didn't look like it'd been restocked in a while, or Fitz had recently hit it. Even odds there. How that skinny Fetch managed to down so much… Rogan shook his head, adding it to the list of recent unexplainable phenomena as he eyed the comeback kid make a beeline for the coffee service.

Rogan grabbed a half-kicked bottle of scotch and sighed, running his thumb over the label. In a weird way, he knew what Flynn was going through. All that talent hollowing him out, losing his mate— been there done that. Granted, Rogan'd never blown himself to shit and come back from the dead, but if Kara and the babies were still alive, Flynn couldn't afford to be anything but on point, no matter how fucked-up his head was.

Especially if the twins had his family. If Elize was involved, then surer than shit, that psycho prick, Enoch, was in on it too, which meant a clock was ticking. The moment he got bored, he'd cut his losses, and Rogan didn't want to think about what that meant for Kara.

He crossed the room to Cal's desk and took a swig from the bottle. Probably not the best time to get drunk, but that hadn't stopped him before. He plunked into his preferred chair and made a point of kicking a bunch of papers onto the floor as he put his feet up.

Cal didn't even bother to glance over as they scattered, his gaze fixed on the salt-and-pepper braid coiled at the center of his blotter.

That was Elize's, all right… Rogan's brow furrowed. He cocked his head, the light sparkling off a simple ring woven into the plait. Holy shit. "Is that—"

"Yeah," Cal muttered around his cigarette. He pulled a slip of paper from his pocket and tossed it at him. "Here. Pretty sure they expect you to be my plus one. And before you ask, all the stones you took off the Sons are dust, too. She never did make anything easy."

Rogan grunted and plucked the note from the desk. Even though he'd expected it, blood thudded through his temples at the double "E" monogram. That motherfucker. "He had the balls to show up here?"

"Dunno." Cal shrugged, watching Flynn stand in front of the coffee service like he had no idea what it was. Kid frowned, then abandoned it to pull out the other chair in front of Cal's desk.

Rogan's brows furrowed as Flynn sat. "You okay?"

Flynn stared at his hands, not giving any indication he'd heard him.

Rogan turned back to Cal and tried to keep his temper in check. Wasn't at Flynn, it was at the situation. "Where'd you get the note and the braid?"

"They were left on Kara's pillow," Cal said after a long moment.

Rogan's eyes narrowed at the way the asshole studiously avoided his gaze, still holding out on him. Christ, this was like pulling fucking teeth—"Okay, so what did Kerns or Fitz have to say? They were up there with her, right?"

"Nothing. Fitz is still sleeping off Nora's bind, dead to the world." Cal snuffed out his cigarette. "And Kerns is just dead." He drew a line across his throat before his fingers drifted to his forehead.

Rogan bit back his rage. He had his own history with that fucking crescent, and all of it was bloody. "Goddamn it, Cal, those two sociopaths need to be put down, and if you're not gonna do it—"

"Who says I'm not gonna do it?"

Rogan barked out a laugh. "Are you for real right now? Uhh…how about me and the last thousand or so years?" He seethed, dropping his feet from the desk to stab a finger at Cal. "The number of times you could've ended this—shit, the number of times *I* could've if you'd just let me—"

"Before or after you decided to hide on your beach for the majority of the millennia?"

Rogan threw up his hands. "Before, after, and at any point in between while you were fucking her. Don't even try to lie to me about leaving the Source to bang that poisonous cunt when all that shit with Kara went down—"

"You keeping tabs on me, McGuire?"

Rogan's knuckles popped, the air wavering above them with heat. "Don't fucking 'McGuire' me, Alister."

"Kerns is dead?" Flynn asked, startling them both.

"Yeah," Cal said, glaring at Rogan. "Her throat was cut."

"By who, and who the fuck are Alister and McGuire?"

"McGuire's me, pre-Firestorm." Rogan swallowed a mouthful of liquor and frowned. Goddamned moniker still tasted bad. "And Caliban's his middle name. Alister is his first, and he hates it. Don't you, Alister?"

"What are you, twelve?" Cal muttered, glaring daggers at him.

"Yeah, and you started it," Rogan spat back before turning to Flynn. "As to who offed Kerns, it was either Elize, Enoch, or a combination of the two. They're the Finders I told you about. Twins. Part of our original seven."

Flynn's brows bunched. "Enoch's the one you tried to kill."

"No, he's the one I'm gonna kill, and this time, Jane's not here to piece his sorry ass back together." Rogan's eyes flicked to Cal at her name, and the bastard refused to meet them. Fuck him. Rogan didn't care anymore. Whatever had gone on the day they'd lost her that made Cal feel so goddamned guilty—Jane was dead, and neither one of them were getting a do-over. It was time to stop treating her memory like some holy fucking relic.

Flynn looked between them, bewildered. "Okay, but why would they take Kara? I figured it would be Titus."

"Don't be so sure he's not involved," Cal said, his voice laden with defeat. "Those coordinates are for the Source."

Now that was interesting. What did the twins have to gain by working with Titus? Rogan cocked a brow. "You really think they've got her there?"

"No, but—"

"Answer the question, why would they take Kara?" Flynn interrupted, whatever had surfaced in the other room back to glare at the two of them. Rogan's hackles rose at the challenge. It was pure Alpha and something else. Something that he wasn't—

The kid blinked, and it was gone.

Cal wet his lips, still trying to prevaricate, goddamn him. "The four of us have…history." He pulled a cigar from his top drawer and lit it with shaking hands. "Suffice to say, the twins've made it their mission to destroy anything we care about."

Rogan swept a hand across Cal's desk, sending a tsunami of paper to the floor. "Fuck your suffice. We're past that. Why does Enoch hate me? Because he's a goddamned predator that won't take no for an answer. He tried to rape me. I tried to kill him. Now he wants to return the favor, but he's too chickenshit to challenge me directly." Rogan upended the bottle of scotch, making a concerted effort not to set the room on fire. He glared at his best friend, wishing he'd hit him harder. "Now, you're gonna man up and spill your deal, or I'm giving the kid my take on it," he growled.

Cal sighed and closed his eyes for a breath, as though disclosing was physically painful. Christ, it probably was. "My 'deal' requires a little more backstory—"

"No, it doesn't. You're just stalling, but if you insist, once upon a time, Elize was a rich-bitch summer boarder, and we were townie trailer trash—"

"*You* were townie trailer trash." Cal's good eye snapped open to narrow at him. "My house didn't have wheels."

"Technically, mine was up on blocks." Rogan threw back another mouthful of liquor. "And yours might as well've been, considering the circles her family ran in." He turned to Flynn. "They were political royalty. Think hill vs. commons. Hands down, I would've been from the seventh rung, but Cal was fifth, at best."

"Fourth," he muttered around a cigar as he lit it. "We had a trade."

"Your daddy was a pig farmer. Hers was next in line for the White House."

"Shitty trade's still a trade." Cal pushed back into the divot in his chair's cushions and crossed a boney ankle over his knee. His left eye was about swollen shut. The other flicked to Flynn. "But the comparison is apt. Every summer, people from the city would come upstate to stay in these big houses around the lake. Town would pander to them. Foo-foo cafes…shops…Main Street was kind of like the promenade. Anyway, I saw Elize at the farmer's market a handful of summers before the Surge and about lost my damned mind."

"You did lose your damned mind."

"Fine." Cal grunted. "I fell hard. Thought she did too. Then the Surge happened. Amplified everyone's natures into talents. Rogan, for example, became even more of an asshole."

"And everything with Cal turned into a state secret," the Breaker shot back. "Meanwhile, the twins were beset with a desire to find and explore every dick and hole in the tristate area, willing or no while society crumbled around us. Not that we found out about that until later. Gimme one of those."

"I'll trade you for the bottle." Rogan handed it over, and Cal tossed him a cigar, then refilled his glass. "Looking back, it was about the thrill for her, but for Enoch—"

"Please. It was a power thing for both of them, and then bodies started showing up." Rogan pulled talent to light his cigar, and the tip burst into flame. He scowled at Flynn's side-eye. "Don't," Rogan snapped, breathing through the influx of talent. Goddamn, he hated how much the possibility of that motherfucker being in the same time zone set him on edge. Enoch was diseased, and Elize was only marginally better.

Cal grunted and went on. "I bonded Elize before any of us knew what bonding was. Asked her to marry me and gave her my granny's ring." He flicked his ash at the coiled braid, and the stench of burning hair filled the room. "Got down on one knee to do it, too. She was supposed to be true." Cal took a long swallow of what was in his glass, then went silent.

"She wasn't," Rogan finished for him, not about to let Cal off the hook.

He sighed. "No, she wasn't. And once we'd bonded, she didn't realize I could feel it every single time she fucked around—"

Rogan snorted. "She didn't care."

Cal glanced at him askance. "Either way, I did what I was best at and disappeared. Jane convinced this asshole to track me down and drag me back, but it took a while." He turned to Rogan. "Elize was what? Seven, eight months pregnant by then?"

"About that." He nodded, remembering how he'd left the three of them that night. Cal and Elize screaming at each other, Jane trying to play peacekeeper… He couldn't—shit had hit too close to home. Besides, if he'd had stayed, would it have made a difference? Christ, he was tired of that keeping him up at night.

"Elize said it was mine, and I called bullshit," Cal continued. "Confronted her about cheating. She denied all of it—lied right to my face—and I pulled my talent from our bond." He finished what was in his glass and sat staring at the bottom of it.

"I didn't know she'd lose the baby. Our baby. Jane tried to save it, but…" Cal shook his head. "Back then, no one knew how it worked, but it didn't—it doesn't—matter. She's never forgiven me. Shit, I haven't forgiven me." He took a long pull on his cigar, and Rogan refilled his tumbler.

"Anytime either one of us finds a modicum of happiness…pride in something…someone…they make sure it gets buried," Rogan murmured, the faces of everyone they'd taken from him playing across his mind's eye. "Enoch slaughtered my entire goddamned House the last time I was up here, save for my boy, Liam."

"Insult to injury." Cal tapped the ash from his cigar. "They leave us with the fuck-ups like Lot and the damaged ones like Jon. The ones that are an embarrassment to our Houses."

Rogan grunted his agreement. "What the twins find best is weaknesses, and collectively, Kara is ours. The babies just up the ante. They're using her to draw us out." His fist tightened around the note. "I'm finishing it, Cal."

His friend met his eye with a kind of sad acceptance and gave a curt nod. Christ, it was about goddamned time he was finally on board with snuffing the psychos. When Cal had rolled over after the Great Incursion, had fucking *begged* him not to intervene, Rogan hadn't thought he'd ever—his eyes narrowed. Wait. Kara's abduction was just a drop in the bucket compared to everything else Elize had put him through. So why the abrupt one-eighty?

"Can you still sense her?" Cal asked Flynn, a bit too eager to change the topic. "Do you have any idea where she is?"

Flynn chewed his lip. Sweat dripped down his neck, staining the collar of his shirt and blooming down his back and under his arms. "I dunno. It's different now," he mumbled after a long moment, then shook his head and pushed a lock of damp hair from his brow. He grimaced. "East? All I can feel—I just wanna go that way. I have to—I can't stay here."

"Agreed," Rogan said, still eyeing Cal. "That craft Titus sent up for Nora. The lightstream. Pretty sure it's right where we left it."

Asshole grunted. "Yeah, but last I heard, Crandall's got it locked down tighter than a virgin during Fleet Week."

"Wasn't an issue then, don't see why it would be now." Rogan laced his fingers together and stretched out his arms, content to swallow Cal's bullshit for the moment. Would be plenty of time to pry the full story out of him on the way to the Source.

Cal's good eye narrowed, and Rogan grinned at the asshole.

"Fitz is still upstairs, right? Have Nora wake his ass up, I'll give him the imprint of Meddleton—"

"Won't work," Cal muttered. "Miriam's got it and the farm warded, and I'm gonna bet she's holed up with the sisters after our last chat. I'd rather not give them a heads up on what we're doing. Damn it, I knew Jon bonding into that family was gonna cause issues—"

"Funny you should mention issues, because there are several."

Rogan's head swiveled at Dorian Blaise's nasal drawl. The scarred blond man limped into the room with the use of a cane, his hands covered by black kid gloves. Aside from hearing that Flynn had saved the Finder's scraggly ass when the two of them had been stationed in Diytan, Rogan didn't know much about him, other than he'd agreed to be part of Flynn's cohort and had some serious beef with Crandall.

Cal frowned. "You don't say."

"Oh, but I do," Dorian guffawed.

Check that. Rogan added not liking him to the list.

"Unfortunately, what Dorian's referring to, is in addition to what one would expect given—well. Given everything, I suppose." Markham huffed, trundling past the Finder. Alice slipped into the room behind them and helped herself to the coffee service. "The first of which is that not everyone was inclined to return with us—Ah, understandably so. Jacques was keen to check in on his wife and the new babe, but promised to be along directly after."

"What about Marcos and Nora?" Cal asked.

"Lady Jester wasn't well, and the Commandant became distraught—"

"Distraught?" Dorian snorted at the big man. "She'd passed out, and when he saw her lying there, he threatened to put a bullet in anyone that came with in thirty feet of them. Lady Carmody requested they be brought to her flat, as opposed to yours," he said, eyeing the Seer distastefully. "And I'm afraid I make it a habit not to argue with witches."

"Pity." Alice smirked around her cup. "We rather enjoy arguing."

"Most women do," Cal muttered, settling back in his seat. He blew out a long stream of smoke. "Right, then what's the damage report; who's about to fuck us and how hard?"

The Finder looked around Cal's study with a frown. "This would be more efficient with a white board, but...I'll start with the good, proceed to the bad, and end on the ugly. First off, you owe Lord Martin a rather nice bottle of wine. Things could've been much worse had he not thrown a cloak over the eastern portion of the wall when it became obvious the situation was spiraling." Dorian hobbled over to the coffee service and began making himself a cup.

"No one from the city saw what happened," he continued. "I can't vouch for what the satellites may've picked up, but worst case, Jacques's cloak has bought us some time before we need to address Laughlin coming back from the dead."

"Thank God for small miracles," Rogan muttered.

"Personally, I'd consider Laughlin's resurrection a rather large miracle, but to each his own." Dorian took a sip of his coffee and leaned against the back of the settee.

Cal's eyebrows shot up. "What's this now?"

"I'll fill you in later," Rogan said, glancing at Flynn. He was staring at his hands again, his shirt soaked with sweat. That couldn't be good. They needed to move this along. "What else?"

"Ah, well, speaking of foresight, I suspect we also owe a bottle of wine to the witches—"

"Really, Dorian, wine is so blasé. I'd prefer an appointment to get my nails done." She waggled her chipped enamel at him and then moued at it. "Dreadful, aren't they?"

"Horrendous," he murmured, "but Alice's manicure notwithstanding, one of them had a vision—"

"Eustance," she interrupted again.

"Eustance." Dorian took a calming breath. "Had a vision. Turns out, the Fixer line was late to the battle because they were reinforcing the structural weaves throughout the city. The damage you see out there is largely concentrated in the Finders' spoke and the southeastern section of the seventh rung."

"Balderdash!" Markham blustered, going over to the window. He craned his neck, the Fetches' spoke barely visible from this vantage. "I can't imagine them making any special effort—"

"Oh, but we did," Alice said, picking at a pastry. "Once the wind clears some of that smoke away, you'll see. But, full disclosure, us saving your spoke was purely a matter of economics. It is where the majority of Glynfyls's foodstuffs and supplies are stored, and we mustn't forget about the importance of the docks." She took a bite of croissant and held up a finger as she chewed, leaving them hanging for the rest of what she had to say.

Dorian snorted and opened his mouth—

"Meanwhile," Alice continued, cutting him off, "the Binders' spoke is where the city's medical facilities are concentrated, we're going to need the Breakers again sooner than anyone thinks, the Shades' spoke was too far from the epicenter to be seriously impacted, and we couldn't ask the Fixers not to protect their own livelihoods, could we? No. I'm afraid it was the Finders' turn to take one for the team."

"I'm so very glad my line could contribute in our own small way," Dorian quipped sourly.

"That look on your face!" Alice laughed. "Oh, it was nothing personal, well, I suppose that's not entirely true. I'm rather tickled that Lord Crandall and his Intelligencers will so busy for the foreseeable future. Deservedly so, in my opinion. They're scrambling after that chasm exposed all sorts of things they'd rather not be brought to light."

"So you're saying we have a window…" Markham murmured.

Alice trilled out a laugh and waggled her finger at him. "Ah, ah, ah, Kyle. I'm afraid the only thing I can say with certainty is that Nora and the Commandant will be staying with Carl and I for the foreseeable future. She needs…space." A look passed between her and Cal.

He pursed his lips and nodded. "Let me know if she needs anything else."

"Of course. Now if you gentlemen will excuse me?" She flashed them a radiant smile as she swept past French on her way out of the room.

"The Jesters' bags have been sent to your flat as requested, madame," he murmured as she did, then turned to them and cleared his throat. "Pardon the interruption, sirs, but a subpoena has arrived requiring Lord Scot to appear before the Assembly to address recent events."

"Ah, that would be the bad, right on schedule," Dorian quipped. "I'm surprised they didn't provide him with an escort."

French's mustache twitched. "They did, but Master Kendall and his outfit arrived just prior to, and are refusing them access to the flat. They've called, ah…dibs on Lord Scot. A handful of them are waiting for you in the parlor, sir."

Flynn blanched whiter. Glass smashed and metal clanged. Behind them, Cal swore. He'd pushed back in his chair, his desk gone. Everything that'd been on it or in it was in a scotch-soaked pile at his feet.

They all turned to stare at Flynn.

"I-I can't." His throat bobbed as he stood and fled the room, stumbling past French. A shadow passed over the butler's face.

"The fuck was that, and what does he mean, he can't?" Rogan pushed out of his chair to go after him.

"I would strongly advise against that, sir," French said, standing in his way.

"Oh, you would, would you?"

"He's right," Cal said, then cleared his throat. "You need to stand down. You won't get anywhere with Flynn when he's like this. He'll either disappear or pitch another fit. Give him time."

Rogan laughed. "We don't have time, unless you've got some bright idea on how to head off the lynch mob we both know is coming? I'm sure they're sharpening their pitchforks as we speak, and Kendall's outfit being here isn't gonna make any part of that better."

"Actually, you've got about an hour," Dorian said, refilling his coffee. "Maybe two, before they come to physically drag him in. The Assembly still has a handful of temperate voices, though Lord Morris has been extremely vocal since last night, and that's only increased in the past few hours."

"Not surprising" Markham murmured, blotting his neck. "Peterli's not one to waste an opportunity, and his animosity towards House Scot has only grown since Laughlin came into power. The blowhard'll use any excuse to push that foul anti-twist agenda of his."

"Yes, especially since his son, Paul, bonded Shelby late last night, further proving dual-Talents' insidious natures and penchant for corrupting the pure of line. He's disowned the boy, and House Morris is up in arms over it," Dorian mused, then glanced around at the abrupt silence. "Oh. You didn't—"

"No." Cal's eyes became hard jade chips. "You wanna repeat that? Because I thought I heard you say that my granddaughter bonded the son of the biggest goddamned bigot in Glynfyls, whose House has been actively working to ruin ours for the past I don't even know how long."

"Ah, yes. I did say that." Dorian's throat bobbed. "Rather *Romeo and Juliet* when you think about it."

"Definitely sounds like a tragedy in the making." Markham chuckled nervously.

Cal pinched a hand across his temples. "Christ, if he didn't have a goddamned reason to hate us before…"

"And how the hell do you know all that?" Rogan asked. Dorian had been up there on the wall with the rest of them, and it wasn't like he'd had time to be briefed.

"I'm afraid that that would fall under 'Finder Business.'" He finger quoted, then brayed out a laugh.

Rogan glowered back. No wonder Flynn called him a jackass.

Dorian cleared his throat. "But all of that only underscores how little time you have to address this before it gets ugly. I need to see to my people, and I suggest you do the same. I'll keep you posted on what I find. Meanwhile, you may have mentioned pitchforks in jest, but take my word for it—they're not. Despite Lady Carmody's assurances that the damage was contained mostly within the Finders' spoke, the agricultural sector didn't fare well. A lot of animals spooked."

"Then I'll make sure I stand sideways while I run interference," Cal said, bending down to retrieve his tobacco pouch from the mess of his phased desk. He sighed as he rose from his chair. "Hopefully while I'm dodging tines, Merchant can slow things down on the legal side of things. Fingers crossed that between the two of us, we can give Flynn enough time to pull himself together before shit completely hits the fan, especially if Morris is fanning the flames." Cal shook his head. "Christ, that entire brood of Miriam's is a pain in my goddamn ass…"

"Believe me, I feel your pain," Markham muttered. "I should, ah, check on where one of them ended up."

"If you're talking about Arileo Prydee, I'd suggest you stop at the coliseum," Dorian said on his way out the door. "They've got him strung up on that yaw of yours. It's quite gruesome, I'm told."

"Good Lord—"

"I'll just bet it is." Rogan stood, smacking the Fetch on the shoulder. "If you're going that way, I'll tag along. With the bomb Marcos plans on dropping, Conclave should be in session, and I need to brief Stonefist before I head out to the craft."

"Ah, yes, about that." Markham blotted his neck. "I couldn't help but overhear your plans as we came in. With the Lady Jester unavailable to wake Fitz, I, ah, owe something of a debt to Laughlin and would return it in kind. I believe securing the means to rescue his lady would go a long way towards that."

"You got someplace off the books to outfit it after it's secured?"

Markham raised an eyebrow. "Several, but the one I have specifically in mind should suit your needs admirably."

"Then let's go." Rogan's held a hand out to the Fetch, ready to shift and wondering exactly what the kid had done to score a favor like that. Whatever it was, he sure as hell wasn't gonna argue. Shit around here was getting dicey, and the sooner they were on their way, the better.

SERRA PUSHED through the tilted doors of the Barris Street clinic with no little savor. The past few hours spent consolidating her position with the Binders guaranteed this would be the last time she ever crossed its filthy threshold again. She seethed at the criminal waste of her ability catering to an endless parade of commoners—half of which hadn't even been talented—and, with her rise in station, she'd be damned before her daughter was forced to do the same.

"Is Tamara here?" The schedule had her on it, but the girl was a bit of a free spirit…

The man at the front desk glanced up at Serra, his expression resigned. "Aye, and if ye've got a moment—"

"I don't." She breezed past him, tossing a writ outlining the new clinic practices onto his desk. There would be no more time wasted on those unworthy of their talent here or anywhere else in Glynfyls. Along with breeding, that was another thing the Source had gotten right and what traditional medicine was for. The huddled masses could figure it out for themselves.

The clinic was small, only two exam rooms and a ward with half a dozen beds in the back, all of them filled thanks to Nora's "restructuring" scattering patients throughout the city. What a waste of time. Serra didn't understand why they didn't just put a bind of heat on the entire facility and be done with it. The writ she'd deposited on the front desk ordered all those worthy brought back and, as soon as someone figured out who was in charge of restoring the power, they'd be getting an earful.

Tamara was hovering over a gurney in the corner of the room with a great deal more attention than was her wont. Serra's brows knit as she approached.

She vaguely registered the patient as one that'd been

unceremoniously dropped at the doors by the constabulary, racked with fever and covered in sores. Serra had kept her distance. Binder or no, it was always best practice to avoid something that might be catching. It was a fact Tamara was well aware of, so why was she so intent?

Tamara glanced up like she'd been caught at something, then breathed a sigh of relief, a hand on the swell of her considerable breast. "Oh, thank Glory, it's you," she whispered, glancing around the room as if there was any one of import to overhear her.

"Yes, it's me." Serra stopped several feet from the gurney, hands at her hips. "And it's time to go."

"No…" Tamara paled. "No, I can't. We have to help him."

"Help him? What's gotten in to you?" Serra chided. "Leave the rabble to—" The man on the gurney groaned and turned his face toward her. Serra felt hers drain of color. She put a hand to her throat. "Otto?"

"Serra…" he murmured through cracked lips.

No. Not him, not now, and not with what he knew. The understanding they'd come to back at the Source was no longer tenable.

He needed to die.

She hurried to his side, pulling talent—

His hand closed around her wrist, and the world blinked.

Serra took a deep breath and smoothed her stomacher, abruptly filled with purpose.

CHAPTER TWO

"I ventured into the ruins today, although I know better. The area where the control room for the collider once stood is a smoking pit, even after all this time. I stood at the fringes of twisted metal, wondering what my father's last thoughts were. If there was a moment when he understood what was about to happen, or if he was snuffed out in an instant.

If he would've been sorry.

I'd like to think so, but the reality is, his only remorse would've been for his inability to continue his research. How he would've loved to study what he'd wrought! Nothing but that horrible woman and his ego mattered once she'd darkened our door…"

– Undated journal entry

KARA WAS GONE.

Flynn took a shaky breath, inhaling her 'lust still subtly perfuming the room and staring at the bed they'd shared not two hours past. Blankets shaped to her body. A dip in the pillow where she'd rested her head.

Empty.

That place within him her presence had warmed, cold. Hollowed out, his insides eaten by what he'd pulled on the plateau, his channel blasted to shit. Scattered and broken like—

… Raw bone and sinew. The nothingness of dust. A sense of intent builds…

No.

He pinched the bridge of his nose. Shook his head, blinking. God, it was so hard to focus, to stay in the now. Those last moments on the plateau something had happened. Had changed. Changed him. Changed *in* him…

His mind shied from the memory, and it was gone. His talent. His rage. The plateau.

Kara.

His fist tightened around the hilt of the tactical knife he'd found at their bedside. He tapped it against his forehead, his pulse mirroring the beat with a throbbing staccato hammer. Was she still alive? Dead? No. Cal and Rogan said she'd been taken. They had coordinates, and he'd felt…something. That was real, right? It was so different, he had no goddamned way of knowing. Jesus. What the fuck had happened?

…the muted sense of her at his back rushes past him, disappearing into the eastern horizon like a shooting star, then winking out…

He snicked the blade open and pressed his free hand to his heart, a dark line seared into his flesh where his wedding band had been and another around his wrist from his cuff. A permanent fucking reminder of all the lies he'd told himself. Of what he'd tried to be.

Everything he'd failed at, indelible.

Flynn slid his palm over his pec to grip his opposite shoulder. Short of breath, he ripped the blade across his forearm, slicing himself to the bone. His teeth clenched at the sharp flare of pain, wishing it hurt more, his eyelids fluttering up at the twisted, euphoric burst of release. Blood dripped from his elbow, spattered to the floor—

…flames consume him, rolling up his body, skin blackening and cracking in their wake. Bubbling liquid running clear, evaporating. The smell…Christ, the fucking smell… Tendons pop, disintegrating, fleshy bark chars away, flaking from his bones…

And reversed. Muscle knitted. Damage from the fire—the knife— undone as the wound closed up, leaving nothing behind but bereavement. The loss of its sweet agony its own hell. A reminder that he couldn't fucking feel her—he couldn't feel *them*.

Kara. Their bond. The babies.

Gone.

Why the fuck would you give her to me just to take her away?

Flynn's breath stuttered out in short, sharp bursts. Head throbbing. What happened on the plateau coming back to him in fits and spurts, like weird stills stacking upon one another to build a scene. Jesus, he was gonna puke. He should've died. Wanted to die—no, he *had* died. Hadn't he? Fuck, did it matter? The blackness of his 'lust had surged up, devouring him, his rage all consuming.

He let out a slow breath. Phantom flames flickered at the edges of the room. Flynn squeezed his eyes shut. Pressed the heels of his hands to their sockets. The plateau. The city. He didn't want to know what was outside. Not yet. He ran a hand over his face, mouth dry. The destruction would be so much worse looking at it from above.

Christ. All that fucking power. What would he have done if Marcos hadn't shot him?

Didn't matter. Something bad had still happened.

…talent rushes through him in an unbridled torrent, ripping through the landscape and reshaping it. The ground splits and water rushes in, the city trembles—

His rage redoubles.

The city. Glynfyls. Gomorrah. If it wasn't such a fucking cesspool, he'd have been with Kara instead of dealing with their shit, and she would've been safe…

Damn it. *He* had fucking happened.

Flynn pinched the bridge of his nose. That was his answer. If Marcos hadn't pulled the trigger, the city, and everyone in it, would've been ash. Flynn slumped, curling forward from the wall. A monster. He was a monster. Devoid of talent, his skin prickled with cold one moment and stippled with sweat the next, his t-shirt dripping. Change. He'd come up here to change.

To Glynfyls, to his room—A laugh burst from his lips. Nothing ever fucking changed. No matter how hard he tried. Willed it otherwise. He was an animal. The prodigal fucking son fucking up some more.

Jesus, she was gone.

It wasn't the city's fault he hadn't been with Kara. It was his. He'd gone out there to answer Beritram's bullshit challenge. Had to people please. To be the big man. Flynn's knuckles whitened around the knife's hilt. And where had that gotten him? He'd lost her, his shit, and everything else that actually fucking mattered.

Head in hands, Flynn slid down the wall to sit on the paint-speckled floor. The thud echoed through the stripped-down suite along with Fitz's snores. Flynn barked out a laugh. Fuck. Kid would be the consolation prize. Everything else was gone. Kara and Kerns. No idea where the fucking cat was… Flynn stared at a knothole just beyond his bare feet. Someone must've shifted the carpet out along with Kerns's body.

Motherfucker. Kerns was dead.

Flynn's head fell back as he absently played with the knife. Eyes unseeing. Staring at the ceiling. He'd failed her. Kara. His mom. Everyone he'd ever been stupid enough to show he'd cared about.

Anyone he'd ever loved.

The elevator pinged in the room behind him, the scent of snickerdoodles and cocoa wafting through the room as the doors slid back. The wheels of French's cart hummed across the scarred floorboards, then came to a stop with a sharp click as he set the brake.

"I couldn't help but notice you didn't partake of anything downstairs. However, I'm afraid you're either going to have to stand up and get it yourself or sit in a chair like a civilized human being," the butler said tersely, preparing his chocolate pot. "It pains me to admit, but my knees aren't as cooperative as they once were. In either case, I'd suggest putting the knife away and cleaning yourself up. You have responsibilities to attend to. Master Scot has gone to face the Assembly in your stead, but that will only satisfy them for so long."

Flynn's head slowly rose. "Cal went?"

"He did."

Flynn just stared at the man as he folded dark curls of chocolate into warmed milk.

The butler glanced at him askance, his mustache twitching. "I believe he's attempting to keep your bits from the fire."

It was too late for that. He'd already burned.

French's words faded, Flynn's thoughts swirling over them. He'd burned and taken all of it down with him. Cal's plans. His mom's memory. Everything he'd worked for since he'd been up here. Everything he'd tried to build for Kara. All of it had fallen to shit, and goddamn if that wasn't a relief on some level.

Sham. Failure. Christ, Lot had called it, it'd only been a matter of time before he fucked it all up. Asshole had to be crowing right about now.

Flynn snicked the tactile blade closed and jammed it into his pocket as he pushed up to stand, then stumbled, falling back against the wall, light-headed.

"Sir, are you quite all right?"

Flames licked up Flynn's wrists, the skin blackening and beginning to bubble—No. He shook his head and they disappeared. No. They weren't real…

Not this time.

"Sir?" French asked again.

Flynn scrubbed a hand over his face, choking back a manic burble of laughter and shook his head. All right? No. There wasn't any coming back from this. Him. House Scot. They were done. Who had he been trying to kid?

"Laughlin? Calm yourself."

Calm himself. Sweat ran down his back and his breath came in short sharp bursts. Fucking hell. He couldn't—he needed to pull his shit together. If Kara was alive—he'd already failed her once. Failed everyone. Nothing he did was good enough. He wasn't good enough. Not enough to keep her safe. Not Kara, not his mom…

"Laughlin! You need to breathe."

He exhaled and raked a trembling hand through his damp hair. God help him, what had he done out there? He didn't remember…just the wounded rage of everything being stripped from him. Laughter erupted from his lips. Happy. He'd been happy. Shit served him right for thinking he could have a family—

He'd deserved to lose them. He'd traded them for Cal's fucking approval and this shit city's fair-weather fealty.

And more people had died.

Flynn rubbed a hand over the building constriction in his chest.

Jesus, what had he done, what had he done? He couldn't fucking breathe. He needed—needed air.

He bolted, fleeing from the room and leaving French behind him, the butler's face pale as milk. Flynn hit the button for the lift, a sliver of guilt for making the old man worry lancing through him. For disappointing him again. Fuck, he was spiraling—he knew he was spiraling—and that look on French's face—

Flynn stumbled through the lift's doors. Weak, he was so damned weak. Yet another reason to hate himself. Laughter burbled up again. Yeah, another. The doors opened at the top floor and he sprinted down the hall, to the roof.

The cold hit him like an icy flail, his skin prickling blue. Cal's shield over the frost-blasted garden had failed. A horrible tingling set into Flynn's extremities, creeping up his limbs. Flesh dying in the intense cold, then reanimating. Pink to gray to black and back again.

His stomach cramped as Kara's bind healed the damage he couldn't shield himself from anymore. Good God, what'd she done to him? He made a beeline for the parapet, dry heaving over its edge, the goddamned drop the least of his worries. Slowly, his gaze slid from the alley below and continued outward to take in the devastation he'd wrought.

Fuck. It was bad. Alice had said it was mostly the Finders' spoke, but goddamn.

A chasm had ripped through their section of the city. Buildings turned to rubble, smoke pouring from the streets, rising into a black haze that occluded the extent of the damage. Pockets of flame flickered, sirens and alarms wailed above the gong of church bells from the cathedral and smaller parishes. His stomach heaved again. Father Benson was gonna have a fucking field day with this. The priest had to be calling for Flynn's excommunication along with his head.

Flynn didn't give a shit about the first, but what was gonna happen when they tried to take the latter and couldn't?

He rubbed his chest, anxiety rising as he turned to the setting sun. It sparkled off inlets of water slicing through the fractured land like fjords. Jesus fuck. How had he—the tightness in his chest rose into his throat, closing it up. He reached for the knife—

"It's quite remarkable, isn't it? Rather pretty, actually. Reminds me of Kintsugi. All that gold binding the slivers of land together," French said from just behind Flynn's shoulder.

A weak cloak settled over him, shielding him from the worst of the cold. Flynn's breath went out in a whoosh, wishing French hadn't wasted his talent on him. Motherfucker, he hadn't even heard the old man come up.

Flynn's empty hand retreated from his pocket. "I don't remember doing any of it."

"I don't imagine that matters." French pursed his lips. "Here. I thought you might need this." He held out Flynn's beanie.

Flynn stared at it for a moment before taking it reverently, his fingers lingering on Kara's lumpy stitches. His brow furrowed. "I thought I wore it out to…"

No. He couldn't have. God, his head—memories—were all fucked up. He pulled it on, settling it low over his ears, his gaze skipping over the devastated portions of the city to the sparkling lochs of gold beyond the wall. How that was still standing, never mind how the shield continued to function…

His eyes went back to the Finders' spoke, not a doubt in his mind that the city would've been flattened if it'd failed and the Fixers hadn't turned out in droves. Flynn ran a hand over his beard, focusing on what was left of the plateau. The way the sun was hitting the inlets was kind of pretty, but fuck glued together pottery, they reminded him of Kara. Her talent. Jesus. If anyone could fix this—fix him—it was her.

He had to find her—goddamn it, how was he gonna find her? The wind picked up, cutting across the rooftop, and he shivered, his breath spiraling to the east.

Damn, baby, where are you? He closed his eyes and tried to push past, past *something*, to find their bond. His brow furrowed, everything muffled. He couldn't feel her. His talent—it was like it was wrapped in cotton. Maybe there was a sense of her, but it was so damned faint…

It would have to be enough. He'd go to the coordinates the twins had left. If they were working with Titus, the consequences be damned.

God, if that son of a bitch had her…

"I need to leave," he croaked around the lump in his throat, his chest tight again.

"Of course you do." French's hand settled on Flynn's shoulder, and he turned to it with a shuddering breath. Allowing himself to surrender to the old man's waiting embrace for a brief moment, desperately wanting to fall apart like he had when he was a kid. To have those fucking snickerdoodles downstairs make everything right again.

They wouldn't. Flynn took a deep breath, trying to center himself. Christ, he couldn't fall apart. He didn't have that luxury anymore. He needed to keep his shit together for Kara and the babies.

He pulled from the butler's embrace.

French cleared his throat as he squared his jacket, his blue eyes uncommonly bright. He whisked a finger beneath one. "I have no doubt you will bring the lady and the babes home safely. Lords Firestorm and Markham have gone to acquire transportation, but in the meantime, you have responsibilities."

"The fuck I do." Flynn glowered, pissed he'd lost his shit and wasn't out there getting the craft with them. Jesus fuck, he was failing her again. "The only responsibility I have—should've ever had—is to Kara. This fucking city can burn." Hell, a huge chunk of it already was. As if to underscore his point, phantom flames flickered in his peripheral. He blinked them away, his anxiety redoubling.

"Mmm. And where did you plan on taking your family once you have them?"

"Anywhere but here."

French moued like that was a load of shit. He stepped back with a curt half-bow. "As you say. However, I'd suggest you speak with Master Kendall before then. I hope I didn't overstep when I sent a missive explaining events and expressing House Scot's sorrow at Mistress Kerns's passing...I also stated your desire to have her interred at Meddleton."

Was that why they were here? Flynn shook his head and ran a shaking hand through his hair. No, that's exactly what he would've—what he should've done. Christ, why was he so fucking bad at this? "Where is she now?"

"At the city morgue. I wasn't sure how services should be handled, or by which party. I suspect there needs to be time for her family to be notified—"

"No. No family. Just the outfit. I'll pay for it. Whatever Kendall wants."

The butler's brows drew together. "I believe what he wants is to see you."

Wasn't gonna happen. "Tell him tomorrow," Flynn said after a brief pause. He'd be gone by then, even if it meant heading out on foot. Flynn turned away, and French caught his arm.

"Then I'd implore you to take tonight to think things through before you set fire to anything else."

Flynn grunted, noncommittal.

"Very good. After all, tomorrow will be a new day. A clean slate, free of today's unpleasantness. Things may just look rosier. Now, if you'll excuse me, I have duties to attend to."

Flynn's spine went rigid at the butler's all-too familiar "new day" mantra as the old man disappeared into the flat. Christ, how long had it been since he'd heard French spout that bullshit? Flynn must've been what? Fifteen? No, sixteen, the last time Lot had beaten the shit out of him…then his mom had died, and he'd started hitting the son of a bitch back.

The door closed behind the butler, and Flynn scrubbed a hand over his face. He pulled the tactical knife from his pocket and flipped it open, thumbing the blade as he focused on that faint sense of something he'd felt earlier in the east.

Where are you, Kara?

TITUS REPRESSED a cackle as he gloated over the Jester girl's inert form. He'd bested Albanach, and not only did he have her and her litter, he was positive Laughlin Scot wouldn't be far behind.

Which meant Salist was going to owe him a great deal of money.

Titus rubbed his hands together, eyes bright as he reviewed the litter's metrics. They streamed across the plaz-screen behind the girl's gurney, already markedly improved from what they'd been. Her talent deficiency had been his initial concern, but once she'd been put into stasis, the metabolic torpor had allowed that to rebound quite nicely.

And, now that her nutritional deficiencies were being addressed, the litter's vitals looked promising, their cellular proliferation off the charts. All but one was meeting its developmental milestones. Titus was confident the treatment he'd proscribed would address any inadequacies, but if by some chance it didn't, he wouldn't turn his nose up at a laboratory specimen.

He pursed his lips, tweaking the formula to bolster vitals as one of his techs administered another round of injections in preparation to stimulate fetal maturation. Typically, in utero development would take twenty-six more days, but given their response to treatment, he was confident he could cut that by a third, if not more.

He frowned as he put the change order through. The caveat to his covetousness was the girl's ability to adapt to the developmental strain. It was going to be a delicate balance considering her already taxed physicals, but not an impossible one. He'd need to monitor her vitals carefully, especially since the divine providence through which she'd managed to continue gestating thus far defied explanation— well, short of the girl's physiology spontaneously regenerating resources. Titus snorted. Though ludicrous, he was unable to fathom an alternative explanation. Given the rate the litter was sucking the life from her, she should've been a withered husk weeks ago.

He ogled several columns of numbers, not quite salivating at the avenues of research that possibility opened up. Regeneration, the ability to share talent, and that blip of power the vectors were unable to identify over the causeway some weeks ago—who knew what else Albanach had bred into her?

A rare smile came to Titus's lips. And it was all his to do with as he pleased, especially if the girl continued to respond favorably to treatment. He made note of the uptick in her metabolic function correlating to the change in meds he'd just prescribed; the numbers further corroborating his regeneration theory.

How exquisite. All that genetic gold wrapped up in a pretty, pretty package. He trailed his fingers beneath the thin sheet covering her breast and pinched a nipple until it pearled. Pity he preferred his conquests to know exactly what he was doing to them. Still…he did wonder just how sensitive her bond with Scot was…

A smile slicked across his face at the prospect of finding out. Oh yes, he had plans for Kara Jester, and none of them involved culling her after she whelped. With all the trouble she'd caused by allegedly "coming back" from succumbing to her bloodlust, there were so many other things he wanted to see if she could recover from. He chuckled. All in the name of science, of course—

"I know what you're thinking," a dusky voice sang behind him.

Elize.

Titus's hackles rose at the intrusion, heads about to roll. He hadn't authorized the twins' access to the gestation chamber. Their security clearances began and ended with the common areas and the suite they'd been assigned.

"You do realize this is a restricted area?" he asked, steeling his nerves at the subtle glow coming from the gem between her brows. It'd been dull earlier and only slightly less off-putting. The random fluctuation of luminescence was disturbing, to say the least.

She shrugged, the bits and bobs twined through her long braids chiming as she came to stand on the other side of the gurney. Her gaze lingered on Kara's breasts in much the same way his had. Unsurprising, considering how thoroughly she'd been enjoying both the consorts and courtesans he kept on staff. Not that it was an apt comparison, the perfection of the Jester girl's form put the rest to shame.

"I'd assumed our partnership extended throughout the entire complex."

"You assumed wrong."

"My apologies, but color me invested." Elize smirked, smoothing the sheet his attentions had mussed. "She's quite the specimen. I can't blame you for wanting to sample her wares, but as long as you have her in stasis, Scot won't be able to sense anything you do to her."

Titus pursed his lips, unhappy she'd been able to read his intentions so accurately.

Elize batted her lashes at him. They were abnormally thick and dark, in stark contrast to the clear azure of her eyes. She nodded at the girl's belly. "How many are we expecting?"

We? His hackles rose at her presumption. "Four."

"Mmm. Quite the brood." She cocked her head, her braids chiming again. "And what of your own progeny, Titus? Do you have a bevy of freckled little redheads running about?"

He raised an eyebrow. "I don't see how that information is the least bit relevant to our business relationship. Shall I ask you the same?"

Elize shrugged, laying a palm flat against the girl's turgid belly—

The gemstone between her brows flared white, and she cried out, snatching her hand back as if burned. Alarms went off, the girl's abdomen writhing.

"What have you done?!" Titus's attention flew to the elevated vitals streaming across the screen, the litter in abrupt distress.

Elize stared at the seething mound of flesh, wide-eyed, that damn rock in her head suddenly devoid of color. She held her hand to her breast, trembling. "I…I don't—didn't—"

"Get out! Out!"

Elize sucked in a breath and sprinted past him, through the double doors. Titus pulled his hair, swearing as the litter's cortisol climbed. Damn that cunt! He was loathe to use a sedative, but if levels increased much more—blast it! He quickly typed in a chemical cocktail to counteract the adrenal response to whatever that bitch had done, incrementally administering it—

There. The numbers slowed their climb, then dipped. He wiped the sweat from his upper lip, backing off the dosage as the girl's abdomen ceased roiling, and the litter's vitals dropped into a normal range…a perfunctory pelvic exam confirmed the dilation and effacement of her cervix remained unchanged.

He snapped off his rubber gloves and raked his hair back, too angry to have enjoyed the intrusion. Whatever that'd been could not happen again. Another spike like that, and it was quite possible he'd lose the entire litter. Partners or no, he refused to let either one of the twins jeopardize all he'd worked for.

Titus's eyes narrowed. The Triam had not been designed with visitors in mind and apparently, coded portlocks weren't sufficient. He'd been lax in not having the retinal scanners and biometrics installed. Foolish of him. That would need to be rectified. So would the slipshod application of his security protocols. An example would be made when he determined who had shared the access codes, and their end would not be quick.

He monitored the litter's streaming metrics for several moments longer. Satisfied they were stable, he left the girl's bedside, barely noting the other gestating bitches as he crossed the room. The lab techs had them well in hand, even with Brix and the rest of his squad contaminating the sanitized space with their "visitor's rota."

Titus scowled. That bit of bargain made his teeth ache. Though necessary at the time, it wouldn't be long-lived. He hung his lab coat on a peg and exited the gestating chamber.

Brix. Without Beritram's Alpha pheromones to keep him in his place, the Elite captain was becoming an issue. The bitch he'd bonded couldn't whelp soon enough. Titus gritted his teeth, eagerly anticipating her succumbing during the throes of labor and tearing the ingrate's throat out as he tried and failed to "bring her back."

Of all the ridiculous notions—Titus took a deep breath, the visual of Brix's demise cheering him as he strode down the sterile hallway to his office. Until then, perhaps he'd use the squad's bizarre obsession with their mates to his advantage. Instead of the ten-minute visits he'd allotted, having them stationed in shifts around the clock abruptly seemed wise.

Titus's stomach clenched at how close he'd just come to losing the litter. Damn that bitch! He should cut his losses and eliminate Elize and her brother—a spike of pain shot through his temples and he winced as he clutched his head.

No. No, this damned partnership had the potential to be far too lucrative to jeopardize it over a single bitch, no matter how exceptional she and her litter might be…and without her, there would be no means of luring in Scot.

Titus blew out another slow breath and continued to his office. With the influx of cash the twins'd brought with them, the facility was once again fully stocked with provisions, and he'd been able to ramp up the breeding schedule to levels predating the dissolution of the Source.

Fingers crossed it continued to be as productive. For all the advantage Titus had with the girl in hand, he didn't trust Scot not to throw some wrench—

Titus paused to collect himself again. No. The Triam's design was infallible. Close to a thousand feet below the surface, the blacksite was completely encased in bedrock. An independent plaz-reactor powered the site, and oxygen generators provided breathable air. The only way in or out was gating via the ring he wore on his pinky or shifting—both an impossibility if one had never been to the location before, and everyone familiar with it had been sequestered inside—

Damn. Yet another reason not to burn his bridges with the twins. His review of the feed from Elize when she retrieved the girl had been enlightening to say the least. Her ability to do so had hinged upon the small white stone she wore upon her person, presumably the same technology as his ring.

A shooting pain flared behind his eyes as he tried to remember where he had acquired it. Blast it—it didn't matter. What did, was that at present they were able to come and go as they pleased, and that was problematic. They'd dropped enough hints for him to suss out that they were the front for a backer. Until he knew exactly who that was and how much they'd disclosed despite their NDAs, it would behoove him not to do anything rash—

"Titus!"

Speak of the devil. Well, one of them anyway. Enoch strode down the hall toward him, running a handkerchief over a crescent blade. Crimson stippled his skin as if he'd been interrupted whilst in the midst of things.

"Have you seen Elize?"

Titus fought the narrowing of his eyes. Shriver had already informed him that Enoch's predilection for blood-play rivaled Titus's own; enough so that the Binder had been kept quite busy of late.

"I have, and if I didn't clearly spell it out before, let me do so now. Your security clearances allot you access to the common areas and your suite. Any other sector is strictly off limits." Defiance sparked within the man's eyes and was quickly blinked away. Not a fan of directives, was he? Titus wasn't terribly sympathetic.

"Oh? And what did my dear sister do to prompt this little reminder?" Enoch tucked the blade away and dabbed the spattered gore from his neck with the blood-smeared cloth. The gem at his brow remained a deep, dull amethyst.

"I evicted her from the gestating chamber." Titus scowled. "Her unauthorized presence triggered a stress response that jeopardized the litter."

"Interesting," Enoch murmured. He folded his handkerchief and slipped it into his pocket. "Well, then I suppose I'll have to have a talk with her myself." He smiled broadly, his shoulder knocking against Titus's as he passed him.

As the shush of Enoch's loafers faded, Titus's bunched brow smoothed with his smirk. Yes. Interesting, indeed. And thanks to the nanobots the two of them had so gleefully infected themselves with, he was positive a revelation was soon to come. Given Enoch's reaction just now, this was something they'd need to report to their mysterious backer, and Titus fully intended to listen in on the call.

ELIZE SOBBED, a crumpled heap just inside the portlock of the suite she shared with Enoch, frantically scrabbling at the ragged pit in her brow. The gem had to still be there, it had to! Her nails scored gory runnels into her flesh, blood streaking to her wrists.

Alone in her mind for the first time in a millennia.

Frenzied, she pulled talent, searching. *Where? Where? Oh! Where are you? Don't leave me! You promised —*

The portlock clicked and rolled open. Rapid footsteps.

"Elize!"

Enoch. He gripped her forearms, pulling her hands from her face and shaking her, the tips of her clawed fingers scarlet.

She struggled against him, pink-tinged snot and tears dripping down her face, diluting the branching trails of gore streaming down the sides of her nose. He didn't—couldn't—understand.

Her chin juddered. "No, no! Leave me be! She's gone, gone! I have to find her!"

Ragged holes left gaping by Mother's absence dotted her memories, her emotions, the taste of abandonment tripping across her tongue—What had she taken? What parts of Elize's past were gone with her? A creeping sense of something important, of something Elize desperately needed to know, of begging…

"How? How are you free?" Manic hope danced in the depths of Enoch's eyes, rivaling her horror. His grip tightened, and she cried out, her teeth clashing together as he shook her. He snarled, feral. "Tell me! Titus said something happened with the girl. Was it her? Did she do this?"

"I don't—I don't know. Jane—Mother was riding me." Elize pressed her lids shut, the room beginning to spin. "S-she touched the girl, tried to use her talent—"

Elize's eyes sprang open at Enoch's strangled grunt. He trembled, his face an enraged purple, spittle foaming at his lips.

Mother had him.

Talent sparked between them. Seething serpents of gold shot from the gem at his brow to twine around Elize and burrow back into her psyche. Her back arched, and she screamed—

Laughter. *There, there, child…*

Black.

Mother paced the dais before her couch, breath coming fast and her halos aglow as she fondled the shard at her brow, reestablishing her dominion over Elize. It slowly regained the deep amethyst of the Finder's talent. Thousands of miles away, the woman twitched as a new gem forced its way out of the bloody hole the old one had left; her will rebound. She lay in a heap, tangled with her brother, both rendered unconscious whilst Mother pondered the unexpected development.

She ignored the seed of fear attempting to root in her belly. Her temporary loss of control was an anomaly. A one off. She'd held the reins of thousands for a millennia without incident.

A frisson of the Jane-that-was rose to the surface, sowing doubts. *Then why was Elize able to slip her leash now? Perhaps we need to reconsider—*

Mother snorted, casting the pale shadow of herself back down. That was rich, coming from the girl that had been so very eager to birth the future. As if she had any right to question Mother's methods now that it was nigh.

Still…she frowned at what her idle curiosity had unearthed, having been wrong about the Jester girl before. The UnMaker, hidden in plain sight. Once again, Mother cursed Cal for pulling off that gambit…but with the girl's pregnancy muting her powers and Mother firmly in control of the other half of the girl's duality, it made little difference. Without the balance of Rebirth, Kara Jester's ability to UnMake was limited at best. She was just a tool to control others; bait for larger prey. Nothing but the means to an end.

…Then how were we rebuffed…?

Mother frowned at the Jane-that-was resurfacing, but she was right. It shouldn't have required any more than an afterthought to access the girl's psyche. The heavy, coma-inducing sedatives administered to keep her in stasis limited brain activity to basic metabolic responses.

The girl should've been an open book.

Instead, Mother had been hit with a wrecking ball of will that had shredded her weaves and sent her reeling across the continent, back into her own mind. She sat, drumming her fingers against her knee, replaying the incident.

Surprise had been what caused her to lose dominion over Elize, not any nuance of power, though there had been plenty of brute force. Now aware of the potential for retaliation, Mother wouldn't be caught nescient again…but with the question answered as to how it had happened, her thoughts turned to the who.

Because with that blast of will she'd encountered, she'd also heard a voice, and it had quite clearly claimed the girl as its own.

MARCOS WARILY EYED the crowd as he pushed through the press into the Marked Man. The Breaker pub was as packed as the streets around it, and that space between his shoulder blades itched.

He was still uneasy about leaving Nora at the Carmody's, for all she'd shooed him out of their new suite, adamant that she was fine, but he had to admit, he glad she wasn't with him in this part of the city.

The damage on the Breakers' spoke had been minimal, but the entire line was in an uproar with the same conversation on everyone's lips. Marcos frowned as he bellied up to the bar. How this damn city was still standing with the amount of division inside it…

The barkeep glanced his way then did a double take before ambling over. They'd met briefly upon the wall, and Marcos let out a breath at Sirrus's familiar face. He held out a hand to shake, and Marcos grasped it.

"Commandant. What can I do ye for?"

"Has Stonefist been by?"

"Aye. He's on the sands. Nash'll take ye below." He glanced down the bar and gave a curt nod. A man finished what was in his tankard and stood, working his way through the crowd, to them.

"Commandant. S'a pleasure, sir." The Breaker tipped his tam with the hook affixed to his wrist.

"Can I get ye somewhat before yer headed that way?" Sirrus offered, plucking a tankard from a line of them dangling from the rafter above. "Bit of the dark's just the thing, if ye want me recommendation."

Marcos paused, sorely tempted—oh, why the hell not? Might settle his nerves a bit while he waited for sunrise. The thought of good men out there, abandoned on the plateau—"Drop a shot into it for me, would you?"

"As ye say." Sirrus grinned, turning to pour.

"Ye hear tell what them hillie fucks is wantin' t'do?" a man asked. Marcos glanced over his shoulder at the irate voice, a group behind him deep in conversation.

"Aye, papers, reels, all of it's rife with their shite," another said. "Bastards is callin' for strippin' the Overlord of his title and exiling him. Say he's gone mad."

"The fuck he has, and over me dead body that'll happen—and I ken I ain't alone in that," growled a third.

"Nay. T'won't," said a fourth. "Thems turnin' their backs on one of our line after savin' their lily white arses ain't gonna fly. And after Scot lost his lady? Man must be a fuckin' wreck, but he ain't mad. City'd be a smokin' pit if he succumbed. Shites is just usin' that as an excuse."

The first frowned. "They exile him, and he'll lose his talent along with his mate and them bairns of his. Ain't no honor in killin' women and the unborn. S'pure evil right there."

"S'fuckin' persecution, pure and simple. Mark me words, the Alpha Prime'll call Conclave sooner than not," the fourth shot back. "Change is comin' and for once, I say Breakers should be leadin' it."

A tankard thumped down on the bar. "Dark with a shot."

Marcos started from his eavesdropping and dug into his pocket—

"Nay, yer money's no good here," Sirrus said, sliding the tankard toward him. "Head on back with Nash, he'll see ye t'where ye need t'be."

Marcos picked up the tankard and nodded his thanks, shaken by what he'd heard. At the Source, if a progenitor was problematic, they'd put them in stasis until the offspring were whelped. Not even they'd indiscriminately nullify a Talent if they were part of a breeding pair. What the hell was the Assembly thinking?

Someone jostled his arm, and he scowled, taking a sip from his tankard as he followed in the Breaker's wake. Damn. If that didn't just hit the spot. It was half gone before they made it to the back of the pub, and Nash rapped a pattern on a door. A moment later it opened, and Marcos was led through.

They descended into a basement far smokier and only slightly less crammed with people, all of them intent on whatever card games were being played at a smattering of tables. Nash ignored them, headed toward an isolated corner of bare foundation, and Marcos's neck prickled, fingers twitching for his sidearm.

Nash sniffed, running a finger under his nose. "Not t'worry, sir. I swear on me mother yer safe as a babe. Stonefist's this way. S'a Northern tradition t'spill blood on the sand if ye ain't spilled it in the field." He approached the corner and pointed out a stone. "Press here, then this, here." Something clicked and the section swung inward on silent hinges.

"Ain't the only way t'enter the sands, but it's the most popular for us commons." The distant sounds of a bout echoed up through a torch-lined darkness, and a wide grin split the Breaker's face. "The general is just through here, payin' his dues."

"I suspect I owe some of those, too," Marcos murmured, trying to tamp down his anticipation at the prospect of hitting someone. He drained his tankard. Damn it, the past twenty-four hours had been a clusterfuck and from what he'd just heard upstairs, it wasn't getting any better.

Nash laughed and slapped Marcos's shoulder. "Sirrus said ye were a good sort. What d'ye say I head up and fetch ye another of these, whilst ye head on down?"

Marcos allowed himself a smile. "I'd say that sounds like exactly what I need."

CHAPTER THREE

"Meskill has become unlivable. The land isn't right. Livestock, small creatures, bugs, they've long since abandoned the area, and those of us that remain are hunted at its fringes. A city in the far north has been proposed. Ri knows the area well, and he and K are confident they can shift in and fix whatever structures we need. The amount of power they're able to channel is astonishing, and the serenity they exude as the nimbus of talent around them grows is awe inspiring.

I admit to being envious, as are others. There are several established couples among us, but none are able to achieve the same. We've taken to calling them a dyad. El thinks it has to do with their talents being a duality. I wonder then, why she and A weren't able to achieve the same?

Perhaps they will when he returns, though we'll have to wait until after her baby comes. She's been unable to pull talent for several weeks. Losing her ability to find has only increased her anxiety. True or not, she's desperate to tell A he's going to be a father."

– Undated journal entry

FLYNN FELL TO HIS KNEES, spitting an odd medicinal funk from his mouth. A foreign anger thrummed through him. Goddamn it, whatever that'd been, it wasn't Kara. He took a deep breath, shaking his head to clear it of the weird lethargy that'd stolen over him along with the hazy impression of a lab somewhere.

Had that been real or was it bullshit? He blinked, then scrubbed a hand over his eyes, surprised to see the last glow of the setting sun behind the mountains in the west and the street lights on below. How long had he been up here? Fuck, maybe he'd dreamt it—

Gravel on the path behind him crunched, and Kendall strode around the bend, his hand cupping the glow of his cheroot against the wind. He stopped several feet away, eyes flicking to the naked blade dangling listlessly from Flynn's fingers, then back up.

Kendall frowned, flicking the ash from his little cigar. "You good?"

Flynn sat, putting his back to the parapet and tipping his head to look up at him. "Not especially."

The old man grunted, sucking on his teeth. "No. Can't imagine so. Rest of us aren't doing so hot, either." He closed space between them and stood at the low wall, looking out, over the city. A gust blasted over the rooftop, and Kendall shivered, his shoulders rising to his ears. "Hell of a view. Could do without the wind, though."

"You get used to it," Flynn murmured, snicking the blade closed and pocketing it.

"About that…" The grizzled man pulled another cheroot from his breast pocket. "Smoke?"

The cellophane crinkled as Flynn took the little cigar and rolled it between his fingers, forearms arms resting on his knees, not sure he could stomach it, or whatever his old CO was about to say. Christ, he didn't want to do this.

"I am truly sorry, son," Kendall began, staring out over the parapet. "We fucked up. It's no excuse, but it never occurred to us that it was possible for someone to just shift in like that."

"Shouldn't have been. Cal…" Flynn shook his head. "It wasn't your fault, it was mine. There was a bunch of stuff I didn't know." And he was sure the twins weren't the last of it. Hell, he'd still be in the dark if Rogan hadn't pried it out of the old man, but Cal was Cal; shady as fuck. The fact that shit from his past was coming home to roost wasn't a surprise, but it was that he'd let Kara get sucked into it. Phantom flames flickered at the corner of Flynn's eye with his anger, and he swept a hand over his face.

Kendall shook his head. "Regardless of quality intel or lack thereof, the job shouldn't have gone sideways. Not to that extent. We were lax. Kerns shouldn't have been alone in that room. At minimum, there should've been another man, if not two, in the living area and a third riding the elevator. It was negligent on our part, and though I understand if you'd prefer to see us on our merry, I'm here to offer up whatever we need to do to help make this right. Any resources I have are yours for as long as you need them, and if that's until those kids of yours are in college, so be it."

What? Flynn stared up at him, speechless. No way was any of this on Kendall or the outfit.

The old man frowned, squinting off into the distance as he smoked. "I told you before that if you wanted us, you had us."

"Kendall, I can't—Kerns died because I didn't—"

"Bullshit. Everything that happened in that room was on her head, and you damned well know she'd say she got exactly what she deserved for letting her guard down—and she'd be right. There was no fight. She wasn't wearing her sidearm. Single, clean slice, ear to ear. Nothing but her own blood on her hands. Whoever killed her took her completely by surprise. Way that suite's set up, she had to've walked right past her attacker for them to get behind her like that. That's incompetence, plain and simple, and she'd be livid at herself."

Flynn swallowed his objections and frowned, but Kendall wasn't wrong.

"What a fucking mess." The CO's gaze swept over Glynfyls again. "Half the city thinks you've gone mad, the Assembly is calling for your head, and none of it would've happened if we'd just done our job."

Flynn stood, the man's logic fucking with him. "No, that's not—"

"I'd go in there and offer mine up on a silver platter if I thought it'd do a damned bit of good—it's turned into a witch hunt, and they're hell bent on seeing you on the pyre, but I swear to God, son, they're gonna have to go through me and my men to do it."

"I can't ask you to do that." Flynn couldn't meet his eye—couldn't see any more people he cared about die because of him. The scent of burning flesh thickened in his nose. He coughed, then spat to the side. Phantom flames skittered along the walkway, and he wet his lips, watching them trail away and flicker out.

"No shit. That's why I'm up here. Bates told me to tell you to stop martyring yourself, and he's right. Take the help we're offering, because in all honesty, you're getting it whether you like it or not. That's what family does, and the last thing we need is Kerns haunting our asses for leaving you in the lurch after her fuck up. Now light your damned cigar." Kendall held up a book of matches between his first two fingers.

She'd do it, too. A knot swelled in Flynn's throat, his hand shaking as he reached out to take the little book. He fumbled and dropped them, blinking back tears.

"Here." Kendall handed him his smoke. "Try that."

Flynn held it to the tip of his cheroot and took a deep drag as it began to smolder, the smoke cutting down into his lungs and grounding him. He handed Kendall's back, then wiped the crook of his arm over his face, trying to pull some nonchalance out of his ass and not see the ghostly flames dancing along the parapet. "So, that island of yours...it a good place to raise kids?"

Kendall snorted. "After what you did out there? I suspect any place is a good place to raise kids if you're the Hand of God. Can't imagine any of the vultures in the Deep South are gonna be hot to wind up like Titus's Elites."

Flynn's stomach flipped at that reminder, but what if he wasn't anymore? He tapped off his ash, feeling sick. His talent was fucked. Whatever he could access now...its sporadic manifestation...shit. What if it didn't come back all the way? How the hell was he going to get Kara back, or his kids? How would he protect them if he did?

"But, that said," Kendall continued, "it doesn't mean they won't still be circling."

No, and just like Cal's fucking twins, they'd be searching for weaknesses, waiting to strike. Titus had seen to that. They'd never be safe. The world knew what Flynn could do. About Kara and the babies. Their potential. The Deep South would be a trap. The anonymity of hiding Outside was no longer an option and heading West…

A desperate yearning knocked the breath from him.

…dust swirls, condensing and fusing into bone. Muscles grow, ligaments and sinew snapping into place, flesh springing into existence, flowing to cover soft tissue, organs, light flares in his skull, and he blinks, colors and patterns falling into place as they register, thoughts ascribing meaning, cataloging and defining the gaping void where she should be…something—he —howls…

"You okay, son?" Kendall asked, snapping Flynn back into the present.

No. "Yeah." His voice cracked. The phantom flames around him flared. Fuck, they weren't real. He knew they weren't real. He took a deep drag from the cheroot, nicotine rushing to his head then landing in his stomach like a lump. A wave of nausea rolled over him, keenly aware of Kendall watching his every move.

Christ. Flynn took another drag, hating himself. Hating that Kendall had seen this before. That he knew what a fucking pussy he was. Fuck, he turned away and dashed a hand across his eyes again.

"You know," Kendall flicked his butt over the parapet, then put his back to the low wall, "best thing to do in these situations is to keep the high ground, and I can't see being much higher than this. Go get your wife and kids. Tonight we're cremating Kerns, and tomorrow we'll run interference and keep the flat secure for you to bring your family back here."

Flynn swallowed the lump in his throat, flames licking at the edges of his vision.

…tomorrow will be a new day, free of today's unpleasantness. Things may just look rosier…

The flames around him surged, licking up Flynn's legs. He broke out in a sweat, stepping back, wanting to run… *They're not real, they're not fucking real…* He wiped the back of his hand over his mouth.

Fuck. Maybe he was mad.

"I dunno. I can't—" Flynn squeezed his eyes shut then blinked, trying to make the flames retreat to the edge of his vision—

Colors ran.

He was back in the bedroom of his suite, his mouth dry as he panted, backlit by the stippled light of phantom flames.

"Fuck!" He tore at his hair and put a fist through the wall. Plaster puffed out, crumbling and pinging to the ground. A sad laugh slipped from his lips. "I can't—can't do this...Fuck. Yes, I can. I will. Tomorrow. Tomorrow things will be rosier..."

He slammed the bedroom door behind him and locked it. Back to the wall, he slid to sit, bringing his knees to his chest and rocking. Chewing the scar on his lip and watching the flames.

FITZ STARTLED from sleep at a loud bang and somewhat furry rubbed against his face. It purred, nosing at him. A rough tongue swept over his cheek, and he frowned, not ready to wake—

Sharp teeth clamped into his brow quick as an asp, and he yelped, hand over his eye and flinched back, tumbling from a couch to the floor. The air went out of him as he hit, and he groaned, rolling to his side on the rough cedar boards. A furry streak of gray-striped malevolence disappeared in the other direction.

Fuckin' cat...the hell had that come from? He blew out a breath, nose wrinkling with the urge to sneeze. Grit beneath his fingers were old and musty, like it'd sat undisturbed 'til now. Shite, the hell with the cat, where the fuck were he? Last thing he remembered, he were looking for Nora Jester after that shite, Leo, had stabbed him...but he'd been at Scot's flat then, hadn't he?

Fitz rubbed his poor abused brow. At least, he thought he remembered that, but wherever he were, he must've found a Binder somewhere along the way. Aside from the throbbing where that vicious beastie had just bitten him, he didn't feel too bad. Channel were sore, but a far cry from the misery it had been, and his side were right as rain beneath—

Right. That were a problem.

Fitz sat up and frowned at the bloodied shirt Markham had lent him, a sticky slick of the half-dried stuff tagging him from armpit to knee. A matching stain ran a good length of the couch. He gingerly pulled talent, wincing as he shifted the mess on him to join it. Weren't no sense in walking around like a horror victim, and them cushions was gonna need attention anyway.

He stared at the sopping mess when he were done. Jesus. All that'd come outta him? Were enough gore to suit a shark bite. How many fucking times could a bloke almost die in a day? Fitz scowled, feeling Cajetan's glee over the near misses.

Wise it, ye shite. If I were done in, who the fuck would ye have t'torment then? he thought at the blessed saint. Coin in his pocket went cold, and he grunted. *S'what I thought, ye bastard.*

And Fitz were positive that it weren't no thanks to Cajetan that he were still this side of the veil. Fitz scrubbed his face and took in the rest of his surroundings, vibe of the place nasty enough to curl his toes. Room were shitty as the rest of the Overlord's flat, but—

His gaze landed on a mess of energy like he'd seen at the Rhineroom—a gate-that-weren't one—on the far side of the room and then a swirl of auric rot by a closed door at the other that meant someone had just been done in.

His stomach heaved at how fresh the signature were. Shite. And him betwixt the two, not a stone's throw from the deed? Weren't no body he could see, but—his hand flattened against the gritty floorboards.

Christ. He'd put money on the corpse getting shifted out with the carpet. And if thems that'd done it was cleanin' up after themselves, meant him being sound weren't a loose end, they was trying to pin it on him.

Right. Time to go—

Fitz froze at the sound of someone moving around behind that closed door. Shite, they was still here?

He swallowed and got to his feet, silently cursing as he scanned the room for his jacket. Were partial to that peacoat and aside from his gran's laudanum, it had a stack of units he'd prefer not t'leave behind —'specially if he were about t'be on the lam—

Another door opened and shut farther in, and then the sound of water kicked on in another room.

Now wouldn't that be a treat. Soon as he got out of here, a wash were at the top of his t'do list. Fitz scratched his stubbly jaw, relaxing a tick as he searched. Jacket had to be somewhere around here…

He headed toward the windows to get his bearings, jamming tails of Markham's shirt into his trousers and missing his skin somewhat fierce. Felt naked without the damned undershirt beneath the rest of his clothes.

Way the vista opened up beyond the thick glass, he were definitely in the—

Jesus, Mary, and Joseph. The fuck had he slept through? Fitz raked a hand through his curls. City thrummed the mustard yellow of fear and the red of anger through billowing smoke, so much rogue energy crazing around the destruction it were making him sicker than anything this side of the glass. Had the Source won? He stumbled back, catching hisself against the door jamb—

His stomach heaved, teeth set on edge.

The ward he'd set on the lady streamed out to the east, and the bit of energy tying him back to Scot through her ended somewhere on the other side of the slab he were leaning against.

Fitz blinked, pinching the bridge of his nose as he staggered, about ready to puke. Following his oath bond to the man were like trying to look through multi-colored wool roving, Scot's energy mashed up with every bond he'd taken, then spun out and amplified like it'd been blown t'shite and were hanging about him in a dense cloud.

Wait. Fitz's throat bobbed. If he were here, and she were there—

Jesus. The lady'd been shanghaied.

He slapped a hand over his mouth and backed from the doorway, stumbling over the damned cat. He swept the beastie up, his pulse thrumming in his ears. A murder, and the city in ruins. He'd bet good money it weren't Titus that'd happened out there. Nah. If she were gone, the Overlord were out for blood.

Were just a matter of time before he tried to collect on Fitz's. Had t'be why the man were here and not after her yet. Fitz froze, his knackers drawing up.

He were next.

*Right, right, right…think, think, think…*He paced the room, absently scritchin' the cat and not quite pissin' hisself. Needed to get his gran square, and then he'd go to ground. If Markham'd turned Leo over to the sisters like he'd been plannin', Fitz probably had a reprieve from them, which meant it were safe to check in with Marl at the pub, then to tend to her.

And if it weren't, with the snaggled mess of energy tying him back to the Overlord peeking though the ward he'd set on the lady—

The blood drained from Fitz's face. Whatever Scot had done, weren't no way to hide that Fitz had pledged now. Shite, if the sisters got even a sniff of that, he were fucked. Needed to cut that connection—

Coin seared so cold in his pocket he yelped. *Shite, ye fuck! The hell ye want me t'do? I can't rightly leave it—*

Cat butted its head up under his chin, and Fitz's brow rose. Now there were an idea…Whether the saint approved or no, the blessed bastard kept mum as Fitz slipped the ward from hisself to the—

Beastie's fur stood on end, and it yowled, scrambling to get away like its tail were on fire. Fitz dropped it, and the thing took off, diving beneath the couch. He brushed hisself off, wincing at the scratches that bit of duplicity'd cost him. Fucking cat. Didn't do it no harm, though he couldn't see how keeping the ward live were doing anyone else any good.

He shrugged, wiping a smear of blood from his hand. Not his problem. Finding his jacket were. He scanned the dimly lit room— there. Had slid off the back of a chair into the shadows. He shrugged into the peacoat and sighed, feeling better with its weight across his shoulders.

Weren't a moment too soon. The water in the next room cut off, and Fitz pulled talent, shifting to the Sailor's Pipe.

Energy of the city hit him like a brick. Fear with an undercurrent of anger so thick he could taste the shite. Fuck. He was too damned sober for this. He winced, channel stinging as he shut his extra down, all the energy in the room snuffing out at once. Christ. Always felt like he were cleaving away a limb. Wanted to puke, and all that back at Scot's flat had already put his stomach on tilt.

Fitz staggered to the bar, not paying much mind to the grumbling of the custom. Didn't look like Craig nor Scotty was there, and Marl weren't at his usual stool. Adelaide weren't workin' the room neither. Fitz's stomach churned again.

"Bottle o' whiskey," he said, resting his elbows on the sticky wood and pulling his hair. Needed somewhat more than an ale to numb the anxious nausea clawing his insides.

Molly came over with a bottle and took a deep breath as she set it before him. "Here…s'on the house."

"No, it ain't." He glared at her through his curls, ego still sore from the dressing down she'd given him in her da's loft. He'd taken her charity once and gotten hell for it, he sure as fuck weren't taking it now.

He reached into his pocket and threw a handful of units onto the bar. She winced at them scattering, his odd, nine-sided coin whirling with the rest. Fitz snatched the scrap of bronze as it came to rest exactly on its edge, image of the saint laughing at him.

"Fitz, I'm sorry for—"

"Don't care. Pamela workin'?" He spun the cap off the bottle and took a deep swallow.

Molly bit her lip and gave her head a shake, eyes all sorrowful as she counted out coins, then pushed the rest back at him.

Fitz grunted and swept them up, his anger faltering, then dying as he caught sight of the reels playing over her shoulder. Jesus fuck. Guess he were right about it not being Titus. He took another mouthful of liquor, watching the account of the devastation.

"S'real bad over on the Finders' spoke," Molly said, fiddling with a bar cloth. She turned to watch the screen with him. "Hear tell it's cracked open like an egg."

"Tis," said someone's missus farther down. "Ye should see the buildings canted over the rend like bridges. S'like somewhat outta a fae tale, man breaking the world for his lover like that."

The women around the bar, and more than a few men, gave a collective sigh. Fitz didn't see the appeal, but t'each his own. He tipped back his bottle, letting the liquor numb him.

"Ain't no chance of Gil doin' the same for ye, Loretta!" a gaffer cackled.

"And don't I know it," she shot back, "but mark me words, the

Overlord'll be bringing the lady and them bairns of his back home, or die trying." She raised her tankard, her and the rest of the bar drinking to that.

"Eh…ye happen t'know how the Pinch made out?" Fitz asked.

"Didna move," another man said, "and sure enough, that's a sign from the Lord above that it truly is rock bottom."

Fitz toasted him; man certainly had a point.

"What I want t'know is how the hell'd anybody get to the lady?" a whore chimed in, fingering a bowl of nuts.

Another slapped her hand away and took some for herself. "Aye, ye'd think he'd have taken precautions."

A still of Scot flashed up on the screen, and the pub raised their tankards again with a cheer.

"I'll bet he did, but with how two-faced them hillies is? Me money's on betrayal."

"Aye." One of the whores tapped the side of her nose, agreeing with the gaffer. "Were probably that shite cousin of his, Arileo. Ye hear tell they stripped his arse and set him t'swing? Wish I'd been there for the deed. Bastard were a right miserable fuck."

"Funny how they ain't took the Scot side of his rhian when they did," a man farther down muttered.

"Scots is Shades," someone else scoffed. "The fuck if they know what leavin' their House tattoo on his back means. Nah, weren't no love lost betwixt them two. I'd put good money on that bein' pure theater."

"Aye, and when Scot tracks down who done him dirty?" The gaffer cackled. "Now that's gonna be somewhat t'see."

Fitz took a long swallow from his bottle and wiped at the sheen of sweat that'd sprung up on his brow. The reel swapped to footage of the front of the Assembly building. Some fat little troll of a lord stood all puffed up in front of a crowd. Looked like that rich frog from the story books that drove cars. The pub broke out in boos, and a rain of peanuts pinged off the screen.

"Hey now, none of that or I'll turn it off!" Molly snapped.

"Better than listening t'the shite that come out of Morris's mouth," the gaffer muttered. "Ye hear on account of that purist prick, they're haulin' in the Overlord for questioning this very minute?"

"So soon after he lost his lady?" a whore gasped. "And they call themselves genteel?"

Loretta snorted from behind her ale. "Heard tell more'n that. Rumors is, thems on the hill is looking t'exile him and kill them babies if she's blessed enough to still be carryin' them. Wanna wipe out his whole House and hers to boot. Can't stand havin' a real man in charge. Would rather listen t'that scrawny Intelligencer telling them it's raining whist he's pissin' down their backs, or Morris spoutin' his hate."

"Monsters."

"Ain't a lick of sense past the third rung," the gaffer muttered.

"Ye serious?" someone else cried. "With all Scot's done for us? Saved our bacon he did. I say we nullify them!" The crowd cheered again, well and truly wound.

Right. Someone's shite were getting fucked up tonight. Another ale or two and they'd be marchin'. Fitz ran a hand over his mouth. That were his cue. "Eh, ye see Marl of late?" he asked Molly.

"Were here earlier. Cleared out after the quakes to check his trawler along with the rest worried about their livelihoods." She glanced at him and her cheeks pinked. Bet she thought it were a right personal failing of his that he had naught t'attend to.

Fitz took another mouthful of liquor, silent as his anger roared back. A muscle in his jaw jumped. This right here. This were why he didn't truck with regular girls. Always came down to shite like this. Shoulda known better than to mess with her.

"Ye know anything about them?" Molly asked, head cocked as she dried a glass.

"Livelihoods? Nah. Prefer to gamble and whore away all me prospects."

"Good man!" the bloke on the stool beside him cried, raising his glass before he threw back what was in it. Fitz toasted him back, downing a mouthful from his bottle.

Molly's cheeks flared from pink to red. Weren't nearly as beguiling as it had been. "I-I meant the quakes. I heard tell ye was workin' for Lord Scot."

"Ye heard wrong." After this, there weren't a chance in hell he were going anywhere near the man. Fitz tapped his knuckles against the bar, contemplating if he were fortified enough to face his gran, since checking in with Marl were a bust. She'd be waiting on her damnable meds, growin' more sour by the—

"Funny, I heard that, too," a bloke with no neck a handful of seats away chimed in. Dopey haircut peaked up high then curled in around his face. Made him look like a peckerhead. Fitting. Fitz were pretty sure he were one of Prydee's boys.

"Ya? And who the hell asked ye?" he shot back. Christ, the man above were hell bent on testin' him today. Fitz took another swallow and grimaced, positive he were about to be found wantin'.

"Who asked me? Ye think I'm one t'wait for an invitation?" Peckerhead pushed his stool back and stood, a fuckin' mountain of a man. The patrons between them grabbed their drinks and made themselves scarce.

Fitz sighed as the behemoth crossed the length of the bar toward him. "I'll tell ye true, friend, I ain't currently in the mood to deal with aught more'n I already am. Ye mind doin' me a solid and fucking off?"

Peckerhead smiled, showin' the gaps in his mouth where teeth shoulda been. "With the size of the bounty the sisters put on ye? Not a chance."

"For fuck's sake—" Fitz capped his bottle and shoved it into his jacket. "Right. Then let's go," he said, motioning for the prick to lead the way.

Peckerhead's brows shot into his too-smooth hairline. He dusted his knuckles across his palm. "Erm…just like that? I'd figured ye was gonna need some convincin'."

"Normally, I'd agree, but this here?" Fitz shrugged. "Seems like the better deal given me current options." Sisters wouldn't piss on him if he were on fire, but they was right misers with what they thought were theirs.

His knackers drew up at the prospect of handing hisself over, but he knew damned well he couldn't dodge 'em forever. Better him than his gran, and Marl'd get word of what went down here and see to her if the sisters messed him up bad.

Wouldn't be nothin' like what Scot were gonna do to him.

Fitz fondled his coin, but the damned thing stayed dead as a smelt for all the blessed saint were so adamant over shite earlier. *Fat lotta help ye is.* Whatever, he were doin' it.

Peckerhead didn't seem convinced either, but fuck him. "Kristine's?" Fitz prompted.

The behemoth blinked at him then gave a halting nod. Right. Good enough. Fitz grabbed the front of the idjit's jacket and shifted them up the hill before he thought better of it.

LORD PETERLI MORRIS sat in chambers, seething along with the rest of Glynfyls's respectable society. The special session he'd instigated wasn't as well attended as he'd hoped, but that was only to be expected. The majority of the Finders were scrambling to save what was left of their spoke, and the bulk of the Breakers were attending their parody of church. The fact that none of the Firsts were in attendance was vexing, but the turnout of the remaining four lines was enough to call and pass a motion, which was really all he needed.

Well, that and Scot. An earlier vote had determined the room wasn't quite ready to haul the scoundrel in by his short hairs, though by now, they might be. Waiting for him to make an appearance was taking entirely too long. That entitled mongrel should've been here twenty minutes ago, trembling before his betters instead of making them wait upon his sufferance.

That backwards attitude needed to be rectified, and Peterli was keen to do it.

Though hardly any time had passed since he'd last checked his pocket watch, he pulled it from his waistcoat, cursing that entire filthy House as he clicked it open—his temper spiked at the laminated still of his wife and son opposite the dial, their smiling faces a dagger to his heart. It was bad enough that Paul had bonded—*bonded!*—that twisted trollop, Shelby Scot, but Augusta condoning the relationship—going so far as to *hide* it from him—

The utter insult of his wife's knowledge of the unhealthy

infatuation seared through him. God forgive him for not following his instincts and forbidding his son to partner with that willowy whore. One year. Twelve whole months Paul had been cozied up to that filthy twist. She was toothsome, Peterli would give her that, but that was how they ensnared you. He didn't blame Paul for taking his pleasure with the little slut, bend her over if you must, but to *bond* her—He might as well have wed his horse for the pleasure of riding it.

Disgusted, Peterli snapped the watch closed, his fist tightening on the case, thinking back to the clues, to the signs that the girl had tainted Paul. The way Augusta had brushed off objections, had cited the girl's ballroom scores as if that justified their familiarity…

… *"Dancing, it's only dancing, Peterli! It's skill that matters in the ballroom, not one's pedigree, and they're both professionals! For goodness sake, how many partners did I have when I competed?…"*

Indeed, he thought sourly. How many partners did you have, Augusta? In retrospect, his son's corruption had been inevitable with such a weak-moraled woman whispering in his ear.

But that didn't excuse it. A Morris should be made of stronger stuff.

Peterli shoved his watch back onto his waistcoat and tugged the mauve silk smooth over his prodigious belly, making an effort to slow the rapidity of his breath. His gaze went from the smattering of irate Finders populating their section to the abundance of the Source's Binders crammed into the gallery above. Here to witness the proceedings and to support Lady Hess, no doubt.

The virago had made quite an entrance earlier, descending into chambers, bold as brass, to take up residence in the First Binders' box. Normally, Peterli would've taken a great deal of pleasure knocking her down a peg by citing Assembly protocol after such an audacious display, despite the fact that none of her line, north or south, had uttered a word of objection. However, given her known disdain for House Scot and the Jesters, far be it from him to remind anyone of procedure. He was willing to let things play out—for now.

Lady Hess glanced up and their eyes met. Her breath noticeably caught beneath his scrutiny. She looked away, a delicate blush staining her considerable bosom. Peterli wet his lips, quite enjoying the exchange. Were the rumors he'd heard true? Talents from the Source were supposed to have sordid inclinations…

She glanced at him again, and this time, she held his gaze.

Brazen of her. Peterli adjusted his crotch, abruptly positive he could count on the Binders for support in his initiative. Though there were far more women in attendance from their line than seemly, if they were anything like their Northern brethren, they wouldn't stand for a mongrel in power, either.

And after Scot's most recent disastrous use of talent, neither would all the bleeding hearts that'd previously been on the fence. How could anyone possibly continue to entrust power to a man who wantonly wreaked havoc?

In Peterli's opinion, there had never been any justification for it, but now that the threat from the Source was gone—a threat that twisted paramour of Scot's had instigated—no rational citizen could possibly support such a monster.

Peterli schooled his expression at the patently false demure nature of Serra's smile. He looked away, coughing into his fist. A slattern indeed, but if he could use her to further his agenda…

He'd been doing his best to fan the flames after the sundering of the plateau and subsequent destruction of the city had terrified the populace, but as stirring an orator as he was, a softer, feminine voice as a counterpoint would be welcome. A carrot to his stick, as it were.

And now that he knew why Augusta had refused to decry that fetid House, he had no guilt filling her shoes with one who would. Nor would she have any right to object. Perhaps the Lady Hess would be so inclined…? The rally he'd scheduled after this was sure to be well attended. He'd have to make sure to extend her a personal invitation.

A low murmur kicked up at the back of the hall, and Peterli turned, his eyes narrowing. That weaselly patriarch of House Scot, Caliban, was descending into the room with a boneless saunter at odds with the seriousness of the charges being leveled against his heir.

Of which, there was still no sign.

Typical. The repellent enabler passed, making his way to the podium at the center of the floor to speak with Riggs. Whatever Scot had to say, it looked like it was being listened to with far more sympathy than it should. Peterli frowned. Amos Riggs always had been a sucker for a sob story. Their little tête-à-tête lasted less than a minute, then they shook hands, and Scot headed for the First Shade's box.

Peterli swallowed the venom poised at the tip of his tongue. *Enjoy it while you can, old man.*

Riggs waited for him to be seated, then banged his gavel, bringing the meeting to order.

"Ah, If I can have your attention? I have…ah…new…ah, dear me. Terrible. It's simply terrible…" He took out his handkerchief and blotted his upper lip, then picked at the cloth with trembling fingers as the room quieted. "That poor, sweet woman." He shook his head, his eyes gone rheumy. "I've just received confirmation that the Lady Scot has indeed been abducted."

"How?!"

"But she's so ill!"

"—And the babies!"

"Laughlin must be devastated…"

"…doesn't excuse it!"

So the rumors were true. Peterli frowned as shock and dismay reverberated through the hall, Scot's knocked-up paramour providing far too sympathetic a figure. Morris's teeth gritted together as his gaze landed back on Caliban Scot, the sag of the man's head between bowed shoulders so obviously pandering to the crowd. Why no one else could see his performance for the theater it was—

"House Scot believes the trauma of the event has interfered with Laughlin's ability to access talent, including the powers of the Overlord," Riggs continued. "He's understandably not himself at the moment, and they've requested that we postpone questioning him until the lady—"

"Preposterous!" Peterli cried, shooting to his feet. "He needs to be held accountable for his actions *today*, not in ten! The chaos and destruction he's caused are grounds to have him immediately removed from office, if not the city! The devastation of the plateau, of Glynfyls— these are not the actions of a stable man. He's gone mad, and letting him retain use of any talent—the Overlord's or that he was born with —is irresponsible!"

"I concur," Lady Hess said, standing as he finished. "He's obviously a danger to himself and others, and as the caretakers of Glynfyls, we have a responsibility to limit his ability to cause harm."

Peterli barely restrained himself from clapping. Remarkable. Now *that* was exactly the kind of woman he needed at his side. Her eyes caught his as she sat, and he tipped his head in acknowledgment of her support.

Riggs pushed his spectacles higher onto his bulbous nose. "Ah, yes, however, based on what we've been told, Lord Scot is currently unable to pull talent—"

"Based on what we've been told," Peterli scoffed. "And with House Scot's history of covering up the boy's malfeasance, how are we to believe anything they say?"

"I say he should be here to explain himself regardless!" one of the few men from the Finders' section yelled. "Our entire spoke has been destroyed, people are missing—dead—we've lost our homes, our livelihoods—one man's upset does not cancel out the suffering of thousands! This cannot go unanswered!"

The room devolved into a flurry of agreement. Riggs banged his gavel for order. Exasperated, he turned to the Shades' section, yelling over the clamor as it subsided.

"Master Scot, although I can appreciate that Laughlin is understandably out of sorts by the loss of his lady, I'm afraid I agree that we are owed answers and entitled to judge whether he's a threat for ourselves." Riggs looked around the room. "I don't believe there's any need for a vote. We'll expect him here tomorrow, nine a.m., sharp."

Caliban Scot pursed his lips and gave a curt nod as he stood, leaving the room with as little reverence as he'd entered.

"Well. I suppose that's it then," Riggs said, banging his gavel again to end the session.

The room slowly started to clear, and Peterli stood. Several people that had previously shunned him came over to speak about his initiative. As he'd expected, today's events more than justified his staunch opposition to half-breeds and exemplified the dangers of allowing them to hold power. The Purist laws on the books were set to protect the decent people of Glynfyls. Current anti-twist legislation should not only be rigorously enforced, but expanded upon. His rhetoric was met with judicious nods and promises of support.

Peterli's chest puffed out as they conversed, keeping watch on the others in the room. Who conferred with who, who left together. Now, more than ever, was the time to make strategic alliances.

And speaking of which…Lady Hess caught his eye as the group around him thinned. Augusta and that twist-loving son of his could hang on the gallows of their own making. Peterli tugged his waistcoat as the lady approached. He was more than ready to make her formal acquaintance.

***

ROGAN SQUINTED up at Leo's body dangling by its ankles from the lowest spar of the yaw. Around the massive pole, the coliseum teemed with people. The party that'd begun hours earlier had morphed into a rally of discontent. Somebody should really kill the reel playing along the far wall. The past footage of Lord Morris calling for Flynn's head wasn't going over well with the commons—

A cry abruptly went up, people yelling and shouting at the projection.

Yeah, that wasn't gonna end well for anybody. Rogan ran a hand down his face, not questioning why he'd returned to Glynfyls anymore, but he definitely hadn't signed up for a revolution. He shook his head and planted his hands on his hips, looking back up at what was left of Leo.

The traitor's corpse spun slowly, giving the entire coliseum a three hundred and sixty degree view of the gaping hole in his chest and the bloody musculature where half the flesh on his back had been flayed. The black glyphs tattooed on the other half stood out starkly against his bloodless skin.

"Let me guess, leaving the Scot side of his rhian is some kind of message."

"It is, and not a favorable one," Markham said at Rogan's elbow.

The big Fetch blotted his neck, staring up at his erstwhile nephew with disgust. "I'm afraid the connotation is that House Scot still claims the boy, and condones whatever actions earned his stripping from House Prydee's roles."

"Lovely. And the hole in his chest? That wasn't made by any weapon I know of."

Markham paused. "No, It's the result of a heart plug being pulled and, quite frankly, that's a great deal more concerning than House Scot's rhian being left behind." He absently picked at his handkerchief as he squinted back up at Leo's corpse.

"Go on…" Rogan prodded after the body had spun another full circuit.

Markham shook his head sadly. "Would that I could, but I'm afraid that's—"

"Lemme guess, a House Matter." A pack of kids ran by, and Rogan swore again. House Matter or not, it wasn't a particularly family-friendly display…but then again this was Glynfyls. "Any reason he hasn't been cut down yet?"

"Other than to continue proving a point that's already been made?" Markham shook his head. "No."

"Then the show's over." Rogan's halos flared, and the corpse ignited, much to the delight of the surrounding crowd.

"Ah…that might not be terribly—"

The rope suspending the body snapped, and it plummeted, landing on the purple pad of ink below with a sickening thump a breath before it went up in a whoosh of flame.

"—wise," Markham finished. The crowd screamed, edging away in rapt horror.

"For the love of—" Rogan's halos flared again, and the flames condensed into a blue white surge of talent that flashed and was gone, leaving nothing but a pile of ash at the base of the singed yaw.

"I rescind my previous comment," Markham murmured. Several people in the crowd applauded before drifting away.

Rogan grunted and stalked over. Not bad. It'd been a hot minute since he'd pulled enough talent to manifest plasma. But then again, he couldn't remember the last time he'd been so fucking irritated with everything for just existing.

Markham sniffed, his handkerchief over his nose as he approached. "Well, I suppose that's the end of it—"

"Hardly. Lord Firestorm, please tell me I did not just see you willfully destroy evidence in an ongoing investigation?"

Crandall.

And today just kept getting better and better. Rogan sighed, fighting the urge to groan aloud. He turned, the oily little Intelligencer flanked by a bevy of his men. "Don't you have enough to keep you busy with the impending revolution and the shit show in your spoke?"

Crandall smoothed his goatee before shoving his hands in his pockets. He laughed, rocking back on the heels of his wingtips. "You'd think that, wouldn't you? And you'd be right, but I find the key to effective leadership is delegation. After all, when the cat's away, the mice will play, now won't they? Rest assured, my captains have things well in hand. Meanwhile, I've been trying to find an opportunity to speak with you, and for whatever reason, this appears to be it. Imagine my surprise walking in on a felony." He tutted, shaking his head.

"I'm sure you're appalled." Rogan's frown deepened as he crossed his arms over his chest and widened his stance. Fuck this guy. "How about you get over it and tell me what you want. I've got things to do."

"Now, now, there's no cause for animosity between us." Crandall smiled. "Especially when I'm about to offer you and yours an olive branch."

"Can't wait to hear what you're gonna want in return."

"Surprisingly, the same thing you do; to get Laughlin Scot out of this city."

Rogan's eyes narrowed. "Keep talking."

Crandall turned to his men and murmured something. They dispersed into the crowd as the Intelligencer came closer. "In case you're unaware, the political climate of Glynfyls has become somewhat charged—"

Rogan snorted. "You don't say?"

"And you've nothing to do with that," Markham huffed.

"I believe we've all played our respective parts, Kyle," Crandall shot back. "Nice work getting the commons to riot the first time, by the way. It took me quite a bit of finding to suss out your hand in that."

"I've no idea what you're talking about," Markham sputtered, indignantly blotting his brow.

Crandall sighed, eyeing the crowd. "Regardless, this time, there is no governor. Rumor has flown far and wide that the Assembly wants to exile Laughlin, and the commons are up in arms over it. Where the hill sees him as a liability hell bent on destruction, they see him as a hero who's just lost his fated love whilst protecting them from certain death—" Crandall ran a hand over his mouth, more flustered than Rogan had ever seen him.

The Intelligencer took a deep breath, collecting himself. "Lord Morris has just pushed through a motion that will essentially put Laughlin on trial tomorrow. With his rhetoric in the forefront of the Assembly's mind, riling up anti-twist sentiment, the probability that the hill backs down like it did last time is slim to none. They will vote to exile him, and the commons will lose its collective mind."

"You're talking civil war," Rogan murmured.

"I am." Crandall wet his lips. "Which necessitates my olive branch. I'm more than happy to look the other way while you take that craft the Source left behind and leave. The commons will settle, content that Laughlin has left on a quest to rescue his lady, and the hill—"

"Will reestablish status quo," Markham finished, looking less pleased about that than Rogan would've thought. "And Kara? His children? You know very well exile will mean him losing his talent, and as soon as he does, they'll die."

Crandall met his eye and didn't answer.

"I see." Markham's lips pursed. "Well, I suspect that's better than the alternative, for you at least, eh, Bart?"

"I've no idea what you're talking about," Crandall deadpanned the words back at him, then checked his watch. "You have one hour to take custody of the craft, signaling your amenability to my terms. Should it still be there after the allotted time, I'll have no choice but to release the paperwork citing Laughlin as a flight risk and implicating him in the murder of Cordelia Kerns. It's quite convenient how people he has umbrage with keep turning up with their throats slit."

"You know damned well he didn't kill Kerns," Rogan growled, struggling not to turn the little shit into ash.

Crandall shrugged. "It's not my job to determine guilt or innocence, only to present the facts…which I'm afraid are often quite subjective. I'd suggest you move before we take him into custody. It would be a shame if during transport some of the more fervent supporters of Lord Morris's rhetoric were to fall upon the Overlord in his weakened state. Heavens knows what could happen."

His smirk widened to a smile, and Rogan grinned back, positive if something did happen, it wasn't gonna end the way this motherfucker thought.

"He's not nearly as clever as he thinks," Markham murmured after the Intelligencer had turned on his heel and was striding through the crowd. "However, I can't help but note that he happened to include you in Laughlin's sojourn."

Rogan grunted his agreement. "That he did, and he'll get his wish…for now. Come on, Conclave is gonna have to wait. Let's get the craft to wherever you were thinking. Our window for departure just got moved up."

SERRA STOOD in the butler's pantry of her new suite admiring how flat all the surfaces were as she waited for her water to boil. The accommodations at the Gilded Pearl had come as something of a shock —as had her and every other House from the Source abruptly gaining a voting seat in Assembly—but she was the last person to look a gift horse in the mouth. Things were moving quickly, and going with the flow was preferable to being dragged under.

Especially since with the addition of House Hess to the rolls, her ascendance to First Binder was all but official. A missive had been waiting in her new rooms informing her that the paperwork would go out in the next few days. Some nonsense about a legal precedent needing to be set, but the deal was done and, as her political star had risen, so had her place in the world. After all, the First Binder couldn't possibly reside in a dilapidated, fifth-rung slum, could they? The very notion was ludicrous.

And apparently she wasn't the only one who thought so, because before she'd even floated the idea of new accommodations, she'd found herself installed in a suite at the most lavish establishment in the Northern Territories.

Serra's smile faltered a fraction, not sure who her benefactor was. Undoubtably, there would be a price to pay for such largesse. She smoothed her stomacher, confident they could come to an arrangement, and if not? Well, then the inroads she'd made today with her line and the bits of gossip she'd been hoarding since her arrival would see that she stayed right where she was.

Regardless of any baggage she might have.

The kettle screamed, and Serra lifted it from the thermocoil. The rooms had also come with a manservant, but Serra had sent him away, cursing Otto with every breath of her being as she did. Grumbling under her breath, she quickly assembled an invalid's tray and carried it into the next room. It had been intended as a small parlor where one could entertain guests of import. Instead, Otto lay on the wide couch, spoiling its purpose.

"Thank you, Serra." He gave her a sickly smile. "I don't know what I would've done had you not found me."

Died, if I'd had my wish. She set the tray within his reach, her lips compressed into a flat line as she methodically set his bed to rights. Not for the first time, she considered ending the man and, as before, a jagged flare of pain shot through her head, stopping her.

She winced, forcing a smile. "Well, I suspect one good turn deserves another, now doesn't it?" Serra helped him to sit and handed him the cuppa.

He took a sip and made a face. Serra hid a satisfied smile that it wasn't to his liking.

"Were you able heal what ails me?" he asked, the cup chittering against the saucer as he set it down.

"I'm afraid not. Without knowing exactly what you were exposed to, I'm having difficulty clearing it," she lied. If he was going to darken her door, he needed a leash. "You'll have to be detoxed regularly, lest you fall into such a state again."

Otto gave her a long look before nodding and taking another shaky sip of tea. "I'm aware of how fortuitous our meeting was. I'm ashamed to say it, but I've never had any skill at healing."

He should be ashamed. All he'd managed to do was make himself worse, though that might've been in his favor. Before she'd cleared the pustules plaguing his body, he was barely recognizable. "Your image is still being circulated throughout the city, and they're actively looking for you. I'm taking a huge risk having you here."

"Indeed. Rather full circle, isn't it? After all I've done for you…" He smiled again, flashing his piggy little teeth. "Where is Tamara? I could've sworn I heard her earlier."

Serra stiffened. "She's seeing to the last of our move while I tend to you." They didn't have much, but Serra would be damned before any of her hard-earned gains ended up in some urchin's grubby hands.

Otto grunted and took a piece of pale toast from the tray. The first of many, she assumed. Serra's frown deepened, already seeing where the majority of her food stipend would be going. She looked around the posh room, fervently hoping food was included with her lodgings. If that was the case, he could have the pittance and choke on it.

Unfortunately, Otto finished his meager meal without incident while she retrieved the paper from this morning. This one lamented the loss of Lady Scot on the front page as opposed to Serra's ascension. Glory. How pathetic that Nora's wretched daughter was the closest thing to royalty this nasty little city had.

Seething, Serra took Otto's dishes back to the pantry and dropped the tray onto the counter with a clash of cutlery. She pressed her palms flat—flat!—against the counter and fought to calm herself. No matter. Let the little slut have Laughlin Scot. Dirty twists the both of them. Serra had never believed the secondary dark ring around Kara's irises was a breeding flaw. She glanced out at the repugnant man already asleep on her couch. She knew exactly how easy it was to modify records with the right motivation.

And Serra would be damned if coming north had changed hers.

The doorknob rattled, and a moment later Tamara came in, arms loaded with bags and her cheeks pink from the cold. She was a lovely girl. Voluptuous, with long, dark brown curls. She set the bags down, the ties on her bodice askew. Serra frowned.

"Such a look for me when I come home!" Tamara laughed. "Have you seen where we've landed? Surely things can't be that bad, and the papers! You should hear what they're saying on the streets!"

Serra sighed, her eyes flicking to Otto. "I have, and things aren't terrible, but they could be better."

Tamara continued like Serra hadn't spoken. "Indira says that she knows a girl Scot was with before he left, and the things she says he tried to get her to do? Twist or not, he's definitely, filthy." Tamara fanned herself and then laughed, adjusting the ties on her bodice.

Serra gave a sigh as her daughter prattled on about Scot's alleged bedroom proclivities, only listening with half an ear. The girl gossiped more than a fishwife. After several minutes Serra cut her off.

"If you heard all of this while packing up with Indira, why are you so late? I expected you back hours ago."

Tamara froze, mouth slightly agape as she scrambled for an answer.

Serra sighed. Lovely, but certainly not quick. She clucked her tongue. "Was it that Pense boy or Gregor Dean tonight?"

Tamara rolled her eyes. "And dally outside of my line? Neither. I've got my hat set for a higher prize," she said smugly, putting the kettle back on to boil.

"Is that right?" Serra asked, her voice laden with sarcasm. Line of talent had little to do with who her daughter dallied with…nor did station, come to think of it.

Tamara took a jar of honey from the counter, smiling slyly as she put a large dollop into her mug. "It is. Lord Saks and I have been spending odd moments together. Miles's House is an Original, and tragically, his wife died in childbirth three years ago. He's not looking for an heir, and the boy is young enough to be malleable."

Serra raised an eyebrow, the situation having more promise than she'd normally give her daughter credit for arranging.

Tamara flicked a curl behind her shoulder. "Miles is quite eager to find the boy a mother. He's a timid little thing. Not too trying to be around, surprisingly," Tamara went on. "It's getting quite serious.

Miles has asked me to dine at one of the supper clubs next Friday night with his mother. When I told him I couldn't possibly go given my current wardrobe, he opened an account for me with one of the designers in the city," Tamara said smugly.

"Then I'd suggest you focus on him and forget the others you've been stringing along," Serra said dryly.

"Well, obviously." Tamara paused her primping, looking shocked that Serra would even suggest such a thing. "The next Lady Saks needs to be respectable, after all. His mother is quite the harridan from what I understand. If there's even a breath of scandal..." She glanced meaningfully toward Otto, snoring away in the next room.

"I wouldn't worry about that. Get your lord hooked and set," Serra said. "I'll take care of the rest."

CHAPTER FOUR

"Refugees continue to flock to Glynfyls and the city has become a haphazard, patchwork metropolis at best, but what are we to do? Even with Ri and K shifting in more buildings, a slum has sprung up along the outer wall. So many more people were affected by the Surge than our small town. Some have halos but are unable to draw talent, others have only the barest whisper of ability.

None of us like it, but a kind of caste system has begun. Those with the strongest talent, able to call on abilities unique to their bloodline, are styling themselves as 'Original Houses' and congregating on the hill at the center of the city. Those with the least are at the fringes with the barest of essentials.

It's not right.

El has proposed continuing the city's growth in rings and having each talent settle with their own line, whereas K thinks they should do so by spoke, radiating outward from the center.

I don't know what the right answer is, but thanks to that same caste system, everyone looks to us for guidance, despite our youth. We all feel A's absence keenly. Until now, I don't think we realized how adroit he is at steering our little group, and without him, we're becoming lost..."

– Undated journal entry

FLYNN WOKE PANTING, covered in sweat, the vestiges of fire still raging around him, his body being consumed—

… hands bubbling black, flesh melts from his bones…

He lunged to his feet, through the bathroom door, vomit spurting from between his fingers as he thrust up the toilet lid. His insides splashed back up at him, and he gagged, another torrent spewing, hollowing his belly.

Fuck…

He fell back against the wall, panting. Pulled a towel from the bar and scrubbed his face.

Flames flickered on the counter. Waiting for him.

Everyone was right. He was losing his mind.

Manic laughter burbled past his lips, intensifying until tears ran down his cheeks.

Then it was just sobbing.

He wiped his eyes, trying not to see the memories playing across his mind's eye. Christ, the fucking memories…

… "What's the matter boy, you went out of your way to earn it, now stand up and take your medicine like a goddamned man, you fucking pussy!"…

Stand up. He needed to stand up. Don't be a pussy. Flynn stumbled to his feet, palms slapping onto the vanity. Flipped on the water and splashed a handful over his face. Beside him, flames lapped up the wall. He squeezed his eyes shut, then forced himself to look in the mirror. Laughed at the madman staring back at him. Fuck, he was fucked—

No. They weren't real.

He'd prove it. He would. *Face your fear, face your fear…*

… "I said stand up!" The belt falls again, and he curls into a ball, hands over his head. Rough fingers pry them away, and a fist takes him in the temple…

He took a deep breath and reached out—

Flames jumped from the wall and ran up his arm. Flynn screamed, falling back and crashing into the tub, the curtain pinging off the bar, crumpling beneath him. He flailed, trying to slam on the tap as fire engulfed him—

The door flung open and Rogan burst in. "What the fuck?!"

Flynn froze. Eyes on Rogan, then his arm. He laughed. "I was on fire."

"No, you weren't. I would've felt it." Rogan kneeled down and shut off the water. "Damn, you look like shit." He sighed and ran his hand over Flynn's forehead like he was checking for fever.

His mom had done that. Everyone else had handed him a thermometer.

A lump rose in his throat, and he covered his face with his hands, breath stuttering. *Keep your shit together, keep your shit together…*

"Christ." Rogan swore. "Come on, let's get you cleaned up."

More water and a towel. Fresh clothes. Flynn sat in one of the chairs by the window in clean sweats, listless. Fitz had disappeared at some point, and French had brought up a cart. Flynn couldn't meet the old man's eyes. Rogan poured a cup of coffee and set it on the occasional table at Flynn's side. Why was the Alpha still here? An odd gratitude that he hadn't left rose in Flynn's throat, choking him.

Rogan poured himself a cup, then took the chair across from him. He sighed, frowning. "I owe you an apology. I listened to that asshole, Cal, and I shouldn't have. You didn't need time to yourself, you needed somebody who gives a shit."

Flynn was silent, watching his fingers blacken.

Rogan's frown deepened. "Why do you keep staring at your hands?"

Flynn glanced up from beneath his brows, chewing the scar on his lip. "I'm burning," he rasped.

"No, you're not…but you did. You remember anything that happened out there?"

He was silent. Waiting for the Breaker to get up and leave.

Why wasn't he leaving?

Flynn shrugged. "Some. Maybe. It comes in spurts." His gaze dropped to stare at his hands again. Shame roiled in his gut. "I saw…I mean I think…" He grimaced, balling up his fists at the sides of his head. "Fuck. I can't—"

He slapped a hand over his mouth, dry heaving.

"Hey, it's okay." Rogan put a hand on Flynn's knee. "Look, it's important you know that you shielded yourself right before you lost control of your talent. If you hadn't, we wouldn't be having this conversation."

Flynn took a deep breath, the Alpha's touch steadying him, giving him space to breathe as he shook his head. "No, it's not okay. Kara… I've got to get her, the babies, I gotta get them back, and I can't get out of my head. I can't…" His gaze returned to his hands. "I think—I think I died." He laughed, the blackness on his fingers spreading to his palms, embers beneath his skin beginning to glow—

"Whatever you're seeing, it's not real," Rogan said. "But I'm pretty sure you're right about dying. Markham, the Commandant, Dorian… we all saw you resurrect from—from dust…I dunno what kind of a weave Kara put on you, but it brought you back, and I'm damn sure that's gotta be for a reason."

Flynn blinked at him. Dust. He hadn't imagined it. His head went light, and he put a hand to his brow, the room spinning. "Then I'm not crazy." Shit. It would've been easier if he was.

"No, not about this." Rogan frowned, sitting back as he helped himself to a Danish. "You ready to tell me what it did to your talent?"

Flynn ran a shaking hand across his mouth. "It's all mixed up. Just kind of comes, then doesn't. It's like I'm wrapped in wool," he mumbled, rubbing his arms and not meeting the Alpha's eye. Rogan saw too fucking much, like he knew about the empty hole inside of Flynn where he'd been shoving shit for as long as he could remember.

"And the flames?"

"They're there all the time. Ever since—ever since I got back." Before. But then it was only when he closed his eyes.

Fuck, he wanted a drink.

Rogan grunted. "You haven't actually tried to pull talent, have you?"

… "How fucking stupid are you? Don't you know how to use a blanket? You hide under your bedsheets enough. Pull one up for me now, genius, let's see how well those fancy test scores work in the real world…"

Flynn shook his head, saliva pooling in his mouth and his guts churning.

"You put out my flames downstairs. Phased Cal's desk. Kendall said you shifted from the roof. It's there, you just need to reach for it. Try it now. I'm here to spot you." Rogan leaned forward, his face intent. "I swear I won't let you burn."

He already had. Flynn's heart rate ticked up. Arms itching, thirsty. Christ, he was so goddamned thirsty…

"Here, cloak this."

Rogan set a unit on the table, and Flynn reached for talent, desperate to distract himself from the sudden sharp craving for a drink. Sweat broke out on his brow, and his halos fizzled verdigris, talent slipping through his fingers, dissipating before it'd formed—

… "Just like I thought. Completely fucking useless." The slap to the back of his head isn't unexpected, but he still stumbles, tears in his eyes, biting back the apology he knows will only make things worse…

Flames leaped around the table, and he flinched back.

"They're not real, Flynn."

Fuck, he knew that, and he knew how to do this, goddamn it. Flynn gritted his teeth and his halos pulsed. The unit flickered, its opacity wavering. He grunted, his insides shredding like they were being peppered with glass—

A wall of flame whooshed up behind Rogan, and Flynn dropped talent, jumping back and scrambling from the chair. It fell to one side and skidded into the wall as he pressed himself into the corner of the room, panting as the fire raged toward him.

"Whatever you're seeing, kid, it's not real." Rogan stood and walked through the flames like they weren't even there—

Because they weren't.

Flynn laughed. Oh, God, they weren't…they weren't… He screwed his eyes shut and fought to swallow, his mouth so damned dry. Fuck, fuck, fuck! He grimaced, sliding to the floor, fists to his temples and rocking again.

Gentle hands encircled his wrists and lowered them.

"Hey," Rogan said, kneeling in front of him. "They're not real, and I'm right here."

Flynn put his head on the man's shoulder and nodded—exhausted. "I kn-know, but I c-can't—" He choked back a sob. What the fuck was wrong with him?

"Hey, it's all right, we'll figure it out." Rogan sighed, pulling him into a tight embrace.

Flynn sniffled; that great, sucking black hole inside of him gaping wide. He needed a drink, a knife.

Fuck, he needed Kara.

"Craft's at an old warehouse Markham recommended," Rogan rumbled, rubbing Flynn's back. "Shot that took out the pilot clipped the control unit for the right wing's stabilizer. He's trying to hunt down someone to fix it. While he's doing that, you need to eat something."

"I'm not hungry," Flynn said woodenly, pulling away. He scrubbed his face. "Talk to Kendall. He probably has a spare of whatever you need." A pang went through his chest. Kerns had been obsessive about squirreling away parts.

Rogan grunted. "Fine, but if you're not gonna eat, then I want you to try to get some sleep. Come on, in bed." He sighed, grabbing Flynn's arm and hauling him up, half dragging him across the room.

Flynn's feet rooted at the bedside, fingers grazing the rumpled sheets where Kara had lain. "I can't...not without her." His face crumpled, and Rogan gripped Flynn's shoulder. Bloodlust, heavy and sweet, filled the room, taking the edge off his anxiety.

"You can, and you will, and then we'll get her back," the Alpha murmured. "I'll be right out that door if you need me. I'm not going anywhere. Sleep."

Flynn slid down the wall, drawing his knees to his chest. He stared at the bed, his eyelids drooping. Rogan went into the other room and came back with a throw. He tucked it around him, leaving the door cracked as he exited.

The Breaker swore, and there was the sound of furniture being dragged around. The low rumble of him talking into the intercom and being answered. Then a chair creaked, followed by the *clunk, clunk* of boots hitting the floor in succession.

Rogan was really going to stay. A lump grew in Flynn's throat. He held the throw close to his nose, breathing in the subtle scent of Kara's 'lust beneath the Alpha's. Giving into the command to sleep, Flynn closed his eyes and drifted off as he silently wept.

CAL SIGHED, his fingers sliding from the intercom in his office. Well, that hadn't been what he wanted to hear. Not that good news had been abundant of late. He ran a hand over his mustache and pushed the call-button for French before ambling over to the makeshift workspace on the coffee table. Cal shot a glance at the empty spot where his desk had been and frowned with a shake of his head. He'd tried to remove Flynn's phase, but it wasn't happening. Didn't know whether to be irritated with the boy for stymying him like that or proud. Equal parts, he supposed.

But hadn't that always been the way of it with Flynn? And as far as the rest of them… Cal's frown deepened to a scowl as he pulled the seams of his trousers to sit.

Tablet was waiting for him right where he'd left it, send button front and center on the screen. A little blinking note above it asked if he was sure with a bunch of the institution's CYA-we're-not-at-fault legalese after. No, that'd be all on him. Was he sure? The fuck if he knew at this point. He hit the damned button anyway, then copied who needed to be copied before shutting it down.

Goddamned bloodsuckers. He tossed the tablet onto the coffee table and sat back, rolling a cigarette and wondering where everything had gone wrong. No, that was a lie. The cause of his current angst definitely had Prydee roots.

Thanks to that goddamned list of Cal's accounts Leo had compiled and apparently shared with everyone and their brother, Cal had consolidated the lion's share of his funds with the intent of redistributing them once he'd set up the proper channels.

And, as of two and a half hours ago, that'd gone to hell.

Every last one of them had been flagged by the international tribunal, and all his assets frozen. Some bullshit about House Scot's culpability in Flynn's alleged war crimes. In reality, it was an outright power grab; the tribunal trying to get their fingers on a hefty slice of Cal's pie. He didn't expect it to stand, but even with his lawyers on it, it'd be a solid week before they released his funds.

And by then, the feint would've served its purpose: leaving him dead in the water while the Deep South made its move to annex the North.

Cal brought a cigarette to his lips, damning those satellites Dorian had mentioned. They hadn't gotten the clearest footage, bands of static and blips of interruption riddling the feed, but it was enough to see Flynn lose his shit, then get hauled out of there by Rogan and Marcos, feeble as fuck.

Which meant blood was in the water. The sharks were circling, and Cal could do fuck all to stop them.

He struck a match and inhaled. Waved out the flame. Wasn't the first time he'd seen his liquidity reduced to what resided in his wall safe. Of course, back then his portfolio hadn't been in the trillions. Oh well. It was what it was, and that was looking pretty damn lean at the moment, especially after sending that last payment off to Salist. Whoever had said loyalty was its own reward didn't know his ass from his elbow, and Cal needed the former patron to keep tabs on Titus and the rest of those jackals on the board.

"Sir?" French drawled from the doorway, making the title sound like an insult.

Cal glowered, not in the mood. "Send a message to Lady Carmody. I don't give a shit how she does it, but Nora's gotta haul her ass back over here. Flynn's in a bad way, and she needs to patch him up so he's functional."

French's lips pruned. "Might I suggest you couch it as a plea instead of a demand?"

"You can do whatever the hell you want, as long as it happens," Cal said, holding out a hand-scratched note. "Here. Rogan needs a part for the craft. He said to ask Kendall if he's got a spare."

"As you wish, sir. I'll attend to both with alacrity." The butler inclined his head and took the sheet, all but broadcasting *fuck you.*

Cal glared at his back as he left. Alacrity my ass. If that prick didn't mean so goddamned much to Flynn…Cal stood, sweeping up his tobacco pouch and a bottle on his way out the door. He snorted at the label. Bushmills. French had to be digging deep into the booze cellar if he was bringing this up. Cal buzzed his lips. Whatever. Shit somehow seemed appropriate, all things considered. Speaking of which, he should probably go see what Flynn's damage was himself.

When he got up to the suite, Rogan was sprawled out in one of the chairs by the window with his feet up on the other. One glance at the blood-soaked couch explained the necessity of that set up.

"When did Fitz clear out?" Cal tossed Rogan the bottle.

"Before I got here." He frowned, catching it, then snorted at the label. "Not my biggest concern. We've got a fucking problem."

"You don't say," Cal muttered around his cigarette. He pulled the chair out from under Rogan's feet and settled into it as they thumped to the floor. "You tell him about the Assembly's mandatory invite for tomorrow?"

"Nope." Rogan raised the bottle of whiskey to his lips, then smacked them after he'd swallowed. "Damn, this shit tastes the same…I didn't tell him because there's not a chance in hell it's happening. The kid's mental state aside, I met Crandall at the coliseum. He's giving Flynn an out by 'letting us,'" he finger quoted, "take that craft, and if we don't use it, an accident's already been arranged."

Cal grunted, not surprised. "What about the boy's talent?"

"Fuck his talent. Kid's a mess."

"Flynn doesn't do loss well," Cal murmured, sitting back in the chair and crossing his ankle over his knee.

"Huh. Wonder where he got that trait from?"

Cal's eyes flicked to Rogan's, ignoring the dig. Asshole should talk. "Flynn never bounced back after Deirdre. Started cutting himself up. Miriam was beside herself."

"I wish I could say I'm surprised, but I'm not, and this ain't that." Rogan frowned, knocking his fist against the arm of the chair. "He's hallucinating, and whatever he's seeing has got him pissing his pants."

"Have anything to do with that resurrection you were gonna fill me in on?"

Rogan gave a slow nod. "Yeah. I think it fucked him up royal. Hell, it fucked me up watching it. He was dust, Cal. Atomized. Then Kara's bind drew all those little pieces back together and reassembled him like it'd never fucking happened."

"She must've UnMade the damage…" Cal murmured.

Rogan went still, the bottle halfway to his mouth. "What's this now?"

"Jesus…" Cal scrubbed his face. "The whole reason Titus was so hot to get his hands on Kara in the first place is based on a hypothesis his father had about bringing another line of talent into being by selective breeding."

"Well, that sounds awfully familiar." Rogan glowered at him. "You wouldn't have anything to do with dropping that fairytale, would you?"

"To what end?" Cal scowled and grabbed the bottle back, not about to tell him Baba Yaga was real. "I spent centuries trying to defund the Source, not provide it with a new revenue stream."

"Ah. So you just cozied up to reap the benefits on the off-shot truth turned out to be stranger than fiction."

Cal leaned forward to snag a glass off the cart French had left. "If you can't beat 'em, join 'em, then steal their work." He poured himself three fingers and handed the bottle back.

"Sounds about right." Rogan frowned. "Roll me one of those, would you?"

"FYI, I got the CliffsNotes of what happened from the satellite feeds being broadcasted all over hell and gone," Cal said, pulling out his pouch. "Doesn't show Flynn atomizing, but it does show him destroying the plateau, then you hauling his ass out of there weaker than a kitten. Coincidently, the tribunal's frozen all my assets, giving the green light for the North's annexation. The Deep South is coming."

"Well, that ain't good." Rogan tipped back the bottle, his eyes flicking to the lift as it pinged. The doors opened, and French came in with another servant. He motioned to the couch and the woman bobbed a curtsey to them before shifting out with the ruined seating. The cat shot from where it'd been hiding and disappeared through the crack in the bedroom's doorway. If the animal hadn't been traumatized before, it was now.

"Pardon the interruption," French frowned after it, "but I thought Lord Firestorm could use more comfortable accommodations."

"I appreciate that," Rogan said, taking a smoke from Cal as the woman reappeared with a blood-free version in beige and orange checkered tweed. "But it sure is fucking ugly."

The butler sucked in his cheeks. "I'm afraid I can't disagree, but I believe it will be a more ergonomic sleeping arrangement," he said, transferring a blanket and pillow from his cart to the upholstered monstrosity.

"You get those missives sent?" Cal asked. What Shane had been thinking bringing that damned thing home…he'd thought it was ugly then, and time hadn't done it any favors.

"I have. Master Kendall believes he has something that should suffice, but lacks a way to retrieve it from his craft at the Manse. However, I believe that's a moot point. Lady Carmody seems to have the task in hand. She replied to my missive with a request that Master LaVeil attend her at her flat and this," French pulled a six pack of porter from his cart and set it on the table between them, "along with the suggestion that you two gentlemen hold on to them whilst you wait."

Rogan lifted a bottle and snorted, cigarette to one side of his mouth. "She wants us to hold her beer? Fuck that, I'm drinking it." He popped the lid and took a swig.

"As you will, sir. Is there anything else you require?" French asked, kneeling to set a plate of shredded chicken to one side of the bedroom door. When he rose, it was painfully slow.

"A reliable Fetch would be nice," Cal murmured, staring at the couch.

"Alas, I don't perform miracles." The butler grimaced as he crossed back to his cart.

"Did you see when Fitz left?" Rogan asked.

"I did not. Shall I send a missive to Lord Markham inquiring after his whereabouts?"

"Yeah. That nephew of his needs to hoof it to the Carmody's." Cal blew out a long stream of smoke as French collected his cart and moved toward the lift. "With the shit the Prydees have been pulling, I don't trust anyone but Fitz to shift Kendall's man out to the Manse."

The butler hit the button and the doors opened. "Then I shall see it done."

"With alacrity?" Cal quipped at his back.

It stiffened. "Of course, sir. What other type of service could you possibly deserve?" French returned curtly before the doors closed.

Rogan snorted and turned to Cal. "What the hell was that about?"

"French's always taken umbrage with my existence."

"He's not the only one."

"No, but he's the only one I employ." Cal pulled a bottle of beer up to read the label then put it right back. Some girly microbrew. "As long as he does his job, I don't give a shit if he likes me. That man's missives can charm the pants off a snake."

"Think you mean skin." Rogan blew a smoke ring, his feet up on the table. "Snakes don't wear pants."

"You been to Assembly lately?"

Rogan grunted. "Point taken."

"What's important is him getting Alice to convince Nora to come back here to look at Flynn. Hopefully, she can patch him up so he's functional. Crandall's death threats and exile aside, I don't see us leaving here without the boy making a very public statement."

Rogan looked at him like he was crazy. "I think you fail to comprehend how fucked up the kid is right now. I haven't seen PTSD like that since the Surge."

"No, I think you fail to comprehend how fucked everyone in the Northern Territories is gonna be if he just up and disappears. Only thing that's gonna give the Deep South pause is if they think he's still capable of doing to them what he did to Titus's Elites. All I need is an hour out of him, and then we can scrape him up and pour him into the craft on our way out the door."

"Unbelievable." Rogan shook his head. "You know, you really are an asshole. You ever stop to think about how he—"

"Constantly," Cal barked. "Where the hell do you think he's gonna go with his family if the North falls? It ain't gonna be to your beach—" He bit his tongue so hard it bled. Shit, it wouldn't be anywhere if he was right about what Jane had coming for them, but he'd be damned if he spilled that this late in the game.

Rogan shook his head again, his arms crossed over his chest as he looked toward the bedroom. "Trust me, you try to parade the kid around, it's only gonna get them up here faster."

"I'd hold your bets until Nora has a look at him." Cal stubbed out his cigarette and started rolling another. "But if he's as bad as you think he is, my lack of consideration is gonna be the least of our problems."

NORA STOOD at the window of her borrowed suite at the Carmody's flat, hair still damp from her shower, eyes dry from crying. She dabbed a bit of scent on her wrists, thanking whatever whim had struck French to include it with her bags. Something about amber had always calmed her, and Glory knew she needed it right now.

She chewed her lip. Alice had assured her that she and Marcos could stay for as long as they wanted, but had she made the right decision accepting the Seer's unexpected hospitality? Nora sighed. It felt like she was running away from her responsibilities, but she just needed… Ugh. She didn't know what she needed anymore.

Aside from her daughter back home and her and the babies safe.

Nora closed her eyes. Everything leading up to that horrible moment when it'd become obvious Kara had been taken, so many seemingly small choices, so pivotal in retrospect… Would staying here become one of them? The last thing Nora wanted was to earn any more of Cal's animosity, but she just couldn't—couldn't *think* in that flat of his. She rubbed her arms, hugging herself. Feeling the censure of invisible eyes, her conscience pricking at her, the last several hours a tumble.

Beritram was dead.

The nightmare well and truly over; she'd thought she'd feel more at his passing. Yes, there was relief—her embarrassing lapse of consciousness at the wall bore that out—but the trauma he'd caused remained. She sighed, parting the sheer white curtains to look down at a picturesque, tree-lined street.

Beyond the neat gothic flats, the darkening gray sky hid the haze of smoke, only the barest glow above the city giving any indication that an entire spoke lay devastated, while the tableau here remained in perfect order. Low granite walls and ornate, wrought iron fences delineated sidewalks free of snow and ice, everything outside the glass fixed to be as meticulous as what was within.

If only her insides were as well-ordered. Nora's thoughts churned, a tumultuous storm of regret and anxiety. Waves broke over her, the reality of her situation and the precariousness of her position not at all what she'd envisioned when she'd chosen this path.

She was losing her line.

The daughter she'd fought so hard for to be free had been taken.

And she had another child on the way.

Her past, present, and future, they crushed down upon her with the weight of expectation. She pressed a fingertip to the windowpane, melting a tiny oval into the gathered hoarfrost at its edge and ruining its feathery swirl as Alice's words echoed in her head:

…*"Three things I see for you. A choice. A sacrifice, and abundance…"*

A choice. Nora's lips flattened. Was that something new, or in reference to the one she'd made all those years ago? It had sounded so simple to bear a child for the Reunification. If she was required to breed, why not do so purposefully? And if that purpose was to reunite Talents from the South with their free brethren in the North, all the better.

She'd dedicated years—decades—of her life to the cause.

To Kara. And now she'd been stolen away.

… She squeezes the bridge of her nose, overcome for a moment. "It really is a girl?"

A smile lights up Deirdre's face, and she nods, her eyes glassy. "Yes. And your job is to protect and prepare her, just as mine is to do the same for Laughlin. There is a future with the two of them out there, but we need to be committed to make it happen, and you have a larger part to play than I…"

Nora closed her eyes and focused on regulating her breathing. Remembering that snippet in time had kept her going for so long…

Had reminded her what was important.

"…the Reunification is only the beginning. Our sacrifice will usher in the bounty for both our peoples. It's up to us to birth the future so that they can shape it."

Deirdre had given her life to do so. Could Nora offer any less? She smoothed a hand over her abdomen and looked at her reflection in the window. At the gray streaking her hair and the swell of new life. Past and future. One was done, and the other yet to be.

What then was she to do in the now?

She brought her hands to her breast, twisting her ring. The subtle scent of amber teased her nose. Her brow furrowed. She raised her wrist and inhaled again. Odd. She'd worn this scent for years, but it smelled so much stronger today. Nora shook her head. Probably because here it wasn't a counterpoint to the ubiquitous stench of Cal's cigarettes—

Her breath caught. Albanach was a thing of the past, too, and as for Cal…what had she said to Marcos?

… *"Wheels within wheels… I've never been privy to his true agenda. Thus far, it coincides with mine…"*

But what if it no longer did?

She didn't owe Caliban Scot anything. For better or worse, she'd been in lockstep with him to make the Reunification happen. Her job there was done, and if now it was time for her to sacrifice? Let Serra have the line and all that went with it. The threat from the Source was over, and for what it was worth, Nora had held the Binders together long enough for them to do their part—

Her eyes flicked back to the reflection in the window as a door at the other end of the room opened. Alice came in with two large, flat boxes balanced in one hand, and a six pack of bottles in the other. She was also wearing the ugliest pair of floral pajamas Nora had ever seen.

"Don't be jealous." Alice smirked as she set the boxes on the coffee table and flipped open the lid of the top one. "I hope you like extra cheese, bacon, and eggplant, because after everything today, I need grease." She plopped down cross-legged on the jacquard settee and twisted the lid off one of the bottles before passing it to Nora. "I don't recommend the second, though you're welcome to it if you're a fan of anchovies."

"I'm not, but thanks." She took the bottle, bemused. "Is this beer?"

"No, you got pop, but mine is a delightful chocolate porter." Alice quirked a brow as she cracked hers and took a sip. "Mmm…but if you don't like cola, I'm happy to drink yours later with ice cream…and eat your half of the pizza. Just don't tell Carl. He's always going on about my cholesterol."

Nora snorted and took a sip as she sat on the opposite end of the couch. "No, I believe I'm happy on all counts."

"I knew I liked you." Alice set her beer aside to pull a slice of pizza from the box. She popped an escaped glop of cheese into her mouth. "Deirdre said I would. It's a pity we won't have time to really become friends."

"And why is that?"

"Preexisting obligations, holidays, opposing soccer schedules for the kids." Alice shrugged and chomped into her slice. "Death."

"Do you have children?" Nora asked, ignoring the last comment.

"I do. A son and a daughter, though admittedly they both hated soccer. Lawrence will make his majority later this year, and my daughter…well, I suspect you'll hear her before you see her. She's a harpist."

"Oh?" Nora struggled to get her slice out of the box. "I hear that's an incredibly difficult instrument to play."

"It is, but you wouldn't think so watching her." Alice dusted off her hands and reached for another slice, stealing all the toppings Nora had left behind. "I probably should've brought napkins…"

"Quite the lack of foresight on your part." Nora bit into her slice. Glory, that was good.

"Har har." Alice rolled her eyes. "So, judging by the changing currents in the aether, I'm assuming you've decided on a path forward. Quicker than I expected, but then you do have that Binder's logic to call upon."

Nora threw her crust into the box and helped herself to another slice. She did, and it was currently telling her that Alice was dropping puzzle pieces for her to pick up and assemble. "What exactly is aether?"

"Now, there's a loaded question. How to best explain…" She took a bite and chewed, staring off into space for a moment. "Aether is all the potential flowing between fixed points in time, every possibility, what could become…"

"Some points are fixed?"

"Many, actually. Most are small, but there's been some boulders to navigate of late…kind of like rocks in a stream. It's also green."

Nora bit into a pocket of molten sauce and fanned her mouth as she fumbled for her pop. "Green?"

"Mmm." Alice hummed around another bite. "The most gorgeous emerald. Working with it is what causes a Seer's irises to change. Getting to that tipping point is a rite of passage for a Carmody. Dubious honor, if you ask me, rather like getting your period but with monthly visions instead of menses." She batted her lashes and laughed.

Nora put a hand to her lips, finishing her mouthful. "Well, if by path forward you mean me stepping down as First Binder and wishing Serra the joy of sorting out the mess they've made of things up here, then yes. I have decided on that."

"Bit of kismet there, since they've just filed formal papers to oust you and install her in your stead, but I can't say that I blame you."

They had? Nora paused, chewing her bite longer than necessary, then shook her head as she swallowed. Idiots. They deserved each other.

"Will you be giving up your spot with the Ladies as well?" Alice asked a bit too nonchalantly.

With reason, Nora was sure. She took another bite to buy time. That she would have to think harder on. "I don't know. I suspect that's entirely dependent on what happens next."

"Oh? What do you plan on doing with your newfound freedom?" Alice glanced up at her from beneath her blunt bangs, a ripple moving through her emerald irises.

The air in the room thickened, and Nora fought the urge to laugh. So many small choices, so difficult to make. How was it that the massive departure she was about to embark upon was so easy? She took a deep breath, feeling her own strength. It was high time for her to pivot from Cal's agenda to her own.

To what was most important.

"For starters?" She tossed her second crust into the box and reached for a third slice of pizza. What the hell. She was pregnant, right? "I need to talk to Cal. I'm accompanying whoever is leaving to bring my daughter and grandchildren home—whether they like it or not."

"They might be more receptive to the idea than you think." Alice smirked as she pulled a missive from her pajama's pocket and handed it over.

Nora flicked it open, her brow furrowing as she scanned the short note from French. Glory, that didn't sound good. She went to stand—

"Mmm, sit down, finish eating," Alice admonished around her bite. "We have time."

Nora's brow quirked, but she suspected the Seer would know. Alice raised a brow at the slice Nora had abandoned, and she leaned forward to retrieve it, a waft of garlic-y fish following her as she settled back. Pregnancy hormones aside, that second pizza smelled horrendous. "Do I want to know why you brought that up if neither one of us is going to eat it?"

Alice smirked around her beer. "Because sometimes, when a current is strong enough, fixed points have a tendency to shift."

FITZ STOOD at the center of Kristine's parlor trying to figure out what the fuck he'd been thinkin' offerin' hisself up on a silver platter. Around the perimeter of the room, several of the more virulent Prydee sisters had appeared after his arrival. They sat scattered amongst the tufted purple upholstery, projecting vicious intent. Way they was lookin' at him could've burned a hole through steel.

'Cept for his ma. She had naught a glance for him, but his half-sisters made up for it with the malice they was shootin' his way. Right cunts, they was.

Only joy he got being there were from the black, cloth-covered cage taking up one full wall, fit t'be a funeral shroud. Felt a tick bad for them birds that'd been offed, but not a wit for the harpy they'd belonged to.

He were pretty sure Kristine knew it, too. She finished yappin' at Giles, that shite butler of hers, then stalked over. Fitz started to sweat, his knackers drawing up.

"Well? What have you got to say for yourself?" she demanded, fists planted on her considerable hips. He about gagged at the wave of her perfume rolling over him.

"Eh…why?" He coughed, eyes watering. "What've ye heard?"

Kristine cuffed his ear. "Mind your tongue before I shift it from your mouth, you pinchling trash! What have I heard? Plenty. I'd thought we'd established quite clearly what would happen if you pledged to the Overlord."

Shite. He bit back a curse, resisting the urge to cup his ear, or wipe at the trickle of warmth riding down its shell to hit his neck.

"Eh…ya—yes, m—*my* lady. Ye—*you* did. " Fitz stuttered, his cant wanting to come out right thick under pressure. He fumed at the way he sounded. Hated it when she put the screws to him, makin' his tongue jump through hoops along with the rest of him. Weren't natural the way it clipped crisp. He wet his lips, sweating for true. "But I dinna…eh, that is *to* say, I haven't. Didn't. I ain't—*aren't*—pledged to nobod—anyone."

"Somehow, I very much doubt that." Kristine scowled, her eyes narrowing as she slowly circled him, reading his energy.

One of the sisters to his left sighed on the harpy's second pass. "There's nothing there and staring at the nasty little urchin isn't going to make it so. You know very well there's no hiding it at this point. The energy of everyone who pledged to the Overlord is in a tangle. This has to be one of the Carmody's games."

"Perhaps, but the fact remains that he's working for House Scot after being told explicitly to stay away." Kristine's lips puckered like an arsehole. She gouged a finger into Fitz's side, then clucked her tongue at his flinch. "Still a bit tender, are you? Pity Arileo couldn't finish the job, but in some respects he was even more disappointing than you. I suspect it's fitting you take his place."

Take his place? Fitz's throat bobbed; weren't no way in hell he were signing up to rat. Words was on the tip of his tongue to tell them he weren't working for Scot no more, and a wave of cold rode over him along with the Cajetan's displeasure—

Sisters pulled back as one, clutching their pearls. "What was that?" one of them shrilled, her breath a puff of white.

"Aether," Kristine spat, stepping closer, her nails digging half-moons into his jaw as she forced him to meet her dish-water brown eyes. "What have you gotten yourself into, Fitzpatrick? Tell me, why are the Seers so invested in having you stay by Laughlin Scot's side?"

Seers? The fuck did them witches have to do with anything? Fitz didn't even try to hide his shock, and Kristine pursed her lips again, calculating this time.

"He honestly doesn't know." One of the sisters laughed. "Idiot."

"Not very happy about it either, is he?"

"Good," said a third.

Kristine's nails clawed his cheek as she thrust him away. He stumbled back, lines of stinging fire scoring his face. Her gaze travelled the room, like she were taking consensus. Each of the sisters nodded back in turn. Shite. Whatever were coming next, he weren't gonna like it.

She finished the circuit and flashed him a nasty smile. "The Seers have called in one of the favors owed to them by House Prydee. As long as you remain in the Overlord's service, we're not to interfere with Delores McCreedy, be it by direct or indirect means. For whatever reason, they've decreed your bloody gran's person sacrosanct...but mark my words, Fitzpatrick, the moment House Scot tosses you out on your ear, I'll take great pleasure in having her take the place of my birds, and until then, you'll report to us every flea bat-mitzvah and cockroach wedding that takes place in that House, understood?"

"Eh, y—yes, me—my lady." Weren't a fuckin chance of that, but he nodded, disbelief rising up with the sick from Fitz's stomach. He eyed the shrouded cage. Harpy would do it, too. Sisters had promised t'leave his gran be before, but crossing them witches weren't somewhat anyone lived to do twice.

His throat bobbed. He had a feeling it worked the same with Scot.

Kristine pulled a small velvet pouch from her skirts and dangled it in front of Fitz. "You're to deliver this to Lady Carmody so she knows we've agreed to uphold our end of the bargain. Giles will give you the imprint." She pulled her hand back as Fitz went to reach for the pouch, her nose wrinkling before she relented and tossed it at him.

He caught the little bag, stumbling as Giles's heavy hand landed on his shoulder, pinching the nerve—

Fitz snagged the imprint of a servant's entrance on some swanky row from the bastard and pulled talent, shifting out before they could add more injury t'insult.

He winced, arm numb and channel protesting somewhat fierce as he materialized into his room at the tenement. Noise from the crowd rallying outside in the street drowned out his curses as he looked around.

Adelaide.

He dropped his jacket over the back of a chair. Fucking place were all tidied and set to rights—vase with posies on the table, bits of maps straightened and tacked to the walls. Christ, looked like she'd had the linens laundered. Were right fuckin' homey, and that were a problem.

Fitz sighed and scrubbed his face. Damned, stubborn, pig-headed —weren't no future betwixt them and never could be. Letting her stay here'd been a mistake. His stomach churned, sick over the fact that he were gonna have to cut her clear before somewhat nasty happened. With Gran off limits, the Prydees would be looking for somewhat new t'hold over him, and he'd be damned before that happened.

He grabbed a skin and a clean set of clothes, tugging his patch as he tromped into the bathroom. Shower were a blessing, lukewarm or no, but it weren't naught he were lingering in. Handful of minutes and he were out. Took longer t'shave around Kristine's claw marks. He breathed a hefty sigh of relief wriggling into his skin, the tight undershirt making him feel like hisself again. Buttoned another over it and mussed his curls.

Right. Now all he needed were a bit of fortifyin' before deliverin' that pouch and seein' to his gran. He shouldered open the bathroom door and made a beeline for the bottle in his jacket. Gettin' killed by Scot could wait. Hopefully His Majesty'd do it quick without technically firing him so the sisters would be stuck keeping their promise to the Seers.

Fitz pulled the roll of units from his pocket and peeled off a generous stack to set in the hidey-hole for Adelaide. He kicked into his boots and frowned, catching sight of a braided rag rug by the bed.

Shouldn't be spending her money on that shite. Had little enough to eat.

He gritted his teeth as he pulled talent, sweat breaking out on his forehead as he shifted a half dozen rungs to a spoke on the opposite side of the city.

Shite. He winced, hands on his knees in the center of a pristine alley, catching his wind. Much more of that, and he'd be taking one of them blighted gates. Where the fuck were Nora Jester when he needed her? Whoever'd bound him up hadn't done shite for his burn, that were for certain. He straightened up, eyeing the servants' entrance at the backend of the brownstone Giles had given him the imprint for.

Little amber lights illuminated a neat path that cut right to the stoop, swept free of snow and ice. Garbage bins beside it was all aligned and tidy; Fitz took another mouthful of liquor and tipped over one at the end as he passed. Shite were too perfect. Made him nervous.

He went up to door and knocked, his other hand tightening around the little pouch. Sweat trickled down his spine. Had cause to be here, he did. Fitz wet his lips, heart thudding. Long glass insets was thick with bubbles, but after a moment, there were definitely someone moving around behind it. Sound of a deadbolt being thrown and the door cracked, a chain drawing taut across the top—

"You!" Sophia glared at him for a split second, then slammed the door in his face.

What the hell were his peach—Fitz stared at where she'd been then raised his fist, knocking again. "Nah, hey wait! It ain't like that—Sophia!" He pounded on the slab—

She ripped the door open, the chain lock thumping at the sudden stop. "Don't! Haven't you done enough without alerting the entire neighborhood?" she hissed through the gap. "I've nothing to say to you, Fitzpatrick McCreedy! Leave me alone!"

She went to slam the door again, and he glanced past her into the marble and stainless steel kitchen, and shifted. He'd almost caught his breath against the counter before she'd thrown the dead bolt and turned on her heel, looking right satisfied with herself until her gaze met his.

Her eyes widened. "What are you doing in here?! How did you

even find me? I told you to leave me alone, I don't want to hear your apologies!"

Apologies? "Eh… What's this now?" Fitz cocked his head. "Ye think that's why I'm here? The hell do I have to apologize for?"

"What do you—" The look on her face were naught but incredulous fury. Sweet Jesus, but she were a treat. "You left me in the men's room!" she gritted out through clenched teeth, balling up her fists. "Do you have any idea how humiliating—"

"*That's* what yer in a tear over?" Fitz laughed, falling back against the counter as he chuckled. He helped himself to an apple from a basket of fruit at his elbow, polishing it on his shirt. "Ye did that to yerself, love. I don't recall inviting ye in, but the offer t'help me hold it stands." His gaze locked on hers, and he look a big bite of the fruit.

Her cheeks flared pink. "But you—you—"

He licked the juice from his lips, still chewing as he watched the flush of color travel down her throat to disappear beneath a white terrycloth robe that ended just above her ankles. Her feet was bare, toenails glimmering with shimmery green paint.

"Ugh! Stop it!" She clutched the collar of her robe to her throat.

"What's that now? I ain't done a thing." He took another bite, slurping. Weren't opposed to starting somewhat, though. Damn, she were fun to rile.

"You are. You're—you're looking at me like that again, and I—I want you to stop it." She huffed, raising her chin with a little stamp of her foot.

And if that weren't the most adorable thing he'd ever seen. He took a step toward her, and a wide grin slid across his face as he munched, finishing the apple. "Looking at ye like what?"

Her blush deepened. "Like you want to eat me."

Laud, she were a sight flustered. Just made him want to rile her more. He tossed the core into the garbage and ran a hand over his mouth, loving the way her eyes followed every little move he made, nervous-like. Her breath sped up, and she pulled her robe closer, her back flat to the door.

"Spoiler, love, that ain't all I want t'do, and ye look like ye'd right enjoy a nibble."

"You're wrong." She swallowed, pulse at her throat a drum. Raven's wing hair were damp and in a thick braid, just asking to be wrapped around his fist.

"Nah, I ain't." He cupped her cheek, running his thumb over its rise. The faintest hint of chlorine teased his nose. Bet she had one of them little suits on. He had a sudden desire to know what color it were. "Ye wearing a one piece under that robe, or is it two?"

"I'm—" The back of her head thumped against the door as she looked up at him, her pupils dilating as he rested his forearm above her, leaning in close. She closed her eyes and inhaled deeply through her nose, then slowly out her mouth before forcing a scowl. "I'm mad at you, and you're not going to charm your way out of apologizing."

"Then I'm sorry I did aught t'offend ye." He trailed his fingers down her throat to the collar of her robe, his grin widening at her quickening pulse, his lips at her ear. Goddamn, if teasin' this little witch weren't his new favorite thing. "I think it's a one piece. Black—nah, green t'match that polish on yer toes."

"You'd be wrong," she breathed, raising her hand to slide up his chest, then hook a lock of hair behind his ear. Her fingers strayed to the scratches on his cheek, and her brows drew together. "And you said you weren't going to touch me."

He nipped at her fingers just to hear her gasp, and his dick jumped. Jesus, that did somewhat to him. "I say a lot of things. Some is even true."

"Are you telling me you're a liar?"

"Depends on who ye ask." Fitz leaned in to trace her throat with his nose, hand at the knot in her belt. He gave it a little tug, loosening it. "Show me?"

Her fingers tightened in his curls. "I'm asking you, and you're not really sorry for leaving me like that, are you?"

"I'll be whatever ye want for a chance t'see what's beneath this robe."

She laughed and pushed him away. "Now I know you're lying. If you're not going to apologize, why are you here? If someone comes down and sees a Fetch in the kitchen..." She tightened her belt and popped up on her toes to peek over his shoulder.

"I got cause." He frowned, taking a step back. Didn't need to read her energy to know the moment were gone. His cock didn't agree, throbbin' somewhat fierce. She glanced away as he adjusted himself, that blush flaring anew. "Sisters sent me to deliver a pouch to the lady."

Sophia's eyes went wide, and her hands flew to her lips. "Then why ever did you come through the kitchen? You should've been sent right up through the front—oh! She's going to be so cross with me!"

She grabbed his hand and hurried past the counter to a set of servants' stairs, pulling him along after her. He dropped back as she started up, gathering the hem of her robe to jog up the flight. He bit back a groan watching her backside sway—

Sophia stopped abruptly at the landing, male voices in the hallway just beyond. She turned to press against him, a hand on his chest and a finger to her lips. Didn't need help skulking about, but damn, she felt good all cozied up. He slid an arm around her waist, way too conscious of her bare legs straddling one of his.

"…legality of what you're trying to do is murky at best. Holding a vote of no confidence so soon after the last clearly goes against Assembly bylaws—I can empathize with your argument, but I don't like it, or its inevitable results."

Fitz's brow furrowed. Where'd he heard that voice before? Another answered it. That one he knew all too well.

"No one likes it, Carl, but it's a matter of public safety, and I need to know I can count on your support," Crandall said, their footsteps coming closer. "We both know Laughlin's never been the most rational of men, and this business with his lady's abduction has pushed him over the edge. He's a become a liability to himself and the city."

Sophia's fingers tightened on Fitz's shirt, her brows furrowed. Shite. if she were thinkin' that hard about somewhat, Crandall were gonna pick it up, and they'd get nicked. Fitz slid his hand from her waist to her hip, easing his fingers wide to cup her rear…

She stiffened against him, and he froze, his cock going ramrod straight. Jesus fuck, as if the swell of her perfect arse weren't enough t' get him all hot and bothered, she weren't wearing a stitch under that robe. His throat bobbed as her gaze locked with his—

And the vixen smiled.

"Our laws exist for a reason," the other voice was firm as it passed by them and continued down the hall.

"So do extenuating circumstances. Sacrifices must be made to ensure Glynfyls continues, and the Northern Territories remain safe…"

Sophia's brow furrowed again, her head moving to follow their voices as they faded—

Fitz pivoted, pressing her to the wall. "The hell do ye think ye were doin' answering the door with nary a stitch on beneath that robe?" he bit out in a ragged whisper.

Her teeth dimpled her lip, and she giggled.

Fitz's temper rose. "It ain't funny! If the wrong man were on the other side of that door—" A growl rumbled in his chest, feeling all sorts of shite he didn't have any damned right t'feel, but if somewhat happened to her—

"I knew it! You do care." Sophia rose up on her tiptoes and kissed his cheek, quick and light as a butterfly. "Apology accepted." She beamed at him, taking his hand and pulling him into another hallway. After a peek in the direction the voices had gone, she led him the other way.

"Nah, I don't, and that weren't an apology," he grumbled, following her.

"No," she said, her voice laden with mock seriousness. "Of course it wasn't."

He opened his mouth to argue, and they were at another door. She knocked softly, then pushed through it.

And there were the queen witch herself and Nora Jester kibitzing over pizza. Fitz sniffed, smelling anchovies. His stomach about roared, and they both glanced up. Alice looked between him and Sophia, and a wide smile slid across her face.

"Eh…" He dropped Sophia's hand to scrub his curls, taking a step away and hunching into his jacket. "Sisters said—"

"You have something for me?" Alice held out her hand and made a come hither motion.

"Eh…that pie got anchovies?"

She flipped up the lid of the box as Fitz wandered closer. Shite. It did. Anchovy, olive, onion, and mushroom with them green peppers ye only saw past the fourth rung. He ran a hand over his waterin' mouth, hair raising on the nape of his neck. How the fuck his favorite were here waiting…

Nah. Were too neat, just like the rest of this place. He took a step back, and the coin in his pocket flared icy. The witch's eyes dropped to it, then moved like they was following somewhat only she could see.

"Decisions, decisions, and how the aether churns about you…what will you do, Fitzpatrick?" Alice asked, the room around them oddly still.

He wet his lips and dug out the pouch, fingers pinching around somewhat hard inside. Felt like a rock. He looked down at scrap of blue velvet, suddenly loathe to hand it to her, even with the blessed saint doin' his mightiest to freeze his bits off—

A hand settled at the crook of his arm, and he glanced over. Sophia clasped her robe close to her throat, eyes shooting daggers at the queen witch.

His brow furrowed for a beat, then cleared. Right, fuck this. She were a Carmody and a lady, to his everlastin' sorrow. Weren't right that a witch should be so tempting.

He took Sophia's hand in his, and dropped the cursed pouch into her palm. Coin flared hot and her eyes went wide as he closed her fingers over it. "S'yer problem now, love."

Sophia looked at him like he'd handed her a severed head. "*My problem…*"

Alice's laugh trilled out as she clapped her hands like a tot, breaking the stillness of the room. Nora Jester frowned, edging back from the open box as she wafted a hand through the air.

"Thank Glory. Now please, take this. It smells terrible."

Fitz rescued the box from between them and pulled out a slice, cheese just gooey enough to stretch. First mouthful were pure heaven. Rest were gone in a blink. "Eh…thank ye kindly," he mumbled around another. "I'll be taking the rest t'go—"

"Yes, you will," Alice said with a pointed look at Nora. She dusted off her hands and stood. "If you'd heal his channel please? I need

Fitzpatrick to take LaVeil out to the Manse, and now Sophia has business there as well. Do get dressed, darling."

Fitz's annoyance with being conscripted for taxi service cut off sharp as Sophia scowled at her and then him before stomping off with tears in her eyes. Shite. He hadn't meant—his bite stuck in his throat, and Alice handed him a beer.

"Don't worry about her or Delores." The queen witch's smirk grew as he started, and she settled back on the couch, taking a sip from her own bottle. "Sophia knows her duty, and we've gotten your gran as comfortable as she can be, all things considered, well, for now at least."

The small hairs on Fitz's nape rose again. Sounded like the witches was takin' over threatenin' her where them harpies had left off. His temper spiked. "Ye've seen her?"

Alice's smirk faltered, her gaze on the door Sophia had not quite slammed on her way out. "Of course. It's my job to see everything."

***

TITUS SAT BACK and stroked a finger over his lips, reviewing footage and comparing it to the twins' metrics again. Curiouser and curiouser. That they were both halo-less Finders possessing off-the-charts ability was the least of the revelations in the current rabbit hole of data he was spiraling down. No. What had Titus riveted was what had occurred following the incident in the gestation chamber.

He checked the current feed, the twins still insensate upon the floor. They could stay that way for all he cared. In fact, he quite preferred it as long as the vitals their bots were reporting remained stable.

The frenzied conversation they'd had he could make neither heads nor tails of, but Elize's brain activity surrounding the exchange was fascinating. Immediately after sending the litter into a crisis state, her hippocampus had become as shriveled as a prune. Now, not quite two hours later, it was as plump as the rest of her gray matter, with synapses lighting it up like a Christmas tree.

In contrast, Enoch's brain chemistry remained relatively stable, save for the region responsible for emotional regulation thudding dully. Titus sipped his bourbon, noting their elevated dopamine levels.

If he hadn't seen the feed, he would've attributed that to some kind of a narcotic, but their systems were clear. What could possibly—

A chime sounded, and a communications orb materialized above Titus's desk. He swept the twins' metrics away. There would be plenty of time to delve into that mystery, now was the time to collect.

"Salist," he said, accepting the call. An image of the dark, robed man resolved. He reclined on his tiger skin couch, packing the bowl of his hookah. "Calling to tell me you've deposited those funds?"

"Absolutely not, you're far too smug already." He glanced up, long fingers still working. "Has your prize whelped yet?"

Titus swirled his glass of bourbon, then took a sip, smacking his lips. "No. Not for several more days, but their progress is promising. They're responding quite favorably to the growth stimulators and are weeks ahead of schedule now. Save for the runt, you wouldn't know that they'd been at a deficit."

Salist cocked a brow and looked impressed, as he should be. "And the girl?"

Titus tempered his frown. "More robust than she has any right to be." It was no longer a question of if she was able to spontaneously regenerate resources; it was a question of how. Nothing in her metrics indicated that she should be capable of such a feat.

"And I'm sure you're eager to test that out," Salist smiled, his teeth a shockingly white slice across his face. "You may have more time to do it than you think."

Titus's mood soured. Damn the man, but he knew something and was about to bleed him. "Oh?"

"I'm assuming you saw the footage of the mess Laughlin Scot made of the North?"

"Oddly enough, yes." Titus sat back in his chair, one ankle upon his knee. "In fact, I seem to remember being there for a portion of it."

Salist's grin widened as he lit his bowl. "Actually," he said, smoke dripping from his lips, "I'm referring to the events after you tucked tail with what remains of your Elites."

Titus regarded him deadpan for a long moment. It must be a juicy tidbit indeed if Salist felt the need to bait him. "If you mean whilst I was securing my prize, then yes. I saw the same footage that everyone else has been agog over." Not that they didn't have good reason to be. The amount of talent Scot had exhibited in destroying the plateau had been shocking, to say the least. A smile slicked over Titus's face.

Too bad the Overlord couldn't take it with him when he left the city.

Salist hummed, a dense cloud of blue smoke wreathing his head. "Then you can understand why there's been quite a bit of conjecture over those last few moments. Per the feed, one can only assume that channeling that much power took quite a toll on the Overlord…as must losing his family in one fell swoop. By all reports, the city is in turmoil with rumors abounding that the man's gone mad."

"Yes, yes, I'm well aware." And completely undeterred in acquiring him to stud. Whatever psychosis Scot was suffering from, it couldn't be any worse than Beritram's had been, and being as mad as a hatter had never precluded his ability to fuck.

"Given he hasn't been seen since the incident, despite that Assembly of theirs issuing a subpoena demanding answers, the overwhelming global consensus is that he's become incapacitated in some way. And with the rest of the city at each other's throats—"

"None of this is news," Titus interrupted peevishly. "I'm assuming next you'll tell me some regime in the Deep South has mobilized—Hexspar, if I had to guess—and I'd wish them luck. No matter how advanced their ground forces, getting anywhere near Glynfyls after what Scot did to the plateau will be impossible."

Salist lipped his hooka's mouthpiece, abruptly silent, and Titus's temper flared.

"How much?" he gritted out.

The former patron shrugged, dallying with the apparatus as if he didn't already have a figure in mind. "Say fifty-thousand. I'll take those funds out of escrow, and we'll call it even."

The amount, once daunting, seemed a pittance at the moment, and if there was one thing Salist was not, it was charitable. Still, Titus couldn't deny the man had him hooked. "Done."

"It's not only Hexspar. Ax'chig and Diytan have aligned for the venture, and the tribunal has finally gotten off the fence. They've frozen every last one of Albanach's assets. Whatever happens next, the old dragon's hands are tied, and I very much doubt the city is in any position to save itself."

Titus pursed his lips, inordinately pleased that someone had finally gotten enough balls to beard the man in his own cave. He swirled the ice in his glass, considering the Southern alliance. It had to be uneasy at best, given Diytan's monotheistic fanaticism and the titular head of Hexspar's practice of Wuism, but Ax'chig ever had been the power broker. Their air fleet in conjunction with Hexspar's ground troops and Diytan's navy had the potential to be a fearsome combination. Still…

"I take nothing at face value where Laughlin Scot is concerned," Titus said after a long sip of his bourbon. "Until I see for myself that the man is a quivering mass, it's just hearsay."

"Hearsay or not, one might conclude that the girl and her litter are safer with you, whilst he deals with the Deep South," Salist said offhandedly.

Titus snorted, his attention snapping back to the dark man, the smoke in the air around him occluding everything but Salist's brilliant smile.

"One would be wrong, but perhaps a reminder is necessary, should Scot be tempted to delay." A grin slicked across his face. "And I know just the memo to send."

CHAPTER FIVE

"Last week it came to a head between Ro and En, and it took all of my talent to save En's life. I question if I did the right thing. After looking through his mind, he's earned the disfiguring scar across his throat and so much worse. Does he know I know what he's done? The monster that he is? I feel no shame keeping a tether upon his mind, if only to assure myself he's not there lurking in the shadows—though, I suppose I don't have to worry. Since the incident, he's returned to Meskill and refuses to leave. None of us know what will happen to him there and honestly, a large part of me hopes something does.

El is devastated, but she and Ri have fashioned a clever white stone that allows someone to find a location with their mind, then shift there without a Fetch. They're calling it gating. We each have one of the stones now, and she's been using hers to visit En daily.

I can't blame her for wanting to get away. So many of the Original Houses whisper behind her back…in the beginning I was glad people had begun to find their faith again, but this new church's teachings worry me. El's become the poster child for original sin. A woman spat at her on the street yesterday. Sometimes I think it might be better if she wasn't so set on waiting for A to return. Perhaps after the child is born she'll follow En wherever he goes…"

– Undated journal entry

FLYNN TUMBLED THROUGH HIS MEMORIES, buffeted and battered by remorse and regret, bruised by loss, rent open by emptiness. He struggled, fighting for the surface, for consciousness—

And was dragged back down.

... Darkness covers him like a shroud, inky and black. Sharp with rust and rock dust and the bitter bite of wet-cold. His breath is loud. The thud of his heart in his ears. Both run counterpoint to the steady, uneven drip of moisture from the stones above.

He holds his chains taut, fighting exhaustion. They'll know if he sleeps. By the clink of metal or the evenness of his breath. Down here you can feel it. The moment someone lets down their guard. The air currents change, and time is measured in heartbeats, waiting for the screams and the sounds of the rest of them feasting...

His stomach growls. How long until he joins them? He squeezes his eyes shut. Not sure why he fights it. He's trapped in the hole, an animal like the rest of them. Blackness wraps around him, the press of earth above his head—suffocating. He crouches to one side of the tunnel, bare toes clinging to slick stone, back against the shale, and listens...

Flynn's eyelids fluttered, desperately trying to wrench his mind from what happened next, the gritty mineral funk of liver on his tongue. His brow furrowed. No. No. He couldn't—wouldn't be that animal again—

... "Only man delights in another creature's suffering..."

No—

Fur. Softness across his cheek. A tiny body against his, wriggling and curling up under his chin. Its gentle rumble vibrated against his throat. Flynn's breathing slowed. His chest rising and falling evenly. The rumble faded away, morphing into a steady beep and hiss...

He was in a sterile white and chrome room.

To either side of him, forms occluded by wires and tubes lay lined up on gurneys, paper drapes over their distended abdomens and clipboards at their feet. Ventilators rising and falling with their chests, numbers scrolling across plaz-screens behind them—

A masked woman in scrubs walked through him, intent on her tablet. Flynn stumbled, turning to follow her...

A gurney separate from the rest. "Jester" at the top of a screen broken into one main section and four below it, one of the columns flagged orange. His feet carried him closer without conscious thought.

Kara and the babies.

He stumbled, breaking into a run—

Something yowled and the wriggling warmth beneath his chin exploded outward with a frantic burst of fur, leaving him bereft, tumbling back into the darkness.

… "Where the fuck you think you're going?"

A meaty hand slams the door in front of him closed, and he falls, skidding across the kitchen floor. His gaze slowly rises. Taking in the muddy boots. Jeans. A belt, buckle hidden by a callused palm, worn leather wrapped once around split knuckles. The rest left to dangle, drawn up and snapped. He flinches, scrabbling back—

"Not so fast, boy. You owe me…"

SERRA TOOK her time as she descended from her suite of rooms at the Gilded Pearl. Her fingers lingered upon the front staircase's inset mosaic banister, bits of iridescent purple and cream shell polished to a mirrored sheen. The inn was purported to be the finest in Glynfyls, and its opulence certainly backed that up.

She crossed the lobby of dark wood and leather, sniffing at the side-eyes from the help, putting a bit more sway in her hips, taking up space—she belonged here, damn it—striding over the herringbone parquet floor of exotic wood, down the hall toward the private theater at the back of the establishment.

Fine art in heavy gilt frames adorned silk-papered walls with floor to ceiling windows overlooking quaint pocket gardens. The gentle murmur of voices rode just above the low music from the string quartet playing behind a painted screen in one of the dining rooms she passed. Warm golden light glinted from crystal chandeliers, stemware, and the jewels adorning the clientele.

Their eyes broadcasted Serra's lack as she traipsed through the lavish space in her borrowed dress. She held her chin higher. She'd earned this, and her fortunes would only continue to rise.

And when they did, she would be sure to remind them who was lacking.

A smile slicked over her mauve-stained lips as she entered the theater. It was much larger than she'd expected, with a wide reception area at the back before the room dipped down. Long, curved rows of seating lined the front of the clamshell surrounding an ornate stage, the venue spacious enough to easily accommodate the several hundred members of Glynfyls's upper crust milling about.

She was unsurprised at the turnout, given the full buffet Lord Morris was rumored to be footing the bill for. Considering the quality of the clothes he swathed himself in, Serra had no doubt he could afford it.

Her brow furrowed before she dismissed the idea of him providing her a suite of rooms. He was much too self-important to think of anyone's situation other than his own. She bit back a laugh at one of the political posters with his image adorning the side of the room. The still did an admirable job capturing his spindly little legs beneath his rotund gut, chin thrust out and hands at his lapels. My, if he didn't have an over-inflated vision of himself.

Serra shook her head. Though it was obvious the city fancied the toady little man as a great orator, she had her doubts. How could anyone that unattractive hold an audience as spellbound as he was purported to? No, his venomous sermons may be currently striking a chord with the city's elite, but she was sure his choice of venue and liberal spending habits were what was drawing such a crowd.

Interesting how many of them were Shades. No one with a Breaker's physique that she could see and only a smattering of tattooed Fetches. All of the Binders from the Source and hill were in attendance. The rest must be Finders and Fixers evening out the rest of the heavy crowd, but despite the press, it didn't take long to espy Lord Morris speaking to Lord Crown. Both were impeccably dressed, though there was no question who wore it better. She swallowed a snicker as she approached. They stood before an exquisite pink marble hearth with a fire burning merrily behind a gilt screen fashioned to resemble a peacock's plumage.

Lord Morris looked over as she came close, his jowls becoming florid. Serra allowed herself a smile, already feeling her fish on the hook. He said something to Lord Crown and the man glanced over, then made his exit, a knowing smile playing at his lips. Serra made a mental note to rekindle their association as she stepped closer to the fire.

"Lord Morris." She inclined her head demurely. "I wanted to thank you. It brings me great comfort to know that my House isn't alone in its concern as to how the state of affairs in Glynfyls stand." She offered him her hand and he bowed over it precisely. My, but he was a dour little troll. Her appreciation for the Source's breeding practices increased another notch.

"Lady Hess. I'm so pleased to see you here. From what I understand, the vast majority of our newest residents share the opinion that Scot has no business being in power," he said, hooking his thumbs into his brocade waistcoat and puffing up like a bullfrog.

Serra inclined her head. "That would be fair to say. His status as a twist makes such a thing unconscionable, and the rumors I've heard concerning his behavior…they're incredibly distasteful."

"They are at that, and I can assure you of their veracity. Scot's history is as sordid as they come. His most recent public records of malfeasance are all right there in black and white." Morris flicked a hand at several stacks of papers scattered along a long table.

"Unfortunately, his wretched House has only facilitated his behavior by paying to have the lion's share of it swept under the rug. They've somehow gotten his early records sealed, else you'd see much the same from his youth."

"It's so sad when elders do nothing to correct their children." Serra shook her head in commiseration. "Forgive me if I'm overstepping, but there's also a more recent, personal element to your crusade, is there not?"

"There is, and I don't deny it." Lord Morris abruptly looked like he'd bitten into something incredibly foul. "The pain of losing Paul is very fresh. Excuse me, please." He took out his pocket square and blotted his brow as he walked away, overcome.

"Of course, you poor, dear man," Serra crooned at his quickly retreating back before making her way to the table he'd indicated. She picked up a random page and scanned it, biting back her smile. My, Lord Scot certainly had a fondness for prostitutes...her mirth faded as she perused his medical records and the amount of damage Kara had healed registered. If not for the x-rays and stills, Serra wouldn't have believed the chit could've...no, there had to be some trick to it. It simply wasn't possible—

"Lady Hess, I presume?"

Serra turned to the extremely distinguished woman that had come up beside her. She leaned upon an onyx cane with a brilliant brass head, one hand atop the other.

"I am, and you are...?"

The woman pursed her lips and raised one slim eyebrow. Her slate gray hair was elegantly coifed and her dress tailored precisely to her sparse form. "Lady Geraldine Saks. Your Tamara and my Miles have been spending a great deal of time together," she said dryly.

Ah. The harridan. "Is that so?" Serra asked, playing dumb. "I'm afraid I've been incredibly busy at the clinics of late."

"So I've read." The woman's tone sent a flush across Serra's cheeks. "But, be that as it may, Miles recently opened an account for your girl with Regina Glass. Pity I had to close it."

Okay...Serra could only smile and maintain eye contact, her mind racing. Had that been a dig, or an opening? The woman was impossible to read, and Serra got the distinct impression that was by design.

Lady Saks let her flounder for several uncomfortable moments before continuing, her enjoyment at throwing Serra off-kilter evident. "The Scots are Regina's biggest clients...or were, and I won't see a single unit given to someone who consorts with such trash. I've had the funds shifted to Luann Melfis. She had enough integrity to turn away their business when the ruffian came back. Money isn't everything, you know. She'll be more than able to clothe both you and your daughter in something suitable." Her quick glance at Serra's dress assured her what she was currently wearing was not.

Serra tapped the papers in her hand square and set them back on the table, ignoring the barb and regrouping. The woman wasn't an ally precisely, but she presented an opportunity to be sure. "Thank you. I appreciate your generosity, and your morality brings me great comfort. It's gratifying to know that Tamara is making the right kind of connections up here. Being so new to the city, it can be difficult to find one's footing."

The woman didn't quite roll her eyes. "From what I understand, Tamara has done nothing but make connections since she arrived. Particularly with that Fixer, Gregor Dean."

"I don't—"

Lady Sax held up a hand, forestalling Serra's protests. "Let me be blunt. My son is intent on bonding your daughter, and I'm not opposed. Their offspring would gain my House the best chance of ascending to First since the Great Incursion, which makes me inclined to support their courtship, and you, by association. I trust your new lodgings will ease whatever financial burdens you may have, and her 'busy nights at the clinic' will stop now."

Serra put a hand to her throat, mortified at the revelation that Geraldine Saks was her benefactress. Worse, that she'd just tied Serra's rising star to Tamara's adherence to Northern propriety…

Glory, she was going to be ruined. There would be no wiggle room, nor any forgiveness should Tamara slip up…*when* Tamara slipped up. Serra smiled, attempting to mask her dismay. "Of course. I'll impress upon her how things stand," she said, fully anticipating she would have to bind her daughter's crotch shut then sit on her until her wedding day.

"See that you do," Lady Saks murmured, thumping her cane against the floor. She turned to go, then frowned at the mugshot of Lord Scot Serra had placed at the top of the pile. "Deirdre was such a paragon, too. It's a shame, but as Paul warned the Corinthians, the devil appears as an angel of light. The same holds true here. No man can be that beautiful and be good as well." She ran her finger down the page and sniffed. "Good evening, Lady Hess."

Serra narrowed her eyes at Lady Saks's back as she moved off through the crowd, mulling over the potential for disaster that meeting had just introduced.

The house lights dimmed and people began to find seats. Serra followed the tide and settled herself upon a clever folding chair of crushed aubergine velvet somewhere in the center.

Lord Morris had moved to the stage. A large screen was behind him. The lights lowered and a montage of the recent destruction began to play behind him in sepia tones.

"Friends," his voice rang out, "like-minded citizens. Today, Glynfyls weeps. The plateau, our city—they lie in ruin. Thousands dead or injured. Homes and livelihoods lost through no fault of our own..." He shook his head, stepping back to watch the screen for a moment. "It isn't right. It isn't fair. And what strikes me as the most unjust?" He struck his palm with a clenched fist and then pointed an accusatory finger in the direction of the city's crown. "That it can all be attributed to that twisted bastard playing king!"

There were cries of agreement and agitated murmurs. Morris acknowledged them with a nod, tugging his lapels square. He began to pace, the images behind him increasingly graphic with Scot's mugshot superimposed over them.

"Laughlin Scot has overthrown our government, threatening violence against law abiding citizens and using his crimes to intimidate us into silence!" He held up a packet of papers and then flung them out at the crowd. "His record Outside. The murders in the tunnels below. Tearing the heart from a man while the world watches! The destruction of the Assembly Hall's west wing, the Judiciary, gone, and what just occurred outside our fair city's gates—" He paused, and the silence hung heavy in the room, the audience on tenterhooks.

Serra glanced around, the shift of power a physical thing.

"Without remorse," Morris rasped, making them lean forward to hear him, moths to his flame. "Without the batting of an eye. But perhaps...perhaps he deserves grace. Perhaps, it's not his fault..."

Serra jumped at the cries to the contrary around her.

Lord Morris held up a hand until they quieted. "Friends, we must accept that there are those amongst us that do not think as we do, nor hold the same values. Instead, they're *twisted*." Catcalls rained down upon him, and he held his hand up again, waiting for them to silence. "It is an established fact 'dual talents' lack the morals that hold our society together. Laughlin Scot is merely a symptom of the disease, as proven by his record of malfeasance. He's unstable, unfit, and unwanted as Overlord and, as such, needs to be expunged!"

The crowd cheered, several of them standing.

"Will you stand idle as a murderer sets himself up as king of our fair city? He's denounced the Assembly, ignored our call for answers—for justice! Grievances and proposals to go through the Firsts and be approved by Quorum," Morris sneered, pacing the stage like a tiger. Flecks of spittle sparkled as they fell to the footlights.

"He's wormed his way into owning that vote! Half Breaker, half Shade, House ties to the Binders and Fetches. The Fixer First owes him his seat! Approved by Quorum? Approved by King Scot! My friends, on all that is holy, the mantle of Overlord must be dissolved, and Laughlin Scot exiled. His nature is anathema, his use of talent, abhorrent. The abuses of power he's perpetrated upon the Northern Territories are reprehensible, and I for one refuse to let that stand!" There were several cries of outrage and a low murmur of unrest amongst those seated.

"Tomorrow…you know what your vote must be." Morris nodded grimly at the crowd. "For Glynfyls. For your children. And for any hope of a bright future. Thank you."

The audience rose to its feet with loud cheers, calling for Scot's head, and Serra sat back blinking. Well. She flicked open her fan. That wasn't what she'd been expecting. The little troll had actually lived up to the hype…

"It'll mean civil war if he pulls that off," the man in front of Serra remarked to another as he tipped his bowler to a woman squeezing past him. "The commons don't give a fig if Scot's a twist."

"It might happen even if Morris doesn't. I hear they're rallying on the lower spokes as we speak," said the other, tugging on his gloves. "Ingrates should've been put in their place the last time they dared to raise a hand against us. Mark my words, one way or another, blood's going to be spilt on the morrow, and I don't intend for it to be from me or mine."

"No, I can promise you the same." Bowler Hat frowned. "The only question is, will he show, or will we have to pry him out of his flat?"

"And risk scuttling what's left of his House?" The man with the gloves laughed. "If I were them, I'd have him hogtied and delivered. One way or another, I have no doubt he'll be there."

Serra sat musing as they left, and the room cleared. From what she'd seen of Laughlin Scot, she didn't doubt he would be there, either…and from what she'd just seen of Lord Morris, she needed to begin reeling him in.

PETERLI MORRIS BLOTTED his brow as he accepted his usual glass of brandy from a waiting servant. These rallies always got his blood up. It was invigorating to see the city come around to his point of view.

The innkeeper, Dorothy, caught his eye as she purposefully crossed the back of the theater. "Lord Morris, this just came for you," she handed him a thick missive, then stood there like she was waiting for him to open it. What cheek!

"Thank you," he said curtly, tucking it into his jacket pocket. "Is there something else?" There were people of importance to speak with, and she wasn't one of them.

"There is. I hope that everything has been to your satisfaction?"

"Yes, yes, everything's exemplary as usual," he said, raising his chin to briskly blot his throat. Couldn't she see he was busy? He hadn't thought her gauche enough to wait for a tip, and after this grasping display, if she'd been expecting one, she could think again. He took another sip of brandy, clearly dismissing her.

"I'm gratified to hear that, sir," she pressed, her voice firmer than its wont. "I'd hoped it wasn't any lack on our part that was preventing you from settling your bill."

The brandy became vinegar in his mouth.

"I've held these rooms for you based on your good name and history with us," she continued, "but it's become a tidy sum, and I'm afraid I'm not going to be able to do so any longer without recompense."

"No, of course not." Lord Morris slowly wiped his mouth, trying to maintain his decorum. He smiled genially at her. "I promise to look into it immediately. I can't imagine what the holdup could be, Davis is usually so punctual."

"Very good, sir, and thank you. I'll expect the entirety of the sum tomorrow, then?"

"Certainly. I'll see it done. Might I have another brandy while you're here?" he asked as she turned to leave.

The innkeeper opened her mouth to say something, then forced a smile and nodded instead. "I'll send someone right in with that."

She left, and he threw his handkerchief to the floor as he retrieved the missive and tore it open. Damn Augusta. That his wife was behind this, he had no doubt. Ever since Paul's betrayal, she'd become completely unreasonable. Peterli ripped the parchment from the envelope, seething. His father had warned him not to lower himself by bonding her, well-off though their House may have been—

His blood pressure spiked at the papers within, eyes widening with fury.

"The cheek of that woman!" She'd sent him a copy of their assets when they'd bonded. In bright red, she'd circled his pitiable net worth at the time, and on the edge of the page in her flowing script:

Not a penny more until Paul is home.

THE DAMNED WOMAN would do it, too. Peterli bit back a curse. One of the stipulations in her father's will was that Augusta retained control of her inheritance; the result of Peterli losing her dowry on several bad business ventures, though the fault clearly lay with his investors, not him.

A girl came in with his drink, and he raised the snifter then drained it, coughing at the liquor's bite. "Another," he said, handing it back to her.

This frisson in his House—in their marriage—was entirely unacceptable. That the shrew was trying to control him with her purse strings went beyond the pale. She should be thanking him for giving her his good name. For God's sake, the woman had been involved with theater when they'd met! The scandal of their bond was the talk of Glynfyls—

He turned at a scuff at the doorway, expecting his brandy. Instead, Serra Hess had appeared like a vision.

"Oh, I'm sorry!" She flicked open her fan and fluttered it coquettishly against the tasteful expanse of her décolletage. "I'd hoped to take just a moment of your time...I thought you were entertaining back here."

He wasn't, but Lord Morris clicked his tongue, inclined to. "If you're willing, I'd enjoy some company."

She looked entirely scandalized—as she should. Damn those brandies. He cleared his throat. "My apologies, Lady Hess, that was untoward. I've had a bit more to drink than is wise, and I've just been dealt a grievous personal blow. Forgive me."

"Of course, and please, think nothing of it," she murmured, an attractive flush staining her cheeks. "It's so rare to find a man of passion in this day and age. I must say it's quite exhilarating. Lady Morris is a lucky woman."

He grunted. Yes, she was, but the she-devil had apparently forgotten that. Perhaps a rival for his affections was what she needed to remind her. He smoothed his waistcoat, not opposed to partaking in some harmless flirtation. "Unfortunately, I'm afraid she doesn't share my convictions."

"How unfortunate." Lady Hess's gaze ran over him as he strolled closer. "It's a pity when people don't appreciate what they have. I've found myself quite envious of your Northern concept of relationships. It's strange to admit that no matter how fine the rooms I've taken upstairs are, they're somehow lacking without a man in my life."

Peterli dabbed his pocket square over his upper lip, suddenly very warm. Her forwardness simultaneously repulsed and attracted him. Apparently, the rumors about Source Binders were true. No lady from Glynfyls would dream of speaking to him so.

"Are they? I don't find that strange at all...you're ah—I was unaware you were lodging here."

Her smile was dazzling. "Yes, it's quite convenient, and I'm ever so fortunate to have gotten a suite with small balcony and separate entrance. Such a blessing when I need to visit the infirmary in the middle of the night. I'd hate to disturb other guests with my comings and goings. Thankfully, they're none the wiser."

What a whore and yet, he couldn't deny he was aroused. Augusta's incredulity faintly registered through their bond. That she would dare to cast further judgement upon him—

Serra waved her fan as if heated. "I won't take up any more of your time, I just wanted to convey my support and tell you how your words have…have touched me." Her cheeks flared as her eyes roamed over him.

"Then we'll have to speak more on the subject," he said, quite forgetting himself.

"Soon, I hope." She smiled enticingly, inclined her head, and left him.

Peterli watched her go, vindicated in his choices. Not only did Lady Hess share his beliefs, she appreciated his conviction. Passion, she'd called it. He ran a hand over his lips, positive the mention of the private entrance to her rooms was an invitation. If that led to anything like the story in the papers had alleged…the thought of her on her knees with that lush mouth wrapped around his member was almost enough to undo him where he stood.

And if the other rumors he'd heard about women from the Source were true…his mouth went dry at the sway of her voluptuous backside as she left the theater.

The serving girl came in with another brandy, and he tore it from the chit's hands, draining a goodly portion as he stared into the shadows. A montage of depravity and degradation ran through his mind, numb to the hurt the reverie was causing his wife.

It served her right for treating him so shabbily.

***

ROGAN NUDGED OPEN the bedroom door and frowned down at Flynn. Kid was curled up on the floor, whimpering in his sleep. Goddamn. What the inside of his head had to be like right now…

The Alpha sighed and eased the door back before crossing to the couch. Didn't want to admit it, but Cal was right to call for Nora. There wasn't a chance in hell Flynn was gonna sleep off whatever he was going through. Rogan plopped onto the nasty checkered cushions and a puff of dust went up along with an alarming creak of protest as his weight settled.

"Christ, at least the last one was solid," he muttered, moving the pillow French had brought up behind him. "This thing sounds like it's gonna collapse."

"Just don't sneeze too hard, and you'll be fine," Cal said offhandedly, eyes on the ruddy glow outside the window as he smoked, empty glass in his hand. "He asleep?"

Rogan snorted. "I guess you could call it that...and for what it's worth, I take back what I said about sending for Nora." He leaned over and refilled Cal's glass. "Kid said he doesn't remember everything, and that's probably a blessing, but something in him is definitely broken."

"He tell you about it?"

"Enough."

Cal grunted and pinched the last of his cigarette between his lips. He took out his pouch to roll another, frowning.

"What?"

"Nothing...he just doesn't usually say a damn thing to anyone other than French. The two of them..." Cal shook his head and sprinkled tobacco along a rolling paper, twisted, then licked the edge of his cigarette closed. He lit it with the smoldering nub of the last one and exhaled a thick stream of blue-gray smoke. "Let's just say Lot and your old man have more in common than I'd like. French was the one that used to piece Flynn back together. Man's of the opinion I should've done more to stop it, and he's probably right."

Rogan grunted, retrieving his bottle. "Then why didn't you?"

"You know damned well why, and I'll maintain the only reason that boy's alive today is because the twins didn't think I gave a shit about him."

"Yeah, but neither does he." Rogan frowned, picking at the label.

Cal took another drag. "I'm well aware, but the best I could do was keep him out of Lot's way."

"Yeah?" Rogan sat back, the couch creaking. "How'd that work?"

"It didn't, and the first time he took a swing back at the man, Lot almost killed him." Cal leaned forward, elbows on his knees. "Deirdre threatened to leave—things got ugly."

Rogan's temper spiked, the scenario hitting him hard, even now. Christ, his past was too fucking close in this city. "There had to have been something—"

"There wasn't." Cal cut off his protest with a look. "Lot was head of House Scot and First Shade. Deirdre was on the cusp of making the Reunification happen. Everything was coming together...we couldn't risk a scandal." He ran a heavy hand down his face. "It kills me to say it, but one sad little boy didn't take precedence."

Rogan's knuckles popped as he made a concerted effort to breathe through the rage that statement sparked. On some level, he'd failed the kid, too. Even if Cal had called him, there was no way he'd have left his beach, and if he had, the twins would've made sure Flynn ended up bleeding out somewhere.

"French always did right by the boy, but the man doesn't have much use for me, and I can't say I blame him." Cal stared into his empty glass, then pursed his lips, thoughtful. "Hopefully, Nora can patch Flynn up enough for him to put on a show so we can get the hell out of here." His cigarette crackled as he took a heavy drag, agitated.

"Patch up? More like perform a miracle," Rogan scoffed. "Because until he stops seeing flames everywhere, he sure as hell isn't gonna be able to hack it in front of a crowd. Christ, I don't even know if he can come back from where he is now."

"Wherever that is, the trip isn't as far as it was to the other side of the grave and back again." Cal sat back and crossed his ankle over a knee.

Rogan grunted, unable to disagree with that. He took another sip of liquor, holding it in his mouth until the burn mellowed. "Any leads on Kara?"

"My contact at the Corporation's confirmed Titus has her, and that he's gotten a sudden influx of cash. Says he's in bed with someone, and it's not any of the usual suspects."

"Then he is working with the twins. Still no clue about the Triam's location?"

"None." Cal ran a hand through his thick white hair. "But I can guarantee you it's underground, and I'm gonna bet the only way in or out is by Fetch."

"Too bad we don't currently have access to one of those." Rogan upended the bottle, the inability to do anything productive making him itch.

"Even if we did, they'd need an imprint," Cal muttered.

Rogan abruptly had the worst urge to pummel the shit out of him. "So we have Dorian find someone who does, then make them scream uncle. Maybe one of those Breakers Titus left behind—"

Cal snorted and held out his empty glass.

"You got a better idea?" Rogan asked, leaning over to refill it.

"Nope."

Asshole. Rogan rolled his eyes and settled back. Something in the couch snapped, and it sank a good inch. Par for the fucking course. "Well, then there ya go."

"There you go," Cal chuckled.

Rogan ran a hand down the side of his head, blowing out a long breath after they'd sat in companionable silence for a time. "You really gonna to be able to do it when you see her?"

Cal looked toward the bedroom, his face stoney. "Yeah—"

They both glanced over at the rumble of the lift and a moment later, Nora stepped out. Physically, she looked beat to shit, but the determined energy about her made Rogan sit up straighter.

Cal must've felt it, too, because he did the same. "Nora. I'm sorry to have to ask you to do this."

"No, you're not. And I'm not here because you asked, I'm here because I'm getting my daughter back, and I need Laughlin to make that happen." She raised her chin like she expected Cal to fight her on it.

He settled back in his chair, an eyebrow cocked as he tongued his cheek. "Is that right?"

"It is. Is he in there?" she asked, her eyes flicking toward the bedroom.

"Last I checked." Rogan slapped his hands onto his thighs. Didn't know what the fuck was going on between the two of them, and didn't particularly care. He stood and crossed to the door.

Flynn was in the same position as he had been, the floorboards around him darkened with sweat. Rogan turned and motioned for her.

Nora slipped inside and crouched down beside the kid. He whimpered, twitching. Her halos glimmered as she gently laid her hand on his head, her frown apparent even in the dim light coming through the shutters.

The angles of the shadows they cast had flattened before she dropped talent.

"Can you get him into bed?" she asked, rising unsteadily as she wiped her cheeks.

Rogan pushed from the wall. "Maybe, if Cal gives me a hand. Kid weighs a ton."

It took some doing, but they managed it. Rogan took one more look at Flynn before easing the door shut and joining them in the other room. Whatever she'd done, he was out cold.

"Well?" Rogan asked, reclaiming his seat on the crappy couch.

Nora stood silent at the window, a hand over her mouth as she gazed out. She looked utterly drained. "Tonight I've learned a great many things about Laughlin Scot I wish I hadn't." She glanced at Cal with such a look of reproach that Rogan wanted to curl up and die on his behalf.

"From what I can tell, Kara's bind was only intended to address physical damage. It restructured his body, but it didn't reorder his mind. Every trauma he's ever suffered has been brought to the surface. His psyche is trying to reprocess decades of abuse on top of losing her. He's—you've no idea how damaged he is, or what he's gone through." She choked back a sob, then turned to glare at Cal. "What were you thinking letting that man anywhere near him?"

"I've made mistakes Nora, I don't deny it," he said, unrepentant.

"Mistakes and years of wanton negligence are two very different things, Caliban Scot." She shook her head in disgust and addressed Rogan. "I'll be blunt. It's impossible for anyone without Otto's extra to overtly influence another Talent's mind. I was able to plant suggestions, but they're just that, and the weaves will shred if they're stressed." Nora took a deep breath before she continued.

"That said, I did what I could to mute his pre-existing trauma, and I purged the residual neurotoxins from the suppressant Marcos shot him with. They could very well have been responsible for any lingering psychosis."

"Will he still see flames?" Rogan asked.

"I don't know, but he should be calmer, which I think will help. At the very least, it should temper his paranoia and any suicidal thoughts." Cal flinched like he'd been struck, and she glared at him. "Don't. You have no right. Not after looking the other way for so long."

She turned back to Rogan. "He's put a major block over what happened on the plateau, and I'm not touching it. He's going to have to come to terms with that and everything else in his own time, and I can't tell you when that will be." She stepped closer, and Rogan stood at the intensity on her face.

"You need to stay by his side until we get Kara and the babies back. Anything I did is temporary and right now, you, Kendall, and French are the only things anchoring him. I'm hoping what I've done will last long enough for him to get his feet under him." She shook her head, whatever verve she'd come up here with gone.

"I'll watch over him," Rogan murmured, catching her arm as she stumbled. "How long will he sleep for?"

She glanced at the bedroom door. "Several more hours. I used the same bind on him as I did on Fitz. It targets metabolic function, not the sleep cycle itself."

"Good." Rogan grunted. "I've gotta run a quick errand. I'll have French sit with him while I'm gone. You should get some rest, too."

"I will." She nodded absently, running a hand over her forehead. "But first, you'll promise that you won't leave to get Kara without me. Swear it, Rogan, because if she and the babies need medical attention—"

"You have my word." He put his hands up in submission and frowned. "But Marcos isn't gonna like it."

She laughed, her shoulders slumping. "There's a great many things I do that Marcos doesn't like, but I suspect my bowing out of politics will soften the blow."

"What's this now?" Cal asked, jolted from whatever funk Nora's censure had put him in.

She smiled smugly at him. "Serra's taken legal action to have me removed as First Binder, and I'm not going to fight her on it. She can have the position with my blessing. I'm done playing the game, and I think you'll agree that I've more than earned my retirement." She dipped her head at Rogan and swept past him, the lift doors opening like they'd been waiting for her when she pressed the button.

"Well, shit," Cal muttered as they closed behind her.

Rogan pulled his boots over. "Why does it feel like you just got dumped?"

"Because I did." Cal sighed and stood. "It's the end of an era."

"Won't be the first you've lived through."

"No, but it might be the last." He looked over at the bedroom door, the slightest tremble to his hand as he raised his cigarette. "You're running out?"

"Yeah, I have to give the Breakers their marching orders before we jump ship. Send French up, will you? I'll wait for him before I go." Rogan sat back to pull on a boot and winced at the sound of splintering wood.

Cal grunted and ambled to the lift. "Will do, and I'll follow up with Markham. Hopefully he was able to track down Fitz. I'd feel a hell of a lot better knowing we had a Fetch in our back pocket."

"Agreed," Rogan said, tying his laces. "And if you plan on keeping him there, I'd suggest you have French pull up a couple more cases of Bushmills."

<hr>

FITZ'S JAW tightened with his frown as he shifted to the Manse, and Sophia hurried off without a word, leaving him with LaVeil. Whatever. Didn't care.

"Damn, yo, she is pissed at you," the red-headed freak chortled.

"Ain't none of yer concern," Fitz muttered, parking his arse on the couch at the side of the stone entry hall with his pizza. He weren't about to let her or playing taxi dim his good mood after crunchin' into them peppers, though LaVeil were workin' his last nerve.

He snorted and shook his head, dreads waggling like eels. "You really gonna park it right there an' wait?"

"That I am." Fitz threw back the lid of the box and mashed the last two slices on top of the other, eating them like a sandwich. "Learned me lesson, wanderin' about, haven't I?" he asked around his third bite, glaring at the man.

"Suit yoself, blondie…" LaVeil's eyes moved to follow Sophia down one of the long hallways. "But FYI, I think Imma be a while."

Fitz tamped down a surge of temper. "I wouldn't suggest it."

LaVeil ran a hand over his jaw, still staring at Sophia's backside as he started after her at a slow saunter. "And I ain't one to take advice…"

Fitz pushed to his feet, still chewing. The hell if he were gonna let that happen. "Fine. I'll find somewhat t'occupy me time. Suggest ye find yer bedeviled part. That way." He pointed down the hallway they'd taken before.

A smile stretched over the pale man's face Fitz didn't much like. "Alright, alright. I gotcha little brutha. All you gotta do is call dibs."

Fitz sputtered. "Nah, *nah*! I ain't—she ain't—"

"Ohhh. It's like that." LaVeil nodded sagely. He clasped Fitz's shoulder. "My condolences. Meet you back here in five." LaVeil smacked his hip and made a face, miming riding a horse to the other hallway before breaking into a jog.

Fitz rubbed his forehead. "Jesus save me from idjits…" He glanced up just as Sophia rounded a corner. He shoved the last of the pizza in his mouth and choked it down before running to catch up with her. "Sophia!"

Shite. If she'd been mad before, Fitz weren't sure what she were now, other than quiet, but he didn't like it. He reached out, and she spun on him as soon as his fingers landed, her glare sending him back a step.

"Please, just…" Wide bands of bronze flickered around her irises, and she closed her eyes, everything around them going unnaturally still for a breath.

A tear slid down her cheek, and Fitz felt like he were gonna be sick.

"Here, now, none of that," he murmured, pulling her against his chest. She sobbed, burying her face in his jacket. Shite. Way she were trembling about broke his heart. "I'm sorry if I did aught t'upset ye—"

Sophia shook her head. "It's not you, it's the path." She threw her arms around his waist, fisting the back of his shirt—

Fitz pulled talent and was halfway down the hall before he'd even thought about it, his flesh crawling at her innocent touch against his spine. Sophia caught herself as she stumbled, sniffling. "W-what happened?"

"Naught." Damn it. His face burned crimson and he turned away, raking a hand through his hair at the reminder of his shame. He jammed his hands into his pockets, slumping. His coin burned cold. Every damned time he thought—didn't matter. "Take care of yerself."

He left her standing there without another word.

LaVeil was waiting for him in the entry chamber, spare part in hand and a waist-high black case with wheels by his side. He snorted and shook his head. "Damn, yo, it went that bad?"

"The hell is that?" Fitz frowned at him.

"This here?" The pale man slapped the case. "Source-issued surveillance tech to keep an eye on all you freaks. Kendall say fuck the plaz, we ain't playin' no more. You got a problem with that?"

That no, but LaVeil were another thing all together. "Let's just fuckin' do this. Ye got the imprint of where we're goin'?" Man nodded and Fitz took it, scowling as he pulled talent again, shifting them from the Manse to a long, low warehouse secreted in one of the hidden coves east of Glynfyls. Weren't one of the usual ones Markham used, though Fitz's da had plenty.

LaVeil left the case and made a beeline for the craft parked at the center of the dilapidated space while Fitz glanced around, kicking at the rotted floor. Pre-dawn sky peered through the holes in the roof and the wind sent loose sheets of corrugated metal flapping. Good possibility ain't no one had used it since. He sure as fuck hadn't been back out here.

Lights in the craft's cabin kicked on, throwing shadows across the warehouse.

"Yo, blondie, you want in on this?" LaVeil asked as he hung out the open door.

Fitz scowled and kept wandering toward the little office at the back of the building. Man didn't need his help replacing whatever part were blighted, and Fitz sure as fuck had better things to do than spend his last few hours on earth staring at LaVeil's scraggly ass shimmyin' about.

Nah. Finding someplace to settle in with a bottle until the mercenary were done were top priority before it were time to head back to Scot's flat and face the ax. Fitz's Adam's apple bobbed. Weren't a fucking chance he were meeting his maker sober.

"Yo! You hear me?"

"Fuck off," Fitz called back, flipping LaVeil the bird.

The pale man laughed. "Suit yoself, little brutha, but don't come cryin' to me after Sasquatch bends you over. This place is sketchy as fuck—"

The craft door hissed as it closed, cutting off whatever else were dribbling out his mouth.

Sasquatch. What an idjit. This far north they was yeti. Fitz shrugged his jacket closer to his ears. Were colder than a witch's—he frowned, rethinking that. Sophia's tits had been right toasty pressed up against him.

His footsteps was too loud kicking through leaves and whatever other shite had blown in as he crossed the rotting space. Christ, but this place were eerier than he'd remembered. Were also fallin' to shite, but the energy out here were a sight easier t'handle than the cluster the city were in.

Were a sight easier t'handle than seeing Sophia's hurt, too. He scrubbed his curls, feeling like a complete shite. Shouldn't give a fuck, but the look on her face after he'd freaked out...Christ. The fuck had he expected? Course she were gonna try to put her arms around him when he were comfortin' her. She were a regular girl, weren't she?

Hugging's what normal people did, and another fuckin' reason why he didn't truck with 'em. Were better this way.

But seeing her standing there, eyes all red and swollen from crying…

Damn it, she were a witch, and he didn't care. His coin flared cold like it were callin' him a liar, and he swore. *Wise it, ye bastard.* Tears always fuckin' got him. Couldn't help it if they made him go all soft—

Cajetan's mirth washed over him, and he scowled again. *Ain't what I meant, and ye know it.* Jesus, the blessed saint were a right prick.

Fitz's scowl evaporated as he palmed the knob for the office door, and it were stuck fast. Shite. Maybe nobody had been there since his da. Quick pull of talent sent the tumblers clicking, and the knob turned.

Door creaked open on a solid rectangle of black.

He focused, callin' up his extra and lines of energy sprung up, outlining the room. Table and chairs three steps from a cot on the other side. Both of 'em bare and a slick of somewhat nasty dripping down the back wall from above. Fitz stepped inside, eyes on the ground as he flipped through his book of memories…

… The heels of his boots clunk out of sync against the cot's rail as he swings them. "Is we pirates, Da? Joey Dashell says his da says we is, an' it makes us filthy."

"Ya? Well, Joey Dashell and his da is a couple o' miserable twats. I look filthy t'ye?" Da holds up a hand creased with engine grease, and Fitz giggles. "Nah. Smugglin's as honest a trade as any, if ye do it right." His halos flare and a chest appears by his side, shifted up from the ground below. He flips up the lid and pulls out a bottle of whiskey, toasting Fitz with it and a broad grin. "And fuckin' with them's a sight more fun than haulin' nets or sitting behind a desk at the customs house…"

Fitz, exhaled, running a hand over his jaw. Picturing the battered chest and pulling talent. He sat heavily on the cot's squealing springs as the wooden trunk appeared in the center of the room, just as he remembered. Tumblers shifted, and he closed his eyes for a tick before carefully lifting the lid.

Case of whiskey clinked amidst a mess of yellowed papers. Fitz slid a bottle free, holding it reverently. "Here's to ye, Da—" He cracked the seal and spun off the top. "I'll be seein' ye soon."

"Though I approve of the toast, I'm afraid I'm going to have to object to the rest."

Shite. Fitz about choked on his mouthful and dropped his head, curls covering his face at his uncle's voice. "Did ye need somewhat?" Words was garbled and thick.

Markham went over to the table and set down his lantern before pulling out a chair. He sighed as he settled his bulk onto the creaking wood. "I'm afraid I do, and it's urgent, else I wouldn't interrupt. Spare me a pull, would you?" he asked, blotting his neck.

Fitz took another swig before passing the bottle over. "Ye'll catch hell if Bernice smells it on ye."

Markham snorted. "I'm catching hell regardless. I might as well go into it well-padded." He slapped his gut as he raised the bottle, "To Denis," and chugged a goodly portion.

Christ. Fitz watched the liquor level drop. Ain't never seen Markham do that before. "Sisters putting the screws to ye?"

"God, you've no idea," his uncle said, wiping a hand over his mouth. "All of them are holed up at Kristine's, and this damned vote tomorrow…" He handed the bottle back and sighed, staring at Fitz.

Shite. Didn't much like that. Fitz upended the bottle, waiting for it.

Didn't take long.

"I'm not privy to all that transpired between the sisters and the Seers, but it concerns me a great deal that you're at the center of it, and blast me if I can see another way to get you clear. In the name of all that's holy, Fitzpatrick, you need to stay in Laughlin Scot's good graces."

Bit late for that. Fitz hid behind his curls and blew out a breath.

"Jesus. What've you done?"

"Eh…s'more like what I ain't." Fitz buzzed his lips and thumbed the mouth of the bottle. "Set a ward on the lady and when it broke, I were goin' at it with Leo. Didn't answer it like I said I would, then woke up with her shanghaied, and a murder done not three steps away."

"Good Lord!" Markham slapped a hand to his breast. "You were there? You're lucky you weren't killed as well! The bastards that took Lady Scot slit that mercenary's throat, ah, Korns—"

"Kerns," Fitz corrected, crossing hisself. Shite, she were the one that were done in? A flare of anger lit him up. Woman were a bitch, but that didn't mean she weren't good people.

"Aye, that was her name. Laughlin's distraught, but he—lord, you don't know him at all do you?" Markham sighed, settling back again. "Laughlin Scot would sooner blame himself for a cloudy day than the heavens. He certainly doesn't fault you for his lady's abduction, nor for the mercenary's murder. I'm here because they've been looking for you; they want your help bringing the lady back." He waved his handkerchief toward the craft. "That's what all that out there is about."

Fitz raised a skeptical brow, not believing it. "Ye serious?"

"I am." Markham ran the cloth over his face. "Laughlin's a good man, Fitz, and you need to make yourself indispensable to him. Something…something's changed with Leo's death. The sisters…" he shook his head. "They're up to something, and I'll be damned if I know what, but with your majority looming—"

"Fuck me majority. Ain't naught gonna happen, 'cause I ain't claimin' shite." Fitz glared at him as he took another swallow.

"So you've said." Markham sighed. "But we both know they're not planning on taking your preferences into account."

"Preferences." Fitz snorted. "Ain't naught to prefer about it. If there were, me preference would be for the lot of 'em t'fuck off, and leave me be."

Markham raised a hand, defeated. "I understand. God Almighty, trust me I do, but the fact remains that you are the only pureblooded male Fetch with a legal claim to House Prydee capable of continuing their bloodline, and unfortunately, Laughlin's recent ascendence to Head of both House Scot and House Firestorm has set a precedent for dual heirships. I can guarantee you the sisters have been exploring the option."

"I ain't a Prydee, and I ain't never gonna be."

"No, but heaven forbid you have a son one day."

Fitz snorted. That weren't gonna be an issue.

Markham sighed, slightly pie-eyed as he took the bottle from him again. Ye'd think with all that weight he could hold his liquor a sight better. "Oh, to be twenty-five again and so sure of how my life would turn out. Did I ever tell you about Letty York? I'd gladly give my left nut, then or now, to be bonded to her."

"She the whore with one eye?"

"No, that was Luz something or other. The Yorks are a respectable Fetch House, and I'd been contracted to Letty for years before—" he hiccupped and passed the bottle back. "Well, until I wasn't. The Prydees had just killed my eldest brother, and my father was desperate. He billed my marriage to Bernice as the only way to end the animosity between our two Houses. In hindsight, he might've been right, but my position as First has given the sisters far more power than the old man envisioned. Instead of outright destroying House Markham, they've leveraged it to further their agenda, which is somehow worse."

Fitz took a swig from his bottle, all the piss and vinegar draining from him as he handed it back to Markham. Man were in even more of a pickle than him. At least he didn't have t'share a bed with one of them harpies. "Sisters want me t'take Leo's place ratting on the Scots."

His uncle hummed his distaste around his mouthful of liquor. "What a foul little shit he was...but their request makes sense. Miriam's so distraught she's become useless to them, and they never did care for Grantham or Shelby. Especially now that they've both made disadvantageous marriages; the sisters have cut that whole branch from the fold. Whether that will be permanent or not remains to be seen, but in the meantime, they must be desperate to have a set of ears in that House, especially now." Markham glanced out the doorway, back toward the craft. "It true that Leo was smuggling bots?"

Fitz nodded, not about to question how Markham had picked up that bit of intel. "Pretty sure he were getting them for the sisters. Dunno why, but I heard tell that's why all their channels was fucked. Know it did mine in, and them bots mess somewhat fierce with the way ye see energy. Makes it all amplified, like."

Markham sat up straighter. "Do you think they were trying to get into the Between?"

Fitz snorted around a mouthful. "I wish." Place would put an end to them right quick. Most Fetches just made tunnels through that bit of space they passed through when they shifted, connecting points, but for the men with House Prydee's energy extra, it let them slip past the tunnel's walls and into what lay, well, between. Didn't know why it wouldn't work for the women, but Fitz were pretty sure that were one of the reasons the sisters hated him.

"Still...I don't like it." Markham rapped his knuckles against the table. "You don't think they know—they haven't asked you to go in again, have they?"

Fitz shook his head. "No, and them maps you asked for is safe."

His uncle blew out a breath and nodded. "I'm more concerned about you. We can hypothesize about the sisters all day, but the Seers? I've no idea what House Carmody's motives are, and I trust them even less, but for whatever reason..." Markham pressed his lips together and shook his head. "I don't care how you do it, but you need to make yourself indispensable to Laughlin."

Fitz scowled. "Before or after they exile him?"

Markham sat back and sucked his cheeks in like he knew somewhat about that. "Trust me when I say that whatever they're planning isn't going to pan out like they think, but you're right. I can't imagine the vote going well. All the more reason for you to stay by him. When he leaves, he'll need as much of a cohort as possible to retain his talent."

"How much of this have ye had?" Fitz sourly eyed the bottle and then his uncle, ignoring the steadily growing warmth of the coin in his pocket at Markham's words.

"Enough to offer you the capital for three trawlers and to bankroll whatever else you need for that fishing venture we've spoken about when you get back."

"Ye mean the one that ye've spoken about." Fitz scowled. He didn't want anything to do with his uncle's grand plans.

"Fitzpatrick, the land this warehouse sits upon, those fishing grounds, they're yours by—"

"Aye, and one more thing them fuckin' Prydees can burn down around me ears." He slammed the lid of the trunk shut and shifted it back to where he'd brought it up from as he stood, riffling his curls.

Out in the warehouse the craft's door hissed and boots hit the ground. Fitz gritted his teeth and glared at his uncle. "For me gran's sake, I'll do what them witches want and make good with Scot—

"On your honor as a McCreedy, swear to me you'll stay in his employ, Fitzpatrick."

"Aye, fine, I swear it," Fitz spat, pacing, "but I don't wanna hear another damned thing about them grounds, land, or me majority. We clear?"

"We are." Markham laced his fingers over his gut, abruptly sober and far too fuckin' satisfied for Fitz's liking. "And, now that I have your solemn word, I suggest you shift that gentlemen back to the Scot's flat, and check in with Caliban whilst I attend to other business." He winked and tipped an imaginary cap at Fitz, and then he was gone.

Fitz's fist tightened around his bottle, staring at where his uncle had just been as the implications of what he'd sworn while his temper were up hit him. That motherfucker.

"Yo, you ready to bail, blondie?" LaVeil called.

Fitz shook his head and killed the flame on the lantern. Aye, he'd bail, but the damned ship were already sunk.

MARCOS SAT at the back of the cavern beneath the Marked Man and picked a bit of crusty blood from his brow. Around him, the chamber teemed with what had to be the majority of the city's Breakers. The 'lust in the room was rank enough to set him on edge even through the swelling of his broken nose. Somewhere around his eighth or ninth bout—or was it his eighth or ninth tankard?—he'd started to get sloppy. He chuckled, then raised his dented mug and drained it, not particularly concerned either way, which was exactly where he wanted to be.

There was plenty of that blasted emotion around him once the sands had cleared and Conclave had begun, and he was tapping out for the night. His position in the hierarchy might've carried over from the Source, but he was still an outsider as far as the North's customs were concerned. Marcos was positive the amount of alcohol he'd imbibed accounted for that not currently bothering him, but it was a strange kind of relief to let someone else drive the transport for once. Unless they solicited his opinion, he was more than happy to sit back and observe.

Especially since he was fairly certain they were debating abandoning Glynfyls, though where they thought they were going to go…

Behind him, the flames burning in the low trough running the circumference of the room flared, and at the center of the sands, Voss Mangleshield's head rose. The Menot scanned the far recesses of the room as he stood in the flickering light, patiently moderating the debate around him. Marcos didn't envy him that, or Rogan once he got here—

A heavy hand landed on his shoulder. "Settling up your debts, Commandant? Must've been one hell of a show. I hear they've named a drink after you."

Speak of the devil. The Alpha Prime sat beside Marcos and handed him another tankard.

He took it, grinning. "Have they?"

Rogan sipped his own. "They have. Henceforth, boilermakers are now a Commandant Special, and the bar's having a run on them. Congrats, there are definitely worse things to be named after." He paused to listen to the debate below for a moment, then, "You talk to Stonefist about those troops at all?"

"I did. He's not opposed, but hasn't brought it up." A Commandant Special. Marcos snorted, dabbing his weeping brow. "Not that I blame him, considering the way the conversation's been going. Something about relocating to the cliffs?" Rogan snorted and Marcos's battered brow rose. "You plan on adding your two cents?"

"Depends, has that been the gist of it?"

Marcos nodded. "They're ready to let the city hang, and it sounds like most of the Breakers from the hill are on board. Exiling the Overlord after what he's done isn't sitting well with any of them."

"No, it shouldn't," Rogan growled. "But tucking tail isn't gonna do a goddamned thing to make the situation any better."

"Did you say something, Alpha Prime?" Mangleshield called out into an abrupt silence, all eyes on the two of them.

"Jesus, I hate that guy," Rogan muttered, pushing to his feet with a sigh. The crowd before him parted, leaving a clear path to the sands below. He started down it, raising his voice to address the assembled Breakers. "I did, and I'll say it again. Leaving isn't going to do a goddamned thing other than fuck every last one of us, but you're right. It's beyond time for the bullshit on the hill to stop."

Mangleshield's brow rose as he leaned upon his staff, a wide grin stretching across his face. "As Sun Tzu said, 'A kingdom that has once been destroyed can never come again into being—'"

"Yeah, whatever. Stop quoting that fucking book, I know what it says," Rogan growled. He took a deep breath as he stepped onto the sands, his gaze sweeping the chamber. "My point is, the Overlord didn't save our asses from the Source just to have the city go belly-up. Not one of you should be surprised he's leaving to go after his mate, and every last warm body inside these walls owes it to him to protect Glynfyls while he's gone." A low murmur rumbled through the chamber and a man in fine silks stood.

"What about the Assembly—"

"Fuck the Assembly." Cheers and hoots echoed through the room. "They didn't grant the Overlord his powers, and I promise you, they can't take them away."

Marcos snorted into his tankard. No, not after what he'd seen…of course whether or not Scot was currently capable of using them was an entirely different conversation.

"Laughlin Scot is Overlord," Rogan continued. "And until the time comes where he steps down of his own free will, he will remain Overlord. No pissant ruling from that squawking body on the hill is gonna change that."

The conversation around the room kicked up, and Rogan nodded at Stonefist; the Northern general returned it grimly. "It's also not going to change the fact that the Deep South is under the false impression that we're currently easy pickings." The focus in the room snapped back to Rogan, rumbles of discontent replacing conjecture.

"But us being at the ready will. The shield wall is still functioning, and the rota for Hexes is in place. Every Breaker is to continue reporting to General Stonefist and fulfilling your assigned duties, or aiding in the city's repair. Additionally, there is only one hierarchy. The Commandant will be conscripting any Breakers left beyond the wall and bringing them into the fold."

The chamber went silent at that, everyone turning to Marcos. Damn it. He stood to address them. "They'll walk the Way, or not at all," he said, parroting back the Alpha Prime's earlier command, though it still stuck in his craw.

"You'll need to prepare to take them in, quietly," Rogan continued. "Markham's on board to make that happen, but the last thing we need is blowback from the other lines on something they have zero understanding of—"

"And where will you be?" a woman at the edge of the sands interrupted.

Marcos started, doing a double take. Was that Phyllis Breakspear? Livid scars gashed her cheeks, and she looked far more haggard than the last time he'd seen her. A younger man bearing her features sat at her side, holding her hand. Her son, maybe? He leaned in, whispering something, and her mouth soured.

"Phyllis," Rogan drew out each syllable in her name as he grinned at her. "I'll be accompanying the Overlord as part of his cohort, and while we're both gone, the hierarchy prevails. If any deviance needs to be made from the plan I've laid out, it falls to Stonefist and the Commandant to decide a new course of action, with Mangleshield acting as counsel."

"And those mercenaries that've been running around?" she pressed.

"Kendall and his outfit are answerable only to the Overlord. They've been tasked with securing his flat. I don't see them leaving the crown, but should there be any concerns, the Commandant will act as liaison. And FYI, just in case it's still not clear, anything spoken about at Conclave, including the integration of any troops from the Source, is Breaker Business. Leave that piece of shit husband of yours, and anyone else, out of it."

She sniffed and ripped her hand away from her son's. The boy sat back with a sigh.

Well, wasn't that just spiffy? Marcos sighed and took another pull of his ale as the conversation below continued, his brief respite of sitting back and observing officially at an end. There wasn't a doubt in his mind that this would be the last Special he enjoyed for the foreseeable future. And as soon as he sobered up, it was time to go to work. He eyed the bottom of his tankard. Hell, maybe before then.

CHAPTER SIX

"He has died. He has risen. Flames flicker as thorns creep across a broken land and the slumbering serpent begins to wake. Too soon. Too late. Probability shifts as the leviathan draws closer..."

– Excerpt from the dream journals of House Carmody

FLYNN'S EYES OPENED, the ceiling above his bed slowly coming into focus. He stared, silent, watching as the shadows gradually faded and dust motes drifted through the beams of early morning light.

... *"You can't do anything to me I don't want you to do,"* she whispers, *her lips teasing his lobe. "I'd be more worried about what I'm going to do to you." He tries to lower his arms, and she laughs softly, keeping him pinned. "Say please..."*

Tears trickled from the corners of his eyes to his hairline. His lids, red and raw, closed, and he let out a measured exhale, right hand twitching, wishing desperately for a familiar weight at his side. Her leg thrown over his. Fingers riffling through the hair across his chest. The feel of her lips turning up into a smile against his shoulder.

Kara.

Flynn blinked, his guts eating themselves, insides an anxious void, waiting for the flames to appear. His brow furrowed when they didn't. He gingerly sat up, scrubbing a hand over his face. Everything that he'd been drowning under yesterday was blunted, the crushing pressure in his chest, distant. He scooped up Kara's pillow, breathing in her scent, not wanting to question the reprieve too closely.

He had it, and now he needed to use it.

Okay, asshole. Suck it the fuck up and pull up your panties. It was time to stop wallowing and get her back. French was right. Today was a new day, and he had goddamned responsibilities.

Which meant he had to man up and face the Assembly.

Flynn threw his legs over the side of the bed. Took a deep breath. Stood, one hand out for balance, eyeing the corners of the room as he crossed it.

The cat poked its nose out from under the bed, but no flames.

Christ, he didn't want to do this. Flynn's hands slapped down on the vanity, and he met his own gaze in the mirror.

He looked like shit.

Dark circles rimmed his eyes, hollowed cheeks, but what the lack of his halos meant—he swore he could still feel—ugh. It didn't matter. Overlord or not, talented or not, he had to play the part. Kara and the babies need a place to come home to, or at the very least, some place to regroup.

He scrubbed his face. Cal had met with the Assembly yesterday. He'd be able to tell him what kind of a shit show he was about to walk into. Flynn sighed. *Fuck, Kara, where are you?* The cat meowed by his feet and rubbed up against him—

The astringent tang of antiseptic filled his nose, the taste coating his tongue…

Flynn stumbled, and Hiss shot back under the bed. He shook his head. The hell had that been about? He pinched a hand across his temples, still tasting medicinal funk as he pushed away from the vanity and passed the bedroom door.

In the next room, Rogan was sprawled out, snoring on the ugliest plaid couch Flynn'd ever seen. Holy shit. The sight of the big Breaker lying there stopped him in his tracks. He'd actually stayed. A weird warmth filled Flynn's chest. He swallowed the lump in his throat and hit the button for the lift. The doors opened and he got in, not sure what to do with that.

First floor of the flat smelled like a house fire, and the carpet crunched beneath his feet. The portcullis had been dropped down over the entrance to the gate's antechamber, and two of Kendall's men sat armed at a card table by it, working with regulated tech. Flynn's brow rose at the module one of them was programming. Shit was definitely Source-issued.

"You putting together a vector mesh?" So much for that no plaz mandate. Crandall was gonna have a fucking bird.

The man grunted, fiddling with parameters on a screen. "Yeah. Kendall wants the building mapped out and online by end of day and then the block reconned and triggered."

"Don't you worry, Yankee," the other chimed in. "By the time we're done, shit around here's gonna be so tight a cockroach won't be able to scratch its ass without us getting a play-by-play, never mind some freak popping in."

Flynn snorted. Yeah, they'd pick up activity along with any use of talent, but the plaz in those modules would guarantee there wasn't a cockroach on the entire hill. Whatever. After the city had been blanketed with fallout, he doubted there were any left in Glynfyls, period.

…*"Do you think that's why Hiss is being so weird?" Kara asks, her voice hopeful.*

"I dunno, maybe…"

At this point, there were no maybes about it.

He pinched the bridge of his nose at the memory. The men looked at him funny, and he forced a smile. "Sounds good." He clasped the first man's shoulder in thanks, then took the hall to Cal's office, shaking his head at the fried plaster and smoke stains.

Christ, he hadn't thought the place could be any more of a shithole. How the fuck was he gonna bring kids back to this? Flynn buzzed his lips, getting ahead of himself. That was definitely a problem for a different day. He needed to survive this one first.

Flynn paused before knocking at the door, someone already in there, despite the early hour.

"Yeah?" his grandfather called.

Flynn stuck his head in. The desk was still missing. He craned his neck toward the sitting area and snorted at Fitzpatrick fucking McCreedy at one end of the settee, sucking down a bottle of whiskey and radiating abject misery. When the fuck had he turned up?

Cal was on the other end, and a trim, red-haired man sat across from them in one of the chairs by the fire. Flynn locked eyes with him. Paul Morris. Asshole looked nervous. He should be after bonding Shelby without so much as a hat tip toward her House.

"You busy?" Flynn asked his grandfather.

"No, Paul and I were just finishing up."

Flynn crossed the room and extended his hand to the prick. "Lord Morris."

"Ah, no, actually," Paul said, rising to take it with a surprisingly firm grip. "Well, not any more. That's one of the things we were just discussing. As I explained to Master Scot, I'd been agonizing over asking for your House's permission to wed Shelby for some time, knowing full well my father would disown me, but all this business with Arileo forced my hand. When I found her at the studio two nights ago…she was in a-a bad way."

"The goddamned sisters made her, Miriam, and Graham watch them strip the rhian from Leo's corpse, then kicked them out of their club," Cal growled around his cigarette, his eyes hard.

"Are you fucking kidding me?" The fire in the hearth flared with Flynn's temper.

"Ain't the worst them harpies's done," Fitz muttered like it was par for the course.

Christ. Leo had been a traitorous sack of shit, but he'd been Miriam's son and their triplet. His death couldn't have been easy for them, and to be forced to watch him being flayed after the fact—

"Unfortunately, no, and I'm afraid that the three of them aren't dealing with it well." Paul frowned. "Graham's not talking to anyone, Miriam's been sedated, and Shelby…" He looked down at his hands. "It was a near thing. If I hadn't gotten there when I did— she's better now. More stable. But the shock of finding her—we bonded through the trauma. I swear to you nothing untoward happened."

Flynn seethed. The fuck it hadn't. The shit the Prydees were pulling was about as untoward as it came, and if he'd lost Shelby because of their twisted—

"Jesus fuck, yer a goddamned walking migraine," Fitz grumbled, knuckling his eyes.

Flynn closed his, breathing through the wave of blackness burbling up and trying to pull zero over it, the air buzzing around him like static. Slowly it quieted, and the darkness receded, taking his anger with it and leaving him exhausted.

He could've lost Shelby. How the hell could the sisters be so fucking cruel?

"…Paul's staying with her up on the fourth floor in Miriam's suite along with Graham and Celine," Cal was saying. His grandfather glanced at him askance, the other two studiously not meeting Flynn's eye as he took a seat in the other armchair, his knees abruptly weak.

He ran a trembling hand over his beard, jumping at the fire crackling beside him and scanned the edges of the room, breathing a sigh of relief that the flames stayed in the hearth. "Yeah, of course… and thank you."

"No thanks needed," Paul said, looking uncomfortable again. "Your cousin means everything to me…I'm sure you can understand."

… She was above him, her forehead to his, lips insistent, the light of her halos gilding him in gold. She bites his lip, and he's overcome.

His chest rumbles, licking his blood from her mouth. "Goddamn, I fucking love you."

Kara laughs, her cheeks wet. "Say it again."

"I love you, Kara Scot. Only you, always you…"

Fitz made a gagging sound, snapping Flynn back. Shit. Paul was still talking.

"…you're looking better than rumors imply."

"Thanks, I think." Flynn shook his head and rubbed a temple. These goddamned memories… He glanced up at Fitz's snort.

"S'a fuckin' lie. Ye look like shite."

Flynn's eyes narrowed. "So do you. Where the fuck have you been?"

Kid took another pull off his bottle, then smacked his lips. "Why, what've ye heard?"

"Doesn't matter, he's here now, and considering the predominant rumor is that you're stark raving mad," Cal flicked his ash, "that's not a compliment."

No, but it might be the truth. "What else is the Assembly gonna hit me with?"

Cal pursed his lips. "Long story short, they want you exiled."

A mist-riddled forest and mossy tumbledown cabin peeking from its edge flashed across Flynn's mind's eye, and he pinched a hand across his temples again.

"And the commons aren't having any of it," Paul added. "They're still agitated from last time, and the thought of cosigning the lady's and your children's deaths—"

… He grins and presses his lips to the top of Kara's head. His hand trails over her abdomen. A kid. He pulls her close, allowing himself to feel the happiness bubbling up inside of him.

Her anxiety became surprise. "Really?"

He laughs. None of this was supposed to happen, not for him, but now that it had… He tips up her chin. Even beat to shit she was so goddamned beautiful. He didn't fucking care if it was the bond. She was his, and she was having his kid. He laughs again at her bewilderment.

"Yeah, really. You gotta understand, I didn't think I'd ever have kids, or find someone like you…"

Flynn shook his head, struggling to remain present. Shit. What were they talking about?

"Not for nothin' but yer da's a right prick," Fitz was saying to Paul. "He steps below the third rung, ye better believe there's a noose waitin' for him."

"Deservedly so, but he'd never stoop to dirtying himself by mingling with those he professes to be so concerned about." Paul snorted. "My father has no idea what his hateful rhetoric is bringing to bear. The city's rife with talk of civil war—"

"Which is why the Breakers are poised to impose martial law," Rogan said, tromping into the room. He stopped, glaring at Paul. "You're in my seat."

"N-no worries. I should be getting back before Shelby wakes.

Master Scot, Laughlin." Paul scrambled to stand and Fitz snickered at the trim man's hasty exit.

"Who the fuck was that?" Rogan asked as the door closed behind him.

"Shelby's new husband."

"Lucky Shelby." Rogan grunted at Cal, obviously unimpressed, and thumped down into the chair, rubbing the back of his neck. "Damn. I've had shittier nights' sleep, but not many. Where the hell did you get that couch? Inquisition tag sale?"

"Dunno, Shane bought it."

"Figures, she always had shitty taste. Roll me one of those?"

Cal raised his eyebrow at the jab and pulled out his pouch. "You know they sell them in packs."

"I only like the ones you lick." The Breaker put his feet up on the coffee table and turned to Flynn. "How you feelin', kid?"

"Functional." Ish.

"Enough so that it sounds like he's planning on going to Assembly."

Rogan shot Cal a look. "Might be easier said than done. You tell him Crandall's got an accident waiting for him? He 'gifted' us that craft with the understanding we'd use it without passing go or collecting two-hundred dollars."

Flynn looked at him blankly. What the fuck was he talking about?

"Crandall would prefer it if we just disappeared so he can control the narrative," Cal translated, tossing Rogan a smoke. "Which is gonna do fuck-all from keeping the Deep South off our backs."

"Pretty sure that wasn't on his radar when we last spoke." The Breaker caught the cigarette and his halos flared as he lit it. "He was too busy spouting some shit about convincing the commons that you've left on a quest while the hill reestablishes status quo, but I suspect with all the shit he's juggling, a little thing like another invasion might've slipped through the cracks."

Fitz sniggered again, and Flynn's brows bunched. "The Deep South is coming?"

"Yep. I got the word an hour ago that Hexspar, Ax'chig, and Diytan have mobilized, and the international tribunal's all but signed off on our annexation," Cal said, trimming a cigar.

Jesus fuck, how much more shit could go wrong? Flynn raked a hand through his hair. How the hell was he supposed to—

"Your job is to get Kara back. The Breakers have this," the Alpha Prime said like he knew exactly what Flynn was thinking. "Marcos is out canvassing what's left of the plateau for survivors with Markham. Best case scenario, they pledge, and there's enough of them to defend outside the wall. Northern Breakers will man it and keep the peace inside. Kendall's agreed to patrol the crown, and if push comes to shove, we can bring in whatever firepower he's got left in his craft."

"And worst case?"

"There won't be a worst case," Cal tapped his cigar against his knee, "because you're gonna make the South think twice about crossing our border."

"Yeah? And how am I supposed to do that while they're exiling me? What the fuck does that even entail?"

"You're a smart kid, you'll figure something out," Cal said around his cigar as he lit it. "And I'm pretty sure all it's gonna amount to is them figuring out they can't take away something they didn't give in the first place. If they had, it'd be a different story. Ask me how I know."

"I'd rather you told me how you got it back," Flynn muttered.

"I did. Time…and I met this Binder—"

Rogan started laughing, and Cal's face broke out in a grin.

"That's how all the best stories start, isn't it?" The Breaker chuckled into his glass of scotch, and Flynn rubbed a temple, not in the mood for this shit. Christ, he'd just wanted a simple fucking answer, not a stroll down memory lane.

"Ginny was something else. She used to do this weave—" Cal glanced at Flynn and cleared his throat. "At any rate, she was able to bind my channel back together enough for it to be functional." Cal took a deep drag and looked at Flynn, suddenly serious again. "But I was invested with those powers by the Assembly."

"I wasn't," Rogan said, leaning forward to tap the ash from his smoke. "And when I left, whatever I wasn't born with faded the farther I got from Glynfyls. Whatever you had, you'll keep, and as long as you have a cohort with you, you should be able to access those other lines as well."

Flynn chewed his lip. "So that's you three." Breaker, Fetch, Shade…

"And Nora," Cal said, staring at him like he was waiting for the fight.

He wasn't gonna get it. "Good. Kara went down in those tunnels to save her ass, she should return the favor," Flynn said, looking away.

"She's set on it, so plan on cutting out right after this circle jerk with the Assembly. City needs to sink or swim on its own merit." Rogan turned to Fitz. "Can you sense Kara through that ward you set?"

Kid squirmed in his seat. "Eh…about that…" Fitz's eyes shot to Flynn, his throat bobbing. "That is t'say, I did. Went east, but I had to, eh, shift it and me oath bond for a spell—But I can get it back," he quickly added at Flynn's growl, "just need t'catch that blighted beastie upstairs."

The three men stared at him.

"What blighted—wait. Are you telling us you shifted the ward on Kara from you to the cat?" Rogan choked out.

"Eh…maybe?"

The two older men exchanged glances, and Flynn ran a hand down his face. How the fuck was that even possible? Christ. Maybe it hadn't been the plaz-radiation screwing with Hiss.

"I don't even wanna know the squirrel cage of logistics behind that, but I'm assuming you had a good reason?" Cal asked.

Fitz thumbed the mouth of his bottle. "Energy's spun up all over the city. Oaths is like wool roving and around him, it's bloody fuckin' painful. Can't use me extra at all." He glared at Flynn then shook his head and slouched into his jacket. "Weren't no way t'hide what I done, and weren't no good gonna come from the sisters seeing it."

"They haul you in?" Rogan asked.

Kid squirmed again, his hand going to his pocket and fiddling. He muttered something unintelligible under his breath, then jerked like he'd been stung. "Aye! Ye fuck…eh…that is t'say, ya. They want me t'rat on ye like Leo done."

"Is that right?" Cal drawled, eyes narrowed as he flicked his ash.

"Tis, but I ain't." Fitz's throat bobbed, and he snatched his hand from his pocket with another yelp. "And if ye want, I'll swear t'ye proper."

His gaze flicked up to meet Flynn's, the kid's weird, splintered halos quicksilver through his irises. He looked sincere, but what the fuck had changed to make him offer that up?

"No," Flynn said.

Fitz's face drained of color, and he wet his lips, swallowing like he was about to be sick. "Eh…right then…but, just t'be clear, I am still in yer employ?"

"If you don't mind working pro bono for the foreseeable future," Cal muttered.

Fitz tugged on the patch of beard beneath his lip, his hand trembling. "Nah, nah…eh…civic duty and all that. Ain't a problem."

"I think it is." Flynn sat forward. "Kid's shifty as fuck, and he's flat out told us the Prydees sent him here to spy on us. Give me one good reason to trust you."

Fitz's eyes darted between them—

"Ah, ye prick!" He jumped up with another cry and ripped something out of his pocket. A coin pinged onto the table, spinning. The wood beneath it smoked. "Fine! Fine, ye shite!" he yelled at it, flicking his hand before sucking on his fingers. "Ye want the meat of it? Witches called in one of them favors they had over the sisters and roped me into it. S'long as I'm in yer employ, they'll keep their claws off me gran, but the minute I'm not, Kristine's gonna cage her, and I'll be damned afore I see them touch one blighted hair on her miserable head!"

"The fuck is that thing?" Rogan asked, his brow furrowed at the coin coming to rest on one of its nine sides. He reached out to it, and Fitz sprang forward.

"S'me lucky coin," he muttered, snatching it back up with a grimace. A black spot had scorched where it'd stood.

Flynn snorted, falling back in his chair. "A lucky coin? That's your nuna?"

"The fuck is a nuna?" Rogan touched the mark it'd left and rubbed soot from his fingers. "How'd it heat up like that?"

"None of yer fuckin' business." Fitz glared at him, pocketing the bit of metal.

"Maybe not, but the Seers calling in a favor is." Cal pursed his lips. "What exactly were the terms?"

"Don't know a damned thing more than what I just told ye, but them, Markham... I swore t'him on me honor as a McCreedy I'd stay in the Overlord's employ. He said ye were a good man and thinks ye can help me get out from under them Prydees," he muttered like the admission had cost him something. He shook out his hand again and winced, his fingertips scalded pink. Kid's expression was pathetic enough for Flynn's conscience to stab at him.

... Kara sighs and settles herself against his chest, a hum growing between them. "You're a good man, Laughlin Scot..."

He raked a hand through his hair. He wasn't, but for her he'd try to be. "Look, as long as you stop disappearing every damned time we need you for something, you've got a job, but I swear to fucking Christ, if I find out you're bleeding intel to the Prydees—"

"Fuck the fuckin' Prydees. McCreedys ain't narcs." Fitz turned his head like he was gonna spit, then thought better of it. "I'd sooner slit me own wrists then meet me maker havin' helped them with aught."

Flynn's brow rose. So the kid did have scruples. Good to know. "Why did I think you were the last McCreedy?"

"Me gran ain't particularly social," Fitz muttered around a slug of liquor. "Trust me, s'better that way. Woman's temperament is as foul as they come."

"Guess we know where you got your people skills from, then."

"And yer a regular fuckin' delight." Kid made a face at Rogan, and he grinned back.

"Touché. French hasn't brought in one of his coffee carts yet?" the Breaker asked, looking around. "There's what, not quite four hours before Flynn's got to make his appearance? You need to eat something."

"Yeah, they want him there by nine, and now that he's up, I'm sure French'll be in here with alacrity," Cal snarked, getting up to hit the intercom.

Audrey answered. "What can I do for you, sir?"

"Coffee service for four, my office. Make sure there's something on there to eat."

"I'll see it done."

Cal grunted and picked his way back around the contents of his desk. "Take your time un-phasing that," he said to Flynn. "Not like it being gone's a major pain in the ass or anything."

Rogan blew out a long stream of smoke. "Exercise is good for you."

"Keep telling yourself that." Cal stooped to snag his tablet from the coffee table as he sat. "Its lack doesn't seem to have cut into my longevity."

"Ground zero exposure to an EMP and sublimating massive amounts of subatomic particulate matter will do that...but that's neither here nor there." He turned back to Flynn. "So. What's the plan?"

"For the Assembly?" He shrugged, still trying to wrap his head around how fucking awful Miriam's House was. Reconciling the dowdy woman that'd raised him with what the rest of the Prydees were capable of... Flynn shook his head. "Now that I know they can't take whatever talent I have left? I don't really have one, aside from showing up—"

"Jesus fucking Christ." They turned to Cal, and he shook his head, a hand over his mouth. He held out his tablet to Flynn. "You don't want to see this, but Titus just copied me on his release of the footage from when you and Kara were infected with those bots."

The sex tape.

Flynn took the device with trembling hands. He'd known it was just a matter of time before that got out, but to see it now...

It was from his point of view, her big brown eyes intent on his as she fellated him. A memo had been sent with it, flashing across the bottom of the screen:

Keep me waiting much longer, and the next reel will have my cock in it whether she's conscious or not.

Static overwhelmed him, loud in his ears, and a tremor went through the room as Flynn powered the tablet down and stood, blackness writhing in his gut. "Tell the Assembly if they want to see me, they'll be there in an hour or not at all. I've got shit to do."

FLYNN STALKED out of the room, and Cal and Rogan exchanged glances, that dangerous part of the boy front and center as he left. The door closed behind him, and they sat frozen for a breath before Fitz and Rogan both grabbed for the tablet. Cal rolled his eyes, sitting back.

"You have any idea how bad he's gonna beat your ass if he knows you're watching that?" Rogan asked, glowering as the Fetch ended up with it on the other side of the room.

"Gotta catch me first." Fitz gave a low whistle, his brows steadily rising. "And if he do, it'll still be worth it. Holy shite, that's fuckin' dirty..." He adjusted himself, leaned back against the bookcases with his prize and turned up the volume.

Cal snorted. "Says the man who was about to do the same thing."

"Doesn't count if I watch it, since I've already been on the receiving end."

"Ye let the Overlord fuck ye?" Fitz tipped up his bottle, eyes glued to the screen. "Huh. Never would've taken ye for a bottom."

Cal snickered as Rogan continued to glare at the kid.

"No, you dumb ass—"

There was a knock at the door and Audrey came in, pushing French's cart. Fitz killed the feed and shoved the tablet behind his back. He nodded at her and she frowned, tidying the coffee table and setting out a continental breakfast.

"Where's French?" Cal asked.

"I'm afraid he's under the weather, but without the lady in residence, I'm at loose ends." She whisked a finger under her ridiculously large glasses and picked up the cafetière. "I'll be attending to you until he's recovered."

Cal's brow furrowed; he was able to count the times French had missed a day on one hand. "Do I need to call a Binder?"

She paused. "I—Yes. I would appreciate that. When I requested one late last night, the waitlist they've put him on is rather… discouraging."

"I'll just bet." With Serra at the helm, Cal imagined anything that even smelled like a Scot could hold their hand on their asses for medical care. "With Flynn moving up the Assembly meeting, we need to get Nora back here anyway." Cal rifled through the papers on the coffee table looking for a blank piece and scribbled out a quick note. He folded it in half and held it out to Fitz. "She's staying at the Carmody's flat. Give her this, and then bring her back here."

The Fetch looked up, startled, halfway through a bagel with more lox than bread. "Now?"

"You working for me or not?"

"Eh…no, actually—"

"Just deliver the goddamned note." Cal pulled it away as the boy went to reach for it. "No detours."

"Sir, yes, sir." Fitz threw him a half-assed salute and scowled as he slipped the note into his pocket along with a Danish before shifting away.

"God, he's miserable." Rogan laughed. "I like him."

"You would."

Audrey handed Cal his coffee. "Is there anything else I can assist you gentlemen with?"

"Yeah. You need to get the word out that the Overlord is calling for the Assembly to convene at seven instead of nine. After what Titus just dropped, if they're not there, Flynn's not gonna wait."

"I'll word the missive accordingly."

Cal grunted, and she curtsied before leaving the room.

"Whelp, we got not quite two hours before we leave," Rogan said, filling a plate. "Other than showing up for that circle jerk, my shit's handled. What about yours?"

Cal tapped the ash from his cigar. "You kidding me? Since when is my work ever done?"

"That's what happens when you're wicked. You gonna be there?"

"At Assembly?" He shook his head. "No. After what happened

upstairs, I don't put it past the twins to offer up my alter ego for shits and grins. It's better I stay out of the public eye."

"You know, now that you mention it, I'm kind of surprised that hasn't already happened," Rogan mused. He popped a chunk of bagel into his mouth. "Or why she never outed you as the last Overlord when you came back."

Because it wasn't Elize he was playing against, and that would've ended the game too soon. Cal took a sip of coffee and shrugged. "I'm assuming it's because this hurts more. Can't crush hope if you have none."

Rogan snorted. "And you've always been the eternal optimist."

Cal shot him a look. "Don't you have a meeting to get ready for?"

The Breaker grinned. "That I do. Make sure Audrey pulls up that case of whiskey," he said, standing. "I got a feeling we're gonna need it."

MARCOS STARED out over the plateau's shattered landscape, trying to focus in on something other than dirt with his borrowed pair of oculars. They had to be close to the edge of this damned thing. He squinting into them against the rising sun's glare, praying for movement. At his side, Markham did the same, looking for the next bit of solid ground.

They'd found out early on that flat didn't equate to safe, and the farther they'd gotten from the city, the more unstable the plateau had become. Freestanding pillars of earth and jagged cliffs dropped off into deep crevasses, the angry sea churning below. The pop and splash of the earth succumbing to its icy wrath punctuated the still of early morning. That Marcos could deal with, but the rumbles of larger masses of stone letting go set his teeth on edge.

"Right. I think that outcropping there should suffice," the First Fetch said, dropping his device to hang around his neck and blotting his brow. "Should it crumble like the last one, I'm going to shift us hard to the left."

Marcos grunted, fisting the back of Markham's jacket. If something went wrong and he lost physical contact with the man, he'd be on his own, and his chances of survival weren't good. He glanced at the plunging drop to his right, his stomach roiling with equal parts hangover and apprehension. He grimaced, missing his antacids.

Colors ran as Markham pulled talent, and they shifted.

Marcos's heart jumped into his throat as they materialized, knees buckling as the earth beneath his feet held. Thank Glory. He let go of the big man and glanced at him askance. Markham did the same, blotting the sweat from his brow. Their eyes met, and they both chuckled at having cheated death for the moment.

"Glad we waited until it was light out, hey?" Markham swabbed his cloth around the back of his neck, sweating profusely despite the windchill adding to the subzero temperatures. It was surreal the way the Fetch shifted the air around them, keeping them from the gale while it battered the landscape.

If there was anyone else out here, they wouldn't be as fortunate.

With that reminder of the task at hand, Marcos gave a begrudging nod. Attempting this after dark would've been suicide—

Something glinted in the distance, and he raised his eyepiece. Tattered camo and broken support rods stuck out of a mound, and behind it, a large berm of earth obstructed all but the wavering tops of the conifers beyond. What could've been a thin stream of smoke rose above it, but with the wind, it was difficult to tell.

Marcos's stomach churned. "Check my eyes. There, on the horizon. Looks like we found what's left of Titus's basecamp."

Markham raised up his ocular, squinting. "The damned angle of the sun…Well, we've definitely hit the edge of the plateau…" The First Fetch fiddled with the controls, focusing the device. His brow furrowed. "Is that smoke?"

"That was my thought."

"Then I think you're right." Markham's lips tightened as he studied the berm. "How do you want to do this? I don't see anywhere I can shift to give them ample time to notice us, and I'm going to assume appearing in their midst unannounced wouldn't be wise."

"It would not, but don't worry about surprising them, just look for some place to shift in safely. I'll let them know we're here." Marcos pulled talent and sent several concentrated bursts of power into the air.

B1 to basecamp. Request to approach. Stand down.

"Morse code?" Markham asked.

"A variation." He waited another moment, then set up the signal again. This time, a quick sequence shot up from the remains of the basecamp in reply.

B2 to B1. Request approved. Standing down.

"Well, I'll be damned…" Marcos sent out another handful of blasts.

B1 to B2. Copy. Approaching from the northwest.

"That should do it. We're clear to come over, if you've found a spot?"

"I'm thinking that berm, there."

Marcos took hold of the Fetch's jacket again, and colors ran.

As soon as they materialized, Marcos started up the crumbling embankment. Beyond, the earth fell sharply away into a massive divot blasted into the side of the plateau. He grunted with approval. Smart move. By hollowing out the frozen earth with their talent and packing themselves inside it like sardines, they conserved what little body heat they had and kept out of the wind. Heart in his throat, his eye trailed over the assembled troops, not believing what he was seeing.

There had to be twenty-five hundred men stranded out here. One and half, maybe two battalions? How the hell could Titus have left them all? Battered and frostbite-blackened, they pushed to either side, allowing for one of their number to step forward.

Pax.

Marcos's jaw tightened, and he rubbed his thumb against his index finger. The beleaguered solider stopped several feet in front of him and gave a sharp salute, any trace of his former arrogance gone as he waited for acknowledgment in his tattered fatigues.

Glory, what the hell did they do to him?

"Status report," Marcos growled around the growing lump in his throat, a strange paternal anger he didn't know he possessed rising up and choking him.

"Sir, yes, sir! Two thousand three hundred eighteen men at forty-seven percent capacity. Three percent listed as critical. Shelter, rudimentary. Supplies, negligible, sir!"

"And your allegiance?"

"The hierarchy prevails, sir!"

Marcos raised his voice. "All of you feel that way?"

A resounding hoo-ha echoed through the ranks.

Marcos blinked away the moisture clouding his vision and addressed them all. "North or South, there is only one hierarchy! The Alpha Prime has decreed that the Breakers of Glynfyls will welcome any willing to pledge their fealty and walk the Way. Those who do will be expected to re-earn their rung, then serve under my command to protect the city as their own. Those opposed won't be leaving this pit."

"Sir, yes, sir!" Pax's jaw worked like he was biting something else back.

"Would you like to add to that, Br2?"

"Requesting permission to speak freely, sir!"

"Permission granted. At ease, solider."

Pax's throat bobbed as he widened his stance with his hands behind his back. "We spent last night hashing this out. None of us would opt to return to the Source, even if it were possible. As you said, there is only one hierarchy, sir, and it's always been here in the North." Pax's gaze hardened, trauma etched across his face and reflected on every man's behind him. He straightened his spine, no longer at ease. "We've seen what a true Alpha is supposed to be, and we want in."

"I'll take that as my cue to bring back reinforcements to get these men home," Markham said softly behind Marcos's shoulder.

"I'd say so." He searched Pax's face, the similarities to his own somehow starker than he remembered. He raised his voice to address the troops—his troops—and a swelling of pride came over him. "In the meantime, let's get you all started by breaking the temperature and taking some oaths. That sound good to you, son?" he asked Pax.

Something in the soldier's eyes flickered at the appellation.

"Yes, sir," his voice cracked. "That sounds great."

MOTHER LAY supine on her chaise, her body in repose, and her mind ablaze with activity. Her consciousness sped throughout her web of power, tending one strand and then the next, curbing one and cajoling another, each abuzz with the doings in the North.

The aristocrat eagerly awaiting the vote on the morrow.

The priest at his lectern.

The assassin escaping from his sundered cell.

Mother gave each a role, tightening the script to speed the final act. That incident in the gestating chamber—the Jane-that-was's whispers and her memories of before—preyed upon her mind, the voice that'd claimed the girl taking on a bizarre familiarity...

Mother's lips whitened. She would not be stopped, and it was time to eliminate any potential complications. Namely, Laughlin Scot. He'd amassed far too much power and needed to be put down. And, by the strength of his bond to the girl, his death would take her and those she carried with him.

Cal and Rogan would still come south for the twins, and Mother had the rest of the Talents right where she wanted them. Though far less satisfying than the drama she'd planned, the last few pieces were almost in place to accomplish her goal.

And once she'd gathered enough talent to reverse the Surge, the nuancing of this stream of aether wouldn't matter when they were firmly ensconced in another.

Mother paused to collect herself, brushing against the corners of Otto's mind. Serra had done well to keep a leash on him, and he'd done a fine job clipping her wings in return. Between the two, Mother's plans for her line in the North were coming along nicely, and would continue to ripen whilst she kept Caliban occupied elsewhere.

Satisfied with her corrected course of action, Mother's consciousness accelerated, gathering intel and filing it away or fitting it to the mosaic within her mind's eye, nudging and negating events toward her desired result.

A member of the Tribunal cross-referencing account numbers and finding a discrepancy.

A Minister of War planning their first airstrike.

A Son watching reels as he sharpened his bolo.

And Titus… Mother smiled at the thought of him poring over data points. Such a diligent boy. She couldn't help being smug as far as he was concerned. To manipulate a being to see itself as autonomous, yet whose will was entirely hers, was intoxicating. He was one of the most clever creatures she'd come across, and it amused her to no end to watch him gradually discover something was tampering with his psyche before plucking the realization from him once again.

Otto had been far too heavy handed with him. The illusion of free will was necessary with the more clever thralls—Titus far more than the others. As long as he had it, he performed admirably. Like his father before him, he was happiest when occupied with something cerebral.

But there were some things children didn't need to know.

She extracted all but the most banal memories of the twins from his mind, and pruned what was left to account for the girl's arrival and their ongoing presence. The entire incident in the gestating chamber and what happened afterwards, gone, along with the footage. His obsessive scrutiny of the girl's metrics Mother allowed. She wasn't ready to write off her expulsion from Kara Jester's psyche as anything other than something Caliban had bred into her, no matter how slim the chance. The alternative—that damned voice—was unconscionable.

Which is why Laughlin Scot needed to be removed from the board, and the girl with him.

Mother's lids fluttered, golden light spilling from her lashes and illuminating the temple around her as she narrowed in on Elize and sent the next imperative.

Awake Enoch and collect the boy. It's time for him to meet Mother.

And on the other side of the continent, the woman's eyes sprang open.

NORA LOOKED up from packing her bag at the quick rap upon her suite door. A moment later, Alice came in. She rested her palm flat against the slab for a breath, the smirk so often gracing the Seer's face noticeably absent.

"The Ladies are here, and they've asked for us to join them downstairs," she said, tucking her bob behind her ears.

Nora put a hand over her stomach, the sick feeling in her gut having nothing to do with pregnancy. She'd hoped to have more time before she faced them again. Abdicating from First was one thing, but leaving the Ladies' little cabal was quite another, and she wasn't sure what the right move was yet. She glanced at the clock. There was a little over an hour before they were scheduled to leave…

"If you're worried about Fitzpatrick, he's quite content to strip my larder while he waits," Alice said, leaning against the door and inspecting her nails. They'd been re-enameled neon orange.

"Then you think I should go down with you?"

Alice laughed. "That's entirely up to you."

"And that's entirely no help."

"I'm aware, but…" The Seer frowned, her irises narrowing to slits and her voice becoming sibilant. "The path clouds, and all I see is mist." She laughed again, shaking away whatever unworldliness had come over . "Which means I've a part to play. Damn, that's inconvenient." She grinned. "But usually entertaining. I suspect I should make the most of it."

The Seer's mirth didn't make Nora feel any better. She took a deep breath, steeling herself for the inevitable. There really wasn't any point in prolonging it. She tucked one more thing into her bag and zipped it up, the note she'd written for Marcos already on the table. She'd hoped he would be back before she left but…they both had their parts to play as well, now didn't they?

"Then I suspect we should get this over with." Her brow furrowed. "Wait. They're here, not at Evie's? Isn't that where you regularly meet?"

"Yes, but apparently she had quite a row with Crandall." Alice's trademark smirk slid back across her face.

Lovely. Nora sighed and motioned for the Seer to lead the way.

They exited into the hall and descended a wide staircase into the foyer. Before they'd gotten halfway down the flight, raised voices drifted up from below. She dropped her bag at the foot of the banister, planning on collecting it and heading directly to the kitchen to meet Fitz as soon as humanly possible.

Alice glanced at her from over her shoulder and disappeared into the parlor. Another deep breath and Nora followed her into the modern, deco room.

Unlike Evie's horrendously styled flat, the Carmody-Klein's home was minimalist, all clean lines and bold colors. Nora found it infinitely preferable to the Crandall's baby blue walls and creme friezes. The last time she'd been there, it'd felt like she'd been stuck in a Wedgwood vase, though she had to admit, the cherubic blonde looked incredibly out of place on the sleek leather divan.

It didn't help that she was sobbing while Phyllis and Bernice shouted at one another, toe-to-toe at the center of the carpet.

"...that grasping, conniving woman is completely unsuitable for inclusion!" the Breaker yelled, her halos crackling scarlet.

"Funny, those qualities never stood in the way of anyone else joining our little group," Alice remarked, sauntering across the bright teal room. "In fact, I was under the impression it was a prerequisite, though I do concur Lady Hess's ambitions are ill-suited to ours."

Nora inwardly cringed, moving to sit by Evie. Did the Seer have to bait them right off the bat?

Evie took Nora's hand and gave her a watery smile as she hipped closer. "I'm so glad you're here. I hate it when they fight," she confided.

Bernice and Phyllis spun from each other to face Alice as she slunk down into a brilliant mustard armchair and sat back with a radiant smile. She crossed her long legs, all but daring them to contradict her.

Bernice's hands fisted at her sides. "And you! Don't even start! Your infernal House knew this was coming! The entire purpose of our partnership—"

"Yes, please remind me of that again, because I could've sworn that the implications of secreting away Julia Cree and allowing her murder, then having Arileo Scot stripped and hung from the yaw at the center of the coliseum would both have far reaching consequences we should've discussed prior to," Alice said, inspecting her nails again.

Oooh… Nora bit her lips, eyes darting between the three. Evie's hand tightened on hers at Phyllis's chuckle.

Bernice gaped like a fish for several breaths. "Those were both House Matters."

"How exactly does that work, since neither of them were scions of House Prydee?" Phyllis remarked, clicking her tongue. Nora averted her eyes from the livid scars scoring the woman's cheeks. That all but screamed Breaker Business, and Nora had the feeling Phyllis was lucky to still be alive.

But by Bernice's glare, if she had anything to say about it, Phyllis wouldn't be for much longer.

"We're getting ahead of ourselves," Evie piped up, sniffling. "Nora hasn't given up her seat at our table." She smiled at her again, and Nora fought to return it.

"Yet she's letting that shrew run riot, playing First with the Binders," Phyllis spat, pacing in front of the window, before turning on Nora. "How can you condone what she's doing with your line?"

Nora's brow furrowed. Glory, what had she missed?

"She's upset about the waitlist Serra implemented for the Breakers at the clinics," Evie stage-whispered to her.

Oh. Well, that was only to be expected. They'd done the same at the Source, but—No. Nora ran a hand over her cheek. It wasn't her job to fix this. She'd earned her reprieve, and her line had earned exactly what was coming to them. They wanted Serra? They were going to get all the nastiness that came with her.

Alice rolled her eyes at Phyllis. "What do you care? You don't like any of the Binders, anyway."

"I care because the system she's put into place is unethical!" Phyllis threw her hands up, then closed her eyes, visibly struggling to calm herself.

"No, it isn't. You're just pissed you can't bully them into treating your line after they beat each other into a pulp," Bernice muttered, flouncing down in another chair with her arms crossed over her breasts. "And it's not just the Binders. Phyllis doesn't like anyone."

"Not true." Alice tongued her cheek. "She's quite cozy with Adlothian Scot."

"Which, along with the state of Glynfyls's heath care, is another problem we don't have time to address," Evie said, dabbing at her eyes with a lacy handkerchief. "Let's cut to the chase. In less than an hour, Laughlin will address the Assembly and, despite my pleas, Bart's moving forward with his plans to exile him. Why that boy didn't take the craft along with the out I arranged for him…" Her gaze flicked to Nora, and she schooled her face. The Finder's halos scintillated purple. "You know something."

Nora laughed. "I know a great many things, actually. Which were you interested in?"

"Why don't we start with why Marcos and Kyle decided to galivant out over what's left of the plateau this morning?" Bernice asked, all saccharine sweet. Her eyes narrowed at Phyllis. "Since *she* refuses to answer the question."

Was that where he was? "That I don't know," Nora said. "I haven't seen Marcos since early yesterday evening."

Bernice huffed like she didn't believe her, and Nora couldn't care less, the anxiety she'd been feeling from him since she'd awoken suddenly falling into place, as did the surge of relief and then the swelling pride an hour or so ago. That it had faded to worry further cemented her belief that not only had he gone out there to find the remnants of Titus's army, he'd been successful.

Which would also explain Phyllis's upset at the Binders not treating her line.

Oh, Marcos… How badly injured were those men? There wasn't a chance anyone on the hill would help, but maybe…

Nora stood. "To answer your earlier question, no. I'm not giving up my seat as one of the Ladies. And as far as Laughlin's visiting the Assembly, the sooner all of you realize that you can't dictate what that man does or doesn't do, the better. Every time he's lost his temper or done something radical, it's been in direct response to someone trying to constrain him, and this will be more of the same. Your time would be better spent curtailing others who don't have the North's best interests at heart." Her gaze landed on Bernice and the woman's face bloomed scarlet.

"Now you see here, Nora Jester—"

"No. I don't think I will, and I'll add your initial support of Serra Hess to Alice's list of things that should've been discussed prior to. If anyone's to blame for her gaining traction in Glynfyls, it's you and your bloody House. Now I have to see to mine. Good day, ladies."

She swept from the room, her heart thudding in her ears, counterpoint to Alice's laughter as she headed toward the Carmody's kitchen.

Fitz was seated at the table, eyeing the other doorway and shoveling some kind of a pie into his mouth. Four empty tins were stacked at his elbow. She stopped short, halfway across the kitchen as the stench of whatever he was eating hit her. Nora pulled her collar up over her nose, gagging.

"Good Glory, what *is* that?"

He froze, then looked around, like he was making sure she was talking to him. "Eh…This? S'a right fine batch of fish pies. Mackerel must've still been floppin'." He glanced down at it, then back at her. "Did ye want some?" He tilted the plate and chunks of gray fish burbled up through a cream sauce.

"No. Please. You finish it." Nora hurried to the sink, her guts heaving and their contents spattering against its stainless steel sides. Glory, she had not missed this part of pregnancy. Had it started so early with Kara? Certainly not, though it had with Riegel—

A wave of elated terror washed over her. Nora ran the water, grateful her back was to Fitz. Could she be giving Marcos another son?

"Here." Fitz came up behind her with half a lemon in hand and offered it to her. "Don't have t'eat it, but smelling it'll help."

She rinsed her mouth and dried off before taking it, the citrus astringency clearing her head. "Thank you."

"Naught to it." Fitz shrugged. "Ginger'd be better or peppermint tea, but I didn't see none of that… Ye sure ye should be going with us, bein' in the family way?"

Nora gave a half-hearted laugh and tossed the towel back onto the counter. She put the lemon to her nose again. "Is it that obvious?"

He scratched the back of his neck. "Ain't nobody losing their guts like that without reason, and me gran were a midwife. Dragged me all over hell and gone to help her when I were little. Come on then, sit for a spell till ye get yer feet back under ye."

Nora sighed and let him lead her to the table. He pulled out a chair for her and got her settled. She was grateful that any trace of what he'd been eating was gone. He sat across from her and pulled a pint from his jacket, checking the entrances to the room. Funny. It hadn't been the first time he'd done that.

"Are you waiting for someone?"

"Hmm?" He lowered his pint and swallowed, his cheeks coloring. "Eh…no. But we should be heading back soon. Pretty sure His Holy High Majesty ain't gonna stay for the full session."

"No, I can't imagine he will, but I need to ask you a favor first."

"Ya?" Fitz raised his brow as he took another swig and looked her up and down. "What'd ye have in mind?"

Glory, but he was a rogue and could certainly pull it off with those silver-gray eyes and curls of his. "I need to make a slight detour. Do you think we can stop at the commons infirmary? It's urgent that I speak with Pithy."

Fitz shook his head and her heart sank. "Won't be there. This time of day he's at his regular haunt in the Pinch…besides, that old hillie said I ain't supposed to—"

"Caliban?"

"Eh…think that's his name. Smoker."

"Caliban." She frowned. "Do this for me, and I'll deal with him. You owe me, Fitzpatrick."

"S'Fitz." He winced sourly, then took one more pull from his bottle and slowly screwed the top back on. "I do at that, but Shilo's ain't exactly the place for a lady."

Nora bit back a laugh. Did he have any idea what went on at the Source? She was positive there was nothing in Glynfyls she hadn't seen before. "I have faith you'll protect my virtue," she said dryly.

Fitz snorted. "First time I've heard that."

She raised an eyebrow and stood, resolute.

He ran a hand over his face before following suit. "Right. This is on you."

"Agreed."

He took her hand and colors ran as he pulled talent.

They appeared in a small, bubblegum pink antechamber. A rigid hide covered the door behind her, and large sequins dangled from strips across a doorway opposite it. The air had a strange acrid tang, and low music thumped up from the floor, resonating in her ribcage.

Fitz glanced at her and then the sequined doorway. "Shite. I can't very well leave ye here…just remember, ye asked for this." His halos briefly flared broken splinters of light through his irises, and the air cleared around her. "Don't need no glimmer in yer system," he muttered with a sigh before taking her hand and pulling her through the shimmering curtain.

The heat hit her first. Musky, damp, and animalistic; her skin took on an instant sheen of sweat, its slickness sparkling in the flickering purple lights. Ahead of her, a mass of scantily clad dancers writhed, strips of neon in their hands and around their limbs, undulating to the waves of sound pounding up from the floor.

Above, orbs of coruscating mist coalesced then rained down upon the crowd, eliciting gasps and moans as it coated their flesh and sent their halos sparkling like a thousand tiny flashbulbs. The dance kicked up into a frenzy of hands, lips, and tongues, couples and groups moving to the shadows as others came and took their places on the floor.

Okay. She took that back. She'd never seen anything like—

Someone pushed past her, and a topless woman in a thong collided with Fitz. He dropped Nora's hand and laughed, catching the woman a split second before her tongue was down his throat, and her legs wrapped around his waist. When they came up for air, he said something in her ear. She glanced at Nora and frowned. He said something else, his forehead to hers as he absently fondled her. The woman rolled her eyes and dropped to the floor. He grinned and smacked her backside as she melted back into the crowd.

He wiped the back of his hand across his lips. "Eh…sorry about that."

"Friend of yours?"

"Acquaintance, more like," he shouted over the music, positioning himself behind her. "She'll have Trick meet us by the bar. Just keep walkin' that way."

They waded through the edges of the crowd, more questing hands than Nora would like traveling over her body. Glory only knew what would've happened if Fitz wasn't directly behind her. When he said this place wasn't fit for a lady, she hadn't expected an orgy, especially given her previous experiences with Glynfyls.

"Where did you say this place was again?" she yelled back at him, imagining Bernice's face if she knew it existed.

"Shilo's? Eh…s'in the Pinch. Moves every so often. Glimmer ain't strictly legal." He wiped a finger over a passing woman's shoulder and held it up, the tip coated with a shimmery residue. "S'an upper."

More like an aphrodisiac. Nora cocked a brow. "You don't say."

He grinned and scrubbed the finger-full over his gums, his halos crackling light.

Her laugh turned into one of relief as the bar came into sight a moment later.

"There's Trick," Fitz shouted in her ear, pointing to the small man in a tam standing to one side of it. Nora sped her steps through the last of the press.

"Fitz! Happy day, happy day, it's been a while, my friend." He and Fitz bumped fists. "For both of ye…somewhat I can help ye with?"

"Lady needs t'see Pithy. He with someone?"

"He is, but I think he'll make time for this one. I'll take ye down, if yer ready?"

"Please," Nora said, her voice more eager than she'd intended.

The little man chuckled and colors ran.

They materialized in a white med-cube, and Nora sagged with relief.

"Shite, ye all right?" Fitz asked, steadying her. He walked her over to the gurney, and she gratefully took a seat, tissue paper crinkling beneath her.

"I am, that was just…a bit much."

"Sure enough it is, it is." Trick chuckled again. "If ye wait right here, I'll be back in a tick with the man hisself." His halos flared, and he was gone.

Nora looked around the room, a strange sense of familiarity coming over her. "I've been here before."

"Brought ye here after we shifted across the border," Fitz said, leaning against a wall.

Nora's brow furrowed. "I can't remember if I ever thanked you for that."

He shrugged, looking up as Trick shifted back into the room with a tall, painfully thin man wearing a lab coat and silvered goggles. Pithy's fingers began to fly as soon as he saw her, obviously not pleased she was there.

Fitz snorted. "Weren't me idea."

"No, it was mine—" Her attention snapped to Fitz. "You can translate?"

Fitz froze like he'd been caught at something. "Eh…"

Nora rolled her eyes. "Could you please give us a moment?" she asked Trick.

"Of course." He bowed and disappeared.

"He's still listening," Fitz murmured.

"Sooner than I'd like, it probably won't matter." Nora turned to Pithy. "I need your help. Marcos, my husband—"

"Knows who he is," Fitz reluctantly muttered, watching Pithy's hands.

"He's trying to save the Breakers that Titus abandoned out on the plateau. I'm sure they need medical attention, and Serra—"

Pithy's gestures became sharper, and Fitz snickered. "Ain't repeating that."

"Whatever it was, I'm sure I agree. I can't tell you how long her and her House have been a plague upon mine—"

"Knows that, too."

"How—" She shook her head. It didn't matter. What did was those men getting care. "I know the commons Binders are already strapped, but—"

"This important to ye?" Fitz interrupted, still translating.

"Extremely." It would destroy Marcos to watch any more of his troops die needlessly.

Pithy's hands went still, then started moving again, his motions deliberate instead of fluid.

Fitz blew out a breath. "Says he already knew about 'em. Lady Breakspear sent someone on the sly to the commons infirmary trying to circumvent the new system Serra's enacted. Says they're only allowed to heal the Talents she approves. Shite, that's gotta be few and far in between."

Pithy nodded, his fingers still moving.

"Says both them bitches can go f—eh, he and the rest of the Binders down here is taking care of their own, but he's got people at loose ends. Ye can have 'em on one condition."

Nora put a hand to her stomach, already knowing what was going to come next.

"Ye gotta take back First."

***

"WHAT DO you mean no funds will be forthcoming?" Peterli Morris blustered, glancing up from his notes. He glared at his wife's secretary, sure the man was partially at fault for Augusta's obstinance.

Davis's throat bobbed, a sheen of sweat dotting his upper lip. "I'm sorry, sir," he cleared his throat, "but I've spoken to the lady, and she refuses to approve the additional funds you've requested to settle with the Pearl… She's also informed me that she's put a stop to payment on what was previously agreed upon."

Lord Morris slapped his pen down and tried to breathe. The vein in his forehead pulsed alarmingly with the sudden spike in his blood pressure. Davis flinched back from the desk.

"Has she now?" Peterli managed through gritted teeth.

"Y-yes, sir. She's firm that there will be none to draw upon until Paul's been recalled."

None to draw upon. Peterli eyed the society page, his temper enflamed. Oh, there was plenty to draw upon. And that she would cut him off, yet squander a fortune on that damn boy and his twisted paramour by buying a theater on the third rung then broadcasting plans to renovate it—The blasted rag had quoted her as saying she was overjoyed at the prospect of her family returning to the stage. The woman had no shame.

Peterli steeled himself; no he couldn't recall Paul. Not now, not ever! A precedent needed to be set. House Morris's reputation demanded it.

"Then what funds do I have available?" He stood and straightened his lapels, glancing at the clock on the mantle. It was far too early to deal with this nonsense, and he had his notes to review before Assembly.

In truth, he never should've left the Pearl last night. Augusta had once again refused to dine with him, and if he was going to eat alone, he could've done that there. In fact, he would've preferred it to choking down overcooked beef Wellington beneath the life-sized oil of his father-in-law presiding over their dining room.

Davis ran a finger under his collar. "Ah…I suppose there's the allowance for your wardrobe—"

"Use it to assuage Dorothy with promise of future payment by the end of the week." He had little doubt the innkeeper would take what she could get for now. "Augusta will relent. She always does, in time."

The man's mouth opened and then closed before he bowed his head and left the study. Peterli glanced at the clock again and shot back the last of his coffee before scooping his notes from his blotter and tucking them into his breast pocket.

He stormed through the flat to the gate. What he needed was a walk to clear his head. He exited on a quiet city street a block away from the Pearl, his feet taking him to its rear. Fie on his wife. If Augusta didn't respect him, there were plenty of others that did.

Several minutes later, he wiped his palms on his breeches before knocking on the private entrance before him, not entirely sure of his intentions—

It opened before he'd lost his nerve.

"Lord Morris?" Lady Hess peeked out at him, a pretty flush spreading over her cheeks. "Is everything quite alright? You look flustered."

"I—might I have a bit of your time?"

"Of course." She opened her door wide, letting him into her well-appointed rooms. "I was just about to have some tea. Would you care to join me?"

"Ah, yes. I believe I would. Thank you, Lady Hess."

She smiled warmly and led him to a wide couch. When she sat beside him, their knees just touched. "Please, call me Serra." She reached for one of the two waiting cups.

"Have I intruded?"

"No, I'd thought Tamara would be here, but she and Miles were invited to break their fast with Lady Saks this morning." Serra poured him a cup and passed it to him.

"Ah. Yes, I heard something about their courtship. Quite an advantageous match for both Houses."

"It is, and I'm pleased there's an element of passion to it. I can't imagine being bonded to someone without finding them desirable. A marriage bed shouldn't be cold."

Peterli's cup trembled against its saucer, and he hastily set it onto the table. "No. It shouldn't. And please, call me Peterli. I-I won't keep you long, I was just thinking about what you said at the rally last night, and wanted to get your thoughts on the Assembly meeting in a few hours."

Serra colored again, and he couldn't help but notice the scandalously low cut of her morning gown. She leaned towards him as if in confidence, and he wet his lips at the deep valley between her creamy mounds.

"My thoughts? You flatter me." Serra put a hand on his knee. "You've no idea the admiration I have for you, standing up to Scot the way you do. You're truly Glynfyls's champion."

Yes, yes, he rather liked that. "I'm only doing my duty."

"Oh, but it's so much more than that," Serra simpered, looking away. "But I must confess, something you said has upset me a great deal."

"It has? I can assure you that wasn't my intent." His thigh grazed hers. "Please, tell me, so that I may address it immediately."

Serra shook her head. "I'm afraid you'll think less of me for it, but I'm rather put out that Lady Morris isn't your staunchest supporter. A man like you deserves better."

"It is quite painful, especially after losing my son in such a fashion." Peterli sighed, placing his hand atop hers.

"I understand. Tamara's father passed tragically, and I've never really gotten over it. Have you ever just wished there was someone you could go to for comfort?"

The look in her eyes left little to the imagination as to what that would entail.

He wet his lips again. "Yes, I do."

She lowered her head demurely, and he couldn't resist the vixen anymore. Peterli grabbed her by the shoulders and kissed her roughly. She made a small sound, enflaming him. Augusta's shock and pain flooded their bond, and he ignored it, Serra's hands already busy at the buttons of his trousers.

CHAPTER SEVEN

"Several days ago Ro gated into the city, covered in blood. K returned to Meskill, afraid he'd gone after En again. She said where Ro's father's trailer and one of the milking barns had stood there was nothing but ash.

No one's seen Mr. McGuire, and Ro's mental state has declined since that ill-fated night. None of us doubt he's responsible. I purposefully brushed over his mind as he slept. To say his thoughts are dark is an understatement, and when I tried to take them, they resisted me. It surprised me so much, I dropped talent and fled.

How is that possible? The question drew me to the Breaker section of the city today. I needed to know if Ro was an anomaly, or if the entire line was resistant to my talent. To my chagrin, it's all Breakers, and their culture is rougher than I could've imagined.

I watched him from the shadows, drinking and sparring with his men. They refer to him as Alpha and are unquestionably his. The sight of him shirtless as he fought...his savagery makes me yearn for things I shouldn't..."

– Undated journal entry

FLYNN SEETHED, struggling to tamp down his rage as he finished tying his cravat, his fingers lingering on the knot—

...he loops it around her wrists and snugs them at the small of her back. "You need to ask me for it," he murmurs in her ear...

He shook his head, the memories that'd assailed him since he'd seen that fucking reel so vivid, he could taste Kara's skin—

Fuck, enough!

He pushed away from the vanity and stomped into the other room. A cart waited for him by the couch. He tipped up the cover of one of the lidded plates. Roast beef, the bloody rare slab at least two inches thick. His stomach churned and he dropped the lid, sick. Why the hell couldn't it've been cookies?

… She laughs sleepily, turning to look at him. "Cookies?"

Christ, he fucking loves her. He bites the thought back, his eyes hot. Her brow creases, and she kisses him before pushing up against his chest to look.

"What kind?"…

"Snickerdoodles," he murmured, turning to the window and pressing his forehead to the frigid glass. Fuck. Beyond the clouding of his breath, the Finders' spoke was a jumble of concrete, and a faint haze of smoke lay over the far reaches of the city.

His pulse quickened. He'd done that and he was going to have to answer for it. Goddamn it. The Assembly's subpoena didn't hold nearly as much terror as it had yesterday, but that didn't mean he wanted to go.

Especially now that he knew they wanted to exile him, fully aware of what that would do to Kara and the babies. Well, what they thought it would do. If he hadn't been planning on it before, he'd come back with his family now just to spite the fucking assholes.

Flynn glanced at the clock. T-minus thirty minutes. He took a deep breath and flipped open the box of cigars on the coffee table, then pulled one out and stared at it for a long moment, waiting for the flames to flicker in his peripheral—

Christ. He grabbed two more and a book of matches. Only a few of those left, but there wasn't a chance he was gonna try to pull talent and wind up seeing that shit again.

Whatever. He needed to cut back on the damned things anyway.

He blew out his cheeks. A half hour. Just enough time to make two quick stops before everything got even shittier than it already was.

The men by the gate's antechamber nodded to him as he hit the button for the portcullis to rise and stepped up to the gate. He vaguely registered it dropping back down behind him as he lit his cigar and entered the opalescent mists.

Flynn stepped out into the entryway of Jacques's flat, and a small boy crashed into him.

"Ow! Who are you? Opi, there's a man here!"

A frazzled maid ran in a second later and grabbed the boy from the floor. "Lord Scot! I am so sorry, sir. I'll tell Lord Martin you're here—"

"No need, Ophelia." Jacques stepped into the foyer and took the child from her.

"He's big, Daddy." The boy hid his face, wrapping his arm around Jacques's neck. Christ, he was a little carbon copy of the man with Bea's red hair.

"He is, and if anything should ever happen to me, you're to go to him. There's no one I trust more in the world than Laughlin Scot. Deal?"

"Deal." The little boy nodded, peeking at Flynn.

His chest ached, mouth gone dry as Jacques turned to him.

"I've been extremely remiss in my duties, and please believe that hasn't been intentional. The Finders' spoke…" Jacques shook his head.

Shit. that was where Bea's House was from. "Her family okay?"

"Yes, but so many others are displaced, and the entire line is fixated on finding every last little—" Jacques frowned. "Suffice to say, her time has been at a premium, and neither one of us are quite ready to let Jamie out of our sight or loose in the city." He tickled the boy's tummy, and the child giggled.

"I believe you two have already met. He's what they call a runner," Jacques said. "I've been assured he'll grow out of it, but in the meantime, it's keeping everyone on their toes."

… A belt cracks. "Get over here you little shit…"

"I can imagine," Flynn said with a catch in his voice. He tore his eyes away from the two, his chest tight as he fought to refocus. "Your office, then?"

A look of pity flashed across Jacques's face before he forced a smile and handed the child back to his nurse. "Of course."

Flynn followed him down a long hall into an office. He stood by the desk as Jacques closed the door behind them.

"I am sorry about that. It's got to be difficult for you."

Flynn stared into the fire, rolling his cigar between his fingers. The flames above the coal basket flared, reaching for him. He moved to the other side of the room, and they snapped back to where they belonged. Goddamn it. Sweat beaded his upper lip. "I'm leaving as soon as I'm through with the Assembly. I need you to administer while I'm gone, and if I'm not back in a week, Glynfyls is yours."

Jacques stared at him, incredulous. "You have gone mad."

"Potentially."

His friend snorted. "What the hell am I supposed to do with the city?"

"Now? Start to rebuild. After a week? Rule it, give it back to the Assembly, burn it to the fucking ground for all I care." Flynn shrugged. "Until then, keep the rest of the cohort in check."

Jacques sighed, running a hand through his dark curls. "That's easier said than done, and you know it."

"I do, but I've got faith in you."

"And I in you. A week then." Jacques held out his hand and pulled Flynn in for a hug when he took it, clasping his shoulders tightly. "You'll find them, Laughlin. You've always had the devil's own luck."

Flynn gave a sad laugh as he left and gated to the Carmody's, needing to know if Jacques was right.

Alice was waiting for him in the foyer when he stepped out of the stone arch.

"I want a reading," Flynn said, cutting straight to it.

"No, you don't. But I'm happy to give you some free advice."

He glowered at her. "Fuck your advice. Did you know?"

"I suspected."

Flynn nodded, having assumed that was the case. He turned away—

"I don't see as clearly as my forbearers, and often not until the branch is upon us."

His temper spiked, along with his anxiety at the tingling in his fingers and that goddamned static—He glanced at the corners of the room, then ran a hand over his face. "Damn it, Alice, if I'd known, I could've protected her!"

"No." She shook her head sadly. "As soon as you bonded the girl you set this in motion, and there was no stopping it. Down every path in which I gave you even an inkling of what was to come, it led to disaster. You had to lose them to keep them. If she stayed, they all would've died."

"This is it then? That thing that you said was coming that I couldn't stop?" He gritted the question out, struggling to keep the churning blackness inside him in check.

Her dark bob swung as she shook her head. "No, this is just on the path to it. Their lives are balanced on a knife's edge. You're going to have to walk it to save them." She laughed. "I honestly didn't think you'd get this far. Death is a rather large hurdle to pass."

...scattered bits of self come together, weighted down and encased as flesh grows up around them, a vessel filled...

He leaned against the wall and slid down it, pinching across his temples. "Don't remind me."

Alice sat next to him and plucked the cigar from his fingers. "Carl hates it when I smoke," she took a couple of puffs, "but it does help with stress, doesn't it?"

"It's better than the bottle," he quipped, wiping his cheeks. That craving still gnawed at him.

She exhaled several small rings. "That path leads to ruin much quicker than any other."

He knew she was right, but it didn't make the gnawing go away. "You said it would all work out in the end, do you still see that?" he asked, running a knuckle under his jaw.

She shrugged and handed the cigar back. "That's entirely dependent upon you. I see a multitude of infinite possibilities. Every decision you make closes some doors and opens others. Even the color of that cravat and what you didn't eat for breakfast. You have the irritating habit of opening and closing extremely large doors, no matter how unlikely they might be. Doors large enough to influence hundreds of thousands of other people's own choices. I can speculate on what you may do and the outcome, but you've proven to be a very difficult horse to bet on, especially when you insist on running upon tracks no one knew existed. When I look into the aether, there are branches that lead to a happy ending, but there's fewer now than there were even an hour ago."

"Then there's nothing useful you can tell me?" He blew out a thick stream of smoke and passed the cigar back to her.

"I didn't say that. Everything I've seen has them safe for the next three days. After that, things start to branch again." She inhaled sharply, her pupils becoming oblong slits. "If you can't get to them by then, you'll lose Kara first, and then the babies."

… "You ever wish on a star when you were a kid?"

Kara looks at him blankly.

"Up here, the first star to show on the horizon every night's the wishing star. It's actually a planet, but when I was a kid—You say this rhyme, and wish for what you want. I always wished for the same thing."

"What was it?"

He bites his lip, his face screwing up. "If I tell anyone, it won't come true."

"I don't understand."

"If I say it, then it's real, and if it's real, it won't last. It'll be like taking the fix off those fucking roses, and before I can blink it, it'll be over." He looks away, wiping his face. "It's stupid. I know it's stupid. But I still can't say it, Kara, I can't take that chance and have it ripped away."

But he had, and it was.

Fuck this, he needed to get her back. He took his cigar from Alice and stood, raking a hand through his hair. She rose with him. "I gotta do this, don't I?"

She reached up and smoothed his messy locks down. "You already know the answer to that."

He did. "Thanks for the advice."

"Any time."

He took her hand and bowed over it before stepping through the stone arch and into the mists again.

The corridor to the Assembly chamber was packed. They all quieted as he appeared, and the sound of the angry crowd outside filled the void. Flynn strode on, people pushing against the walls, parting like the Red Sea as he swept down the hall. Sweat broke out on his forehead, his anxiety churning. No fucking fear, no fucking fear... Christ, they'd eat him.

...scuff of flesh on stone and a chain rattles. He slows his breathing, pushing back into the darkness, praying that they'll pass...

Fuck, that didn't help. He shook the memory away. Behind him, the tide of people clashed together in his wake, whispers and catcalls riling the small hairs at the back of his neck. Down the hall, the main doors leading outside thudded, and a group of security pushed past, grimly headed in that direction.

Flynn paused at the main chamber's entrance, looking in. The entire Assembly was present, along with every single Binder from the Source, and Serra fucking Hess sat in the First's box looking way too goddamned smug. Christ, he'd never thought he'd miss seeing Nora there. She was a bitch, but this cunt definitely wanted him dead.

He should've let that mutie eat her.

Morris looked pleased as fucking punch, too, despite Lot sitting in the council's chair, glaring at him. The rest of the Shades ran the gamut. Sympathy and concern from Jacques and Charles, to outright hatred from Horace. Flynn sighed. No surprise there.

Finders definitely wanted to fuck him up as badly as he had their spoke, and it was obvious Crandall had called first dibs. The man's face was livid and became more so as he caught sight of Flynn.

Guess that was his cue.

He started down the wide steps into the amphitheater, the silence cloying. In the center of the floor, a chair had been placed upon a dais. Christ, Kendall was right. This was a fucking witch hunt. All they needed was the pyre. Flynn focused on his breathing and tried to ignore the sweat running down his spine as the room closed in on him, the tension amplifying as he approached its center.

To his left, Markham's pained expression clearly broadcast that the Prydees had his nuts firmly in a vise and were twisting. To Flynn's right, Carl and the rest of the Fixers were far more stoic than usual. God only knew what he could expect from them, and in the section dead ahead, the frown on Rogan's face wasn't giving Flynn warm fuzzies. Shit. Anxiety crested over him as he glanced at Riggs. The speaker looked like someone had run over his dog.

Flynn's throat bobbed. Yeah. He was fucked. *Well, let's just get right to it then…*

"That for me?" he asked, motioning to the chair and trying for some levity. It fell flat, and he blew out a thick stream of smoke. A woman behind him coughed pointedly. Whatever. Fuck her and the rest of them.

"Ah, yes, if you would be so—so kind as to have a seat." Riggs shuffled his papers with trembling hands. "I'd like to begin by thanking the Breaker line for maintaining order outside. I don't think any of us are eager to have a repeat of the last time our city was at odds…"

Flynn ascended the dais, but didn't sit, his pulse racing as Riggs droned on. Another bead of sweat ran down his back to pool against his waistband. Right. Just give the South a reason not to come, avoid a civil war, and then rescue Kara. That's all he had to do. Jesus. He bit back a laugh. How the fuck was he gonna do any of it?

… "It's just—it's like there's two of me. Regular me and this other guy that comes out whenever someone pushes me. I lost it today. Told the entire Assembly that they were a bunch of fucking pussies."

Kara laughs. "I bet that felt good."

"I suppose. I don't… Kara, I don't know what the fuck to do. How am I gonna be what all these people think I am?" Christ, did he really give a shit?

"I can't tell you that, but whatever it is, they've seen it in you since you've come back, just keep doing what you've been doing."

He laughs. "Great, so lose my temper and act like an arrogant prick."

"Sounds about right…"

He blinked the memory away, trying to pretend he wasn't a cunt hair away from losing his shit. The lights flickered, and his gaze snapped to the news crew in the gallery. Just fucking great. They were streaming this live.

"Laughlin?" Riggs pushed up his spectacles, the room waiting, tension so thick it pressed against him with claustrophobic intensity. "Ah, if you, ah, would have a seat? We've convened to—to ask you some questions." He forced a smile, and Flynn read the lie beneath it.

How fucking stupid did they think he was? He wet his lips. Didn't matter. It was time to play the game and give them front row seats to the Lord Laughlin Scot show. They already hated him. Why not be an asshole and bring the bravado?

His throat bobbed. Because the shit wasn't gonna work, and they'd see right through him.

Fuck it. He couldn't think of anything better.

"Thanks, but I'd prefer to stand." Flynn took a deep breath, pasted an arrogant grin across his face, and flipped the hair from his eyes. "Well, here I am, as requested. I appreciate you all accommodating my schedule." He spread his arms wide and turned in a slow circle. "As you can see, I'm alive and currently in control of all of my faculties. I'm also kind of crunched for time, so if we can speed this up, that would be great."

The static in his ears got louder. Dear, sweet baby Jesus, please speed it the fuck up before they called him on his bullshit.

Riggs opened his mouth and then closed it again several times.

Lord Morris shot to his feet. "Just spit it out, Riggs! We've called you here for a vote, Scot. I've entered a motion to remove from you the title of Overlord and its associated powers. Your use of talent is reckless to the extreme, and Glynfyls won't stand for it!"

What a fucking asshole. Flynn laughed. "It won't, huh? And here I thought those powers were the only reason it is standing." The room was silent, and he laughed again. Why was he arguing? Christ, he needed to let them get on with this shit and—

"Look at you," Morris sneered. "Not a care in the world, nor a thread of conscience."

"Actually, I was going to point out that you've already called for a vote on this, and doing so again without first having the motion vetted and approved by Quorum violates Assembly bylaws—"

"No rational person would think double jeopardy applies, this is clearly based upon a separate incident!" a Finder yelled.

"Circumstantial evidence and supposition don't overrule procedure," Flynn shot back. "Additionally, as head of House Scot and First Shade, you were required to send me a packet outlining the proposed legislation in advance of the vote. Failure to do so also invalidates the motion, but fine." Flynn put the cigar back his mouth and shrugged. "Go for it."

Morris looked at him like he was insane. Shit, maybe he was.

"Ah…ar-are you seconding that the motion go forward?" Riggs asked, glancing between the two of them.

Fuck it, if it got him out of here faster, let them do what they had to do. Flynn looked around the hostile room, silently wishing them luck when the Deep South got up here. *Yeah, that's right, fuck every last one of you* ."Sure. Let's vote."

Riggs gingerly set his papers upon his lectern and regarded Flynn over the tops of his spectacles. "Ah…all right then. Our bylaws state that an Overlord's power can be revoked with a two-thirds majority vote of no confidence, however, if you recall the last time this matter was on our docket, it was settled by Quorum—"

"Exactly, it has been settled," Lord Klein stood with a quick glance at Crandall. "And Lord Scot is correct. Everything about this motion goes against Assembly protocol. If we can't follow our own rules, how can we expect anyone else to abide by them? I'll agree that his use of power was extreme, but I don't believe it was malicious. In that moment, I don't know that any of us would've handled ourselves differently, and until a proper fact-finding motion executed per our procedures crosses my desk, the Fixers will be abstaining from this farcical nonsense."

Flynn snorted as whispers filled the chamber. Holy shit. Leave it to Carl's line to muddy the waters with protocol.

"Well said, Lord Klein. I couldn't agree more." Riggs sniffed. "Ah… Lord Crandall? You look like you have something to add?"

Actually, he looked like he was up to something, but whatever. The weaselly Intelligencer stood, gripping the rail at the front of his box. "I'll agree that the legality is murky, but we've also never been in a position where the Overlord has turned the people's own powers against them, causing widespread death and destruction. And I'm afraid I don't agree with Carl's summation of Lord Scot's intent. Aside from the plateau, the rest of the city is relatively unscathed, whereas the Finders' spoke is completely devastated. Given his animosity toward my line, I can't help but wonder if that was intentional—"

"Are you seriously alleging profiling?" Carl sputtered. "You know very well that was due to *my* line, and if it hadn't been for the Fixers, the rest of the city would've been in the same condition!"

"Oh?" Crandall smoothed a hand over his mustache.

Lord Klein opened his mouth and then closed it, seeing the trap too late.

Crandall smirked. "As Overlord, Laughlin Scot is a threat to us all. Finders vote yea."

"So noted…" Riggs said, flipping through his papers then scanning the Binders' section. "Ah…I don't see Lady Jester…"

"No, you won't, as I've taken her place," Serra said, sinuously rising to her feet and flashing a viper's smile.

The speaker's brows drew together. "I'm afraid I don't have any record of that change…"

"That's because the paperwork is still in process—"

"Then you can sit back down," Riggs interrupted, more sternly than Flynn thought him capable of. "If the paperwork hasn't been signed, then Lady Jester is still First, and without a writ of proxy, I'm afraid the Binders are locked out of the vote."

"But that's absolutely ridiculous—" The look on her face was priceless, shock and rage in equal parts as the objections from the Binders and the majority of the Shades filled the room, ignoring Riggs striking the lectern with his gavel for order.

"No, that's the law," Carl shouted over them.

"Why start following that now?" Rogan called back.

"Agreed," Flynn boomed, stunning the room to silence. "Let them vote. I wanna see exactly where I stand."

"Well, I—a-are you sure, Laughlin?" the speaker stammered.

Flynn chewed his cigar, meeting Serra's eye. "Yeah. If we're gonna do this, let's do it."

Serra sniffed, drawing herself up. "Then the Binders vote yea."

He grinned back at her. Of course they did.

"So do the Shades!" Morris yelled from behind him.

Riggs gaped at him for a moment, exasperated. "I-I'm afraid you can't—Laughlin is still First—"

"Then put me down for a yea," Flynn said, locking gazes with Morris.

"B-but you…you could recuse—"

"If that's what my line wants, I won't stand in their way."

Riggs swallowed heavily, abruptly intent on shuffling his papers, their crackle very loud in the ensuing silence. So was Rogan's chair scraping against the floor as he pushed it back and stood.

"You're all fucking idiots. Especially you for going along with this bullshit," he said, glowering at Flynn. Shocked cries echoed through the room, and Flynn didn't bother to temper his grin. "Laughlin Scot is Overlord. Breakers vote nay."

"Ah…yes. Thank you for that…and it seems that leaves the deciding vote to the Fetches…ah, Lord Markham? If you please?"

Markham sighed heavily, his expression dour as he stood. "Might I just start by saying that as much as it pains me to admit, I agree with everything Carl said, and I shouldn't have to remind you all what happened the last time we allowed someone not duly-elected to shape policy," he said with a nod to the Binders' section as he mopped his brow.

"All of that aside, I can't stomach the possibility of bringing harm to Lord Scot's unborn children. If this matter is to be taken up in truth, it needs to happen after the lady gives birth. Until then, the Fetches also abst—"

A deafening crack echoed through the chamber, and Flynn fell back a step, then twice more as he was struck in succession. An otherwise nondescript man with a Glasgow smile and a rolling blink was tackled by security in the gallery, a spray of bullets peppering the crowd as he disappeared beneath the two big men.

The room dissolved into chaos.

Jesus fuck, had that been Barton? People screamed, and Flynn staggered, fixated by the bright patches of red blossoming across his torso. What the fuck? Crandall was supposed to have Titus's assassin in a hole somewhere.

… They're scrambling after that chasm exposed all sorts of things they'd rather not be brought to light…

Flynn wavered, putting a hand to the too-warm, sticky, scarlet ebb of life. Assembly members alternately scrambled for the exits or froze, unable to tear their eyes from the slick of blood saturating his shirt.

"Dead! She's dead!"

"I need a Binder!"

"It's everywhere, get it off me!"

"Good God, he's bleeding out—"

Flynn swayed, then fell to a knee, emotions and memories washing over him again in a wave of static.

… Flames surround him, searing vortices tearing the flesh from his bones, ash spiraling away. He opens his mouth to scream…

A bind snapped over the crack in his psyche, and the memory became remote, his fear replaced by panic.

That wasn't one of Kara's.

The feel of it similar, but not…his vision tunneled.

… "You let one of them touch you, and they'll know. What you are, all the dirt and filth inside you, they'll see it all, boy…"

Nora Jester had been inside his head. She knew, had fucking seen—

… "Stand the fuck up, you goddamned pussy!"…

… Viscera coats his hands, thick and mineral. He sniffs at it, licks it clean…

… He slides the tip of his machete beneath the Talent's skin…

Flynn grimaced, his initial shock gone, his body finally registering being shot. He cleaved to the pain, burying everything from his past and riding the agony back to the present.

He'd deal with Nora later.

"Fuck, that hurts." He coughed, one hand clutching his chest and blood at the back of his throat. His cough turned wracking, gore spattering past his raised fist, over the dais. Static drowned out the screaming crowd as he retched and spat out a gob. A bit of metal pinged out with it and rolled away. Christ, that had to be one of the bullets. Probably too much to hope one of them had taken out fucking Morris. The static surged again, and he shook his head. Goddamn. What the hell was that?

A woman screamed.

"Dear God!" someone yelled.

"Where's the shooter?"

"They have him in the gallery!"

Flynn's eyes rose to meet Serra's, and she cocked a brow back at him, her nails still clicking against the rail of her box like she was waiting for him to hurry up and die. His temper spiked, the darkness in him rising.

Not today, bitch... He grinned back at her and licked the blood from his teeth—

... he grapples with another, pulling him from the corpse and slamming him against the tunnel wall, teeth biting, tearing into his throat, the filth and sweat of skin washed away with a clean, coppery heat...

A searing stab of pain lanced through him, and he fell forward, coughing again.

The last two slugs pinged onto the floor.

"Good heavens—did you see that?" a woman cried, hushing the one beside her.

Great. Just what he needed, a goddamned audience. Flynn grunted, sweeping the bits of metal up as he pushed back onto his knees. The slick of blood soaking his shirt receded, flowing back into his body. He cracked his neck, strength returning, and stood, rolling his shoulders, bloodlust thrumming through his veins, feeding on the trauma.

"He's—he's not pulling talent—" the other shrilled, garnering more attention. It spread like wildfire, and the Assembly went still, transfixed to find him standing.

"His shirt...how is that happening?"

"He should be dead."

"Why isn't he dead?"

...they wave fists full of money, staring and pointing at him as he enters the ring opposite a feral mutie. The shrieking squeal of a silver whistle slices through his brain and he charges, howling...

Flynn blinked the memory away, pinching the bridge of his nose, pheromones thickening the air around him. He tamped them back, struggling to find zero. Goddamn it, this was not the time to lose his shit... The blood spatters across the dais evaporated, and a crimson fog swirled up his body, taking what was left on his shirt and leaving it pristine. His eyes closed, and he inhaled, pulling it and his 'lust back into him as muscle, skin, and bone re-knit. His wounds itched, and then it was like they'd never been.

He looked down and fingered one of the holes above his heart, the darkness inside him surging and suffusing his senses, looking for the enemy as it bolstered him, pushing the memories down. Static hissed around him, crackling.

He opened his palm, slugs glinting silver. His eyes flicked to Barton. Two Breakers held the assassin. He stood between them gazing back at Flynn deadpan from the gallery—

Static surged through Flynn's mind, and his palm was empty.

The assassin's head cracked back, the top blowing off and spattering across the gallery's friezes. He slumped between the Breakers, two bloody holes in his forehead.

The Assembly gaped, the room dead quiet.

"What the fuck just happened?" Lord Klein asked into the heavy silence, every face in the chamber, pale.

Flynn rode the wave of otherness flowing through his body, oddly euphoric.

And the cameras in the gallery were still rolling.

He snorted. What'd just happened? He'd given whatever news outlet that was a full frontal of him cheating death then murdering his would-be killer. His gaze dropped back to the Assembly—

Jesus. The darkness faltered.

Lord Morris's body was splayed back in his chair, the right side of his face a ruin. Flynn's stomach dropped, feeling somehow responsible for the man's death. Behind the corpse, Charles hyperventilated, hand clamped over his arm, spattered with gore, his shirt a sodden crimson beneath his fingers. A lady lay still on the marble steps, face down, another beside her sobbing. Others stared back, shell-shocked.

Flynn sucked in his cheeks, the darkness in him rising again at the judgement in their eyes and their armchair quarterback morality. This was nothing compared to what would've happened if he hadn't dealt with Titus's legion of Elites, and they wanted to strip him of his talent and murder his family for keeping theirs safe. Their horror abruptly rang hollow. He wasn't going to save them from themselves. Not anymore.

He was done.

He turned to Carl. "What just happened? An unnecessary tragedy,

Lord Klein, as it appears that ousting me from my position, by vote or assassination, is outside of the Assembly's purview."

"Y-you killed him…" A woman wavered and another steadied her.

Flynn just stopped himself from looking at what was left of Morris. The assassin. She meant the assassin. "I did, and my only regret is that I wasn't able to do it sooner. Is there any particular reason there isn't a Binder attending the wounded?"

Serra's eyes blazed as the room turned to her. She made a motion and several of her line dispersed to the other side of the room. "I-I'm afraid we're all in shock."

"Really?" The lie riled the small hairs on the back of Flynn's neck, the darkness inside him too close. "Because from where I'm standing, the lapse seemed intentional, as does the appearance of an assassin the Intelligencers had presumably incarcerated."

"Unfortunately, the damage to the Finders' spoke included the penal facilities." Crandall snapped as the woman who had been face down was revived. She didn't look like she'd been shot, just fainted. Did that make Morris the only fatality? Somehow that didn't make Flynn feel any better. He focused back on Crandall still trying to spin his fuck-up. "…currently re-securing inmates, but it is a process—"

"There's more criminals loose?" a woman shrilled.

Crandall's eyes flicked to her. "Few of which are of danger to the public, madame."

"That one certainly isn't anymore," Markham quipped as the Breakers hauled away Barton's corpse.

"But the Gorer is! That monster hasn't been brought to heel, and I want to know what you're doing about it!" A dowager spat.

"Everything in our power, madame." The Intelligencer's gaze returned to Flynn's. "I can assure you, he'll be brought to justice soon, and believe me, Laughlin, if I wanted you dead, you would be."

"You sure about that?" Flynn pulled a cigar from his breast pocket and frowned; a bullet had clipped it in two. He snorted as he tossed it onto the chair and fished out another. "If I didn't know any better, I might think I've been given this position by divine right."

He paused to light it, and Crandall glared at him, an island of animosity amidst a sea of shock.

Blasphemy had a tendency to do that up here.

Flynn paced the dais, addressing the entire room. "Now here's what's gonna happen. I'm going to bring my family home, and while I'm gone, Glynfyls will be administered by my cohort. That's Carl, Markham, Jacques, Dorian, and the Commandant. The Binders can go fuck themselves." He ignored their outcry, raising his voice to speak over them.

"The cohort will oversee the restoration of Glynfyls and the Flats beyond. I expect everyone to lend a hand to this initiative. Those that do will be compensated accordingly. Those that do not will be dealt with upon my return." He paused to looked directly at the cameras above. "And I can assure you, justice will be swift. If by chance a regime decides to try and poach what's mine in my absence, the condition of the plateau will pale in comparison to what I visit upon whatever country they slithered out from."

"That's—that's provocation," a man cried.

"No." Flynn's eyes snapped to the asshole. "That's karma, and going forward, I have no issue being the hand that deals it out. You try to take my shit; I'm gonna fuck yours up." He stepped off the dais and started up the steps.

Crandall sputtered, spittle flecking his lips. "So you would hold us hostage—"

"I would keep this city safe!" Flynn roared, a wave of his 'lust putting everyone in the chamber on their knees. "Especially from all of you."

He spat the last of the blood from his mouth as they cowered beneath his gaze. Fuck this and fuck them. He had somebody's shit to fuck up, and Barton was only the beginning.

THE LIVE FEED from Glynfyls went black, and Titus sat silent for a moment before sweeping the holo away, echoing Carl's sentiment, whoever he was.

What the fuck *had* just happened?

From the vantage of the camera, Scot seemed to completely reverse being shot thrice in the chest, and something other than Binding was definitely responsible. And as to the aftermath…Titus wet his lips, positively feral for the litter to be born, and a titch apprehensive over that little "reminder" he'd sent to Scot, but what was done, was done.

Titus pulled up a communications orb, its pulsing blue swirl barely into its second rotation before Salist answered.

"My, that was quick." The dark man laughed.

Titus glowered at him over the rim of his bourbon, not amused. "Yes. I'm eager for you to tell me more about your source that claimed Scot was…how did you put it? Oh yes. Incapacitated.'"

"Mmm." The dark man took a sip from an effervescing flute and tapped a finger against its cut-crystal stem. "I don't believe I said I had a source. I recall citing global consensus, and there's no way anyone could've anticipated that turn of events. I've certainly never seen the like, though I'd wager however he cheated death, it's legitimate given the collateral damage."

"Would you now?" Titus seethed, unable to disagree and thoroughly sick and bloody tired of Scot and his surprises. "Forgive me if I don't take you up on that, considering the last fifty thousand units you weaseled out of me was based on nothing more substantial than hearsay."

"Oh, come now," Salist grinned, "it wasn't my intent to mislead you. I'm happy to offer recompense. That concubine of yours I have on contract, Vignette. She's paid for through the better part of the year, but someone else has caught my eye, and I'm afraid I've become quite neglectful. I'd be willing to return her early to smooth things between us."

Titus swirled the ice in his glass, not having to crunch the numbers. If he'd been inclined to whore out Kara Jester's lookalike, he could make that figure back within the hour, depending upon the level of depravation requested. He wasn't, but depriving Salist of the pleasure suited Titus's current mood admirably. "Fine, send her to the drop, and I'll have someone retrieve her."

"Consider it done." Salist raised his glass in salute, and the communications orb blipped out.

Titus glowered at the space it had occupied and drained his glass.

He cracked it down onto his desk, then called up Kara Jester's metrics and that of the litter. Based on data points from weeks ago, he'd already proven out that the Jesters were able to share their talent. Might the girl's ability to regenerate be something she was pulling from Scot?

It seemed as likely an answer as any, especially since her health had continued to improve despite the additional strain of the litter's expedited developmental schedule. In fact, they'd been responding so well to the proscribed treatment, he'd been toying with the possibility of increasing the amount of accelerant being administered and having her whelp within the next day or two. A bird in the hand and all that. Physically, the litter was developed enough to survive…

Titus's mouth pursed, well aware he was on a slippery slope. With the current levels in her system, the birthing process would be particularly violent. The last thing he wanted was to lose any further opportunity to study her and relinquish his leash on Scot.…but if that wasn't as foolproof as he thought, there needed to be alternate arrangements.

Yes. The sooner she whelped the litter, the better.

Because the man was definitely coming, and while Titus couldn't anticipate what Scot would do when he got there, he was overwhelmingly positive the blasted man wouldn't endanger his so-called family.

And regardless of whether or not she survived, Titus planned on making very sure that even after the birth, their continued existence depended entirely upon his sufferance.

CAL SAT in front of the fire, a cigar clenched between his teeth and an empty bottle at his side. His thumb worried the edge of a blurry photograph. It curled with age despite the fix keeping it from turning to dust. A glimpse of the future in the past. The night had started out idyllic, then it'd fallen to shit, as per usual.

Nothing with Elize had ever been easy, but he'd be damned if it wasn't repeatable.

He stared at the frozen relic of time, remembering. In it, he stood in a rented suit on the front porch of the farmhouse he'd grown up in. At his side, Elize was a vision in a deep blue gown. Happy. Christ, they were so fucking happy—well, he had been. She'd been playing the part. He'd known it, and hadn't cared.

The color accentuated her burnished skin, her azure irises popping behind heavy, kohl-lined lids. Dress had probably cost the same as his daddy's mortgage. The tiara atop her elaborate braids definitely had, and then some.

So had the contingent of body guards that'd shadowed their limo.

Senior prom. He blew out a long stream of smoke and picked a bit of tobacco from his lip. Never did ask her what her father had asked her to do in exchange for that little slice of freedom. In retrospect, Cal probably didn't want to know, but he was certain it wasn't disappearing with Stacy Lee and Joey Harris under the bleachers.

No. That'd been all her, and he couldn't blame her any more then, than he could now.

Cal ran a hand over his face. Why he hadn't put an end to it—to all of this—sooner…

He snorted, reaching for the bottle and cursing when he found it empty. He tossed it aside and sat back with a huff. Why. He was all too goddamned aware of why. His lips tightened. He was a coward. A selfish piece of shit as opportunistic as Leo had ever been.

More so, and a hypocrite to boot. Maybe that's why the boy's betrayal cut so deep.

Cal saw himself in it, and the reflection hurt. Each one of his wounds self-inflicted.

His gaze fell back on the photo. God, he loved her.

And it hadn't fucking mattered. Then or now. Happily ever after wasn't what Elize had signed up for, and despite the Surge flipping the script, that'd never changed. Cal took another long drag, damning himself for wanting more than she could give.

Then ripping it away from her when she was ready to try.

But how the hell had he known? Everything with Elize was always a goddamned test, and there wasn't a damned bit of difference between passing and failing.

Nothing he could give would ever be enough. The hunger inside her, the void. That'd been the one hole she couldn't fill.

He swept up the coiled braid at his side and pulled out his pocket knife, slashing his granny's ring free. It sparkled dully, the filigree around the stone caked with a millennium of deceit.

Shit. It'd been longer than that.

He'd just never wanted to see it. Now he couldn't look away, neck deep in the same web of lies. Didn't matter. He needed to finish what he'd started, regardless of the bridges he was gonna burn.

Rogan had been pushed to his limit. He wouldn't let Elize walk again, not with Kara in the mix, and not with Enoch taunting him to boot. Taking her had forced Cal's hand, and the writing was on the wall. Jane was giving him one last out. One last chance to come clean.

Or one last chance to bury his sins.

Wasn't a choice. The end was too goddamned close to risk losing the game now, and Jane knew it. She had to be betting on breaking him, and damn her…he scrubbed his face. Damn her, but this would.

It shouldn't. God knew it shouldn't. Elize…it wasn't her anymore. Jane had pruned and twisted her into a goddamned construct. Made her a victim. Christ, it was no more than a continuation of what he'd started but—

He had to end it.

Her. His Lizzy.

He buried his face in his hands. Could he? Despite what he'd said to Rogan, despite every goddamned thing she'd done…it'd all been on him. Cal knew what she was going into it and loved her anyway, God help him. He'd forgive her in a heartbeat to feel her by his side again.

To be happy.

He never would. She wouldn't—couldn't—goddamn it, she shouldn't—forgive him for what he'd done in turn.

Jeremy. Jane.

He'd never forgive himself. No one would. This entire clusterfuck was on him, and it was too late to admit he'd been wrong on either count. He'd opened the door to it, and it was on him to set it right. He flung the photo and the coil of hair into the fire. The flames lapped at them eagerly, blackening and curling the last lingering keepsake from his first—his only—true love.

Cal stood, unsteadily gripping the back of the chair. It was time. On the coffee table behind him, his tablet pinged. Another message from his lawyers. Another ill-concealed inquiry into his mental health. Was he certain on the allocations and changes to his trust? He swept it up, trying to focus on the legalese and snorted, forwarding it to Merchant. The little barrister knew where he stood. Flynn could have it all.

Cal didn't plan on being around to need it.

"HERE KITTY, KITTY, KITTY..." Fitz lifted the fabric flap across the bottom of the couch and squinted into the musty darkness beyond. The previous travesty of comfort Scot'd had up here were ugly, but even blood-soaked, Fitz would've taken it over this monstrosity. The shite rich people spent their money on...

He eyed the broken, splintering slats across the bottom. S'what ye got for using cheap wood. Ain't nobody cared about craftsmanship no more. The one in his gran's hovel were thrice as old and twice as sound, lumps and all. He sighed and dropped the flap as he sat back on his heels. No cat. Where in the hell...

He scrubbed a hand through his curls. Beastie had to be in the bedroom. Weren't nowhere else for it to hide. Fitz stood and made his way over, poking his head in before the rest of him followed, then shut the door in case the rotten animal made a break for it.

Huh. He took in the surprisingly spartan space. Had pictured His High Holy Highness's boudoir a tick more opulent. Bevy of cloth-o-gold throw pillows, a plush throne...weren't naught but a bed, dresser, and a vanity. One door that probably led to the closet were shut tight and another left open for the washroom.

And right next to the bed, one of them energy tangles. Fitz rubbed his brow, wincing. Even without usin' his sight, this one were a doozy, and he didn't want no part of it. He shivered, the resonance curlin' his toes. Soon as he caught that beastie, he were out of here, and the sooner he did that, the better.

Weren't room for a cat to get under or behind anything but the bed. Fitz crouched down and peered beneath it.

Two narrowed green eyes glared back at him.

He grinned. "There ye is…" He rubbed his fingers together and made stupid kissy noises at the blighted thing as he stretched out on his belly, wriggling closer. "Kitty, kitty—"

Beast bared its fangs and hissed at him, backing away.

"Aw, now ye don't mean that…come t'Fitzy…" He reached, out and the cat swiped at him, growling. "Jesus, Mary, and—fine, ye shite, have it yer way." Fitz pulled talent, planning on shifting behind the miserable beast—

The cat bolted.

Fitz lunged, snagging the furry bastard by the back leg, and the cat flailed directly into—

"Shite! Nah! Stay away from—"

Colors ran.

Somewhat clattered above him, and he glanced up just as a vase toppled over the edge of a prissy white table. He swore, letting go of the cat to catch the heavy crystal, and the miserable animal dove under the lacy white duvet of the bed beside him.

"Christ, ye fu—"

"Gemma, is that you?" a lady's muffled voice from another room called out. A door on the other side of the bed opened, whoever it were close enough to hear their skirts rustle.

Fitz froze, clutching the vase to his chest, a mess of dried petals and dust still floating down. Shite. His nose crinkled, resisting the urge to sneeze.

"Huh."

The door closed and he let out a slow breath, sniffling. Christ. Where the fuck were he? Pulling talent around that goddamned energy tangle must've been like pokin' a light socket with a fork, though where the hell it'd blown him…

Right, had t'be somewhere he'd been. Shiftin' didn't work no other way, unless his talent were fuckin' with him again…which were more probably than he liked. Damn it. He sat up and peeked over the side of the bed, taking in the lady's room of pinks and white. This definitely weren't his usual haunt, and it weren't ringing no bells, neither.

Luggage were all over the room, dainties hanging from drawers and spilling from the closet. Bed the cat'd dove under were one of them poofy pillow-tops, with curtains of silk gauze around it.

Hill. He were definitely on the hill. Floor so clean ye could eat off it, planked with wide, warm oak and walls the palest pinky peach, some shimmery design on 'em where the light from the window hit just right.

A seat were built below it between two overflowing bookcases and a prim desk catty-corned to one side. French doors the lady had come through faced the end of the bed. Fitz could just make out a couch and a hearth through the bubbly glass.

Shite. Had he been here on a drunk? Nah. Knew better even then. He ran a hand over his face, positive his fuckin' talent had dumped him somewhere random again. He scowled, feeling the blessed saint's amusement. Whatever, wherever it were, he weren't stayin' any longer than it took to catch that blighted cat.

Fitz pulled at his patch, weighin' his options. Hadn't used his talent to shift the beast like he done the weasel on account of knowing Miriam and them shite kids of hers was in the same flat, but here...

Christ, for all he knew it were one of his half-sisters in the other room, and then he'd be well and truly fucked. He eyed a silky pair of knickers hangin' from a drawer and got the creeps, hoping to hell that weren't the case. Ain't nobody needed to see that.

Fuckin' cat.

He crouched back down at the side of the bed, keeping an ear cocked for any clue the lady were coming back. Needed to be long gone before—a door creaked, and he peered beyond the bed skirt—Jesus fuck!

That stripy little bastard'd pushed open one of them French doors and were strutting right into the other room with its tail held high, flashin' Fitz its asshole.

"Oh! Hello...where did you come from?"

Fitz's stomach dropped, and he sprang to his feet. Shite. Knew that voice. *Ye gotta be fuckin' kiddin' me.*

The feeling of Cajetan's merriment grew.

Fitz's throat bobbed. He went to pull talent, and his coin seared ice through him, breaking his concentration. *Fuck, fuck, fuck, ye fuck—*

"Fitz?"

Sophia stood in the doorway, holding the cat, her mouth a small round 'o'.

"Eh...ya?" he croaked out, his brain short-circuiting.

Heaven fucking help him. He must've caught her changing gowns. Her hair were done up all proper with combs, and she wore a long silky robe over her petticoat and chemise. That'd slipped, baring one smooth shoulder, and her feet was bare again, peeping out from her hemline. Fabric were so fine, the light behind her lit the whole ensemble like somewhat worthy of a peep show. His Adam's apple bobbed, and she ducked her head, a blush coloring the downright indecent expanse of her bosom. He wet his lips, his pants growing tight—

Knew he shouldn't have taken that finger-full of glimmer.

"What are you... Is he from you?" She snuggled the beastie closer, ruining his view. Cat smirked at him like he knew it. Bastard.

"Eh, what's that now?"

"The cat. Did you bring him for me? To keep?" It butted up under her chin, purring. "Oooh, what a precious baby, yes, yes you are..." she cooed back at it.

Fitz scratched the back of his neck, the coin in his pocket growing warm as inspiration struck. "Eh...more like it's on loan from the Overlord while he's gone. I thought ye could use a friend." He jammed his hands into his pockets, remembering Craig spouting a similar line of horseshite to one of the barmaids he were trying t'bed.

A radiant smile broke across Sophia's face, and somewhat in Fitz's chest somersaulted. She cuddled the beast closer. "You did, really?"

Christ, he'd tell her he brung the moon if it meant having her smile at him like that again. He swallowed the lump in his throat and nodded, owing Craig a pint. "Eh, ya. Do me a favor, and hold him so I can say goodbye?"

"Of course." She came farther into the room, and he kicked the door shut as he met her. Weren't about to chase the miserable animal again.

He ducked his head, hiding behind his curls as he pulled talent, taking back the ward and his oath to Scot. "Eh…behave yerself there, Pumpkin." Patted the beast on the head, and the shite tried to bite him.

"Pumpkin?" Her brow furrowed. "Why would you call a gray tiger cat Pumpkin?"

Shite. "Why do ye fuckin' hillies do anything?" He scowled. "Ye should see the couch the Overlord's got in his suite. S'fit t'turn yer stomach."

Sophia laughed as the beast growled, hissing at him. "I know, Fitzpatrick has the same effect on me, but I don't think he's all bad, even when he tries to be." Sophia kissed the cat between its ears and set it on the bed.

"S'Fitz," he muttered.

She popped up and kissed his cheek, her arms around his neck. "Fitz. Thank you. This is the nicest apology I've ever gotten. No one's ever stolen a cat for me."

"Ain't stolen—"

"There's no way his name is Pumpkin."

"Animal's name is whatever ye call it." He huffed the curls from his eyes. "And it ain't stealin' if ye plan on bringin' it back." His hands found her waist and settled on her hips. Sophia melted against him. Christ, she felt a treat—his brow furrowed. "Eh…apology?"

She nodded, sliding a hand down his chest. "For abandoning me like that at the Manse. You have no idea how much I hate it there, and now that I have to move in—" She made that little gasp in the back of her throat as her palm grazed over his nipple ring. He bit back a groan as she paused to outline the silver hoop, her big doe eyes rising to meet his. "Did it hurt?"

His head dipped, gaze on her plump lips. Fuckin' glimmer. He needed to walk away. She were a lady and a Carmody t'boot. Ain't no good were gonna come of havin' his hands on her like this… He slid them to the small of her back, drawing her closer. "Not as bad as others."

"These?" She trailed the fingers of her free hand over the rings studding the shell of his ear before sinking them into his curls, the other still playing with the ring.

"Nah. Not those."

That saucy glint in her eye he'd seen when they was in the stairwell were back. "Where else do you have them?"

Shite. If she weren't doing things to him… "Ask nice and I'll show ye."

She colored again, and he chuckled. His nose brushed hers, and he cupped her rear, her wholesome flesh dimpling beneath his fingers like a dream. His length hardened against her belly. Damn, she were a treat, and there weren't no time to enjoy her proper.

"When do ye leave?"

Her eyes were on his lips. "As soon as I finish packing."

"Will ye be back?" The hell were it about her? Glimmer shouldn't be messin' with him this bad. *Christ…Fitzy, snap out of it, she's a Carmody, a fuckin' witch…* He cursed hisself, well and truly under her spell and happy as a goddamned clam to be there.

Her pupils blew out as his knuckles traced the line of her throat to her sternum and he smoothed his thumb across the curve of her breast. "Not until I—N-no. Not for a while." Sophia swallowed, her breath coming fast. "Six months. Maybe a year."

His stomach lurched same way it did when he cut off his sight.

"W-will you kiss me goodbye?"

If he weren't gonna see her again? "I'm set t'do a sight more'n that." The Overlord and all the rest of 'em could fucking wait. A flicker of silver flashed at the corner of his eye as he lowered his lips to hers—

"Sophia!" The door in the other room opened, and they sprang apart. "I've got those boxes you asked for—"

Fitz pulled talent and were gone.

He appeared back in his tenement with a raging hard-on. Motherfucker. Of all the goddamned times to interrupt a bloke—He frowned at Adelaide asleep in bed and stomped into the bathroom. Slammed the door closed behind him and pulled his cock out, stroking. Weren't gonna take long to set hisself right. Woman got him hotter than a pair of whores going at it after stiff dose of crash—

"Fitz? Is that ye?"

He grunted, one hand on the wall, fist pumping below, remembering the way Sophia's softness felt in his hands. Imagining spreading them cheeks apart, her bent over, him on his knees behind her, spearing into her with his tongue—goddamn, what did a girl like her taste like—

Door rattled behind him. "Fitz?"

"Busy!"

Bet she'd make that little gasp, and he'd have to grip her hips while she squirmed, all wet and slipping over his face, then pressing back, smothering him as she came—he bit his lip and groaned, cum spurting over the sink and coating his hand.

"Ye alright?"

"Ya." He snorted, looking at the mess he'd made. Alright? No, he weren't alright and oddly unsatisfied. He slapped on the water, rinsing down his spunk, out of his goddamned mind for jackin' off to a witch when he could've fucked a willing whore not a handful of steps away. He cleaned up and splashed a handful of tepid water over his face, staring at hisself in the mirror.

What the fuck is wrong with ye, Fitzy?

He sighed. Whatever it were, it were done. Aside from figuring out how to get that cat back, didn't sound like he were gonna see Sophia no more. Stomach churned like he'd eaten spoiled pie, but it were better that way. Ain't no good could come from truckin' with regular girls, and even less if they was a hillie witch.

He turned the water off and shouldered open the door.

Adelaide sat at the edge of the bed, a ratty throw around her shoulders. "Aught I can do?"

"Eh...nah." He rummaged in a drawer and pulled out a knapsack. "Somewhat I ate."

She raised her brow, all but callin' him a liar. "Were it now?"

Sure as hell wished so. He shoved some clothes into the bag. "Ye find the rent?"

"Aye, but ye left a fair bit more'n that..." She paused as he grabbed his toothbrush and razor from the bathroom. "Ye going somewhere?"

"Am. Keep whatever's extra."

"Where?"

"Dunno."

"When will ye be back?"

…Six months. Maybe a year…

"Eh…" He cinched the top of the knapsack tight. "Dunno."

She crossed her arms over her breasts. "Were ye gonna say goodbye?"

"I'm here now, ain't I?"

Adelaide shrugged her narrow shoulders, lookin' away.

Christ. Fitz raked a hand through his curls, feelin' like a right shite and not sure why. Didn't owe her a goddamned thing. "I'll see ye when I get back, ya?" She nodded, and he sighed, putting an arm around her as he sat.

Adelaide snuggled against his chest for a long moment. "I'll miss ye."

"Shouldn't be long. Stay here 'til then?" She nodded, and he kissed her temple before he stood and pulled talent.

He appeared back in the parlor at the Scot's flat feeling even more like a shite and made a beeline for the sideboard. Dealin' with women were gonna drive him into an early goddamned grave. He swiped up a bottle and tipped it back, ears perking at his name mentioned amidst some commotion coming from down the hall. Probably should go see who else he'd disappointed of late. He traded what he'd been drinking for a fuller bottle and stomped toward the ruckus.

Servants was adding to a pile of gear in the middle of a room that looked more suited to an opium den than the Overlord's flat. His High Holiness were front and center, flipping through a journal, and that willowy sister of Arileo's, Shelby, were at his side with Kendall.

"…I know it's going to be a big job, but I can't—I need to do something to keep busy, and now that Paul's mother has recalled him as heir…" She put a hand to her throat and shook her head.

Scot sighed and hugged her. "I'm not sorry Morris is dead, Shelby, but I am sorry for their House's loss."

She gave a sad laugh and pushed away, wiping her eyes. "Then you'd be the only one. Augusta was finalizing papers for divorce this morning. It's sad, but this works out best for everyone, well, not the late Lord Morris, but he was an awful man. No, I'm just…" She shook her head. "Audrey and I were talking, and you can't bring Kara and the babies home to this. The theater can wait."

Scot looked at her for a long moment and then returned his attention to the sketch book in his hand, reverently turning a page. "These are really all Kara's drawings?"

Shelby nodded. "She started them when she was waiting to be Introduced. Miriam had said something about redecorating Meddleton, but most of them are from when she was here."

"I didn't know…"

"She didn't like to share them, but Kara was a really talented artist."

Scot's knuckles whitened, and his head bowed over the little book. "You mean she is."

"That's not—You know that's what I meant, Flynn."

"Yeah…" He ran a hand down his face and handed the journal back to Shelby. "If it's gonna help you get through this, gut it, burn it, I don't give a shit. Do whatever you need to do. Anything's better than what it is now."

"And I'll make sure there aren't any more surprises," Kendall said. "Mesh found a hidden staircase running the east side of the building with access points on each floor, and someone had used it recently."

A muscle in Scot's jaw ticked. "I didn't know about that, but there's several levels below the servants' quarters used for storage. French or Audrey can help you get into those."

Shelby threw her arms around him. "I won't let you down."

"No." He hugged her back, looking like a schooner after all the wind had gone out of its sails—adrift and sad. "You never do—" He caught sight of Fitz, and the bluster were back. "There you are. Where the fuck is Hiss?"

He looked at him blankly. "Hiss?"

"Kara's cat."

Definitely a more fitting name for the beast than Pumpkin. Fitz scratched his jaw and shrugged. "Eh…on loan."

"On loan?" Scot glared at him, and Shelby stepped away, scooting from the room. The servants followed suit, clearing the way between them as the man stalked closer. Kendall and the two guards at the gate looked like they needed popcorn. "What the hell is that supposed to mean?"

"Means the wretched beast's being cared for. Or would ye rather it up there all by its lonesome while yer gone and the place's being torn apart?" Fitz asked, holding his ground as he spun off the bottle's cap.

Man went to say somewhat then stopped hisself. "Like you give a shit," he grumbled.

"S'fair observation, but not the one I were going for." Fitz took a swallow and smacked his lips at the overwhelming taste of rye. Should've kept what he had. "The fuck's up yer ass all of a sudden?"

The Overlord glared at him for a breath and then started laughing. "What the fuck's up my ass? Didn't you watch the feed from Assembly?"

Fitz took another swig of liquor, and the Overlord's eyes followed the bottle. "Why would I wanna do that? Ain't seein' ye in person miserable enough?"

Scot scrubbed his beard. "You get what you needed to?"

"Aye. Ye want the lady's ward?"

Panic flitted over Scot's face, and he licked his lips. Man looked sorely conflicted, but shook his head. "Keep it for now. I'm so fucked up... You feel her though? The babies?"

"Eh...just the lady somewhere t'the southeast. We ready then?" Fitz asked, hoping the man weren't gonna get all girly on him.

Scot gave him a look like he knew what Fitz were thinking and scowled, ashing his cigar on the filthy carpet. "Yeah, we were just waiting on you and Nora. She's supposed to be taking a look at French." He glanced over Fitz's shoulder at voices coming closer.

That woman with the big glasses were listening to somewhat the lady in question were saying, though Fitz hardly recognized her decked out in Breaker's gear. Nora Jester looked weird in pants. The two of them stopped to speak in quick whispers, then they hugged. Fitz's eyebrow rose, and he adjusted hisself. Maybe all that with Sophia were the glimmer if he were already rarin' for round two—

Scot smacked him. "Seriously?"

"Were at a rave earlier," he muttered.

"Tell me you didn't leave the cat there."

"Wrong kind of pussy for one of them."

The Overlord snorted as Nora joined them. He edged away from her, his face a thundercloud. Hers went pale. Fitz tipped back his bottle, and plopped down on one of them couches to enjoy the show.

"How is he?" Scot asked, voice gruffer than usual. Wouldn't look at her.

"Old," she said with a sad smile. "And not interested in extending his life outside of what nature intended. I've done what I can to strengthen him, and advised he stick to light duty while we're gone. Audrey's working on convincing him to hire someone to help for when we return."

"Good luck with that," Flynn muttered.

"Indeed. Caliban, Rogan." Nora inclined her head at the two men as they joined them, way too fucking excited to see the bastards in Fitz's opinion.

The big Breaker nodded back then turned to him. "You do what you needed to?"

"Eh…ya," he said, eyeing a case of whiskey the man were carrying. Fitz's mouth watered. Looked like a straight-up barley malt—

"Shift first, booze later," the Breaker said. "You ready?"

Fitz stood up and scowled. Like multi-taskin' were an issue. "'Course I'm fuckin' ready."

Colors ran as he pulled talent.

<hr>

ROGAN FLICKED THROUGH the lightstream's controls doing the final systems check before takeoff. Behind him, Flynn stowed the last of the gear and crammed himself into the co-pilot's seat. The craft was definitely not made for comfort and space was gonna be at a premium, especially on the way back up.

"We good to go?" Flynn asked, his eyes flicking to the side like he was seeing shit again.

"Yeah, she's checking out fine. You?" Rogan wasn't gonna bring up what happened at Assembly, but if the kid wanted to talk about it…

Flynn chewed his lip and ducked his head, shrugging. "I saw

Jacques's kid…Jamie. You know we only named one of ours? Kara wanted me to pick the rest. She said it would make it more real, but I…" He shook his head. "It's already too real."

Wasn't where Rogan thought this was gonna go, but okay. "Waiting isn't uncommon. We didn't name the twins until after they were born. Maria said it'd be bad luck. She wanted to meet them first." Hadn't made a damn bit of difference in the end, but Flynn didn't need to know that.

Kid nodded, glancing out the cockpit's transparency at the warehouse beyond. Cal was pacing, sucking down as many cigarettes as he could before he had to go cold turkey, and what a fucking joy that was gonna be. Couldn't see Fitz or Nora, but they were both out there somewhere.

"When can we leave?" Flynn asked, scratching his jaw. His hand trembled, and he jammed it into his pocket. Shit. That wasn't a good sign. Whatever Nora had done must be fading.

They needed to move.

Rogan hit the ignition. "Now, actually."

Outside, Cal took one last drag before heading in their direction, already looking surly.

"Is there someplace particular I should sit?" Nora asked as she climbed aboard. Fitz stumbled out of a ramshackle office across the warehouse, and staggered toward them.

"Nope," Rogan said, watching the kid's negligible progress. How the hell he'd managed to get that plastered in the fifteen minutes they'd been here…

"I call the back row." Flynn hefted himself up and ducked down the length of the craft to the bench seat along the back. He put his back to the wall of the cabin and stretched out, pulling a battered beanie from his coat. Kid tugged it on, low over his ears, closed his eyes, and hunkered down, arms across his chest.

Good. He could use some more sleep. Nora slid into the row in front of him, and Cal took a seat in the co-pilot's chair. Even better. Rogan grinned at him. When the asshole got too pissy, he could just reach over and knock him the fuck out.

"Where the hell is Fitz?" Cal grumbled, pulling out a pack of nicotine gum.

Well, that didn't take long. Rogan rolled his eyes. "Can you at least wait until we take off before you start bitching?"

"And miss ruining your day from the jump? Not a goddamned chance." His two fingers moved toward his mouth, and he scowled, shoving his hands into his armpits.

Great. Rogan looked over his shoulder at Nora. "Is his bullshit something you can bind?"

She shook her head. "It's behavioral."

"Lovely."

"So, where the hell is he?" Cal barked.

"Ri' h-here, ye shite," Fitz muttered at the hatchway. "An' ain't nobody said naught,"—he hiccupped and fell back a step—"about me havin' t'go anywhere in one o' these fuckin' contraptions."

Rogan tongued his cheek, sympathetic but not. Fetches didn't tend to do well with methods of travel other than their own, but getting shitfaced wasn't gonna help. "Suck it up and do it for your gran."

Kid shot him a look that came close to striking him dead. He climbed into the seat closest to the hatch like it was the electric chair.

Rogan closed the craft up and hit the button for suspension before the kid made a break for it. The craft lurched, hovering a few feet off the ground. Over his shoulder, Fitz went green, white knuckling the armrests. Oh yeah. This was gonna be bad—no check that, between him and Cal, it was gonna be downright fucking painful.

"Barf bags are in the seat back. I'm ready to get out of here when you are." Rogan sighed. "Shift us out over the cove and I'll do the rest."

Fitz grunted, leaning forward to fish a bag out, and colors ran.

A moment later, they were outside, poised above the water, and the kid was heaving. Rogan said a quick prayer, engaged the thrusters, and they were off.

CHAPTER EIGHT

"My hand shakes as I write this. A returned and discovered El's condition. He flew into a rage and—dear God...

The look on both their faces with their dead child between them will haunt me forever.

Yet as I recount the horror, all I can think of is the night of the explosion. Looking up into that great tear in the sky and watching the ribbons of light flow down to us. Seeing what was behind them. The velvet blackness studded with points of light and the scent of petrichor and green things. The power behind all the others...the child reeked of it..."

– Undated journal entry

MOTHER SAT up and slid her legs to the edge of the chaise, running a finger across her bloodless lips, intrigued. Barton had performed his directives flawlessly. She'd witnessed it firsthand through the assassin's eyes and then again countless times via the multifaceted lens of her legion. From every perspective, at every speed, then was privy to the analysis that'd followed. In any other world, Laughlin Scot would've been dead and taken his family with him.

*He's more than you give him credit for...just like Rogan...*the Jane-that-was whispered, rising to the surface. She'd been doing that more of late, listening at the doors and peering through the windows, adding unsolicited commentary.

Mother snorted. It had nothing to do with him and everything to do with a bind of uncommon skill running through Scot's being. That it was laced with UnMaking was a complication Mother had not anticipated.

Yet, it tracked. Considering his conception defied natural law, why should the rest of his existence be any different? That penchant she attributed solely to his mother.

Deirdre Scot had been a wild card. How an unaffected unknown had managed to galvanize the city and crossbreed with a Talent to produce a fecund son of Laughlin's caliber still eluded explanation. Mother sniffed. Perhaps his assertion that he'd been gifted his position by divine providence held merit.

She came very close to laughing, having long since given up that particular fairytale. As with everything else, it came down to genetics, and Titus would suss those out soon enough, for what it was worth. Undoubtably, Laughlin's escape from death would've given any other pause, but it only served to increase her determination.

She would *not* be stopped, and in the grand scheme of things, the boy mattered very little. Sending Barton had been a knee-jerk reaction based on old fear. There was no place for that here. She pushed down the Jane-that-was, the echo of the girl she'd been too close to the surface of late.

And that was entirely thanks to Kara Jester. Mother's thoughts turned to the insensate woman back in Titus's gestating chamber. Not a pawn, but a queen in her own right. Mother started at a frisson of jealousy running through her and quashed it. Another emotion that harkened back to the Jane-that-was, and it was as useless now as it had been then.

Especially with an UnMaker of her own now in hand. A smile tipped up Mother's lips. Whatever had or hadn't been bred into Caliban's protégés at this point was moot.

Mother stood, descending the hundred steps from her dais to the temple's ground floor and passed through its pillared length. She'd chosen her adversary well. Caliban Scot was nothing if not devious.

He'd certainly attempted to stack the deck with the girl. The rare urge to laugh burbled within Mother's breast again. Let him and his progeny strive to thwart her. It would come to naught.

She exited her temple, the tropical air balmy against her pale flesh. She maundered through her garden, the crepitation of tiny shells beneath her feet loud in the predawn silence. A smile played over her lips at her measured tread grinding the bones of the sea closer to dust.

She stopped to stand at the low wall, looking out over the city and past the ocean, to the horizon. Her sightless eyes took in the energetic play of night's UnMaking and the rebirth of day. She never tired of witnessing the universe's daily battle of power beyond the stars. So few had any idea just how perilous their trip around the sun truly was.

Even less had the ability to turn that power to their own devices.

She had both. UnMaking and Rebirth—the fourth duality—firmly in her grasp.

The other pairings, Finder / Shade, Fixer / Fetch, and even the Breaker to her Binder, paled in comparison. Perhaps that's why there was only ever a single pair born in each generation, and then only if the stars aligned properly and a certain concentration of talent was met.

That it had happened as a result of the fallout between Laughlin and Arileo over Julia Cree was a delicious irony. A Fixer / Fetch duality, their bonding after Laughlin's unceremonious abandonment of the North had been a surprising kismet of genetics.

The universe, once again, striving for correction.

Mother sighed. So much time had been squandered. In their ignorance after the Surge, purity of line was lost, dualities no longer diametrically opposed enough to create the same storm of warring genetics.

A correction had been needed. First at the Source and then in Glynfyls, a strict adherence to purity of line. Her whispers worked to condense what had been scattered, binding the pieces back together to ultimately return them to the reality the Surge had thrust them from. It was so close, she could taste it.

Judgement Day was coming, and the bounty was at hand.

Mother swept her fingers across the top of the parapet as she continued on her way, her jewel-encrusted rings tinging over stone. Each gem a Talent she'd bound, adding their power to hers.

She entered her private demesne, leaving the garden and the susurration of the surf behind. The whirl of wide-bladed fans stirred the air and sent the low flames of lamps inset along the walls flickering. She paused at a doorway to a small room and regarded the huddled form on the bed.

The child glared at her from behind his lank, black hair; his halos still a muddy ring around his cornflower blue irises. His wide mouth turned down, petulant as he rolled over, putting his back to her.

Mother chuckled, nature versus nurture as much of a tangle as correlation and causation, but she could say with one hundred percent certainty that one axiom was true in regard to Henry Prydee-Scot-Cree.

Like father like son.

SERRA IDLED on a couch in the back room of the Pearl, staring into the fire. Behind her, servants silently took away the remains of what should've been a celebratory luncheon. She was positive it would be the last bit of House Morris's largesse the inn would see. The city was already rife with rumors that Peterli's widow was less than saddened by today's tragic events.

Serra couldn't blame her for not mourning the toady little man's demise, but it was incredibly inconvenient on her end. She still couldn't get the feel of his sweaty hands off her, and to have it come to naught? What a waste of time. Though it was barely noon, she raised her glass of Chablis, fervently wishing she was drinking to Laughlin Scot's death.

Damn that man and whatever deal he'd made with the devil. She fumed as the retreating servant's footsteps rang through the empty room like a premonition. All the support Peterli had garnered that she'd hoped to turn to her own purposes, undone in a moment. The lion's share of the movement's supporters had been cowed into silence, too frightened to continue the work that had been started or further associate with anyone who would.

Spineless fools, all of them. Serra took a mouthful of wine, and grimaced. She tightened her fingers around the stem of her glass, wishing it was Scot's throat. Whatever he'd just pulled in front of the Assembly, she'd like to see him try to do it again with a nullifying noose around his neck.

The image calmed her as she stared into the flames. If only she could recover the groundswell of support Peterli had drummed up to make that happen…

A serving girl approached and set a sumptuous charcuterie board at Serra's elbow. She ignored it as her due, and the girl left her.

Scot would misstep, Serra was sure of it. She just needed to make sure she was ready to capitalize on it. Based on what she'd seen at the Assembly, gaining Lord Crandall's confidence seemed the obvious move forward, as long as she was discreet.

She tore a grape from the cluster. It would also be interesting to hear what Father Benson had to say about Scot's blasphemy. It was common knowledge that the priest had been reluctant to support the movement before, but after that declaration of divine right?

Though she didn't understand the intricacies of the North's farcical belief in a higher power, the opportunities it presented couldn't be overlooked. Not with the streets already humming with warring explanations for Scot leaving chambers unscathed while so many were wounded and Peterli lay dead. A miracle. Blasphemy. Resurrection by God's hand versus the Devil's, or was it some trick of technology he'd brought up from the South? Who was to say?

Serra was inclined to believe the latter, but as to the rest of them? The church would be forced to weigh in, and from what she'd heard, Father Benson and Laughlin Scot were far from friends.

She pursed her lips, about to pluck a strawberry from the plate, when a soft knock at the entryway commanded her attention.

The innkeeper, Dorothy, made a quick curtsey. The mousy little woman certainly wasn't anything to look at, but Serra had to admit she was good at her job. "Pardon the interruption, Lady Hess, but a missive just arrived for you." She placed a small white envelope on the table beside her, and exited the room.

Serra's eyes narrowed at her back. The wealth of information that woman must have between her ears… It was absolutely infuriating that she refused to part with any of it despite Serra's best efforts. She sighed, counseling patience. At some point, there would be something that she could hold against the innkeeper, and then all the woman's secrets would tumble from her lips.

On that happy thought, Serra pulled the typed note from the envelope, her brow steadily rising. That sham of a government Scot had just propped up was due to meet in two hours' time in General Stonefist's private offices. Serra flipped the page over, then the envelope. No identifying marks to speak of. She pursed her lips, wondering if it was one of her current contacts or someone new that had sent this juicy tidbit along.

But regardless of who, she was grateful that they had. Keeping the Binders from their little boys' club wasn't going to happen, and every last one of them would rue the day they tried to disregard Serra Hess.

MARCOS CROSSED the sands gripping a bloody cloth. After taking the combined oaths of the Breakers from the plateau, the wound across his palm throbbed all the way to his shoulder.

And he reveled in every beat, proud of his troops.

Each man had unquestioningly sworn fealty the Overlord, pledging to their squad leaders, who in turn had passed their oaths up through the ranks to the captain of each company, who had then passed them to Marcos. Zero hesitation, zero fuss. Exactly how he expected his troops to function. Glory, but he'd forgotten the thrill of having a well-oiled machine beneath him. The reminder was well worth the shredded mess it'd made of his palm.

He'd intended on asking Pithy to bind it, but Marcos slowed as he got closer to the side of the cavern where the emaciated Binder stood closeted with Mangleshield. By the speed of their fingers, the two were deep in discussion, and Marcos didn't want to interrupt them. Especially if they were coming to an agreement on how to further treat the Breaker line.

Not an hour after flat-out denying Phyllis Breakspear's request for help, Pithy had appeared in the pub upstairs with a contingent at his back and made it clear that they were there to work. He'd also made it clear that the only reason they'd come was because Nora had cut a deal on Marcos's behalf.

He put a hand to his breast pocket, the letter she'd written him crinkling within. Damn it. He understood why she'd gone after Kara, but it turned his stomach that Caliban Scot was with her and he wasn't. The deal she'd struck with Pithy Marcos liked even less, though he understood the necessity.

Wrestling back control of the Binder line when she returned would be a colossal undertaking and far more dangerous than he was comfortable with. For her and the baby. Nora's ability to use her talent was going to suffer with the pregnancy, and that wouldn't deter Serra from playing dirty. He frowned, not opposed to doing the same if his family was at stake.

Damn that woman. Marcos popped an antacid.

"You feeling all right, Commandant?" Jolie asked, coming up beside him. "I know that look, and it says indigestion."

"It'll pass," he muttered, crunching on another chalky tablet. Thank Glory he'd been able to finally get ahold of some, his stomach was a mess.

She frowned at his hand. "Maybe, but how about we take care of that? Nora'll have my hide if I let it turn green and fall off." Her halos flared, and his flesh bound together, leaving a tender pink scar.

He grunted, glad she'd left one.

"Please." She huffed, rolling her eyes. "I know how you Breakers do. That, and I'm about tapped. I couldn't make it pretty right now if you paid me."

"I've got no complaints."

Her brow rose. "Now that's a damn lie."

"I was talking specifically about my hand." Marcos chuckled, shaking his head. Pithy bringing Jolie and several other Binders from the Source to help had been a surprise, but apparently one of the first things Serra had done was purge the ranks. Anyone not willing to kiss her ass had been summarily demoted to the commons, and considering Jolie was Nora's best friend, she'd been at the top of that list.

Which also put her first in line to do whatever she could to piss Serra off. His fingers brushed over his service weapon, seriously considering putting a bullet in the woman and damning the consequences.

"Yeah, well, I suspect you take what you can get when the rest is a complete shit show." Jolie sighed, looking out over the crowded cavern.

"How are they?"

"The troops?" She cocked a brow. "You mean other than something I'd normally wanna take a bath in?" She barked out a laugh. "Glory, the look on your face…yeah, you know I heard about you."

Marcos felt his color rise, and Jolie laughed again, turning her attention to the Breakers congregating with their squads. Most were working through bowls of gruel Mangleshield's wife and the other Banes had whipped up. Visually, it was incredibly unappetizing, but he couldn't say it didn't smell tempting. For men that hadn't eaten in days, it was like that fairytale about manna falling from Heaven. Marcos had seen more than one take their ration with tears in their eyes.

Those not eating had curled up on the wide stone steps under blankets that'd been distributed. Even with their combined body heat warming the cavern and the flames roaring around its edges, they couldn't seem to shake the plateau's chill.

Jolie sighed again beside him, her levity gone. She rubbed a hand over the dark frizz shadowing her scalp. "I'm not gonna lie, they were in rough shape, and most still are. Frostbite's bad enough since binding can't regenerate tissue, but radiation poisoning? That's no joke, and the Binders up here definitely don't have the same oomph as us Sourcies."

"Too bad there aren't more of you here."

"Give it time," Jolie said, looking awfully smug about something. "Regardless, we got another day, probably two, before all but the worst cases are resolved. Mental health notwithstanding, as of right now, I'd release a little less than a quarter of them from a clinical setting, though where they're gonna go…"

"Markham's working on shifting in temporary housing and more supplies," Marcos said. "I don't foresee any of them returning to active duty before the Overlord returns." After being pushed to the breaking point, what they needed was rest. In past ops, Marcos had used twitching as a benchmark for recovery. There wasn't any reason for the men not to accept the same now. They could all wait to re-establish their rank in the hierarchy and meld with the Northern troops later.

Jolie shot him a side-eye. "Where do they plan on setting that up? With the Finders' spoke in shambles there's not a wall in the city without a lean-to."

"Last I heard, they were going to repopulate the Flats, but we needed to enlist the Fixers to make sure the ground's stable first. I was supposed to check in…" He glanced at his watch, and swore, overdue at the meeting Jacques had called.

"Go on, we got this," Jolie said, her eyes intent on his face.

"Thank you. I appreciate your help, and I know they do, too."

"You can pay us all back by keeping Hexspar off our doorstep. One of my first assignations was down there, and the list of things I would rather do starts and ends with anything but." She shivered, rubbing her arms.

Marcos gave her a curt nod. "I'll do my best."

He jogged out of the cavern and back up through the pub, nodding to Sirrus as he left. The nearest gate was half a block away. Marcos made for it, eyeing the street warily. Jolie was right. Any kind of shelter that could be cobbled together against the existing buildings had been. Despite that, the city was oddly subdued, especially after how riled its denizens had been not even four hours ago. He suspected seeing the Overlord cheat death then exact justice was largely to blame, but the change raised the small hairs on the nape of his neck. Something was brewing.

The Assembly Hall wasn't any better. The normal murmur of afternoon business was absent, and the corridors glaringly empty. Even the rotunda was silent, vendor's carts shuttered and the food court abandoned.

Marcos took the steps two at a time up to Stonefist's office, frowning at the muffled voices coming from the other side of the door. Marcos paused at Crandall's. He wasn't supposed to be here.

"...ludicrous to think that I or my Intelligencers would purposefully release any of the individuals we have in custody—"

"Forgive me if I'm skeptical after that little 'accident' comment you made back at the coliseum," Markham said, cutting him off.

"Kyle, you know damned well that was entirely anecdotal, and given the climate of the city at the time, completely warranted!"

Marcos popped another antacid as more voices chimed in, talking over one another. He sighed and let himself in, then fought the urge to head right back out.

Jacques Martin sat at the table's head, clearly flustered and rightfully so. The Shade slumped against the back of his chair with two fingers pressed to his temple and frowned past the rest of the cohort at Serra Hess. She sat smiling at the other end of the table with Crandall beside her.

Well, it didn't look like they'd be discussing the status of the troops they'd taken in. Marcos could only imagine what Serra would do if she found out a portion of her line was actively disobeying her orders and using their talent to heal them.

"Ah, Commandant." Crandall smiled at him. "I was wondering when you'd show up. Are we all here then?"

"Actually," Jacques leaned forward and addressed the opposite end of the table, "there are rather more of us here than there should be."

"You mean far fewer." Crandall frowned. "Glynfyls remains a democracy in spite of Lord Scot's declarations. This meeting should be opened to the entire Assembly."

"I concur." Lady Hess studied her bejeweled nails, rhinestones dotting the midpoint of each long, curved talon. "And with Scot gone, do we really need to entertain his ridiculous mandates? I vote we return to business as usual."

The others at the table stared at her, incredulous.

"Pity you don't have a vote, nor any right to sit at this table," Dorian said. He turned to Jacques. "Isn't there something in the bylaws about the exclusion of non-voting members and their forceable removal if non-compliant?"

"If there isn't, there should be," Stonefist growled. "And here or not, *Overlord* Scot's word is law. We do as he's instructed."

"Just because you Breakers are a bunch of mindless thugs following the biggest lout amongst you, doesn't mean the rest of us are," Lady Hess snipped back, regarding him as if he were filth. "None of my Binders voted for Scot to stay in power, nor do we plan on supporting his seizure of it. Especially if he's not here to enforce his ill-gotten rule."

Lord Klein gritted his teeth. "Regardless, the rest of us did vote for him to retain his office. That ill-conceived motion didn't gain two-thirds majority. Therefore, General Stonefist is correct, Laughlin Scot *is* Overlord, and that's *exactly* how a democracy works. What you're talking about is insurrection."

"And he doesn't need to be here to enforce his will, we'll do it for him." Stonefist glowered. "Even if that means detaining you so we can do it."

"Is that right?" Serra smiled, her halos glimmering. Stonefist growled, the room thickening with 'lust as his flared in kind—

"Enough!" Jacques stood, slapping his hands onto the table. "I won't have infighting. Lady Hess, I know you're new to Glynfyls, but threatening to draw talent on another is extremely poor form." She sat back with a huff and crossed her arms over her bosom. Stonefist continued to glare at her, and Jacques shook his head at the both of them. "The Overlord has asked me to administer the city with the rest of his cohort's assistance until his return. If that doesn't happen by the end of the week, we can reassess."

Serra perked up. "A week?"

"Yes. Surely we can wait that long before contemplating sedition," Jacques snapped sourly, straightening his lapels as he took his seat again with an eye on Serra and Crandall. They unapologetically stared back.

Jacques sighed. "Commandant, won't you join us?"

Marcos snorted. The hell if he would. "I'll stand, thanks. Any chance I can get a quick estimate on when Fixers can be allocated to secure the terrain outside the city?"

Carl glanced over at him. "It's already in the works. After Laughlin's mention of compensation for efforts going toward rebuilding the city, I have more volunteers than I know what to do with. Crews are reporting that most of the land around Glynfyls can be stabilized fairly easily, with the exception of a large patch by the east gate and along the bay. I should know more in the next hour or so, but I've given the go ahead to do what they can now."

"I don't see the point if the rumors of another invasion are true," Lady Hess sniffed. "Shouldn't they be focusing on repairing the Finders' spoke?"

"Shouldn't you be focused on healing everyone in need?" Stonefist growled.

Serra glowered back. "Don't tell me how to administer my line."

"Then don't tell him how to allocate his."

"We've already established that housing is the main concern there as well," Jacques said, pinching the bridge of his nose, "and we've all agreed that restoring the Flats is the quickest way to do that."

"And your rumor mill is running a bit slow, Lady Hess," Dorian said. "The Deep South's alliance seems to have fallen apart after Laughlin's very public resurrection, not that I blame them for their change of heart."

"Oh?" Crandall's gaze snapped to the other Finder. "And how would you know that?"

"I'd imagine the same way you do, Bart. We each have our little birds, don't we? I'm just judicious enough to share their song." Dorian turned to the rest of the table. "From what I understand, Diytan's alliance with Hexspar and Ax'chig wasn't entirely on the up and up to begin with, and now that they have visual confirmation of what they're classifying as something between a miracle and divine retribution, they're adamantly opposed to pissing Laughlin off."

"Probably wise, considering what he already did to their country," Marcos murmured.

"A miracle," Serra scoffed. "More like smoke and mirrors!"

"Smoke and mirrors don't blow the back of a man's head off. You would do well to take heed."

Serra's eyes narrowed. "Are threatening me, Lord Blaise?"

Dorian brayed out a laugh. "Me? Most assuredly not. Consider it a friendly overture of lessons learned. Those that stand at cross-purpose to Laughlin's will don't do so for long."

"Overture indeed. I refuse to bow before that tyrant, and his threats will only further sour the rest of the world toward our kind!"

"Actually," Markham said, blotting his brow. "The majority of Glynfyls's trading partners have reached out to offer aid along with no few others. If I had to guess, I'd say the interpretation of who Laughlin expected to aid in the city's reconstruction has become rather broad. It, or perhaps the second half of that imperative, has gained us a bevy of new friends, fair weather though they may be. I'm certainly not opposed to taking them up on their largesse while it lasts. Building supplies and foodstuffs are being shifted in as we speak."

Serra's face soured, but she didn't comment.

"Well, that's encouraging." Jacques sighed, sitting back. "Let's hope that trend continues, and we have a moment to catch our breaths. Does anyone have anything else?"

Carl cleared his throat. "There is the matter of the assassin's death…"

"What of it? He got what he deserved," Markham said. "No one can debate he shot Laughlin Scot three times in front of the entire Assembly, killed Lord Morris, and wounded a dozen more. There's hundreds of witnesses, and the fact that he was killed by the very bullets he used…quite fitting in my opinion."

"I don't think anyone would debate his guilt," Lord Klein conceded, "but he should've been tried for his crimes…especially since there's questions about his escape. His execution sets a precedent I'm not comfortable with," he glanced askance at Crandall, "as does his being held for this long without due process."

"Due process is an entitlement given to those not categorized as enemies of the state."

Lord Klein's brow rose at the Intelligencer's assertion. "Oh? Curious how you didn't make that argument for the Sons on trial several years back after the riots on the lower rungs. You can't pick and choose whom the law applies to—"

"Be that as it may, Lord Klein, as the man is dead, it's a rather moot point, now isn't it?" Jacques interrupted. "As I understand it, the Overlord's word is law. I'm assuming that includes the sentencing of criminals. If you feel an inquest is warranted, by all means, initiate one."

Lord Klein bristled, but held his peace with a curt nod of his head.

"Wonderful." Jacques forced a smile. "If we're quite finished? I'll bid you all a good day, and I'll see you tomorrow." He gave a shallow bow and exited the room as quickly as possible without breaking into a jog.

Serra and Lord Crandall followed after, their heads closer together than was seemly as they walked.

Marcos's brow rose at the latter, and Dorian's gaze caught his. The Finder gave him a subtle nod, his eyes flicking to the pair. Good. He's seen it too, and would no doubt keep his ear close to the ground. Nothing wholesome could come of Serra having her sights set on Lord Bartholomew Crandall.

TITUS SIPPED HIS BOURBON, intent on the live footage of Vignette lingering in the Laborium's hall. The courtesan had been returned only a handful of hours ago and had spent most of them fixated on what was going on beyond the windows of the gestating chamber.

He pursed his lips; her fascination was bizarre, to say the least. The females at the facility were under no illusions what being bred meant. Subsequently, they'd contrived a ritualistic rite in which whatever goodbyes they deemed necessary were said before the bitch was removed from the general population and sent into stasis. After which, it was as if she ceased to exist.

And none of them ventured into this part of the facility.

But Vignette had been occupied for some time now. Titus could only imagine she was enthralled by her lookalike beyond the glass.

Though, side by side they would never pass for one another. That they shared genetics was apparent, but Kara Jester had something about her. Perhaps it was that her features weren't quite as stark, or the fuller curve to her lips. It could be that the tilt to her eyes was more pronounced or that her skin tone was a bronzed almond as opposed to ivory, but whatever it was, Vignette was decidedly lacking it.

Titus swirled the ice in his glass and took another sip. What could she be thinking, standing there, and just watching her half-sib's chest rise and fall—

The courtesan's hand rose to press against the glass and then pushed away. She glanced around as if she knew she was being watched. A moment later, she sprinted down the hall and was gone.

Titus's eyes narrowed, positive the bitch was up to something. That would need to be monitored. He pressed a panel, summoning Brix. The man must've been already en route, knocking at Titus's door only a moment or two later and looking more dour than usual.

Titus pushed back, ankle upon his knee as he spun his glass on the arm of his chair. "Do you have a status update?"

Brix grunted the affirmative. "Something crossed into our airspace from the north about four hours ago. If it's the lightstream we lost trying to collect the Commandant and they fly straight through, they can be at the Source in another six."

"I'm assuming you've made arrangements for that eventuality?"

"I have men stationed, but the place is crawling with civs. Something's happened topside. Sons, scabs, rival gangs, anyone left Outside is converging on the site."

"Then I fully anticipate having ample warning if Scot retained his talent," Titus said, leaning forward. "The twins have assured me he'll be neutralized away from Glynfyls, but Scot's defied reason too many times to take that statement at face value. Let him run the gauntlet before you engage."

Brix grunted, something stuck in his craw. "The twins..." He ran a hand over his bald pate. "Their interaction with my men is causing problems. The woman's inciting dissent. Three of them came to blows before she convinced them to share her yesterday."

Titus nodded, having watched the incident several times. As

enticing as it was, it did set a bad precedent. Sex as a tool to establish dominance over one's troops was one thing, for pleasure it was quite another. Her sampling would need to stop, as would Enoch's. The last man he'd dallied with had to be put down, and Titus didn't have the troops to spare.

"I'll speak with them. Separate the men involved into different squads. I need you to find Vignette and meet me in the hall by the gestating chamber in an hour."

Brix grunted then paused. "Tonya...have you been able to tell yet?"

Titus templed his fingers, briefly debating the merits of withholding the information.

"Yes," he finally said. "She's set to whelp a litter of three."

Brix grunted, a self-satisfied smile turning up his lips.

Titus pursed his own. He might've felt compelled to do something about that bizarre attachment if he wasn't so sure she was going to rip Brix's throat out after she gave birth. Titus frowned at the Breaker's wide back as he exited the office.

Hopefully his demise would serve as a cautionary tale. The other Breakers that'd returned to the Triam seemed to share the same affliction. If their delusions persisted, Titus would lose all of his prime breeding stock, and that simply would not do at all.

CHAPTER NINE

"Glynfyls has gone from a symbol of hope to a stinking cesspit of humanity. I have trouble even walking the streets as I used to. God, the vile thoughts I pick up from those that brush past me as they go about their dreary lives…their echoes live inside my head, the strongest melding together and feeding a consciousness separate from my own, and what she says…

I wish I could refute it, but I can't.

I call her Mother because she treats me like a child, and though I do my best to act as though nothing has changed, my dewy-eyed sympathy for the plight of the unwashed masses has vanished. Increasingly, she turns my thoughts to that poor dead babe—to the powers we have not yet accessed—and whispers of what could be.

The rend in the sky, the points of light beyond…another duality lies beyond the three the Surge created. I'm convinced A and El's child would've been the first half of a fourth duality; creation and destruction. It feels so right that it be born into this world instead of being thrust into it as the other talents were. My gut says it must be conceived between the seven of us, and with El's inability to have more children and Ri's sterility, only Ro and I have any chance of bringing it into existence.

I can't help but wonder at the limits to such power. Would there be any at all? Could it be possible to reverse—to UnMake—the Surge? To Rebirth the world we once knew? Mother is adamant that it is so, and I…I yearn for how things were, for how idyllic our lives were in comparison to the harsh reality of now. But to make that happen, how can I justify those means?

Her whispers tempt me with the ends, preying upon where my heart lies..."

– Undated journal entry

FLYNN STARTLED FROM SLEEP, the nape of his neck prickling at the hazy memory of a woman who looked eerily similar to Kara. What a weird fucking dream. He pulled his coat around himself, shaking. She'd just stood there, staring at him through a window like she wanted to tear him apart. Shit shouldn't creep him out as much as it had, but holy fuck.

He ran a trembling hand over his face and pushed his beanie back, trying to focus on the muffled hiss of the craft heading south. Outside, it was full dark. However long he'd slept, he was glad he wasn't anymore. Christ—that dream—he couldn't stop shaking—

"You awake, kid?" Rogan asked from the front of the craft.

Flynn sat up and ran a hand under his nose. "Yeah. What'd I miss?" Craft stank like whiskey and vomit. Nora was curled up in her seat, and Fitz and Cal were snoring. Per the clock on the dash, they'd been flying for the past ten hours.

"After Fitz regurgitated the entire food pyramid, Nora took pity on him, and put him out. Cal bitched himself to sleep, and while I appreciate not having to listen to him, it did keep me awake." Rogan yawned. "We're gonna have to stop so I can get in a combat nap, unless you feel up to taking over? Skies are clear."

Under normal circumstances, it wouldn't have been an issue, but right now? Flynn tightened a trembling fist, his nerves raw. A cloying sense of dread churned in his stomach. Everything that'd happened at Assembly—putting those bullets through Barton's skull—shit, through Morris's—Jesus, he didn't understand how he'd done that. He hadn't pulled talent, it was like he'd just...just willed it to fucking happen.

And he wasn't sorry. The euphoria that'd come with it...that always came with it.

He'd wanted more. To rip the man apart and feel his entrails burst beneath his fingers. To hear his screams.

… *"Only man delights in another creature's suffering…"*

He had. He did. And he'd do it again. Wanted to.

Fuck. His stomach roiled, sickened.

He was a monster.

The tremors in his hands intensified.

There was no way he could pilot a craft. Shit reminded him of DTs. Anxiety prickled up his spine, and he swallowed as he glanced at his peripheral, expecting flames. Feeling them waiting for him. Whatever Nora had done to him was fading, and he was an accident waiting to happen, regardless of how clear the skies were.

… His clothes are torn and spattered with blood. Jaw set, he stares blankly out over the hillside. Kara stops just out of arm's reach. A frisson of uncertainty crosses her face, and then she laughs, the air spiking with her perfume. Something in him relaxes, gravitating toward her like a magnet as she closes the distance between them.

"Flynn… Hey, who am I?" She searches his eyes, her thumb running over his cheek.

"Our mate." Another's words rumble up from his chest, spoken with his tongue.

Her brow furrows like she knows it. She reaches up, trailing her fingers across his forehead. "Flynn, I need you here, with me. Let me in, love…"

Love.

But she'd seen. Him. What he turned into. What he could do… A desperate fear consumes him—guilt, shame, and a horrible self-loathing oozing beneath it all.

Her arms float around his neck—a calm to his storm—and the desire to let her in, to—

No. If she knew all of it, she'd hate him. His gaze slides from hers. "You saw."

"Enough." Kara burrows into his coat, close against his chest, and the emotion she sends to him through their bond…

He hugs her close, undone. Goddamn it, he wants to be the man she thinks he is, but… She looks up, her breath catching as their eyes meet. "I won't let anything happen to you Kara. I-I won't lose you…this…"

But he had, and now he was right back where she'd found him. Worse.

"I don't think that's a great idea," he said, unable to meet the Breaker's eye. Fuck. He needed to pull himself together—

"Then you got any suggestions where I can put down without scabs or Sons converging on us? Cal's got a cloak up, but it's gonna reek like hot plaz while the thrusters cool, and you know that'll draw anyone out there like stink on shit."

"Yeah, I dunno, maybe. Where are we?" Flynn pulled himself up between the seats to look at the GPS. Shit. He rifled his hair. They were almost to Greyburn, because of course they were. He sighed, wanting to know but terrified to find out what'd happened to the coop since the Source'd had its way with it.

Unfortunately, the same reasons he'd been able to stay there for as long as he had made it the perfect place to take a breather. The next site that might work was an hour farther south, and Rogan didn't look like he had it in him. Flynn sighed, reluctantly entering the rough coordinates.

"Look for a clearing to the west of Route 32. Best case, there's a barn and an outbuilding approximately thirty miles south of Greyburn. Worst case, it's a smoking pit, but either way there'll be room to land," he muttered.

Rogan cocked his brow. "Do I wanna know?"

...the door blows inward off its hinges, an icy blast of air following in its wake. He flattens Kara beneath him, praying the stacks of books are enough cover to keep their heat signatures from being picked up by the thermal sensors embedded in the troops' face shields...

Flynn shook his head to dispel the memory. "Coop's where the Source found me and Kara holed up. They ransacked it and left a body. I dunno what they did when they went back to retrieve it." He let out a slow breath, sweat pebbling his brow, and his stomach churning as their destination crept closer.

"Well, I guess we're gonna find out," Rogan said, dropping the craft below the clouds and beginning their descent. He checked his instrument panel and swapped between the night-vues and thermals. The moon hadn't risen yet, and it was pitch black. He swore. "Or not. I don't know how the hell we're gonna find it. The night-vues in this thing aren't updating for shit, and everything down there is frozen solid."

"Not everything," Flynn muttered. He tapped two faint lines in the southwestern portion of the grid. "Head there."

Rogan squinted at the screen, the lines resolving into rectangles as they got closer. "What the hell is that?"

"Battery bank for the coop is full, and the solar panels are backfeeding."

... "How does all that work in there? The bathroom, I mean," she asks.

"Pump runs on solar. Battery bank's in the barn...radiant water heater doesn't work so good in January, and the propane's about out, but I could, did you...ah..." His dick throbs at the thought of her showering. Please say no, please say no...

"Oh, no. I mean, yes, but no, I'm okay..."

Fuck. Flynn pinched the bridge of his nose. Losing it. He was fucking losing it... Rogan grunted, the man's side-eye more than a little concerned as he maneuvered the craft to skim the trees. A few minutes later, the sharp lines of the barn's roof came into view, and he banked around it to land in the yard.

As they thumped onto solid ground, Fitz jerked awake, whipping a nasty little dagger from his jacket. "Shite..." he muttered, unapologetically tucking it away. "We there?"

"No." Rogan switched on the cabin lights. "We're just making a pitst—"

Kid shifted and reappeared outside by the barn's listing doors. Flynn chewed his lip, watching him poke around in the dim light spilling from the craft. Place looked deserted. The front entry was a gaping black maw, wide open to the elements, and piles of books and gear littered the yard between it and the craft. The weather hadn't been kind to any of it.

"He's got the right idea," Cal muttered, a cigarette already clamped between his lips. He grabbed a plaz-lantern from an overhead bin and flicked it on. Flynn blinked at the harsh white light. "Lemme out of this sardine can."

Rogan dropped the hatch and the flat, dead smell of the Outside rolled through the cabin with a burst of cold. Flynn's nose wrinkled. Christ, he'd forgotten about that…but it also meant they didn't have to worry about disturbing any animals denning inside. At least not the four-legged kind.

Nora stretched her arms over her head. "Where are we?"

"A waypoint," Rogan said when Flynn didn't answer. "You coming in, kid?"

"I don't—no." He shook his head, turning from the window.

Rogan shot Nora a look Flynn was pretty sure he wasn't supposed to see, and the two of them left, closing the hatch behind them. His curiosity satisfied that the coop was still standing, he sighed, sitting back with his eyes closed. Wasn't a chance in hell he was going inside…

… "You know, sweetheart, it'd be a lot easier talking to you if I knew your name."

"Kara." She blushes and thrusts a pair of forks at him.

He bites back a smile. Damn, when was the last time he'd been able to fluster a girl like this? Shit did something to him. "Thank you for doing the dishes, Kara."

Her breath catches as he purposefully steps into her personal space, and that fucking scent—her perfume—coils around him. His mouth waters. He sniffs, then shakes his head to clear it. Doesn't help. Christ, whatever that was lit him up. The shit he wanted to do to her…he traps her gaze with his, and her pupils blow out as his fingertips graze her cheek. Would her lips taste as sweet? He wets his as she leans into him…

Flynn's eyes snapped open at the hiss of the hatch. Nora climbed back into the craft and sat down, facing him. His stomach cramped. Hadn't this bitch fucked with his head enough?

She smiled. "So, this is the coop."

Really? That's what she was gonna lead with? He grunted and took out a cigar. Should've had Rogan light the damn thing before he left, the book of matches was kicked. Flynn rolled it between his fingers, and a heavy expectancy gathered around him, like his talent was just waiting for him to pull—

Yeah, not happening. He pinched the bridge of his nose, blinking it away.

"Believe it or not," Nora said, still blabbing, "it's not bad inside, just a little damp. I bound the door back onto its hinges, and Rogan started a fire. He thinks it should warm up pretty quickly."

Good for Rogan.

"Laughlin?" She chewed her lip. "I need to...to—Kara's bind only addressed your physical wellbeing..."

He didn't fucking care. Flynn went to get up, and Nora put a hand on his knee—

He ripped his leg away and focused on his breathing, his voice thick. "Don't."

She went very still. "You already know."

"Yeah, and if you touch me again, I dunno what that's gonna look like, but it won't be pretty." His rage—Christ, the fucking static in his ears, the pressure building around him—he put a hand to his temple, trying to breathe through it. Zero. He needed to pull zero. No matter how much he wanted to end this cunt, if he did something to Kara's mother...shit would not be well received.

Nora's lips whitened, and she gave a curt nod. Bitch should be running. "For the record, Cal asked me to bind your memories, but that's not a skill I possess. Instead, I did what I could to facilitate your recovery and dampen any psychosis you may be experiencing."

He laughed, static filling his ears. May be experiencing. Bound, dampened, whatever the fuck she'd done, he was still fucking living it, and her being here wasn't doing jack shit to make that better.

Fuck, being here in general wasn't making it better.

She wet her lips. "I-I purged the last of the suppressant from your system and remoted your memories, but the weave is extremely fragile. From what I could tell, your mind is very busy trying to reprocess anything of—of significance you've experienced for the last thirty-six years."

Of significance, huh? Flynn met her eyes, and she couldn't hold his gaze.

"Yeah? And how much of that did you see?" His anger licked at him, and he let it. It was better than the shame waiting beneath it.

She worried the ring on her finger, staring at her lap. "Enough. Too much."

Fuck. He knew exactly what she'd seen. What had come after.

Kensbot.

… The guards are mute in their crow's nest above the yard. He kneels amid the carnage, fingers laced behind his head, eyes on the ground. The red pinpoints of their laser sites lost against the gore coating him. His chest heaves. Breath loud in his ears.

A metal door opens above. The warden steps up to the rail. Is silent. Then, "Thirty days in the hole with the rest of the animals…"

"You tell Cal? Rogan?"

"No, and I won't."

"What about Kara?" he growled. "You gonna tell her what a fucked up monster I am?"

"You're not a monster, Laughlin, but you were certainly raised by one."

She met his gaze squarely, and this time, he looked away; his stomach flipping at her allusion to Lot. Shit, he hadn't had a reaction like that since he'd been a kid. Flynn wiped his sweaty palms against his pants, gaze jumping at a flash of something in his peripheral—

"You persevered through circumstances that would've crushed anyone else. What I saw was exactly why Kara loves you. Why your mother fought so hard for you two to be together, and why I'm going down there to help you bring Kara back." Nora's voice caught, and he glanced up, surprised to see tears rolling down her cheeks.

"That's my daughter they have. My grandchildren." Her knuckles whitened as she fisted her hand. "All I've fought to keep from the Source, Titus has taken, and I'll be damned if I let him get away with it."

… "Everything I've seen has them safe for the next three days. After that, things start to branch again…If you can't get to them by then, you'll lose Kara first, and then the babies…"

He shuddered, pushing out of his seat and past her, his emotions churning. "I can't do this. I can't…I can't afford to remember—to feel anything right now." Couldn't lose his shit—

Flames flickered at the window of the coop.

Christ, he was losing his shit.

"You're wrong," she called after him. "You think it's a weakness, but it's one of your strengths, Laughlin. I've seen how you love Kara, those babies, and that's what's going to get them back, not whatever talent you can or can't pull."

Sure. Whatever she needed to—

He stepped out of the craft, through Cal's cloak, and stumbled, his awareness of Kara—no, of his kids—hitting him like a wrecking ball.

Fuck, they were close.

He pulled his beanie lower and took off, into the woods.

NORA WIPED the tears from her cheeks as Laughlin broke into a jog, heading away from the craft, into the darkness. Remotely, she felt Marcos's anxiety over her upset, but it was so very faint… A sad smile tipped up her lips, reminded of when Titus had deployed him to the Deep South when she was pregnant with Riegel. That had been six months of nothing but the faintest suggestion of a bond, only to have all of Marcos's emotions crash in around her, and then be ripped away two days after their son's birth.

Glory. She wiped her face again. This wasn't the time or place to think about that.

Nora exited the craft and picked her way across the yard's frozen ruts, piles of ruined books open to the sky. It was so sad that Laughlin's sanctuary had been violated like this. All this additional trauma…no wonder her binds on his psyche were disintegrating so quickly.

Not that she was doing much better. The closer she got to the Source, the more she questioned her resolve. The implications of returning to that place, all the ghosts there…

Nora paused for a breath with her forehead to the door before she opened it. She could do this. The only ghosts occupying the Source were the ones in her memory, and she'd be better off worrying about who was living. The facility would've been a juicy target, and had to be crawling with scavengers after Titus had abandoned it with the gates open wide.

"Not a bad setup for a little rich kid out of Glynfyls." Rogan's voice rumbled from within the coop, jogging her from her thoughts.

"Agreed. It's nice to see he was actually listening to some of what I taught him at the farm," Cal replied. "Sure as hell could've fooled me, considering his attitude at the time."

Nora frowned as she opened the door, knowing that attitude had been warranted. Cal and Rogan turned to look at her expectantly, and she shook her head.

"Didn't think you'd be able to get him to come in," Cal said, leaning back in a battered recliner with his cigarette. "Boy never does anything he's not good and ready to do."

"Can't imagine where he got that gem of a personality trait from," Rogan muttered.

Nora ignored the byplay, taken aback by the sheer number of books in the tiny room. "The bind I put on him is fading faster than I anticipated, and I don't think landing here is helping." She picked her way through the toppled stacks to right a chair in front of a listing cupboard, its contents heaped and scattered across the floor. What she assumed had been the table was in pieces.

"We'll go as soon as I catch a couple hours of shut-eye," Rogan said, dropping the mattress back onto the bed frame. He tossed Cal a vial of Jesse's pills. "I just took one of those and make sure you both pop one before we leave. We got no idea what we're about to walk into."

"Yes, mom." Cal downed one then handed the vial to Nora before he pulled out his pouch and began rolling another cigarette. "Well, I suspect there's plenty to read while you do. Boy managed to amass quite the eclectic library, I'll give him that."

Nora frowned at the pills but took one, then handed him a chipped mug. "And if you ash on the floor, you'll end up burning it down."

Cal grunted and set it in his lap. "Anyone see where Fitz went?"

"Nope, but I can't imagine there's much out there for him to get into."

"I wouldn't tempt fate if I were you," Cal said to Rogan as he licked his cigarette closed and lit it. "From what I can tell, he doesn't need to look for trouble to find it."

Nora frowned, pushing the cupboard back against the wall and binding it into place. Sadly, she agreed with Cal. Fitzpatrick definitely held the record for near death experiences of late. She crouched down, sorting through the mess at her feet and setting things back onto the cupboard's shelves. Tea, cans of soup, a half crushed package of weird, flat crackers, and a vat of peanut butter… Considering the condition of the rest of the place, it was an exercise in futility, but she was too keyed up to be idle, and Cal's smoking was riding a nerve she didn't know she had. Glory, but she was on edge. She picked up a canister, and her brow rose at the label.

"There's tea, and this says it's coffee if anyone wants some, though it's not in any form I've ever seen…"

Rogan snorted as he glanced over. "They're freeze dried crystals. You dissolve them in hot water. A sink's through there, and I think I saw a kettle behind Cal's chair."

He had, and Nora retrieved it. She went through the doorway into a dismal little bathroom, scrunching her nose at the faint scent of animal urine coming from a pile of filthy laundry. Glory, that was unappealing, the semblance of indoor facilities not much better than squatting in the woods. She approached the rust-stained sink and turned on the faucet, then off and on again.

"There's nothing coming out," she called back to Rogan.

He came in with the plaz-lantern. "Kid said something about solar batteries, so I'm assuming there's a—ah." He crouched down and did something below the sink. A faint hum kicked on, and after a moment, water spurted from the tap.

Nora stepped back in surprise and laughed, filling up the battered kettle. She left him inspecting the set up.

"Shit, Cal, you should see what the kid did in here."

"I'm sure it's impressive," he said dismissively, ashing into the mug. "Flynn's always had a knack with things like that."

No thanks to him. For the life of her, she couldn't understand how Caliban Scot had turned a blind eye to what was going on in his own home. She knew him far too well to think the abuse had flown under his radar. Nora set the kettle to boil and searched the mess on the floor for more mugs, biting her tongue.

Rogan came back into the main room and shot him an incredulous look. "A knack? That's not a knack, that's savant material." He grabbed a handful of books off the floor and set them on top of a haphazard pile. "*Applied Differential Geometry, Walden, The Dialogues of Plato…* Who the hell is this kid?" he asked. "You couldn't even finish *The Catcher in the Rye* and paid Suzy Fallon to do your algebra homework. His 'knack' sure as fuck didn't come from your gene pool."

"I'm well aware," Cal muttered. "He's always been an odd duck."

"Deirdre used to call him an old soul." Nora said, feeling abruptly maternal. She put two mismatched spoons with the rest of the cutlery she'd found. Still no other mugs.

"That she did," Cal said, staring up at the rafters crisscrossing the ceiling. His gaze dropped as Rogan grabbed a book off the pile and headed out the door. "I thought you were sleeping."

"I can wait, but I don't think this can."

The door closed after him and Cal exhaled a long plume of smoke into the air. He watched it dissipate, a heavy silence settling with it for a handful of heartbeats.

And then his eyes were on her.

"Well? You ready to chew my ass, or were you planning on stewing some more?"

A clipped laugh escaped Nora's lips as she tidied the last tumble of books by the cupboard. She righted the chair and sat, her trousers pulling. Glory, she missed her gowns. "I have nothing to say."

He glowered at her from behind his cigarette. "Bullshit."

"All right then, I have nothing to say that will constructively add to the situation at hand."

"You know…" A muscle in his jaw jumped and he shook his head, looking away. "I wish to God you didn't have to go through any of what you did."

"And if wishes were horses, beggars would ride." She smoothed a hand over the crease in her pants. "I've made my choices, Caliban, as have you. I expect mine are somewhat easier to live with."

He grunted. "You might be right, and you've got Marcos and a new family to look forward to." His eyes dropped to her abdomen, and she fought the urge to cover it. "Quite the full circle."

"If only it hadn't taken thirty years to get there."

"A drop in the bucket." His gaze frosted jade. "Be thankful you've got the time you have. Anyone I ever gave a shit about is dust and ashes…or is about to be."

"Elize?"

"How about you tell me about these retirement plans of yours."

And that was the end of that discussion. "Would that I could." She sighed, not particularly interested in discussing anything line-related with him. "You of all people should know that some plans are more fleeting than others. Unfortunately, that was one of mine. As soon as we're back, I'll assert my claim for First. Serra's already done a fine job of ostracizing all of the Binders in the commons, and she's ousted her political enemies from the Source. Save for a select few, I have a feeling that the rest of the line will have had quite enough of her by the time we return."

"You know she's not going to give it up willingly."

"No. I can't imagine she is." Nora worried her ring, a shiver of anxiety running through her. "Which is why I'm going to formally challenge her to a Binder's duel."

Cal's gaze flicked to her abdomen. "That's a damned fool move."

That was the price for Pithy to treat those Breakers. "I've already agreed to it."

"Then you're letting Flynn phase your pregnancy, because that's the first thing Serra is going to go for."

A smile tipped up Nora's lips. "Oh, I'm counting on it."

***

ROGAN CLOSED the door behind him and scanned the mist-riddled darkness. The moon had risen enough to light the horizon, but the landscape was still occluded within a shadowy murk. Aside from what was highlighted by the rectangle of light thrown by the coop's sole window, it was impossible to see more than a few feet in any direction. Shit. He ran an hand down the side of his head, frowning. How he was gonna track down Flynn out there—

A bottle sloshed to his left, and Rogan jumped. Fitz snickered, loitering in the shadows. Jesus. Faint jags of light splintered through his irises like something out of Cal's crappy B-movies.

"Don't fucking do that!"

The little shit snorted. "Right creepy around here, innit?"

Rogan glowered at the Fetch. Him included. And as far as the Outside was concerned, historically, Rogan had done his best to steer clear. No bugs, animals, the weird weather patterns…reminded him too much of Meskill after the Surge. The pervasive silence alone was enough reason to avoid the place.

"Yeah…why the hell aren't you inside?"

"Ye really askin' that, considering what ye looked like coming out? As fucked as the energy to this horror show is, it's preferable to whatever's going on betwixt them two in there."

Rogan grunted. Kid had a point.

"All ye fucking hillies is cause for a migraine." Fitz tipped his bottle back, then smacked his wide lips. "Ye lookin' for His High Holy Majesty?" He wiped off the mouth of the bottle with his sleeve and offered it to him.

Rogan shook his head, trying not to stare at the kid's weird irises. "Yeah, you see where he went?" What the fuck had happened that'd fractured his halos like that? Rogan'd never seen anything like it. No wonder the kid was always hiding behind that curly mop.

"Yer loss. And it depends." He spun the cap back onto the bottle and tucked it away. "If I says yes, what're the chances I ain't gonna end up holdin' yer hand to track him down?"

"Nil, but you won't have to hang out with Cal once Nora tosses his ass out."

Fitz tugged his patch. "S'tempting argument right there…" He buzzed his lips, muttering something. His hand jiggled in his pocket, and then he sighed. "Right. Last I seen him, man were on a mission. He were takin' off at a clip to the southeast, and it didn't look like company'd be welcome."

"He'll get over it." Rogan stepped to one side and swept out a hand. "Lead the way."

Fitz sighed, his hand still busy in his pocket and arguing with himself. After a long moment he pushed off the barn. "Fine, but this shite's on ye."

"Perpetually," Rogan muttered, trying to keep track of the Fetch as he disappeared into the murk. Damn. He'd hoped his vision would've adjusted, but he was just as blind as when he'd come out here, though Fitz didn't seem to be having any trouble navigating through the bracken. Whatever he'd said about the energy out here being fucked, that had to be how he knew where to put his feet. "Your extra lets you see in the dark?"

"Eh…nah. Just used to moving around at night."

"Yeah? You make it a habit of going for midnight hikes through—" A branch whipped out and smacked Rogan in the face. He fell back a step, a hand across his mouth. "Jesus! Watch it!"

"Sorry," Fitz called back, still moving. "Didn't see that."

Rogan wiped a bit of blood from his lip. "The fuck you didn't."

"On me mother's grave, s'the solemn truth. Maybe ye should shut yer fuckin' trap so I can concentrate."

Shut his fucking…Rogan glowered at the kid's gangly silhouette, barely discernible against the trees. He'd stopped at the top of a wooded rise.

"Isn't your mother still alive?"

"Aye, but here's to wishful thinking." He raised up his bottle, and Rogan shook his head as he caught up to him. This fucking kid…

"Shit." He stopped beside Fitz. The tree line ended abruptly at a rocky ledge that ran a good hundred and some-odd feet higher than the heavily forested valley below. Rogan scanned the moonlit ridge. Whether Fitz was using his extra or not, there was no way they were gonna rely on it to pick their way down—

Something glinted.

A stone's throw away, Flynn sat beneath the trees.

"Stay here," Rogan murmured to Fitz.

He gave a half-assed salute. "Aye, aye, Capt'n."

Rogan shook his head and made his way over to Flynn, grateful for the moonlight illuminating the rise—shit. The glint had been the blade of a tactical knife. Flynn clicked it closed, dropping it into the pocket of his big barn coat as Rogan got close. That was gonna be a problem.

The kid sighed, not bothering to look his way. "Aren't you supposed to be sleeping?"

"Why *Walden*?" Rogan asked, tossing the book into Flynn's lap.

"Why not?" He snorted softly, riffling the pages with his thumb. "What do you want me to say? 'I went to the woods because I wished to live deliberately, to front only the essential facts of life, and see if I could not learn what it had to teach, and not, when I came to die, discover that I had not lived,'" he recited blithely as he tossed it back.

Rogan caught it and turned the beat up paperback over in his hands. "That what you were doing out here?"

"No." Flynn pulled out a cigar. "Can I get a light?"

Rogan's halos glimmered, and Flynn took a deep drag.

"You still seeing flames?"

Kid didn't answer. Rogan was gonna take that as a yes.

"Coop's pretty impressive. That's a gray water system back there, yeah? Solar panels powering the submersible? It's a sleek little set up."

Flynn grunted, still staring out over the valley. Kid was pulling on zero so hard Rogan could taste it.

He leaned against an outcropping of stone. "You know, it took me a long time to come to terms with the fact I was a hell of a lot smarter than where I'd come from, and that it wasn't something to be ashamed of. People think Breakers are all big dumb thugs, and I'll be the first to admit, it's a perception I've encouraged—"

Flynn gave him an odd look, and Rogan shrugged.

"Our talent freaks people out enough as it is. Before the hierarchy was established, the other lines banded together and hunted us." It hadn't helped that a bunch of assholes had taken it upon themselves to terrorize the general populace… Rogan spat to the side. What it'd taken to bring the line under him still put a bad taste in his mouth. "It's easier not to be afraid of something if you don't think it can tie its own shoelaces," he finished lamely.

Kid snorted. "That's bullshit."

Rogan wet his lips, wishing he'd taken up Fitz on that drink. "I said it was easier, not that it was always possible. My daddy was dumb as a box of rocks but you better believe there was a stretch of time I pissed myself whenever he came home from work. Man used to beat the ever-loving shit out of me."

"Yeah. What happened to him?"

"He got off too easy," Rogan muttered, breathing through the minefield of emotions the subject of his father's death still dropped him into. "After, I needed to disassociate myself from the entire McGuire clan and everything that came with it." Guilt did that to you, along with a bunch of other shit.

"That why you changed your name?"

"It is. You gonna tell me why you're out here?" Rogan looked out over the valley, watching the sickle of moon creep above the trees. Their branches were stunted, twisted things, clawing toward the inky sky.

"My bond came back," Flynn said after a long silence. "At first it felt like they were so close, but from up here…they're still out there, past the horizon. I-I can feel the babies, but Kara…she's not there, Rogan."

His stomach dropped. "If Titus has her in stasis—"

"Alice says if I can't get to her in the next two days I'll lose her." Flynn's voice broke. "And whatever Nora did, it's not…fuck. I am so fucked…"

"No, you're not, and we'll find her. We're not gonna lose any of them, but in the meantime, you need to eat something. You look like shit."

"I'm not hungry—"

"Jesus, Mary, and Joseph, enough. I fucking am," Fitz grumbled, appearing between the two of them. "The two of ye done braiding each other's hair yet so we can go? Couple of fucking pansies…"

Flynn was on his feet faster than Rogan could credit, jacking the Fetch up against a tree by his neck. "Couple of what?"

"Pansies," Fitz choked out, lighting flickering through his halos as he grappled with Flynn, pulling talent—

A burst of white light sent Rogan reeling. He landed on the ground hard, blinking as his vision slowly returned. "Jesus fuck. What the hell—"

The two of them were gone.

FITZ GROANED, flat on his back in an alley. Christ, not again… He pushed hisself up onto his elbows, frowning at Scot doing the same beside him. Fitz put a hand to his bruised throat, annoyed with the handful of imprints he'd accidentally pulled from the man. Jungle somewhere, fancy conservatory with a pond, loft full of kittens, and some creepy white and chrome facility. Didn't want none of it mucking up his book of memories. If he'd had his druthers, he would've dropped the shitehead in the reeking dumpster across the way when they'd shifted and had done.

"The fuck are we?" His High Holiness bitched, rubbing the back of his neck as he sat up, wincing. Headache would serve the rotten prick right.

"Dunno."

Scot's aura pulsed, angry. Christ, that fuckin' hurt—

"What do you mean you don't know? You're the one that shifted."

"Wise it, ye fuck," Fitz snapped, cradling his poor, throbbing head. "I were pullin' talent, but it were that mess of energy around ye that directed the shift, same as the tangle in yer bedroom." Or maybe it were Cajetan. Seemed like somewhat the blessed bastard would do.

Coin were suspiciously noncommittal on the subject.

Scot looked at him like he were crazy, his auric storm a-whirl. Man's moods was a fuckin' problem, his energy sucking in then expanding outward. Wool roving turned to eiderdown and back again, bits of it spinning off and away like it were being stirred by some cosmic fuckin' breeze. Fitz pinched the bridge of his nose, not nearly drunk enough to be seeing shite like that.

"What tangle in my bedroom?"

"The one they shanghaied the lady through," Fitz muttered, glancing around the alley. Weren't no place he'd ever been, and way too clean to be Glynfyls. Everything were creepy quiet, and the only sign of life were the flickering light from a lantern in the window across the way. Nah…surer than shite, they was still south of the border the way all the energy were dead flat.

Except around Scot, and that were a right nightmare. "You know how they took Kara?" he asked. He got to his feet and held a hand out to Fitz.

He eyed it like a snake. "That for me hand or me throat?"

"Look, I'm sorry I lost my temper," Scot gritted out, his tone to the contrary, "but it would help if you didn't go out of your way to be such a miserable prick all the time." He frowned, scuffing out his cigar.

"Psh. I'm a goddamned delight." Fitz stood, dusting hisself off. "And for the record, I don't go out of me way for naught but pussy, pie, or the pub."

"Pie?"

"Mackerel's me favorite, but I won't say no to a good bit of mutton." His stomach growled. "Eh, speakin' of which, what'd we bring to eat?"

Didn't need light to tell Scot rolled his eyes at that. "Not a clue. Tell me about the tangle."

"Eh…were like a gate, but not." Fitz pulled at his patch. "Left a right mess. Shite's dangerous." So were what Scot had goin' on around him. Man needed to figure hisself out.

"If you say so." Scot sighed and stepped back, his focus snapping to the lantern across the way. "Fuck. We're in Lyden."

"Where's that?"

"Twenty minutes south of the coop, and someplace we don't wanna be." Anxiety spiked around him as he stared out the mouth of the alley, and Fitz knuckled an eye.

Of course, by the time Scot did figure it out, between him and all the fuckin' plaz resonance, Fitz'd probably be in a migraine-induced grave…fuck it. He sent a puff of talent to scatter the energy build-up, the line between his brows smoothing as it dispersed. Wouldn't last, but being next the man were right painful otherwise.

"You feel that?" Scot asked, turning back to him.

"What? The wind? Course I did. Weather's positive shite down here."

Scot's brows furrowed. "No, it wasn't—"

"Any particular reason this ain't someplace we want t'be? I'm assuming it's got somewhat to do with the residents havin' made yer acquaintance." Fitz pulled out his bottle and sadly downed the last of it. Needed a refill, stat.

Scot shot him a look. "Yeah, you could say that."

"Who'd ye fuck over?"

That earned him another look. "Underhill. Gang's like a mini version of the Sons, and that bar's where they hang out."

Fitz tugged his patch, jiggling his coin and grinning at its growing warmth. "That bar right there?" *Wonder if they served pies…*

"Don't even fucking think about it," Flynn growled. "If your halos don't give you away, that Northern cant will. Come on, we need to get back."

"That a fact?" Fitz asked, more than thinkin' about it. He ambled closer to the dumpster; bar looked like a likely establishment t'him, and seein' how his bottle were tapped…

His coin flared hot, and that sold it. He tossed his empty into the dumpster. It landed with a godawful clang, and he bolted.

"Christ, what the—Hey! Where—Fitz!" Scot hissed after him.

"Just popping in for a pint," he called over his shoulder.

"The fuck you are!" Scot's heavy tread pounded the cracked pavement behind him, and Fitz laughed, sprinting across the road and ducking through the door.

He paused for a breath, and Scot plowed into his back, pushing him forward. Fitz stumbled and turned to glare over his shoulder, but there weren't no one there. Not that anyone without his extra could see at any rate. Nice to know the fucker could still pull a cloak.

Fitz turned back around and made a show of warmin' hisself up, blowin' on his hands as he ambled toward the bar. Place were dead, but it were pretty obvious that were a recent development. Bunch of empty tables was strewn with cards and tankards, chairs all askew, and the sawdust on the floor were rucked up like there'd been a rush to leave.

A lone whore were taking her time cleaning up, collecting the empties on a battered tray. She blew a gray-streaked tendril of hair from her eyes, so high on sear the whites shone blue from clear across the room. Fitz looked away, taking a hard pass on whatever she had to offer.

"We're closed." A stocky man behind the bar growled, packing what were left of the bottles on his shelves into straw lined crates.

"I ain't in a mind t'stay," Fitz said, moving to the bar's far end. Weren't about to put his back to the whore. Last thing he needed were her tryin' to cozy up. "Eh…how much t'take one of them bottles off yer hands?"

"You're a fucking idiot," Scot muttered behind him.

The bartender froze, then gently set the bottle in his hand down and turned. Across the room, the whore disappeared through a ragged curtain. "What the fuck did you just say?"

"Damn it, Fitz, we need to go," Scot hissed, tugging at Fitz's jacket.

He sighed, buzzing his lips. Christ, for someone that'd sent the entire city shakin', the Overlord were fuckin' milquetoast when push came to shove. Coin in Fitz's pocket flared hot, agreein' with him. They'd leave when he had what he come for and not a tick prior to.

"How much for a bottle?" he enunciated like the bloke were an idjit.

The bartender's eyes narrowed, and his hand drifted to the pistol at his belt. Looked like a well-kept weapon. Fitz figured he probably knew how to use it.

"Jesus, Fitz—"

"Just how far North are you from, friend?"

"Far enough t'know fifty-three words for snow." Were actually fifty-six, but the coded response fell from Fitz's lips before he'd thought about it.

The bartender's shoulders dropped, and he ran a hand over his face. "Christ, it's about time they sent someone down." He set a bottle of twenty-five year malt on the bar, then pulled a brick-sized package from under it. "I haven't been able to get a message through in weeks and wasn't keen on sitting on this for much longer. Man who brung it said not to get it hot."

"You gotta be fucking kidding me…" Scot muttered.

Fitz grinned, sweeping the package into his jacket pocket, his coin flaring warm against his leg again. Not a fuckin' clue what it were, but that weren't neither here nor there. It were saint approved, which meant it were somewhat good.

Well, maybe not good, but usually entertaining.

"Bottle's on the house for whatever information you can give me about how things stand in Glynfyls," the bartender said. He flicked his hair behind his left ear, the half-dozen gold hoops studding its shell connected by a curved bar.

Fitz perked up. Man were the hub for the smuggling ring in this area. Well, well, well…coin kept burning, egging him on. "That's a shite show to be sure—eh…"

"Tibbs."

"Right." Fitz cracked the cap, and there weren't never a sweeter sound. "City's a mess, but I figure Markham's calling in what aid he can. Ye want an in, he's your man. Tell him Fitz sent ye, and he'll give ye a proper cut."

"Markham…ain't he the big man? My last contact told me to steer clear."

"Then yer last contact were fleecing ye."

"Ask if it was Leo," Scot growled behind him.

Fitz coughed into his hand to hide his incredulity. Ask it if were—Jesus, Mary, and Joseph. Didn't the man know how this worked? "Eh…lemme guess, greasy little fucker with too-big teeth?"

The bartender's eyes narrowed again. "Yeah, that's him."

Scot swore, pacing.

"Ah." Fitz ignored His Majesty's fit of temper and shook his head remorseful like, not a doubt in his mind Tibbs's outfit weren't sanctioned. Leo'd been running the network rogue, or worse, for the sisters. Shite would've gotten him keelhauled if the bastard weren't dead already. Markham were right particular about getting his cut.

Fitz spun the cap off the bottle, thoughtful-like, his coin still warm. "That son of a bitch were sent swinging not two days past for pinchin' from the till. S'why they sent me down personal, like, t'check in. Get in touch with Markham—and only Markham. He'll cut with ye clear."

"I ain't surprised. Never did like that fucker," Tibbs muttered. "Fitz, ye said?"

"Aye." Loopin' in a new ring would earn him brownie points he were sure he'd need at some point. He took a pull from the bottle and murmured a prayer. Jesus, that were smooth. "Eh, what about here? Seems a bit quiet."

Tibbs snorted. "Ever since the Corporation abandoned the Source, scabs have been flocking to it, abandoning the dead towns. It's turning into a proper city, like the ones they got down south. I'm packing up to join 'em. Only people left in Lyden for the past few weeks have been Underhill, and that's only because the Sons claimed the facility." The bartender paused to draw hisself an ale. He took a sip and made a face.

"Then a couple of hours ago, call comes through that the Overlord's en route, and if anyone wants a piece of the son of a bitch, that's the place to do it. You wouldn't know anything about that, would you?"

"Not a blessed thing." Fitz smacked his lips, enjoying the vintage more than what were proper in public. "Hear tell the man's a right bastard, and rubbing elbows with His High Holy Majesty's a sight above me pay grade."

Scot growled behind him, and Fitz swallowed a grin.

"That reel of him at the big meeting…was that legit? He really die and come back?"

"Haven't seen it meself, but seems t'be the general consensus, and the man's ego's certainly big enough to float him back from the afterlife."

"Fuck you," His High Holy Majesty muttered.

The bartender grunted. "Well, if he shows up at the Source, he's gonna need to do it again. Word to the wise, steer clear of the place. It's not just Underhill that got the call. The Fuil cut some kind of a deal with the Sons, and between the two of them, they've absorbed every other gang large enough to show colors."

Scot made a pained noise behind him and grabbed Fitz's sleeve. "We're leaving, now."

"Will do," Fitz said, capping his bottle on the way out. "Best of luck to ye."

The bartended grunted. "And you."

As soon as the door closed behind them, Scot snorted, corporeal again. "I swear to God, you're the luckiest prick I've ever met."

"Ye say that, but here I am, stuck with ye." Fitz knuckled an eye, the energy around the man swirling again. Christ, that hadn't taken long.

Scot sighed, pinching the bridge of his nose. "Can you shift us back to the coop or are we gonna end up somewhere fucked up if you try?"

"Dunno." Fitz shrugged, his stomach growling as he reached for talent. "But wherever it is, fingers crossed there's pie."

CHAPTER TEN

"My course of action set, I asked Ro to escort me to the festival at the coliseum. He was reluctant, but finally agreed. As we took in the sights, I tried to speak to him, but he's never been one for words. Throwing caution to the wind, I took his hand in mine, and with that brief touch, I felt his lust for me. It lasted only a second before he pulled away and left me there in the crowd.

But my hope that we could be together—could become a duality like the others—rekindled. I'd felt his want, was so sure I could make it happen…

I was so stupid.

I waited for him in his rooms. He staggered in late with some woman, the both of them drunk. I hid, watching the two of them pleasure each other, then snuck out as they slept. I'm shaking as I write this, wracked with lust and envy. To be touched like that by a man…by him…

I hate them. Every last one of the whores that have tasted what should be mine."

– Undated journal entry

FLYNN LET out a sigh of relief as they materialized in front of the coop. He let go of Fitz's jacket, and the kid ambled over to the door like he'd never had any doubt they'd get back—

No. It was more like he didn't care where he ended up. Flynn could relate. It was easy not to when there wasn't any place you felt like you belonged.

Or anyone you felt like you belonged to.

"Ye comin'?" Fitz asked over his shoulder, hand on the knob.

"No."

"Suit yerself, but if there's pie, I'm eatin' yers."

"Go for it."

Fitz grunted and went inside.

Flynn stood there for a breath, the night closing in on him—

…"When we reach the border, we're in the North?" Kara asks.

"Not really, but we'll be out of the territory controlled by the Source. I mean, technically, yeah, it's the North, unless you're from the North." He smiles, feeling her frustration at his answer, but it was true.

Almost home.

Shit. It hadn't been home for eight years, and hadn't felt like it for a lot longer. He knew exactly what she was talking about and was just as scared.

Walking into the unknown had been easier…

"I—actually, yeah," he said just before Fitz closed the door. As irritating as the kid was, Flynn hadn't had one flashback while they were in Lyden.

Maybe Fitz was as lucky as his stupid coin.

"I'm still eating yer pie."

He was welcome to it. Flynn's stomach dropped as he stepped over the threshold, and he ran a hand over his face.

Christ.

Half his books were missing, the others jumbled in mismatched piles. What was left of the table had been stacked next to the potbellied stove to burn. Rogan was snoring on the bed, and Cal was in the recliner, the air dense with smoke. His eyes flicked up from Flynn's copy of *Flowers for Algernon.*

"I don't know how the hell you read this shit."

"Hitting a little too close to home, Professor Nemur?" Nora asked him, stepping out of the bathroom as she dried a pot.

"Hardly." Cal snorted.

She rolled her eyes, and Flynn's stomach heaved, the mannerism too similar to Kara's. "There anything to eat?" he asked.

Cal looked at him like he had two heads. "You're hungry?"

"No, but Fitz is, and I'm tired of listening to him talk about pie."

"S'a delight, but I ain't picky." The kid wandered over to a stack of books. He pulled out an oversized atlas and plopped down onto the floor, thumbing through it.

"Good, because the only thing in here are cans of soup or peanut butter." Nora said, picking her way back toward the stove. "If that doesn't suit, Rogan said there were MREs in the craft."

Fitz looked between them. "What's that?"

"Meals ready to eat," Flynn murmured. "I'd take the soup if I were you."

Nora set the pot to heat and frowned at the mess still strewn about the room. "That's what Rogan said, but I can't find the can opener…"

… "Here, just—no, not like—come here." He moves behind her, adjusting her grip, and firmly clips it onto the side of the can. Damn, she smells good. As in there-goes-taking-a-piss-right-away good.

"Go on, turn it." Her fingers are long and slender beneath his. Smooth.

"Like this?" she asks, peeking over her shoulder at him, all innocent and sexy as hell. Her perfume twines around him in a heady musk. Flynn's eyes drop to her lips—…

The tang of aluminum filled his mouth, and he fought the urge to spit. He glanced over at Fitz, totally engrossed in a full-color map of Xian. Well, guess that answered that question. Goddamn it. Lyden must've been a fluke.

"Have Fitz shift it out," Cal muttered around his cigarette.

"What's that?" the Fetch asked, glancing up.

"You wanna eat, you gotta shift your dinner out of the can."

"And how the hell do ye expect me to do that?" he asked, setting the atlas aside. "Ye can't shift what ye can't see, ye idjit."

"Then I guess you're not eating."

"Ye know, ain't none of this were stipulated in me onboarding."

Cal licked his finger and turned a page. "I don't recall per diem being discussed."

"The fuck it weren't," the kid shot back. "I negotiated room and board, but there weren't no mention of travel—"

"The can opener's under the recliner." They stopped bickering to look at him, and Flynn sighed. "Seriously, move your boney ass and look."

Cal glowered at him for half a breath and stood. "My boney ass is about to whip yours if you keep it up," he muttered as he tipped the chair to one side, then reached down to grab the opener. "So what's that make?" He tossed it over, and Flynn caught it with a grunt. "You put out Rogan's fire, phased my desk, shifted from the roof, found the can opener, and if I had to guess, I'd say that was a rebounding bind that put those bullets through Barton's skull, which just leaves fixing."

"It's not..." Flynn turned the can opener over in his hands. "Yeah, I guess, but I didn't do any of it intentionally. I didn't pull, it just... happened."

"Well, that sounds familiar." Cal plopped back into the recliner, his brow raised. "Why am I getting flashbacks of you going through puberty?"

... *"Just fucking pull! Christ, you're so goddamned stupid. You've got a channel, use it!"*

He swallows, his mouth dry, not understanding, and terrified he was gonna do it wrong. Sweat beads on his forehead and slicks down his back. A meaty hand cuffs him upside the head, and he bites back a cry, his ear ringing.

Across the room, a curio cabinet flickers in and out of existence. He opens his mouth to say something, but it's too late, knuckles drive into his gut...

Nora plucked the opener from Flynn's hand. "Thank you."

Her eyes caught his. They were warm. Understanding, like his mom's had been.

And Nora knew.

"I can't do this." He swallowed the lump in his throat and made for the door.

It slammed behind him and cool air hit his face. He breathed it in, trying to slow his rapid heartbeat, old hurt and voices clamoring in his head. His fists rose to his temples, and he bit back a whimper—

A match flared behind him.

"Need a light?"

Flynn straightened up, panting. Struggling to bury shit enough to function. He licked his lips, his clouded breath spiraling away. What he needed was a bottle like Fitz's to fucking drown himself in—

... *"That path leads to ruin faster than any other...'*

Fuck. It did, he knew it did, but...no. He drew in a deep breath. He didn't need it. Could do this. Had to keep it together. For them. Kara, the babies...he felt them out there, reaching for him. They needed him.

God help him, he needed them.

He wiped his face and turned to Cal, pushing everything beneath zero again. Playing the fucking part. "Yeah. You got a smoke?" His voice cracked.

His grandfather held out a cigarette like a peace offering. "Those cigars you like are in the craft."

So was the case of whiskey.

"This is fine," he said, taking the cigarette with a trembling hand. "Thanks."

Cal grunted, staring out into the darkness. "I don't—" He shook his head and kicked at the frozen ground. "Sorry about that quip in there. I'm not good at whatever this is," he said waggling a finger between them.

He was sorry? Flynn barked out a laugh. That'd be a first. "Clearly."

The old man glanced at him askance. "Doesn't mean I don't give a shit. Elize...if she thought I did, you'd be dead, and I couldn't let that happen. Not again and not after Deirdre. Your mother...I loved that girl like she was my own."

Flynn went very still. "You think Elize had something to do with that?"

"I can't rule out the possibility, especially considering she's in bed with Titus. Woman's probably riding his dick as we speak," he muttered, cupping his hand over his cigarette to light it. He blew out a long stream of smoke. "When we get to the Source, you need to keep your wits about you. She'll find your fears—your weaknesses—and twist them to get what she wants. It's what she does...what she's always done."

"Yeah? And what do you think it is she wants?"

Cal shook his head. "I dunno, but I can promise you that this time, she's not gonna get it." He wandered off a little ways, lost in his thoughts.

Flynn rolled his cigarette between his fingers. "Fitz says there's a tangle of energy in my bedroom. A gate that's not a gate. I thought you shielded the flat. How was she able to get in?"

"I did," his grandfather sighed, "but her extra is the ability to find paths and move between them. All those gates around Glynfyls? Her and Richard created them. He fixed her talent into arches. The seven of us each had a bauble that could do the same. Called them gating stones."

"That was what Rogan was yelling at you about the other day… said his fell apart."

Cal nodded. "So did mine and all the knock-offs we'd collected from the Sons. I'm assuming she pulled her talent from them. Though why she decided to do it now…" He frowned again, ashing. "As far as the flat goes, I never could keep her out of someplace she wanted to be, and the shield wall wouldn't have stopped her, either. Woman's a bulldog. She would've found a way around it." A smile ghosted over his lips before he shook his head and flicked his spent cigarette into the darkness. It arched, falling like a shooting star—

Flynn wavered, overcome by a flash of a sterile white room and a visual of that fucking woman from his dream, staring at him again. What the fuck—

"When's the last time you ate something?" Cal asked, gripping Flynn's shoulders to hold him upright.

"I—no—I'm not, I think…I think it's Kara," Flynn muttered, light-headed. Fuck, what the hell was that?

"Your bond's back? She okay? The babies?"

"Yeah…but there's something…I can't explain it." He ground the palms of his hands into his eye sockets, anxiety cresting over him. "We need to go. Alice said I had three days, but we're running out of time, I can feel it."

Cal's jaw tightened like he was biting back questions, then he grunted with a curt nod. "I'll rally the troops, and we'll meet you in the craft."

Flynn concentrated on his bond to Kara. The white room and that spooky bitch flashed before his mind's eye, and then he was deeper, with Kara. She was there, but not. Rogan had to be right about Titus putting her in stasis. Pushing further, he moved to the babies.

A sob burst from his lips, and he crumpled, emotion bringing him to his knees.

They knew him, and they were thriving.

Flynn tamped down the deluge of guilt threatening to drive him back into his body. He hadn't realize how weak they'd been before—

… *"You had to lose them to keep them…"*

God, he hadn't believed it but… Two of them, girls, drifted in and out of slumber. The larger curled protectively around the smaller. Damn, she was so little…the other two, another girl and a boy, were alert. Too big to tumble about, they flexed against the darkness surrounding them—

A creeping sense of menace assailed Flynn, and all four went still.

His consciousness rose to meet the threat, and he was in the white room again, that cunt still standing there. Her face had morphed into a rictus snarl, crimson scintillated around her irises—

Oh, hell no.

He pulled talent, ripping it from the mess surrounding him. Static surged, crackling in his ears, and a wave of talent shot through his bond to Kara. It sliced through him, and he screamed, throwing everything he had into bending the power to his will. It writhed, fighting him like a living thing, then snapped into place around Kara and the babies a heartbeat before a blast of Breaker talent hit the gurney, jolting the equipment around it across the room. Behind it, electronics fizzled and an alarm went off—

Talent recoiled, tearing him away from his family and slamming him back into his body. He hit the ground seizing, voices around him faintly registering.

"Jesus fuck, Cal, what the hell was that?!"

"Don't look at me, he was fine when I left him!"

Hands turned him over. Fingers lifted a lid. Faces a blur—

Golden light filled his vision, bringing him back, then receded.

Kara. His kids. They needed him, and they needed him now.

He staggered to his feet, bloodlust dank with fury seeping from his pores. Cal and Fitz eyed him warily, and Nora stepped back, a hand at her throat.

Rogan swiped beneath his nose, sniffing. "You good, kid?"

Flynn didn't bother answering as he turned his back on them and boarded the craft. No, he wasn't good. He was fucking pissed.

———

ELIZE STABBED her needle through the fabric of her embroidery hoop and pulled the strands of crimson floss taut, riding a thread of tranquility coming from Mother. A vague recollection of the anxious creature she'd been in another lifetime flitted across her mind's eye and was batted away as she worked.

There was no one she needed to please in this one but herself. No one's approval she needed to whore herself out for. Daddy dearest was dead, and her pleasure was her own, however and whenever she chose to take it.

She stabbed through the her fabric again, idly counting stitches, irked that Titus had put a moratorium on that particular form of entertainment. The consorts and courtesans he kept on staff were skilled but about as entertaining as pudding. They couldn't hold a candle to the thrill of goading Titus's troops into sharing her and then pleasuring each other. She wet her lips at the jump of heat in her core the memory incited. That had been absolutely intoxicating.

And was apparently off-limits now.

She frowned, tying off her crimson floss and rethreading her needle with a wheaten gold, glad Mother had assured her they wouldn't be here much longer. The ennui of the utilitarian suite they'd been relegated to was praying on Elize's mind, the bland decor straight out of one of her father's campaign offices.

Her gaze flicked to her twin in the arm chair opposite the exaggerated "U" of the low coffee table. Ever since Titus had very firmly suggested they stay out of the barracks, Enoch had been pouring over the Jester girl's metrics, though what he found so riveting—

She shook her head. As much as she loved her brother, being in the

same room with Enoch for more than an hour or two was usually…
intense. Especially when he lacked an outlet. His current equilibrium
was suspect, to say the least.

"Are there any consorts left in Titus's stables?" she asked.

"Weak mead," he murmured. "And as to the rest, although the
temptation is significant, I've managed to control myself," he finished
dryly.

She snorted and set another stitch.

"Mother asked me to read the dice again," he said a moment later.

Elize dropped her embroidery hoop in her lap. Mother kept a tight
leash on Enoch's extra, only allowing him to find probability at her
behest. "What did you see?"

"Cal and Rogan are both en route."

Her chest tightened. He was coming… "And the outcome?"

"There's still a tangent that ends in a void—" A small gasp of
surprise left his lips, and he leaned closer to his tablet, intent.

"What is it?" she asked, taking up her hoop again.

Enoch furrowed his brows. "That Breaker whore that came in with
the last supply shipment…she just attacked Kara Jester."

Elize paused, her hand outstretched, floss pulled tight. Mother had
instructed her to peruse the girl's file when she'd been delivered, the
potential of a doppelgänger too tempting to ignore. Unfortunately, the
reality didn't live up to the hype. "Did she?"

"Yes, but that's not what—" He cocked his head as he pulled up
something else on the tablet. "I'll be damned."

Elize stabbed the needle through the fabric and set her hoop aside.
Enoch rarely was intrigued without reason.

He glanced at her as she came to stand behind him. "The Triam's
vector sensors are picking up an unconscionable amount of Shade
talent around the girl."

"He's here?" Elize's halos flashed and her head tilted to the
northwest. "I don't understand. Cal's void around the craft hasn't
reached the Source yet."

Enoch drummed his long fingers against his lips. "Come, let's take
a walk. Titus's suggestions be damned; I want a closer look at this."

As do I… Mother whispered within Elize's mind. *Go.*

Unable to ignore the imperative, she followed her twin as he strode from their suite of rooms and into the stark white corridor. Faint alarms grew louder as they neared the gestation chamber, then abruptly shut off, the sound of hurried boot-falls striking linoleum replacing them.

"It appears my summation of the situation was correct," Enoch murmured. "Quite the beehive, isn't it?"

It was, from what Elize could see of it past the two hulking Breakers standing guard over the scene. She craned her neck, peering around them. The big windows had been blacked out with security film, and the whore was on her knees between another pair of the big men, her wrists drawn tight against her back with nullifying manacles.

Titus stood before her, glowering. He glanced in their direction, his annoyance evident.

"Something you wanted?" he snapped.

"Just checking on our investment." Enoch smiled.

It wasn't returned.

Approach her, Mother's voice commanded, sliding further into Elize's consciousness. *I would speak to this would-be assassin.* The weight of her regard descended, crushing any free will Elize might still have.

She slithered between the guards and went to Titus's side as a vessel—Mother's words upon her lips, her limbs responding on puppet's strings. "If I may?"

She put a hand on his arm, a tendril of talent snaking between them.

Titus's eye twitched. He raised a hand to his temple, then begrudgingly stepped aside. "Of course."

She lifted the girl's chin. Her eyes were a blue so pale they were almost white, leaving her thin red halos to float around her pupils. She attempted to flinch from the touch, and Mother's laugh echoed in Elize's skull.

"Ah, ah, ah…" she tutted, clenching the girl's jaw. "Let her go," she instructed the Breakers. They glanced at Titus, and he waved his permission, holding his head as if it pained him.

Mother gazed at the girl through Elize's eyes. "Vignette, isn't it?

Tell me…what were you thinking? Surely you knew you couldn't get away with it."

"I-I just wanted to see her," Vignette said, wetting her lips. Her eyes darted to Titus and then back again. "The one that everyone says looks like me."

"And what do you think?" Mother asked, her voice deceptively soft as her consciousness pushed Elize's aside, and she stepped fully into her skin. "Does she?"

"N-no. Not really."

Mother's smile curved Elize's lips, and the girl shrank back again. This time, Mother let her. She dusted off her palms. "No, she doesn't, though from what I understand, you've suffered quite a bit of attention based on that passing likeness, treated as nothing but a consolation prize while she lies there, breeding."

Mother circled the girl, her steps slow and deliberate. "Such a shame she doesn't share your flaw." She brushed Vignette's hair back. It was a lovely chestnut color. Mother began to braid it, and the girl trembled beneath her ministrations. "It must be infuriating to be barren in a world that only sees the value of your womb."

Vignette's shoulders sagged, and Mother smiled as that dart hit. She wrapped the girl's braid around her fist and slammed her forward, driving her face against the floor, then snapping her head back. Vignette cried out, her breath stilted.

Mother's lips brushed her ear. "But there are larger things at play than your quest for vengeance, and you've overstepped yourself. Her fate was not for you to decide, and now you've forced Scot's hand, limiting mine." Mother thrust her down again, leaving her bound and heaving upon the floor.

"But don't worry, child," she said, straightening back up. "I have every confidence you'll redeem yourself after you've done penance. I think you need to work off some of that angst in the barracks." Mother's eyes flicked to Titus, and his spine straightened.

"Agreed," he intoned, motioning to his Breakers. "Use her as you see fit until I send for her. She's to remain nullified." He dismissed them with a flick of one hand as he massaged a temple with the other.

The Breakers hauled her up between them and dragged her away, sobbing.

Enoch cleared his throat, and Mother raised a brow. He returned her gaze deadpan, wholly aware that she was riding his twin. "If you're quite done with the whore, can we address what's been done to the Jester girl?"

Titus made a pained sound, and Mother pursed Elize's lips, his struggle against her dominance amusing. Although she'd plucked the incident from his mind, she had little doubt his reticence was due to the last time Elize had been in the gestating chamber. It was fascinating how the subconscious retained instinctual reactions even after she'd removed the core memories that had formed them.

Mother put a hand on Titus's arm, and a muscle in his jaw twitched. "The last thing we want to do is endanger our investment, but perhaps we can shed some light on the use of talent." She steered Titus to the chamber's doors, and he shot her a look before entering his code.

Mother was surprised to see the Jester girl still in the same gestation bay, the plaz-screen behind her shattered. Small pricks of light scintillated through the cracks as the circuity worked to repair itself. "You haven't moved her?"

"No. She and the gurney have been fixed in place, but what's of larger concern is that neither she nor the litter are receiving their nutritionals." A muscle in his jaw ticked, and he raked a hand through his hair.

"How long can they go without?" Mother asked, wondering if Scot had just become a self-limiting problem.

"With the protocol I had them on? Another two days, max," he seethed. "That cunt's threatened everything!"

"Fascinating," Enoch murmured, his halos glowing softly. "The girl's completely shielded from my talent. Let Elize try to find a way in."

Do as he suggests. Mother stepped back, allowing Elize to access her power. It rebounded, and her eyes narrowed as she cast her weave wider.

Nothing.

How was that possible? She searched, trying to find where the shield had originated from. There was the faintest sense of something to the northwest, but the energy was strange, staticky, for lack of a better term. She couldn't lock in on anything.

"I can't," Elize reluctantly admitted. "And if I didn't see her, I wouldn't know she was here. My talent's useless." And it was going to drive her mad until she figured out how—

"Caliban's work?" Enoch asked.

"I don't know," she spat. "He's always kept his secrets close. I've never been entirely certain of what he can and can't do, but this…" She shook her head, absently playing with a braid. Enoch raised his brow at her show of agitation, and she dropped it in annoyance. "After his exile, he shouldn't be able to cast a shield of this magnitude."

"Then it has to be Scot," Enoch said, echoing Mother's thoughts.

Try again, she urged.

Elize probed the shield around the girl a second time. "I can't fathom a working like this at any distance," she said as her talent slid off it, unable to find purchase. "But there's few candidates. It has to be either him or Cal." And one of them had to be responsible for the void Enoch's dice had sensed. He grunted, as if to agree with her unspoken conclusion as she turned to Titus.

The nasty little man had been listening intently to their conversation, though how much of it he'd be allowed to retain was anyone's guess.

"Then I suggest we prepare for the inevitable," Mother said, cresting to ride Elize again. "Laughlin Scot is coming, and I'm certain he'll be here soon."

ROGAN GLANCED BACK at Flynn glaring out one of the lightstream's apertures, his arms crossed over his chest. They were a little less than ten minutes from the Source, and if Rogan could've flown faster, he would've. The 'lust coming off the kid was making him mental. He couldn't figure out if he wanted to give Flynn a hug or beat the crap out of him.

The inside of the craft started to heat up, and his inclination went to the latter.

"Cut the shit, Flynn," he barked. "You burn this craft up, and we'll all be walking."

The temperature slowly dropped, and Rogan grunted. Nice to know the kid had some semblance of control, even if he didn't look the part. Whatever had put him on the ground back at the coop had left dark circles under his eyes, and his cheeks were sunken and waxy. The fact that Kara's bind wasn't healing him the way it had been wasn't something Rogan wanted to dwell on, and no one else was mentioning it either. Kid needed to eat.

Between them, Fitz snorted in his sleep, almost as annoying as when he was awake. He, on the other hand, needed to stop putting shit in his stomach until he could keep it down. They were never gonna get the smell of vomit out of this craft. The bind Nora had him under was preferable to him adding to the ambiance, but Christ, the Fetch could saw logs.

"We almost there?" Cal asked for the umpteenth time.

Rogan glanced at him askance, his irritation echoed by Nora's huff from the back. "Ask me again and I'll turn this thing around."

"Asshole."

"That's me, and we should be coming up on it in the next few minutes. We got a plan for when we get there?"

"We find someplace to hunker down and get the lay of the land," Cal said.

Rogan grunted, his eyes flicking back to Flynn. Pretty sure that wasn't gonna work for the kid. "You think he'll eat something when we do?"

"Not likely," Cal snorted. "When Deirdre died, Miriam ended up shifting food directly into his stomach. Dropped enough weight to scare the crap out of everyone."

"What snapped him out of it?"

"He picked up more bouts in the city, started drinking like a fish and fucking anything with a pulse."

"You know I can hear you right?" Flynn growled.

"If you'd put something in your goddamned mouth, you wouldn't have to," Cal shot back.

The comment was met by silence, and Rogan frowned as a steady glow popped up on the horizon. He checked the instrument panel. "We're coming up on the facility now."

Four tall white towers appeared in the distance, looming equidistance around the circumference of a large industrial facility, save for where a fifth should be. There, a broken, burned out shell hunched beside the others. So much for staying in Cal's tower.

"Looks like we're gonna have to find an alternate landing site," Rogan said, eyeing the flickering lights throughout the complex. Somebody was home.

"To be expected, I suppose." Cal sighed. "Question is, where's the least probable place to put down now? Enoch would've rolled those goddamned dice of his, and although I'm sure they're gonna wait for us at those damned coordinates like they're holding court, I'm gonna bet they'll have people waiting—"

"If they don't, the Sons will," Flynn muttered from the back. "Somehow they got word I'm en route, and they've called in anyone who's got a beef against me. Underhill, the Fuil, they're all in there, waiting."

"Yeah?" Cal turned around to look at the kid. "And when did you pick up that little tidbit of information?"

"When Fitz shifted us into Lyden and decided to go bar hopping."

Rogan snorted. "That's where you two went when you ditched me in the woods?"

"Yeah. I mean, he said he didn't direct the shift, whatever that means. Wasn't my idea. Little prick bolted, and we ended up in the bar Underhill usually hangs out in. They'd literally just left. Don't ask me how, but that shithead somehow managed to get in good with the proprietor, picked up a package I'm pretty sure was waiting for Leo, and get a heads up about the Source in under five minutes flat."

"Fitzpatrick tends to have an uncanny amount of luck," Nora said.

Cal narrowed his eyes. "What was in the package?"

"Dunno, but if you're looking for a place to land, I'd wake his ass up and have him pick."

"If you're gonna do that, I'd make it quick," Rogan said.

They'd gotten close enough for the details of the facility to sharpen. Lights flickered around the complex, backlighting the multitude of bridges and walkways connecting what was left of the buildings. Large portions had been blown to hell, and sickly, pale purple clouds of plaz-contamination drifted throughout.

But by the prevalent signs of habitation below, it was obvious that the intel they'd gotten in the bar was accurate. Smoke from cook fires and barrels burned at street corners. Lines of hanging laundry and piles of garbage. Gang signs and colors sprayed across the white stucco facades. Rogan supposed the city repopulating was unsurprising, considering the wealth the place represented. Scavengers could retire on what was embedded in some of the walls, and gangs would want a piece of that action.

Nora made her way to the front of the craft with a fresh barf bag in hand. Her halos flared, and Fitz groaned.

"Jesus fuck, ain't we there yet?"

She held the bag out to him. "We are, but we need you to tell us where the best place to land the craft is."

"I look like a fucking travel agent? How in the hell would I know?" He snatched the bag with one hand, the other over his mouth.

"Please, Fitzpatrick, if you could just look out the window—"

Kid doubled over, dry heaving.

"Well, that sounds promising," Cal muttered. "Christ. There. See that building up on the right? It's got a helipad, and there's corporate suites below, one of which I own. Hopefully Titus forgot about it while he was busy blowing up my tower."

"It's gonna be tight…" Rogan grimaced, a copter was half the size of what he was flying. Sweat pebbled his brow as he maneuvered through the gauntlet of bridges and walkways to set down on the helipad with an ominous groan. Shit was not designed to accommodate a craft this size. Rogan wouldn't be surprised if the roof caved in when they went to take off again. He cut the engines and stared at the access port through the transparency, suspecting that wasn't the most immediate of their problems. "Hey, Fitz—"

He turned, and the kid was already gone. A second later he appeared out on the roof, spread eagle, groaning up at the stars.

"Never mind." Rogan hit the button for the hatch, and Cal and Flynn were out of the craft in quick succession. Rogan waited for Nora. "You okay?"

A sad smile crossed her face. "No, but I hope I will be soon. Shall we?"

He motioned for her to go first, and they exited onto the roof. "You think you've got enough juice to phase this?" he asked, catching up with Cal.

"I'm gonna say no, but I don't know that it matters much. Titus will have seen the void already and know we're here, which means so will the twins." He looked up from lighting his cigarette and glanced at Flynn. Even from across the roof the kid looked like he was barely keeping it together. "Lock it up and hopefully no one stumbles across it with a nullifier. Best case scenario, we're in and out before the Sons know we're here."

Rogan cocked a brow. Hoots and gunfire echoed in the streets below. Farther away, tires squealed and glass breaking shot through the night. "We both know that's not happening."

"Now who's the eternal optimist? Come on, let's see what it looks like inside. I for one wouldn't mind a nap in an actual bed somewhere that doesn't smell like a vomitorium before we go any farther." He started walking toward the access port. Nora stood to one side of it, and Flynn was pacing at the other.

"What do you want to do with him?" Rogan asked, looking at Fitz still spread eagle.

"I'm assuming he'll move as soon as he hears that there's food downstairs."

Kid's head popped up, glaring. "Better not have t'shift it out of a can."

"No promises." Cal exhaled a plume of smoke.

Rogan shook his head. He'd never met someone so motivated by his stomach. The Fetch was worse than Pavlov's dog.

"It's locked," Nora said as they approached the port.

Fitz shouldered them aside and reached for the panel, muttering about energy as his halos flared. A series of rapid clicks followed, and the portlock rolled to the side. Rogan blinked, trying to work out how in the hell the Fetch had shifted an electronically coded door. Tumblers were one thing, but—

"What?" Fitz scowled at them, his stomach gurgling loudly. "Why are we waiting? Didn't ye say somewhat about food?"

Cal eyed the kid the same way Rogan had been. "I did." He entered, descending the staircase beyond. The rest of them followed. Cal had Fitz open another of the round doors two flights down and muttered something about waste as he went in.

Rogan echoed the sentiment. The place was trashed. Wires hung from the ceiling and the floor was covered in shards of chunky, blue-tinted glass. Art shredded, furniture lay in pieces, and holes gaped in the walls. Shrapnel from the destruction was blown everywhere. Definitely Breaker work.

Cal ducked through one of the gaps, bypassing the portlock blocked by an upended file cabinet and a mangled bronze statue. In the next room, graffiti had been sprayed liberally over a long wall of inlaid stone and syringes littered the floor. Flynn stopped, staring at the glyphs before catching up to them again.

"You know what they say?" Rogan asked.

"Yeah," he muttered, not elaborating, but the way the tremors in his hands ticked up, it couldn't be anything good.

They passed through several more rooms of the same to a large portlock at the end of a hallway. It looked like it'd been hacked with an ax and set on fire, but it hadn't been opened, and the gilt crest on its face was still recognizable.

"Pretentious much?" Rogan snorted.

Cal turned to smirk at him, his halos flaring. A panel phased, and he put his palm against the biometrics scanner inside. Something clicked, and the portlock rolled to one side. Rogan gave a low whistle as they entered the room. As modern as the flat in Glynfyls was antiquated, everything here was clean and sleek; all leather and chrome.

The portlock clicked shut behind them, and Cal made a beeline for a plaz-screen set into the wall. He scrolled through several menus, and the windows blacked out and the lights came on.

"Right." He blew out a breath and ran a hand over his mustache. "I'll see what I can suss out as far as the facility's concerned. Should be able to tell where the concentration of squatters and contaminated sectors are, minimum. Plan on hoofing it to the coordinates we got from the twins as soon as it's light. There's a couple of bedrooms back there, and a kitchenette through that door. Make yourselves at home. Hopefully we won't be here for long, but in the meantime, this suite's as secure as they come."

Fitz was already in the kitchenette, and Flynn disappeared into one of the bedrooms. The portlock clicked closed behind him. Cal glanced at Rogan askance, and he sighed.

"He's pushing everything down, using zero to try to disassociate. If he doesn't address it, he's gonna blow, and it's gonna be ugly."

"Then hopefully he's in the middle of a bunch of Sons when he does," Cal said, lighting another cigarette and retrieving a tablet from a drawer.

Rogan exchanged a look with Nora, and Cal snorted, settling into a chair.

"The two of you need to stop with the loaded glances. It's gonna be what it's gonna be. I told you, the boy doesn't do anything until he's good and ready. Leave it alone, and he'll figure it out. Push him, and we're gonna have problems."

Rogan shook his head and went into the kitchenette. Fitz was bent over, waist-deep in the cryocase, cackling as he pulled out everything from lasagna to stuffed Cornish hen.

Rogan clicked on the coffee maker and sat at the table, trying not to think about Flynn in that room alone and failing miserably. He sniffed, kid's bloodlust already permeating the suite, and what was seething beneath it was straight-up fucking scary. Rogan couldn't put his finger on what the hell it was, but it had a wildness to it that he hadn't felt since the Surge.

Damn. That had to be what had him so on edge. Those first few days after...they'd been a lot like what Nora said Flynn was experiencing. Rogan rapped his knuckles against the table and watched the coffee drip, remembering how fucking raw he'd been. All of his repressed anger and hurt, years of being marginalized and beat on brought to the surface. His rage had been a tangible thing and when he'd sent it out—

Yeah. Nothing good had come from it, and nothing good was gonna come from letting the kid stew in there, either.

Rogan ran a hand over the side of his stubbly head. He'd give him an hour. Maybe find a razor and clean himself up. Short of that, he could head out and do some recon, maybe suss out what the twins had waiting for them at those coordinates. Guaranteed the assholes had the high ground, and weren't gonna leave it to come to them—

Fitz staggered back from the cryocase with his arms full and dropped a half-dozen prepackaged meals on the table. He turned to the wall of appliances and scratched his head. "Eh…"

"That one there." Rogan pointed to the microwave. "Scan the code on the top, then take off the lid and pop it in. It'll bing when it's done. Do me a favor and pour me a cup of coffee while you're over there."

Kid grunted and started looking for mugs—

Both their heads snapped to the bedroom Flynn had claimed. A surge of Breaker talent built and then faded away, something off about it.

"Guess His High Holy Majesty's figured out how to light his own cigars," the kid said, closing the microwave's panel and taking a mug down from a cabinet. "Jesus fuck." He winced, clenching his jaw and glowering at the appliance as it powered on.

Rogan's brow quirked that the Fetch'd been able to pinpoint the line of talent. Kid was a hell of a lot cannier than he looked. "I guess so. How does it feel to you?"

"Tainted, like every other thing in this fuckin' place," he muttered.

"How so?"

Kid scratched the back of his head. "S'the plaz. Shit resonates wrong. Makes me fuckin' teeth ache and wanna hurl. Cars ain't as bad as that damned tin can we come down in. S'fuckin' torture, that." He looked around the kitchenette. "This ain't much better."

No surprise there. There was a reason plaz was banned in seventy-five percent of the world, and the rest was a wasteland. "No, I meant Flynn's talent."

"Like I said. Tainted."

Rogan rolled his eyes, but Fitz was right, the shit Flynn had just pulled didn't feel like pure Breaker talent, but Fitz dancing around the answer made Rogan want to pummel the kid. It was as bad as talking to Cal. "Tainted by what?"

Fitz shrugged, still grimacing behind that curly mop of his. The microwave binged, saving him from answering. His shoulders relaxed a fraction, and he brought his meal to the table along with Rogan's mug of coffee, then sighed and loaded the appliance with something else. The Fetch tensed up again as it began to run. He sat, staring at his plate for a long moment, frowning, then his halos pulsed, and he picked up his fork.

Rogan sipped his coffee, watching him shovel food into his mouth. "What did you just do to it?"

"This twenty fucking questions?" Fitz glared at him through his curls, chewing.

"You sure you aren't part Shade?"

"Fuck off," the kid mumbled around a mouthful. "Weren't right. Now it's passable."

Didn't smell or look it. Rogan hoped the brown goop tasted better. "What is it?"

"Eh…said eel kabayaki. S'not bad. Ye want some?"

"No. What I want is for you to tell me what you think Flynn's talent is tainted by."

Kid's chewing slowed. "All the rest," he finally said, pushing away the empty container and retrieving whatever else he'd cooked up. A third meal went in before he sat again.

"As in the rest of the talents?"

Fitz gave something between a nod and a shrug, pushing around a bunch of nefarious saucy chunks with his fork. "S'like he ain't got a channel no more. Swirls around him. He's just pluckin' shite out of the aether. Ye and the rest of the Breakers, ye can see it, a constant flow. Rest of them, s'like turning on a tap from elsewhere, but it's always a straight shot. Before, he were the same, now he's a right fuckin' mess, all that churning about him, screwing with his aura. S'all tangled."

Rogan bunched his brows at the Fetch, and the kid paused again with his fork halfway to his mouth. "What?"

"Can all the Prydees read energy as clearly as you?"

"Dunno. I ain't a Prydee." Fitz scowled.

Both their eyes flicked back to Flynn's room at another rush of talent.

Fuck this.

Rogan pushed up from the table and stalked into the other room. "Flynn?" He knocked on the port, then hit the panel to open it. Surprisingly, it did.

Room was dense with 'lust, and the kid was sitting on the edge of the bed with an unlit cigar. "Cal figure shit out yet?"

"He's working on it. How are you?"

Flynn snorted and looked away.

Rogan closed the portlock behind him. "You know you can only hold zero for so long, right? You're real good at disassociating, but it's gonna bite you in the ass. All of it comes out one way or another, and if you need to talk, I'm here."

Kid wouldn't look at him. "You done?"

Rogan frowned. "No. Fitz says it's like your channel got blasted to shit and now you're just pulling talent out of the air." He called flame, and Flynn went very still, watching him manipulate it, changing its shape and intensity until he held a steadily glowing orb in his palm. "That's exactly how our extra works. Breaker talent's the catalyst, and your emotions will feed it, but the flames originate from manipulating the innate energy in the physical world."

Flynn wet his lips, his gaze flicking from the orb to the edges of the room. Sweat broke out on his forehead. "So, what are you trying to tell me?"

"I'm not trying to tell you anything, but maybe all those flames you keep seeing are."

The kid snorted and turned away.

"Look, when you use it, you can bury anyone I've ever met with sheer power, but you're constantly holding yourself back. Breaker talent is the chaos side of the coin, kid. We're supposed to break shit up, smash things, and blow everything to hell, but you're so fucking afraid to lose control, you bury it and then end up leveling city blocks."

Flynn didn't say anything, staring at the cigar in his hands.

"And that's on Cal and me for not getting you a damned Menot." Rogan sighed. "You try doing sparks yet? That's usually how this lesson starts." It was twenty something years too late, but the fuck if he was gonna let the kid keep fumbling.

Flynn shook his head, the temperature in the room increasing along with the amount of tainted Breaker talent. "No, and every time I try to pull it's like I'm channeling broken glass. I can fucking feel it, like the shit is taunting me, but I can't fucking use it—"

The dresser across the room imploded, and Rogan's talent met the spray of splintered wood. A haze of ash filled the room. "No, you can't direct it," he said, not batting an eye. "And that starts with breaking off bits of what's moving through you. Fuck your channel, you don't need to pull. It's already there. Make it do what you want." Rogan flicked his fingers and a shower of tiny lights fell from his hand. "Your will is the blade, sharpen it against the flow."

The kid chewed his lip, looking at the blast mark where the dresser had been. The air tinged with his anxiety.

"You need to get a handle on this, Flynn. If the flames come, I'll deal with them, and if you fuck up more of the facility, no one here's gonna give a shit."

Flynn's eyes met his, and he took a deep breath. Seconds ticked by, then minutes before sparks fizzled between them, dying out before they hit the ground. He did it again, his brow furrowing as a sloppy ball of flame condensed in his palm.

Rogan couldn't help the shit eating grin that split his face. Kid was a natural, and if calling flame didn't stamp him as blood, nothing else would.

CHAPTER ELEVEN

"It is not possible to overstate my humiliation. I waited for Ro to return from maneuvers, knowing his blood would be up. When he saw me lying on his bed, he paused at the threshold. I touched myself, bathed in the half light of the moon as he silently watched. When it became obvious he wasn't going to come to me, I stood, my nipples tightening as his eyes slid over my body, but before I was halfway across the room, he was gone, slamming the door after him.

And when I'd collected myself enough to leave, I saw him mounting one of his whores. Am I really so repugnant? I—It doesn't matter…not any more.

What I once naively assumed to be divine intervention—these talents—are nothing more than an infectious disease unleashed upon an unwary populace. We continue to spread the contagion with every squalling brat that comes into the world. The fact that I know what the cure is and am unable to implement it is infuriating. I can't pretend anymore, and I know the others are watching me. I feel their eyes and hear their what their lips don't say…not to me at least.

But Mother hears everything. She told me this would happen, and now we'll do things her way. Ro's whore will be the first of the Talents we harvest.

– Undated journal entry

FLYNN MANIPULATED a ball of flame in his palm, trying to shape it to his will. Rogan made it look so fucking easy—flames danced in Flynn's peripheral and he broke out in a sweat. He dropped talent, and it lashed back through him as it recoiled, rejoining the stream he'd taken it from. He stared at his trembling hands.

… Flesh peels back and falls away into greasy black ash as flames lick his bones. Searing, all-encompassing agony ravages him, and he screams, sucking the inferno into his lungs…

"Excellent," Rogan said, snapping him back into the here and now. "You've just passed the first test we give every eleven-year-old, and your final exam in one go, which means you get the lecture…"

Flynn shot him a sour look and tuned out, his temper roiling. A test? He'd come in here because he was about to lose his shit, and he didn't need a fucking test or a goddamned lecture. What he needed was to be was with Kara, and not sitting in here on his ass—

Fuck. Calm down. He fought to pull up zero again. It wasn't gonna do anyone any good if he ran off half-cocked. Cal was right. They needed to find a secure route to the coordinates the twins had left and play Titus's fucking game. Cal had said daybreak, right? That was only a few hours away.

And Kara had less than forty-eight of those left.

"…a big dumb thug, and that comes down to getting a handle on your emotions." Rogan stopped talking and looked at Flynn like he was waiting for an answer.

He didn't have one.

The Breaker glowered at him, hands on his hips. "You didn't listen to a fucking thing I just said, did you?"

Flynn stared back. His throat bobbed, seeing a different man standing there.

… "Are you even fucking listening? Christ, you're fucking useless! What good's a Talent that can't figure out how to pull?!" Knuckles drive into his temple. He falls and a boot catches him in the gut. "Pull, you fucking loser, pull!"…

A cloak settled around him, the blanket of talent bringing him back to himself. He pinched across his temples, the memory of a pained gasp at his lips—

Rogan threw up his hands. "Fine. I'm in the next room if you need me." He left, closing the portlock after himself.

Flynn dry-heaved, shame and self-loathing churning through his gut, darkness writhing within him. Feeling it surface and bleed throughout his being. His heart rate increased and sweat dripped from the tip of his nose.

Shit, if he kept this up, bad things were gonna happen.

Fuck, lock it down, lock it down…zero settled over him, and he reveled in the numbness. He'd already lost control and let the power consume him. Shame ate at him that in that moment; he'd welcomed death. If it hadn't been for Kara's bind… Christ. Even when she wasn't with him she was still making him do the right thing. Making him a better man.

He had to get her back. Flynn raked a hand through his hair, trying to dispel the cloak around him.

It wouldn't budge.

He laughed. God had to love fucking with him. Jesus fucking Christ, he'd done it without even thinking back in Lyden, when he'd pulled it just now, how in the fuck—

Weak. He was fucking weak. He tore at his beard, hating himself, how goddamned pathetic he was under everything, the rest of it a bullshit act.

No. He could figure this out. He had to.

He mopped his sleeve across his forehead and directed talent again like Rogan had shown him. An orb sprang back into existence, steadier this time. Flynn wrestled with the power, fighting to bend it to his will —it slid from his grasp, the rebound flaying his insides as the orb winked out.

He shot to his feet and hurled the lamp from the bedside table against the opposite wall. Why was this so fucking hard?! He swore, rifling his hair. He didn't have fucking time to learn how to use his talent all over again—

No, you know what? Fine. He slowed his breathing. Fine. He would start from the beginning. Rogan had just gone over Breaker 101, might as well take a refresher in Shade. Flynn took a deep, crackling drag of his cigar—

When had he lit that?

He closed his eyes and exhaled a stuttering breath. Nope. Not going there. Didn't matter. Shade talent, Shade talent…

... "You're so fucking smart, how do you think you pull talent, hot shot?"...

Fuck. Or not. His fingers itched for a bottle, something, anything to bury that particular memory down deep. He ran a hand across his beard, his stomach churning.

Hot shot.

He broke out in a cold sweat. The last time someone had called him that, he'd gone to jail for two years. Fuck Lot. Cal. Start with what Cal had taught him.

Flynn took another drag and closed his eyes again. He opened himself up to the talent that'd been swirling around him, taunting him. It was all jumbled. Christ. Before when he'd reached for talent it was just there, a stream he could tap into and divert to use the way he wanted. This was like trying to separate out different densities of liquid as they boiled.

... "Not so fucking easy is it?" A blow strikes him across the face and he reels, slamming against the wall. A fist drives into his stomach. Vomits spews from his mouth. Lot bellows, blows rain down...'

Flynn's eyes sprang back open, and he wiped the sweat from his brow. The cloak around him fizzled away. Christ, that'd been bad.

He'd pissed blood for a week.

Fuck this, and fuck his fucking talent. Flynn dragged a hand across his face, his shirt soaked. He paced the room, trying desperately to achieve zero state and failing. Why the fuck was this so fucking hard?! He pulled over another dresser and ripped a painting from the wall, snapping the canvas over his knee—

The portlock rolled aside again.

He whipped the painting across the room, a corner of the frame embedding into the wall. His chest heaved. God fucking—"What?!"

Rogan's gaze swept the room before focusing on him. Seeing too goddamned much. "Come on, I need to get some air, and so do you."

Flynn glared at him for half a breath, then grabbed his jacket. What the fuck. Maybe that was what he needed. He followed Rogan through the main room. A surge of anger seared through him as he passed his grandfather, 'lust potent enough for the old man's head to jerk up. Their gazes met, and Cal's face paled—

"Flynn."

Rogan was holding the port for him.

Flynn stalked through it, into the hallway and slammed his fist through the wall. Once, twice…

"Come on, kid. You want to hit something? Let's go up top where we'll have some room."

He swallowed, breath coming fast, and wet his lips. Grunted.

Rogan led him back through the building and up the stairs. Above the rooftop, the sky was that funky shade of gloaming, and the temperature straddled the line between cold and balmy. A thick fog snaked around the buildings, insulating them from the rest of the city.

Rogan stood by the helipad. "You need something to hit? Let's do it."

Flynn took a drag of his cigar, his emotions warring between wanting to pummel the man and terrified of what would happen if he did.

"I warned you, kid. It all comes out sooner or later."

"The fuck would you know about it?"

Rogan laughed. "You got no idea. After the Surge, all that power laid me open. I did a lot of stupid shit trying to bury it again. Shit that took me lifetimes to crawl back from. You don't have the same luxury. You need to handle your trauma, now. People are depending on you."

"Right, yeah, lemme get on that." Because it was totally more important than figuring out his fucking talent. Flynn glowered, raking a hand through his hair. Deal with his trauma. All he could see was his fucking trauma. His stomach clenched again, and bile rose into his throat.

…*"Not so fucking easy, is it?"*…

Flynn slammed his fist into the bricks beside the port, bones cracking, trying to drown out Lot's goddamned voice. Christ. Flynn closed his eyes, savoring the pain of his joints resetting. He ground his palm over his busted knuckles, drawing the process out. The flares of agony cleared his head enough for him to slip into zero state again. It settled over him, and he gave a shaky exhalation.

"Your father really fucked you up, didn't he?" Rogan spat. Flynn tensed, but didn't turn. "And I bet Cal just disappeared. Must make it worse, that he knew and didn't do anything about it. I'm not surprised you looked like you were gonna murder him just now."

Flynn shoulders tensed. He clamped the cigar between his teeth and forced himself to shrug as he turned back to the Breaker. "I dunno what you're talking about."

Rogan stood in that widened stance of his, arms crossed over his chest and snorted. "Don't try to bullshit me. I've heard enough since I've been up here to know Lot beat the fuck out of you whenever he felt the need."

Hitting Rogan abruptly didn't seem like such a bad idea. "That's none of your fucking business."

"Anything that affects your ability in the field is my fucking business. I came down here to get Kara, not to worry about you losing your shit."

Phantom flames licked around the rooftop. "If you left me the fuck alone, it wouldn't be a problem. None of that matters, what does is—"

"You mean you didn't matter."

Flynn's temper flared, burning off some of the fog. He laughed, pacing. Fucking Rogan. Alpha Prime, therapist. "Fine, you want the sob story? No. I didn't matter any further than being a warm body. Heir to House fucking Scot. Aside from that, nobody gave a shit. Not Cal, not Lot, and not anybody else." He ran a hand over his mouth, dying for a drink. Felt like a fist had settled in his chest, squeezing.

"That's bullshit. I know for a fact your mom did, and French would go to war for you. That they couldn't do anything to stop it's an entirely different issue."

"It's not something we talk about," Flynn murmured, the old mantra springing to his lips.

"What's that?"

Fuck. Flynn shook himself. His past was too goddamned raw. He ran a hand up the back of his neck, biting the scar on his lip hard enough to taste blood. "I don't wanna talk about it."

"That's not what you said. Why aren't you supposed to talk about it? All that shit's gonna to poison you. Sometimes you need to lance the boil."

Flynn chewed his lip, not used to having anyone ask questions or anyone look past what he wanted them to see. No one had ever really bothered, for the most part. Or if they did, they didn't stick around for too long after. It would be easier if the man just went away, but—Flynn took another drag, his emotions warring. He glanced at where the lightstream sat cloaked, a case of whiskey inside. His mouth watered, and he spat to the side.

… "That path leads to ruin faster than any other…."

Christ, he was done with this shit. "Just drop it. It was my fault, I never tried hard enough."

Rogan laughed, and Flynn's temper jumped again. "That's the biggest line of shit I've heard in years. You were a kid. There wasn't a fucking thing you could've done to keep that man off you. It sure as hell wasn't your job to make him behave. I bet he beat your mamma, too."

…her skin is sallow beneath the bruises. Eyes puffy and lips cracked. She's bleeding; he can smell it soaking the bedsheets.

"Let me get French."

She stops him, her voice so sad. "No, baby. There's nothing he can do. There's nothing anybody can do…"

"I didn't see them together much," Flynn muttered. He took a slow drag of his cigar, his stomach clenching, gaze drifting back to the lightstream. His hand shook as he ran it over his mouth. Fuck, this was as bad as his first week drying out in Kensbot.

"You didn't answer me."

"Did you ask a question?" Flynn snapped back, the phantom flames around the roof flickering closer.

Rogan snorted.

Jesus fucking—"What the hell do you want from me, Rogan? Yeah. He hit her when he wasn't beating the shit out of me, and I made sure I kept him busy. You want all the nasty details? Honestly, they all kind of bleed together. He was real good at making you fucking hurt without leaving marks where people could see them."

"That why you've won't spar with women?"

"What? No, I—" hadn't ever thought about that, but fuck him, it wasn't, that wasn't—Flynn clenched his jaw, unable to meet the asshole's gaze. "Whatever, it's a fine fucking line, because I love to make them cry." He got in Rogan's face. "You wanna hear about how fucking hard I get when they're screaming around my dick? I like that even more than beating the shit out of people."

Rogan pursed his lips as he looked away.

Good. Let him see what a twisted fuck he was. Maybe the prick would leave him the fuck alone. He turned towards the lightstream to find that bottle.

Fuck it.

"What about Kara?"

Flynn froze, his stomach dropping at her name. "Kara begs me for it," he snapped, flinging the butt of his cigar over the side of the building.

... "Does it hurt enough, baby? Or do you want more?"

"More," she chokes out, the scent of her 'lust twining around them.

He picks her up and flips her over, slamming her against the wall, plaster cracking. Her eyes are deep pools of smoldering need. She wraps her legs around him, lowering her bound wrists around his neck. Christ, the shit he wants to do to her—primal and dark, his desires churn inside him. Needing to claim her. To break her into little pieces and remake her as his...

She kisses him. Her lips the barest brush of flesh. Soft. So fucking soft. His insides melt. He'd do anything for this woman.

"Hurt me, Flynn. Please..."

He crumpled to sit at the edge of the helipad, his rage deserting him.

"She's the only one who's ever asked me to. Fuck." His voice broke. "She hurts me back." Kara gave him everything. Was everything. Sated him. Loved him for him, none of the other shit mattered. He closed his eyes and scrubbed his face, hands trembling.

"Sharing pain is part of the domination and submission our line needs. You find your true mate, she'll give it as good as she takes it. Shit, Maria used to beat the hell out of me." A broad smile split Rogan's face. "As far as the rest...you're Alpha. I am a little surprised at Kara, though. She was all Binder when I had my chance at her."

Flynn took a deep breath, the admission somehow comforting. Kara...she'd shown him. Only him. Had opened herself up and laid her soul bare. She was his. The question that'd plagued him fell from his lips before he could think about it. "Why didn't you try to bond her?"

"Cal," the man said flatly. "This Reunification of his...the only reason I touched her was because of that fucking coercion program. She was spiraling, drowning in some asshole's memories. Shit's evil. If a Binder can't compartmentalize what they take, it corrupts them. Changes who they are. She's lucky she was able to come back from it, not everyone does."

... Kara looks down, playing with his shirt buttons. "When they come back... I'm there again. With them. It's everything, not just emotions. I—I feel their hands, taste—" She shivers, her voice very small. "Will you make it go away? Help me forget, just for a little while?"

A tear rolls down her cheek, and he brushes it away, wanting to hunt down and eviscerate anyone who'd ever hurt her...

He still did, but surprisingly, Rogan wasn't one of them.

Flynn's brows furrowed, confused. He still didn't like that they'd slept together, or Rogan in general, but...Christ, maybe he just had more important things to worry about. He scanned the edges of the roof, the fog dissipating and slowly revealing the city around them, the murky facades of buildings poking through.

Rogan scratched his stubble. "I pains me to admit, but Cal was right. You two bring out a light in each other I haven't seen since Richard and Karen. As much as you need her, she needs you, and I swear I'm gonna do everything in my power to get her back."

"Richard and Karen?"

"Part of our original seven, the Fixer and the Fetch. Only couple I've ever known to become a dyad." He scratched his stubble again. Man was making him itch. "No idea how that worked, but the talent they could pull...if anyone's got a chance of doing that again, it's you and Kara. Now tell me you've got a plan for swiping her out from under Titus's nose."

Flynn frowned. "We're not gonna be able to just take her. Back at the coop, I saw—Titus—he's the only reason they're alive right now. I need to know how to keep them that way, and I'm gonna have to play his game to do it."

"You know where she is? You get an imprint Fitz can shift to?"

"I think so, but that's the nuclear option. The safer Titus feels, the safer Kara's gonna be, and right now he thinks he's holding all the cards. We shift in there, and I dunno what he'll do, especially if the twins are as batshit as you keep saying."

"They're worse, and if we don't show up at those coordinates soon, I've got no idea what's gonna happen, other than it's not gonna be good," Rogan murmured. "So you're just gonna offer yourself up?"

"Basically. Look, whatever you and Cal have going on with the them aside, Titus's end game has always been genetics. I should be relatively safe as long as he doesn't think I'm a threat."

"It's not a terrible plan, but I would feel better if you had a handle on your talent," Rogan said, running a hand down the side of his head.

"Yeah, so would I." Flynn closed his eyes, feeling the jumble swirl around him, somehow less tightly coiled than before. Damn the man, but he'd been right about spilling shit. "It's—I dunno. Like Fitz said, all mixed up."

The big Breaker stared up at the sky. Despite the fog around them, above them was dawning a clear, soft blue. "You know, I've always thought of talent as light, and that our channels act like prisms, breaking it into wave lengths we can manipulate. It sounds like whatever you've got going on now isn't separating it into a clean spectrum."

The theory made sense. "Yeah, that's pretty much how it feels," Flynn grumbled. "If I try to channel, it fucking hurts, then it comes as easy as breathing other times."

"So stop thinking about it." Rogan shrugged. "Sounds like a mental block you're trying to force. You grip a weapon too tightly, it becomes harder to hold onto than if you'd been relaxed."

Flynn snorted. "Kind of hard to relax when Titus has my family, and I've got all this shit clanging around in my head."

"True, that." Rogan crouched down and palmed a handful of pea stone. "You'll bring her back, but in the meantime, you can't let a shitty upbringing consume you. It will if you let it, and vengeance never feels as good as you think it's gonna."

"Isn't that what this is about for you and Cal? I thought you wanted to put the twins in the ground."

"Oh, I do." Rogan grinned. "But that's not gonna be vengeance. That's karmic fucking retribution."

"There's a difference?"

"Yeah." He chucked a couple of pebbles and blew out a breath. "Vengeance is going back and beating the shit out of the man who made your life hell until he's not breathing and then beating him some more."

Flynn chewed his lip. "I dunno, that sounds pretty cathartic to me."

"Maybe at the time, but pounding my daddy into ground chuck didn't change a fucking thing other than make me feel like an even bigger piece of shit than I already did. I still wake up some nights thinking about it." Rogan sat, chucking the rest of the pebbles in his hand away. "How his blood spattered. How sticky my knuckles were…" He absently swept them against his palm and looked out over the city. "It was all I could smell for weeks, shit, sometimes I still do."

… His bolo slides between skin and muscle and the man screams; horror, then recognition flickering through his eyes.

"Y-you…but y-you're a T—" the word trails off in a gurgle, blood bubbling up around his severed trachea.

He licks the spatter from his lips. He wasn't. Not anymore, and the lot of them could go fuck themselves…

"So what about ending the twins makes it karmic retribution?" Flynn asked, pinching the bridge of his nose, too many memories best forgotten roiling to the surface of his mind.

"My father was a piece of shit, but he wasn't evil. I've got a pretty good idea why he did what he did, not that it excuses it. The twins hurt people because they can, and they like it. The fucking mind games they play…that's why they're waiting for us to deliver ourselves to those coordinates and not here already. They're rabid and need to be put down like the sick animals they are." He dusted off his palms and sighed, scratching his stubble. "Damn, I need a razor. I don't know how you stand it."

"It's better than seeing Lot every time I look in the mirror. I don't really think about it anymore." Flynn ran a hand over his beard and scratched under his jaw. "Kara likes it."

Rogan grunted, standing. "We should go in." The fog had burned off beneath the early morning sun, leaving them exposed. Flynn got to his feet.

"If things go the way I hope, I'll bring Kara back here as soon as I find out what I need to know. Keep Fitz close. He might have to shift her to Glynfyls."

"How do you plan on getting her out?"

Flynn ran a hand through is hair. "My talent…I think it will come if I need it. Back in Lyden, I was freaking out about being seen, and it cloaked me just before I went into that bar. I think…I don't think it will abandon me."

Rogan considered him for a while. "Okay, but give Fitz the imprint of whatever you got and have him put a ward on you. If you need an extraction, break it…and if you see the twins, tell them I'm inviting them to a hunt."

"A hunt?"

"Yeah." Rogan's face was hard. "Whatever they've got waiting at those coordinates for us can go fuck itself, and Enoch won't be able to keep to the script after that."

Flynn nodded, the two of them silent as they walked back to the door. Rogan went to open it and paused, lifting up a finger.

Faint voices came from the other side.

"Shit," Rogan murmured, scanning the barren rooftop. "If your talent's gonna pony up, now'd be a great time to do it."

Sweat broke out over Flynn's brow, trying not to reach for talent. *Please, please, please, please…*

A misty tingle swept around them as a cloak settled. *Sweet Jesus, thank you.* Rogan grunted, backing around the side of the port. It opened a moment later and three men came out.

"He said two guys were up here," a bruiser grumbled, holding a cudgel in his hand.

Fuck. They were Sons. That was one of the larger chapter's enforcers, Hoyt. Flynn ran a hand down his face and just shook his head at Rogan's side-eye.

"Then there was. Sam don't imagine things." A lanky man Flynn didn't recognize walked out toward the center of the roof, dangerously close to where the craft was cloaked. A couple more feet, and he was gonna smack right into it.

Another unknown with a blue beanie hawked and spat. "You think it's Bento's crew?"

"After last week? Not a fucking chance." Hoyt chuckled, slapping his cudgel against his meaty palm. "Besides, Sam said they were big, like Breakers."

The lanky man walked back to the others. "Been plenty of them lately."

"Yeah, around that building five sectors over. What the hell would two Breakers be doing in this one, alone? Assholes don't go anywhere without an entire squad."

"Maybe there ain't enough of them after they got spanked up north," Blue Beanie said, looking around like he was nervous.

"You're an idiot if you believe that." Hoyt snorted. "S'all propaganda. An army of Peacekeepers would fuck that place up."

Blue Beanie shrugged. "Just telling you what I heard."

"You hear a lot of shit, and ain't half of it true. Come on, let's see if the guys downstairs found anything and report back to Sam." They followed Hoyt back through the port, leaving Flynn and Rogan alone again.

"Give it a few minutes," the Breaker murmured. "Friends of yours?"

"No, those tags downstairs—it's the Sons. Specifically, the assholes that irradiated the plateau. Christ, I'd hoped they'd nuked themselves in the process."

Rogan snorted. "Word to the wise? Unless you personally finish the job, don't ever assume it's done." He pushed away from the wall. "Come on. Cal's gotta have whatever intel there is to be had by now, and after seeing your talent cooperate, the sooner we get you to the rendezvous point, the better."

Flynn grunted. He couldn't agree more.

MARCOS JOGGED down the Carmody's front steps into the foyer, stifling a yawn. He'd been at Conclave all night acclimating the troops, and as exhausting as that had been, he couldn't deny a newfound sense of purpose. A grin broke over his face as he made his way to the kitchen, hoping to snag a cup of coffee and a plate of something. That, along with the shower and clean shirt he'd just grabbed should see him through the morning.

Though dawn hadn't quite broken, there was an impressive spread of pastries and a pair of chafing dishes set up on the counter. Marcos bypassed them for the carafe of coffee and poured himself a cup—business before pleasure.

A few minutes later, he set himself up at the kitchen table with his second cup and a heaping plate of sausages and eggs. He busied himself with it, distantly sensing Nora's angst. Glory but that killed him. He sent what reassurance he could. The last time they'd been in this position, feeling the brush of her regard had gotten him through the tougher aspects of his deployment down in Hexspar. What a stinking swamp—

A door to his right cracked open, and a gray striped cat sauntered past his ankles, voices filtering in behind it. His ears perked up at Phyllis Breakspear's rich alto.

"...have a responsibility to the people of Glynfyls."

"Yes, to them, perhaps, but not to all that riffraff Titus discarded on the plateau—"

"Funny, weren't you in that exact same position not so long ago?" Alice asked, cutting Serra off. "You'd think you'd be a bit more empathetic."

They might, but they'd be wrong. Glory, what was Serra Hess doing here? Marcos's chewing slowed as he made a concerted effort to control his bloodlust. By what was coming through that cracked door, Phyllis was not. He leaned back in his chair, just able to make out the three of them in the other room and the skirts of two others.

"I don't see how that's the same thing at all," Serra shot back. "We were brought up here specifically to become citizens. Those Breakers came to rape and pillage! They're animals without purpose. Why we're discussing how to feed and house them—"

"We're discussing it because every last one of those *men* have pledged fealty to the Overlord, making them citizens," Phyllis said through gritted teeth. "A better question is why Bernice felt the need to include you in our discussion."

"Nora's not here, and the Binders need to be looped into our efforts," Bernice returned sourly. "If you know of a more qualified candidate, I'm all ears, but the fact of the matter is, Serra is currently acting as First."

Marcos snorted around his mouthful of eggs at that ringing endorsement.

"I'm not acting as First, I *am* First," Serra spat back. "And if you want my line's cooperation, I suggest you show the appropriate amount of respect."

"Perhaps we would, if you contributed to something other than your ego," Alice drawled.

"Beginning with a recall of that writ you sent out. Your line's sworn to heal those in need," Evie Crandall's voice pipped up. "You can't just sashay into that box at the Assembly and re-write the ethos this city was founded upon."

"Rewrite the city's ethos?" Serra laughed. "You would accuse that of me while you endorse a man who's dissolved your democratic system and opened your gates wide for the enemy—"

"Have you ever heard of the phrase, don't poke the bear, Lady Hess?" Alice asked. "As amusing as it seems to be for you, I'd suggest you desist in baiting present company. Those Breakers are not our enemy, and I can promise that the city will be very glad to have them in the not-so-distant future. However, your inclusion in this little sorority is solely dependent upon our good will and, quite frankly, you're doing little to nurture it."

"Oh really? I was under the impression that my status as First determined my eligibility for the Ladies," Serra shot back. "And if I read your bylaws correctly, none of you have any say in who the Binders elect."

"The bylaws are as you say, dear." Lady Crandall tittered. "Yet, I would advise caution. The North is a very different arena than the one you're accustomed to playing in. For example, it would be a shame if rumors began circulating about your daughter's fertility, or lack thereof. According to those same bylaws you just mentioned, the First of a line must be able to prove their House fecund. If your only issue is barren, I'm afraid that disqualifies you…unless you have plans to try again?"

Marcos froze, his fork poised at his lips. Impossible. The Source culled infertile Talents.

Phyllis tsked. "I can't imagine anyone spreading such hurtful rumors…but, this is Glynfyls." She sighed. "Not to worry though, if something like that did happen, a public inquest would be opened and the matter definitively put to rest…one way or another."

Her words hung in the air, and Marcos's brow furrowed at Serra's silence. Could it be true? If it was, their entire House would be discredited, and Nora—

"I didn't come here to be insulted!" Serra blustered, the swirl of skirts coming from beyond the door. "My writ stands, and if you expected me to be cowed by your vicious lies, you're sadly mistaken!" Her footsteps clacked against the floor as she stormed from the room.

"Well, that was a bit heavy handed," Bernice huffed as they faded down the hall.

"Oh, please." Phyllis snorted. "Do you really think she'd be swayed by subtly?"

"I didn't expect her to be swayed at all, but after her reaction, we've no choice but to put it out there and pressure her line to remit their election."

"Alice is right," Evie said. "I'll talk to Bart, and until there's proof to the contrary, neither Hesses will be aspiring to First. Do you really believe that Binder…what was her name?"

"Jolie, and yes, I do." Phyllis sighed. "Granted, she seems to have a grudge against Serra, but I can certainly understand that. Evie, did you glean anything from her?"

"Not much. These Source Binders have more mental training than the ones up here. Fear was what I found foremost in her mind, followed by desperation. Beyond that, I couldn't say, but questioning her daughter's fertility definitely hit a nerve. Someone needs to keep an eye on her. Something about that woman isn't right, but I can't put my finger on it."

Marcos agreed and had heard enough. He quietly pushed back from the table and brought his plate to the sink. If what the Ladies had just threatened Serra with was true…he frowned. That had to be what Jolie was so smug about earlier, but discrediting Serra was only going to make her more dangerous. Her being disqualified for First wasn't going to do a damned thing to keep Nora safe, and knowing Serra, it would probably put her in more danger.

For the first time since Nora had left, Marcos was relieved she was gone. She was safer at the Source.

SERRA STOMPED BACK into her rooms at the Pearl and flung her wrap onto the couch. She snarled at the crumpled blanket Otto had left on the floor and kicked it, wishing it were one of those miserable cunts. The Ladies. Ugh! How had she managed to misread that situation so badly?

She ground her teeth in frustration, but it was her own fault. This damned city, all the politics…she'd been too bold—moved too quickly —and the old guard had smacked her down for it. Damn it, she knew better, but the opportunity to oust Nora had been too ripe not to exploit.

And now it had been squandered.

Serra bit the inside of her cheek, her eyes closed tight, the urge to scream overpowering. She'd been so damned careful, here and at the Source. The lengths she'd gone to—everything had been to protect Tamara. Was it something the girl had done? Something she'd said? How had that fat bitch ferreted out the one thing that would destroy them both—

Serra's hands fisted at her sides. Bloody Finders. All her work, her sacrifice, her opportunity! Gone in an instant—and the way it'd just been blatantly laid on the table…. Serra collapsed onto the couch and cradled her head in her hands. She wouldn't cry. She wouldn't!

"Serra, is that you?" Otto called from the other room, the repugnant little man's footsteps shuffling closer.

Damn him. "Yes," she wiped a hand over her cheeks, quickly pulling herself together. "I'll call up a tray for you in a moment."

He appeared in the doorway and leaned against it, breathing heavily. Serra frowned, he should be able to dance into the room en pointe considering how much talent she'd been pouring into him.

"No, no, don't trouble yourself, you were right, I need to move around more so I can regain my strength." He hobbled over to a chair and sat down with a sigh, eyeing her wrap. "Oh my. That's white ermine, if I'm not mistaken? I seem to recall that being quite expensive up here. I hope that means you've run into some good fortune?"

"Up until a day ago I would've said so," she muttered, absently stroking the garment. It had been the most expensive thing in the couturier's shop, and barely dented the allowance Lady Saks had allotted her and Tamara.

Serra frowned, certain the woman's largesse was about to come to an end. She turned back to Otto, not in the mood to prevaricate. "Unfortunately, Evie Crandall has somehow sniffed out Tamara's deficiency, and I'm sure by now the entire city's gotten an earful. Once word reaches Lady Saks, we'll be ruined." Tears pricked Serra's eyes as she looked around the posh suite.

Otto clucked his tongue. "Not necessarily." Her gaze jumped to meet his, and he smiled, flashing those blunt, piggy teeth of his. "Apparently our fates have entwined once again. I seem to remember helping you out of a similar situation once before, and there's no reason why I can't do so again…as long as my fortunes continue to increase with yours. My body may be ravaged, but my talent is unaffected. Might I suggest you request to have tea with our benefactress, and we can put any rumors she might have heard to rest?"

Serra went very still. If he could use his talent to persuade her the way he had the records office at the Source…a smile lit up her face at the prospect of out-maneuvering those vicious bitches. "Yes, I think that's a wonderful idea."

FITZ SAT at the kitchen table playing stab scotch, tryin' to keep his mind off the energy currents throbbing around him.

Shite weren't working.

He huffed the curls from his eyes, speeding up the thrust of the blade betwixt his spread fingers. Resonance from all the plaz in this place were puttin' his teeth on edge somewhat fierce. Christ, it were as bad as when all the sisters was on their rag.

"You know you're fucking up my table," that old hillie—Eh, Cal— said, coming over to sit with a glass of somewhat amber. He lit another cigarette and blew out a cloud.

"D'ye really give a shit?"

"Nope."

Fitz grunted and went back to playing for all of a breath before giving up and slapping his pigsticker down. Man's energy were riot. Probably had somewhat to do with the way His High Holiness were looking at him on his way out the door. Ye'd think the man had killed his kitten or somewhat.

Shite. Fitz tugged his patch, then shook his head. Nah. Sophia'd take care of the beastie proper. It were probably all snuggled up against her right now, nuzzling against that white throat of hers. He scowled, imagining the furry fuckin' bastard pressed up against them soft breasts—

Christ. It were a sorry state of affairs when he were jealous of a damned cat, and the lack of Cajetan's mirth over it weren't helpin' none. Were like the blessed bastard couldn't get through all the Christ-begotten noise, and his silence were more'n disconcerting. Fitz'd heard tell the Source were Godless, but he didn't think that extended t'saints. Though if he'd had his druthers, he wouldn't be anywhere near this shitehole either.

Nah. He'd be cozied up to them breasts, and the cat could go fuck itself. Fitz snatched up his pigsticker and tucked it away, muttering as he shifted the gouges he'd made to the underside of the table.

Cal snorted. "What's her name?"

"What's whose name?"

"Whoever you're pining after." Cal ashed into one of the empty food containers Fitz'd piled to the side. "Man doesn't get that expression on his face unless a woman's involved, and he's in deep."

"Ain't no woman," Fitz muttered. And there weren't never gonna be, more's the fucking pity. His scowl deepened, his chest going tight. Jesus, Mary, and Joseph, why he couldn't get that ripe little peach out of his head—

He should've kissed her.

"Whatever you gotta tell yourself." Cal chuckled.

"Fuck off," Fitz snarled. Chair screeched against the floor as he pushed it back in a right foul mood. "Ain't ye supposed to be looking for a route or somewhat? I ain't keen on lingering in this miserable shithole." Energy were getting harder to stomach by the moment.

"That makes two of us, but we've got some time to kill. How about we spend it opening up that package you intercepted?" Man's eyes were hard, like it weren't a request.

Fitz dug into his jacket pocket and tossed it on the table between them. "Have at it."

Cal stared at it for a spell before he picked it up, turning it over in his hands. Brown paper were stained and battered like it'd been through the mill a time or seven. "They say anything when they gave it to you?"

"Not t'get it hot."

Old man grunted, pulled off the string and tore the paper. Were three layers deep before he hit a hinged black box. He wet his lips and tipped the lid up. His face went soft before it hardened again, and he tossed the box back at Fitz. "Take 'em."

Fitz's brow creased as he picked it up and looked inside. "Chocolates?"

Cal grunted. "Truffles out of Xian, one of the few countries that refuses to trade with Glynfyls on pain of death. Their empress has got a real stick up her ass about Talents. Miriam's birthday is next week, and those are her favorites. I'm sure that's who the little shit intended them for."

"Eh...then shouldn't—"

"Hell no," the man barked. "The last thing she or anyone else needs right now is to remember any of Leo's redeeming qualities, few though they may've been. They're all yours."

Fitz snorted. Weren't a chance in hell he were touchin' any of it. Shite fucked with him somewhat fierce. He pushed the box back. "Don't eat chocolate."

Cal's brow quirked, his eyes flicking to the pile of empty trays. "Good to know there's something on that list." Fitz scowled, and the prick smirked at him. "Then give 'em to that girl you don't have. I don't care as long as I don't have to see them."

That weren't happening, but Gran would probably fancy 'em. Old bat'd eat 'em out of spite once she knew where they'd been bound, and she could use somewhat in her stomach. He begrudgingly re-tied the string around the box and slipped it back into his pocket. He got that shite on his fingers they'd blister so bad he wouldn't be able to wipe his arse for a week.

The portlock clicked in the other room, and Rogan and His High Holiness strode in. Thank fuckin' God the man's energy were more settled.

"Just missed a group of Sons on the roof," the Breaker said. "They searched the rest of the building on the way out. We need to move. What've you got down here?"

"No good news." Cal pulled out that pouch of his, eyeing the doorway as Nora joined them. "The sector the laborium's in is completely nullified, and the Sons have men patrolling the streets that haven't been cordoned off by plaz-contamination. If we somehow manage to get past that, Titus has Breakers stationed around the coordinates the twins left. I don't see how we're getting past them without one hell of a brawl."

Rogan scratched his jaw. "Think we can get them to engage with each other and slip past when they do?"

"Normally I'd say yes, but I'm gonna bet there's a reason they haven't already." Cal's eyes flicked to the Overlord. "We're better off shifting in. Give Fitz some of those bots—"

He shot to his feet, his chair slamming into the wall behind him. "Nah, ain't doin' that!" Energy around here were intolerable enough. He took one of them pills, it'd do him in.

"I have to agree," Nora said from the doorway. "The past two times I've bound Fitz's channel after he's taken those, it's gotten progressively worse. At this point he'd be running the risk of losing his talent."

Everyone's gaze slid to the Overlord. He raked a hand through his hair, face a thundercloud. "Well, isn't that just fucking dandy," His High Holiness muttered, storming from the room.

The old hillie lit another smoke. "I take it that means he doesn't have a handle on his talent yet."

"Nope." Rogan sighed and retrieved a pint from the other room. "But he's closer."

"Only counts with horseshoes and hand grenades."

"I'd say Laughlin qualifies for the latter." Nora's brow wrinkled as she stared at the door he'd disappeared behind.

Rogan cracked the bottle open and took a long pull before handing it over to Cal. He did the same and passed the half empty bottle back, sucking air through his teeth with a little cough. That were one way t'kill a bottle.

Nora frowned as she turned back to them. "Do you two really think drinking is wise considering our situation?"

"Well, Nora," Cal smacked his lips, "I figure if we get too plastered, you can just sober us up with a bind. Until then, I'm gonna make use of our downtime."

She crossed her arms over her breasts. Look on her face said she were more apt to let 'em hang. "Oh, I can, can I?"

"Be a waste of a perfectly good drunk right there. Give it here, I ain't got no place t'be." Cal considered him a moment before passing it over. Fitz downed a goodly portion and handed it back with a suppressed belch. "Laud, that's smooth."

"Should be, considering it's pre-Surge," Rogan said, killing the rest of it. He tipped the corner of an empty container toward hisself. "There anything left in that cryocase?"

Their gazes landed on Fitz, and his throat bobbed. "Eh…"

A cry came from the room Scot were in, and Fitz sighed, slumping into his chair as everyone's attention snapped to it. His High Holiness bellowed again. Talent surged—erratic— and were followed by a drawn out groan and panting.

"What the hell is he doing?" Cal asked, fingers pausing around his rolling paper.

"Jackin' off?"

Old hillie snorted at Fitz. "If that's the case, he's doing it wrong."

Rogan went over and knocked on the door. "Flynn? You alright in there?" A shield snapped up, knocking the big man back a step. "Okay, then—"

A muffled scream cut through the room then everything went silent.

Fitz ran a hand over his mouth, nauseous with the play of energy ticking up through the suite, spinning like they was at the edges of one of them suck-holes in the middle of the ocean. He swallowed heavily and cradled his head against the table, groaning. Why the fuck he'd ever agreed t'stay by that maniac's side…

And then Scot started to laugh.

TITUS STROKED a finger across his lips, head tilted as he tried to make sense of the Source's vector readings. That a craft had entered the facility wasn't in question, but the rat's nest of talent it was carrying—

He pushed back in his seat, not doubting that Laughlin Scot was responsible. What it meant, however, was an entirely different quandary. For an exceedingly brief moment, Titus actually considered summoning the twins to pick their pointed little brains on the subject —No, he didn't need the two of them interfering.

A dull ache began behind Titus's eyes as he wondered once again why he'd allowed Elize to dictate Vignette's continued existence. As entertaining as the holo of the Breakers putting the whore through her paces in the barracks were, the bitch should've been culled for inciting his current predicament.

Titus stared at the churning maelstrom centered over a building containing corporate suites. If memory served, Albanach owned one of them. Titus frowned, annoyed he'd left a bolt-hole, but in a facility so large, it'd been bound to happen.

Unfortunately, the various gangs and indigents swarming the streets promised to make Scot's journey to the rendezvous point difficult, if not impossible. Titus tapped his teeth, reconsidering his previous directive for Brix to nullify the area. That Scot had retained his talent was clear, though how much of it he could bring to bear, or would be willing to…

Titus rubbed his brow and pulled up a holo of the lab, considering the gestation bay where Kara Jester lay sedated. With the screen behind her shattered and the bitch wrapped in talent, he had no way of monitoring her or the litter. Despite that, it was obvious she was declining. Her cheeks had lost the healthy flush they'd so recently gained, and her skin had gone sallow. The physical indicators of deterioration were concerning, but of more import was how long she would remain in stasis.

The drugs keeping her under had been administered intravenously along with the nutritionals Titus had prescribed, and now neither were flowing, thanks to Scot's shield. The cocktail had a half-life of several hours, but the tail-end of that was quickly approaching.

And Titus had no idea what it was going to look like when she regained consciousness. If it was anything like the fury his other bitches exhibited when revived, she'd be a threat to the litter and anyone else in the vicinity. He'd preemptively cleared the chamber, but it was of small comfort.

The litter was the prize, and after the changes he'd made to their protocol, their birth was imminent. Damn it, he needed Scot here, now.

Titus pursed his lips around a mouthful of bourbon and quickly typed out a revised directive to Brix, pulling the nullifiers for the time being. Once Scot shifted in, the behemoth could shackle him in nullifying cuffs to be brought down. Those were non-negotiable. There was no way Titus was allowing the man anywhere near the Triam with access to his talent unless it was to remove that blasted shield.

But once here, he'd have no choice but to be amicable to the terms set forth, the girl's fate and that of the litter entirely dependent upon Titus's good will. His brow furrowed as he slowly spun his glass of bourbon on his knee, trying to foresee the complications that would no doubt arise. The precariousness of their positions aside, he had no illusions that Scot would be easy to tame. Not for the first time, Titus questioned the wisdom of allowing the man into the Triam. A lancing pain shot behind his eyes, and he put his hand to his temple—

Above his desk, a holo pinged with Brix's acknowledgment of the order to desist nullification topside.

Titus grimaced, sucking his teeth as he finished what was in his glass. It was done, and second guessing himself now wasn't going to do a bit of good. The plan was set, and he needed to ride it out, for better or worse. He called for another bourbon then sat back, watching the maelstrom of talent swirl over the Source, gaining momentum.

There was nothing left to do but wait.

MOTHER WITHDREW from Titus's mind with the implementation of the new directives she'd seeded. She lay back on her chaise, caressing the cuff of stones at her wrist. The tiny bumps of crystalized talent hummed beneath her fingers, the Talents within becoming restless at her touch. As were the twins to play their part.

"Soon," she murmured, to herself and them. Everything was almost in place.

But is it? That storm—

Is nothing in comparison to what I will bring to bear, she snapped back at the Jane-that-was. She had centuries worth of talent to draw upon, encapsulated and removed from the collective to fuel her machinations. What was out there, swirling above the Source? The last dregs of what once was.

You're underestimating him…them…Ro needed to be backed into a corner to see what he was truly made of, maybe Laughlin does too, and if he and Kara become a dyad…

Mother scoffed. The only dyad in existence currently graced her brow, their power hers to call upon, and with what Titus had done to the girl, she wouldn't last long enough for them to reach that point. And should Mother be proven wrong about Kara Jester's impending demise, the mechanics of becoming a dyad made the chances so slim they were laughable.

It could have been us...we could've had that...after the First Incursion, if we'd just come back...told Ro we were alive...we could still tell him—

No. They couldn't. Not then and not now, not after she'd—Rogan's response to her supposed death was an anomaly and too little too late. A pang of remorse flitted through her breast, and she snarled. The course they'd set out upon would lead them back to that night in the quarry, back to the lives they should've been leading—

Enough. Mother slapped the Jane-that-was down again, banishing her to the depths of their shared psyche. Her delusions had no place here.

But her whispers persisted.

CHAPTER TWELVE

"Several weeks ago, I made my first harvest. The weave Mother devised to bind another's talent to my own condensed the whore's essence into a small gemstone the same shade as her halos. I smile at her sparkling upon my finger as I write this, drinking in her despair that she'll never feel Ro cover her again.

The success has improved my outlook considerably, and I almost feel my old sense of optimism. Several times a week I venture down to the lower city and harvest another to add to my collection. They're not dead in the traditional sense, so my conscience is clear. They're serving a higher purpose, as am I.

I've had the gems mounted on a cuff I wear around my upper arm, safe from prying eyes. Only the newest protest, the rest seem content with their fate once Mother explains it to them. At the edge of my consciousness, I hear her murmuring, taking bits of them to add to herself and quieting their cries..."

— Undated journal entry

FLYNN PULLED TALENT, panting as phantom flames engulfed him. He pushed down the terror churning in his gut, teeth chattering. Rogan was right. He needed to deal with his shit, and he needed to do it now.

Kara needed him. This fucking block had to go.

The smell of burning flesh ripened in his nose, crackle of heat searing his bones. He leaned into it, whimpering. Reliving his body disintegrating, ashes spiraling away, consumed by the vortex inside the shield containing the power he'd unleashed—

Then everything winked out.

… Buoyed by darkness, pinpricks of light surround him, distant but closer than thought. Liquid velvet sound, felt more than heard, holding his consciousness in its womb. Music fills him, suffusing his being with an overwhelming sense of peace. He floats, the moment eerily similar to when he'd bonded Kara—

Kara.

Panic lances through him. He gropes blindly for their bond. Please God, please, please, please—Talent pricks his senses as he catches the last fraying threads linking him to her—

Searing white light rips him from the darkness, and he screams. It becomes a wave of force blasting out, past his shield, across the plateau, his body making itself anew—…

He'd been reborn.

Flynn's eyes flew open, his chest heaving. Jesus fuck. He reached for a cigar, his hands trembling so badly he could barely hold the damn thing. It began smoldering as he brought it to his mouth, and manic laughter burbled from his lips.

He licked them, his heart pounding, wanting a drink so goddamned bad…

Kara's bind wasn't what brought him back.

It'd been talent, but nothing like he'd ever felt. Shit. What had Rogan said? It was light and they were prisms. So what the hell had come through? Flynn closed his eyes and concentrated on the maelstrom swirling around him. His throat bobbed. Right. Don't pull. It's already there. But how…? He ran a hand down his face. Christ, if it would just show him what the fuck it wanted him to do—

Talent surged into him like it'd been waiting for the invitation.

His eyes flew wide as it filled him with power, the jumble overwhelming. He gritted his teeth. Light. Think of it as light, and he was the prism, breaking it up. He laughed again. Shit wasn't what was about to break. Sweat stung his eyes, and his stomach cramped. He took a deep breath. Let go, let go, let go…

Bad things happened when he let go.

… Darkness licked up through the void where his emotions should be, filling him with black fury. Righteous and divine, his eyes rolled back as he breathed it in and held it, savoring its seductive pull until it felt as if his lungs would burst. Then, with a great outpouring of breath, he welcomed the animal…

Damn it, not this time.

He forced himself to relax, and power swept through him like when he channeled Breaker talent. His breath stuttered, he tried to focus…

Shade talent was the first to coalesce around him in an undulating green mist, then Finder found him, a violet satin lining to the underside of his cloak. As it settled, exhaustion swept over him, gray pricking the edges of his vision—

No. Kara needed him.

Flynn fought oblivion, his bloodlust surging, clearing his head with a rush of adrenaline. He strained, sweat dripping from his nose, pulling—bright silver sparks of Fetch talent flashed like minnows, slipping between his fingers, mocking him, the talent's sharp edges slicing. He gasped, blood welling—

… "You grip a weapon too tightly, it becomes harder to hold onto than if you'd been relaxed…"

Fuck. Pulling. He was pulling. Talent was already here. He dropped it, and the power whipped away, ripping through him, shredding his shirt and gouging chunks of flesh and slivers of bone from his chest. Agony seared through him, a wash of blood and serrated muscle—he screamed, flesh flaying from him in long gory strips. Kara's bind struggled to piece him together, slow—too fucking slow—his vision grayed…

Flynn panted, blinking as it cleared. If he fucked up like that again, he had a bad feeling her bind might not work at all.

Motherfucker. He retrieved his cigar from where it'd fallen to the carpet. The room stank like BO, burnt wool, and charred plastic. He raked his fingers through his hair and sat on the bed, head hanging. How the fuck was he supposed to… When Markham had called the storm, what the hell had he done diff—

Shit. He'd *called* the storm.

A prism didn't pull light into itself, it just was. Flynn ran a hand over his torn shirt, wincing as he brushed against the raw ruin of his chest, still oozing where it'd been ripped apart. He wet his lips. Right, so call talent. Christ, don't fuck this up, don't fuck this up—

Come…

A flood of Fetch talent slammed into him, hurling him against the wall. He bellowed beneath the slippery silver assault and threw his arms up over his face. Fish! Fish, it was like drowning in fucking— *help!*

Bronze sparks of Fixer talent stacked through it, pinning the stream to either side of him. He stood rigid, trying to catch his breath in the center of the deluge as it slowed to a trickle with the distinct impression it was fucking laughing at him.

Motherfucker…he let out a shaky breath. Four down, two to go.

Phantom flames crackled around the room, eager.

Flynn wet his lips again, stomach churning. The wound on his chest stung, throbbing with the elevated beat of his heart. Right. Don't think about that. He could do this.

And if he couldn't, they'd all be greasy smears.

Fuck, he couldn't do this.

He didn't have a choice.

He closed his eyes, bile searing the back of his throat. It was now or never. Kara, the babies, they were running out of time. He held out his trembling hand, palm slick with sweat, and envisioned an orb like Rogan had made.

It came with a surge, flames flaring up around him. He sprang from the bed, the mattress engulfed. Shit! No, that's not—

The flames died, talent still pricking at him. He swept the sodden hair from his eyes, coughing, the room filled with smoke. He waved a hand in front of his face. Jesus Christ, he'd just wanted it to come—

The air scintillated, crimson curtains of sparks undulating through the fug. Waiting.

He panted, eyeing it warily as he searched the room for its duality. Where the fuck was Binder talent? The others had just shown up…

The barest streaks of gold striated toward him, so faint he could hardly sense them. They teased around him, ropy scars forming across his torso. He exhaled slowly as the pain receded, laughing at the ugly mess. He'd never been able to figure that talent out. Kara was the Binder.

And he needed her back. Shit, it felt like *it* needed her back.

His head tipped against the wall as the two talents dissipated, the room still heavy with expectation, another force churning behind it all. No. Not yet. He pushed it away, his stomach cramped with fear, not ready to deal with it. He had what he needed.

Flynn closed his eyes and followed his bond to Kara. The babies' anxiety was palpable. Their consciousnesses clung to his, crying for him. A sense of foreboding tightened in his chest. She was still in stasis, but felt closer…like she was waking up.

He needed to be there when she did.

NORA SAT at the kitchen table, her brow knit. She absently played with the tag on her tea bag; what was in her cup long gone cold. Her gaze drifted to Laughlin's room. "He's been pulling a great deal of talent."

Two of the three men at the table grunted, which was more than she'd heard from any of them in some time. Cal sat chain smoking, busy on his tablet since Laughlin had locked himself away. Rogan thumbed through a paperback he'd taken from the coop, and Fitz had his face buried in his arms and was uncharacteristically silent, his leg jiggling beneath the table at odd intervals.

None of them had wanted to talk.

Men. She rolled her eyes, although she supposed she had to give them some credit. All of them save Fitz had given up drinking, and even he seemed surprisingly sober. She glanced at the portlock again. Their devil-may-care attitudes from earlier had definitely waned as the sounds of whatever Laughlin was doing in there increased.

An abrupt rush of Binder talent ruffled the small hairs on the nape of her neck, and she shivered. Glory, was he able to pull that, too? She'd been under the impression dealing with her line's talent wasn't something that came easily to him. Not that the rest seemed to be cooperative of late—

The shield around the room abruptly winked out, and it became oppressively silent.

Fitz's head jerked up a moment before the bedroom door opened, and Flynn strode into the kitchen, shirtless, looking like he'd been through a war. Soot streaked his face and horrendous scars marred his torso. Nora twisted her ring, ill with anxiety. Kara's bind had to be failing if it'd left that mess behind. What that meant for him—for Kara and the babies—Glory.

Laughlin headed for the sink, a horrific stench wafting in with him. Nora put a hand to her nose.

"What the hell've you been doing in there?" Cal blustered as Laughlin scrubbed himself down.

He shrugged, finishing up before he grabbed a hand towel, then turned to lean against the counter as he dried off. "I had some stuff I needed to work out."

"Like what? A kidney stone the size of Ayers Rock?"

"Told ye he were jackin' off," Fitz muttered. Rogan went to cuff him upside the head, and the Fetch shifted to the other side of the room before the blow landed. Nora sighed. It was no wonder that boy needed patching up so often.

"I'm assuming all that was you getting a handle on your talent?" Rogan asked, breaking off glowering at Fitz to address Laughlin.

"Kind of. That prism thing helped." He chewed his lip. "Kara's talent. UnMaking. What's its duality?" He looked between Cal and Rogan. "Christ. Fetch / Fixer, Binder / Breaker, Shade / Finder. All of the talents have a duality, so what's hers?"

The two men scowled at each other. Cal shook his head and lit another cigarette.

Rogan's frown deepened. "Jane called it Rebirth, though none of us ever saw it. Hell, as far as I know, no one's ever seen UnMaking until Kara. Why?"

"Because her balance has to be out there, and I'm pretty sure that's what brought me back. Kara's weave is one thing, but that…that was totally different."

"Jesus." Rogan scrubbed his face. "During the Surge—I dunno what I saw, but Jane was convinced there were powers beyond ours that could be harnessed. A fourth duality—"

"Yeah, and at that point she was certifiable," Cal muttered.

"Was she?" Rogan shot back. "She was right about Kara's talent, and so is Flynn. There has to be another power out there to balance hers."

"Well shit, McGuire, next you'll be telling me we can use them to reverse the whole damned cataclysm and forget about the past thousand years. I'll be due to clock in at Micky D's after class, and you'll be off fucking Lucy Wells in the milk shed before football practice."

Rogan stared at him for a long moment. "You know, you really are an asshole. Then and now."

Cal shrugged. "At least I'm consistent."

"To a fault."

Laughlin pushed off the counter. "So, neither of you knows shit about it."

"Not anymore than he's spilling," Rogan said sourly, looking at Cal. "Regardless, you think you've got enough of a handle on things for that plan of yours to work?"

"Yeah. I think so. You said you have bots?"

"I do. They're in the craft—"

"Wouldn't," Fitz blurted from by the port. He shrank back after the outburst, rubbing his forehead.

Nora put an arm across the back of her chair to face him. "Why not?"

"Eh…" He frowned, swallowing like he was going to be sick again. "Energy—talent—around him's still fucked and from what I seen, them pills amplify it. Dunno what that'll mean, but, eh…probably ain't gonna be good."

"It's also not going to be necessary," Cal said, setting his tablet down. "For whatever reason, Titus has stopped nullifying the laborium where the rendezvous point is. Pretty sure that's as close to an invitation as you're gonna get."

"More like he's baiting a trap." Rogan snorted.

"Doesn't matter. I'm positive Kara's waking up, and I need to be there when she does." Laughlin tossed his towel into the sink and met Nora's gaze. "I need an imprint of the laborium, and the rest of you to stay here."

Cal was oddly silent at the declaration, and Rogan ran a hand down the side of his head. He frowned like he wasn't comfortable with the idea. Nora wasn't either, but Laughlin's expression quashed any argument. She went to him, and gave him the imprint of the birthing facility's central courtyard.

"Now get Fitz to put that ward on you," Rogan said when they were done, "give him the imprint of where you think she is, and you're taking some bots with you, regardless. You get into a jam, use 'em."

The Fetch frowned. "S'a bad idea. Them fucking pills...even if ye don't take 'em and implode, Titus gets his grubby hands on 'em, and there'll be hell t'pay up north."

"He's got a point," Cal murmured.

How convenient that he abruptly had an opinion. Nora was sure it'd come about exactly at the same moment he'd figured out how to monetize the technology.

"Whatever happens, I can promise you Titus isn't gonna be a problem." Laughlin growled, the temperature in the room jumping several degrees. "Whether it's me imploding or tearing out his black heart, one way or another that fucker's dead."

"As His Majesty decrees." Fitz twirled his fingers near his brow in an irreverent salute and Laughlin glowered at him. The Fetch rolled his eyes. "Gimme yer hand." He took it in his and muttered something about a blessed saint as his halos flared. "There. Snap yer fingers t'break it."

Laughlin's brow cocked with a glimmer of amusement. "Snap my fingers?"

"Aye. Snap yer fingers, and I'll come running to save yer sorry arse." Fitz scowled. "They get ye in restraints and yer not gonna be able t'do aught else, ye idjit. Now gimme the fucking imprint—Christ, that's fucking depressing."

"No shit, you got it?"

The Fetch nodded, his jaw set.

"Then it's settled," Rogan said, slapping his hands on his thighs as he pushed his chair back and stood. "I'll run up with Flynn to get the bots, Nora, you and Fitz stay here, and while we're waiting on that ward to break, Cal and I've got some hunting to do."

Laughlin nodded, leaving the room. "Lemme get a shirt, and I'll meet you by the port."

"Are you really sure this is wise?" Nora asked when he was out of earshot.

"No." Rogan laughed, pulling on his jacket. "But it's all we've got at the moment, and besides, this kind of shit always makes the best stories."

Nora twisted her ring, staring at the Alpha's broad back as he went to join Laughlin. That may be true, but you had to be alive to tell them. She shook her head and went over to the counter to make herself another cup of tea. Maybe she'd actually drink this one.

Fitz was staring at the glowing strip of plaz running beneath the cabinets and grimacing. He chewed his lip, his halos scintillating with jagged flashes of light. She watched him askance as he murmured to himself, his fingers twitching closer to the strip.

"Didn't anybody ever tell you not to play with plaz?"

The Fetch jumped at Cal's question and jammed his hands into his pockets with his back to the counter. He ran a hand over his mouth and tugged the little patch of hair beneath his lip. "Eh…no?"

Nora huffed out a laugh. How he could look so guilty just standing there…

His eyes flicked to her, and he frowned. "Ain't never seen this shite up close before, and it's a goddamned nightmare. Were trying to figure out why it's so miserable."

"Because mellitic anhydride is an anomaly to begin with, and irradiating the shit out of it then spiking it with God knows what didn't do it any favors," Cal murmured, scrolling through his tablet. "Humanoids are typically immune to the field it puts out, though. Resonance usually only bothers lower life forms." He raised a brow at Fitz.

"Huh, and here I were thinkin' the contrary."

Cal snorted, his attention going back to the screen—"Shit."

"What is it?" Nora asked as he tossed the device on the table and pushed from his chair.

"A nullifying field just killed my shield over the craft." He stood and grabbed his jacket. She hurried to do the same. "Nora—"

She spun on him. "Do not even begin to think that you can dictate to me anymore, Caliban Scot. I'm going with you. Whoever's up there I can gain intel from, and I'm perfectly capable of taking care of myself." Her halos sparked, not above throwing a very specific bind over him to prove her point.

He held up his hands like he knew it. "Fine, but I'm cloaking you." He shook his head and turned to Fitz. "You want in on this, too?"

The Fetch was back to staring at the plaz strip. He absently shot Cal the bird and then glanced at Nora. "Eh…that is t'say, I'm fine here, thanks."

"Christ, hell must've frozen over when he's the only one showing any sense," Cal muttered.

Nora frowned, glancing back at Fitz as they headed out the port. Whatever the Fetch was up to, she doubted sense factored into any part of the equation.

MARCOS STEPPED through the gate and into the Assembly Hall, heading for Stonefist's office. The complex was just as empty as yesterday, but this time he attributed it to the beehive of activity outside the city.

Supplies had poured in throughout the night, and the speed at which things were happening was astounding. Talents, the unaffected, all of Glynfyls had pulled together to work toward the Overlord's directive.

Well, everyone except for the Binders loyal to Serra.

Unfortunately, that made up the lion's share of the hill and everyone from the Source, but the results were never-the-less impressive.

A rudimentary tent city had sprung up, and more permanent housing was being erected at a surprising pace. Unlike before, the Flats were being laid out beneath the Fixer's sharp eyes, with two clearly delineated rungs echoing those inside the city and a secondary, outlying wall being planned.

"Commandant, a moment?"

He turned and stopped, waiting for Markham to catch up with him. He was surprised the Fetch hadn't just shifted to the meeting. The big man huffed as he approached, mopping his brow. Dark circles rimmed his eyes. "Kyle. Busy night?"

"Indeed. I'd be lying if I said coordinating my line wasn't like herding cats, but they've finally got their marching orders."

"I'm assuming issuing them was the easy part."

Markham chuckled as they continued down the hall. "You'd be right. I'm afraid, as a whole, we don't tend to take direction well, but the Overlord's promise of recompense is a rather strong motivator. Before we get in there, I wanted to ask how your men are getting on with the Binders."

A broad smile bloomed over Marcos's face. "Better than expected, considering all the troops have been through. Pithy's released a few squads to help outside the gate. I'm just coming from introducing them to Stonefist. All of them are eager to contribute."

"Mmm. I can imagine." He ran his handkerchief over his lips, Marcos's response furrowing his brow.

"Something else on your mind?"

"That obvious is it?" Markham frowned. "I must admit, I'm a bit concerned about how Fitzpatrick is comporting himself."

"Poorly, if I had to guess. He's your what? Nephew?"

Markham sighed. "Yes, through marriage. He's Bernice's youngest sister's son, from her first marriage, and Laughlin's second cousin. The boy…" He paused as if trying to find the right words. "Fitzpatrick can be difficult."

"More like straight-up insubordinate." They both chuckled, and Marcos shook his head. "The way you keep track of relations up here is mind boggling."

"An entirely different mindset from the Source, I gather. I'm assuming you have children…forgive me if I'm overstepping, but I'm as flummoxed by your practices as you are by ours. Do you know any of them?"

"A few." Marcos prevaricated, starting up the steps. He wasn't about to claim Riegel, but... "Pax is the eldest of my living offspring that I'm aware of. He came in with the Breakers Titus left on the plateau."

"A son! How wonderful, you've an heir to your House."

Marcos's foot faltered on the next step, not having thought about that, but the warmth that accompanied it...he bit back a smile. "I suppose I do." Too bad he had no idea what his House actually was.

"Have you spoken to him about it?"

"No. Not yet. He stepped into my shoes when I fled the Source and has enough on his plate with the men right now." And from what Marcos had gathered, was the reason so many of them were still alive. Pride swelled his chest as he held the door to Stonefist's office open for the Fetch.

"I'd make it a point to. We never know how much time we've been allotted," Markham said in passing.

Marcos grunted in agreement, following him into the room and taking a seat.

As before, Jacques, Dorian, and Carl were there. Unfortunately, Crandall also sat at the table. Marcus adjusted his jacket, surprised not to see Serra after what he'd overheard this morning. It wasn't like her to concede defeat—

"Commandant," Jacques nodded his head in greeting. "Glad to see you; I heard you had a long night. How are the Breakers transitioning?"

Marcos fought the urge to glance at Crandall, not sure how far in bed he was with the rotten woman. There was no hiding the troops were up here, but as to the Binders' involvement... "Well. The most fit have been assigned to work crews and are eager to assist with the reconstruction of the Flats."

"Twitching already, are they?" Crandall asked.

And that answered that question. Marcos sucked in his cheeks at the jab. "I'd attribute it more to them recognizing their civic duty and not wanting to be a drain on society like some others I could name."

"Right, yes, moving on," Jacques said hurriedly. "Shall we—"

"From what I've seen, the lack of Binders engaging hasn't made much of a difference," Dorian interrupted. "Nor has the lack of Intelligencers beyond the wall." He didn't quite bat his lashes at Crandall, but it was close.

The man bared his teeth in return. "That's gratifying to hear, as we're quite busy dealing with the large uptick in crime. In fact, since you and that pathetic little network of yours have nothing better to do than lurk around job-sites, why don't you lend a hand and take over fielding all the missives from Madame Wence and her compatriots? She and the rest of the hill are up-in-arms over the current influx of petty crime and street walkers."

"Unfortunately, I agree that it is an issue," Carl said. "Someone knocked over a garbage can outside my flat, bold as brass. Can you imagine? Their gall is appalling."

"Street walkers? As in prostitutes?"

Crandall broke off scowling at Dorian to address Marcos. "The lower rungs of the Finders' spoke housed the city's former pleasure district, and it's been all but wiped out. There's nothing but a gaping hole where the Painted Pony used to be."

"Oddly apropos..." Jacques murmured.

Markham snickered, then swallowed it at Crandall's glare.

The Intelligencer took a deep breath and tongued his cheek. "We've also been looking into the inquest Carl filed regarding the assassination attempt on the Overlord, and I should mention that I've found an inconsistency of some note."

That got everyone's attention.

"An inconsistency?" Markham irritably blotted his chins. "The man attempted to murder the Overlord and was put down in his stead. Seems rather cut and dry to me."

"At first glance, perhaps." Crandall pursed his lips as he fiddled with a pen. "However, I find it interesting that Laughlin was shot thrice, yet only two of those bullets made it into the assassin. I also find it very interesting that the trajectory of Lord Morris's wound came from below, as opposed to above like the rest."

"I don't," Marcos said, reaching for his antacids. "Bullets ricochet."

"They do," Crandall nodded, "but rarely with enough force to blow apart a man's skull, go through the arm of another, and then imbed three-inches into the hardened maple rail behind him."

The men around the table fidgeted in their seats. Marcos popped a chalky tablet into his mouth and crunched it. Glory knew that toady little man had deserved to be shot, but to accuse Scot? He'd been bleeding out when Morris was struck. Marcos opened his mouth to say it wasn't possible, then bit his tongue. Who the hell knew what Scot was capable of?

And that was the problem, wasn't it? None of them could rule it out, and considering the animosity between the two men, Scot certainly had motive. Marcos ran a hand over his jaw. But then again, so did half the damned city given Morris's political views—

"What exactly are you alleging?" Carl asked, bringing Marcos's focus back to the table.

"Not a thing." The Intelligencer shrugged, the insincerity of that statement laughable. "I think I mentioned before, it's my job to present the facts, not to cast judgement."

"But you're perfectly fine with sowing incrimination, now aren't you?" Dorian glowered. "And what, might I ask, do you plan on doing with this 'inconsistency?'"

"Aside from conveying it to all of you, nothing for the moment." Crandall smiled. "I wouldn't want to do anything that might impede the city's newfound sense of solidarity."

"My God, you're a scoundrel," Markham spat.

Dorian snorted. "I'd go with something that's four letters and starts with—"

"Didn't you just recently protest the Overlord 'holding us all hostage?'"

Crandall's smile widened at Jacques. "The irony doesn't escape me, but think of it as quid pro quo, and as long as I remain an equal member at this table, my suspicions will remain my own."

Glory, he was repellent. Marcos popped the last of his antacids. He'd need to buy a case of them at this rate.

"Well, then," Jacques said into the loaded silence, "if Crandall's done swinging his dick around, how about we discuss what we came here for? Ah, Carl. I believe you're overseeing logistics?"

The Fixer turned from Crandall, shaking his head. "I am," he said. "We've been able to stabilize the land around the city and throughout the Finders' spoke. The supplies coming in are being utilized almost as quickly as they arrive. If we continue at the same pace, and barring any unforeseen calamity, I'm estimating that the need for housing will ease significantly within the next couple of weeks."

"Wonderful," Jacques said. "And has the damage report to the city been completed?"

"It has," Dorian answered with a quick glance at Crandall. "And as anticipated, the worst of it is on the lower rungs. Above the fourth, it's mostly cracked windows and broken china, unless you believe House Inasoll's claim that it caused a catastrophic leak in their fountain—"

Markham scoffed. "That eyesore's been leaking since I was in the Academy."

"You mean since you and your friends tried to blow it up."

"That's entirely hearsay," Markham shot back at Crandall.

The Intelligencer rolled his eyes.

"Aside from the numerous insurance claims on the hill," Dorian continued, glancing between the two, "on the municipal side, only minor street repair will be necessary. Below the fourth however, it's an entirely different story."

"Well, I suppose no good crisis ever goes to waste, now does it?" Markham said, eyeing Crandall.

"No, and if I might make a suggestion?" he asked. "With the amount of skilled labor we've drawn to our shores, it might be wise to offer an additional stipend for any that would take on an apprentice."

Marcos turned to look at him along with the rest of the table, wondering what'd motivated that bit of altruism. Was this the carrot after the stick?

The weaselly Intelligencer shrugged. "As much as I hate to admit it, the reconstruction of Glynfyls has the potential to be a boon for our lesser-served population. We might as well take advantage of it and perhaps lure some of them to more honest trades."

Markham frowned. "Yes…and secure their favor while we're at it, aye, Bart?"

"Aren't you the one always cautioning about riling the commons? It seems to me that economic stability would go a long way to smooth their feathers."

"And where do you envision these funds coming from?" Carl asked.

"I'm sure a fund could be set up, short of that—"

Jacques held up a hand, cutting Crandall off. "I know where this is going, and although I'm sure the Overlord would espouse the spirit of the initiative, I don't believe we should be eyeing his coffers to finance it."

"You didn't let me finish. I was going to say I see little reason not to gut the Binders' funding to do so." Crandall met the rest of their gazes squarely. "If they're not serving the populace, they shouldn't be receiving their tax dollars."

The rest of the table stared at him like he had two heads, and he blithely returned their stares. What game was he playing? After the way he and Serra had left the room yesterday, Marcos was sure they were in cahoots—

"Forgive me if I'm suspect of your motives," Markham finally said, breaking the silence.

"You're not the only one." Carl scrubbed a hand over his face, exasperated. "What the hell are you up to, Bart?"

Lord Crandall sucked in his cheeks. "I don't—"

"It's not him, it's the Ladies," Marcos said, putting two and two together. "I overheard them meeting with Serra this morning, and she basically told them all to pound sand when they asked her to toe the line."

That got everyone's attention.

"Well, then she won't be First for much longer," Jacques said with an air of finality. "And good riddance." The other men around the table murmured their agreement.

"Perhaps not, but given Serra's ambition, I don't expect her to go quietly," Crandall said sourly, not denying Marcos's allegation.

"Really?" Dorian asked. "Was that what the two of you were discussing when you left here yesterday?"

"Amongst other things." The Intelligencer sighed. "Now that she no longer has Morris's coattails to ride, she's looking for a new mark to manipulate. Apparently, I drew the short straw."

"Funny, I heard she was riding something else entirely," Dorian quipped. "Looking for sloppy seconds?"

Crandall snorted. "Hardly, but according to Lady Morris, you're not wrong, which is in large part why Evie's pushing for the apprentice program to come from the Binders' budget. Her and Augusta are quite close from their theater days."

Carl drummed his fingers against the table. "If the Ladies are behind it, I have to say I'm more in favor of the motion…at least until Serra's unseated. I'm fairly certain there was legal precedent set for reallocating funds during the Uprising."

"There was," Markham agreed. "And that should provide enough seed money to get the program off the ground and limit her influence."

The rationale was met with a volley of agreement, and Marcus couldn't help but chuckle imagining the look on Serra's face when she found her line bankrupt, but without her here to challenge their decision—

His smile faded as he glanced at the seat she'd claimed during the last meeting. Whatever she'd deemed important enough to keep her from it this morning, he was positive it was going to bite them.

SERRA SAT PRIMLY in her chair, dredging up the etiquette classes she'd largely ignored back when she was a pre-pube. Glory. If she'd know that she would need them now…there had to be some kind of manual for all this nonsense. She made a mental note to ask one of the servants back at the Pearl once she returned.

In the meantime, she needed to step carefully.

Lady Saks's morning room was a massive, echoing chamber of coffered dark wood ceilings and marble walls lined by tapestries. Serra had very little doubt they were pre-Surge. A dozen tall-backed chairs surrounded an elegant table set with silver and a tiered tray at the far end displaying a fine, if sparse, selection of pastries.

None of which had been offered to Serra.

Her stomach burbled, and she prayed no one heard it. Damn her nerves, but she hadn't been able to manage a morsel of her breakfast, and now she was paying the price.

If Lady Saks had heard it, she gave no indication; instead her laser-focus lay on a very pale young woman adding an exacting amount of sugar to the cup of tea before her. The harridan was completely serene, and apparently perfectly content to let Serra's agitation at her indifference grow. That was most assuredly by design, Lady Saks had used the same trick to disconcert her back at the theater.

Serra's nails dug into her palms as she fought to match the older woman's poise without letting her exhaustion show. Her eyes flicked to the hallway where propriety had relegated Otto to remain. Yet another lesson learned too late. Outfitting him as her manservant had done nothing to win him entry into the meeting, his sex barring him from inclusion. So much for exhausting herself healing him last night so he could pull off the role. Why he responded so poorly to her talent—

Lady Saks's gaze abruptly met Serra's before she murmured something to the girl. She curtsied in acknowledgment and used a pair of silver tongs to place a piece of shortbread on a plate, then added a dollop of ruby-red jam.

The harridan pursed her lips as it was set before her, as if loathe to begin discourse.

Serra could relate. It had been far too easy to secure an invitation to the woman's home, and the speed in which it was granted implied that what had tripped off Evie's foul tongue had already made it to Lady Saks's ears.

But how inclined would she be to believe rumor?

"I don't think I have to tell you why I've agreed to meet with you today, Lady Hess," Lady Saks began, dispensing with any pleasantries. "Disturbing rumors have reached my ears, and as I stated previously, my largesse is based solely upon your daughter's ability to further my House's goals."

"Yes, you were quite clear on that point, which is why I'm here." Serra fidgeted beneath the woman's steely gaze before she could stop herself. "These vile rumors circulating are incredibly hurtful. I've no idea why Lady Crandall would feel the need to spout such hatefulness."

"I can think of several reasons," Lady Saks deadpanned, using a knife and fork to dissect her shortbread. "And I've never known Evie to make a false accusation. If it were up to me, you'd already be out on your ear by virtue of her word alone." She took a delicate bite, and Serra was abruptly glad she hadn't been offered anything. There was no way she could've kept it down.

"However," Lady Saks continued, "Miles is besotted and being quite unreasonable. He requires absolute proof, so I've had my solicitor set up a fertility test, discreetly, of course. I would advise you to make sure Tamara is available. I want this settled by end of day."

"Of course." Serra smiled, the situation similar to what Otto had helped her circumvent at the Source.

Lady Saks's eyes narrowed. "I will also mention that your dalliance with the late Lord Morris did not go unnoticed—" She held up a hand cutting off Serra's protests. "From what I've been told, such behavior was not uncommon down south." Her lips pruned as she paused to flick her gaze over Serra. "But up here, enticing another woman's husband into your bed isn't something that is done." Her expression soured further. "Nor is being accompanied out and about with a manservant. It would serve you well to be more cognizant of our social forms, lest you unintentionally ostracize yourself from polite society. Culture shock only lasts for so long before it's willful dissent."

"Of course." Serra ducked her head to hide the gritting of her teeth and attempted to look contrite. "It won't happen again."

By the expression on Lady Saks's face, she shouldn't have bothered. "I should think not." She blotted her thin lips with a square of starched linen and looked to the wan serving maid. "Pru, please provide that odious little man in the hall with the appointment details as you show him and Serra out. I've correspondence to attend to."

Serra's eyes narrowed at the woman's abrupt dismissal, but she stood and curtsied. "I look forward to our next conversation, Lady Saks. Have a pleasant day."

The harridan dismissively flicked the fingers of her free hand, already skimming a missive from the pile of letters at her elbow.

Serra seethed as she bustled from the room. Otto stood just outside the door. When they reached the gate in the foyer, he collected an envelope from another serving girl, then helped Serra into her wrap. She gritted her teeth at the ermine as if it were somehow to blame for her situation then stepped through the cool stone arch and came out back at the inn.

She managed to maintain her decorum until the door to her suite closed behind Otto. "The nerve of that woman! How dare she talk that way to me, a Hess, and the First of my line!"

"There, there, Serra, I can't imagine she'll be dictating to you for much longer," Otto said, taking her wrap and brushing it out. He was a surprisingly efficient manservant.

"Why, what do you know?" she asked tearing the missive open. Glory. Tamara was expected on the other side of the city within the hour. Serra's gaze went to her daughter's bedroom, trying to remember if she'd come home last night. Damn Geraldine to Hell!

Otto hummed, scratching his patchy beard. Between that and the weight loss from his illness, she barely recognized him as the man on the "Wanted" posters still plastered about the city, and even less as the Binder she'd struck that fateful deal with back at the Source.

"I don't know for certain, but her voice was familiar. I think it's quite possible she was one of Titus's moles. I know he had several agents up here, though not who, specifically. He liked to keep us ignorant of each other."

"Is that so?" Serra plopped onto the settee. She fanned herself with the letter, her mind racing and coming up blackmail. "Then I propose you deal with the solicitor, whilst I handle Lady Saks." Serra smiled. "I can't begin to imagine what rumors of treason would do to *her* House's reputation."

Otto gave a small smile of his own and went to hang her wrap.

FITZ VAGUELY REGISTERED that the portlock had closed in the other room, his attention square on the clashing bits of energy pinging through the fixture in front of him. Gah, that were naught but bottled fuckin' misery. Chewin' his lip, he pulled more talent now that he were by his lonesome.

The shite were drivin' him mad.

He scratched his nape, brow furrowed. Energy-wise, everything had a pattern to it. This weren't no different, but laud. Chains was long and complex as hell, moving faster than they had any right to at cross purposes. Reminded him of one of them symphonies his da had taken him to up on the hill, but the strings was sped up t'sound like chipmunks on repeat and someone were playing a trumpet flat when it shoulda been sharp, half a beat too late.

That fuckin' bastard had t'go.

He reached out and tweaked the son of a bitch.

Soon as he did, a godawful hum kicked in, amplifying as the plaz surged, light flaring like a supernova. Fitz threw an arm over his face, stumbled back, then slapped his hands over his ears, light blinding white through his lids—

And Cajetan's laughter rippled through Fitz's mind as he were wrapped in velvet night.

CHAPTER THIRTEEN

"My foresight has paid off. I used the stone El left me to visit the twins in Meskill, presumably to check on En's progress. While I was there, I reinforced the tethers I'd made to their minds when I healed them previously. At the time, I told myself it was so I'd know if they tried to self-harm, but If I'm being honest, that was just an excuse to leash them. The twins are dangerous, their thoughts unbalanced cesspools of depravity.

What does it say about me, that I profess to be their friend?

I asked En to use his talent and find several probabilities for me. He's assured me I'll have a son with the ability to harness the fourth duality. Unfortunately, there are too many branches for his dice to determine the absolute success of resetting this reality. That will take more dedication, but the possibility is enough. Mother was speaking the truth, it can be done, if only I have the fortitude to see it through..."

– Undated journal entry

FLYNN KNEW something was wrong as soon as they opened the port to the roof. Seeing the lightstream ransacked and cloak-less confirmed it. Christ, shit was strewn all over the helipad.

"So much for Cal locking it up," Rogan muttered, striding over to the craft. He came out a few second later, swearing. "It doesn't look like they damaged any of the flight controls, but the cabin's been scoured, and the case with the bots is gone."

Flynn raked a hand through his hair. Goddamn it, he didn't have time for this shit.

"Go get Kara," Rogan said, like he'd read his mind. "I'll haul Cal's boney ass up here, and we'll take care of it. Worst case, I'll get Fitz to—"

A series of nullifiers kicked on, and Flynn flinched. The low hum of static that'd been at the edges of his consciousness rose up to meet it, muddling the screeching dissonance and drowning it out. He blinked hard, a hand at his temple—

"Wolf! That you, you stupid motherfucker?"

Jesus fucking Christ. Flynn stiffened at the voice, growling as he turned. The hard clack of guns racking followed the motion. Forget about Titus setting a trap, they'd walked right into this one.

"Victor." Asshole must've been waiting right by the port, the stupid thing still gaping wide. Aside from a weird rock stuck to his brow, the son of a bitch didn't look any worse the wear for having gotten bathed in his own fallout on the plateau. In fact, he looked fucking hale.

Man only came up to Flynn's breast bone, and he was easily as wide, that neon green mohawk of his standing straight up from his head like a shark's fin. A handful of Sons flanked him. How many men...talent prickled, and he spat the taste of chew from his mouth, finding more of the assholes on the surrounding bridges and rooftops—

Wait a minute, if a nullifier was running, how—

"That all you got to say?" the prick asked, pulling his bolo out from its harness and teasing the edge as he strode closer. The hate in his eyes was feral.

… *"What, no wiseass comments?"*

"Why bother? Half the time you're too fucking stupid to understand them."

"That a fact?" Victor grins, stepping toward him. Several hammers cock and his smile grew bigger. "Funny, I'm not the dumb fuck who just delivered himself to the chopping block." He sticks the point of his knife up under Flynn's chin. It slices into him, dull enough to sting. "But you always were

an arrogant son of a bitch. Tell me, shithead. How the fuck do you plan on getting out of this?"...

Flynn blinked, talent gathering around him, waiting.

... "Take the help we're offering...you're getting it whether you like it or not..."

Help. Where the fuck was he gonna get... He shook his head at another influx of static.

... "I'll be right out that door if you need me. I'm not going anywhere..."

He glanced at Rogan. "Actually, I got something to ask." Flynn wet his lips, calling a shield to protect himself and Rogan. The Breaker's gaze snapped to him as it settled over them, despite the nullifiers running. No clue how the hell that worked, but Flynn wasn't about to question it. "You got this?"

Rogan nodded, his grin vicious. "I do. Go get her."

Flynn called talent again, and shifted.

He materialized in a stark white hallway lit by flickering lights.

What the—he called talent again, and the shit laughed at him. Fucking Fetch—Goddamn it! Was this what Fitz had meant earlier about not directing the shift? No wonder that line was so fucking unreliable. Flynn tore at his beard, swearing. He blew out a breath and hung his head, hands on his hips.

How the hell did—fuck. It didn't matter. He just needed to find that courtyard and hoof it.

Little help?

Nothing. A laugh burbled from his lips. Great—no, fucking perfect. Just what he needed. To be lost somewhere in the middle of the goddamned Source with talent fucking with him. Christ. The universe did hate him. He raised his fingers to snap for Fitz and just stopped himself at the tromp of boots and low murmur of voices farther on.

The cadence of both was definitely not from the Outside.

A group of Titus's Elites rounded the corner farther down the hall. The hair on Flynn's nape rose at the biggest of them, his gut telling him to run, but there was nowhere to go.

Which left bullshit.

"Gentlemen," he said, spreading his hands at his sides. "I believe you were expecting—"

Faster than he could credit, they were around him. A meaty palm smashed his face into the wall, then wrenched his arms back. Shackles snapped around his wrists, hot breath searing across his cheek…

… A knife slides down the side of his face, his limbs held prone by Peacekeepers. He knows better than to struggle. His eyes stay on the one with the wine-colored birthmark wielding the blade. "You're awful pretty, Inmate 5462. Let's do something 'bout that"…

"Scot. Fancy seeing you here." Brix laughed. "Tell me you're gonna make this difficult, sweetheart."

Christ, he wanted to.

Flynn swallowed his 'lust, the phantom scar along his temple aching. He fought to pull zero, burying his clawing rage beneath it, the darkness in him howling. Kara. He had to cooperate to get to Kara. But as soon as he had her… "I'm here for my mate. As long as you're facilitating that, we're good."

"I wouldn't go that far," Brix drawled, running his tongue over a sharpened canine. He had plugs shoved up his nose. Christ, they all did. To mitigate pheromones, maybe? Was that even possible? "But we got time. Squeak! Let's take him down."

Two of the Elites spun Flynn around and jacked him up between them. A skinny Fetch slunk around the Breakers, and his halos flared.

Colors ran.

They shifted into a sterile white room, Flynn's sense of Kara overpowering. He turned toward it, and the Elites jerked him in the opposite direction.

"Not so fast, lover boy. Titus wants to see you, and I'd suggest you play ball if you want any hope of seeing your bitch." Brix grinned, thumbing his tactical knife. "Not that I'm opposed if you don't."

A growl welled up in Flynn's throat at the slur and the 'lust the prick was putting out.

No. Kara. He was here for Kara.

"Then let's get the meet and greet over with," he gritted out.

Brix's smile widened as he turned on his heel. They traversed two more hallways before stopping at a portlock. Brix scanned his barcode, and after a moment it rolled aside. The Elite ducked through the port and was in and out in under a minute, waggling two fingers for Flynn to follow.

… They lead him to a door in the bowels of the prison, the chains around his wrists and ankles clanking with each step. The damp is pervasive, iron-tinged and cold. His breath fogs as they pause, fingers on triggers. Another unlocks a cell with a round, reinforced port set into the floor. They push him in and slam the bars behind him. A lever is thrown, and the port rises. He gags. God, the smell…

Guns rack.

"Down you go, 5462. Thirty days starts now…"

Flynn blinked the memory away, his biceps trembling beneath the Elites' grip. One of them glanced at him askance, a bead of sweat tracking down his temple. Flynn laughed. Asshole was looking at him like he was a bomb.

Fuck, he wasn't far off.

No. Flynn blinked hard again. No, damn it. Play along, play along… Bile seared his throat as he stepped forward, ducking through the port like Brix had.

Titus lounged in his chair behind a Lucite desk, ankle over his knee with a crystal cut glass of something mahogany-colored. The red-headed asshole smiled and took a sip as Flynn came in. Man was far too fucking confident of his personal safety.

Titus grinned, just asking for a fist through his teeth. "Overlord Scot…or may I call you Laughlin?"

"It's Flynn," he growled, his control over his bloodlust slipping as he struggled to maintain zero. He glanced at Brix, but the Elite didn't so much as sniff. Had to be the nose plugs. Flynn took a shallow breath, not afforded the same.

The room reeked with the Elite's challenge, eroding Flynn's restraint. The darkness in him surged, fighting for ascendence, testing the cracks, pushing… Jesus, how many times had he thought about what he'd do if he had five minutes with either one of these assholes? It sure as fuck wasn't discussing his preferred nominative.

Blackness churned in his guts, whispering all the fucked up shit that used to get his dick hard. Talent swirled around him, at the ready—

No. He blew out a shaky breath, knuckles cracking. He needed to know what Titus had done to keep Kara and the babies alive. Until then, he had to play the prick's game.

"Flynn," Titus rolled the name around in his mouth like he was savoring it and adjusted his cock. Christ. Flynn snorted and looked away. Windows lined the far wall of the office, and he caught Titus's reflection in the glass, smirking.

"Brix, release his wrists, we're all friends here."

The Elite's expression said something entirely different, but he unhitched the mechanism keeping the manacles pinned behind Flynn's back. They snicked apart, and he rolled his shoulders, not bothering to test the cuffs for give. There wouldn't be any. He reached into his jacket pocket and pulled out a cigar, taking petty pleasure in Brix tensing up.

"Got a light?"

Titus motioned, and a wall panel slid to one side. A nude woman wearing a ball-gag hastened over, offering a book of matches. Jesus. That couldn't be comfortable. Flynn averted his eyes as he took them and grunted his thanks.

He lit his cigar and waved out the match. "What do I need to do to take my wife and kids home?"

"Not much for foreplay, are you?" Titus moued.

"I don't plan on getting fucked by you, so no." Flynn wandered over to the windows. Beyond them were vast subterranean fields, cultivated gardens, and sprawling trees. A sparkling ribbon of water snaked through low hills.

Damn. If it hadn't been for the plaz-lighting above, he would've sworn they were on the surface somewhere. The amount of capital and engineering this had to have taken was mind boggling. That Titus had done it entirely under the Corporation's—under Cal's—radar? Christ, it wasn't possible…but somehow, here it was.

And it was filled with female Breakers.

"Ah, I see you've found the Triam's bounty." The pride in Titus's voice turned Flynn's stomach. "Impressive, aren't they?"

"Sad, actually. In a perfect world, they'd be free."

"But this is my world, and the only thing it lacks is you studding for me." The man grinned. "Choose as many as you like. They're all at your disposal."

"The only woman I'm interested in is my wife, and I want to see her, now." Flynn growled. Christ, that this piece of shit could offer up people like fucking property—

"About that..." Titus threw up a holo of Kara's metrics. "When she arrived she was in a critical state; nowhere near the established baseline for successful gestation. If she'd remained in the North, she'd be dead and the litter with her. Frankly, they should've been weeks ago."

...*"You really believe it, don't you? That you're gonna die."*

She couldn't hold his gaze. "I...there's no balance to this, Flynn. It feels wrong..."

Flynn chewed his cigar, fighting to keep his expression bland. Kara had been right, and he hadn't listened. Hadn't wanted to. Guilt ate at his insides, but seeing it all laid out in black and white aside, the prick wasn't telling him anything he didn't already know on some level. He shoved down his pang of conscience to refocus on the here and now.

"So you're telling me that if I walk out of here with them, they'll die."

Titus's grin widened. "I find it fascinating that you think you can just walk out of here, but yes, that's what I'm saying. Neither her nor the litter will survive without the continuous medical intervention that only I can provide, and I've already incurred substantial overhead whilst doing so. The cost of their nutritionals alone would bankrupt a small nation, but up until your shield interrupted delivery, they were meeting their developmental milestones. Now..." Titus templed his fingers and shrugged.

Flynn's eyes narrowed. "Now?"

"Now we negotiate terms."

"Not until I see—"

The portlock rolled to one side, and a dusky man with close-cropped white hair strode in with a tablet, followed by a woman with long, chiming braids. That had to be the twins.

"Titus, have you seen the readings coming from the Source? The facility's plaz-reserves—oh, hello..." Enoch stopped dead in his tracks, his odd, azure eyes sweeping over Flynn.

... Guards open the gate for the yard, and the barrel of a gun presses between his shoulder blades. Another racks close to his ear. "Get in and present your wrists through the bars."

He does as he's told, and they release his manacles. From across the yard, there's a low whistle...

Flynn took another drag of his cigar, pushing down the darkness rushing to meet Enoch's predatory gaze. Rogan hadn't been kidding. The last time a man had looked at Flynn like that, it hadn't ended well. If he'd laid one finger on Kara—

Elize sauntered closer to Flynn and raised her hand to his cheek.

He stepped back. "Don't."

"No?" She quirked her brow, a coy smile flitting over her lips. Both the twins had one of those weird crystals set into their brows like Victor, but his had been a funny yellow. These were purple, like Finder talent. What the hell was that about?

"No."

"Pity. You are extraordinary." She circled around him, her braids chiming, tempting him to wrap them around her throat and pull. His knuckles cracked, the darkness in him rising again, static crackling...

... A body lies at his feet. Dark fingers trail over his blood stippled skin. Lush red lips at his ear. Her hand drops to stroke him, and he groans.

Her lips quirk. "Good boy..."

Flynn pushed the memory away, the hair on his nape rising as Elize stopped before him, eyes knowing, like she'd seen what'd just played through his mind.

"You don't look a thing like Alister, though I can see plenty of Rogan. Don't you think so?" she asked Enoch over her shoulder.

"I do," he purred, sending another chill through Flynn. Rabid didn't come close to whatever Enoch had going on. "Where are our old friends? I can't imagine why they'd spurn our invitation to come down and play."

"They asked me to deliver one of their own. Something about a hunt back at the Source."

Enoch laughed, flicking a crescent blade from his belt, and Flynn bit back a growl. Dude was feral as fuck. "How delightful. Well, no time like the present. What do you say, Elize? Do you think we can get permission from Mother?"

Flynn's brow furrowed. What a fucking weirdo.

"Mmm." Elize hummed, running her fingers over the gem at her brow. Amethyst halos shimmered around her irises, and a whisper of a Finder talent skittered over Flynn. A shield rose up to meet it before he could react, and she pursed her lips, but didn't out him.

Not yet anyway.

Titus cleared his throat, his eyes narrowing. "We can continue this later. Brix, show Scot to the gestation chamber. Make sure Yu explains the precariousness of the bitch's position to him." Flynn bristled and Titus smiled.

Great. Couldn't wait to find out what that was about. Brix headed to the port, and Flynn grunted, following in the Elite's wake.

"I don't have to tell you that their survival is dependent upon your good behavior, do I?" Titus called after him.

"That was implied," Flynn said, the spot between his shoulders itching as he put his back to the twins. The port closed behind him, and he breathed a sigh of relief. It wasn't long-lived. Ahead, Brix lumbered down the sterile white hall, his 'lust leaving a foul trail Flynn could've followed with his eyes closed.

He ran a hand under his nose and frowned, keeping pace with the prick. They retraced their earlier steps and passed the room where they'd come in. Another turn and Brix pushed through two double doors into a hallway lined with silvered panes of plex. He stopped to scan his barcode at another port, and it rolled aside.

"In here," he growled, ducking through.

It was the room Flynn had gotten glimpses of, but the plaz-screens lining the walls were dark and the gurneys with Breaker females gone, save for one at the far end of the room.

Kara.

He pushed past the Elite and went to her. She lay prone amid a jumble of tubes and wires, her face serene. Flynn pulled over a wheeled stool, the shield around her dissipating and his stomach wrenching as he took her hand. A machine sprang to life and the steady beat of her heart punctuated the silence. He kissed her knuckles above an IV port, his eyes closing at the scent of her skin. Jesus fuck, he'd missed her…

"I'm here, baby. I'm here," he rumbled softly, feeling eyes on him and not caring. "I'm gonna make this right, I swear I am." He lay his palm on her distended abdomen, biting back a sob as the life within rocked against it, wrestling to be closer to him.

God, the babies felt strong. Whatever Titus had been doing, he needed to keep doing it until they were here. Flynn's gaze traced the myriad of tubes. They ran to a bank of monitors, lights flickering, and the hiss of pumps actuating behind panels. A bank of IV bags hung to one side, just beginning to drip.

… He stands in the mud, grass trampled beneath the ebbing crowd. Rain patters over the sea of black umbrellas surrounding the casket. A rising staccato percussion, one last song, a dirge. Her voice teases the edge of his hearing, weaving an aria in accompaniment —

He'd never hear her sing again…

His grip on Kara's hand tightened, emotion undoing him. He sniffled, pressing her palm to his cheek, then kissed it. This. This was why he had to play Titus's game. He wouldn't lose anyone else.

He couldn't.

Flynn turned at the hiss of the portlock opening. A rotund, older woman wearing scrubs and a lab coat and bustled in.

"Ah, BrE2. I've been told to advise you your lab privileges have been revoked. Your bitch's levels crashed after your last visit, and Titus isn't willing to sacrifice a litter for your whims. If you have issue with that, I suggest you take it up with him."

Brix grunted and stormed out.

The woman's eyes flicked to Flynn's, then back to her tablet. "Mr. Scot, I presume?"

He wiped his face against his shoulder and blinked the tears from his eyes. "Yeah."

She nodded curtly. "Doctor Yu. I'm supposed to tell you how lucky you are she was brought in, but I'd hazard that's a given." Her gaze roamed over his face and lingered on his beard. "Interesting. I've never met a wild Talent…not a male one at any rate."

Flynn frowned, letting that last comment slide. "What is all this she's hooked up to?"

"Nutritionals, mostly. Growth stimulant. She was severely malnourished when she came in, and the litter wasn't meeting its milestones. You're fortunate Patron Titus deemed her worthy of his attention. She wouldn't be alive, otherwise."

"So I've been told."

"Then I suggest you show some respect." Yu raised a steely brow. "I've been doing this for well over forty years, and I've never seen a bitch this deficient keep breathing, never mind support a pregnancy on so little reserves. Patron Titus's breadth of knowledge, his skill—no one else could've done what he's doing here. I would've culled her and not even attempted to save the litter, then or now. With what the greedy little things are pulling from her, her physiology is too unstable."

Flynn gritted his teeth at the fan-girling cunt. There was only one bitch in this room, and it wasn't his wife. "Her name is Kara."

"I'm aware." Yu made a few entries into her tablet, and a nearby screen lit up, populating with the babies' vitals and Kara's metrics. "And as much as I appreciate the opportunity to observe Patron Titus's skill, I very much doubt this litter will be as robust as it could've been. You've only yourself to blame for that."

"As you can see from the x-ray, the joint is completely crushed. You'll never walk again. You need to take quality of life into account. What can yours possibly be? The Outside is no place for a cripple. Euthanasia is a valid service we provide free of charge through a grant from the Source…"

Shit hadn't been true then, and it wasn't true now.

Flynn bit his cheek so hard it bled, breathing through his fury at the woman's callousness. The temperature in the lab rose, a sensor by the door flashing orange. It was mirrored on Yu's tablet. She frowned at it and made another entry.

"So…forty years, huh? All of that here?" he asked, struggling to keep his tone neutral and tamp down his temper. Calm. He needed to stay calm. The babies were vibing off him, and the plot showing their movement had started to look like a seismograph. The woman's sharp eyes caught it and made another note.

"Mmm." Her fingers flew across the screen, and the numbers on the monitor jumped. Pumps actuated and a steady hum kicked on in the background, the babies settling.

Jesus, that she could do that so goddamned easily…bile rose in his throat again. "How long will she need to stay on all this?"

"You ask a lot of questions for someone being granted a privilege contingent upon good behavior. That includes not making a nuisance of yourself."

Flynn's knuckles whitened, the urge to rip the good doctor's throat out overpowering. He breathed through his rage, hoping to hell she didn't pick up on how close she was to being eviscerated. "I'm trying to understand the precariousness of her position," he bit out.

She stared back at him like he was a specimen she was having trouble categorizing.

"I thought I was clear," the woman finally relented. "With the amount of accelerant she's on, I'd imagine she'll whelp within the next day or two, and then that will be that."

Dread lanced up Flynn's spine, not wanting to know what "that" was. "Accelerant?"

"Mmm."

God, he wanted to fucking strangle her.

The temperature jumped another several degrees, and she furrowed her brow at him. "Fascinating. Is temperature manipulation something Shades do? I must admit, I've never seen one of your kind. I can't wait to get you up on the examination table."

He snorted. Fat fucking chance that was gonna happen.

"To answer your question, accelerant essentially makes the third trimester unnecessary. The caveat is that she and the litter will require exponentially higher doses of nutritionals until she whelps…" Her brow knit again, and she made several more entries, then shook her head at the numbers scrolling across her tablet. "What is Titus…this does not fall into best practices. We're going to need a Fixer down here on call…"

Fuck, that didn't sound good. Flynn took a deep breath, trying to swallow his rising panic. "Why's that?"

She shot him an irritated glance. "Typically, these levels of accelerant aren't used so close to birth, but it's a fine line. The half-life needs to last long enough to bolster the litter's development once out of the womb to reduce the need for incubation, but its effects on the host are…rather spectacular. The continuation of the protocol in her chart—"

"It will kill her, won't it?" Flynn growled, a black rage washing over him with his certainty. That motherfucker.

Yu took a step back. "No, Mr. Scot. Whelping the litter will do that."

"No, that's what you'll do, because Titus fucked with their genetics and keeps them from their mates!" he roared. Where the hell was that prick—"Titus!" Flynn yelled, sure the asshole was listening.

There was a long pause, and a communications orb sprang up. The patron's disembodied voice pulsed out of the swirling blue mist. "Laughlin. Have you seen enough?"

"Yeah, and I want Kara out of stasis." The babies needed her. He needed her. And he'd be damned if he let this shit show go on any longer. He was done trying to play Titus's game. He'd had it rigged, and Flynn wasn't about to let the motherfucker win.

… *"Source Breakers don't survive pregnancy, Flynn. Rogan said—"*

Rage contorts his face, and she flinches back. "You did this because of that asshole filling your head with shit? You're a Binder, a Breaker, a goddamned UnMaker, the fuck you're gonna die! I brought you back from the bloodlust, and I'll be damned before I believe that goddamned prick or anyone else. Christ, Kara, there's never been a Talent like you, how the fuck can anyone apply a blanket statement like that? How can you believe them?"…

He didn't. Wouldn't. He was gonna make this right, and between him and Nora, they'd figure it out.

Yu chuckled, snapping him back then caught the look on his face. A look of alarm passed over hers. "You're serious? Impossible. She'll become uncontrollable, if not when she wakes, as soon as slide kicks in."

"No. She won't. Wake her up, now."

"I really must object—"

"Wheel her into one of the birthing cubes and give her a dose of 45r3-18," Titus said over the woman's objections. "I'm curious to see what will happen."

The woman stood with her mouth open before shaking her head like she'd bitten back another protest, then made several entries into her tablet. She shot Flynn a dirty look and began unhooking Kara from the machines. "As I said earlier, you've only yourself to blame. You can at least help me push her."

Flynn took the head of the gurney, his conviction growing that Nora would be able to handle things if Titus was amiable to taking Kara off of whatever she and the babies were on. He and Yu wheeled the gurney down the hall into an empty square room. A piece of two-way mirrored plex took up one wall, and a drain was in the center of the floor. Static rose around him at the discordance of a nullifier, drowning it out.

Yu injected something into the IV port on the back of Kara's hand. "She should wake in the next few minutes," she said, quickly backing from the room. "It's a pity, you're a handsome one. I'll enjoy doing your autopsy."

Not as much as he was going to enjoy putting Titus on a slab.

The port closed, and the rapid thud of security bars dropping followed in its wake.

Flynn sat on the side of the gurney and took Kara's hand, his thumb sweeping over her knuckles. Her expression tightened, like she was having a troubling dream. Emotion began to filter through their bond again, fractured and frantic.

…"Kara…" He puts his hands on her cheeks and searches her eyes, trying to make her see him.

The rage of a trapped animal glares out.

He chokes back a sob. "Christ, you need to snap out of it! Don't…don't leave me." He presses his lips to her forehead, sending emotion through their bond…

No. Not again. He wasn't going to lose her to bloodlust. He pushed her the waltz playing in his head, his love, his concern, a constant stream of emotion for her to hold on to as she found her way back to him. Her breathing sped up and he leaned closer, smoothing the little triangle between her brows. "Shh…it's okay, baby. I'm here…"

He held his breath as her lids fluttered. They snapped open, and he bit back a sob at the recognition in her eyes. "Flynn? Oh Glory, where

—" Her gaze dropped her abdomen, then darted around the room. Anxiety flooded their bond.

"Shh…it's okay. We're in the Triam."

"The Triam!" She went to sit, then cried out at the sudden movement, a hand on her abdomen as he helped her struggle upright. "No! We can't, Titus—"

"Is watching and listening to everything we're saying." Christ, her terror and confusion—but the feel of her again—static picked up, tangible against his skin and she paled, her hand to her mouth like she was about to be sick. The scent of her bloodlust thickened with her panic.

He gripped her shoulders, his 'lust rising in response. "Kara—Kara! *Look at me.*"

Her gaze snapped to his at the Alpha command, breast heaving and eyes wild. That darkness he knew all too well flickered in their depths. Not a chance it was fucking taking her again. He ran the back of his hand down her cheek, leaned in, and kissed her.

Flynn groaned at her little gasp, her lips so sweet against his, opening to accept his tongue. The taste of her…He tangled his fingers in her hair, reveling in the feel of her, her emotions steadying. The flavor of her 'lust changed, edging from the darkness. His cock stirred as her arms wrapped around his neck, nails teasing his scalp—

Christ, he'd missed her, but this was not the time or the fucking place to do all the shit he wanted to. Reluctantly, he pulled away, his forehead resting against hers. She gazed into his eyes, so fucking beautiful, so goddamned trusting.

He wasn't gonna fuck this up.

"Tell me what happened."

Flynn took a deep breath, and began.

ELIZE WATCHED the exchange between Scot and the girl with a hollow pang, Mother's presence suspiciously absent from her mind after giving her consent for them to go topside. Something about the way Scot held the girl, how he looked into her eyes…

Enoch cleared his throat, and she glanced up to see his raised brow. She scowled, flicking her braids over her shoulder.

"Are you quite done ogling the man?" he asked.

"Oh, fuck you."

Enoch grinned. "Crass. I like it."

She shook her head. Heaven help her, but Laughlin Scot was exquisite. They hadn't run across a Battle Shade in over seven hundred years, and he was a prime specimen. She'd always found it to be an intoxicating mix, and with Rogan's looks and Cal's charm? Scot definitely ranked as one of the most attractive men she'd seen throughout her very long lifetime.

Why shouldn't she be a bit enamored? And despite his nonchalance, by the way Enoch's hand was straying to his blade, he was as well. The throb of his pulse was evident from across the room. He wanted the boy even more than she did.

"I suppose I'm just surprised," she said with a laugh. "I thought he was going to roll in here in a cloud of fire and brimstone."

"Laughlin Scot is a great many things but stupid isn't one of them. He's well aware her survival is at my sufferance—even so, I will admit, his compliance is concerning...among other things." Titus frowned at the holo.

The metrics streaming from the girl had abruptly gone dark after a wash of talent had ridden over her. Now she was curled against Scot's chest, her eyes closed as he murmured in her ear. Something in Elize rose up, choking her. Not a memory, but—

"He dispersed the shield in the other room," Enoch said, disrupting her musings. "Don't you have him nullified?"

"Yes, and there's additional units running in the birthing cube." Titus sipped his drink, seemingly unconcerned. "But I'm assuming they'll be just as ineffective, considering he's just managed to clear my bots from the girl. I can't say that I'm surprised. Scot delights in defying expectation."

Elize's gaze flicked to the holo with the numbers from his vector sensors fluctuating wildly. That storm she'd sensed back in Glynfyls... it was here, and all that was left for it to do was break. Her eyes narrowed. She didn't share Titus's indifference, but his nonchalance did peak her curiosity. "That doesn't concern you?"

"No. Not with what I've set in motion."

Elize shared a glance with Enoch before their eyes went back to the holo. Scot's voice rumbled as he tenderly brushed the girl's hair back from her face, his cheeks wet.

Titus scoffed and called for another drink.

"Something else amiss?" Elize asked.

"All that power, and he sets it aside to chase after a spent bitch."

Something in Elize's breast tightened. "He's in love."

"Useless emotion," Titus muttered, a finger over his lips. "It's a weakness the next iteration won't be bothered by."

"I'd advise you to rethink that." Elize's brows furrowed, remembering the chaos after the Surge. That particular breed of Breaker had been hunted down and snuffed out early on. That Titus wanted to bring it back… "Their humanity is the only governor they have. Without it, all that's left is bloodlust."

"With the proper Alpha at the helm, I don't see that as an issue."

But it would be, because the hierarchy didn't work without honor. Elize held her tongue and refocused on the holo. Once Mother reset the Surge, it wouldn't matter.

"He is totally devoted to the girl, isn't he?" Enoch remarked. "You're right, it is his weakness. The one most easily exploited, at any rate." He stood, stretching. "Good luck with that. We've a hunt to attend. Are you ready Elize?"

"I am." She smiled at Titus, wondering at Mother's absence. "Don't wait up for us."

Titus snorted, still scowling at the holo. Elize tapped her lips with the tip of a braid, taking one last look at the scene playing out. The sentiment on Laughlin's face was wrenching. Cal had never been so easy to read.

Enoch was right. This boy's emotions would be his undoing. Just like Rogan's had been.

ROGAN GRINNED at the Sons surrounding him on the roof. The look on their goddamned faces when Flynn shifted out... Shit, where the hell was a camera when you needed one?

"The fuck did he go?" the dopey one in a blue beanie asked.

"He had more important shit to do," Rogan said, cracking his knuckles and ignoring the red laser points clustered over his chest. "Now, what can I assist you ladies with?"

The one Flynn had called Victor laughed, flashing gold-foiled canines. Rest of his teeth were stained shit brown, probably from the chew bulging his bottom lip. Rogan's eyes narrowed at the crystal between the prick's brows. Where had he seen something like that before?

"None of you dirty fucking Talents got any idea who the hell he is, do you?" The man grinned, and it wasn't pretty.

"You might be surprised," Rogan said, collecting the power that was streaming through him. If not about Flynn, they'd definitely be surprised when their nullifiers didn't work. "Why don't you tell me who you think he is?"

Victor spat out a stream of noxious brown sludge, splattering Rogan's boots. Asshole. "Wolf?" The men around him snickered. "Before he turned coat, motherfucker used to scourge for us. You know what that means, Breaker boy?"

Rogan grunted. He did, and his heart hurt for the kid. Scourges were the Sons tasked with hunting down and exterminating Talents. Damn. That kind of self-hatred never sat well. No wonder Flynn was such a fucking mess.

Been there, done that.

"I do, and can't say I particularly give a shit. We finished?" Rogan's eyes flicked to the open port, the barest shadow of movement catching his eye. No shit. He bit back a smile at Cal joining the party. Damn, it'd been ages since they'd worked a crowd together. Asshole better not've lost his edge.

"Finished?" Victor teased the edge of his bolo, the rest of the Sons tightening their circle around Rogan. "No, I'm pretty sure this is the part where you start screaming."

"And I'm pretty sure your ability to read a situation is for shit."

Rogan pulled talent, sending curtains of flame around the rooftop and surrounding buildings. Sons panicked, scattering from the blaze. Victor snarled, lunging forward, and Rogan threw a punch, cracking the prick's head back.

As he staggered, two of the other Sons rushed Rogan. He disarmed one and snapped the neck of another, flipped the gun the Son had been holding and fired, blowing a hole through the second, then another through the lone sniper left on a far rooftop. Two more tried to disappear down the fire escape, and bounced off Cal's shield. A pair of bullets put them down.

The last fell to his knees, eyes wide, clutching his chest before he pitched to the side and lay still.

"Goddamn it, I forgot how messy that is," Cal bitched, popping back into view with the Son's heart in his fist. He dropped the gory organ and bent to wipe his hand on the fallen man's shirt.

Rogan snorted, scanning the rooftops above the flames. Whatever reinforcements had been there, weren't now. "Bigoted cowards—"

A high-pitched scream split the air, then cut off sharply.

"Who the hell was that?"—Shit, Victor wasn't with the men that they'd ended—

"That?" Cal lit a cigarette and blew out a cloud of smoke. "Don't know his name, but I'm pretty sure Nora's responsible."

"Nora?" Was he fucking joke—Rogan did a double take as she pushed the whimpering man out of the port in front of her, her mouth pressed into a thin line. Victor screamed again and collapsed, spasming.

"They have no idea what they took from the craft, but unless someone's moved it, it's piled in the next building's auditorium," Nora said, huffing an errant strand of hair from her eyes. "He has more men over there, and there's several hundred stationed throughout the Source. More are en route." Her halos flared, and he screamed again, vomiting and clutching his nuts. "This was going to be the Sons' new base of operations."

Damn. Rogan blinked. This was a side of Nora Jester he hadn't seen before. No wonder Marcos was so whipped. Shit was hot as hell. "And Fitz?"

"Still downstairs. When the Sons' nullified my cloak, he opted to play with the lights, but she refused to stay put," Cal muttered, visibly agitated. He exhaled another plume. "Some shit about gathering intel."

Rogan's gaze dropped to the nasty little prick at her feet. That weird crystal that'd been on his forehead was gone, a bloody hole gaping where it'd been. His gaze skipped over the roof. Must've fallen off...but damn. Something about that... "There was a rock on his forehead, some kind of crystal. You know anything about it?"

"Yeah, Elize's got one. Some new-age religious thing out of the South," Cal spat, his lips pruning. Rogan grunted. Sounded about right. The twins had always been into hippy-dippy ohm.

"There's gaps...holes," Nora said, bringing their attention back to her. Woman's expression was ice, her halos glittering. She frowned. "Recent ones. His mind's been tampered with, but..." She dropped talent and rubbed her brow.

"But...?" Rogan prompted.

"It's like memories were torn from his head just now, but there's no one else here, and I didn't sense any Binder talent being used. Whoever did this couldn't have expected him to function after, and the bits of coercion that were left..." She shook her head. "The signature of the constructs are similar to Otto's, but they're far more refined than his work, which means there's a rogue Binder out here, blood-related to him, and they're far more skilled than I."

Rogan did a double-take as Cal paled in his peripheral. "You got any idea of who—"

"No, but thanks to you lighting the beacons across the Rohim or whatever the fuck it was, they know right where to find us." Cal's eyes flicked to Nora. "We need to get her inside."

Rogan grunted, toeing Victor. "I'm assuming you're done with this?"

"I am," Nora said coldly, not flinching when Rogan sent a bullet through the Son's skull.

Cal paused with his cigarette half way to his lips. "You hear that?"

"Hear wha—"

A hum like enraged bees grew to swallow all other sound, every light in the facility flaring a thousand times brighter—

Then died. An unnatural silence followed, every system in the Source completely defunct. The three looked at each other, then spoke as one.

"Fitz."

HIS EYES FLEW open at his name.

Shite.

"Oh, thank the Gods." A vision in white looked down at him.

"Sophia?" Where the fuck has his peach come from? He raised a hand to tuck a tendril of midnight hair behind her ear.

A delicate blush stained her cheeks, then she scowled. "What did you do?"

"Eh…Dunno? What've ye heard?" Christ, what had he done?

Sophia pushed back on her knees. "Nothing, it's what I saw. The paths were fixed, and then all of a sudden a new path shot out, and—and here you are!"

He winced, his head aching somewhat fierce. Above them, the branches of a massive tree spread in a vibrant canopy. Colors too damned sharp, and somewhat off with the sky beyond. Black were too inky t'be natural, and it felt like all them little points of lights was lookin' at him. He sat up wincing, a hand to his head, and shot them the bird.

Sophia shoved it down with a little gasp, and he grinned. Liked that, but where the fuck was they?

Save for the tree, weren't naught else t'be seen but wide stone pavers, and a broken arch just beyond. Thick, green mist flowed around them in sluggish currents, the faint scent of licorice teasing his nose. His throat bobbed. Couldn't say he missed the racket he just come from, but damn, it were quiet. Wherever they was, he'd bet good money it weren't no earthly realm. Messin' with that plaz must've blown him to straight to—nah, it'd be a sight hotter, and not a chance his little peach'd earned that hereafter.

"Where are we?"

"The astral—" She clammed up quick, glancing around and stood. "Someplace you aren't supposed to be, and you need to go back, now."

Fitz got to his feet, light-headed. "Sec." He wobbled, woozy. "The fuck do ye have on?"

She flushed again, her arms wrapping around herself and perking up them generous breasts of hers. "Initiate's robes."

His gaze ran over her. The hell if that were any robe he'd ever seen. Were like someone had cut arm holes in a gossamer bed sheet and crisscrossed it over her body, the back draped down low, just brushing the top of her rear, and the fabric in the front were so sheer he could see the pink tips of her breasts and the dark triangle betwixt her thighs. He wet his lips, not much caring where they was anymore.

"Stop looking at me like that," she huffed, hooking that tendril of hair behind her ear again, the rest done up all fine with combs. "It's ceremonial. No one's supposed to see it."

"Ain't no way I'm gonna unsee it," he murmured, pulling her close. With that visual in his book of memories, he could die happy…or be happy he were dead. "Eh…ye said astral, that like a dream?" His hand smoothed down her bare spine. This sure as hell were fulfilling one of his.

She made one of them little gasps again, and his dick jumped. Christ, she were beautiful. He ran his hand over the curve of her hip. Lush. Soft in all the right places.

"K-kind of? We're not physically here, just our consciousnesses."

"Then this ain't real…" Which meant he could have his cake and eat it, too. Weren't like he were breaking his rule about hillies. Dreams didn't count, and if he bent her over here, maybe he could get her out of his mind when he were awake. He lowered his face to hers, more than ready to taste a piece of this little witch.

"Yes, it—Fitz?" she whispered, looking up at him all winsome, hands flat against his chest. "Are you going to kiss me?"

"Nah, love, I'm gonna eat ye up."

Jesus, Mary, and Joseph, that fuckin' blush killed him. He pressed his lips to hers, and it were like fireworks went off in his brain. Soft. Her lips was so damned soft. She fisted his shirt, and gave a little moan that about made him lose all reason.

Fuck, he had lost all reason; he were kissing a witch.

Were a dream. Didn't count.

He swept his tongue over the seam of her lips, and she pulled back a tick before parting them for him. Fitz groaned, swallowing her gasp as he licked into her mouth, his fingers in her hair and dimpling her rear. He pressed his cock against her belly, and she gave another little cry. Bet she were a screamer. Jesus fuck, he wanted to find out.

Her breath sped, kisses unsure, then firmer. Her tongue met his, and he deepened the kiss, moving his hand to cup her breast, nipple hardening against his palm. He tugged it, wishing it were his teeth. Christ, she made him crazy—

She pushed him away panting, her pupils wide, and put a hand to her lips.

Shite. He struggled to slow his own ragged breathing. "Ye alright?"

Sophia nodded. "I-I just...I've never been kissed—um, like that before, I mean."

He wet his lips, gaze dropping to the pointed tips of her breasts poking up that gossamer robe, screaming his name. Fuck, he wanted his mouth on 'em. "Good, 'cause I'd be scrambled ham if ye did." This little witch...the thought of some other bloke's hands on her made him mental. Nah, fuck that. He ducked his head back toward hers, needing to claim her mouth with his, shite, needing to claim all of her—

"Scrambled ham?" she asked, stopping him.

"Eh...out of me mind."

Sophia looked oddly pleased about that, then pulled farther away, her eyes narrowed. "Are you lying?"

"Nah, love. I'd kill the fucker."

She laughed like he were joking. He weren't. "You're trouble, Fitzpatrick McCreedy."

"S'Fitz," he murmured, stealing another kiss and a handful of bliss. Damn, her tits was perfect. Wanting this woman were gonna kill him. What the fuck were it about her? He couldn't get enough. "And I think ye like it."

"I think I like you," she said, removing his hand. "Despite my better judgement."

He put it right back, a wide grin split his face. "Ya?"

"Yes." She ran her fingers through his curls, and he about purred like a big cat. Jesus, this woman… He chewed his lip, pushing down the part of him that were screaming at him that she were a witch—a hillie!—and he were out of his damned mind. Knew it. Didn't care, and it were a dream right? Didn't matter if he acted a right fool, she'd never know.

"You really can't be here, Fitz. You need to go home."

"Tell me ye'll see me again," he murmured, his forehead to hers.

Sophia laughed. "I don't think I could keep you away if I tried."

She weren't wrong, and dream or no, he had the abrupt urge to keep tabs. He grunted and shifted one of the tiny hoops from his ear to hers, warding it. She put a hand to it, her brows furrowed. Looked right fetching, it did. "In case one of them hillie fucks tries t'kiss ye. Twist that thrice, and I'll come beat their arse."

She bit back a smile. "You're sweet, but no one is going to try to kiss me, and if they did, I'm pretty sure my brother will be first in line to put them in their place."

Fitz scratched the back of his head. "Eh…he a big bloke?"

Sophia laughed. "His shoulders are broader than yours, but he's not as tall. Don't worry, I don't make it a practice to tell him who I'm kissing, and there's only one person on that list."

"For true?"

"For true." His lips met hers again, and then she sighed, reaching up to brush the curls back from his face. "Goodbye, Fitz."

She tapped two fingers against his brow and everything went emerald.

CHAPTER FOURTEEN

KARA GAZED down at her stomach in horrified wonder as she snuggled against Flynn's chest, letting the rumble of his voice soothe her. So much had happened. She ran a hand over the bulge. The babies squirmed beneath her palm, and tears pricked her eyes. How did they get so big? Ugh, how did she get so big? Glory, she'd missed so much…

"Hey." He leaned back and tipped her chin up. Her gaze flicked to his, and was trapped.

Concern etched his features. He'd lost weight, and dark circles rimmed his eyes. He hadn't told her everything—she knew he hadn't, not here, he couldn't—but something, something had changed. He felt different, their bond, the few emotions coming through it. He was blocking them from her again, but what she could feel was lighter and heavier, and she kept getting glimpses of a creeping dread in his eyes.

She swallowed, her mouth dry, wishing she could ask him—no. Goosebumps rose on her skin, and she wished she had more than a flimsy sheet covering her. Titus was watching them, she was sure of it.

"Hey." She forced a smile, and he sighed, kissing her forehead. "So, what now?"

"I'm gonna make things right, and that starts with getting you someplace safe so I can deal with things. You need to trust me, okay?"

"Always." She ran a hand down his cheek, and he turned his head to kiss her palm.

Flynn scooped her up, and something—static?—prickled around them. He gave a pained grunt, sweat beading across his forehead as he wet his lips, then blew out a breath and shook his head. His face screwed up like he was in pain, and that sense of static increased—

Colors ran.

They appeared in a darkened room, lit by an orb of flame flickering through a doorway farther in.

"The fuck?"

Kara was thinking the same. How had he pulled talent in a nullified room?

The question was forgotten as Flynn set her on her feet, steadying her as she found her new balance, all her weight dragging down her middle. A cramp shot through her back, and she put a hand to it, struggling to straighten up. Ugh, that was horrible. She gathered the sheet closer to her throat as Flynn helped her to the couch. You'd think she'd be tired of sitting, but—Oh, Glory, that felt better.

She sighed, looking through the backlit doorway. Rogan, Cal, and Nora were clustered around someone on the floor in the next room—

Whoever it was took a heaving breath and shot up to sit like a defibrillator had been used on them—Fitz. She bit back a laugh, because of course it was.

He coughed, and green vapor puffed from his lips.

"Jesus. The hell did you eat now?" Rogan asked waving it away.

"Better question is what the hell did you do?" Cal barked. "The entire facility's down."

The Fetch scratched the back of his head. "Eh…"

Nora sighed and pushed up to stand. She caught sight of them and gasped. "Kara!"

Her mother ran from the kitchen and caught her up in an embrace. Kara held her as she cried. Glory. She could understand why everyone was so upset, but having slept through it, it was hard to be emotional.

Nora stepped back, her halos flaring as she looked Kara over. "You're well, the babies—"

"You done here, then?" Cal asked Flynn, lighting a smoke.

"Not until they're born," he growled. "Titus has her on some kind of fucking accelerant speeding up the pregnancy, and the only way she's going to survive is if I can get to what's in his head."

He and Nora exchanged a look, and she nodded curtly. Kara tried not to gape at their détente. That was new.

"Whatever needs to be done." Nora's gaze went back to Kara, concern marring her brow as her halos glimmered again, then flared with her frown. "Most of the compounds in her system aren't something I'm familiar with, but it looks like prostaglandins were recently introduced—"

"They gave her a shot of something before she woke up," Flynn growled, his rage tangible. Kara tucked a tendril of hair behind her ear, a sheen of sweat across her skin. When did it get so hot in here?

Nora nodded, sitting beside Kara on the couch. "Prostaglandins stimulate labor, and it was a potent mix. I've bound and removed what I could, but they were there long enough to have a residual effect. As to the rest…I have no idea what half of them are for, or what removing them would do."

Kara ran a hand over her abdomen, the babies' lack of movement more ominous than before. "They're coming—now?"

"No…but sooner then they might've," Nora said, taking her hand.

Kara bit her lip, fighting back tears. How was this happening to her? She closed her eyes, taking comfort in Flynn's rage searing through their bond. It was better than feeling her own fear.

Rogan swore. "You think you'll be able to coerce him to fix whatever the hell he did?"

"If she can't, I'll beat the fuck out of him until he does," Flynn muttered.

Cal snorted. "You do that, and he'll keep mum just to spite you. My money's on Nora."

"I'm not sure that's a wise investment." Nora twisted her ring. "My skill has never been in influencing thoughts, but I am adept at reading them. I should be able to flip through his memories enough to see what he's given Kara and why, then hopefully reverse engineer it. If I can implant a suggestion for him to do it himself, I will."

Kara wiped her eyes then took a stuttering breath, pulling herself together. None of this was a surprise, not really. Once she gave birth, she was expendable. If that didn't kill her, it tracked that Titus would've built contingencies into her care nasty enough to leash Flynn. She put a hand to her abdomen, numb. Glory, she missed their squirming…

"What about the babies?" she asked. "Did he do something to them, too?" Ugh. That was a dumb question. Of course he had. It was more like what. Her temper spiked, sick and tired of her physiology being manipulated like a lab rat's. It needed to end, and if Flynn didn't beat the heck out of Titus she'd be more than happy to do it.

Flynn's eyes snapped to hers. He ran a hand under his nose and edged closer, putting his hand on her shoulder. She reached up and grabbed it. "We don't know."

"But we will," Nora said firmly.

"Eh…question." Fitz leaned in the doorway to the other room, swirling a bottle. "Don't the shite know that if the lady goes, that bond of yers will take ye with it?"

"I very much doubt Titus believes that will happen." Nora sighed. "The Source has had its share of difficult breakings, and his Binder, Shriver, is one of the more adept Talents at preventing bond-related fatalities."

"And if it did, I'm sure he's still counting on harvesting genetics from the babies," Cal added. "They're his contingency plan, and his goal has always been to perpetuate the breed."

Kara turned to Flynn, tears welling in her eyes. "Flynn, you can't let him—"

"Shh…I know," he said sitting beside her and tucking her head beneath his chin. He stroked her hair, an odd hum prickled over her skin, lulling her. "That's why I've taken all of you out of the equation until I get answers…but unfortunately, it's not just all of you. The Triam's full of Breaker females, and I can't leave them there either. They need to come home with us." Flynn looked at Rogan before his eyes flicked to Fitz. "We're gonna need more Fetches."

"We'll take care of it." The Breaker widened his stance and crossed his arms over his chest. "What about the twins?"

"They're coming."

"Then we need to get that case of bots before they're here."

Cal grunted and stubbed out his cigarette, eyeing Fitz. "Your dumb ass is gonna have to shift us out. Whatever you did, nothing powered by plaz works anymore, portlocks included."

"Dunno what makes ye think it were me," the Fetch grumbled, following them to the port. Kara laughed, and he glanced at her through his tangle of curls, the corner of his lips twitching up.

"Wait—" Flynn took a deep breath and closed his eyes, a frisson of uncertain fear shooting through their bond. Beads of sweat broke out on his forehead, then light flared through his lids as he pulled talent—no. It was different—he pulled it from the static surrounding them. It surged, and he staggered beneath the weight of it.

Fitz knuckled his eyes, swearing under his breath. What was that?

"I've cloaked everyone in this room and shielded the building. They won't be able to find any of you as long as it holds, and Elize shouldn't be able to use that fucking gating stone to get in here," he said, looking at Cal.

"You sure about that?"

"I am." Flynn swept a hand across his brow then wiped his palm against his pants.

Kara wet her lips, her anxiety rising at the tremble running through his body. Something was wrong with him—with his talent—she could feel it as clearly as the exhaustion already creeping up on her. Another cramp shot along her midsection, and she rubbed it. What had happened when she'd been taken? He'd glossed over so much…

"They couldn't get past what I set on Kara earlier, and this one's a variation. If it works the way I want it to, we're the only ones that should be able to get in and out." Flynn glared at the Fetch. "Stay with her. Any sign of trouble, bring her back to the coop—"

"That's three hours by craft. You sure he can shift that far?" Rogan asked.

"Bet me, ye shite." Fitz scowled, and his halos sparked as he pulled talent then disappeared. Minutes ticked by before he was back, muttering. "Done."

Flynn's eyes narrowed. "Why'd it take you so long?"

"Eh…no reason."

No one looked like they believed him.

Flynn raked a hand through his hair. "You're not to leave her side, and I swear to Christ, if I find out you stopped anywhere for a fucking pint—"

The Fetch rolled his eyes and pulled a fresh bottle from his jacket.

Flynn growled, and Kara couldn't help but laugh. He turned to her, and his expression softened as he slid from the couch to kneel before her, a hand on her abdomen. Fitz went over to Cal and Rogan and disappeared with the two, shifting from the room.

Kara ran her fingers through Flynn's hair, then trailed them down his jaw. His beard had gotten soft, but the sharp emotions warring inside of him were anything but. "Stop," she said. "I'll be fine. I'm more worried about you."

"Don't be. Now that I have you back, the only person that needs to worry is Titus," Flynn murmured, kissing her palm. He hooked her hair behind her ear, his gaze so intense…

"Get a room," Fitz muttered as he reappeared and stalked back into the kitchen.

Flynn stood, glowering at the Fetch's back. "I swear I'll make this right, Kara. You ready?" he asked, directing the last to Nora.

She nodded, taking his outstretched hand as static surged again, and they were gone.

TITUS TAPPED HIS LIPS, eyes lingering on the holo of the now empty birthing cube before sliding to a snapshot of metrics his system had collected from the Jester girl before Scot had cleared her bots. A smile slicked across Titus's face, not expecting them to be gone for long.

Between what the litter was pulling from her and the cocktail he'd instructed Doctor Yu to introduce into her system, Scot would have no choice but to return the girl to his care when she went into labor. Perhaps a bit more dramatic than he'd originally intended, but the man retaining his talent despite being nullified had forced his hand.

And after that pathetic display in the birthing cube, Titus was confident Scot would do all he could to keep his bitch alive. He'd slipped the net only to entangle himself in Titus's noose. Any negotiations the man had anticipated would be held in Titus's court.

He turned his attention to the readings Enoch had barged in with earlier, though Titus sourly conceded that there'd been just cause. The Source had gone completely dark. He was unable to access any of its systems, the only feedback was from what was streaming down from the vector satellites high overhead.

As much as he'd like to attribute it to Scot, for once he didn't think the man was responsible. The storm of churning talent had only recently returned to the facility with his departure from the Triam, its edges just visible beyond a massive void that had sprung up over a quarter of the Source.

Titus swirled the bourbon in his glass, intrigued. Plaz didn't just "die," but that's exactly what the vectors were reporting—even its heat signature was gone after an abrupt burst, and now the facility's temperature read several degrees below ambient.

His brow furrowed. What had—the storm disappeared and movement across the room caught his eye. He looked up to see the Scot staring out of the office windows at the fields beyond.

"Reconsidering my offer?" Titus asked, unable to hide the smugness from his voice. He pushed back in his chair and placed an ankle over his knee.

"No. I'm leaving here with my wife and children. Additionally, I'll be taking whatever Talents are here with me."

Titus snorted at the man's delusion—

Fingers grazed his temples, and the world blinked.

NORA SLID into Titus's mind and almost dropped talent in shock at the intricately crafted web of suggestion and directive lacing through his psyche. She'd never seen anything like it. His mind had been shaped and pruned like a garden, his persona cultivated over several decades to suit the whims of whoever had done this.

A vague impression of a woman lingered within the weaves, but trying to pin it down was like smelling perfume on a windy day. Her essence was everywhere, yet undefinable at the same time. Something about his mother? No, that couldn't be right, Titus was a lot of things, but talented wasn't one of them, and neither was the auburn-haired woman that'd birthed him.

But one thing Nora did know was that whoever it was, the talent signature was the same as the one responsible for manipulating that Son on the roof. Glory, the experience that this would've taken…the sense of time behind the weaves…the only other instance she'd felt that weight was around Cal's talent.

Could it be one of his contemporaries? Rogan, the twins…Cal had never discussed the fates of the other original seven, but was it so far-fetched to believe that the Binder of their group was still out there? Nora didn't expect him to be forthcoming about it, but maybe Rogan would. It was the only thing that made sense. What had been done to Titus would take lifetimes to learn.

Nora delved deeper to his core memories. Perhaps there was some clue there…

One point in time stood out with crystalline clarity. A female Breaker's death—no, her abduction. That had been the impetus for Titus taking his father's place and the Triam being built. Titus's mind had been bombarded with a flurry of directives, and the imperative to perpetuate the breed escalated to a kind of mania. Everything prior to that single point was hazy and muted, overwritten with the need to perfect the Breaker line—

An associated memory caught her attention. The development of the accelerant they'd used on Kara. It had been in response to litters being born sickly after modifying gestational speed to fill quotas. The risks to the women were dismissed, since they'd be culled after whelping anyway.

Glory, she felt ill. Nora's talent wavered as she took it all in, compartmentalizing it to go through later. Hopefully, she'd be able to make some sense of it, but now wasn't the time. She'd lingered in the past long enough.

The present was more fraught. Numbers, charts, and codes—what this man had done to keep Kara and the babies alive...despite Nora's extensive medical background, she faltered beneath the amount of technical information. Glory, she didn't even know if Jon would understand half of what Titus was doing.

Nora's talent wavered again, and she rushed to gather anything even remotely related to Kara's care, then fled his mind.

She came back to herself blinking, her fingers still on Titus's temples, keeping him serene. Exhaustion weighed on her.

Across the room, Flynn's gaze was intent. "You have what we need?"

Nora shook her head, unable to trust her voice. She cleared her throat. "I don't know. I've learned what I can, but the scope of what he's done—I don't fully understand it, and as far as coercing him...his mind is a construct. I can't risk tampering with what's there." She chewed her lip. "Back on the roof...there's a rogue Binder out there, and they've completely rewritten Titus's psyche. His obsession with perfecting the Breaker line was seeded."

Laughlin's brows furrowed. "Seeded?"

"Suggestions implanted then nurtured over a period of time to become a subject's own," she clarified. "His cultivation has been going on for close to a century. Someone has been using him to push their agenda, and they have ties to the Sons as well. I found the same trace of talent in one of their minds."

"A Binder?" The crease between his brows deepened. "Why the

fuck would a Binder want to deal with any of those assholes—why would they want Kara and my kids?"

Nora shook her head. "I don't know…but Cal and Rogan might. This talent, it feels akin to theirs."

"Great." Flynn snorted and ran a hand over his beard. "So even if I kill this piece of shit and get my wife and kids out of here, they're still not gonna be safe." The temperature in the room began to rise.

"One step at a time," Nora said evenly. "We need to get Kara back here before she gives birth. She and the babies are going to need intervention and as of right now, Titus is the only one that can provide that."

"Of course he fucking is." Laughlin's knuckles popped, the expression on his face murderous.

"It gets worse," Nora ventured, not wanting to set him off. "The Triam's operations are keyed to the biometric data streaming from the bots in his system. If he becomes incapacitated or his adrenal levels exceed certain preset thresholds, it all goes dark. The oxygen generators will shut off, and everyone down here will die."

"Motherfucker—" Laughlin raked a hand through his hair, the air roiling with 'lust so dank she wanted to crawl under the desk and hide. He ran a heavy hand down his face, the inevitable etched over it.

"Then that's it. I have to agree to his terms."

ROGAN JERKED his blade as it caught at the edge of a Son's trachea. Damn, he always forgot how much of a bitch those rings of cartilage were to slice through. If you didn't hit them just right… He glanced over at Cal. "When's the last time we did this?"

"You ask that like you miss it," he bitched, his halos shimmering olive.

Rogan grinned, not denying it. They'd cut down at least a dozen of the Sons on their way to the auditorium where Nora had said the loot from the lightstream was being held. Despite the Sons' numbers, their security was for shit, and what they could see beyond the oversized portlock looked like a flop house. The big room flickered with rudimentary torches and was teeming with the assholes, a bunch of whom were very busy trying to chop a hole through a wall.

"So much for using the breaker bars on the fire exits," Cal murmured, watching them through the portlock's windows. "Idiots."

"You think you can pull enough to phase us through these doors?" Rogan wiped his blade on the dead Son's shirt and dragged his body into an alcove, heaping it with the other.

"Not if you want me to be any use inside. Phasing into the suite right after that stunt on the roof about drained me. If I'd known about the Overlord's power filling you back up, I'd have been a hell of a lot less judicious using it."

Rogan rolled his eyes, doubtful that was actually the case, but God forbid there was something Cal didn't know. "You'd still be holed up in your office chain smoking."

"That's not the point," Cal muttered.

"That's entirely the point. Phase us through, and I'll take care of the rest."

"Fine. It's on you." Cal's halos flared as they stepped through the portlock.

The room was filthy and stank. Greasy smoke drifted through the space and large sections of seating had been ripped out and thrown into haphazard piles. A lot more men than Nora had mentioned were standing around picking their asses as they grumbled. Shit. How were he and Cal gonna get anywhere without tripping over shit or bashing into someone—

"Well, you're up," Cal said, shooing him. "Take care of it, Firestorm."

"Did I say I miss this? I don't miss this," Rogan muttered, glaring at the man. "Oh wait, no, it's you I don't miss."

Cal grinned at him. Asshole.

Rogan snorted. "Let's just find the damn case."

"How big was it?"

"Same size as that Hello Critter lunchbox you hauled around all throughout middle school," Rogan muttered, trying not to kick shit out of his way. The amount of garbage in here was ridiculous. How the fuck were they supposed to find anything?

"You mean kitty, and that wasn't me, that was my sister, and if memory serves, you stole it to keep your weed in."

A wide grin broke across Rogan's face. "I did at that."

"Is it pink?"

"Is what pink?"

"The case we're looking for," Cal said, sidestepping a snoring man.

"What? No, it's gray. Why the hell would you think it's pink?"

"You're the one that brought up that lunch box."

"It wasn't pink, it was blue."

"The hell it was," Cal muttered.

They picked around the edge of the room toward the stage, trying not to upset the copious amount of shit strewn everywhere or the groups of men. Had to be at least a hundred Sons in here milling about, all of them pissed they couldn't leave.

"Christ, the goddamned directions are right there on the port," Cal bitched. "Hit the bar, and roll the thing aside—"

"Literacy is probably a factor."

"There's a pictogram beside it on the—" Cal grabbed Rogan's sleeve and pointed at a little case beneath a mound of random spoils. "That it?"

"Yeah, go grab it."

"And have the whole damn pile come down as soon as I do?" he asked sourly. Rogan shrugged and Cal scowled at him. "Fine, I'll run point, but why don't you make yourself useful and set a couple more fires to keep them busy?"

Rogan frowned, scanning the auditorium for a likely pile of shit to burn. He definitely had plenty of options. His halos pulsed, and a moment later, a thick plume of smoke rose up in the far corner, followed by several more before someone finally noticed.

"Fire!" one of the Sons bellowed, grabbing his kit and making for the port.

He was about halfway out of the auditorium before the rest of them registered what was going on and began to scramble. Flames caught the material lining the walls and whooshed up to the ceiling. Sons grabbed what they could and bolted for the exits, pounding on them.

Miraculously, one opened.

Cal pulled out the case, and the mound collapsed with a godawful racket. No one noticed, the flames growing higher as the last of the men fled the room—

The sprinkler system kicked on, dousing the room in a frigid deluge.

Cal dashed the water from his eyes. "Guess that's not plaz dependent."

Rogan shot him a foul glare. "Lucky fucking us. Damn it, I hate getting wet," he snarled, headed for the port.

"Afraid it's gonna ruin your man bun?" Cal asked, trailing behind.

"It's a top knot."

"It's a goddamn bun. My grandma used to wear her hair like that, same color too."

"You're such an asshole."

"Must have to do with the company I keep."

Rogan snorted. "Hold up." He put the case down to check inside. All the vials were there, and thank God for that. "Right, let's get this back to the suite. Twins have gotta be here by now… You really think Flynn's shield is gonna keep them from finding us?"

"It pains me to say that what that boy threw over us, I wouldn't be able to put over a potato in my heyday."

Rogan's brows rose. "That tight?"

"That tight," Cal said with a ghost of a smile as they made their way back through the building.

"You gonna be ready for this next bit, or you need a nap?"

"What I need's a goddamned cigarette," Cal muttered pulling out his pouch. "So you got any idea how this hunt of yours is gonna go, or are we just gonna run around the facility like we're LARPing?"

"Aside from visions of cutting out Enoch's shriveled little heart and feeding it back to him, I'm open to suggestions," Rogan said, running a hand down the side of his head. Stubble was making him nuts. Wasn't a fucking thing like Cal's grandma's. All her stubble had been on her chin along with a godawful mole. A man bun. Fuck him. They crossed the street to the corporate building. "I should've killed that fucker the first time."

"Mistakes were made. If I'd kept my temper, we wouldn't be in this mess." Cal slipped in through the half-open portlock on the ground floor and stopped to light his smoke.

Rogan squeezed through after him. "Nah, pretty sure it would've happened sooner or later. You were never able to think straight when Elize was involved, and she got off on making you lose your shit."

Cal shot Rogan a side-eye. "Sounds like someone else I know, and I was never able to think straight because she kept fucking anything with a pulse—including my best friend," he said, starting across the lobby. A hole in the wall led to the stairwell.

"If it makes you feel any better, I didn't touch her until after you broke your bond."

"Well gee, buddy, thanks for that."

"No problem," Rogan said jogging up the first flight of steps. He turned to wait for Cal's emphysemic ass. "Can't blame me for wanting to know what all the fuss was about, and I still can't say I understand it. You know, you look like shit. You sure you don't need a nap?"

"Fuck you," Cal huffed. "Let's just get this over with. I swear she's so close I can hear her goddamned braids chiming."

<hr>

MARCOS WINCED at the clang of rebar being shifted in as he jogged up the steps of the platform overlooking construction outside the eastern gate. Thankfully, the next wave of workers were due. The Talents currently out there were reaching their limits.

Markham shouted something from the platform's rail, waving his handkerchief in the air. The group of Fetches stopped what they were doing and popped from sight. A moment later, another group shifted in, picking up where they'd left off.

Marcos crossed the platform to join Lords Blaise and Klein under a makeshift roof where a table with a map had been set up. The two were poring over it as they flipped through a pair of clipboards thick with notes, the both of them haggard. Dorian's Finders had been working overtime trying to put order to the supplies being shifted in, and Carl was attempting to oversee it all. The sheer amount of material was overwhelming, but as Markham said, they needed to take advantage of it while they could. From what Marcos had heard, promised goods were already being reneged on or meeting mysterious delays.

"We've got plenty of I-beams, and now that the rebar's been shifted in, we should be able to begin raising the wall on our eastern flank," Carl said pointing to a section of the map before glancing up at Marcos. "We underestimated the work ethic of your men. They've already cleared the area, and the footings have been completed for this entire section. I wasn't aware that they had construction experience."

Marcos swallowed the wide grin threatening to split his face. "None of them are going to be able to put up a house, but walls, dikes, and bridges are standard instruction…or were."

"All skills we're currently in desperate need of," Dorian mused.

"It's not the only one," Markham huffed, blotting his brow as he joined them. "This would go a hell of a lot faster if we had someone to bind these godforsaken bundles of material."

Carl grunted his agreement. "Pithy's assured me of his assistance as soon as the rest of the Breakers his people are treating stabilize. He released another group about an hour ago, and I've had Stonefist send them to the western side of the city. There's a ridge we need cordoned off," he said, pointing to the map. "We lost what little space we had to bivouac the herds with the quakes, and that should provide a natural windbreak, which puts the lion's share of our agricultural concerns… here."

Marcos nodded. "You've verified the land's stable in that direction?"

"Most of it. I'm planning on heading out there myself in the morning…their captain, Pax, said it would take them that long to get out there and establish a base camp."

"They're not shifting?" Dorian asked.

Carl shook his head. "No. I got the impression they were looking forward to the run."

Marcos was positive they were. He chuckled, and Dorian and Carl's gazes jumped to him. "I don't think you understand what was expected of those boys down south. Being at loose ends isn't going to sit well." Marcos allowed himself a small smile, knowing exactly how they felt. "It'll take some time for them to find their balance up here."

Dorian snorted. "Well, not for nothing, but while they're finding their balance, we're being run ragged trying to keep up."

"The loss of roughly half of the Original Houses to their country estates certainly hasn't helped on that front." Markham frowned, picking at his handkerchief. "Without Laughlin here to put the fear of God into them, their initial support is already lagging."

"They might feel differently if the rumblings I've heard of Hexspar and Ax'chig continuing their alliance hold true," Dorian said. "I'll also add that Diytan's warships are still anchored off the Northern Territories' coast."

Marcos frowned. "Then it's probably safe to assume that they're waiting to see how this plays out."

"Agreed. Somehow Laughlin's self-imposed timeframe of a week has gotten out. I've very little doubt that if he isn't back in the next few days, they'll be here in force."

Marcos snorted, positive there was no somehow about it, and that Serra was—his breath caught as the nasty bitch sashayed up the platform steps holding a goddamned parasol of all things. Lord Crandall followed in her wake, like a bad smell. He went to the rail of the platform, looking out over the construction as she approached the table.

"Gentlemen," she drawled after a perfunctory glance at the headway being made, then flicking her gaze dismissively over the map. Marcos had the worst urge to fold it up and hide it from her prying eyes.

"Lady Hess," Carl greeted her tightly. "My, you're looking well-rested. What can we possibly do for you?"

Marcos sucked his teeth, trying not to grin at the Fixer's all but outright hostility.

She sniffed. "I've come to clear up a clerical matter. Imagine my surprise when I went to draw on my line's funds, only to find the scheduled deposit from the general ledger had been withheld."

"Mmm. Yes, just imagine," Markham murmured, his expression

just shy of vicious. She narrowed her eyes at him and went to open her mouth—

"Unfortunately, Lady Hess," Carl intervened, "the law is very clear, and a stipulation to receiving public funding is actually serving said public."

"Yes," Dorian chimed in. "It would be extremely helpful if your line participated in rebuilding the city that has so generously offered you succor, instead of just feeding off it like bloated ticks."

Her color rose as she drew herself up, the fit of her gown not doing anything to dispel the imagery. "And I thought I made our position very clear," she hissed. "We have no desire to support Lord Scot or his vision, and as far as serving the public—your wall wouldn't have been functional without our binds, and the Infirmary—"

"You mean the one that's currently at a fraction of its capacity?" Markham asked.

"No, I think she was referring to the clinics that have been instructed to turn people away," Carl mused.

"How I administer my line is my prerogative!"

"And how the city's funds are distributed is ours, unless you'd like to challenge that in court?" Carl asked. "Feel free to do so, though I will mention cases are currently being scheduled out to sometime next year. I'll also mention that the Source Binders signed contracts upon their arrival which stipulate their use of housing is in exchange for serving the populace via their talent. Violators will be receiving notices later today. It would be a shame if those finding their footing were displaced due to any misunderstanding of obligation."

Serra's face twisted into something decidedly unattractive, then smoothed. Her serenity was somehow more frightening. "I see. Well, I appreciate you keeping everyone informed of their duty. If you'll excuse me, I need to attend to mine. Bart?"

"I've still some business to discuss," Crandall said, turning from the rail. "You don't mind, do you?"

"No, not at all. I'll see myself back."

Marcos bit back a snort, her expression saying otherwise.

They watched her go, a pall settling in her wake.

"Bart?" Carl asked the Intelligencer as he ran a hand through his dark hair. His normally slicked-back locks fell to frame his face, mirroring the exhausted set to his shoulders.

"Over familiarity is part of the seduction process," Crandall muttered, coming over to join them. "The woman is like a terrier with a bone, and as much as I'm loathe to admit it, I've gained quite a bit more sympathy for Laughlin's temper over the past few days."

Dorian snorted. "I believe we all have. Serra's elitism is infecting the other lines, emboldening those that otherwise would've done as expected. The hill leaving the city is a prime example, and without them, it opens all of us to risk. Her faction is becoming a danger to Glynfyls's stability, politically and otherwise."

"Agreed, and if the trend continues, we'll need to bring in machinery to stay on target," Carl said, looking out over the construction. "Our finances have already been extended beyond what I'm comfortable with. The last thing we need is to default and be beholden to foreign creditors."

"One way or another, the sharks are coming." Crandall pursed his lips. "In retrospect, we never should have allowed that feed. My sources are divided as to whether the shooting and its aftermath were doctored, but the fact that Laughlin's left isn't in dispute. We need to get the wall up, the sooner the better, and Serra's not budging."

"So we saw." Marcos's jaw ticked. "How would you suggest we proceed?"

Crandall's brow rose. "That's a dangerous question to ask me, Commandant." He ran a hand over his goatee. "Let me ask you something before I answer. If Lord Scot returns, how confident are you in his ability to rule? Despite that bit of theater he pulled at the Assembly, I've confirmed the rumors of his, shall we say, 'delicate' state of mind."

Marcos's thumb worried his forefinger, all too aware. He reached into his pocket for his antacids. "*When* he returns, it will be with his family, and I have every confidence his state of mind won't be an issue once they're safe." The other men around the table grunted their agreement.

Crandall's gaze flicked over all of them. "Don't you think it rather dangerous to back a man whose mental stability is dependent upon the presence of a woman?"

Marcos met the Intelligencer's piercing gaze, the man's halos glimmering, finding the truth of their words.

Markham cleared his throat. "I think you're oversimplifying the situation—"

"Perhaps. Still, my question remains."

"Then I can understand your concern, but nothing I've seen leads me to doubt the Overlord's abilities," Marcos said.

"Agreed," Carl chimed in. "If he said he'll be back with his family, he will, and when he returns, it will be to resume administering this city, and this goddamned wall had better be up."

A hint of smile crossed Lord Crandall's lips.

"Then I would advise making the additional costs of the project known, and the impact of that on the hill's taxes. I'd wager we'll know very shortly who would rather contribute physically versus with their wallet. And as far as the Binders are concerned, we all need to pray that Nora Jester returns very soon. Now if you'll excuse me..." He inclined his head and started across the platform.

"What would you have advised if we'd doubted Laughlin?" Dorian called after him.

Crandall didn't stop. "More prayer, gentleman. As I said, the sharks are coming."

Marcus watched the man descend the steps and crunched into an antacid, certain they were already here.

CHAPTER FIFTEEN

"I've modified the tethers to El and En with a new bind of Mother's design. It's quite clever. The resulting crystal allows complete dominion over their psyche while they retain their forms. En fought me, but with all the talent I've harvested, his submission was a forgone conclusion.

El was more amiable to wearing a leash after I returned some of the memories I had taken from her. She burns to make A suffer almost as badly as En wants to see Ro dead. I feel the echoes of their ire upon my own heart. Not for the first time, I wonder what this ability is doing to me, and if it really matters anymore."

– Undated journal entry

FLYNN CALLED talent and shifted himself and Nora back to the Source. Construct or not, leaving that fucking asshole still breathing at his desk was the hardest goddamned thing he'd ever done. *Fuck, fuck, fuck!*

Flynn swept a pile of magazines off the coffee table and upended it, winging it across the room. It hit the wall hard and shattered, glass shards shimmering in the ruddy glow of the orb Rogan had left as they peppered the carpet.

"M'guessin' it didn't go well," Fitz said around a mouthful of something. He leaned in the kitchen's doorway, chewing, fork busy in another one of those meal containers.

Flynn rounded on him. "Why the fuck aren't you with Kara?" he roared.

Asshole didn't even flinch. "Figured Yer High Holiness's commandment didn't extend t'keeping her company in the bedroom. Not that I'd be opposed…"

"Laughlin—" Nora stepped between the two of them a breath before he lunged at the little fucker. "I'll take care of Fitz. Go talk to Kara."

"I'm gonna fucking kill you," Flynn growled, stabbing a finger at the Fetch as he stalked to the bedroom.

Fitz snorted, going back to his meal.

Flynn swore again and ducked past the portlock that'd been partially shifted to the side. The room Nora had been using wasn't quite pitch black. Christ, he couldn't see—another orb of flickering flame materialized before he'd finished the thought. He raked a hand through his hair. Shit was just fucking weird. Kara was curled up in the center of the bed. Goddamn it. He pushed energy towards her—and she didn't need it.

He swallowed a laugh and hung his head as he sat beside her. No. She wouldn't, would she? Fucking Titus had cured her goddamned deficiency so he could murder her. Flynn swallowed the spike of fury lancing through him. How he could be so fucking indebted to a man he wanted to eviscerate—

"Shh. Stop being rage-y and come be the big spoon." Kara's fingers grazed over his lower back.

"The big spoon?" Flynn snorted and climbed onto the bed behind her. His temper mellowed as soon as his arms wrapped around her, and he sighed, nose brushing against her nape. The static in his head mellowed to a low hum.

"Mmm. Yes. Big spoon." She wriggled her backside into his groin, and he bit back a pained moan. God, he'd missed her. "I like your nightlight. When did you learn to do that?"

He glanced at the orb. "Like an hour ago," he murmured, breathing her in. She must've showered. Her hair was damp, and the antiseptic smell from the Triam was gone. Somewhere she'd gotten a new sheet to wrap up in, this one with armholes. He fingered one of them. "Where'd this come from?"

"Linen closet and Fitz's pigsticker." She laughed, and he held her tighter. Christ, he'd missed that, too. "The holes were his idea. Now I don't have to worry about holding it up."

Flynn didn't even know what to stay about that. Fucking kid. He smoothed a hand over her abdomen, and his brow furrowed at the babies' subdued movement. "How are you feeling?"

"Crampy and huge. That's why I came in here to lie down… I have to go back, don't I?"

"Yeah," he said, his voice breaking. "Nora was in Titus's head. She said you and the babies are going to need intervention, and that he's the only one that can do it."

"Then you have to agree to his terms." Kara turned to look at him over her shoulder, her halos back to the wide golden rings they'd been when he'd first met her. Her emotions were oddly flat. "Flynn, he's going to want you to—"

"Stud for him. I know." Flynn rolled onto his back, sick about it. "And if I don't, I'll lose you."

A shadow passed over her face. "If you go through with it, you will too. I won't share you, Laughlin Scot, and you gave me your word I wouldn't have to."

He had, and he'd be damned if he fucking broke it. "No. It won't come to that. I-I'm gonna lie to him, Kara."

She looked like she'd been slapped. "But…you don't lie."

He grunted, hating the position he was in, but the alternative was so much fucking worse. This was about saving his family, not his bullshit honor, and Titus sure as fuck didn't have any.

"How long have I been asleep?" she asked, incredulous. "Flynn, you let Crandall put you in jail over semantics—"

"I did, and the papers broadcasted it far and wide. If I give Titus my word, he won't question that I'll keep it, but it will only get us so far. We have to figure out what's gonna happen after the babies are born."

Kara chewed the side of her thumb, and he swore he could feel her

Binder's intellect pinging through their bond. "Well, If I'm dead, it's one thing—"

"Jesus, Kara—"

"Shut up and listen to me," she said, squirming around so they were face-to-face. "If I'm dead, you need to do whatever it takes to get the babies out of there. But if I'm still alive, he's going to have to wait before he tries to break our bond—" She winced and put a hand to her abdomen with a long exhale.

"Is it starting already?"

"No, I'm fine." Her nose scrunched up as she grimaced again.

"The fuck you are," he growled, going to the port and calling for her mother.

"Since when are you two so chummy?" Kara grumbled.

"We aren't, we just have a common goal." He stepped back as Nora came in. "Can you look at her? She's having cramps."

Nora's halos flared as she put a hand on Kara's abdomen. "She's starting to dilate, but that doesn't necessarily mean anything…it could be false labor pains, they're common at this stage." She brushed back Kara's hair. "Breathe through them instead of clenching up. I'll get you some water. Staying hydrated will help more than you think, but if they get worse you need to let us know."

"See, I told you I was fine," Kara muttered as Flynn helped her sit up against the headboard.

He kissed her forehead and settled beside her. "And now I believe you."

"Jerk." She smiled as Nora came back with a bottle of water then turned to leave. "Wait, you know more about this than I do. How long do you think Titus will wait to break our bond?"

Nora smoothed her pants. "I can't tell you that, but thirty-seven hours is the earliest it's ever been successfully attempted. There was a study—" She shook her head. "Anything sooner resulted in dual fatalities, and with only Shriver in attendance, it will push that timeframe out. How far, I can't tell you."

Kara chewed her thumb. "Okay…that's a decent window, and Titus doesn't know you've been in his head. I'm assuming you riffled through his memories of my treatment plan?"

"I did, but I'm not going to lie, it's a lot to unpack. I'm going to start assimilating them, but I don't know how long that will take."

"It'll go faster if you're in the environment where the memories originated. If we take you back with us, and you can gain access to his lab, there's a better chance you'll figure out what he's done and how to mitigate it, and if not—"

"Hold on," Flynn interrupted. "That's a lot of fucking ifs." He turned to Nora. "Does Titus know you're here?"

She shook her head. "No, not unless he reviews the footage of his office, which isn't something he'd do without reason. If he did, he'd see something was amiss, but you cloaked me, and I erased any memory of our visit."

"Then let's keep it that way. If he knows you're here, he'll try to leverage it. If not with the breaking, then with something else."

Kara huffed. "But then how—"

"His memories, can you give them to me?" Flynn asked.

Kara and Nora stared at him.

"I could," she said slowly, "but you wouldn't have any of the medical context to make sense of them. I can't even make sense of them right now."

"I'm talking about the technical information. Logins, passwords, anything on how the Triam works. If I can keep the facility from crashing without that prick at the helm, then you'll have access to his tech and time to figure out how to use it."

Nora let out a long breath. "Laughlin, I don't think that's wise, given—"

"I didn't ask if it was wise. I need you to do it."

"Given what?" Kara asked glancing between them. Shit.

Nora's lips thinned, and she looked away. "I'll give you two a moment."

"Flynn?" Kara's big brown eyes went to him and he couldn't meet them. "What aren't you telling me?"

Goddamn it. He ran a hand down his face at the jump in her anxiety streaming through their bond. "It's not—fuck. Can we talk about this later?"

"What? No. Tell me now."

"Kara, it's gonna upset you, and you don't need—"

"Oh, I'm already upset," she said with a sweet little smile and batted her lashes. "But go ahead, keep telling me all about what I don't need."

Damn it. He sighed, and tipped his head back against the wall, staring at the ceiling. How was he supposed to—fuck, he didn't want to do this. "When they took you…I died."

She blinked at him. "Excuse me?"

"I lost control of my talent. Blew myself up, the plateau, part of the city—"

"I don't understand, my bind is still there. It would've UnMade the damage."

"It did and didn't. Your bind worked, but—Rogan, Marcos, shit I saw myself disintegrate into ashes. Something…something else brought me back. I think it was Rebirth, the duality to your UnMaking."

Kara shook her head and wiped her cheeks. Goddamn it, he knew this shit was gonna upset her. "I still don't understand…"

"No, neither do I, but it fucked me up. My talent, my memories… Nora did something so I can function, but my head's still not right. Shit that happened gets triggered, and I'm in that moment. It's been better with you here, but I can feel them, Kara. Like they're waiting for me, and I keep seeing flames—"

"That's why she doesn't want to give you what she took."

Flynn nodded. "Yeah."

"What about your talent?"

"I can't pull like before," he muttered. "It got all twisted up, and either shit just happens, or it's like I gotta ask permission to use it. If I don't, it fucks me up." He dragged his shirt up over his head and tossed it aside. She gasped, her hand going to the nasty clumps of scar tissue across his torso. "That's the last time I tried to pull Fetch talent. It flayed me open."

"It did this?" She bit her lip. "My bind should've erased that, Flynn."

"It healed some of it, but it's getting weaker. If I fuck up again, I don't think it'll save me."

Her face paled. "Does Titus know that?"

He shook his head. "No, I'm pretty sure him and the rest of the world think I'm still bulletproof." Her eyebrow cocked, and he sighed. "After I blew myself up, I might've gotten shot in the middle of Assembly during a live feed."

Kara laughed, then slapped a hand over her mouth. "Glory, you're not joking, are you? Wait—who shot you?"

"Barton—"

"Barton!"

"Yeah, it was a whole thing," he said, running a hand over his jaw and trying to downplay it. "Whatever, I'm still alive and he's not." Neither was Morris, but there was no way he was getting into that right now.

"You're as bad at staying out of trouble as Fitz," she muttered, fitting herself into the crook of his arm, her head against his chest. She sighed, snuggling close. Their bond rife with her concern. Shit, he wasn't exactly carefree either. "How are we going to do this, Flynn?"

"I dunno, but we are." He kissed the top of her head, drawing circles over her bare shoulder. "I need those memories, Kara. Titus has gotta have contingencies built in. There's no way he'd run the risk of being trapped down there, and—"

"No, but if you fry your brain trying to figure out what those are, it's not going to do anyone any good." She grimaced, rubbing at another cramp. Flynn looked pointedly at the bottle of water Nora had brought in, and Kara scowled before cracking it open and taking a sip. "I just have to get through the birth. After that, if Nora can't figure out what Titus did to me and the babies, I think there's a chance I can UnMake it once I have my talent back."

He grunted at that thin thread of hope. "I don't think we can afford to leave either option on the table. There's too much at risk, and all those other females down there…all the kids…they're important," he said, his voice cracking.

She looked up at him, her forehead furrowed. "So are you. Glory, I hate this."

"Trust me, I know. You think I wanna bring you back there?" He reached up to smooth his thumb over the little triangle of worry between her brows, then cupped her cheek and kissed her. "I just want to keep you here, with me."

Kara laughed. "I can think of better places."

Flynn smiled. "I can, too…we stopped at the coop." He trailed his knuckles over her jawline and down the length of her throat. She was so damned beautiful.

"Did you?" she asked, her head dropping back.

"Yeah." He kissed along the path his fingers had just taken. "It's trashed, but standing. We could go back someday."

Kara threaded her fingers through his hair, pulling him closer. "I like someday."

Their lips met, softly, then insistent. Her tongue dueling with his as he swept it through her mouth. He groaned, cupping the back of her head. Fuck, she was here. His. He didn't want to ever let her go. Her 'lust threaded around them, muting the static and mellowing his nerves. His rose to meet it, their bond thrumming with desire, resonating with the growing hum in the air around them.

Across the room, the portlock clicked closed, and Kara laughed. "Was that you or Fitz?"

"I don't know, and right now, I don't care."

"Good, then kiss me," she said, abruptly teary.

"Tell me why you're crying first."

"I'm not crying." She sniffled, then scowled at his raised brow. "Okay fine, I'm crying, it's just…" She choked up again, her sorrow drowning him with its intensity. "I'm scared, Flynn. What if this time is the last time?"

Cold sweat prickled over him, followed by a wash of rage, phantom flames flickering in his peripheral. Didn't matter. Nothing but her did. He kissed her forehead and smoothed back her hair, taking her cheeks between his palms as he met her teary gaze. "Then I'll burn this world down until I find you in the next."

She bit back a sob and kissed him fiercely, their bond rife with joy and fear. She nipped at his scar as he pulled away, then kissed her again, teasing her lips open with his tongue and sliding it along hers. Goddamn, he fucking loved her. The hum around them intensified with their 'lust, dank ribbons of desire twining around them, tangible; they swept over their skin, raising gooseflesh in their wake.

Kara moaned as he cupped her breast, flicking his thumb over her nipple. He swallowed her cries, finding the part in the sheet surrounding her and running his rough palm over her smooth skin.

She arched her back, drawing in a quick breath as he inhaled along the deep valley between her breasts, kneading, then lowered his mouth to suckle.

"Damn, baby," he murmured, nosing a taut peak. "You feel so fucking good."

"So do you," she whispered, her nails teased his scalp, urging him on. He latched on again, gently tugging, pebbling her nipple between his lips as he lapped over its tip, exploring her new fullness. She cried out pressing against him, so damned sensitive, and reached down to stroke him through his pants.

He groaned, hips reflexively thrusting against her. Jesus, it'd been so long…her hands were at his buckle, reaching inside—a growl rumbled through his chest at her fingers sliding around his aching cock and swirling the bead of moisture at its tip. He claimed her mouth again, running his hand over the wide curve of her abdomen. How the fuck was that so goddamned sexy? She was a goddess, and all he wanted to do was worship her.

Talent prickled around them, surging, its hum deep and resonant, reverberating through them. She pushed back, her halos scintillating, the room awash in gold and verdigris, their bond rife with too many damned questions—

"Later," he murmured, pulling her to him. The talent could do whatever the hell it wanted. Christ, he needed this woman like his next breath. Her fingers tightened around him, and he groaned, his desire surging—

Her abdomen rolled beneath his hand, and he jerked away like he'd been burned.

"Shit—"

"It's okay." She laughed, and nipped at his ear. "Just be gentle. I know you can." Her hand pumped over him steadily, driving away reason.

His throat bobbed as she kissed along his Adam's apple, sucking. He squeezed his eyes shut. Fuck, she was killing him. What if he hurt her, the babies—"Kara…"

"You won't hurt me. Do you need me to ask for it?" Her breath tickled his ear. "I want you, Laughlin. Please? I miss your mouth between my legs, nice and slow…"

He groaned, sliding off the edge of the bed and kneeling as she wriggled toward him. He wet his lips as she parted her thighs, folds already swollen with desire. She trailed her fingers along her glistening slit, her gaze hooded.

God. Fucking. Damn.

He met her eyes as he took her foot in his hand, kissing along her instep, the hollow at her heel. Suckling at her ankle bone, then sliding his tongue along her calf to linger and nip behind her knee. He grazed up her thigh to her apex and paused to inhale, breathing in the scent of her, the taste… His dick throbbed. She was so fucking sweet, her 'lust heavy and ripe. He swept through her dewy folds, tasting, teasing, lapping into her.

Kara cried out as a groan rumbled from his throat. He bent to the task, feasting. Reveling in her gasp at the rub of his beard. Her fingers buried in his hair. She rocked against him, moaning as they struck a rhythm. Damn, the little noises she made lit him the fuck up. He pleasured her with long, firm strokes, drawing her into his mouth, and gripped his cock, stroking himself at the same pace.

She tightened her hold, nails an exquisite drag across his scalp as he flicked her clit with his tongue and sucked, slowly teasing her entrance with a finger. Her thighs quivered, hips beginning to rock—

"Oh Glory, please, Flynn. Please…"

"You said slow," he rumbled, then dipped his tongue into her sweetness.

She whimpered, pushing against him, panting, knees hooked over his shoulders and her heels digging into his back. "Please…"

Christ, he loved it when she begged. He chuckled and lightly slapped her clit, his dick jumping at her gasp. "You want me, baby? Tell me you need my cock. If you promise to be good, I'll give you half of it."

"Half?!"

He kicked off his pants and leaned over her, hands to either side of her head. "That back-talk?"

"No," she huffed, and his gaze dropped to her pouty lips as he licked her desire from his, a grin replacing it.

"Good girl, now ask me for what you want."

She pulled him down and kissed him, her tongue flicking out to sample her essence from his beard. "Love me."

"I do love you," he rumbled.

"Then show me. Make me feel it. Break me into pieces and make me yours."

Jesus fucking Christ, this woman…

"Yes, ma'am." He kissed her, then leaned back and slicked his crown through her wet cleft. God, he'd missed this…her…"Slow," he growled, gazing through his fall of dark hair to meet her eyes.

"Slow."

He pushed into her, and the world fell away.

Velvet heat gripped him, familiar and not, the weight of her pregnancy pressing down. Jesus fuck. He fought to find a rhythm, overwhelmed. Half…he wasn't gonna…

He wasn't gonna last.

Kara let out a long, guttural cry and wrapped her legs around his hips, urging him deeper. He fell forward, one knee on the bed, and shoved a pillow under her backside, groaning at the new angle.

"This okay?"

"Glory, yes…" She nodded, raising her arms up over her head and arching, so damned gorgeous. Her halos shimmered, the talent in the room ticking up, that hum vibrating against his skin, 'lust thick in his nose.

Christ, she felt so fucking good…he circled his thumb around her clit, her walls tightening along his length, fluttering. He groaned, his forehead beading with sweat…gaze dropping to watch himself slide into her, slick with passion, her flesh clenching his—shit, he was definitely not at the halfway mark anymore.

"Oh, yes…" She dropped her hands to her breasts, smoothing up their sides, pressing them together and tugging her nipples. Lips parted, her breath quick, their bond pulsed carnal with shared sensation.

Him feeling her, feeling him.

The slide of her silken softness against his hard flesh. The delicious stretch of him filling her and then taking himself away. The building heat between them, their connection intensifying. Talent plucked at them, where he stopped and she began, indistinct. The hum blurred their edges, prickling, teasing, wanting more, their beings becoming one—

No.

Christ. He shook his head, breath ragged, jolted out of whatever the fuck that'd been. Kara whimpered, head back, shoulders rounding off the bed. Close, she was so damned close…

"Eyes on me, baby," he panted, wetting his lips. Fuck. He wanted— no, needed—to see her break into pieces as badly as she wanted it. "Come for me. Show me what I do to you."

Her pupils dilated, a flush traveling from her chest to her cheeks, those beautiful almond eyes widening with a catch of breath. A tingle started at the base of his spine, and he gritted his teeth, then gasped, hips driving forward as he came, his vision tunneling with his release. Kara cried out, her walls clamping down, her climax milking his, filling her with his seed.

"Jesus fuck…" he panted, wiping the sweat from his eyes. "I didn't mean to—you okay?"

She laughed, running her hand over her abdomen. "All things considered? Yes."

Flynn climbed into bed beside her and tucked her against his chest. "I love you."

"I know." She smiled. "I love you, too."

He kissed the top of her head and closed his eyes, allowing himself a moment of happiness and praying to God it wasn't the last.

FITZ SLOUCHED against the couch's cushions, muttering to hisself and playing with his coin. Nora were in the kitchen trying to work with them memories she took, and between the talent she were pulling and the psychedelic porno going on in the bedroom behind him, he were in a foul mood.

At least the energy from the plaz driving him mental were gone, but the silence in its wake weren't no comfort. Stupid fuckin'—if it hadn't been so damned miserable, he never would've done what he done. He cursed hisself, and reached up, fingering the rings along the shell of his ear, the fifth one missing and a ward streaming out in its place.

The fuck had happened? All that shite with Sophia couldn't have been real. No way he'd really kissed her. Were supposed to have been a damned dream, but this fucking ward—his head fell back, and he groaned up at the ceiling.

Jesus, Mary, and Joseph, he'd kissed a hillie witch.

Worse, he were keen t'do more of it—had asked t'fucking see her again like he were gonna come courtin'. What in the ever lovin' fuck were wrong with him? Nah. Ain't somewhat that were in them witches' godforsaken cards. Not now, and not ever.

More's the fuckin' pity.

He sucked his lip, scowling at Cajetan's merriment. Prick. Whatever. He'd just pretend it didn't happen. Weren't like Sophia were gonna be back anytime soon. A year were a long time. She'd forget about it. Him. He could break the ward, and that'd be—

Coin seared cold across his fingers, and he swore as he dropped it. *Gah, ye fuck!* He shook out his hand. Blessed fuckin' bastard—

Somewhat thudded against the portlock, and Fitz swept up the rotten round of metal, scowling as the thud came again. "For the love of fuckin'—" Like being a goddamned taxi weren't bad enough, now he were a fuckin' doorman.

"Please tell me that's Cal and Rogan," Nora said from the doorway of the kitchen, rubbing her temple.

Fitz's halos flared like he were gonna shift, peering through the window in his mind to the hallway. "Ya, it's them," he grumbled, stalking over. He slapped a hand against the metal and shifted it aside.

"And?" Rogan asked.

Cal stubbed out his cigarette before coming through the port. "And I woke up at the Red Skirt."

Rogan laughed, following him in. "How many trips to the Binder did it take to clear up that case of the clap?"

"More than I'll admit to."

"Why the hell didn't you go to the Pony?"

Were a valid question. Fitz raised a brow, waiting for the answer. Goin' to the Red Skirt were just askin' t'get VD. No one with any sense dipped their wick into that dirty hole. Barris Street were cleaner by comparison.

Old hillie went to answer, then caught sight of the lady. "Nora."

"Caliban."

The big Alpha snickered and threw a case onto the couch as he glanced at the bedroom's closed portlock. "They in there?"

"Yes, Laughlin and I got back from the Triam about an hour ago," Nora said, still frowning at Cal.

Didn't seem t'faze him. "And?"

"And she has to go back," Nora said. "Titus has her on accelerant."

The old hillie pulled out his pouch of tobacco. "Which is?"

"Exactly what it sounds like. It essentially replaces the third trimester and boosts growth for the first few weeks after birth, but it destroys the mother's reproductive system." Nora twisted her ring. "The births during the trials were incredibly violent, and if a female managed to survive, she was culled directly after. There's no research on what happens past that."

"Sounds about right." Cal spat a bit of tobacco from his lip, his gaze lingering on the bedroom's port. "You think you can get her through it?"

"I don't know… I wish Jolie was here. She has far more experience with this than I do, and with the babies to contend with as well… I'm going to need help."

"Flynn wanted us up there to bring back more Fetches," Cal said. "No reason we couldn't throw a Binder into the mix."

Everyone's gaze landed on Fitz.

Shite.

"How long would it take you to shift to Glynfyls and back?" Rogan asked.

Fitz tugged his patch. "Eh…dunno. Half a day? More, mayhap. Depends on how fucked them Breakers left where I got imprints." Or he could slip into the Between, be there in a blink, and have time to grab a pie and a pint with no one the wiser…his coin flared hot, and he bit back a grin.

The big Breaker caught it and ran a hand down his face. "Why do I feel like letting him go by himself is asking for trouble?"

"You're not the only one, but we don't have an extra body to babysit," Cal muttered, lighting his smoke. "Luckily, I do have incentive. Extra thousand units if you go straight there, pick up Markham and Jolie, and come straight back, no—"

"Ya, ya. No detours. Ye said already." Shite, he'd have done it for half that. Fitz got to his feet, and Rogan scowled.

"That. Right there, that fucking look."

"What look?" Fitz wiped the smile off his face. "Ain't no fuckin' look."

"I'm sure Fitz understands how important this is," Nora said, scribbling out a note and folding it in half before handing it to him. "Give this to Jolie. Last I knew, she was at the Breakers' Conclave. You're going to have to go to the Marked Man—what?"

Fitz's throat bobbed and he tugged his collar. "Eh…naught. I just ain't, eh, exactly welcome at that particular establishment."

"Jesus Christ, what the hell did you do?" Rogan crossed his arms over his chest, like he were just waitin' for it.

"Had a slight disagreement over cards. Me luck were runnin' higher than it aught, and the table took umbrage." Fitz smoothed his patch. "'Specially one prick in particular."

The big Breaker rolled his eyes. "So you were stupid enough to cheat and got caught."

"Nah, ye fuck." Fitz scowled. Cheat? Like he needed to fucking— "A McCreedy don't cheat, and I swore it on Cajetan hisself. Cards is somewhat of a sacrament to the blessed saint, and ain't no good comes from crossin' divinity."

Cal snorted. "Bet that oath went over well."

"Nah." Fitz snapped his lapels square, riled. He were a lot of things, but a cheat weren't one of 'em. "Man were out for blood and mine were up…might've run me mouth then sliced off his ear."

Rogan barked out a laugh. "Tell me his name wasn't Sirrus Fastblade."

"Dunno, but weren't the quickest I've seen…eh…why? Ye know him?"

"Yeah, I know him, he's the proprietor. Shit, no wonder you're not welcome. A skinny little shit like you besting him in his own damned house? I guarantee you he doesn't give a fuck about his ear, but his pride's another matter." Rogan pinched the bridge of his nose. "Jesus, kid. You step a toe in there, and he's gonna challenge to regain his honor."

Fitz grunted, well aware. Them Breakers was a touchy lot.

"Then hopefully Jolie's with Pithy or at the Academy where they're housing the children. Take this imprint," Nora said. He did, a mental image of a comely dark woman searing into his book of memories. Fitz went to take the paper from Nora, and she pulled it back a fraction. "The money aside, you need to come back as soon as possible, Fitzpatrick. If Jolie's not here for Kara when the babies come, I-I don't know what will happen…" She bit her lip and turned away, teary eyed.

Christ, that got him every damned time… Fitz scowled and took the note from her, tucking it into his pocket. "Ye have me word, there and right back," he muttered. She sniffled and nodded as she went back into the kitchen, leaving him feelin' like a right shite.

Rogan grunted, watching her go. He blew out his cheeks. "And if Jolie is at Conclave, find Marcos or Stonefist to take you in. If someone higher on the hierarchy vouches for you, Sirrus might not kill you on sight."

"I'd like t'see the prick try—"

"Do me a favor and don't." Rogan scowled, shaking his head. "That leaves us to settle with the twins. You ready?" he asked Cal.

"Ready? I was waiting on you."

"The fuck you were," Rogan snorted. "Let us out?" he asked Fitz.

Jesus, they was worse than his gran's dog. He glowered and went back over to the port, shifting it aside with a half-arsed bow. The Breaker muttered somewhat unflattering and pushed past him with the old hillie smoking in his wake. Two of 'em started blatherin' like a couple of fishwives before they'd cleared the hall.

Fitz shifted the portlock back into place and craned his neck toward the kitchen. By the play of energy, Nora were right back at it, sortin' them memories, and His High Holiness and the lady were still fuckin' their brains out.

A smile slid across Fitz's face as he opened his sight wide to the planes of energy weaving around him. He might not have all the imprints heading north, but surer than shite someone had been that way, and as long as they was fairly recent…

Christ, sure enough, there was a mess of 'em big enough to sail a schooner through. Must've been from them Breakers on the march. He took a deep breath, sending talent betwixt 'em like an arrow through a hula hoop and aligned them, tethering hisself to a path.

He licked his lips and took one last glance toward the kitchen before shifting a bit of reality to the side, then grinned as he dove into the tear.

MOTHER SAT upon the bench in her garden, face lifted to the noontime sun, her halos aglow. She swept through Titus's mind, the small signs of intrusion disappearing beneath the tines of her talent like footprints from a sand garden. A dry, rasping chuckle slipped past her bloodless lips at the boldness of Nora Jester's intrusion, but like so much else, naught would come of whatever breadcrumbs she'd gleaned from Titus or Victor.

Not now, and not after what was to come.

The strands of talent connecting Mother to the twins thrummed with anticipation, and she smiled at the gambit about to play out amid the ruins of the defunct facility. The beginning of the final act. The two of them stalked the streets of the Source, and regardless of how

Enoch's dice may fall, she was confident of the outcome. She would win, and Cal would lose.

Perhaps that's why she'd chosen to indulge the Jane-that-was, letting her run through memories typically locked away. The silly girl took them out like baubles to see them sparkle, ignoring the grime of reality caking each of her precious moments.

A Christmas eve with family—the last before her mother's fatal crash.

A kitten—gone with the arrival of her father's new paramour.

And Rogan. So very many of him.

Tall and broad with a thick mane of fiery red hair, his cheeks and forearms burnished by the sun—Mother frowned, suffering through the montage. She was certain that the rekindling of the Jane-that-was's obsession with the big man was entirely due to the holo of Laughlin in the birthing cube.

The scene had made her more unstable than usual, bringing up emotions Mother had thought long dead. But, as much as she hated to admit it, the parallels between the two men were difficult to ignore. Especially with the Jane-that-was harping on them. Mother frowned, not understanding the desire to self-flagellate. One would think the sting of Rogan's chronic rejection enough…but apparently it wasn't.

The way Laughlin spoke to the Assembly before he left, didn't it remind you of Ro after the First Incursion?

No, but him destroying half of Glynfyls did, she returned dryly.

The Jane-that-was laughed. *God, how I ached for him after that…*

That was true. It had led to their first battle for dominance. Mother smiled. Victory had been sweet, and Jane knew her place now.

Unfortunately, there were others that chafed at their roles.

Mother's smile evaporated, leaving her alter ego to reminisce and following one of her threads leading north…

Lady Geraldine Saks swept in to her solicitor's office, half an hour late, and didn't bother to remove her hat or gloves as she settled onto a chair. Mother smirked from the edges of the woman's mind at Serra's sniff of impatience. It was nothing compared to Geraldine's annoyance that she had to deal with the shrew, and it had only been at Mother's behest that she'd lowered herself to do so.

The solicitor stopped staring at Serra's breasts long enough to hand Lady Saks the findings of Tamara's fertility test. Geraldine snapped the report open and scanned it with a smug little smile—

Serra plucked it from her hand and tore it into two long, thin strips. Lady Saks bit back her outrage at Mother's unspoken command, the sonorous ticking of a wall clock and the crackle of the fire in the hearth the only sounds in the room.

Serra passed the strips over her shoulder to Otto, and he obligingly fed them to the fire. Mother sent a tendril of talent-laden suggestion to Lady Saks, and the woman's face twitched as it took root.

"I believe Lady Hess and I need a moment," she said.

Otto gave her a sly glance before he bowed, then followed the solicitor from the room.

The door closed behind them, and Lady Saks peeled off her gloves. "There were no surprises in that envelope, were there, Serra?"

"No, Geraldine, there were not."

"And what do you hope to gain from this shameful display?"

"Hope to gain?" Serra laughed. "Oh no, I fully *expect* Tamara and Miles to be bonded as soon as possible."

"You're quite bold, aren't you?" Lady Saks snapped incredulously. "I can assure you that if that were to happen, I would disown Miles, then take guardianship of his son and make him my heir."

Serra's eyebrow rose. "No, you won't. The boy will remain with his father. Miles and Tamara will raise Owen as the next Lord Saks. You'll instruct your solicitor to draw up an agreement between our two Houses to include a generous stipend and housing arrangements for myself. I'll also need several thousand units deposited into my account by the end of day."

Lady Saks's temper rose, and Mother soothed her a fraction. *Play along…* she whispered into the woman's mind.

"And why, pray tell, would I ever I do that?" Geraldine asked tartly.

Serra smiled at her. "Because I have irrefutable proof you've been working with a certain person in the South."

"Oh, you do, do you now?" Lady Saks scoffed, a sliver of anxiety riding beneath it.

"I do, and it would be a shame if it should get out you've been feeding Titus information."

Mother bit back a chuckle as Serra overplayed her hand. *Agree to her terms, you'll be rid of all of them soon enough…*

The woman frowned, shaking with rage as she smoothed the kid gloves on her lap, as if mulling Serra's demands over; though there really was no decision to be made. Not after Mother's conditioning. Getting rid of the Source trash sullying their city was Lady Saks's civic duty.

"Well, then I suspect in exchange for your silence, your terms are acceptable," she said, pursing her lips sourly. "And with the coming nuptials, you and Tamara should retire from the city to Jarlsford, our country estate. Living at a hotel is rather gauche…"

Excellent. Pleased with the results of their meeting, Mother slid from Lady Saks's consciousness and jumped to a nearby strand. She stayed at the edge of Otto's mind as he removed his hands from the solicitor's temples.

Mother pursed her lips in approval. What a good boy, doing as he was told. He waited for the solicitor's eyes to refocus on the room. Once they did, the solicitor's brows furrowed for a beat before he turned on his heel and headed directly to the water closet, his backside clenching beneath his trousers.

Otto chuckled and turned to the sideboard to make himself a cup of tea. Mother waited until he was done to strum his consciousness, and his spine straightened as he lowered himself to sit.

Have the twins been set to their task? he asked, settling into a chair before the small hearth and blowing across his cuppa.

They have, and now it's time for you to escalate on your end.

What about Scot?

He's not your concern. Otto's annoyance flared and was quickly quashed at the lash of agony she sent through his temple. Mother tsked as he put a hand to it, his teacup rattling on its saucer—

"Bring my wrap, Otto, it's time we left," Serra said, breezing into the room.

Mother withdrew enough for him to do as he was bid. Through the doorway beyond, Lady Geraldine Saks's expression was akin to someone's who'd bitten into rotting meat. But that was to be expected. Serra was nothing if not predictable, and she'd made an art of alienating people.

Otto fetched her wrap, and they exited the solicitor's office. The gate was a few blocks down in the center of a landscaped square. Mother rode with them as they waited to pass beneath the milky arch. It began to snow, and Serra pulled the swath of ermine closer around herself, muttering. Mother smiled, wondering if the tropics would appeal. If all went to plan, she'd find out soon. She nudged Otto, and he sighed.

"How did it go?" he asked Serra.

She looked down her nose at him. "Better than with Scot's damned cohort, but funding is no longer an issue. You were right about her affiliations. We're to move into her country estate as soon as possible. No one who's anyone is staying in this cursed city, and half the hill is already gone. I'll need you to make arrangements."

"Of course." Otto paused as if something had just occurred to him. "You know, I've been thinking about the notices sent to the Source Binders regarding the violations of their housing contracts. It seems rather discriminatory to me. I think you could have a viable lawsuit on your hands…"

He shivered as Mother left him, stroking her approval over his hypothalamus in her wake. Another strand of her web had begun to thrum. Her attention was needed elsewhere.

ELIZE PAUSED at the mouth of the alley somewhere deep within the Source. It vexed her to no end, but she wasn't able to find her way into the building where Cal and Rogan were holed up. She pulled talent, getting her bearings and searching for her erstwhile lover. Her eyes narrowed as she ran into a wall of static, her talent dispersing beneath it. She gritted her teeth, unable to find Rogan either.

Enoch broke his stride to turn back to her. "Issues?"

"They're cloaked the same way the girl was back at the Triam," she huffed, plaiting her braids together to mute their chime. The streets were too quiet. The last thing she needed to do was parade down them with a bell around her neck.

"It doesn't matter. We know where they landed. They won't be far, and I'm eager to get on with this." He pulled his crescent blade from his belt, knuckles whitening around its leather wrapped hilt.

Elize blew out a fitful breath and nodded, swallowing her anxiety. She reached up to caress the gem at her brow, a wave of calm breaking over her. Her anxiety faded beneath Mother's attentions. Enoch was right. They needed to make an end of this.

The thought sent an unexpected pang through her chest as she followed her twin out onto the streets. Once pristine, they were now littered with broken glass and debris. The late afternoon sun rode low on the horizon, casting the ruined facility in shades of gray. "What about probability? Can you use your extra to find their location?"

"No." Enoch's mouth soured. He moved to keep within the darker shadows. "Not since the facility's power went down. All probability ends in a void."

"Well, that's less than ideal." Elize chewed her lip. "Do you think this is it? The tangent you saw?"

"I can't imagine what else it could be."

She frowned, grazing her hand over the swirls of the engraved revolver riding on her waistband beside her own crescent blade. She eyed the way Enoch was gripping his. "Do you really think Rogan will let you get close enough to use that?"

"Of course." Her brother smiled at her, flipping the wicked little knife around his fingers. "His honor will be his undoing. I found that fate written for him long ago. All that remains to be seen is if that night is tonight."

"And if he kills you?"

"Then pray Jane's mad scheme actually works, and we wake up in our summerhouse swathed in silk sheets with a beautiful, clueless boy between us."

"It will work." It had to. She sniffed, and held her head higher.

"Are you afraid?" he asked a moment later. Elize shook her head, and he scoffed. "Liar."

"Fine. Of facing Cal? Yes. Of dying? No."

"I don't see why." Enoch scowled. "He never deserved you."

And Cal hadn't deserved what she'd done to him in return but then, they'd both been adept at hurting each other. Fuzzy bits of memory teased the edges of her mind, familiar and not…

Something was there that hadn't been before. Dry leaves skittering on a chill wind and the moon riding low in the sky. She shook her head, the crisp autumn breeze of upstate New York against her skin instead of the hollow dankness of the Source. "Next time will be different."

"Doubtful," Enoch snorted. "If none of this ever happened, then we're all bound to repeat—"

She spun on him, revolver in hand, and jammed it beneath his jaw. His pupils expanded and he wet his lips. "Next time will be different," she gritted out.

Enoch smirked, his Adam's apple rising to kiss the barrel of the gun as he swallowed. She narrowed her eyes, finger on the trigger. Whatever was about to come out of his mouth—

A harsh cry echoed through the streets behind them. Another answered it, and then a third. They weren't the only ones hunting in the city tonight.

Enoch lowered her arm and started down the street again. "Let's go. As much as I enjoy you threatening me, it will have to wait. I'd prefer not to be held up by other matters."

Damn him, but he was right. She slipped the gun back into her waistband and followed him through the deepening shadows. He paused at the end of the block, frowning as he considered the barren intersection ahead. It was too quiet. Expectant. The hair at Elize's nape rose. Something man-sized darted between the buildings and they froze, listening.

The barest scrape came from behind them, and she plastered herself to a wall as Enoch ducked and swung, taking their erstwhile assailant in the gut. He clamped his hand over the thug's mouth and slashed across his throat, then lowered his corpse to the ground as he bled out. Murmurs rose from the surrounding buildings.

"Run," Enoch hissed.

Elize sprinted across the intersection to the next patch of shadow, her heart in her throat, its beat choking out the manic laughter rising and the strike of footfalls behind her.

The hunt was on.

CHAPTER SIXTEEN

"Mother has become a constant whisper in my ear, and my mania to reverse the Surge laid plain to any who know me…who knew me…I-I am not the Jane I was, or perhaps I am, and she is not me? I try to temper myself, but Mother's words slip from my lips unbidden. The looks on Ri and K's faces when I tried to explain about the fourth duality, how all of the squalor and suffering will disappear as if it had never been—

The pity in their eyes—it's not there now. No. Now I hear them crying out in my mind with the others. Bargaining and cajoling. Claiming friendship, to help…but I see their minds too clearly. They would turn on me, just like Mother said.

Like A when he saw me…her…what we've become.

The rage I felt wasn't my own, yet how it burned! An amalgamation of all the wrongs and slights I've taken from others' minds—all Elize's pain at his betrayal—I see it too late. There are more of them than me, and their fears and the blackness from their souls has grown into a separate thing.

She hates. Hungers. Is me, and I am she riding roughshod over the Jane-that-was and all the rest that we've harvested. Nothing remains but our goal, and I will have what I've lost…"

— Undated journal entry
Final entry

FLYNN OPENED HIS EYES, slowly remembering where he was. Shit. He scrubbed a hand over his face. He hadn't slept that well in days. Just sweet oblivion; not one fucked up dream or memory. Kara made a little noise and scooched closer to him. He tightened his arms around her as she sighed, nestling close. Contentment streamed through their bond, and her breath steadied as she slipped back into sleep.

He dipped his head to breathe her in, the babies a slow churn beneath his hand. Around them the air hummed, heavy with that sense of expectation that'd been growing ever since they first crossed the border. Flynn frowned at the new thread of urgency lacing through it. That he could do without, but whatever the hell it was, it'd mellowed the static, and he felt more whole than he had since the plateau. He was gonna take that as a win.

Kara murmured in her sleep, and he smiled, kissing her temple. It wasn't the only win he needed to celebrate. Her, the babies, he had them back and wasn't letting them out of his sight. He sighed. Now he just had to get them through the rest of it, which meant they needed to move.

"Wake up, baby," he murmured.

She frowned, her nose crinkling as his beard tickled her skin. "No."

Flynn chuckled. "Yes, brat."

"No," she said, rolling to nuzzle against his chest, face still heavy with sleep. "Not until you tell me what you think that hum is."

"You hear it?"

She cracked an eye and looked at him like he was an idiot. "Of course I do. And you do too, don't tell me you don't...I felt it. We both did." She sighed, her breath warm against his skin. "It's like before, but stronger."

"Yeah." He tucked her hair behind her ear. "But I dunno why."

"I think it's trying to tell us something."

Flynn snorted. Great. Just what he needed. One more thing to add to the list of cryptic messages. Like phantom flames and talent fucking with him weren't enough. "Then it should speak the fuck up instead of sending smoke signals."

"Careful what you wish for." She yawned, pushing up on an elbow, a hand over the "o" of her lips. Her hair fell forward to frame her face, and he cupped her cheek. Damn, she was beautiful. She tucked a lock behind her ear. "Ugh. I feel like I could've slept for hours. How does that even make sense if I've been in stasis?"

"Because your body's working overtime." And that was exactly why they had to get back to the Triam. Doctor Yu had said Kara and the babies were gonna need extra nutritionals, and he believed her. "Come on, Rogan and Cal have gotta be back by now."

Kara sighed but let him help her up, scowling as she got to her feet, a hand at the small of her back. "Glory, I hate this," she muttered, doing a double take at his smile. She smacked him. "It's not funny!"

"I'm not laughing," he said, laughing. "I think you look beautiful."

"Yeah, well, you've also decided to start lying," she grumbled.

He hugged her and kissed her forehead. "Not about that, baby. Never about that."

She bit back a smile and huffed, trying to play it off. God, she was fucking adorable. He helped her to the port and brushed his fingers over the metal. *Little help...?* It rolled to the side, and he let out his breath. Thank you, sweet baby Jesus.

The main room was empty, and only Nora was in the kitchen. Well, that didn't bode well. Where the hell had that shifty Fetch gone now?

"Where's Fitz?" he asked, coming to the doorway.

Nora dropped talent and opened her eyes. "He's on his way to Glynfyls."

"Cal and Rogan with him?"

"No. They left to take care of the twins."

Jesus fuck. Flynn riffled his hair. She had to be kidding. "You're telling me they sent him up alone?" Nora nodded and he swore. "What the fuck were they thinking? There's no way that little prick's gonna make it back in time to shift anybody out of the Triam—if he comes back at all. Shithead's probably at a pub somewhere."

Nora drew herself up. "I don't think you give Fitzpatrick enough credit. He gave me his word he'd be back as quickly as he could."

Flynn snorted. "Yeah, I bet he did." Which would be after the fact, blotto and stinking like fish. Flynn's knuckles cracked, ready to make good on his threat to beat the shit out of the kid. Christ, he knew keeping Fitz around was gonna fuck him.

"Hey." Kara put a hand on Flynn's chest. "It will be okay."

"You're right, it will, because Nora's giving me those memories." With Plan B off on a bender, they didn't have any other choice.

Kara chewed her lip. "Flynn, I don't think—"

"It's not open for discussion," he snapped, trying not to wince at her hurt anger searing back at him. Damn it. "Look, I'm sorry, but I don't see any other way to do this."

Her gaze locked with his, emotion flying between them. Kara's jaw tightened, and she shook her head, looking away. "Fine. Then that's what we do, but you're an idiot."

Nora sighed like she was in full agreement. "I figured you wouldn't be dissuaded. I've done what I can to process them...but I'll warn you, they're still fragmented, and I have no idea how your mind will respond."

Hopefully better than last time. Couldn't be worse, right? "I'll make it work."

Nora glanced at Kara before rising to put her hands on his temples. "You're sure?"

"Just fucking do it."

Nora's lips whitened and her halos flared. Flynn stumbled, wincing as codes and protocols meshed with odd bits of info flooded his psyche. He inhaled sharply and gritted his teeth, trying to—fuck, how the hell was he gonna do anything with this shit? The way it was ordered...goddamn Binder logic...he couldn't make heads or tails of why she'd grouped things together and other things floated free—

Nora dropped her hands and stepped back. "That's all of it."

Christ, it better be. Flynn rubbed the heel of his hand across his forehead and fell back into a chair. He rocked forward, gripping his head. Felt like it was gonna split in two—God, that fucking hurt. "Shit. You weren't kidding."

"No, I wasn't." Nora spun that stupid little ring of hers. "I'm hoping because it's information as opposed to suggestion your Breaker psychology won't reject it...but this isn't something I have any experience with—"

"Yeah I know. You can't predict how it's gonna affect me," Flynn said sourly, cutting her off. Spoiler, so far it sucked. "You got any aspirin?" She nodded and hurried into the next room. Fuck, the pounding behind his eyes was awful, and he was abruptly freezing.

Nora back came in, and he took the bottle from her, downing two of the little white pills dry and shoving the rest into his pocket. He ran a hand over his face and pinched across his temples. Wasn't anything for it. They had to go. He'd figure shit out while they were there.

"Right. We're out. When Rogan gets back, ask him about that rogue Binder. We both know Cal won't say shit. You ready?" he asked Kara.

She stepped away from her mother's embrace, tears in both their eyes. Nora gave her a curt nod and Kara turned to him. Her lips were pressed into the same white line as Nora's. "Are you?"

"I have to be," he muttered, fighting a wave of dizziness. He stood and put an arm around Kara. *Triam?* he asked, calling for Fetch talent.

Talent flared silver and colors ran.

Flynn staggered as they materialized back in the gestation chamber, and Kara steadied him. "Sorry, my head's killing me," he said at her look.

"No shit," she muttered.

He snorted at her cursing and immediately regretted it.

Around them, the hiss of pumps actuating was louder than it should've been, and halos bled out around the low pulse of lights. He blinked, and they stubbornly persisted. Christ, that wasn't good.

The other women on gurneys had been moved back into the room, easily a dozen of them in various stages of pregnancy. Doctor Yu was at one of their consoles. She finished what she was doing and turned to them like they'd been expected.

"Mr. Scot," Doctor Yu said. "I was starting to think you'd decided to decline Patron Titus's generous offer. Wise of you to return." She turned to Kara, and Flynn caught site of a smaller woman in scrubs across the room. She looked up, her bronze halos catching the light. That had to be the Fixer Yu had wanted on-call.

"Your gestation bay is there." Yu pointed to where Kara had been when Flynn had first arrived, the screen behind it repaired. The doctor went over and made several entries.

He stood rapt. The flash of menus and codes she was entering triggered what Nora had given him, associations building between the free-floating snippets and information extrapolating. It was like an operations manual had opened in his mind's eye, the information on the comms system and facility protocol abruptly available. Jesus. A dull throb began in his temple.

"I've let Patron Titus know you've returned," Yu said, frowning at him. "I'm sure he'll send someone shortly to show you where you'll be staying."

"I'm staying with Kara."

Doctor Yu's frown deepened and she shouldered past him. "You'll have to take that up with him. My concern begins and ends with this litter, which by now will be in desperate need of nutritionals—"

Flynn's bloodlust surged, another data dump unfolding. He grabbed the woman by the throat. His breath stuttered out as he fought against the overwhelming urge to crush her larynx. It would be so fucking easy…her eyes bulged, tablet clattering to the floor, hands scrabbling at his forearm—

Bronze light flared and he gritted his teeth, static eating the Fixer's talent before it reached him. Kara's surprise filtered past his rage. Fuck. What was he doing? He breathed through his 'lust and eased his grip a fraction.

"Only nutritionals," he growled. "No accelerant, and if I find you trying to pull any shit like you did with those prostaglandins, I will inject you with the exact same cocktail then take you apart piece by piece as you writhe on your own fucking autopsy table—got it?"

She nodded, her face purple. Flynn released her, and she dropped to the ground sucking wind. Kara put a hand on his arm as he rubbed his temple. Christ, he couldn't remember the last time he'd lost his temper like that. He shook his head at Kara's concern.

Across the room, the portlock rolled to the side and a scantily clad Breaker female strode in. Her nostrils flared, and she ran a hand through her thick blonde locks, nipples pearling beneath the gauzy fabric of her chiton. A wave of her 'lust answered his. He pinched it from his nose, the shitty perfume magnifying his headache. Christ, she was eyeing him like—

Kara growled, blackness churning through their bond. She stalked forward. "He's mine."

Shit.

"Not for long," the blonde pipped, her gaze slid to Kara's abdomen, her lips curling into a dismissive smirk before coming back to eye-fuck him.

A dank cloud of Kara's fury filled the room, devouring the female's 'lust. She took one step back, then another, and her legs gave out. She fell to her knees, prostrating herself. Her shock and sour fear spiked the room.

"I'm sorry!" she squealed, her high, flute-like voice cutting through Flynn's skull. "I didn't—Patron Titus assigned me to escort him to the glade and see to his needs. Nothing was said about a-a *mate*," she spat out the word like it tasted bad.

"Surprise," Kara said sweetly.

Flynn's balls drew up. Shit. Things were about to go downhill fast. "Tell Titus to fuck off," he said, sliding his arm across Kara's chest and holding her against him. "Shh…calm down, baby," he murmured into her hair. "The only thing I need is you."

She growled. "Calm down?" Her 'lust churned blacker. The blonde coughed, gasping. Alarms went off throughout the room, the vitals of the women in stasis rising. Pain lanced through Flynn's head with the noise, and he swallowed bile.

Kara's gaze flicked to him, then back to the blonde. "Get. Out," she seethed.

The woman frantically nodded, struggling to rise, then gave up, scooting backwards on her hands and knees. The port behind her opened. She fell through, then was up and running.

Kara shivered, coming back to herself once the female was out of sight. She put a hand to Flynn's temple, her brow furrowed—

"Fascinating," Doctor Yu murmured, scribbling notes on her tablet.

Kara's head whipped around, and Flynn took her hand. "Ignore her. You okay?"

She nodded, but her expression said otherwise. "You're not leaving me."

"No." He kissed her palm. "I'm here, and I'm yours. Let's get the babies what they need, then we'll deal with Titus."

Kara gave a curt nod, but her gaze lingered on the port.

ROGAN CROUCHED in the shadows of a balcony three stories above street level. Below, Enoch dispatched thugs as they trailed after Elize. He'd sent her running, flushing out the members of the gang that'd been stalking them. It'd been smart distracting them with what they figured was easy prey while he methodically picked them off from behind.

Rogan studied the man. He hadn't been this close to the feral prick in centuries, and Enoch had definitely upped his game. His kills were quick and efficient, and he was adept at using that fucking crescent blade of his.

He sliced the throat of another thug, and Rogan grunted, standing. In another few minutes Enoch would be at the front of the building, and Rogan wanted to be downstairs to greet him.

He ducked through a shattered window and made his way through the ruined convention space to the floating, gilded staircase leading to the vestibule. Above, a massive starburst chandelier glinted in the dying rays of the setting sun. Amber light pinged from its facets, stippling the room's burnished walls and the intricate mosaic floor below.

Rogan sat on the steps facing the blasted frame where the rotating door had been. Only the metal struts of the windows facing the street remained, thick mounds of shattered glass littering the room and the pavement beyond.

He threw up an orb of flame, highlighting the destruction and sending long shadows streaming from the tumble of ruined couches and chairs.

A handful of minutes ticked by before Enoch resolved from the darkness across the street, his pressed chinos and white button down spattered with gore. Even from afar, an unholy gleam lit his eyes.

Rogan stared back, his face blank. Enoch smiled and crossed to the building, glass crunching beneath his loafers.

He stepped into the room and looked around. "Is this where you want to do it then?" The hair on Rogan's nape rose at the man's silky, cultured voice. Enoch had always been too damned smooth. "I suspect it's as good a place to die as any."

"Is that the end you found for me?" Rogan asked, running a hand over his stubble. He leaned back onto his elbows, and Enoch's grin widened.

"You know it doesn't work that way. I find probabilities, not certainties, and tonight is a blank slate, which makes it all the more exciting. It really is quite tedious when things are set, but lately I've had as much fun as in the beginning of all this." He ran his thumb over the sweep of his blade, tonguing the corner of his lip. "How would you like to begin? I think a challenge seems apropos. No talent, my blade against yours."

Rogan stared at him for a long moment.

"Was it you or Elize who slaughtered my boys in Tribeca?"

A sly smile flitted about Enoch's lips. "Oh, that was me. The elder died well. He reminded me so much of you, I made sure he lingered. As for the younger…well. He just cried."

Rogan nodded, silent for a breath before his halos flared.

The dusky man collapsed into a boneless pile on the floor, a cry of outrage reverberating through the room, his upper vertebrae atomized. Rogan leaned forward, savoring the struggle on the prick's face. The finality of what was about to come gradually set in, and Enoch's expression smoothed to a simmering hatred.

Rogan pulled his own blade, thumbing its edge. It'd gone dull from all the use he'd gotten out of it earlier, but was still sharp enough to end this.

"There was a time when I would've taken a great deal of pleasure in beating the shit out of you," Rogan said softly. "Now, I just want it done, and you dead."

Enoch laughed. "Where's your honor, Rogan McGuire? You, who used to be so fond of lecturing me on the subject. You'd cripple me then finish the job when I'm defenseless? You're no better than I am."

Rogan stood and crossed the floor. He crouched in front of Enoch and raked his head back to bare his throat.

"You're right, I'm not. Any honor I had you killed with my boys in that fucking desert."

He ripped his blade across the feral prick's throat, doing what he should've centuries ago. Color bled from the gem at Enoch's brow. It crumbled as a wash of blood surged over the floor's tiny tiles, racing through the grout lines and spiking the air with the sharp mineral tang of copper.

Rogan drew in a stuttering breath and closed his eyes. His throat bobbed. It was done.

He dropped the waste of meat, the thud of Enoch's head a dull echo throughout the blasted space. Rogan stepped back. He killed his orb and sat on the steps, watching the mosaic disappear beneath the creeping black slick.

Remembering.

Then his halos flared, and there was nothing left of his enemy but ash.

ELIZE SPRINTED through the shadows laughing, her halos aglow as she found ways to elude the men on her trail. The footfalls behind her slowly reduced in number, silence surrounding her as she stopped to catch her breath. She scanned the street, waiting for Enoch to appear, grinning and blood spattered, as he had so many times before.

Five minutes, ten... Her throat bobbed as her breath slowed, and she tucked a stray braid behind her ear. Where was he?

You know the answer to that, Mother whispered. *Now remember the rest...*

Elize cried out as memories flooded her, the holes in her mind abruptly filled with what had been.

Cal.

Walking at his side, her hand in his. Their bond. Feeling his love and dragging it through the mud just to prove it was real, then punishing him for it. Her past rearing between them, too ugly to escape.

Everything before the Surge, before it all went wrong—she laughed, slumping against the building's facade—no, it had never been right. She'd never been right. There was too much there. The things she'd done in her father's name—in her own to spite him—she'd never meant to love the pig farmer's son from Meskill. Had never meant to hurt him…but couldn't stop from doing either.

And Cal'd just taken it, damn him…until he hadn't.

Autumn leaves skittered through her mind. Her abdomen heavy. Words shouted that could never be taken back. Lord, how they'd fought, how he'd raged, how she'd purposefully goaded him, drinking up his pain along with her own—

Then choked on it.

Jeremy. Their boy. So little. So perfect and so still. Her midsection a ruin of red along with any chance of redemption she might've had, and Cal…

He couldn't let her die, goddamn him. He'd begged Jane to heal the gaping wound, to make her forget. To take the only thing she had left of them.

Her memories. Her emotions.

She'd never hold a baby. She'd never gotten to hold her son.

She wished she'd been buried with him.

But no. Jane had saved her. Cursed her. And Elize had revisited that on Cal in turn.

Her hand shook as she clamped it across her smile, everything that had happened after playing out in graphic detail. All the deaths at her hand. His sweet pain at her betrayal time and time again, and it still wasn't enough to balance the scales. It never would be.

How dare he make her feel.

And each time Mother took her memories away only to return them again; Elize's hatred burned anew, as fresh as the blood dripping from his elbows that night—

Familiar hands closed around her shoulders, and she choked back a sob as the scent of tobacco surrounded her with his cloak. She leaned into him, her backside aligning with his groin, her head tucked against the underside of his chin. A perfect fit—like they'd been made for each other.

On the outside at least.

Cal let out a slow breath, hot and scotch-laden, across her cheek, his arms tightening around her. "Don't," he whispered in her ear, his voice cracking.

"Since when have I ever listened?" She arched her neck and offered him her throat, needing to feel the brush of his lips. He hardened against her, and she smiled as his fingers strayed to brush against her breast. His weakness had always been her, and no matter how toxic, some habits were too hard to break. She gasped the way he liked it, and he pushed her against the side of the building.

"I said don't, Elize. This needs to stop." He panted, his hands at her hips saying otherwise.

She laughed at him over her shoulder, her nipples pebbling against the gritty brick. God, she loved it when he was riled, the way his eyes turned to jade ice. "There's only one way that will happen."

"No. You could walk away."

Mother laughed in the depths of Elize's mind, echoing the one coming from her lips. "We both know that's not true," Elize murmured. Cal stepped back, and she slowly turned to face him. "There's no coming back or moving forward. Not for us."

"I made a mistake, Lizzy, and we've both made plenty since. Walk away."

The pain in his voice warred between a tightening fist in her chest and the growing heat between her thighs. Wanting to destroy and devour him and hold him to her always—*Sick, this is sick*, a distant voice screamed inside her—

Then end it… Mother whispered, quashing it.

"I can't do that," Elize said, not sure who she was answering.

Cal closed his eyes for a long moment. When he opened them, they glistened in the moonlight. She reached up and ran a hand through his thick, snow white hair, remembering it as the color of burnished wheat. Alister Caliban Scot. Tall and golden with those great big green eyes and a grin that made you want to drop your panties there and then. Not the most handsome man in the hollow, but so damned charming. Laughlin had that. Would their son have as well?

"It will never go back to how it was," Cal murmured.

"No. But it can be better." She gave a sad laugh at his frown. "Walk away. How could I have walked away when those women…your *wives*," she spat, drawing out the word, "had everything I ever wanted and could never give you or anyone else."

Cal ran a thumb across her cheek and leaned in, kissing her softly. Her lips trembled against his. How long had it been? God in heaven. No one kissed her like he did.

"I would've loved you for however long we were set to walk this world."

"Then you can love me again in the next."

"I don't believe that," he said, shaking his head, "and I can't let you do it. Jane's playing with shit she doesn't understand, just like her goddamned father—"

"If that was all it was, you would've told them by now." Elize laughed softly at the look of pain that crossed his face. "My onion man. All this time and still so many secrets. Are you that afraid to die?"

"No." Cal frowned and cupped her cheek, drawing her closer against him with the hand gripping her hip. "You warm up to the idea after your heart's been ripped out a time or seven."

She laughed and tilted her chin, kissing beneath his jaw and down his throat, her fingers drifting to the gun at her waistband. He gave a low moan, the air between them thick with everything still unspoken.

"I would feel you in me one last time before the end," she whispered.

"You will." He captured her lips with his and kissed her like it was already upon them.

Elize jerked twice—his phased hand closing around her heart and twisting. The revolver fell from her grip, discharging as it hit the ground.

Cal sank to the pavement with her corpse in his arms, silent and still while the moon rose. Then he sifted through her braids to find the milky stone entwined in them, and gated away.

KARA FLINCHED as her vein rolled for the second time, and the bruise beneath her skin bloomed darker. She breathed through her 'lust, Doctor Yu muttering something and jabbing her with the butterfly needle again. This time, she managed to do it correctly and set the IV port into the back of Kara's hand. The chill burst of saline flushing through it was a welcome distraction from what'd just happened.

Kara chewed her lip. Glory, this was going to be harder than she'd thought…but that female…she closed her eyes and took a deep breath. She had nothing to worry about. Flynn was hers, she knew that, but the shock of being slapped with the Source's culture after Glynfyls's was akin to jumping into Casmot's Bay.

There was so much more danger here than Titus. The female would've killed her and the babies in a heartbeat to get to Flynn. Kara took another slow breath. She shouldn't be surprised, the competition for the status second brought had always been vicious. She chewed her lip as her gaze moved over the women in stasis lining the room. But why would anyone want to sign up to be a part of this living morgue? Status couldn't be a factor, so why the heck—

Kara shook her head. Whatever weird subculture they had didn't matter. She couldn't show the slightest inkling of weakness, but relying on her 'lust was a slippery slope. If Flynn hadn't been here…

But he had been, and he promised he wasn't going to leave her. He squeezed her hand as he stood beside the gurney, giving her no reason to doubt him. He ran his thumb over her knuckles before raising them to kiss, his hazel-green eyes laden with worry.

Crap. He'd felt how close she'd been to letting the 'lust get the upper hand. She needed to manage it, but it was so close to the surface, and he wasn't doing much better. The darkness she'd felt when he'd grabbed the doctor by the throat—

Kara winced as Doctor Yu tugged on her IV to hook her up to the bank of machines behind the gurney. Not that she could blame Flynn. The woman's bedside manner was sorely lacking, but since all of her patients were comatose, it probably wasn't something she had to work on. A pump actuated, and Kara shivered at the cold stream running up her arm.

"Can she get a blanket?" Flynn asked.

"That usually isn't an issue—"

"And that wasn't a question. Find one," he growled.

Doctor Yu glanced at the Fixer, and the slight woman hurried from the room.

Another pump engaged, and a searing burn replaced the chill in Kara's veins. She winced as the ochre solution disappeared into her body. Glory only knew what it was. "I wish Nora were here."

Flynn grunted, more fidgety than usual. He watched everything Doctor Yu was doing like a hawk. His forehead was lined and the pulse at his temple throbbed. Kara hoped that meant the memories Nora had given him were assimilating.

He glanced at Kara. "How are you feeling?"

"Okay, but I could ask you the same thing."

His face darkened, eyes flicking to the bruise at Doctor Yu's throat. A wave of self-loathing cresting through their bond. "I need a shower and to stay out of my own head," he murmured.

The port to the gestation chamber rolled to the side, and the Fixer came back in with a blanket. She handed it to Flynn, the thick fabric trembling as she held it out to him.

"Thanks," he said, taking it and spreading it over Kara.

"You're welcome." The woman's throat bobbed. "When you're done, I'm to escort you to the glade to join Patron Titus for dinner."

Flynn grunted, his eyes flicking to Doctor Yu. She was busy making notes, tight-lipped. He rubbed his forehead. "How long is this gonna take?"

She huffed, finishing what she was doing before answering. "The levels are right there on the screen. There and there. She's almost done for this round, but the litter's vitals have suffered from your little sojourn. Ideally, she would stay put, but given your lack of concern for their welfare, I'll need her back here within the hour to get them caught up."

Flynn's jaw tightened, and Kara put a hand on his arm. Glory, did this woman not understand how close he was to the edge? A machine beeped, and a light on the screen flashed green. Good. They could get out of here.

Flynn grimaced, scrunching his eyes shut for a breath. "Fine. She'll be back then."

"Fine." The doctor disconnected the IV and pointed at the port. "That stays in."

"Of course," Kara said. After the botched job the woman had made of replacing the first one, there wasn't a chance Kara was letting her do it again.

Flynn helped her up, and she bit back a wince at the dull cramping in her back, equally terrified and hopeful it was an early sign of labor. As it was, she was ridiculously close to thanking Titus for speeding things up. It was awful being pregnant.

She chewed her thumb, trying not to scowl as they followed the Fixer from the gestation chamber and passed another Breaker female eyeing Flynn. Kara reached for his hand, swallowing a growl. Glory, she felt like a cow.

"You're more beautiful than any of them," Flynn murmured, pausing to kiss her temple.

"Let's just get this over with," Kara muttered, waddling deeper into the Triam.

TITUS LOUNGED beneath the twisted boughs of a live oak, ankle over his knee. The massive tree pushed up through the stones at the edge of the glade, dwarfing those around it and shading the manufactured oasis from the harsh plaz lights above. He picked at a plate of fruit and cheese at his elbow, having already cleared it of its array of cured meats. Waiting was not his strong suit, and typically he would've dined an hour ago.

Bourbon in hand, he sourly observed a group of females playing pétanque. Their capering did little to distract from the fact that Scot had returned with Kara Jester, and for some inexplicable reason, it was not amidst the throes of labor.

Titus frowned, unable to justify that or how the prostaglandins in the cocktail Doctor Yu had injected were now suspiciously absent from the girl's system. Whether Scot had access to Binder talent or not, one would think removing them beyond his expertise.

Which meant that Scot hadn't been the only Talent to come south, and Titus's money was on Albanach's erstwhile paramour, Nora Jester, being back at the corporate suite. He dusted a finger over his lips, considering the implications. Regardless of whether or not he could get his hands on the bitch, her meddling was cause for concern.

A communications orb materialized to his left, interrupting his thoughts. Doctor Yu's voice came from the swirling blue mist. "Patron Titus?"

He swirled the ice in his glass. "Yes?"

"I'm sorry for the intruding, sir, but you wanted to know when Mr. Scot was en route? He and his bitch have just left the gestation chamber, and you should know, there was an incident—"

"I'm aware." Of both Scot's threats and the little pissing match between the females. Normally he'd let the latter play out, but with his cocktail compromised, the Jester girl's survival had abruptly become a dice roll.

Titus frowned, ending the communication at the low whir of a personnel transport in the distance. It irked that he had no idea what the girl's reaction to the rest of the reagents in that shot would be, and betting on her regenerative abilities seemed foolhardy…but what was done was done. As long as a portion of the litter survived, he was still ahead.

And Scot could always breed more.

A smile slicked across Titus's face as the whir of the transport grew louder and he glimpsed the vehicle through the trees. It followed the serpentine path through the little wooded valley and coasted to a stop at the glade's entrance.

The females paused their game to stare as Scot exited the vehicle. With reason. Titus's own pulse ticked up at the play of muscle beneath the man's shirt. He motioned for another bourbon as Scot helped his bitch stand. She took a moment to catch her breath, and then hung on his arm as he escorted her to the table. A sub hurried over with a third chair and another followed with an additional place setting.

"I'm assuming your return means you're acquiescing to my terms?" Titus asked.

Scot frowned. "About that." He got the Jester girl settled, then pulled his seat closer to hers. The females on the other side of the glade whispered amongst themselves as he sat. "I have some caveats."

"Oh?" Ballsy of him, but then Titus had expected as much. He swept up a handful of almonds, noting the youngest female disappear between the trees. If the rest of them weren't already on their way here, they would be soon to inspect their new Alpha. Thanks to Vignette running her mouth, they all knew Scot had put down Beritram, and that Brix would be displaced was a foregone conclusion.

Titus popped a nut into his mouth, unabashedly inspecting Kara Jester. The females were doing the same. They were quite territorial, and the incident in the gestation chamber had yet to play out. Until then, she would be considered a threat.

He frowned. Although obviously uncomfortable, she looked more hale than she had any right to be. Perhaps he should be betting on her ability to regenerate. Titus's mouth watered at the potential of breeding that into his other bitches. He dabbed his lips with a napkin to hide his smile, already crunching the numbers. His production rate would skyrocket.

"Right. We're here. Now what?" Scot growled.

Titus returned the napkin to his lap. *Now you comply.* "Anything to drink?" he asked as a sub approached the table. "Our meals will be out shortly."

Scot glanced at the girl, and she shook her head. "She'll have a water," he said, lacing his fingers with hers and kissing her knuckles. The sub bowed and left them.

Titus bit back a scowl at the display of affection. "You said something about caveats?"

"Yeah. I'll take your deal, but until I'm broken from her, Kara is mine. I'm not leaving her side, and whatever shit that was with the female in the lab, stops."

"I've no idea what you're referring to," Titus lied. His lips pursed around a sip of bourbon as the girl's beverage was delivered. Leaves rustled beyond the glade, more females arriving by the moment. "And

I'm happy to provide a suite." Whether or not the girl ever set foot in it remained to be seen. The way she kept rubbing her abdomen, Titus very much doubted that would be the case.

"Let me be clear," Scot said, squarely meeting Titus's eye as if he hadn't spoken. "I'll stay, but after the birth, Kara and my children will be returned to Glynfyls—" He squeezed the girl's hand at her cry of protest, and she looked away, her expression murderous. The females across the glade and those hiding beneath the trees went very still.

"And if she dies," Scot continued, "so do you. I will peel your skin from your sorry carcass, grind what's left in rock salt, set it on fire, then tear you open with my bare hands. Once I've pissed on what's left, I'll lay waste to this entire facility then hunt down anyone that shares a drop of your fucking blood and do the same to them."

Titus shivered, a delicious chill traveling up his spine. "Been thinking about this for a while, have you?" he drawled, his pants growing tight. If Scot had meant to dissuade him, he was going about it the wrong way. That was exactly the type of visceral savagery Titus meant to populate his ranks with.

A trio of subs approached with carefully plated potions of steak au poivre. Titus traded his bourbon for a knife and fork as they set it before them. He took an appreciative bite, savoring it along with the moment as he chewed.

Across the table, Scot glowered at him, and the girl was very busy trying to manage her 'lust. The females across the glade had resumed their game and were flashing far more skin than they had been. Titus ran his napkin over his lips, assuming that was intended to antagonize. If so, it was working.

"I must admit, I've thought about your return quite a bit as well, which is precisely why her and the litter's continued survival is subject to my goodwill," he said, carving off another forkful. Neither of them had touched theirs. Probably wise with the amount of Zanthium he'd instructed it to be laced with. "I'm afraid returning them north is impossible if you wish them to continue breathing. But I'm a reasonable man and more than willing to continue supporting their existences—on two conditions."

"Which are?" Scot growled around his cigar.

"First, you'll sign a contract giving me your allegiance and agree to breed whatever bitches I select, in perpetuity. In return, you'll become the Triam's Alpha and have access to all that entails."

A muscle in Scot's jaw jumped, apparently not impressed with the generosity of that offer. "And Kara and my kids?"

Titus popped another bite into his mouth and shrugged. "I'd expect that's largely dependent upon your behavior and hers." He ran his gaze over the seething girl. My, but she lovely when thirsting for blood. "In anticipation of your demands, I've already arranged for her next stud."

Scot's face contorted and the air grew heavy. The girl put her hand on his arm, his struggle to control himself apparent. The females across the glade darted into the trees to join the others, the air gaining an anticipatory vibe.

"No one touches her."

"Mmm." Titus hummed around his mouthful. "I don't believe you're entitled to that prerogative anymore, and without that as part of the agreement, the rest is void." He swept a forkful of meat through a slick of sauce, completely unconcerned that Scot would cave.

He and the girl stared at each other, some unspoken communication passing between them if their facial expressions were anything to go by.

"Fine," Scot finally gritted out. "But I swear to Christ, if—"

His nostrils flared, and he shot to his feet as footsteps pounded down the path the transport had taken earlier. Brix burst into the glade, a dank cloud of 'lust billowing in around him.

"Scot! You'd challenge me in my own house? I'm gonna fucking kill you!"

CHAPTER SEVENTEEN

Glynfyls's golden age is rife with fantastical tales, however the legends surrounding Pans are somewhat of an anomaly. The mythical Fetches were purported to be able to translocate objects remotely, harness the power of flight, and shift vast distances. Yet, unlike the other lines which revere their most powerful members, Pans are always portrayed as despots. Without exception, the stories surrounding them deride their powers and laud them being outsmarted by the line's common element, ultimately resulting in them being expunged…

– Lord Talos, Preceptor of History,
Academy of Glynfyls

"…A contract signed under duress negates consent and renders the stipulation of use of talent in exchange for housing void. This is an egregious example of pay-to-play, taking advantage of my clients' unfamiliarity with the North, and an abhorrent attempt to exploit a subset of an emerging community. Ergo, we're demanding redress…"

– Atty. L. Watyr for the Plaintiff
Class Action Lawsuit, Hess v. Scot

FLYNN'S HAND closed around the tactical knife in his pocket, static surging around him as Brix stalked closer. Christ—he blinked hard, his vision swimming as he rose to stand between the prick and Kara. Goddamn it, his head was already pounding from all the new info cramming his brain and Titus's shit. The Elite's twisted panties were the last fucking thing he wanted to deal with.

"If you kill him, I'll be displeased," Titus said, the ice in his glass clinking.

Displeased? Was that motherfucker talking to him or—

Brix threw out a burst of talent, making the question moot. Flynn's shield met it, and another formed over the table to keep Kara and that red-headed asshole safe. He grimaced at the surge in static, but thank God his fucking talent was cooperating. As much as he wanted to see Titus dead, they needed him alive—for now. There was still too much of what Nora had bound into Flynn's brain that he had no idea what to do with.

Brix laughed. "Is that how you beat Beritram, you twisted fuck? Couldn't face him like a Breaker?"

Flynn winced, not in the mood to trash-talk. "You've got one chance." He growled, losing the fight to push down the rising darkness in his gut and leaking 'lust. Kara's concern twined through the sticky strands, grounding him. He held on to them for dear life. "Stand down and submit."

"Fuck you." Brix lunged, and Flynn dodged to the side, slamming his fist into the Elite's face. Blood sprayed from his nose, and he fell back, ripping the dangling plug from his nostrils as it began to smoke. It bounced across the ground and burst into flames.

Flynn pushed out a cloud of 'lust, and the Elite's knees buckled. "Submit!"

"Overlord," Brix sneered as he struggled to keep standing. He swept the back of his hand through the slick of crimson painting his face and laughed. "You still hit like that pussy I took apart in Kensbot." He cracked his nose back into place, then spat out a gob of gore.

...the blade flashes at the corner of his eye, molten warmth dripping from his jaw, agony building, searing, as the Peacekeeper slices him wide...

The darkness inside Flynn surged, clawing for release. He shook the memory away, his headache receding beneath his hate and the Elite's challenge, Kara's emotions distant. His focus narrowed, centering on the bigger man. The static in his head pitched to a shrill whine, and he bared his teeth. "Yeah? Wanna try it again?"

"Gladly, and after I put you on your knees, I'll do the same to your bitch. I bet she's gonna look real pretty with my dick in her mouth."

A torrent of blackness screamed through Flynn, devouring his reason.

He sprang, and the Elite fell back beneath the ferocity of his attack. Talent laden blows rained between them, the reek of singed flesh and blood flooded the glade. Bone cracked, and Flynn went down, his ankle crumbling, and his tentative hold on the beast inside him slipping.

He hit the ground hard, the Elite on top of him. Brix's fist took him in the jaw, wrenching it askew. Flynn yelled, sending out an onslaught of flame. The Breaker scrambled off him, screaming, his face an oozing blistered mess; one lid melted wide with horror and what'd lain beneath it a charred, milky ruin.

Flynn slowly got to his feet, swiping blood from his eye. Motherfucker had split his brow. He struggled to maintain his balance, hobbling as Kara's bind struggled to reverse the damage to his ankle. Claws scrabbled at his insides, begging for release. He slammed his jaw back into place and rode the pain to maintain his dominance over the darkness within. Grimacing, he held a hand to his face as it swelled, panting and blinking away the gray tunneling his vision.

"Submit," he garbled out as his chest heaved. "I. Am. Alpha."

Brix laughed, his 'lust turning sour as he clambered to his feet. "Doesn't matter. When we left that field up north...there is no hierarchy. Not for us."

"Yeah, and what about your mate?" Flynn spitballed, remembering the man's face when Yu cut his access to the lab.

"Don't fucking talk about her!" Brix charged, and Flynn met him, digging in his heels as he was pushed back, the Elite's fury fueling his strength. Brix lashed out, gnashing his teeth and ripping off a chunk of Flynn's ear.

He bellowed, the beast inside him answering the assault, and the world washed crimson.

WOLF SURGED FORWARD. Time sped and slowed, his senses gaining a predatorial sharpness. His body exploded into motion, reflexes automatic—

Sweat slicks, fingers dig, slipping, he claws at the man and jerks his knee into his groin. Agony blooms amid the ruin. Sweet bliss. Musk, heavy and dank twines around them. Wolf revels, panting, wanting to roll in it like spoiled meat. He throws the man, and his spine cracks against an outcropping of stone. A scream splits the air, and Wolf shivers with pleasure.

The knife from his pocket is in his hand—flicked open. He stalks closer, his prey's remaining eye wide with fear, the stink of it a foul ribbon of shit splayed through the air. He rips at the ground to escape, pulling himself toward the trees, his legs a dead weight.

A cruel grin slice Wolf's face, lupine and mocking. He grabs an arm and flips the man onto his back, breath speeding. Tendons strain, bones offset. A slow creak—sharp crack—guttural shriek, shards of white shrapnel arrow from within. His fingers slick with blood—

"Flynn."

Wolf's head jerks up. The growl in his throat dies.

His mate crouches on the other side of his prey. Reaches across. Her hand on his cheek.

"He's had enough. I need you to come back to me."

KARA.

Her emotions poured into him; love, concern…he flinched, waiting for the disgust, for the judgement in her gaze—

"Please. Come back."

No. She didn't, she couldn't—

She'd fucking seen.

She is our mate.

Flynn's pulse sped, the animal retreating, pushing him forward. He rocked back on his heels, clenching his fists as his mind cleared, hands sticky.

He stared down at the mutilated man between them, the barest rise and fall to his chest. Shit. That was Brix.

Flynn's bloodlust left him. He stood as Kara came to his side, pushing beneath his arm. She took the blade from him. Closed it. He pulled her close, grounded by her touch. His mouth dry, he swallowed. What the fuck had he just done?

Around them, the glade was silent, but there were people beneath the trees, the air heavy, humming—

They'd all fucking seen.

Memories assaulted him, jumbled and incoherent, his headache roaring back. His knees threatened to buckle, and Kara steadied him as he began to shake.

Play it off, play it off…fuck. He needed to keep his shit together—

"Laughlin Scot is Alpha!" she cried, that hum around them increasing, her strength pouring into him through their bond.

Goddamn it, she didn't have it to spare. He forced himself to stand taller, feeling like a complete asshole. Around the glade leaves rustled, and a crowd of female Breakers stepped forward—shit, how many of them were there?

"He is Alpha," they intoned, falling to their knees.

Jesus fuck—

Slow clapping came from behind them, and Flynn bit back a growl. "My, you're quite the showman, aren't you?"

Fuck Titus and fuck this shit.

Flynn lifted his chin, ignoring the prick and taking the ball Kara had given him. He needed to run with it. "Stand up, Breakers don't kneel."

Furtive glances shot between the females as they reluctantly complied. What the fuck had Titus done to these women? Flynn's 'lust jumped again, and Kara's arm tightened around his waist. Whatever their conditioning was, it stopped now and so did them fucking with her. "I am Alpha, and Kara is my mate," he shouted loud enough to reach the far edges of the crowd. "You obey her as you obey me."

"And you'll both obey me," Titus said from the table. "My second condition is that you submit to any and all testing I deem necessary to catalog and replicate those delightful genomes of yours."

Flynn's stomach dropped.

… *"You let them touch you, and they're gonna see it, all the black and evil you've got inside…"*

And now Titus wanted it.

Flynn closed his eyes, his headache ticking up a notch as his shredded ear throbbed. He pinched across his temples. Of all the fucking places to lose his temper—Christ, he'd fucked up.

Beside him Kara faltered, snapping him back into the present. He scooped her up, streaking the sheet around her crimson. "Where can I clean up?" he asked ignoring the ultimatum.

Titus smirked from behind his bourbon and motioned to one of his servants. The man cautiously stepped forward and bowed before leading them back to the transport. The crowd of females silently parted for them, every eye glued to Kara, the stench of their challenges clinging to them as they passed.

KARA BREATHED THROUGH HER RAGE, her arms tightening around Flynn's shoulders. The transport had carried them back through Titus's weird underworld and let them off at the double doors leading to the facility. Flynn had refused to put her down, and despite her token protest, she was glad. All of those females—ugh!

Her bloodlust was screaming at her to beat the hell out of every last one of them, but physically? There was no way she could take any of them on in her present state…at least not without hurting the babies. She closed her eyes, another cramp rippling through her abdomen. Glory, she was so done with this pregnancy.

The sub led them to a port just past a set of double doors not too far from lab. He scanned his barcode, and the portlock rolled aside. He stepped back to let them through. Beyond was a cookie cutter version of every suite in the Source. The aperture closed behind them, the click of a locking mechanism absent. Glory, the fact that anyone could just walk in here made her skin crawl.

"Fucking Titus," Flynn swore, setting Kara on her feet. The static around him ticked up. His halos flared plum, then crimson, tiny pops sounding around them and the smell of burnt electronics threaded through the remains of her 'lust. Cameras, she assumed. He collapsed onto the couch, pinching across his temples with a bloodstained hand.

"Why don't you take that shower?" Kara said, trying to keep the fury from her voice and failing miserably. "Let me go make sure there's no one in there waiting for you."

She headed to the bedroom before he could reply. The portlock rolled to the side, and she laughed. The bed was a leather covered mattress, and the rest was set up as an S&M dungeon. She shook her head at the low contoured couches and the flails lining the walls. Well, she suspected whips and chains tracked, now didn't they?

"Seriously?" Flynn's sigh came from behind her, and she glanced at him. Her 'lust waned. He looked terrible.

Kara put a hand to his swollen cheek, her heart hurting for him. All the self-loathing and disgust churning through him... Glory. He wouldn't meet her eyes.

"Why don't you go first?" Flynn mumbled, dabbing at his split brow. "I-I think I need to lie down. Maybe I can start to make sense of what Nora dumped into my head." He turned away—

"Flynn, stop. You did what you had to."

"Did I?" He snorted, flexing his knuckles and dusting them over his palm. Bits of gore flaked to the carpet. "I wasn't gonna stop, Kara. I didn't want to. Fuck, I wanna go back out there and finish it."

She drew in a slow breath, fighting to push emotion into the sucking black void that'd opened inside him. "Neither one of us is at our best right now. That's not who you are—"

"No?" Flynn's laugh was cruel, tinged with the same dark fury he'd expelled on Brix. "What if it is? What if that is who I really am, and the rest is just fucking window dressing?"

"So you're saying when I succumbed, that was the real me?"

"No, but I didn't—that out there wasn't—Jesus fuck, Kara, even before I fucking split—it's more than that. Something in me...shit like that just now? It lights me up." His face contorted and he tore at his hair, pacing. "I used to make a ton of fucking money doing it for hire, and I'd laugh my ass off every payday because I would've done it for free."

Kara narrowed her eyes at the mix of longing, satisfaction, and contempt for himself roiling through their bond. "That out there was you claiming Alpha. From what I've seen of those females, they wouldn't have accepted anything less, and you and Brix have history —he tried to peel your face off when you were in prison!" she gritted out through clenched teeth, her 'lust seething at his myopic view of himself. "You gave him the chance to submit, and he didn't. He deserved everything he got. That darkness might be a tool, but it isn't you."

"A tool." He ran a hand over his beard and laughed again.

"Yeah, and you're acting like a huge one right now." Glory, why couldn't he just—*ugh!* She wanted to shake him! "Didn't you tell me I could be whatever I wanted to be? That the past didn't define us? You weren't that man when I met you, and you're not that man now."

He looked away. "If that were true, I wouldn't have done the same thing to those Sons after the train wreck, or gutted the Breakers in the tunnels. Fuck, Morris would still be alive—"

Her fist took him in the face.

He fell backward, tripping over a low couch and landed on the floor.

"And here I am, a breeder. How dare you, Laughlin Scot? How dare you think the same rules don't apply? If that's the case, then I guess I'll just accept my fate and bend over for the next stud in line," she hissed with cold fury.

Darkness flickered around them, like tinder trying to catch. Hers or his, it didn't matter. He'd put this thing between them.

He slowly got to his feet, teeth bared. "That's not what I—"

Kara backhanded him. "That's exactly what you said!" Blood sprayed from his lips, and her pulse jumped in response, an all-consuming need to hurt him thrumming through her veins. Golden light flickered through the room. Had she called talent? It didn't matter. She knew what to do with it.

Flynn grunted, hunching over with a pained gasp, his eyes level with hers as he cupped his groin. "Kara—"

She bit her lip and reached out, gently stroking his battered cheek. "Is that what you want? For me to do the things with them I do with you? Will you watch when Brix puts me on my knees and shoves his dick in my mouth?"

Flynn growled and grabbed a handful of her hair, his 'lust flooding the room. Talent hummed around them, pulsing, filling her with power. She laughed and tightened the bind on him. He huffed, shaking.

"What's the matter? I was meant to be a breeder, so what do you care?"

His halos flared scarlet, breaking her bind, and he spun her around, pinning her arms, his lips at her throat. "You're not a breeder, you're mine," he snarled.

"Then prove it to me."

"I don't want to hurt you, Kara."

"That's too bad, because I'm going to hurt you."

***

TALENT SURGED, slamming Flynn back against the wall. Golden binds spread him eagle, snaking around him. He writhed, the pressure in his nuts dancing the knife's edge between pleasure and pain. He gasped as it pulsed, and his dick jumped in response. What she was pulling...no, she wasn't pulling. It was from that mess of static around him, but how the hell—

She drew from the mess of talent, his clothes shifting to the floor. He shivered, his desire coiling with hers, their need shared. The bonds restraining him tightened, digging into his skin. His nostrils flared, her 'lust tipping toward chaos. Flynn wet his lips, anticipation dampening his spine, craving...needing...

"You want to be punished?" she asked, plucking a flogger from the wall and running the leather falls through her fingers. "You're such a bad man...I'll punish you." She snapped them straight between her hands then trailed them along his shoulders and down his chest. His head fell back, cock bobbing as she teased around it... Jesus fuck, this woman...

"Kara, I—" He cried out as she flicked the falls across his engorged shaft, leaving little burning echoes in their wake. Flynn groaned, the softness of her palm following over it delicious torture against his abused flesh.

"Is that what you want, baby?" she crooned, stroking away the sting.

No, it was what he needed. He choked down a sob. "Yeah."

"Ask me for another."

"Another, more," he panted. "Please..."

She lashed him again, his thighs, his chest. Little red ribbons raised over his body. He groaned, his tip dripping as her nails scored down his rigid length. Kara traced up his slit, gathering the seeping moisture.

"This is mine." She met his gaze and sucked her finger clean. "I won't share you, and I won't be passed around. I am not a breeder, no matter what my past might've dictated, and you are not your darkness. Understood?"

"I—"

She lashed him again, and he screamed.

"Understood?"

"Yes, ma'am." Flynn's throat bobbed, his body aflame from the flogger. The subtle air currents laden with the scent of her arousal prickled against his skin, and that fucking hum between them was going straight to his cock. It throbbed, his crown an angry purple. Christ, he needed her. More than the blood in his body or the breath in his lungs, she was his soul. His light. His fucking everything. She held his goddamn heart.

He'd be anything she wanted, or die trying.

"Say it."

For her. He could do this. For her.

His head hung, throat bobbing. He inhaled, breath shuddering over cracked lips. A fist tightened in his chest. "I'm not my darkness."

"No...you're not." Their bond thrummed with her satisfaction at his submission. It soothed her 'lust, blunting the edge screaming for his blood. The dark tendrils softened, her talent caressing away and healing his wounds. "Do you need me, Laughlin?" she purred, close against him.

So fucking bad. He strained against her binds. "Please, baby…"

"Please what?" She traced the pulsing ridge of his crown and looked up at him through her lashes. "How can I make it better?"

Goddamn, she was driving him insane. That vision of her with Brix —"Suck my dick," he rasped.

She laughed and dropped to her knees, kissing along his corded shaft before taking him into her mouth.

"Oh, fuck, yes…" Flynn groaned, eyes rolling back into his head. The hot, slick velvet of her cheeks pulling on him, the flick of her tongue as she built a rhythm with the twist of her grip… Pressure from her bind flowed from his sac to his pucker, teasing around his asshole—

Her fingers dug into his thigh as he tensed, eyes raising to his, so fucking beautiful as she swallowed his cock. Sweat dripped town his torso, his breath coming fast. Her brow quirked, and he gave a halting nod.

The thread of talent expanded, pushing inward to his gland and began to pulse as she worked his length deeper into her mouth. Waves of pleasure coursed through him, short-circuiting his brain, the tingle in his spine immediate—

He bellowed, coming so hard he saw stars. Hips jerked forward as he emptied himself into her throat, his legs turning to rubber. He sagged against the binds. They dissolved, and he sank to the floor.

"Jesus fuck, woman…"

"Wow. You liked that, huh?" Kara laughed, still on her knees before him.

Had he liked it? Flynn snorted and pulled her against his chest, kissing her forehead. Shit had fucking rocked him. "Yeah, I liked it… what about you?"

"Raincheck…" She frowned at the ear Brix'd gnashed. "But can you please stop being stupid now?"

"I dunno if that's possible," he rumbled, fingering the wound. Top was tender and new, her weave struggling to repair it. He hoped what that fucker ate made him sick. Flynn sighed, smoothing back her hair. "But I'm yours…" She grimaced, and he leaned forward, searching her face. "You okay? Shit, you were using talent—"

Kara waved him away. "I'm fine, just crampy—that talent wasn't mine. The hum…the static past it. It was weird. I was so upset with you, and then it was just there for me to use…is that what you meant about not pulling?"

Flynn shrugged, running a hand over his face, then grabbed his shirt. That motherfucker's blood was still all over him. "Maybe? I mean, it sounds like it, but how—"

"If Titus cured my deficiency, then my extra would've let me share your talent," she said, biting back another grimace. Flesh rippled across her belly, like a shark preparing to crest. Her hand followed it. "Something's different. It's been building since this morning, I can't explain it, but I think the babies are coming soon."

Which meant he was running out of time to figure things out. He hugged her tight, then lurched to his feet and offered her a hand. "Go ahead and take the shower first, maybe it will help with your cramps. I'm gonna lie down and try to sort shit out."

She nodded, wincing as she stood, and trundled into the bathroom. It was surprisingly normal considering the room it was connected to. He pulled a thick white robe from a hook on the wall and set it on the vanity.

"Just call if you need me."

"Okay. I won't be long."

Flynn grunted and headed to the leather mattress. He tossed a bolster onto it and flicked out the folded silk sheet at its foot. Christ. He snorted as he climbed in, but he'd definitely slept worse places.

The low hum of ultrasonics pulsed on in the bathroom as he lay down, throwing an arm over his face. He exhaled, grimacing at the low-grade migraine creeping back. The sooner he made sense of the information messing with his mind, the sooner they could get the hell out of here.

FITZ SHOT out of the Between and landed face down his old bed, his heart goin' gangbusters and his body abuzz. Christ, that were always a rush. He rolled onto his back and frowned up at the pristine ceiling. Last time he were here, cobwebs had hung thick in the corners.

Shite. That didn't bode well. He sat up, stomach dropping. Rest of the room were neat as a pin. Odd piles of crap he'd pulled from his pockets over a decade ago were lined up on the dusted dresser, and the change of too-small clothes tossed over the chair, gone.

His throat bobbed as he glanced at the slick of silver coating him, listening hard. Didn't hear aught, but thank Jesus the liquid talent were sucking into his skin faster than usual. Must be on account of him not streaming in a dog's age. Usually took a good half hour before he were fit to be seen.

Which was why he always came out of it here where there weren't chance of him being happened upon. At least there hadn't been. He ran a hand over his mouth and crept toward the door, inching it open.

Big room beyond were just as tidy. Place had been cleaned, wall of windows overlooking the city washed—Jesus. He moved closer to the glass, talent flickering through his halos in the reflection. A sea of lights surrounded the dusk-cloaked city where the Flats had been, skeletal buildings going up at a furious pace and what looked like the beginnings of a second wall just past 'em. How all that'd been done since they'd been south...

Fitz shook his head and turned away, pausing by the sunken couches. The desiccated cheese board and the two crystal cut highboys was gone. He frowned, an ache in his chest at the remains of that last night with his Uncle Ian being cleared.

Fitz's hands fisted by his sides. Fuck them fuckin' Prydees. Knew it'd been them. His uncle had bequeathed the damned flat to him—not that it would've stopped them from havin' their way with it.

He closed his eyes. Done. It were done. Let them harpies have it. He never wanted it anyway. Just meant he had to find a new place to come out of the Between, and now weren't the time to do it. He scratched his stubble, glancing back at the window. Halos had about stopped flickerin'. Needed t'get the lay of the land, and the best way t'do that were to find a chatty whore. If he were lucky, Adelaide'd just be getting up.

He pulled talent and shifted to his tenement, swearing as he tripped—

"Fitz?" Her voice filtered through the washroom door as he kicked a box aside, scowling. She came out, pinning up her hair.

"What the hell's in there?"

"Naught," she said, hurrying to push it beneath the bed. "When did ye get back?"

"Just now, but I ain't stayin'. Ye know where Markham is?"

"Ain't ye even gonna say hello?" she huffed, all gussied up in her Sunday best, arms crossed over her chest, pushin' up what little were there to an advantage.

He wet his lips. "Eh…hello?"

By her smile, she'd caught him lookin'. She strolled over all coy and cozied up, fiddlin' with his shirt buttons. "Markham's down at the wall, most like. There's a big platform where all them Firsts is overseeing the build."

Fitz grunted. Then that's where he'd head next. "Why ye in yer church clothes?" he asked, resting his hands on her hips. Had she always been this slender? Didn't feel right, his fingers aching to sink into somewhat…nah, someone. Christ, he needed to forget about that little witch. "Ye get canned?"

"Worse. Pony were done in by the quakes. Ain't naught left but rubble, and the city's awash with tail. Me and the other girls is takin' turns staking out the pubs and workin' the fourth rung. Ain't no money t'be made below, but if them Intelligencers see ye up there regular-like, they'll haul ye in whether they catch ye soliciting or no."

"How much ye need t'stay here?" He frowned at her furrowed brows, but the last time she'd gotten picked up, bastards had beaten her bad while takin' liberties. She'd been abed for a week even after he brung her to Pithy. Some shite the Binder couldn't heal. "I don't want ye anywhere near the hill, 'Laidey. It ain't safe." Especially with them Prydees on the hunt. Her face went soft, and he looked away, her aura way too fuckin' rosy. Damn it. "Look, ye do what ye want. I'm only offering 'cause of what they done before."

"Fitz, I can't keep takin' yer money—"

That were a new one. He snorted and pulled out what were left of his units, peeling off enough t'keep her set for a spell. "Oh, ye'll earn it..." She smiled, reaching for his cock, and he twisted his hips from her. "Nah, ain't got time for that...need information, and maybe a favor. Ye know where I can find a Binder named Jolie?"

"No," Adelaide said too quick, her face a careful blank, tellin' him aught he needed to know. Only time she clammed up tight were with Breaker Business.

"Good." Adelaide would be able to get in and out of Conclave without anyone battin' an eye. "Then I need ye to give her this." He pulled out Nora's note.

"The fuck I will." She huffed a strand of hair from her face. "I ain't exactly welcome after vouching for ye to get in on that card game. Sirrus's still scrambled ham about his ear." She shook her head. "Nah. I'd rather take me chances with them Intelligencers."

Damn it—wait. His coin warmed as inspiration struck. "Eh... Never did say I were sorry about that." Mostly 'cause he weren't, but she didn't need to know that part. "Here," he said, pulling the box of sweets from his pocket. Hadn't been keen on carryin' around an anaphylactic attack anyways, and his gran'd probably feed 'em to the damned dog. Didn't need that vet bill.

Adelaide's brows knit as she took them. She unwrapped the bit of twine, her breath catching as she opened it. "Fitzpatrick McCreedy—y-ye got me chocolates?"

"S'Fitz," he muttered, rubbing his jaw at her eyes welling up. Shite. "Eh...know how ye fancy 'em. They're them Deep South ones hillies smuggle in special. Ain't got a drop of wax—" He shoved his hands into his pockets and scowled. "Whatever. Eat 'em, sell 'em, I don't care."

Her big blue eyes met his, all winsome. "Ya, ye do."

Fuck. He turned away, running a hand up his nape. Should'a fed them to the dog hisself and paid the damned vet. Woulda been cheaper than what this were gonna cost him.

"Gimme the note. Ye want her back here?"

Fitz paused, and she snatched it from his hand. "Eh...ya?"

Adelaide nodded and tucked it into her bodice then popped up on her tiptoes to kiss his cheek. "Gimme an hour. I ain't back by then, ye better come callin'," she said, shoving the box of chocolates under the mattress on her way out the door.

It closed after her, and Fitz stared at the warped planking for a breath before raking a hand through his curls. Fuckin' woman had been lookin' at them damned sweets like they was a ring—

Markham. He needed to find Markham…then deal with Adelaide, after.

Didn't have an imprint for the platform she'd mentioned, but knew the wall well enough, and then it were only a matter of jumping line-of-sight. His uncle were right there front and center waving his arms every which way. Fitz shifted to the rail at the man's elbow.

"Eh…"

His uncle started, spinning around with his hand pressed to his chest. "Good Lord, Fitzpatrick, I wasn't expecting you!" He grabbed Fitz's sleeve and hurried him beneath an awning where the First Fixer, some lord with dark curls, and a blond man was standing around a table.

Shite. Hadn't seen them.

Fitz shrank back, and his uncle tightened his grip on his arm. They stopped talking soon as they saw him, suspicious-like. Markham smiled and shook out his handkerchief before he coughed into it, clearing his throat.

"Ah, Carl, Jacques, Dorian. You gentlemen remember my nephew, Fitzpatrick—

"S'Fitz."

"—he recently accompanied the Overlord south," Markham finished, his clamped fingers all but screaming at Fitz to behave.

Fitz's throat bobbed at the hope that bloomed across their faces.

"Laughlin—is he back?" the curly-haired lord—eh, Jacques—asked.

Fitz wet his lips, glancing at Markham. His uncle nodded at him. "Eh…nah. Sent me back t'get help. Found the Triam. He's with the lady, but the place is full of Breaker females and kids. Said he needs Fetches t'get 'em clear…" Fitz glanced at Markham again. "Asked for ye, particular."

"Damn it, the timing is terrible," the big man murmured, his gaze flicking out to the construction. "How many of us do you think he needs?"

Fitz shrugged. "Dunno. Ain't seen how many there is…send down a dozen, mayhap?"

His uncle grunted. "When does he want us there?"

"Sooner than naught. I can give ye the imprints t'follow. Gotta t'bring back some Binder, eh, Jolie, for the lady tonight."

Markham chewed his lip. "Yes…following's best, it will take me some time to—"

"A Binder?" the Fixer First asked. "I thought Lady Jester went with the Overlord."

"Eh…ya." Somewhat about him were familiar, but Fitz couldn't place it. "Needs help. Lady can't leave until she has them babies, and Titus did somewhat to 'em."

"Jolie…" the horsey-looking blond man murmured, his halos glimmering purple. "She's working with the Breakers in Conclave—"

"Oh no. Fitzpatrick's not getting anywhere near there."

Markham frowned at Fitz, and he shrugged. What he'd done, he'd done. Usually weren't no skin off his nose—or his ear.

"What do you think the chances of Marcos and Stonefist still being at the ridge are?" Markham asked the others.

"Poor." The blond man frowned, his halos flaring again. "That was hours ago, and I'm certain—yes. They're at the Marked Man now, and without a Breaker to vouch for you, you won't be able to set foot inside." He drummed his gloved fingers against the table.

"Perhaps Lady Breakspear?" the Fixer First asked.

The blond man snorted. "I believe she's quite busy at the moment. Your notice to the Source Binders in violation of their housing contracts was not well received. Serra filed suit and the idiots decided to take the matter up with Lot since he's the only Scot currently in residence."

Fitz glanced between the four lords. Whatever that meant, by their expressions it weren't good.

Jacques snorted after a heavy silence. "I'm assuming that didn't go well."

"Ah, no." The blond man guffawed. "Words were exchanged, Lot hit one of them, and the Intelligencers hauled everyone in, including the lady. He's being charged with assault, and it's becoming quite the circus. I'm assuming that's why Crandall's not here."

"Damn. As Laughlin's proxy, I should make an appearance." Jacques swore again. "Who else can we get to vouch—"

"Already took care of it," Fitz murmured, itching to be done with this. He jammed his hands into his pockets as their attention focused back on him. He shrank back behind his curls. Christ, he hated dealin' with hillies.

Markham froze mid-blot. "Tell me you didn't send Adelaide."

"Eh…"

His uncle shook his head with a long-suffering sigh.

"Who's Adelaide?" Jacques asked.

"The Breaker whore Fitz gave Sirrus Fastblade's ear to after he sliced it off."

MARCOS BELLIED up to the bar at the Marked Man and ran a hand over his close cropped hair, sighing. What a damned day. He caught Sirrus's eye through the crowd and held up two fingers. The barkeep nodded and reached for a pair of tankards.

"You a regular here?" Pax asked, scanning the crowd.

The pub was quite a bit fuller than when they'd come up from Conclave earlier. Glory, had that only been this morning? Felt like a solid week had passed. Despite his exhaustion, Marcos bit back a smile. "I wouldn't say so, but they do know who I am."

"Sounds familiar," the boy murmured, his gaze lingering on a pair of females. He smiled as they giggled and turned away, then focused back on the conversation. "North or South, everyone knows the Commandant."

"Do they? Because I can't say I know myself since I've been up here. The learning curve is steep, especially when it comes to familial connections—the Houses, and all they entail."

Pax tensed, and Marcos's palms grew slick, wondering if he'd pushed too far too fast. When the hell had it become so important to assert his paternity? Pax probably didn't even care that he was his son. Marcos let out a sigh at Sirrus coming over with their drinks, saving him from the awkward moment.

"Commandant," he said, setting them on the bar. "Two Specials. Can I get ye aught else?"

"We're good for now, thanks."

The one-eared man grunted and went to tend the rest of his custom.

Pax claimed a tankard and took a sip. He grunted appreciatively and licked a bit of foam from his lip. "The men were wondering about that…the House thing…how it's gonna work. City doesn't have barracks like the Source did."

"No, not at present, though it's something we can make happen—"

"Get yer hands off me, ye shite! I've a right to the sands, same as any of ye."

They turned at the commotion, a waif-thin blonde glowered back at three hulking men by the door. Her hands were planted on her hips, and her halos sparked scarlet.

"Now there's a spitfire," Pax murmured into his tankard.

"No, there's a very stupid whore," Sirrus growled from behind them. "Adelaide! The fuck are ye doin' in me pub?"

The blonde huffed one more time at the trio, then stomped over. "All I want is t'get downstairs!"

"Ya? And all I want's me goddamned ear back. Chances of either happenin's nil."

"Ye can't keep me from Conclave. Ain't legal."

"Watch me," he growled, looming over the bar.

"Rather not." She sniffed. "Already seen it, and ye ain't that impressive."

Pax spit out his mouthful of ale, and Sirrus's glower deepened.

"That sack o' shite send ye in here t'rile me? Where is that blighted little prick?"

Adelaide glanced at his trousers.

The crowd around them edged back, and Marcos tensed with them, ready for the man to go over the bar.

"Yer friend," Sirrus gritted out. "Where is he?"

"Which one?" She moued, despite his 'lust saying she was a dead woman. Girl had a pair of balls on her, that was for certain. "I got a fair number of 'em."

"Need another?" Pax asked, the air around him thick with pheromones.

She eyed him, tonguing her cheek. "I do at that."

"The hell ye do—where's McCreedy?" Sirrus roared, the entire bar going still.

"Him? Dunno." She fluffed her hair as she took Pax's arm. "Ain't seen him of late. I'm here t'pray, and ye can't keep me from me devotions. Escort a lady to the sands?" she asked, batting her lashes at Pax, a tendril of her own 'lust promising more than a walk. The burst Pax sent back drowned out Sirrus's protest. The barkeep scowled, but stood down, the crowd going back to their own conversations as the hierarchy prevailed.

Pax grunted and downed his beer. "Commandant."

"Pax." Marcos raised his tankard.

"Slippery bitch." Sirrus snorted, watching them cut through the crowd. "Twists the truth just like that fuckin' Fetch of hers."

"Seems to be a common theme with that line, though I'll admit I don't know many of them," Marcos said, then took another hefty swallow. His anticipated heart-to-heart with Pax a bust, he should probably turn in and get some sleep while he could.

"That First of theirs, Markham, ain't bad, but if I ever see that nephew of his again..."

Marcos almost choked on his mouthful as he made the connection. "Fitz?"

"Aye, that's the prick," Sirrus muttered, narrowing his eyes. "Ye know him?"

"Well enough that I'm not surprised you want him dead."

Sirrus snorted again. "From yer lips t'God's ears, but I ain't gonna hold me breath. Never seen a body move so fast. The little shite put me House name t'shame." He fingered the scar at the side of his head and pursed his lips. "Nah. The devil take him, but Fitzpatrick McCreedy ain't half of what he seems and a sight more dangerous. Can I get ye another?" he asked, nodding to Marcos's tankard.

"No, but thanks." Marcus threw a handful of units onto the bar. "Tomorrow comes early."

"That it do, every mornin'," Sirrus said, sweeping them up. "And from what I hear tell, big doins is afoot. Might not need them barracks if Scot has his way."

"The Overlord?" Marcos's heart leapt. "Is he back?"

"Nah, not him, the elder, Lot. Got into it with them Sourcies, and I'd bet me other ear he's gonna make 'em bleed for it. Fuckers ain't got no idea the power that House's got in this city." He grinned. "And without the Overlord or the old man t'gainsay him, they're about to find out."

MOTHER MEANDERED through her garden as the twilight came alive around her. She paused beside a spray of Epiphyllum oxypetalum, the Queen of the Night's heady essence perfuming the balmy air.

A scrap of memory from the Jane-that-was flitted through her mind. Daubing the scent at her wrists…behind her ears…making sure her hair fell just so…

A smug smile played over Mother's bloodless lips as she moved on. As savory as its bloom was, it didn't hold a candle to Caliban Scot's expression as the light had left Elize's eyes. No. That had been pure ambrosia.

He was broken, and Mother's victory assured.

Within the diadem at her brow the twin's talent pulsed, harvested at the moment of their deaths before it could disperse back into the cosmos. Her attention free from leashing them for the first time in a millennium and Caliban off the board, her focus wandered to her remaining thralls. Sifting through their strands, she idly pruned the dead ends.

The Assassin. The Son. A handful of others, all of lesser consequence.

Those that remained were more important pieces in what was left to play out. Caliban's adroit theft of the Source Binders still needed to be remedied, and time was of the essence to bring that final piece into play.

She continued to a bench beside a gurgling fountain and sat, the stone cool beneath her. A cecropia moth flitted past. Silly fleeting things. Void of mouthparts, it intently searched for its mate—its only purpose to breed, then die, the next iteration doomed to repeat the cycle.

She would break it.

An anticipated thread of talent reverberated, calling her attention, and she sped its length, a hallway in a neoclassical mansion resolving in her mind's eye. Mother sifted through the forefront of Otto's thoughts and chuckled as he knocked upon a paneled door. Serra wasn't wasting any time, was she? Her voice within bade him to enter, and a pale maid opened it before he could reach for the handle.

Their new accommodations at Lady Saks's country estate were quite posh, if a tad ostentatious for Mother's taste. She rode Otto's mind as he strode through the sitting room toward the dressing chamber. He smirked at the maid's gasp of impropriety behind him, his thoughts trending to how she'd be doing that again for him later.

Mother frowned at the lascivious image his imagination supplied and she sent a needle of pain through his temple.

He broke stride and put a hand to it, wincing, his thoughts still tinged with filth. *Mother. You're here sooner than I expected.*

Obviously, she thought back dryly. *You've made progress with the Binders?*

His smugness was answer enough.

"Lady Hess," he said, sweeping into the next room. She sat before a vanity, her generous backside swallowing its tiny tufted stool. Another drawn maid added a jeweled clip to the Binder's elaborately coifed hair, then positioned a hand mirror for Serra to see the back.

"Master Perkins." Her gaze slid from her updo to meet his in the reflection of the ornate mirror. "Leave us," she commanded. The maid gave a quick curtsey and scurried from the room.

Ottos eyes followed the sway of her skirts until the door closed firmly behind her. Mother's lips pursed, his appetites far too similar to his father's.

"Well?" Serra said, turning to him as the latch clicked into place. "Spit it out, I've dinner plans."

"Unfortunately, I think you'll be late. It seems that after we brought suit against the Scots, the Binders who received notice of their pending evictions went in force to protest. In the Overlord's absence, they demanded to see Lord Scot's father." His face became positively gleeful in the mirror behind Serra. "The man flew into a rage and attacked one of them. Everyone involved has been arrested and charges are being filed."

"Oh my." Serra's eyebrows rose with her smile. "And here I'd thought the rumors about Adlothian Scot's temper were exaggerated..." She abruptly stood. "Go, collect my wrap. As First, I should be present."

Otto gave her a mocking bow and left the room.

Your doing? Mother asked.

Of course, he thought back smugly.

He collected Serra's fur from the closet and hurried down to the gate. She met him a moment later and in another breath, they were at the hill's constabulary.

A group of agitated Binders crowded the lobby. As soon as they saw her, everyone began speaking at once.

"Please, one at a time, I've only just heard—Lord Crandall!" she called out, across the room. The Intelligencer stopped short, then slowly turned, his smile an obvious fabrication. Mother chuckled at the obsequious little weasel's ill-concealed contempt.

"Lady Hess."

The crowd parted for her, and Otto trailed in her wake, taking far too much pleasure in flaunting himself beneath the authorities' noses. Crandall's brows knit as they got closer and a tingle of Finder's talent brushed against Otto's mind. Mother batted it away. *Nothing to see here...*

"What can I do for you?" Crandall asked Serra, turning from Otto with disinterest.

"I heard my line was involved in an altercation?"

"They were..." Crandall's lips pursed as he rocked back on his heels and tapped a sheath of paper against his palm. "Follow me.

Perhaps you can talk some sense into Lord Preston, because there's none to be had from Lot."

Otto trailed behind them to a small conference room. A public defender sat on one side of the table beside a Binder nursing his eye. Otto bit back a snicker at that bit of drama, and Mother had to agree. Was the man actually holding an ice pack to it?

Across from them, Scot sat between Phyllis Breakspear and another solicitor. The similarities between him and Laughlin were striking; enough so that the Jane-that-was burbled to the surface to watch alongside Mother.

The door behind them opened again, and Jacques Martin came into the room.

"What's this nonsense now, Crandall?" he asked, pulling off his gloves and stuffing them into his bowler hat.

"Yes, I'm curious to know as well." Serra sat primly in one of the hard wooden chairs as Otto hung back by the wall.

"On a normal day? Lot lost his temper again. Today? Assault and Battery. Lord Preston here is very firmly set on pressing charges." Crandall frowned, obviously displeased.

"The man is an animal, he attacked me without provocation!" the Binder bristled. Lot growled at him, not helping his case.

"Actually," his solicitor cleared his throat, "we have witnesses that you made several rather inflammatory and threatening remarks, and if you proceed with this farce, we'll be entering a counter suit for defamation, intimidation, and extortion."

"Is all this really necessary?" Lord Martin asked with an exhausted sigh. He ran a heavy hand through his springy black curls. "The terms of your contracts are more than generous. All that's required of you is to use your talent for the betterment of the city—" He shook his head at Lord Preston's indignant glower. Jacques sighed, his gaze moving to Lot. "And what do you have to say for yourself?"

Lot's lips tightened into a sour line.

"My client regrets his part in the escalation, and is prepared to forget the entire affair ever happened if the charges against him are dropped," the solicitor answered for him.

Mother snorted. Adlothian looked like he was going to chew through his lip.

Jacques sighed again. "I'm assuming that's not going to happen?"

"Not unless Lord Preston wants to retract his statement," Crandall said, handing each of the solicitors a copy of something. "Charges have been filed."

"As anticipated." The solicitor beside Adlothian pulled several sheets of paper from his briefcase and slid them across the table. "Consider yourselves served. Your act of aggression has violated clause 9.c of your housing contract, voiding it effective immediately. Any and all of the involved parties listed are hereby ordered to immediately vacate any property owned by the Scots, their subsidiaries or holdings, and remain at a distance no closer than five hundred feet per the terms of the restraining order."

Jacques sputtered. "Jesus, don't you think that's a little extreme?"

"No," Lot spat. Lady Breakspear put her hand on his arm, and he bit back whatever else he was going to say.

Their solicitor shot him a look. "Given that my client was accosted at his home, I have to agree. I've taken the liberty of compiling a map of the aforementioned properties with the calculated buffer notated in red. We wish to be quite clear so that there are no future incidents."

"Well, then I suspect there's nothing more to be done." Jacques shook his head in disgust as he pulled his gloves back on. "Lady Hess, I'll leave it to you to try to find adequate housing for the displaced. Quite frankly, I can save you the time and suggest you head out to the Flats and attempt to requisition something. Good luck with that." He looked at Lord Preston squarely as he put on his hat. "I would think very carefully about how you want to proceed."

"Shall we?" Lord Crandall asked Lot, motioning to the door. "You know the drill."

Scot rose, and the rest of them followed after, leaving Otto with Serra, Lord Preston, and the solicitor.

"Explain to me what just happened," Serra said to the solicitor.

The man blew through his mustache. "That idiotic rally and pressing charges has started a war. I'll tell you bluntly, it's not one you can win." He snapped the map open, cutting off her protest. "These are properties you've been banned from."

Serra's eyebrows rose to her hairline. Once the private residences and businesses were taken out of the equation, it was easily half the city. "All of that?"

"To say that the Scots are wealthy is a grievous understatement." The solicitor frowned and scribbled over several other sections until only a handful of blocks remained open at the very edges of Glynfyls. "And what I've just filled in has either been destroyed by the quakes or is Breaker owned. I can assure you, your line won't be welcomed by them either."

Serra's hand rose to her throat. "He wasn't kidding about putting in a requisition..."

"No," the solicitor said with a humorless laugh, "and since all the tents would be coming from the Breakers' supplies, I very much doubt you'll be able to use them at all..."

Mother withdrew from Otto's psyche. A girlish giggle escaped her, and she stood, the Jane-that-was surging to the forefront and spinning around in a circle, her arms wide. Soon! It would be soon! Everything was falling into place, and now that trap was set, all that was left to do was dangle the bait.

CHAPTER EIGHTEEN

talent drunk [talənt drəŋk] noun

1. *The state of being exposed to an excessive amount of talent resulting in a temporary, euphoric high. Negative side effects include compromised faculties, cognition issues, and the temporary loss of control over one's talent.*

– Excerpt from Glynfyls: A History

"ALTHOUGH THE BREAKER *hierarchy lends itself to external control through their Alpha, their clannish idiosyncrasies present issues. The most notable of them is the concept of 'Breaker Business,' in which their behavior is not discussed outside the line. Save for rare instances, re-education efforts have had no effect, and those that break their silence are swiftly silenced themselves.*

Expunging this doctrine via quarantined populations has also proven ineffective, the trait manifesting regardless of generational disconnect. One has to wonder if it's somehow tied to their innate morality, and if so, perhaps the solution lies in the manipulation of their world-view..."

– L. Merkel, Head Geneticist, The Source

SERRA STORMED through the gate and into the Saks's country estate. How could this have happened? Not three days ago everything she'd ever wanted was within her grasp, and now the better half of her line had been evicted from the city. She couldn't—*ugh!* She grabbed an urn from an occasional table and dashed it to the ground, the splintering porcelain and whomp of ash doing little to assuage her anger.

"Oh my, I believe that was a Pre-Surge death urn..." Otto said, coming in behind her. He waved a hand in front of his face and coughed.

"I don't care!" she shrieked. "The whole bloody North can go up in ashes, along with the rest of my plans!" Otto tsked and the urge to bind his wretched tongue to the floor surged through her. She kicked at the shards peppering the inlaid hardwood, taking small satisfaction in the gouges the impact had left. "Why are things this difficult? All I want is what's mine by right!"

"And you'll get it...though perhaps the North isn't the place to do it," he said, leaning against a silk-papered wall.

"Please." She shook the remains of—well, the remains—from her skirts and frowned at the chaise's narrow cushions. Like everything else in this place, it'd been designed to suit that acerbic stick, Geraldine Saks. Serra barely had room to fit half her backside on anything.

And that was the issue wasn't it? She didn't fit in the North, and they refused to make room for her. The entire populace could hang for all she cared.

She huffed as she sat, balancing on one cheek, and focused on Otto again. "As Nora so gleefully pointed out when we arrived, there are no other places for Talents to go."

The vile little man looked pensive, as if he wasn't sure he should speak. Serra's eyes narrowed. What did he know?

"That's not entirely true..." he said after a weighted moment. "Titus had a connection in the Deep South. Off-books of course, but there's a small city-state on the western edge of the continent populated by Talents—Halja, or something like that." He frowned and ran a hand over his scraggly goatee, the name coming out somewhere between a cough and a sneeze.

"But regardless of my pronunciation, they regularly paid him a great deal of money to retain their anonymity and sent up, ah, tributes, if you will, from their criminal element to further his research."

Serra's brow cocked at the obvious fabrication. An entire population of Talents hidden from the rest of the world? "How is that even remotely possible?" The idea was ludicrous.

"My particular skill set isn't so rare as you might think," Otto said, brushing off his sleeve. "And when one has a legion to dampen the memory of its existence..." He shrugged. "Unfortunately for them, my existence made doing the same to Titus impossible, and they were forced to come to terms."

Serra sniffed at his smugness, although that would explain his favored status back at the Source. She drummed her nails on the arm of the chaise, having often wondered at the laxness of the leash Otto wore in comparison to Titus's other Talents. An arrangement like that would definitely justify special treatment...

No. Serra huffed, not believing a word. If nothing else, Otto was a practiced liar, but—Damn him, all of it was plausible and certainly distasteful enough for the Patron to be involved in. "Did they now?" she asked, attempting to sound noncommittal.

"Mmm." Otto hummed. "I'm assuming communications are still open. If you'd like, I believe I could get in contact with them...perhaps cut a side deal and see if they'd be open to receiving expatriates."

Serra narrowed her eyes, not wanting to be any more beholden to the odious man than she already was, nor did she trust one word out of his mouth...but if what he said was true, and there were greener pastures elsewhere...

"Fine, but this Halja of yours needs to be vetted before I agree to anything. I won't be put in the same position as here. If we go, there will be no strings or conditions attached."

"Of course," Otto agreed, not questioning the stipulation. Serra sucked her cheeks, his lack of argument suspect. He glanced at the clock on the mantel. "I'll look into it first thing in the morning. If you have no further need of me?"

She waved him away and rang for a servant. As much as she'd been looking forward to dining at the Park Club, it would be unseemly given the majority of her line was currently being evicted from their lodgings.

Glory, where would they all go? She looked around her spacious accommodations and frowned at the fleeting thought of sharing them. No. They could fend for themselves. If Halja was all Otto seemed to think it was, she wanted her line ready to jump at the chance. If they thought they could slide into a cushy nest like this, there would be resistance, and she'd had quite enough of that.

TITUS SIPPED his bourbon as the crowd of females that'd gathered at the glade drifted away in small groups. He motioned for several of them to restart their game, and they reluctantly collected their boule, far more interested in gossiping. That something momentous had just occurred he had no doubt. Unfortunately, its implications were murkier.

Especially where the Jester girl was concerned.

Rack his brain though he might, Titus couldn't recall an instance of a stud declaring his bitch an equal, the idea ludicrous on multiple levels. Having to rank in their hierarchy aside, every last one of them was disposable, existing only to become a vessel for the next iteration. For them to think otherwise was exceedingly unwise.

Scot had set a dangerous precedent, and his rhetoric needed to be curbed. Titus drummed his fingers against the table, ultimately deciding to let them chew on what they'd seen for now. When he made an example of the girl, they'd no longer harbor any fantasies. Despite his mention of assigning her a second to rile Scot, and if she somehow miraculously survived the birth, Titus fully intended for Kara Jester to disappear from the population. The rooms for her to receive his personal attentions had already been prepared.

He clunked his empty glass onto the table and sucked air through his teeth as he leaned forward, inspecting what was left of Brix. The Elite's chest stubbornly rose and fell, but given the extent of the damage, it was only a matter of time before that ceased to be the case. It was too bad his mate hadn't whelped yet. Until then, Titus needed him alive.

"Another bourbon," he said to the handful of subs awaiting his pleasure. "And find Shriver to heal this lump of meat."

With the twins gone, the Binder certainly wouldn't have anything else pressing to attend to. A sub handed Titus a fresh glass, and he took a sip, enjoying the Elite's struggle to breathe almost as much as the vintage. He smiled as blood bubbled at Brix's nostrils with each disturbing wheeze.

Titus idly tapped the rim of his glass. It took a great deal of skill to inflict that much damage without killing a man, leading him to believe that Scot'd had considerable practice. What had he been doing for those unaccounted years before he was incarcerated in Kensbot?

A Fetch shifted into the glade with Shriver by his side. The thin man nodded at Titus, then knelt by the fallen Elite. His halos flared for a long moment.

"How far?" Shriver asked, his face devoid of expression.

"How bad is he?"

"He won't die from any of it, but will wish he had for quite some time."

Titus smiled to himself, Scot's value continuing to climb. "I want him to be able to chew his own food and shit where he's supposed to. The rest he can suffer through."

Shriver nodded, his halos burning as he turned his attention back to Brix. The Elite coughed, then groaned, curling onto his side with a small whimper.

Titus smirked into his bourbon. It was always so satisfying to see the big men brought low. "Well, that was entertaining. Care to explain what just happened in those quaint Breaker terms of yours?"

Brix's shoulders heaved. He struggled to sit, muttering something too low to hear.

"Care to repeat that?"

The Elite grimaced, his face a horror of weeping tissue. It took several tries for him to gain control of his jaw, very obviously in a great deal of pain. Titus's smirk grew. How delightful.

"He is Alpha," Brix finally managed.

The females playing pétanque all turned at his admission.

Titus's eyes flicked from them back to the Elite. "Which means…?"

Brix attempted to shrug and cried out, the bulge of a misaligned clavicle appearing beneath his shirt. Titus didn't bother to hide his grin as the man wept. Shriver would have to do something about that later, but it was certainly amusing now.

Titus motioned to one of the females, admiring her exquisitely turned calves as she crossed the glade with her head bowed. She stopped to stand before him instead of groveling as was proper, her insubordination no doubt in response to Scot's little proclamation.

"On your knees and approach," Titus commanded.

She hesitated for a breath before complying, crawling to kneel between his thighs. Titus tilted up her chin. Her bone structure was marvelous. "What did you think of Lord Scot?"

"He is Alpha," she said without pause.

"Do you want to fuck him?"

"Yes."

"And what of his command that you obey the female with him?"

Her eyes darted back toward the others, no longer intent on their game. "She is his mate," she said, nervously wetting her lips.

Titus snorted and shoved her face away, annoyed, but he didn't breed them for their brains. He tried again through gritted teeth. "That's not what I asked."

"I—that's Breaker Busin—"

Titus backhanded her before she could finish speaking, unable to leash his contempt. Breaker Business. Those two damned words were the bane of his existence. How that odd bit of their subculture had survived this long… He raked a hand through his hair as the bitch lay where she'd fallen, wise enough not to move without his permission. The others stood solemn, eyes lowered.

"Whether Scot is Alpha or not, *my* word is law, not his. Br4Ef!"

A buxom female with a glorious mane of thick black hair dropped her boule and ran over, prostrating herself. Titus's breathing smoothed at her show of subservience. "Well? What's your answer?"

The female kept her face in the dirt. "She needs to be challenged."

Titus grunted. Finally. "Rise." She pushed back onto her haunches, and he swept a finger over his lips. This one wasn't quite as fair as the other, but her breasts were exquisite. "And are you willing?"

"Oh, yes." The female smiled, her eyes darting to the frowns on the others' faces.

"Then do so. I need an example set. Make sure she and the litter survive, but I care little about the packaging." She bowed her head, and he flicked his hand, dismissing her before turning to Brix. "You'll be in my office within the hour ready for duty, or I'll have you culled."

Titus rose from the table and caressed the milky white stone on his finger, gating back to his desk. He wasn't quite sure how, but it abruptly felt like Scot had gained the upper hand, and that wouldn't do at all.

FLYNN WINCED as snippets of complex technical information filtered to the forefront of his brain. Trying to figure out how the Triam operated was a shit show, and it wasn't the content that was killing him, it was how Nora had packaged it. Each bit was a new goddamned puzzle to assimilate, and with each one he opened, the sicker he felt. His stomach wrenched, and he swallowed bile as he tried to process the cold logic, other bits and pieces intruding.

The Merkels specialization with Breakers, their obsession with contracting a Binder from an Original House to breed. The conviction there were other talents that hadn't been accessed and the belief they needed a duality to get them.

Threading through it all was their animosity toward Albanach—Cal—for blocking them at every turn...until Nora. Why had the old man given in then?

Memories rose up, twisting and tangling with the odd bits of information, one settling at the forefront of his thoughts.

"... *Riegel was one side of the coin, nasty business. Kara here...she's the other, what we'd been looking for...*"

Flynn's thoughts froze, fixating on that snippet of conversation. What if Cal hadn't been talking about Titus—

That motherfucker.

Flynn's eyes snapped open, and he groaned, struggling to sit. The silk sheet clung to him, soaked with sweat. Christ, his fucking head… He shook as he moved to stand—so fucking weak—and fell against the bedside table, taking it down with him. The room spun above him. *Fuck. Don't move, don't move…* Sprawled on the floor, he squeezed his eyes shut, swallowing bile. Felt worse than that one time he'd come off a shotgun hit of sear from a prostitute in Malai.

"Flynn?" The bathroom door opened and Kara padded in.

"That other Binder Nora sensed…Cal knows," he slurred, his mouth sticky and tongue thick. His stomach heaved, and he gagged, dry-heaving.

"I don't—Glory, you're burning up," Kara said, her palm ice against his forehead.

"I just need a couple of aspirin," he rasped out.

She shook her head, and his vision swam as he retched again. "I'm pulling talent."

"Kara—"

Her halos flared, and he cried out, slamming his eyes shut, tendrils of golden light streaking behind his lids. He whimpered as they eased into his mind, soothing the sharp edges of thought.

"There's a buildup of residue from all the compulsion Titus is under. Your body can't process it and is treating it like a tumor," she murmured, her voice still too loud. "Stay still, I'll UnMake it."

He fought the urge to laugh, he couldn't have moved if he wanted to. Gradually, the pain faded to a manageable level, and her palm slipped from his skin. He opened his eyes. Fucking hell.

"Did you get all of it?"

Kara shook her head and leaned back against the bed, looking as beat up as he felt. "No, and what I did will probably come back. You're right about my weave. The UnMaking is getting weaker…I don't understand why it isn't working like it should." She winced, rubbing her side.

He leaned forward and grabbed his pants, fishing for the bottle of aspirin and chewing two before fighting to pull the fabric up over his bare ass. A pained chuckle rose in his throat. Christ, what a fucking pair they made.

"Something funny?"

Flynn just looked at her. She snorted, then grimaced, gripping her side again. Shit. "Do we need to get you to the lab?"

She shook her head. "Not yet. Did you figure things out?"

"Some of it—" The portlock in the other room opened and closed. Christ, without the ability to lock that, he should've fucking fixed it shut. He sighed, staggering to his feet and zipping up his pants. "Stay here. I'll take care of whoever it is."

A raven-haired female stood in the next room.

"Titus says his word is law, not yours. That woman isn't fit to be your mate. I'm to see to your needs."

Flynn pinched the bridge of his nose. Jesus fucking Christ, he didn't have the bandwidth to deal with this shit or her cloying 'lust. It swirled around him, turning his stomach. He slapped a hand against the wall, gagging. God, she fucking stank—"I don't give a fuck what Titus says, or what you think. Get out."

She shrugged her shoulders, and her skanky little dress fell to pool around her ankles. Was she fucking serious?

"I can make you forget all about her..." Her hips rolled as she sauntered close and reached for his groin. He intercepted her hand, the bones in her wrist cracking as he wrenched it away. She let out a shrill scream, and pain shot through his skull. He clenched his jaw, head throbbing—

Binder talent twined with dank 'lust flooded the room. The female's scream abruptly cut off, a weave slapping over her mouth, and her arms wrenched behind her back.

Shit. His gaze snapped to the bedroom.

"Stay out of this," Kara snarled before he could open his mouth. She pushed from the port and grimaced, gripping her abdomen. The air crackled with bloodlust, the hum between them feral.

He stepped back, his balls drawing up at the menace she was putting out. Stay out of it? Gladly. There wasn't a fucking chance he was getting involved.

Kara clenched the knife she'd taken from him back at the glade. She stalked toward the woman, talent surging again. Another bind slammed the female against the wall, her eyes flying wide on impact. She panted, her chest straining as she struggled to breathe.

Kara ran the blade up the woman's bare sternum, a line of weeping red in its wake, her voice deadly calm. "Am I fit now, bitch? You should've run while you had the chance. Did you really think you'd win if you challenged for him? Surprise..." She smiled serenely and sliced the woman's cheek open to the bone, then softly kissed the other. "You lose."

Tears leaked from the female's eyes, the rest of her paralyzed. Flynn could sense her frantically trying to pull talent, but Kara had bound her channel tight.

"This is the second time one of you have disrespected me," she said, weighing one of the woman's thick raven locks in her hand before raggedly sawing it off. She pursed her lips at the hank then dropped it, methodically moving to another. "It will be the last. I don't need the Alpha to declare my position as his mate, it's mine by right, and the next to challenge me for him or it will die."

Kara hacked through the last of the female's hair and ran the blade up the nape of her neck and across her stubbled scalp, shaving a messy stripe bare. "Now be a good girl and tell me what your designator is," she crooned, the bind from the female's lips dissolving.

"B-Br4Ef."

"You mean Br5Ef. Have I made myself clear?"

"Y-yes, my queen. I am Br5Ef. My rung has dropped. I challenged and lost. You are his mate. I-I will obey, and tell my sisters."

"Good." Kara dropped the rest of her binds, and the female collapsed onto the hair-strewn floor at her feet. "Clean up your mess. I don't care what Titus does to you, I see you again, and the next thing I slice will be your throat."

She turned her back on the female as she scrambled to collect her shorn hair, pinning the hanks against her chest with her broken wrist. When she'd gotten the last bit, she scuttled from the room, the portlock clicking closed behind her.

Flynn fixed it shut, the silence in the room deafening.

Kara sat on the couch with a pained exhale and put a hand to her belly. Damn. He wet his lips as she settled. The female had called Kara a queen, and she was right. A grin slid across his face, his pants tight. His woman was fierce as fuck.

She sighed after a moment. "I had to do it."

"I know." And there were three other females above the one she'd just bested. Knocking that one from her rung would only push them to challenge until the hierarchy was settled again. Kara leaned against him as he sat, and he kissed the top of her head. Now that her bloodlust had left her, she radiated exhaustion.

"I think I need to get those nutritionals now."

Flynn nodded. A shower would have to wait. "Lemme grab my boots and a shirt." He went back into the bedroom and rifled through the drawers—

His head snapped up at Kara's burst of anxiety.

"Flynn?" The quaver in her voice sent ice down his spine. "Can you please hurry?"

He kicked into his boots and ripped on a shirt, rushing back out to her. "What happened, you okay?"

She looked at him wide-eyed, and her throat bobbed. "I-I think my water just broke."

He glanced down at her stomach, light-headed, and stumbled back a step. "Now. You're having the babies now?"

"No, it doesn't necessarily mean right now—" Kara bit her lip and grimaced. "But they're definitely coming."

They were coming. Definitely. Shit, Nora. They needed Nora. Flynn fumbled, trying twice to snap his fingers before it actually happened. He broke the ward to Fitz—

Nothing happened.

He laughed. Of course nothing was gonna happen. His bloodlust surged, clearing his head in its wake. If Fitz wasn't back at the bar in Lyden, then he was halfway to fucking Glynfyls—

Flynn made himself take a breath. Fuck, he needed to calm down. He could do it. He could get Nora. "I'm gonna—"

"Don't you dare leave me!" Kara growled. "It could still be hours before anything happens. Fitz will get Nora here. Just—just take me to the lab—"

She cried out, and Flynn's guts cramped, feeling the echo of her pain through their bond. He had a bad feeling it wasn't gonna be hours. Jesus fuck, how—

"Flynn!"

Shit, right. He hurried to the couch and scooped her up. Christ, her water had broken, her bottom soaked and a visceral salinity spiking the air. Another rush of liquid splattered the floor as he hurried to the port. She bit back a moan and pressed her face to his neck.

"Almost there, almost there," he murmured, not sure if he was talking to her or himself, but he did know that if Fitz didn't show up with Nora in time, that motherfucker was dead.

FITZ PACED HIS TENEMENT, the pint in his hand doin' naught to quell his growin' anxiety. Somewhat were happening down south, and him still being here were an issue. Scot had broken the ward, and what Fitz were feelin' from him and the lady made his stomach churn.

He upended the bottle again, then swore and whipped the empty against the wall—

Rapid footsteps sounded through the tinklin' of glass, and the door flew open. Adelaide hustled in with a tall, dark woman in scrubs. Right, she matched the imprint in his book of memories, now they needed to go.

"Jesus fuck, took ye long enough!" he muttered, reaching for Jolie's arm.

Adelaide batted it away, her halos sparkin'. "And yer very welcome, ye shite! Why I even bother with ye—"

"Yer right. Ye should stop." He hustled her back out the door—

"Fitz!"

"Later, love, shite's hittin' the fan. Owe ye a pie, ya?" He slammed the door on her protests and turned to Jolie.

She looked him up and down, hip cocked, and her brow raised. "You're Fitzpatrick McCreedy?" she asked, arms across her chest and looking thoroughly unimpressed.

Way she said it put his back up. He squared his lapels, his eyes narrowing. "S'Fitz...why? What've ye heard?"

"Not a damned thing. You're just taller than I expected. Way that note from Nora read, I figured you for an alcoholic twelve year-old."

"Nah. Were just a hobby 'til me early twenties," he snarked back. "Look, yer delightful personality aside, we gotta go. Somewhat's happenin' with the lady."

Jolie's expression lost its edge. "Fine, but I don't know what good I'll be able to do by the time we get there. Unless you're a super Fetch, it's gonna take us the better part of a day to shift all the way to the Source."

Fitz scratched his jaw. "Eh...Ye ain't wrong, but we ain't exactly shiftin'." He swallowed, despite his coin flaring hot, egging him on. The Between were a House Matter of epic proportion. If aught were gonna get him stripped, it'd be crossin' the Prydees on this. Not that they'd allowed him t'claim their Christ-forsaken rhian t'begin with, but that weren't gonna stop 'em from flayin' him outta spite.

But if he fucked this up, it were his gran that were gonna pay.

Ya, that weren't happenin'. Fitz wet his lip and tugged the patch of beard beneath it. So how the fuck were he gonna do this? He held out a hand. "Right. Ye need t'bind yerself t'me."

Jolie looked him up and down again. "Excuse me?"

"Just—I ain't got time t'explain, just put yer arms around me neck and do it," he muttered.

She smirked, shimmying up to him bold as brass. Her brow raised as her halos flared, pressin' up against him familiar-like. She traced his sideburn. "Damn, if you aren't just pretty enough to be from the Source. You know, I got a thing for blonds..."

"Eh...congratulations?" Fitz's throat bobbed, not sure he were keen on the way she were lookin' at him. Normally didn't have an issue with older women, but tangling with this one made him nervous.

She laughed. "You wanna help me celebrate?"

"I...eh..." His coin burned cold, and he swore. Damn it. He swallowed again. "Maybe later. Right now, I need ye t'give me yer solemn word yer gonna keep yer eyes closed and ain't never gonna tell a soul about this next part."

"Keep my eyes closed?"

A growl escaped him, and she laughed again. Shite. Been hanging around His High Holiness too much of late, that was for certain. "Ya."

Jolie wriggled closer. "Mmm. Purr for me again, pussycat."

Jesus fuck—"Would ye just give me yer damned word?"

Her lip poked out all coy as she raised her right hand and crossed her heart. "I promise."

Fitz blew out an anxious breath. Her sincerity left more'n somewhat t'be desired, but his coin were flaring, urgent. "Fuck. Gimme a sec…"

"Issues?"

"Nah, I just…" He scowled. "I ain't never done this with nobody, nor so soon after I been through once before."

"Worried you won't be able to perform?" She ran her fingers through his curls. "Don't worry, boo, I haven't ever let a man down."

Fitz opened his mouth then closed it again, and she started laughing all over again. Right, that tore it. Fuck this. His halos flared, retracing the path he'd made up here and securing his tether of talent. Woman were still cackling as he shifted a bit of reality to the side, then grabbed her around the waist and dove into the Between.

ROGAN SQUATTED beside a bloody patch of concrete, turning a gun over in his hands. There was only one person on the planet that owned an engraved Remington Rider pocket revolver with a mother-of-pearl grip, and Elize wouldn't have willingly left it behind. He chewed his lip, eyeing a gory handprint. Hopefully the combination meant Cal had gotten her before she'd gotten him, and the bitch was dead.

Rogan's jaw tightened as he stood, jamming the little revolver into his waistband. On the off-chance Cal hadn't, she would be when she came looking for it. Meanwhile, where the hell the two of them had gotten off to was a better question. She would've had her gating stone on her, so that could be anywhere, depending on which one of them was still breathing.

Rogan couldn't see her hauling Cal's body off unless it was part of a fucked up game. Christ, for all he knew his best friend's corpse could be propped up waiting for him somewhere. Rogan grimaced, starting back toward the corporate suites. Last thing he needed was to open up a door and find that, but it would track—especially after offing Enoch.

And if Cal had been the last man standing? Rogan sighed, looking up at the stars. Cal would want to give her some kind of proper burial, bless his poor, abused heart. If that's what was going on, the chances of him coming back anytime this century or the next were slim to none. He'd be in the wind, and good fucking luck tracking him down until he was ready to be found. Then the asshole would pop up like nothing had happened, and the fuck if he'd open his mouth about anything that had.

Rogan crossed a shadowed street, gnawing on his lip. No. Then it'd be just like when Sarah and the kids were murdered during the Second Incursion. Or worse, when they'd lost everyone in the first. Cal had stayed just long enough to deliver the news then disappeared, leaving everything he'd worked so hard to build and Rogan with the fallout.

Fuck, that'd been bad. Cal didn't process loss—he abandoned everything that reminded him of it like it'd never been. Rogan shook his head and squeezed through the port into the lobby, certain that's how this was gonna play out. Goddamn it. Rogan ran a hand over his face. He should've fucking ended the bitch years ago and done the stupid asshole a favor. He would've been rip shit then, but at least he would've been here now.

Maybe.

Whatever, it was what it was. Rogan jogged up the steps, headed toward the helipad with a pang in his chest. Cal was gone and that case of whiskey was calling Rogan's name.

The expanse of the roof was a relief after the closeness of the stairwell. The lights that'd been on when they'd landed were dead, the dim flickers of flame dotting the facility. In the distance, gunshots rang out and a woman screamed.

Rogan shook his head as he strode to the craft. Christ, he was done with this fucking shit show. He slapped the panel to open the hatch—

And it didn't move.

You gotta be fucking—he jerked the manual release, and it moved about an inch, a rime of ice coating the gasket. *Are you fucking*—nope. The plaz-powered hydraulics were frozen. Rogan laughed. Well, wasn't this the fucking icing on the cake? He leaned forward, smacking his head against the fuselage. *Fuck, fuck, fuck.*

Dead. The craft was as dead as everything else. He was gonna kill that fucking Fetch when he got back—if he got back. In the meantime, they were stuck here and their only means of transportation was useless as the rest of the goddamned—

Honk.

The fuck? Rogan pushed back from the craft and looked up. A V of geese flew directly overhead. He stared at them as they disappeared to the north, a shiver traveling up his spine.

What the hell had Fitz done?

Rogan ran a shaking hand over his mouth and wedged his fingers into the hatch's crack, hauling it open. Now he really needed a drink. Thank God the Sons hadn't found the cargo bay the case was in. He jammed it under his arm, took one more look at the skies, and headed back down to the suite.

NORA DROPPED talent as something slammed against the suite's port. She pinched the bridge of her nose, shaking away the memories of medical data she was trying to assimilate from Titus. Something slammed against the port again. She pushed back from the table and stood, her mouth abruptly dry. If that wasn't Cal or—

"Nora! Open the fucking door—port, whatever the hell this goddamned thing is…"

Rogan.

"Just a moment!" She hurried across the room and hit the breaker bar, trying to remember the trick to it…there. The portlock sank a fraction, and she began to roll it—

It abruptly slammed into the pocket hard enough to bounce back. The Alpha Prime's hand shot out and stopped it before it could close again. He came in, then rolled it shut with exaggerated care and paused, hanging his head, the case of whiskey from the craft tucked under his arm.

Glory, he looked defeated. A icy sliver of dread went up her spine. "Is everything all right? Is Cal—"

"Enoch's dead, Cal's gone, and not a fucking clue how it went down with Elize." Rogan threw his knife onto the table, and Nora jumped as it landed. "That fucking woman's been devouring his soul since the day they met, and however tonight shook out, I'm pretty sure she finished the last of it." He sighed, bottles clinking as he dropped the crate by the couch, then pulled a revolver from his waistband. He frowned at it, then set it beside his knife. "You hear anything from Flynn?"

"No," Nora said, blinking to keep her tears at bay. She was still angry at Cal, but if something had happened to him...

Rogan flopped onto the couch and grabbed a bottle. He cracked the lid and up-ended it. The level dropped by half before he lowered it and wiped his mouth on his sleeve. He frowned at what was left. "Christ. What I wouldn't give for a still of rot-gut right about now. If ever there was a night to get black-out drunk..."

"Are you celebrating or mourning?"

"In my experience, neither's mutually exclusive." He took another pull and smacked his lips. "I'd offer you some, but..."

Nora smoothed a hand over her abdomen. "Regardless, I'm afraid I'm not much of a drinker."

"Never met a Binder that was," Rogan said, putting his feet up on the coffee table and muttered something about control freaks. Ruddy grime spattered onto the tabletop, his boots caked with Glory knew what.

Nora sat in one of the chairs beside the couch, trying not to focus on the mess or lump all Breakers together as barbarians. No matter how much some of them acted like it. "Speaking of Binders, both the Son on the roof and Titus had a very specific talent signature—like, like a fragrance—laced through the compulsions riddling their minds." She twisted her ring. "Cal never spoke about—"

"Anything he wasn't good and fucking ready to?" Rogan finished for her, raising the bottle to his lips.

She frowned. "No, he doesn't, which is why Laughlin wanted me to ask you about the Binder that was part of your original seven."

"Jane?" Rogan ran his thumb over the label. "She died in the First Incursion. Why?"

"Because it's not possible for anyone to have learned to do what I saw in Titus's mind in a single lifetime, and the talent had the same feel to it as yours and Cal's—"

"Not possible." Rogan snorted. "If Jane Young were still alive..." He shook his head and rubbed a hand over his sternum. "No."

"But—"

"It has to be someone else, and Cal would be the one to ask. The way they figured out how to extend life at the Source—rejuvenation, Binders were always his thing." Rogan killed the rest of the bottle and grabbed another. Granted, Breakers had a much higher tolerance for alcohol than other people, but still...

"Do you really think that's wise?"

"Absolutely not." He twisted off the cap. "You know what I just saw?"

Nora paused. "Do I want to?"

"Geese."

"Geese?"

He nodded. "A fucking V of geese flying directly over the Source, heading north."

That wasn't possible either. The field of radiation plaz put out—she glanced at the dead lights above. No. It still wasn't possible. Even when it wasn't energized, plaz repelled lower lifeforms. "Is that the only bottle of whiskey you've drunk tonight?"

"Cute." Rogan snorted, lifting it up. "I'm as positive I saw that as I am that our craft is as dead as everything else plaz-dependent in this place."

Nora put a hand to her throat. "We're stuck here?"

"Yep. And between that and the possibility of being the last of my generation, I really don't give a fuck if getting drunk's wise or not. Do me a favor, if my liver decides to give up the ghost—let it."

Nora crossed her arms over her breast and sat back, not particularly keen on watching him give himself alcohol poisoning, and not ready to drop the subject of Binders either. "Why do you think that was?"

He glanced at her askance. "Why was what?"

"Why Binders? I don't understand why Cal—"

"Christ, you're as bad as a fucking Finder." Rogan blew out his cheeks. "Fine. You wanna know all the dirt? Sure. Why the hell not? We've got time, and tonight's the goddamned night for it, so I'll say this once, and then it's done." He took another slug of liquor and held it in his mouth for a moment, staring at a point across the room before he swallowed.

"Yeah. Jane was the Binder in our group, but she shouldn't have been. Only reason she was in the quarry that night was because I'd begged my buddy's girlfriend to talk her into it. I was obsessed with Jane, but she..." He shook his head like the memory pained him.

"She was too good, too smart. Her family was a bunch of scientists. Moved up when the Corporation built that fucking facility outside of town. Rest of us were delinquents, but she had everything planned out and a full ride to college. Wanted to be a botanist like her mother." Rogan sighed, swirling what was in his bottle.

"Whatever. She got caught up in it. Her talent...how everything went to shit...she couldn't handle it. She wasn't..." He shook his head again. "She wasn't made for life after. Was too kind. Gentle. All she wanted was to help people, and she couldn't even help herself. The Surge broke her, and there wasn't a fucking thing any of us could do to make that better." He scrubbed his thumb over the bottle's label. "No one understood what using compulsion was doing to her until it was too late, and by then, she wasn't Jane anymore."

"I lost my mother the same way," Nora murmured, thinking about Veronica. Her personality had totally changed, taking on aspects of all the memories she'd held. "They hide it well, but there's a tipping point..." And once you reached it, there was no coming back.

Rogan grunted. "Then the Source attacked. We were woefully unprepared. I was pinned down with the rest of the Breakers trying to hold the front line. Karen and Richard, our Fixer and Fetch— everything the records say about dyads is true. The two of them could do some crazy shit together. They went after the Source's air power and got eighty-sixed taking out one of the main crafts. Jane tried to save them and got clipped. Cal found her as she was bleeding out, which in retrospect was probably a kindness, but I sure as fuck didn't think so at the time."

Rogan took another pull from the bottle and frowned. "Before she died, she made Cal promise to watch over her line. I don't have any other details. He disappeared right after, and it's not something we talked about when he resurfaced, but I've never had any reason to doubt him. He sure as hell mourned her like she was dead along with the other two, and I haven't caught wind of her in the hundreds of years since."

"But you never saw a body?" Nora pressed, unconvinced.

Rogan slowly shook his head. "No, but not for lack of trying. I burned down half the fucking city searching through the rubble…" He ran a hand across the side of his head, his expression pensive, then he swore. "If that fucking asshole lied…"

"Maybe he didn't. Could she have manipulated Cal's memories?"

Rogan went still, his face pale. "I don't—"

A scream cut through the air as a flash of silver flared from the bedroom Kara had been using, then faded to a steady glow.

Rogan was on his feet, knife in hand, and at the port quicker than Nora'd thought possible given how much he'd drunk. He pulled up short at its threshold. "Jesus."

She hurried to his side, her hand flying to her mouth. Fitz lay on the floor in a puddle of liquid metal with Jolie sprawled on top of him. She gasped like she was coming up from deep water and scrambled off the prone Fetch, splashing through the rapidly diminishing puddle beneath him in her haste to escape. Her back hit the side of the bed, and she panted, face ashy as the bits of metallic slick splashed over her streamed back to him.

He groaned and curled onto his side, his entire body shimmering with the stuff.

"What is that?" Nora whispered hoarsely. Fitz groaned something, pulling his arms up over his head, and scrunching into a tighter ball. His body flickered in and out of existence before it wavered and held solid. Glory, but he looked miserable.

"Concentrated Fetch talent," Rogan murmured beside her. "A shit ton of it."

Nora wet her lips. She'd seen people talent drunk before, but had never heard of it physically manifesting like that. It looked like liquid mercury. "How is that possible?"

The big Breaker crossed his arms over his chest. "Pretty sure it's because he's a Pan."

"What's a—" The room abruptly prickled with tension, Nora's question dying on her tongue.

Fitz pushed up to sit, his head hanging between his knees for several breaths. His body flickered again, and the air vibrated ominously. She took a step back. Glory…but that…Fitz wasn't…

He slowly raised his face, glaring at Rogan from beneath his curls. Lightning crackled through his weird splintered irises. "That ain't an allegation t'make lightly," he said, his voice dripping with menace.

The Breaker's hand tightened around the hilt of his knife. "No, and it won't leave this room. Your line's a bunch of fucking idiots, and as far as I'm concerned, this never happened."

Something passed between the two, and Fitz looked away, a muscle in his jaw jumping.

"But—"

"No buts," Rogan said, cutting Nora off. "He just outed himself to help Kara, and all of us owe him in kind. If his line catches wind of this, he's a dead man. Both of you are gonna swear to keep your mouths shut, or I'll shut them permanently."

Fitz's head jerked up at the declaration, the tension in the room breaking with his surprise. "Ye serious?"

"If I don't do it, I have a feeling Markham will."

"Is that true?" Nora asked Fitz. "Markham knows about…this?"

"Where is he, anyway?" Rogan asked.

"Following. Figure him being here tomorrow night, mayhap?" Fitz riffled his hair and blew a stray curl from his eyes. He flickered again, frowning as he solidified. "S'far as the rest, eh…s'House Matter."

Which meant Markham did know about whatever this Pan-thing was, and the last thing they needed was the First Fetch's animosity, but even without that in the mix, she'd grown oddly protective of Fitz. "I swear I won't say anything." Nora glanced at Jolie, her friend's eyes still on the Fetch. "Jolie?"

She took a deep breath, her color slowly returning. "He already made me swear. I ain't saying shit about shit. All I wanna know is where Kara's at. You said it was time."

"'Tis." Fitz grunted, pulling a pint from his jacket as he wobbled to his feet, there and then gone and then back again. Nora put a hand to her stomach, not understanding how riding in the craft made him ill, but he seemed unaffected by that. In fact, his rakishness had returned in spades.

Rogan swore as the Fetch flickered again. "How talent drunk are you?"

"Not as drunk as I could be, talent or otherwise, but gimme a minute, and I'll catch up," Fitz said, spinning off the cap to his bottle and taking a hefty swallow. "Eh…ye ready?"

"Eh, no." Jolie crossed her arms over her breast. "You're gonna shift us straight into a damned wall. Where the hell do you even go when you disappear like that?"

"Dunno. Never really thought about it. In and out?" He shrugged, which didn't make Nora feel any better. "And I ain't about t'do naught of the sort. In me experience, the fastest way t'sober up yer talent's t'use it…just might take a couple jumps t'get it square." He flickered again. "Eh…maybe more."

Nora and Jolie exchanged a look.

"You really think you'll be able to safely shift us to the Triam?" Nora asked.

"Eventually." The Fetch capped his bottle. "Ye can always wait here while I—"

"Not a fucking chance," Rogan said, lunging for Fitz's arm while he was still corporeal.

He winced as the Breaker's hand closed around it. "Not so hard, ye brawny bastard!"

"We're going with you."

Fitz sighed. The two of them disappeared for a split second, and Rogan staggered as they came back, looking green. "Suit yerselves, but I'd suggest ye bind on. I ain't responsible if ye let go."

"Nor in general," Nora murmured, her halos flaring as she grabbed onto Fitz's belt then sobered Rogan up. He grunted his thanks, and Jolie snorted as she took hold of the Fetch.

He grinned, his halos still crackling. "Ye say that like it's a bad thing, love." Fitz looked around, craning toward the kitchen. "Where's the old hillie?"

"MIA," Rogan said, his expression going hard. "But if that sack of shit's still alive, he owes me some answers. Fucker would disappear now. Let's get going. I'm not gonna be able to track his ass down until this shit is settled, and the longer he has to go to ground, the harder he's gonna be to dig up."

Fitz grunted, pulling talent, and Nora braced herself for the ride ahead, agreeing with Rogan. If there was one thing Caliban Scot excelled at, it was disappearing.

CHAPTER NINETEEN

"...The success of a Talent's gestation period is entirely dependent upon receiving an adequate amount of talent, and to that end, subject to three rather restrictive caveats. The inability to culture specimens in a lab, the fetus's reliance upon their progenitors' bonds remaining intact throughout the pregnancy, and the requirement for vaginal delivery.

Though the last would seem innocuous enough, performing a cesarean or attempting to shift offspring from utero inevitably results in loss. Interestingly, postmortem exams find no trace of ability in that subset, whereas stillbirths and aborted material typically retain traces of a developing channel..."

– L. Merkel, Head Geneticist, The Source

KARA PUSHED her face against Flynn's sweaty neck as he hurried down the corridor to the lab. Her cramps were getting worse, and she couldn't shake the feeling that something was wrong—

No, she just needed to breathe. Nora had said that right? To breathe through them? Of course, she'd also said to drink water, and Kara hadn't done that either—

She bit back a cry as the dull pain that'd been plaguing her all morning sharpened, shooting through her lower back and down her thighs. What the heck? That wasn't even where the stupid babies were!

Her eyes widened. Was that normal? It couldn't be normal. Oh Glory, why were they there? Was something really wrong, or was she just freaking out?

Maybe she was freaking out because something was really wrong, and her stupid bloodlust wasn't helping. All of that with the female still had her on edge, and now it coiled in her gut, feeding on the pain and growing stronger, harder to ignore…

"Almost there, almost there…" Flynn murmured, sharing her anxiety.

The port to the gestation chamber rolled open as they approached, and Doctor Yu stood at the threshold. She opened her mouth, and he steamrolled past her.

"She needs to be in a birthing cube!" the woman shrieked.

"The hell she does!" Flynn shot back over her protests. He set Kara down in the empty gestation bay. "All the equipment's here, now help her!"

Doctor Yu laughed. "Exactly what do you expect me to do? Push for her? Aside from monitoring them, females are fixed to their gurneys and nature takes its course…"

Kara tuned out, her breath hissing through her gritted teeth. Her 'lust rose, the woman's voice inciting a wave of rage. The suggestion of whispers rode within it, the dark murmur just out of hearing. She struggled to pull zero, gripping the edges of the metal gurney beneath its thin padding. Darkness bit at her as she fought to rise above its licking tendrils. *Breathe, breathe through it. Ascend your platform, it can't touch you there…* Her nostrils flared. In and out. In and out…

"…on the verge of succumbing!" Yu shrieked. "You're endangering every female in this room—"

Kara laughed through the cresting blackness, the doctor had no idea…the urge to destroy, to tear someone limb from limb—

"Then move them!" Flynn bellowed. He turned his back to Yu and took Kara's hand in his, kissing her knuckles. His gaze locked on hers. "It's okay, baby, I'm here. Stay with me."

Behind him, spittle flew, the doctor's face purple. "Titus is not going to be happy when he sees this!"

"Fucking—Fuck Titus, and fuck you!" Flynn roared, throwing out talent.

His halos flared like they had back in the suite, and a flurry of tiny pops followed, drowning the doctor's gasp of outrage. Kara laughed again at the look on the awful woman's face as the scent of burnt electronics drifted through the air. Guess Titus wasn't going to see anything. Glory, the chaos—

"Hey. Stay with me, Kara." Flynn grazed his thumb over her dimple, his face intense as he cupped her cheeks between his palms, forcing her to look at him. "Stay with me and ignore the rest. Tell me what you need. What can I do?" His sincerity overrode the darkness's glee, and she latched onto it, grounding herself.

She swallowed her mania and nodded, fighting to stay with him. "Sensors." She blew out a long breath as her cramping began to increase again, the pain in her back a low throb. "To monitor the babies."

She pointed to the bundle of wires hanging beside the console. The doctor huffed as he handed them over. She made an entry on her tablet, then started unplugging the nearest woman from her bay.

The monitor at the head of the gurney began to trend as Kara affixed the little pads, the steady beeping soothing her nerves. She was okay. The babies were okay. She affixed the last one and lay back, her eyes on the ceiling as another wave of cramps—ugh, contractions—threatened then passed…

It was happening. The babies were coming.

Tears pricked her eyes, and she blinked them back, not ready. Glory, she wasn't ready…No. Don't think about it. Think about— another contraction hit, and she gritted her teeth—Contractions. She was supposed to do something with contractions…count them, or was it the time between them? Nora would know. Why wasn't she here?

She would be. Fitz wouldn't let them down. Kara knew he wouldn't.

Would he?

She dashed a hand over her eyes. In her peripheral, Yu muttered darkly as she wheeled out a heavily gravid female. A bevy of techs came into the room as she left. They hurried to disconnect the other women, casting fearful glances in Kara's direction. She choked down a laugh, way too tempted to say "Boo!"

Flynn ran a hand under his nose, sniffing. He glanced at her and then focused on the graphs trending, his grip on her hand tightening. Being in the same environ where Titus's memories had originated should help put them into context…at least it would for a Binder. Unfortunately, the more of them Flynn accessed, the faster that residue from the compulsions would build, and if she couldn't UnMake it…

No. She couldn't think about that, either. It had to be the pregnancy. She still didn't have access to her talent. As soon as the babies were born she would, and her UnMaking would work the way it was supposed to. It had to.

Glory, please let that be true.

You know it's not…

Her stomach dropped at the cruel whisper of her 'lust. She flailed at it, pushing the encroaching darkness away. Too close, it was too close…it pushed back, rising up to lap at her resolve. Her heart rate jumped, the beat a rapid staccato throughout the room. She wouldn't succumb. Not again. Never again—Glory, she said that but—

laughter

"Is that helping you assimilate things?" she asked, trying to distract herself from its licking tendrils. Her fear spiked through their bond. Sweet bliss help her, her 'lust was right. She would cave and then it would have her… What if Flynn couldn't bring her back this time? Her brow knitted, his face so much grayer than even a moment ago. How many of Titus's memories were left?

Too many…

"Some," he murmured. "It would be easier if this shit was labeled."

Blackness rose into her throat, and she choked it down. "Go use the console."

Yes, send him away. Run, rabbit, run…

Shut up! Kara thought back, her breathing ragged.

He glanced at her and then at the remaining techs wheeling women out. "I'll wait."

She gritted her teeth at another contraction pushing a wave of 'lust before it, her temper jumping. Glory only knew what he was feeling from her right now, she couldn't feel anything past the blackness stalking her psyche, just waiting for her to let down her guard... *Go away!* she screamed at it. "They're not going to steal me, Flynn. You'll be, like, three feet away, I think it's safe."

Safer for him...

"And losing you isn't a mistake I'm gonna make twice." He growled at a tech that was dumb enough to make eye contact, the scent of Flynn's 'lust a counterpoint to hers. The man paled and hurried out.

Kara's retort was cut short by another lancing pain. A line on the graph spiked as she bit back a cry.

"Guess I know what that one's for," he murmured.

She glared at him, hissing air through her teeth. "Do you now?"

The portlock closed behind the last tech, saving Flynn from answering. He kissed her knuckles and went to the console, slogging through the first few menus and then gaining speed, his pallor growing by the moment.

He was doing this for her—poisoning himself with Titus's memories. She sent a wave of UnMaking to break up the gathering residue—and blanched, the talent she gathered dispersing as another contraction ripped through her, 'lust lashing in its wake, the madness promising to make everything go away... She squeezed her eyes shut against its siren's call. It would be so easy to just give in...

No. She needed to focus, to stay in the now. She wet her lips. Glory, they were dry. What she wouldn't give for one of those frozen lemonades Nora and Albanach would bring back for her whenever they went on a picnic... A shiver went through Kara. Ugh, she could practically see the stupid thing. She focused on the image, all the little details, trying to stay sane—

Flynn staggered at the console, and she fought to gather enough talent to help him, her bloodlust working against her, only wanting to harm. Talent fizzled around her. She bit back a sob, giving up.

"Are you okay?" It was a stupid question, he obviously wasn't, and neither was she, but the gritted determination on his face was terrifying.

"I just need..." he grimaced. "Christ, where the fuck would Nora have put Titus's admin override?"

Kara shook her head, struggling to stay calm. The code. Where would it be? She was pretty certain that if Nora had gotten that, it would've been front and center. "Maybe it's not there," she panted.

Flynn ran a heavy hand down his face. "I've got everything else, at least I think I do, but..." he frowned, then glanced at the screen again and started pulling up different menus.

"You find it?"

"No, but if I dig through my head much more, I'm not gonna be functional," he muttered, his fingers trembling as he typed. "I might have a work around, but I need to figure out a way to get him..." He chewed his lip then grunted, making more entries.

The plex windows facing the hall shimmered to a mirrored surface, and Kara's anxiety eased a fraction at the illusion of privacy.

No one else to see what you'll become...

"Better?" Flynn asked her over his shoulder.

No. "Yes. Thank you...is that my treatment plan?" she asked as he closed out of whatever he'd been in. Her name was at the top, but the rest was unfamiliar codes and strings of bastardized medical shorthand. What it said was beyond her. Titus definitely had his own system in place, and it wasn't the same one she'd learned at the Source.

Flynn grunted again, his dark brows bunched as he scanned the chart. Glory, he didn't look well.

Her anxiety ticked back up. "Is there a problem?"

"Yeah, Fitz isn't fucking here, and Nora needs to be."

Instant cold sweat. "You're not leaving me."

"Kara—" He broke off at her glare and raked a trembling hand through his hair, sighing. "Ten more minutes. If he's not here by then, I'm getting her even if I have to shift you and the gurney back to the Source with me."

With the amount of compulsion his mind was trying to process, she doubted he'd be able to stand in ten minutes, never mind shift. She went to say as much, and another cramp ripped through her, not letting go. Something inside—she screamed, frantically trying to bind the damage. Flynn was back at her side as her vision tunneled...

"Okay," she panted when it cleared.

"Okay?"

"Ten minutes." Kara nodded, pacifying him as another wave of pain built along her spine, the fragile weave over a tear in her uterus straining…she clenched her jaw, the dampness between her thighs too sticky to be amniotic fluid. He was right. She needed Nora, but Kara was pretty certain it was already too late.

<hr>

TITUS RAN a finger over his lips, watching the live feed of the females' dormitory. Br4Ef had returned significantly worse for the wear from her visit to the Scot's suite. Now she knelt, her raggedly shorn head bowed within a circle of the others as their fingers moved rapidly.

He frowned at the use of their coded language, not a clue what was transpiring, though it didn't look good for Br4Ef. Admittedly, he'd been negligent in snuffing out its use, but it hadn't been high on his list of priorities.

Apparently that would have to change now that Scot was instructing them in insurrection. Titus raised his glass to his lips and paused for a brief moment at a chime announcing Brix's arrival. The Elite hobbled in, his right arm in a sling and his face a mangled mass of glistening, raw tissue. How marvelous. Titus enlarged the holo of the females.

"Br2E. Tell me. What exactly am I seeing here?" he asked, motioning with his drink at the scene playing out. Br4Ef had risen, her head bowed as the women surrounding her turned their backs on her one by one.

Brix stared unblinkingly ahead, his left eye socket a gory sunken pit. "Breaker Business."

Titus put his drink down and slowly rotated the glass. "It's irksome how you and your ilk delight in using that phrase to obstruct my will. I'm well aware that you have no qualms about me punishing you for your insubordination, so let's do it this way. If you don't answer my questions, I'll remove your bitch from stasis and let both her and the litter die."

Brix stood straighter. "Dying is also Breaker Business," he said roughly. "Her honor and mine demand obedience to the hierarchy."

"Honor?" Titus laughed. "What honor do you have? You abandoned your precious hierarchy when you left the battlefield at my behest. The only obedience you owe is to me."

Brix's gaze was serene. "That's Breaker Business."

Titus ripped open his desk drawer and pulled out a pistol. He racked it, and pointed it at the Elite's head. "Say it again."

Brix stared at him, disturbingly calm. "He's already won, Titus. Whatever you do, he'll roll right over—"

The bullet took the Elite in the forehead, and he toppled backwards, splintering a chair beneath him. Titus tossed the pistol back into his drawer, eyeing the spatter of gray matter and gore peppered over the far wall. A bit too evocative of Jackson Pollock for his taste. He reached for his bourbon, his gaze drifting back to the holo still playing, the females' dormitory now empty. Hmm. Where had Br4Ef gotten off to…he tapped through several screens—

And stopped. What was this? Doctor Yu was setting up the gestating females in the overflow chamber. He swapped to the room they'd been in and was met with static. He scowled. All his damned feeds had been cut, but the lack of visuals aside, the data streaming more than made up for it.

A grin slicked over Titus's face. Scot's bitch was in labor. How very excellent. He typed out a quick missive alerting the techs preassigned to care for the litter. They'd require immediate attention once they were whelped, and a transport needed to be readied. There wasn't a chance they were remaining here with Scot in residence.

Titus couldn't possibly imagine the man's promise to agree to his terms would hold once he had an inkling of what was in store for them. Especially the runt, should it survive…or not. Either way, its ultimate fate lay in several different specimen jars swimming in formaldehyde with its ribcage pinned open like a butterfly.

Titus glanced at his shelf in the corner of the room, imagining the aesthetic in tandem with his Picasso. Something about displaying the preserved remains of one of Scot's offspring beside "The Weeping Woman" just spoke to him. Titus shivered at the artistry of it.

Ah! Which reminded him, where had he left off... His gaze returned to his feeds. He cycled through the facility and came to a stop in the lower grotto, a body floating face down in its still waters.

He sighed. There wasn't a doubt in his mind that Br4Ef's death had been self-inflicted. It wouldn't be the first time he'd lost a female that way, nor would it be the last. Yet another annoying Breaker predilection he hadn't been able to stem.

Titus took a long swallow of bourbon, unable to see the point of the deluded practice. He pursed his lips at the waste of fuckable flesh before ringing for maintenance.

"There's a corpse floating in the lower grotto. Fish it out and deliver it to lab twelve," he said when they answered. It hadn't been there long, perhaps Doctor Yu could still salvage something of worth. Titus glanced at what was left of Brix. "And then do the same with the one in my office." That would be a total loss as far as he was concerned, but the good doctor had a fondness for taxidermy, and he was certain portions of the former Elite would be put to good use.

Titus cut the call, his attention going to an uncharacteristically short missive from Yu, marked urgent. His frown deepened as he read through it. Scot chasing her from the gestating chamber was preventing the girl from receiving the injections she'd require to survive the birth after the cocktail Yu had given her earlier—

The entire sector abruptly stopped transmitting data, the feed going dark.

Titus's eyebrows rose with his temper. Oh no. This wouldn't do at all. He threw back the last of his drink and strode out of his office, grinding his teeth. His annoyance didn't abate as he was stopped at the access port leading to the gestating chamber's hallway and forced to enter admin credentials. How Scot had managed to tamper with the security clearances...

Titus seethed as he punched in his override code, and the port opened. He stormed through, his fury redoubled in the mirrored plex lining his path. Another setting Scot shouldn't have the ability to access.

The techs he'd summoned stood in the hallway outside the chamber with the litter's incubation units. They stopped their hushed conversation as they caught sight of him. Titus didn't bother to ask why they weren't inside, and his attempt to open the port confirmed his suspicions. He stabbed in his override code again, irate.

The portlock rolled aside, and he stepped through, marginally pacified by the pained moans from within, then pulled up short as he caught sight of Scot. In the few hours he'd been closeted in his assigned suite, dark circles had rimmed his eyes. He leaned heavily against the room's console, typing rapidly and very obviously ill.

Well, wasn't this an interesting turn of events? Lord Laughlin Scot didn't look like he should be standing, never mind engaging in a pissing contest. His face was positively gray beneath the bright plaz-lights.

The girl screamed and his face paled further. Titus grinned. Her panicked cries were delightfully visceral, the air heady with the scent amniotic fluid and gore. He motioned for the techs to set up their equipment and chuckled, his good mood restored as he snatched a pair of blue latex gloves from a dispenser and shook them out.

"You look like you should be in bed, preferably with one of my bitches." Titus snapped on a glove and frowned at Scot's broad back, the man ignoring him in favor of typing. "Short of that, I'd suggest you begin explaining exactly what you think you're doing frittering around with my facility's settings—"

"You mean *my* facility's settings," Scot said, making a final entry then throwing out a wave of talent. "I appreciate you entering your codes. You've just become obsolete."

FLYNN'S HEAD POUNDED, static hissing around him as he sent out a burst of Fixer talent. It hit Titus, and he froze from the neck down, his outstretched fingers worked halfway into his second glove. Impotent rage seared over his face.

"How dare you!" he sputtered, the cords in his throat standing out as he strained against the fix. "Release me at once!"

Flynn turned to the four techs cowering by the equipment they'd rolled in. "I'd leave now, if I were you." They didn't argue, hurrying from the room. He pushed away from the console and staggered to Kara's side. She gave a pained whimper, the air thick with bloodlust. It churned, his own answering it and clearing his head. Darkness flickered behind her eyes, losing the battle—

"You're not touching her."

"You fool," Titus seethed. "You'll kill them all! Without my intervention, that litter is going to rip her apart, and she'll take them with her!"

Flynn's temper surged. It was Titus's fucking intervention that'd put them in this place to begin with. Everything Kara had suffered through—all of the shit at the Source and everything since—was because of this fucking asshole. Flynn growled, baring his teeth.

It needed to end.

"Flynn?" Kara panted as she met his gaze, her breath choppy. Their bond thrummed with her repressed 'lust, toxic and black, begging to be used. She couldn't keep fighting it and concentrate on having the babies. His fucking head—he didn't know if he could bring her back. Flynn grabbed a cloth from the gurney's side and swept it over her sweat-beaded brow.

"I love you," he murmured.

"I love you, too." Tears spilled down Kara's cheeks, the finality in her gaze wrenching. She put a hand on his cheek. "Baby, we both know it's too late."

A fist settled around Flynn's heart, and phantom flames sprang up to lap at the corners of the room. "Then I'll burn it all down," he choked out, "but before I do, he's yours."

Kara's eyes darted to Titus, then back to Flynn, and he gave a slow nod. Another time, another place, he would've torn the fucker limb from limb, but she needed this, needed to make the motherfucker hurt for everything he'd put her through.

And he was pretty sure whatever she'd do would be worse than dismemberment.

It ended now.

The prick watched them, his gaze narrowed. "I don't know what you hope to gain by this little power play," he spat.

"Closure," Flynn said, stepping aside as he took Kara's hand.

And they'd find that together.

Her lids fluttered as she gave in to the darkness and 'lust coursed through the room, heady and black. The jagged cloud of talent around them surged, the undercurrent of malevolence it rode upon buoying them. He knew that darkness, felt it as his own and welcomed it. They pushed it out together, releasing it before it devoured them.

Tiny blue particles streamed from the tips of Titus's outstretched fingers like mist rising, the plaz-lights refracting rainbows. They wafted in the current from the overhead air duct, then dispersed into nothingness.

Titus stared at his hand, the whites of his eyes huge. His glove thinned and faded from existence, followed by the smattering of hair on the back of his hand and knuckles. "W-what are you doing? What talent..." His face contorted, ribbons of skin flaying into the atmosphere, leaving gory tracks stippling his outstretched arm. The pitch of his voice rose, frantic. "What talent is this?!"

"The one you've been looking for," Kara said, her voice saccharine.

Titus ripped his gaze from himself to settle on her. "You—this is what you pulled at the lake. This, this—"

"UnMaking," she purred, her satisfaction edging on obscene. "And you've more than earned it."

Understanding dawned over Titus's face, his cheeks blistering red and the skin peeling back. His nails sloughed off and his flesh sagged. He screamed in abject horror, his jaw distending, dripping down his chest as he disintegrated, his being eroding like a pillar of salt in a windstorm. His expression rapidly tipped toward agony, his gaze losing focus—

Kara cried out and grimaced. Behind her, the graph trending her contractions spiked again. She curled toward her belly, panting. Gold scintillated through her halos, her brow dripping sweat.

Phantom flames at the edges of the room rushed in, becoming corporeal and igniting Titus in a pyre.

The sour mineral funk of viscera cooking lanced through the air. Creamy yellow globules of fat crackled and spit, clear juices running. Raw muscle browned and blackened, flaking away in the relentless heat to reveal withered sinew, and charring tendons from bone.

Kara's hand tightened in Flynn's, her face a rictus. The fix holding Titus's corpse upright failed, and what was left collapsed into an incinerating heap. The flames intensified, building on themselves and shot up like a roman candle, scorching the ceiling tiles. Greasy smoke hung lank in striating garlands—

Alarms went off and a cloud of white suppressant dispersed, then a surge of talent went through the room clearing it away—

"Jesus fuck." Fitz swore, riffling the powder from his curls as he eyed the smoking pile. "The hell is that?"

NORA FLINCHED CLOSER to Fitz as he swore. She cracked an eye and choked down the bile at the back of her throat as they lingered in the space instead of shifting away. Were they finally where they were supposed to be?

The room swam as she gripped the Fetch's shoulder for balance, trying to make sense of their environ. Glory, it still felt like they were moving…but no, they'd stopped. So where…she let out a breath at the bright plaz-lights above and harsh lines of the room around them.

A lab. They were in a lab. She bit back a sob. Not waist deep in swamp water, or falling to their deaths, or in the dusty back room of some questionable establishment, or in any of the dozens of other rapid fire places they'd shifted through before Nora had screwed her eyes shut in an attempt not to vomit.

At her side, Jolie hadn't been as successful, and Fitz's jacket had borne the brunt of it.

"Jesus fuck is right. What is that?" Jolie whispered, her face agog at something past Rogan's bulk. Whatever it was smelled horrible, but Fitz and the big Breaker blocked Nora's view and didn't seem inclined to move.

"Don't know and don't fuckin' care," Fitz muttered, pulling talent again. "Christ, ye got any idea how hard it is t'get the smell of vomit out of wool?" His halos flared and the mess from his jacket and everything else they'd picked up along the way shifted onto the scorched linoleum at their feet with a wet—

"Where's Nora?" Laughlin's voice cut through the last of her disorientation, and she dropped her bind on Fitz and stepped away from him. Her gaze skipped through the haze of smoke and the horror in the center of the room to the woman on a gurney beyond.

Kara.

Oh, Glory. Her face was contorted with agony as she gripped the sides of the metal cot, panting, a trail of crimson dripping from its edge.

Nora grabbed Jolie's arm and hauled her around Fitz and Rogan, giving whatever that smoking pile was a wide berth. She had a feeling that up until a few moments ago it'd been breathing. Nora kicked a tooth from her path, any doubts she'd had on that count gone.

"Sweet bliss, remind me not to piss the Overlord off," Jolie muttered as she went past.

"Then we better get started. You triage, I'll pull up Kara's treatment plan." If Nora had learned anything from Titus's memories, it was that he'd purposefully developed his coding system to confuse anyone but him and a chosen few.

Jolie's gaze whipped from the smoldering heap to Kara and caught on the growing pool of crimson at the foot of her gurney. "Oh, hell no." She took off at a sprint, and Nora headed for the console.

Jolie reached Kara's side and placed one palm, then two, against her abdomen. Her halos flared for a long moment and sweat stippled her brow before Kara's grimace eased.

Laughlin held her closer as a sob broke from her lips. "Shh, it's okay. See, it's not too late. Nora's here now. It's gonna be okay."

"I c-couldn't bind it. My 'lust..." Kara grimaced again, the graph behind her spiking.

"No, I know, baby girl, but now we got you," Jolie said, frowning at the sloppy port in the back of Kara's hand, then nodding at Laughlin before she turned to rifle through the medical cabinet. She pulled out a tubing kit to run an IV. "And the first thing you need are some fluids."

Which was Jolie for, *I have no idea what to do and need to buy time.* Nora glanced up, and Jolie met her gaze, the concern in hers apparent as she mouthed the word, *"Breech."*

Damn it. "Saline is over here," Nora said, flipping through Kara's chart. She paled reading over the final cocktail Kara had been injected with. Prostaglandins had been the least of it, and by removing them, Nora had done more harm than good. If she'd understood what the Rebytrol was doing to her…

The drug was just short of miraculous for lung development, but had been pulled after finding it decayed the musculature of a woman's uterus, increasing the chance of rupture by a staggering amount. Glory. Even with a weave reinforcing her womb, palpitating Kara's abdomen to turn the breeched baby would be incredibly risky.

And they were running out of time.

Kara screamed, back arching and eyes rolling as Laughlin fought to keep her calm.

Nora pulled up Titus's notes, confirming her fears. If Kara had gone into labor hours ago like he'd intended, this wouldn't have been an issue, but now? Nora chewed her lip. There was a final entry with what looked like counteractive measures, but did she trust it? Two of the compounds on the list she had no memories of.

"Protocol?" Jolie asked, adjusting the saline's drip.

"Gamalit." Nora nodded to a locked plex cabinet. It wouldn't fix the damage already inflicted, but it would hopefully slow further degeneration. She read over the final entry again, not knowing what to make of Titus wanting to test Kara's regenerative abilities… Why would he think she had the ability to regenerate?

Nora shook her head. Who knew what else that Binder had implanted in his mind? They were beyond evil, and for whatever reason had a vendetta against Talents. The realization decided her. She closed out of the note, not willing to put Kara any more at risk. At this point, she needed to keep calm while they addressed what they could.

Nora took a deep breath and rattled off the code to open the cabinet. "Start with thirty-two milligrams," she said to Jolie.

"What does that do?" Laughlin asked, his face haggard. He looked worse than Kara did as she breathed through another contraction. Nora's stomach sank, sure the memories she'd given him were responsible for his current state.

"It counteracts something Titus had her on." Jolie flicked the air from a syringe she'd prepared and injected it into Kara's port.

She whimpered, the graph behind beginning to spike again. Contractions were less than a minute apart and gaining in intensity. Nora's halos flared. Kara was fully dilated, eight and a half centimeters...and thanks to Titus's protocols, this was going to go faster than it had any right to.

"I want to push—"

"Not yet," Nora said more quickly than she probably should've.

Laughlin tensed, picking up on it. "What's wrong?"

"Baby girl's in there tryin' to come out ass first," Jolie said, frowning. "We gotta turn her, but Kara's womb is compromised."

"Oh Glory, I knew something was wrong—"

"Shh...save your strength and let us deal with it. Your job is just to breathe. In and out..." Nora prompted, trying to buy time. How were they going to turn this child without risking another rupture? Kara's uterus was dangerously thin, even allowing her to push would be a risk.

Jolie glanced at Kara's abdomen, no doubt thinking the same thing. Her lips thinned. "You going in or am I?"

Nora shook her head, her eyes sweeping the room—

And landed on Fitz.

FITZ WINCED at the damn plaz-resonance screaming through his head, but he weren't about to fuck with it and blow hisself t'hell again. Though, now that he knew what to expect, maybe he could—his coin burned cold at the idea, and he sighed, resignin' hisself to a migraine, damn it.

The lady let out another cry, and Christ, if it didn't raise his hair. Hated this fucking part, waiting around for the miracle to happen and not bein' able t'do a fucking thing to speed it on its way. He eyed the portlock, wonderin' if he could make a break for it. Weren't like they needed him for aught.

He pulled the bottle from his jacket, focusing on what were left of a corpse smokin' in the middle of the room instead of the lady's distress.

Jesus, Mary, and Joseph, but that smoking pile made him right nostalgic for the lower rungs.

"Who do ye think it were?" he asked Rogan, then took a pull from his bottle and winced at the lady's pained moans.

"Titus, if God is good." He glanced from the corpse to the rest of 'em.

"He ain't, but even an addled rat sometimes finds cheese."

The Breaker snorted, then ran a hand under his nose, sniffing. "That they do."

Fitz took another pull from his bottle. "Eh...any reason ye ain't flappin' around over there with the rest of 'em?"

"Yeah. One, I'd just get in the way, and two, with the amount of bloodlust in the room, the last thing I need to do is anything that can be even remotely perceived as a challenge. Neither one of them are thinking clearly, and it'd go bad quick." He blew out a breath and glanced at the portlock, cringing as the lady cried out again. "What are the chances you can shift that open that one like you did back at the Source without fucking with the plaz?"

"Fair, but the hell do ye mean about fucking with the plaz? That right there is slander, and I ain't done a damned thing t'deserve it."

Rogan just looked at him—

"Fitzpatrick!"

He flinched, then glowered through his curls at Nora. "S'Fitz."

"You said your grandmother was a midwife."

Shite. Cold sweat prickled over his body. Him and his big fucking mouth...he rubbed a hand across the back of his neck, not excited about where this were going.

"Did you ever help turn a breeched baby?" Nora asked, not waiting for his answer and the hope on her face just about killin' him. Wait. She didn't—Fitz blanched. She had t'be fucking jokin'. That weren't—she couldn't be serious—

"You gotta be fucking kidding me," Scot blurted, shooting to his feet and coming up short, the lady's fist grabbing his shirt in a death grip. He glanced down at her and then glowered back up at Fitz. "No. There's no goddamned way he's touching—"

Jolie smacked him upside the head, and His High Holiness

whipped around to glower at her. She glared back. "Sit your ass down. It's the best option. One of us tries, and there's a good chance she'll rupture and bleed out."

"Listen to them, Flynn," the lady panted. "It doesn't..." she sobbed, "it doesn't feel right."

Scot paled and sat his arse back down, but he sure as fuck weren't happy about it.

Fitz wet his lips. "Eh...mayhap I seen it done, but—"

"But nothing." Nora beckoned him closer. "Kara and the babies need you, now."

Scot's growl rumbled through the room, and Nora put a hand to her throat, glancing at him askance. His glare burned through Fitz, the man's lip curled over a canine, his knuckles gone white on the bedrail.

"Good fucking luck with that." Rogan jerked the bottle from Fitz's hand. "No sudden movements, don't touch her any more than you have to, and don't make eye contact with either of them."

The lady screamed, and Fitz's throat bobbed like that graph running behind her. Rogan pushed him forward, and Fitz stumbled across the room to her bedside. Fuck. Didn't wanna do this...

He raised a hand over the lady's belly, and Scot let out another growl that made Fitz's knackers wizen. How the fuck did they expect him to shift somewhat he couldn't see? Blight the harpy, his gran could do it in her sleep, but...damn it all t'hell. She weren't here, he were, and if she caught wind he'd sat around with his thumb up his arse, he were a dead man...course, he might be anyway with how Scot were lookin' at him. No goddamned pressure. Right, eh...think she started by puttin' a hand on each end...

He glanced up, and Scot's gaze caught his. Shite. Weren't supposed t'do that...

The lady whimpered, and Scot's glower intensified—

Yep, he were dead. Fitz stepped back, his hands raised. "I ain't touchin' her."

"Why the fuck not?" Scot growled again, edging forward like he were ready t'come over the gurney at him. Jesus, man were scrambled fuckin' ham—

"Please, Fitz," the lady panted, her face slick with sweat. "It hurts…"

Christ, he couldn't say no t'that, but fuckin' Scot…blight the prick, but this shite were hard enough… Fitz riffled his curls. Goddamn it, fuck him. "Fine, but—swear ye'll name one after me House."

"Done!" she gasped.

Scot blinked and pulled back. "What?"

"Eh…ya. A little McCreedy Scot." Fitz said, his hands settling on the lady's abdomen. Felt fevered. "That's me price."

His High Holiness sputtered. "Name my kid McCreedy? Are you out of your goddamned mind? I'm not naming one of my kids after you. That's fucking awful—"

"Ooh, and Laughlin's a right prize of a name," Fitz muttered trying to figure out where the little bugger beneath his hands started and stopped. Think that were a head. Shite, he hoped so. Never saw Gran turn a breech with multiples… He glanced at Nora, and she set her hands atop his as her talent flared.

"Cal would approve," Rogan said from across the room, capturing Scot's attention as it wandered to what Fitz was doing and a growl started in his chest again.

"Yeah, and where the fuck is he?"

"S'it the same one?" Fitz hissed at Nora while Scot were distracted.

She gave a quick nod. "Yes. Use my talent to guide you. Head over teakettle, quickly now…"

"Eh…bet me I can't do it first."

"What?"

"Just…it's a luck thing." He blinked the sweat from his eyes. "Bet me."

"I…bet you can't turn the baby?"

Christ, Cajetan, ye better pony up, ye fucking prick, and prove her wrong… Fitz's throat bobbed, followin' her talent like she said and pulled a quick burst of his own, flipping the problematic little bundle. The lady screamed, and he flinched back like he'd been burnt, Scot lunging at him.

"The fuck did you just do—" He were abruptly in front of Fitz, gripping his lapels as he slammed him against the far wall. Jesus fuck! His teeth clashed together and stars burst behind his lids—

"No, it's a good thing!" Nora yelled. "Laughlin, stop! The baby dropped—it's coming!"

"Flynn!"

His head whipped around at the lady's voice, and he abandoned Fitz.

Fitz blew out his cheeks as he slid down the wall and hit the floor, nauseous, the ceiling slowly coming back into focus.

"Told you not to make eye contact." Rogan crouched down and held out a hand, helping him up he exchanged a quick glance with Nora and she nodded. "Come on. Let's get out of here. I wanna go take a look at the rest of the facility and figure out what we're dealing with before Markham gets here."

Still had plenty of time before that happened, but Fitz weren't gonna argue. He wobbled to his feet and staggered to the portlock, gingerly touching the goose egg blooming at the back of his head. Fuck that'd about scrambled him.

"You did good back there," Rogan said at his side. "I don't think I could've gotten him to stand down."

Psh. Whatever. He'd still gotten his arse beat. He'd make the fucker pay for it later. Fitz grunted and shifted the portlock's circuits. It rolled to the side, letting them out of the fuckin' mad house.

The Breaker chuckled as he stepped through. "And I sure as fuck couldn't have gotten him to name one of his kids after me."

"Were just bullshit t'distract him," Fitz grumbled, jamming his hands into his pockets as the portlock rolled shut behind them, cutting off the lady's distress. "Ye really think he'll do it?"

Rogan passed him back his bottle. "They come through this, nothing will surprise me."

CHAPTER TWENTY

THE CONTRACTION HIT KARA HARD, a burning ring of fire blooming at her core. She screamed with the need to push, squeezing the side of the gurney. The sheet metal buckled and bent. Flynn moved behind her, supporting her against his chest.

"I got you, baby…breathe…"

Fuck him and fuck breathing. Kara gnashed her teeth, trying to focus on Titus's corpse smoldering against blackened linoleum, the stench cutting through the cloud of 'lust and sticking to the back of her throat. She gagged. The reflex pulled on her abdominals, and she cried out, the pain too sharp. Even after Fitz had turned the baby, something was still wrong—Oh Glory, it was wrong—she could feel it.

Nora handed Flynn a damp cloth, and he put it against Kara's brow. "You have to breathe through them, Kara," she said, pulling over an instrument tray. "Jolie, you have the carts?"

"We're good." Her mother's best friend wheeled over the last of the incubation units the techs had brought in and switched it on, warming it. "Nutritionals are already loaded…not for nothing, but they're set up for a good forty-eight hours. If I didn't know any better, I'd say Titus planned on transporting them somewhere."

"Good, then they're set to head north," Nora said, her voice perfunctory as she pulled out the stirrups and lifted Kara's heels into them. She moved to her side, her halos flaring to a steady glow, palms slick against Kara's abdomen. Binder talent laced through her, maintaining an even pressure around her womb. "Now we just need to get the babies into them safely…"

Whatever else she said was lost beneath Kara's next contraction. She rounded over her abdomen, teeth gritted as she screamed. Sweat stung her eyes. *Get it out, get it out, get it out!*

laughter

"One more push Kara, the baby's crowning!"

Flynn's breathing sped with hers, his terror pervasive, fingers stabbing points of pressure at her shoulders. She growled, jerking from him, her world condensing and burning away beneath the onslaught of pain consuming her. Darkness flickered, pushing her into the maelstrom, urging her to accept the chaos…

"Stay with us, Kar-bear," Jolie forced a smile. "Things are about to get heavy, but we got you and all four of these little angels. Sooner we get this done, sooner you get to meet them."

We? Kara didn't see anyone else being ripped in two. She hissed air through her teeth, glowering at the woman through the lank strands of her sweat-soaked hair. The bitch laughed.

"Yeah, that's it, game face on. Big breath, then hold it, and push with the contractions."

Breathe, don't breathe—the next wave built on the heels of the last, and an animalistic howl tore from Kara's throat, darkness overwhelming her and stars pricking her vision—

Something broke through, sliding free, and a fierce wail split the air—

"Oooh, little girl's got her daddy's fire," Jolie held up a tiny wriggling form caked with white and smeared with crimson. Behind Kara, Flynn's fingers found her shoulders again, his breath bursting out in a sob—

And then the next contraction hit.

Burning pain, deeper this time—something tore—Kara screamed, agony lancing through her—Nora's halos brightened in response, and it dulled—flared. Stabbing pain shot through Kara's hips and back. No, no, no, no, no….

Yes…give in. Let me take it from you…

Kara moaned. Tempted, so tempted…her 'lust licked around the edges of her consciousness, slowly enveloping her and drowning her resolve…

Flynn tensed. His lips at her ear. "Fight it, Kara. Don't leave me, don't leave us…did you see her?" His voice caught. "That's Aurora…"

Aurora. "I hate that name," she growled.

Jerk laughed and kissed her temple.

Jolie got the baby settled in the first incubation unit, the plex dampening the baby's wails, and Jolie rushed back to add her talent to Nora's. Kara whimpered, crying in relief as the pain receded, her bloodlust ebbing.

Another contraction and that horrible burn rushed in on hits heels.

"Glory, number two's already at the chute. Goddamn that fucking bastard, women are not made for this rapid fire shit," Jolie muttered. "No rest for the wicked, baby girl. Big breath and then ride those waves."

Kara's tears fell faster. Ride the waves? She could barely keep her head above—

A contraction ripped through her and a pop came from deep inside. Kara heaved, vomit spattering with the sudden influx of pain, that ring of fire surging wide, her vision tunneling—

Nora's halos blazed, throwing shadows into stark relief beneath the bright plaz-lights. Warmth spread through Kara's hips and abdomen, slowly binding the damage. Another warbling cry joined the first as the darkness receded. Nora dashed the sweat from her eyes, stumbling.

"Nora…" Jolie's face was pale.

Nora shook her head. "I'm fine. The baby…?"

Jolie's halos scintillated as she made for another incubation unit, a tiny arm waving as she clutched the child to her chest. "He's good. More even tempered than the first, if I had to guess."

Flynn kissed Kara's temple again. "Halfway there, Kara, you can do this…"

No, she couldn't. She bit back a sob, her consciousness tunneling black and darkness surging, swallowing her—

Another wave of pain engulfed her, and her world shrank to encompass it and the certainty that she was going to die.

Flynn laced his fingers through hers, raising her hand to kiss her knuckles. "Stay with me, stay with me…" She gripped back desperately, her face streaked with tears.

"Don't let go!"

"No, baby, never, I promise, I'm here—"

She screamed again, her bloodlust surging with the contraction. Nora's halos flared, weaker this time, the edge of agony Kara was riding on barely blunted.

Jolie's hands slapped down over Nora's, augmenting her talent again. "You need to stand down, before you burn yourself out," she said through gritted teeth.

"No, I need to do this," Nora spat back.

Jolie's eyes flicked to Nora's midsection. "Nono, you gotta think about your own—"

"Alice said I had a choice to make, and I'm making it!" Her face contorted, and she bit her lips. "Marcos…he'll understand. I can't—I won't trade the certainty of my grandchildren for another potential Riegel."

Kara blanched. What? No… Nora couldn't—

The burning in her groin surged, and Kara screamed, the darkness pouncing and dragging her under.

DARKNESS FLICKERED in Kara's eyes, and Flynn's hair rose as the wave of 'lust swallowed her.

Fuck.

The change was immediate, her pheromones blackening, tinged with something corrupt. She struggled to rip her hand from his, and he gripped it tighter, her bones grating beneath his fingers.

"No. I promised I wouldn't let go…"

Kara screamed in fury instead of pain, her 'lust feeding off it, lending her strength. She thrashed, and Nora fell back against the console, striking her head. She sagged against it, dazed.

"Damn it! You need to keep her still," Jolie yelled. "Fuck, fuck, fuck—the next one's starting to crown! Nono, I need you!"

Shit, the Fixer, where was the—he needed to fix—the static around them hissed, a living thing in his ears—

Everything in the room froze.

Goddamn it. No, not, just—the fix eased around them, and Jolie shot him a dirty look.

"The baby's gotta come out, genius."

"No shit." He glared at her, his gaze going to Nora as she gingerly shook her head and came back to Kara's side.

"Wait…" she set a trembling hand on Kara's abdomen, too pale. "Help me reinforce the weaves first…"

Jolie frowned, but did as Nora said, their halos flaring in tandem. "That's not gonna hold. There's nothing—"

"As long as I'm standing, it *will* hold," Nora hissed. Her glared leaped to Flynn. "Do it now. Ease the fix."

He opened his mouth and then closed it again, bracing himself as talent ebbed, trying to find the line between keeping Kara restrained and able to push—

She lashed out at him, pulling from the static around them. He bellowed, his bloodlust flaring at the crippling pain lancing through his bones. His hand shot out, and he fisted her hair, pulling her against him, a lethal growl rumbling through his chest as he tightened the fix, blocking her from attacking him again.

"Give. Her. Back."

"Make me." The creature Kara had become laughed, the challenge burbling from her lips with unholy glee as she squirmed, her hips lifting from the gurney.

"Sweet fucking bliss, nothing's ever easy." Jolie threw out a bind, and Kara screeched as she was bound to the metal, her abdomen hardening with another contraction.

"Push!" he growled, sending out a cloud of 'lust with his Alpha command.

Her eyes rolled back into her head, lids fluttering over the whites as a scream tore from her lips, no option but to comply—

A reedy cry threaded through the room as the third baby slid into Jolie's waiting arms.

Recognition flickered over Kara's face for a breath and was lost, her attention back on fighting his fix. Her halos began to glow, and he doubled down, pushing her emotion and drowning her in his 'lust.

She screamed in frustration, her cries rising above the newborns' as her fury ticked up, her pheromones thickening to compete with his. Jolie swore, stumbling from the cart, and the tremor in Nora's hands became a palsy.

Fuck. Flynn gritted his teeth and focused on their bond, pushing Kara emotion, the barest trickle eking through. "Listen. You hear that, baby?" he murmured in her ear. "They're calling for you. They want their mom. They need you. I need you. Follow it back to us..."

Kara spat at him.

Damn it—

"One more," Jolie said, her eyes on Nora. Hers were closed, lips moving in prayer.

A shrill alarm sliced through the air, and Kara laughed.

The last baby was flatlining.

SHE WAS LOST in a stifling tomb of darkness. Sticky tendrils encased her, lashing and teasing, blocking her senses, feeding on her pain and lulling her with chaos. There had been something—a cry—she'd tried to rise with it, but then the moment was lost, and the madness had swept back in around her.

Its whispers were drowning her, dragging her under and shoving her down. She flailed, not knowing if she was cresting or swimming deeper. *Oh Glory...please help!*

There is no Glory, and your man's abandoned you...they all have... Her 'lust laughed, taunting her. *You'll never be free...*

No! It lied, she knew it did. Flynn would never leave her, but he'd been so ill…Glory, he needed her, the babies, they needed her—

And to save them, she had to save herself.

Her resolve hardened. She could do it. For them. She'd come back before, and Phyllis had said it was easier each time. She just needed something to show her the way, which end was up, something, anything—

There. Ever so faintly, buried within the shrieking caterwaul of her 'lust, a piercing beep rode above the maelstrom.

Kara fought against the malevolence churning around her, throwing off the shackles of madness to ascend through the murk, and rose.

NORA PANTED, her channel straining as she sent more talent around the last child. After the third, Kara's womb was gone, completely disintegrated thanks to that damned drug Titus had pumped her full of. And now, without anything to push it through, Kara's baby was dying.

And Nora's was already lost.

Her choice. The sacrifice Alice had seen…not her damned position as First Binder, but her child and Marcos's. Their second chance. What would she tell him? What would he say?

Glory help her, but she couldn't think about that right now, and it wouldn't be for naught. Kara's child would live.

She bit back her guilt with a ragged sob, positioning her weave and praying she could simulate the motions. If Cal was right and there was a God…oh, sweet bliss, please let this work… Pain sliced through her being, bits of her channel fraying—

A wave of Jolie's talent washed over hers, weak from stabilizing the other infants, but just enough to buttress the bind. "You know I got you," she gritted out through her clenched teeth, sweat streaking her face.

A smile flitted over Nora's lips. "Always. Ready?"

Jolie grunted, and Nora closed her eyes, pulling one last shock of talent and palpitating the weave to push the child through.

Her talent faltered as the last little bundle slipped from between Kara's blood-slickened thighs. Glory, it was so tiny. So still. The alarm cut off, and Jolie's talent flared again to stimulate its heart, its breath, she swore, rubbing its little blue limbs. "Damn it, come on…"

A frail voice broke the silence.

"Give her to me."

Kara.

FLYNN DROPPED THE FIX, the corruption in Kara's 'lust gone and the lingering traces fading like a bad smell. Kara collapsed against him as she opened her arms for the last of their children. Her face was drawn but determined, and her gaze clear. The hum of talent between them strengthened, their bond wide open, flooded with emotion. Devastation. Guilt. Anger. They blurred into a deep shared sorrow, one in their loss.

Jolie hesitated for a breath, her eyes flicking to his. He gave a defeated nod, cringing at the static surging at the back of his brain. He couldn't deal with it right now, Christ…he couldn't fucking deal with any of this…

Jolie brought the child over and placed her lifeless body on Kara's breast. Flynn cupped his palm over the little girl's dark, damp frizz, his fingers tingling. Would it have been wavy like his? His heart ached for all the might've-beens. Kara took a little hand in hers, curling the baby's slender fingers over one of her own. Jesus Christ, they were so fucking tiny… His arms closed around them both with a heaving sob, breath stuttered, his face damp with tears.

Kara looked up at him, broken. "I-I can't UnMake this."

"No, baby," his voice cracked. "No one can."

Her gaze dropped from his, back to the child in their arms, and his temper surged. Why the fuck did she have to go through this? Why did any of them? After everything—he clenched his jaw so tight his teeth popped. Fuck, why bring him back—

He froze, and Kara glanced back up at him, a question in her eyes. Something had brought him back.

The static around them grew tangible, the room heavy with expectation, that other force…the one churning behind it all. His stomach cramped, he hadn't been ready to deal with it before, but he had a sinking suspicion it was now or never.

"Flynn?"

He took a deep breath. "No one can UnMake it, but I think I can make it right." He closed his eyes, and focused on the static, opening himself to it and inviting it in.

Please…

The hum between him and Kara grew louder. She tensed against him, the tingle in his fingers a slow trickle, spreading to his palm, the small hairs on his arms rising, resonating with a vibration beyond hearing. The effect spread to her, and she gasped. Something like music flitted past his ears, and a soft glow shined through his lids.

He opened his eyes. Talent streamed around him like before, but this was a brilliant, feathering opalescence smoothing to starlight as it was drawn into an umber spiral fading to nothingness. UnMaking and Rebirth, the two danced together in an eternal harmony.

His throat bobbed as it swirled around them, backing Jolie and Nora against the console. They trembled, arms around each other, lips parted, and eyes wide. A plume slipped between them, brushing over Nora's abdomen and disappeared. Her hand followed it, and surprise bloomed over her face. She let out a choked sob, staggering against Jolie and then falling to her knees.

"Abundance…" Nora whispered past her shaking fingers. "Oh Glory, she saw abundance…"

"Shh…I got you Nono…" Jolie crouched beside her, trembling. The swirling power retreated from them and extend to the incubators, the babies' cries calming to coos.

The suggestion of music grew louder…no, closer, as the spiraling opalescence feathered toward the gurney and swirled over Kara's body. Voices? A language familiar and not, almost understood. The susurration of a dinner party heard from behind closed doors. A intimate whisper two rows in front of you at a crowded theater.

They weren't alone, and somehow…the talent was alive, sentient.

Kara's brow knitted, listening, then smoothed as if she understood. She lifted a hand to Flynn's temple, and he groaned, his shoulders sagging as the residue from Titus's memories was UnMade. Fucking hell, that was sweet relief…

"It's Mina's turn now, Help me?" She dipped her head and kissed the baby's brow. "We both need to call her back."

Mina. He choked up, cupping the baby's head again and dipping his to kiss the spot Kara had, willing her to live with all of his being. *Please, please give us this…* "Wake up, little beauty…"

A sigh went through the room and talent flared around them, the opalescence a swirling storm of feathers blowing away the stench of Titus's death and Kara's remaining 'lust. Petrichor and the scent of green things filled his lungs, and Kara let out a gasp.

Flynn swallowed a sob. Mina's little fingers had tightened around Kara's.

The baby opened her eyes, silently regarding them with a knowing gaze the dark velvet of night, studded with stars. She gave a slow blink, and it was gone, replaced by irises of watery gray-blue.

The opalescence surrounding them drew into the umber spiral, and was gone, taking the static around them with it, and leaving behind the smell of rain and the memory of song.

"I dunno what the fuck is in the water up north, but I'm tapping out," Jolie said, breaking the spell it'd cast. "I see one more miracle, and Imma lose my shit."

Flynn's brow knit. He drew Kara and the baby closer. "What do you mean one more miracle? What the hell else happened?"

Jolie waved a hand, shaking her head as she staggered to her feet. "I need to go find Fitz and his bottle."

Flynn glanced at Nora. She sniffled as she wiped away her tears, then bit back a laugh, a wide smile on her face. "No, what we need to do is get the babies back to Glynfyls and settled. It's going to take time for Jon to figure out their nutritionals, and we only have forty-eight hours of whatever's in those units."

Jolie snorted as she headed for the port. "Color me optimistic, but I don't think you're gonna need whatever's in those units."

Flynn was pretty sure she was right, but he didn't have any desire to hang around and wait for her to come back from her stroll. "Once Nora gives the okay, we're leaving. If you're not here, you're gonna have to shift back with Fitz or Markham." Flynn glanced at the time ticking away on one of the plaz-screens. "And he better be here soon."

"Or?" Kara turned to look at him, and he chewed his lip.

"I couldn't completely bypass the biometric security clearances required for the Triam's operations. We've got five days before it goes dark and maybe another two before the oxygen reserves are tapped. Everyone has to be out by then."

"Fitz said Markham should be here by tomorrow night, but you do know that crazy-ass Fetch broke your craft along with the rest of the Source, right?" Jolie asked, cocking a hip.

Flynn opened his mouth and then closed it, somehow not surprised.

"Mmm hmm," she continued. "Way I heard it, nothing plaz-dependent's working."

"She's right," Nora said, "and Rogan told me he saw a V of geese fly right over the facility."

Geese? There was no way. Flynn's doubt must've shown on his face, because Nora huffed out a sigh as she stood.

"He swears it's true, but I don't understand how it's possible, either."

"It's because your Uncle Fitz is a menace," Kara murmured to the baby. "Hopefully your brother Mac doesn't take after him."

Nora made a noise that sounded suspiciously like a snort. Flynn narrowed his eyes at her as she pulled talent and began looking Kara over.

"He's not Uncle fucking Fitz," Flynn blustered, "and I'm not naming my son McCreedy."

"Oh, but you are, because I already promised," Kara said sweetly, batting her lashes. "Besides, Aurora is vile, and if I have to deal with that, you can deal with McCreedy."

Flynn glowered at her. "Middle name."

"Nope. McCreedy Cornelius Scot. Done deal."

Goddamn it. Using French's given name was just playing dirty. She smiled at him, knowing full well he couldn't say no to that.

"Right, that's three out of four, but can we play the name game later?" Jolie asked. "With the craft out of the picture, aren't you gonna need Fitz to get us out of here?"

Flynn scowled at her. "No. I'm pretty sure I can shift to the coop from here, and then through the safe houses we stayed at with Graham and Leo." He chewed his lip. "Crossing from the last one to the farmhouse might be dicey." He ran a hand over his face. "Shit. Miriam warded it and the Sons left Hamlin a smoking ruin…"

"Please tell me we don't have to stop at the Pinion," Kara moaned.

"Considering that was in flames when we left, I don't think that's an option, but there's a town not too far away—or was." He shook his head. "We'll figure it out when we get there. Fitz needs to stay with Rogan, at least until Markham gets here. Even with Titus dead, this place isn't safe, and he needs a way out." He turned to Jolie. "Make sure you tell them they've only got a few days to get this clear of this place."

"Will do, Daddy."

Daddy. Flynn snorted, unable to stop the stupid smile spreading over his face.

Kara yawned and snuggled against his chest, exhaustion coloring their bond. Mina was fast asleep, her cheek smooshed against Kara's breast, lips parted. He slid his hand to cover Kara's against the baby's back, so fucking grateful for the soft rise and fall of breath beneath their palms. He frowned as he eyed the incubators. They needed to get somewhere with a bed big enough for all of them.

And they needed to do it soon. He couldn't shake the feeling that they needed to be back in Glynfyls. He turned to Nora checking over the other three. "Are they good to travel?"

"Yes, as soon as we get Mina into—"

"No," Kara's eyes flew open. "Pack her nutritionals with the others, but she stays with me." Her halos flared as she situated the baby higher up on her shoulder and bound her there. "Hand me that blanket?"

Jolie grabbed it and tucked it around the two of them like a shawl. "You got this?" she asked Nora.

"I do. You have Fitz and Rogan?"

"Not yet, but I will." Jolie smirked, licked a finger and flicked it over her cocked eyebrow as she sauntered to the port.

"Glory." Nora sighed, snapping the units together to create one and hitting a button. A low hum engaged, and the wheels folded up. It rose to hover several inches above the floor. "Leaving her to chaperone those two is probably not the wisest choice," she said, pushing the incubators to the bedside as the portlock rolled closed behind Jolie.

Flynn frowned, in full agreement as he stood with Kara in his arms. "No, but that's what's happening. We ready?"

Nora nodded, and he called for Fetch talent to take them to the coop—

"What's wrong?" Kara asked after a long moment.

Flynn shook his head and laughed, the air silent and still around him. Fucking talent. "Not a damned thing." The static was gone and his channel right back where it should be. He puffed out his cheeks and pulled, power filling him the way it was supposed to.

Something at the edge of his understanding laughed, and colors ran, shifting them away.

CHAPTER TWENTY-ONE

"The origin of talent is a topic of heavy debate. Creationists believe it to be a gift from God, Evolutionists opine it stems from the genetic mutations necessary survive in a post-apocalyptic world. However, what both agree upon is its abrupt manifestation.

And therein lies the crux.

It is a fact that at some point, the entire Northern Hemisphere went dark. Yet, given only those in a small pocket of the northeastern portion of the continent were affected—or infected—with talent, it stands to reason that somewhere Outside is a proverbial ground zero from which it spread. Our talent is not due to God, nor evolution, but something created. A man-made catalyst—unleashed intentionally or no—which propelled us into this new age, and changed humanity forever..."

– Lord Talos, Preceptor of History,
Academy of Glynfyls

"HOW'S YOUR HEAD?"

Fitz paused fiddling with the massive goose egg Scot had given him to glance over at Rogan. "Eh...I've had worse."

"Not what I asked," the big Breaker said, craning his neck around the same corner for the third time. He frowned. "Christ, all these fucking hallways looks the same..."

Fitz lifted his bottle and grunted, agreeing with him. Were because they'd been walking in ramblin' circles for the past half hour, but he weren't about to break it to the idjit if he couldn't figure it out hisself. Granted, they was all white and chrome with them damn plaz-lights running the length, but the number of doors and how they was laid out should've been a giveaway.

That and the number of lefts they'd taken.

Rogan huffed out a breath before turning right, and thank Christ for that. Ye'd think he were heavy on the port side.

Fitz rubbed his head again, wincing. Weren't just because of the ache. Breaker had done him a solid, and he weren't quite sure what to do with it. Owed him now, and it chafed somewhat fierce. Man were right about the rest of Fitz's line risin' up against him if they knew what he were, what he could pull… It were a shite hand that Rogan'd sussed it out, but the man would keep his word about not spilling. Breakers was good like that. Were pretty sure Nora would, too, but that other one…he thumbed his pigsticker, not opposed to making certain.

"Eh…question. Ye really mean what ye said earlier?"

"I did." Rogan glanced back at him. "No one's gonna touch you for being a Pan, but your fucking mouth's on you." They walked in silence for a spell more, the clomp of the Breaker's boots echoing down the hall and not another body in sight. He glanced over his shoulder at the mouth of another branching corridor. "That what happened to the rest of your house?"

"Nah. Fuckin' Prydees is what happened to them," Fitz muttered, raising his bottle.

Rogan grunted, taking the detour. "They know?"

"Dunno." Fitz shrugged, but were pretty sure he'd be at the bottom of the bay if they did.

"Then what the fuck do they have against you?"

"S'complicated."

Rogan paused at another T. "I'll bet…right or left?"

"Right," Fitz said before he'd really thought about it. The doors was spaced farther apart that way, and the air felt different. More humid. "Regardless, I owe ye."

"Good. You can pay me back with a road trip."

Fitz paused. "Eh...what's that now?"

Rogan turned to look at him again. "Once we get everyone back to Glynfyls, you and I are going on a walkabout. I need some answers, and the only way I'm gonna get them is if I can track down Cal."

"Good fuckin' luck with that." Fitz snorted. The old hillie weren't exactly forthcoming and Shades was slipperier than snot. 'Specially *that* Shade.

Rogan grunted like he agreed. "Luck's not gonna have anything to do with it. There's only so many places he'd go to ground, and I'm pretty sure I know where the lion's share of them are. Unfortunately, without my gating stone, getting to them's gonna be a bitch." His jaw tightened as he met Fitz's eyes. "And I'm not willing to just give anyone the imprints."

Fitz nodded and looked away first. Tit for tat, the man were squarin' up. His secrets in trade for Fitz's. Well, for some of 'em. He frowned, the bottle of laudanum in his pocket heavier than it should be. Christ, his gran were gonna skin him alive for not checkin' in... "Right then, s'long as I stay in Scot's employ."

"I don't think that'll be a problem. He's gonna have plenty to keep him busy."

Fitz didn't doubt that, and diaper duty were the last thing he were interested in. In fact, the longer he thought about it, the better a trip sounded, and his coin were warmin' up like the blessed saint agreed.

His gran aside, the less he had to deal with Adelaide after givin' her them damned chocolates, the better. Way she were lookin' at him after made him itch, and if she knew he were helping with littles...nah. That shite always made women broody. Why she couldn't get it through her thick head that there weren't never gonna be naught between 'em...

They rounded another corner and the hall opened up, the far wall lined with windows. Rogan stepped up to one and swore. Fitz joined him and almost dropped his bottle.

Beyond the plex, an entire world opened up. Grass, trees, hills rolling into the distance, were like they'd stumbled upon one of them fairy mounds in his gran's stories.

And the entire place were full of nymphs.

ROGAN GRABBED Fitz's sleeve and pulled the kid away from the window. The entrance had to be somewhere around here…ah. Jackpot. "Open it," he said, stopping before a wide portlock.

The kid glanced at him, but didn't argue for once. His halos flared, and after a long moment, the portlock rolled aside. A burst of warm, humid air poured out, tinged with 'lust. Rogan grunted at the punch of it, his dick twitching. Jesus fuck, the shit was like catnip.

He adjusted himself and stalked through, sending out a cloud of his own. They stopped at the top of a rise, looking out over the rolling hills. The atmosphere grew dense, and beside him, Fitz knuckled an eye.

Christ, Rogan couldn't believe what he was seeing either.

Breaker females streamed through the trees, a crowd cresting the hill to surround them. His mouth went dry. He hadn't seen so many since after the Surge, and they definitely hadn't look this good then.

They hadn't all been primed to mate either.

He ran a hand over his mouth. Focus. He needed to focus.

Rogan cleared his throat, their 'lust thick upon his tongue and raised his voice to reach the back of the crowd. "Listen up! Titus is dead, and this facility needs to be cleared—"

"By whose order?" a voice carried over the murmurs his announcement had caused, silencing them. Females stepped to the side and a statuesque blonde strode through the press.

Lord have mercy.

Her wheaten waves were held back by a leather thong and fell down her back. Toned, bronze skin, legs that went on for days, and a pair of tits the likes of which Rogan hadn't seen since watching *Baywatch* reruns.

"Eh…he's Alpha Prime." Fitz elbowed him, and Rogan grunted, not sure how long he'd been staring.

"*The* Alpha Prime?" Her moss green eyes crinkled in amusement, and she crossed her arms under her breasts, cocking a hip. Goddamn…

he shook himself as she laughed. Christ, he hadn't been this dick-dazzled in centuries. "And who does that make you, Fetch? The Builder of Cities?"

Rogan's stomach dropped at the moniker. How the fuck would she know about Richard?

She turned to glance at the giggling crowd. "Huh. The old tales say you're short, with dark hair, and you…" She tsked, sweeping her eyes over Rogan. "You, old man, are definitely not Rogan Firestorm. Would you like to try again?"

Try ag—wait. Old man?

Fitz sniggered, and Rogan growled at the little prick.

The female's brow cocked in challenge, and the crowd behind her went silent and still, save for the rapid movement of their fingers—Rogan started. *You gotta be fucking kidding me…* He watched them for a moment longer until there was no question they were using a form of the battlefield sign language his Valkyries had. It was a hell of a lot more fleshed out, but the bones of it were there.

Shit. That had to be how they knew about Richard, about him…or who he was. That form of sign language, what they were talking about, all of it spanned back to the First Incursion…but Marcos hadn't had a clue about any of it. Rogan's brow furrowed. He knew for a fact that the Source had done its damndest to erase any knowledge of the North, so how had these females retained their history?

It was a question for later. Right now, he needed them to comply.

"Your lore's a little outdated." Rogan crossed his arms over his chest and widened his stance. "And I am Rogan Firestorm, the Alpha Prime." He sent out another puff of 'lust, this one tinged with warning.

"More like past your prime," she drawled, ignoring it.

Fitz just about choked, and her lips twitched into a half-smile as the rest of the crowd tensed. Rogan wasn't fucking amused, his 'lust creeping darker. The females around her shrank back.

She shrugged one slim, bronzed shoulder. "And as far as our lore being outdated, you might be surprised."

He growled, not sure what she was playing at. Whatever it was, he didn't like it, and the urge to put her over his goddamned knee sure as fuck wasn't platonic. He gritted his teeth, ignoring the jab to address the others. "Fetches are on their way to bring everyone back to Glynfyls, so I suggest you start packing." He ran his eyes over her short chiton. "You're gonna want to dress warmer."

"There's a lot of things I'd like to do," she said, sliding her gaze over him in turn. Then it hardened. "But packing isn't one of them. I'll ask you again. Who are you, really?"

"You'll just have to wait and be surprised." Rogan grinned at her scowl. "Meanwhile, how about you tell me your name, princess?"

She narrowed her eyes at him. "I don't know what that means, but I don't like your tone."

"And I don't like your fucking attitude." He glowered down at her, somehow toe-to-toe.

That half smile twitched up her lips again, and he growled, getting the distinct impression she was baiting him on purpose and enjoying the fuck out of it. Two could play that game, and he'd been at it for a hell of a lot longer.

Her nostrils flared at the abrupt change in his 'lust, her smile slipping as what he was putting out became predatory. He leaned forward and she took a step back. A chuckle rumbled through his chest.

"What's the matter, princess?" he asked softly, wetting his lips. Her gaze darted to them, and the pulse in her throat jumped.

His own sped to match it, anticipating the chase. How long had it been? She took another half step back from him, the tension between them coiling like a spring. His 'lust ripened, and the barest tremble went through her as he stepped forward again.

"You're not worthy." Her spine straightened, and she raised her chin in defiance.

"No?" Rogan's grin widened. She was putting on a good show, but it had to be killing her not to turn and run. He dipped his head, inhaling along her shoulder and pausing at the crook of her neck to breathe her in. Damn. There it was. Her pheromones were definitely telling him to fuck off with a side of spank-me-daddy.

And if that just wasn't his favorite scent…

A rumble of pleasure went through him, and the air spiked with her desire. She gave a sharp gasp and pulled back, her fist taking him in the face before she bolted, running back down the hillside.

That's it princess, make me earn it... Rogan's grin went feral as he took off after her, deaf to Fitz's protests, and totally consumed by the chase.

———

NORA SHOOK out another blanket that'd been trapped beneath a bureau and bound it with heat before draping it around Kara and the babies. The stove was taking longer than she'd like to get to temperature, and even with Laughlin's shield, the little room was cold.

She sighed. The coop wasn't ideal, but it was better than the alternative. All of them needed to rest before they went any farther, and she wasn't the only one glad to see the last of the Corporation's facilities. Glory forbid she ever had to set foot in one of them again, and sweet bliss willing, none of her grandchildren would either.

She tucked in the edges of the blanket, beaming down at them, her smile growing wider as she watched the little ones nuzzle against Kara in their sleep. It made her heart so full; she couldn't remember the last time she'd been this happy.

She gingerly sat beside them and ran a hand over Mac's pale fuzz, wondering if he would become as golden as his namesake, or if it would darken. Both Kara and Riegel had been tow-headed when they were born, but hers had darkened to chestnut, and his had become honey-blond like Marcos's.

Nora's smile faltered, and her hand went to her abdomen, remembering what a beautiful child Riegel had been—and the rotten core that beauty had covered.

She shivered. No. This one would be different. She could feel it. Being touched by that strange power had removed her doubts. She and Marcos would have the family they'd only dared to talk about in whispers. A child they could be proud of. She blinked the tears from her eyes, her entire being overflowing with gratitude. Glory…she was so damned grateful…

"Are you all right?" Kara asked, her voice muzzy.

"I thought you were asleep." Nora laughed, dashing a hand across her eyes. "Yes. I'm…I'm the best I think I've ever been. You?"

"Same, but exhausted," Kara sighed, smiling down at her brood. "And starving. Tell me I'm not imagining you're cooking over there."

"I wouldn't call it cooking, but I am heating up some soup. I can't vouch for how appetizing it's going to be." Though she did have to admit, it smelled better than it looked. "And without Fitz here, there should be plenty."

Kara laughed. "Don't be so sure, whatever was in those nutritionals Titus had me on, I'm pretty sure they bypassed my stomach. I think I might be able to put his appetite to shame."

Nora chewed her lip, not quite knowing how to broach the subject, but it needed to be said. That same power that had given Nora back her child had healed Kara from the damage the birth had caused, but it hadn't restored her womb. "Kara, the protocol Titus had you on—"

"I know I can't have any more children," she said matter-of-factly.

"You do?"

Kara nodded. "Considering how it felt? I'm assuming I just had the equivalent to a chemical hysterectomy." She yawned. "And I'm fine with it. Relieved, if I'm being honest. I'm done with being a breeder hanging over my head. Now I can just be me."

Oh. Nora glanced at the door, not sure how much time they had before Laughlin came back with more firewood. "What about Laughlin?"

Kara's brow furrowed. "We talked about it. He knows I didn't want any more after this."

"Wanting and being unable are two very different things," Nora said, rising to tend the soup. "You need to tell him."

"Tell me what?" he asked, coming in on the tail end of the conversation. He kicked the door closed behind him, then cringed at the resulting bang. "Sorry." He set the load of wood he was carrying down with exaggerated care, grimacing at the babies' fussing the noise had set off.

"The protocol Titus had me on," Kara said, soothing them. The largest, Aurora, already had a tendency to fuss.

"What about it?" Laughlin asked over his shoulder as he fed the stove.

"I can't have any more children."

He went still for a breath, then shrugged, jamming more logs into the fire. "Well, I guess that makes things easier. I thought we'd agreed this was it anyway."

"We did, but—"

"But?" He stood, turning to look at her as he dusted off his hands.

"But the abstract is always easier than the reality—Glory, come take this child," Kara huffed. Aurora's unconsolable wailing was upsetting the others.

A wide grin split Laughlin's face as he waded through the mess still strewn over the floor. The baby immediately quieted in his arms.

"Someone's a daddy's girl," he murmured, swaying with her, his lips at the top of her head.

Nora's heart melted watching them, but Kara snorted. "Only until she figures out you were the one who named her."

"You think that's a crappy name? I'll take Aurora—Rori—and raise you a McCreedy," he frowned, settling next to her with the baby on his chest. He reached past Mina to the other tow-headed infant. "What do you think of Diandra?"

Kara cocked a brow. "Instead of Deirdre?"

"Yeah, I mean, Diandra's still a nod to my mom, but I think she'd want the baby's name to be her own." He chewed his lip. "When all those memories came back...I'd asked her once why she named me Laughlin, and she said it was because names had their own music, and no one should have to share a song."

Glory. Nora turned from the murmur of their voices, feeling like she was intruding. That was something Deirdre would say. She wiped her eyes and tried to concentrate on stirring the soup, although what she was going to serve it in—

"Nora. I need to say thank you." Laughlin's voice rumbled out, startling her.

She put a hand to her throat as she turned. "I-I'm sorry, what?"

He frowned, his head hanging for a beat before he looked at her.

"Kara and the babies would've died without you there. I would've died. What you did…risked…thank you."

"Of course, it wasn't—no thanks needed," she said, flustered by his sincerity.

"You've got it anyway."

"Any chance bowls come with it?" she quipped, trying to lighten the mood before she started bawling.

Laughlin's halos flared. "Behind the stove and at the end of the dresser—no. Never mind, that one's busted." His halos flared again. "There's a mug at the foot of the bed and another jammed into the side of the recliner's cushions."

That's right. Cal had been using it as an ashtray. Nora moved around the room gathering them. "I'll just wash these," she sniffled, still shaken, "and then I suppose dinner is served."

KARA'S BROW knitted as Nora bustled past them and into the bathroom with the dishes. She'd never seen her mother so emotional, and it was definitely not something Kara was used to. Her gaze dropped to the babies draped over her and Flynn, and she bit back a laugh. Glory. None of this was what she was used to.

"You really don't mind I can't have more?" she asked him.

"I just said so, didn't I?" he murmured, his head back and his eyes closed as he stroked Rori's back. Gah, that stupid diminutive wasn't much better than Aurora, but something about seeing him hold her made Kara inclined to give the jerk a pass.

That, and she couldn't help but smile at his contentment streaming through their bond. "Yes, but you've also started lying."

He cracked a lid to look at her. "Technically, I never agreed to Titus's terms."

Kara rolled her eyes. "But you were going to."

"Intent isn't action."

"And if that isn't Glynfyls double-speak, I don't know what is." She laughed. "You sound like you're already prepping for the Assembly."

He frowned, pinching the bridge of his nose. "No, but I probably should be. I didn't exactly leave under the best circumstances, and I can guarantee you there's a shit ton of those fuckers who would be thrilled if I never came back."

"You're not alone," Nora said, heading to the stove with her cleaned dishes. She ladled out portions of soup and brought them over. "Sorry, I couldn't help but overhear, and you're right. Serra and her sympathizers aren't going to make it easy for either of us."

"I wish the Assembly would do something useful for a change and exile her," Kara murmured blowing over her cup.

"Mmm," Flynn murmured, already devouring what was in the bowl Nora had brought him.

Kara laughed. "Good?"

"Needs hot sauce. What?" he asked at her eye roll. "I told you, everything's better with hot sauce."

"If you say so." Kara took a sip and grimaced, resigned to choking the rest down. Maybe he was right. "Glory, this is foul. Sorry, Nora."

"You're not getting an argument from me," she said frowning at her spoonful.

Flynn tipped the bowl to his lips again and shrugged. "I've had worse. No, what I was going to say was I've been thinking about that. The Assembly. When Titus was coming, I told them Glynfyls was no longer a democracy, and when we get back, it needs to stay that way. That rogue Binder has to be dealt with and the last thing I need to do is worry about all those idiots. I've got a really bad feeling that putting Titus down wasn't the end of whatever else is going on. We need to get back to the city."

"There's a woman out there," Nora said at Kara's look of confusion. "By her talent signature, I'm certain she's from the same House as Otto. She's been using coercion to manipulate the Sons and was responsible for seeding Titus's obsession with the Breaker line. I think she's the reason you were taken."

Kara swallowed the lump in her throat, suddenly not hungry anymore. She handed back her half-eaten cup of soup.

Flynn grunted, agreeing. "And Cal knows who she is."

Nora put a hand to her throat before she took the cup and Flynn's empty bowl. "Are you certain?"

"No, but he sure as fuck knows more about it than he's saying. He made a comment about Kara being the one they were waiting for. At the time I didn't question it, but now I don't think he meant him and Titus. I think he meant him and this rogue Binder. For whatever reason, they've both been looking for someone that can pull from the fourth duality, and I'm gonna beat his ass until he spills why."

"You're going to have to wait in line," Nora said. "I asked Rogan about the Binder from their original seven, Jane. He said Cal told him she died in the First Incursion—"

Flynn snorted, and by Nora's expression she felt the same. "My thoughts exactly, and I don't think Rogan's sold on the story anymore, either. When we last spoke, he was adamant about hunting Cal down and getting some answers. He disappeared after whatever happened with Elize."

Flynn's halos flared, and he frowned. "Wherever he is, he's cloaked. I can't find him, but if anyone can, it'd be Rogan."

"Do you think this Binder can influence Talents like Otto can?" Kara asked.

"From what I saw in Titus's mind, I'd say it's a safe bet." Nora frowned, fiddling with her ring. "The weaves...I've never seen anything like them, and it would take lifetimes to become that adept. It has to be Jane, or another of their contemporaries."

"Having Otto running around the city was bad enough, but if she's able to influence Talents too, that's even more incentive to shut the Assembly down...unless you can tell who's been compromised?" Flynn asked.

"I can for the rest of your cohort, but everyone else?" Nora shook her head. "It would take too long, and if people found out what I was looking for—Glory, if Serra did—"

"People would freak," Kara finished, chewing her thumb.

Nora nodded, sighing. "And whatever this Binder has been working toward, I can't imagine Titus's death has put an end to it. The way she uses her talent is unscrupulous. If she figures out we're looking for her or Cal—who knows what she might do?"

"Cal would," Flynn growled, scrubbing his face. "Christ. That motherfucker would disappear now. Rogan needs to find the prick, stat. Until we know who she is, and what the hell she wants, we've got no way to combat her next move."

"We don't need to, we just need to buy enough time for Rogan to find Cal without tipping her off." Kara yawned, her eyelids heavy as she idly stroked Mina's dark fuzz. "He's the missing link."

"He's the missing something," Flynn muttered. "Look, we can figure it out after we see what's going on up north. The Deep South could've razed the place for all we know. We all need to get some sleep. The sooner we get up there with the babies, the better I'll feel."

"Agreed. Every minute we tarry is another Serra can use to dig herself in," Nora said, shaking out another blanket from the floor and curling up in the recliner.

Flynn scooted Diandra across his chest to lay next to Rori and raised his arm for Kara to snuggle closer with the other two babies. His halos flared, and a cloak settled around them. He sighed, kissing the top of her head, their bond replete and talent humming around them.

"Why do you think it does that?"

"I dunno," he said, his eyes already closed.

She sighed, not knowing either, but for whatever reason it felt like it was important. Kara yawned again, too tired to put much thought into it. "Thank you."

"For what?"

"Coming for me in the Triam, and then not letting go."

"I'll always come for you, Kara, and I'm never letting go," he rumbled. "Nothing will ever take you from me. Not Titus, not this fucking Binder, and not your 'lust. You're mine. All of you are mine."

A soft smile crossed her face as she snuggled closer. That they were, and so was this place. "When we leave, will you put a shield over the coop? I-I don't know if we'll ever have the opportunity to come back, but I like knowing it's here waiting for us."

"I was thinking the same thing." He smiled. "This is our place, Kara." He kissed her softly. She smiled and brushed his hair back from his brow.

"I love you, Laughlin Scot."

"And I love you, now go to sleep. We've still got a long way to go."

Kara settled back against him, her cheeks dimpling at how far they'd already come.

"The end begins with life, and life begins at the end. A serpent eating its tail. It hungers, devouring, time etched upon its scales. Judgement day is nigh…"

– Excerpt from the dream journals of House Carmody

CAL STOOD on the low rise, a fresh mound of raised earth at his feet and beside it, a much smaller, time-worn depression. What a goddamned waste. He brought his cigarette to his lips, nails broken and caked with dirt. Nothing but the blood on the stone he'd used to scrape out the shallow grave and memory to mark either of them.

Prayers eluded him, just like the last time he'd been here. But that felt right. Invoking God's name in the place where you've buried your own soul seemed somehow hypocritical.

Sun rise, sun set. He looked out over the unchanging vista.

Jane could fucking have all of it.

He was done.

DYAD

THE PRICE OF TALENT: BOOK SIX

"A person often meets his destiny on the road he took to avoid it."

— *Jean de La Fontaine*

Outside of Time—The Astral Plane

SOPHIA SEETHED AS she stared past the ever-shifting currents of time to the fixed paths they flowed through. The half-moons of her blunt nails dug into the dampness of her palms as she willed herself to see whatever it was she was here to see. Stupid initiation.

Ugh! More like stupid Fitzpatrick McCreedy. Why did he have to hand her that damned pouch?

She scuffed her toe against one of the wide gray flagstones of the ruined courtyard beneath the Astral Plane's great tree, completely beside herself. Four more years. She'd had four more years until her majority and—and *this*.

She frowned. Okay, technically that was true, but not really.

Not when you were a Carmody and had your life pre-ordained in bullet points somewhere in a dusty tome written before your grandmother's grandmother had been born.

Sophia wet her lips, closing her eyes as she swallowed, well aware of the lousy fate the coven had seen for her. This was just one of the immutable points along the way, which was exactly the way her line liked things—fixed.

She couldn't—what was the point when you knew how it all was going to play out? It was so unfair. Life should be more than a series of checkboxes. She huffed, shaking her hands out and wiping them between the gossamer folds of her gown. Serene. She was supposed to be serene.

Come on Sophia, play the part. Shoulders back, chin up—she straightened her stance by rote, then buzzed her lips and slouched. Gods, what a joke. She sighed, pinching a hand across her temples. But really. Like the aether cared what her posture was. If this point was fixed, she could be pirouetting on her head and it would still happen.

The thick green mist flowed around her in sluggish, knee-high currents, the faint scent of anise turning her stomach. Wasn't like time was gonna stop until she got with the program. She was destined to become a Seer whether she was ready or not, regardless if that's what she wanted.

She hugged herself, rubbing her bare arms as her gaze swept over the flat expanse of wide stone pavers to the broken arch just beyond, her gut roiling. It wasn't what she wanted, but fate was gonna run her right over, doing its own thing, and drag her along for the ride. She sighed, resigned to her role. What was the point of kicking and screaming?

As if in response to the question, the currents around her slowed and condensed, the heavy scent of anise cloying—

A new path shot out before her, reassembling or truncating all of the existing probabilities after that point, the future completely reordered. Sophia gaped at the altered vista, aether churning, occluding what was to come.

Her hand rose to her throat. But that…that wasn't…didn't…

Something thudded against the stone behind her, and she spun.

Mist puffed away from a body on the flagstones, like it'd been dropped there.

Gods…She rushed over—

Fitz?

She fell to her knees beside him and raised a trembling hand to brush back his wild curls. Was he—? No, he was breathing. Lord, his hair was soft...she shook herself at the errant thought and frowned. She should be more concerned with how he'd gotten here. It wasn't possible—her gaze flicked back to the settling aether. Neither was an entirely new branch forming so abruptly. Granted, when a current was strong enough, sometimes fixed points shifted, but that was within pre-established channels.

Sophia went hot and then cold. What was out there was new. Fate...destiny. Hers and countless others' could've all been rewritten, and she had zero doubt that Fitzpatrick McCreedy had something to do with it.

The coven was going to have kittens.

Good. It served them right. She grinned, her fingers straying to the sharp angle of Fitz's sideburns against his cheek, stubble encroaching on the clean line. What had he done? She steeled herself. It didn't matter, he needed to go back and mooning over him like a school girl wasn't going to help.

"Fitz..." she lightly slapped his cheek. "Fitz..."

His brows furrowed, a frown marring his generous lips a moment before his eyes flew open and set on her.

"Oh, thank the Gods," she breathed.

"Sophia?" Her stomach flipped at his rolling cant. *S'feeah.* Why the way he said her name gave her butterflies... He raised a hand and tucked a tendril of hair behind her ear, shooting tingles across her skin.

Her cheeks heated, and she scowled at her reaction to him. "What did you do?"

"Eh... Dunno? What've ye heard?" A roguish smirk spread across his face, and she could just kick him.

Oooh! He was infuriating! She pushed back on her knees. "Nothing, it's what I saw. The paths were fixed, and then all of a sudden a new one shot out, and—and here you are!"

He winced, his gaze going to the branches of the Astral Plane's great tree spread over them in a vibrant canopy. His brow furrowed again, and her breath hitched as he took in the blackness of eternity beyond with all the little points of light studding it—its denizens, watching. How was she going to explain—

Fitz sat up with a hand to his head and shot them the bird with the other.

She blanched, gasping at his impropriety, and he grinned at her. Gods, she shouldn't encourage him, and Cybil was right; he was a rogue, and that wasn't going to win him any points, especially not here.

He wet his lips and looked around, his brows furrowing deeper as he did. "Where are we?"

"The Astral—" Damn it. She glanced around and stood, hoping nothing had heard her slip. No one was supposed to know the Astral Plane existed, never mind that House Carmody could access it. "Someplace you aren't supposed to be, and you need to go back, now."

Fitz got to his feet. "Sec." He wobbled, like he was light-headed, then did a double take, his eyes widening. "The fuck do ye have on?"

Oh Gods. Her cheeks heated again, and she wrapped her arms around herself, wishing the fabric was thicker as her nipples pearled. *Please don't notice, please don't notice…* "Initiate's robes."

If the look on his face was anything to go by, he noticed. His gaze ran over her, heated trails searing in its wake. He wet his lips again, stepping closer, and her thighs clenched.

"Stop looking at me like that," she huffed, mortified, and nervously hooked an errant tendril of hair behind her ear again. "It's ceremonial. No one's supposed to see it." Especially not him.

"Ain't no way I'm gonna unsee it," he murmured, pulling her against him. "Eh…ye said astral, that like a dream?" His hand smoothed down her bare spine and she gasped, not used to being touched, and never by a man. He skated his palm over the curve of her hip, and she trembled, laying her hands against his chest to try and maintain some propriety. Didn't seem to make much difference to him, and for whatever reason, she couldn't say she was overly upset about that.

"K-kind of? We're not physically here, just our consciousnesses." It was more than that, but he didn't need to know the details. Gods, his irises were such a brilliant steel gray, striated with shimmering bits of silver. She gazed into them, losing herself, her breath coming fast. Her heart pounded. The way he was looking at her…

"Then this ain't real," he murmured.

"Yes, it—Fitz?" she whispered as he lowered his face to hers. Was he—"Are you going to kiss me?"

"Nah, love, I'm gonna eat ye up."

He pressed his lips to hers, and Sophia's fingers tightened on his lapels, fisting them. What was she supposed to—? *Ugh! Stop thinking about it! Just follow along. Pretend you know what you're doing…*Gods, the way he teased her lips with his… She chased them, melting against him. This wasn't what she'd imagined. He was so—so gentle. Like he cared about her.

A moan rose in her throat, and his lips quirked against hers, smiling.

"That's it, love," he murmured, pulling her closer and swept his tongue over the seam of her lips. She jerked away, startled for a breath before parting them. Fitz licked into her mouth, and groaned, swallowing her gasp, his fingers tightening in her hair and squeezing her bottom. He pressed his growing hardness against her belly, and she gasped again, sure she was bright red.

Her temper jumped. She shouldn't be embarrassed. Every other girl her age had let a boy kiss them. There wasn't any blasted reason why she shouldn't—or why she shouldn't kiss him back. Emboldened, her tongue met his, and the length against her belly went rock hard as he deepened the kiss, moving his hand to cup her breast. Her nipple tightened against his palm, and he tugged it, a line of heat shooting from it to between her legs—

She pushed him away, panting, and put a hand to her lips. Okay, maybe that was a little more than a kiss, but still…

He swore and scrubbed a hand through his curls, his chest heaving as he took a step back and adjusted himself. "Ye alright?"

Sophia nodded, her cheeks on fire. "I-I just… I've never been kissed —um, like that before, I mean." There wasn't a chance she was giving him the satisfaction of letting him know he'd been her first.

He grinned, coming closer again, his gaze dropping to the pointed tips of her breasts. "Good, 'cause I'd be scrambled ham if ye did." He ducked his head back toward hers—

"Scrambled ham?" she asked.

"Eh…out of me mind."

A smile tipped up her lips, but—she pulled back to look at him, narrowing her eyes. "Are you lying?"

"Nah, love. I'd kill the fucker." His irises crackled, dead serious.

She laughed. "You're trouble, Fitzpatrick McCreedy."

"S'Fitz," he murmured, stealing another kiss and his hand cupping her breast again. She shivered, enjoying his touch far more than she should. "And I think ye like it."

"I think I like you," she said before she thought better of it. Crap. Now he was going to think she was some silly—*ugh!* She removed his hand. "Despite my better judgement."

He put it right back like he hadn't heard that last part, a wide grin on his face. "Ya?"

Wait, did he like her too? Her stomach flipped again. "Yes." She brazenly reached up and ran her fingers through his curls. Gods, they were sinful. He closed his eyes with a blissful expression, like when that whore'd had her mouth on him. Sophia had the worst urge to do whatever he wanted to keep it on his face.

Lord, what was wrong with her? He was a Fetch for heaven's sake, and from a disgraced House at that, without a unit to his name. He was also trouble. Pure, unadulterated trouble and he would drag her into it with him, especially if she was already contemplating such wicked acts. She'd never be able to look Father Benson—or her own—in the eye again. She didn't need to be a Seer to know that as clearly as her own name.

"You really can't be here, Fitz. You need to go home."

"Tell me ye'll see me again," he murmured, his forehead to hers, those big gray eyes beseeching.

Sophia laughed. Lord, this man was the devil. "I don't think I could keep you away if I tried." And she didn't think she wanted to.

He grunted and little lightning bolts shot through his irises as he pulled talent. What? Where were his halos? The question died on her tongue at a quick pinch to her ear. Her brows furrowed as she fingered an unbroken hoop now threading through its shell. He grinned, looking pleased. "In case one of them hillie fucks tries t'kiss ye. Twist that thrice, and I'll come beat their arse."

She bit back a smile. "You're sweet, but no one is going to try to kiss me, and if they did, I'm pretty sure my brother will be first in line to put them in their place." More like Lawrence would beat them bloody. Both he and her father were incredibly protective of her. Overly so, in her opinion.

Fitz scratched the back of his head. "Eh…he a big bloke?"

Sophia laughed again. "His shoulders are broader than yours, but he's not as tall. Don't worry, I don't make it a practice to tell him who I'm kissing, and there's only one person on that list."

Fitz's face lit up, and her insides melted. He did care. "For true?"

"For true." His lips met hers again, and then she sighed, brushing the curls back from his face. "Goodbye, Fitz."

She tapped two fingers against his brow and the aether rose up around him.

Then he was gone.

Sophia sighed again, her hand drifting to her lips. They curved into a soft smile.

"Well done."

Her smile faded as she turned to face Alice stepping from the mists. "I told you, I'm not doing anything."

"Not intentionally, perhaps, but destiny has a way of tipping our hand whether we're a party to it or not." The Seer's gaze lingered on the ring in Sophia's ear, and she fought the urge to hide it. "And your destiny lies beyond that arch. It's time."

Sophia put a hand to her stomach, abruptly ill. "So soon? But I thought—"

Alice's laugh trilled out, too loud in the stone courtyard beneath the great tree. "Yes. So did the coven. And that, my dear, is entirely the point."

WANT MORE?

DYAD, the final volume in The Price of Talent,
is coming soon.

BREEDER

WHAT YOU DON'T KNOW CAN KILL you…

Before Kara met Flynn, she was property of the Source. The genetic research facility owned by a powerful international conglomerate dominates the Northern Hemisphere. Valued solely for her DNA when she receives her summons to breed, she panics.

Rescued from the brink of death, she's offered the chance to escape and find her own destiny. But the journey through the desolation of the Outside is fraught with peril, and the golden halos marking her as a Talent also paint her as a target.

Kept ignorant of everything beyond the facility's walls, Kara grapples to survive in the hostile wasteland. Humanity purists and roving gangs are only a fraction of her problems, because the Source, and Riegel, her contracted mate, aren't just going to let her walk away…

CONSPIRATOR

Twenty-eight years before the events in *Breaker*, Nora Jester will do anything to aid the Reunification of her people. Conceiving a female heir to marry their two cultures together shouldn't have involved her heart. But her feelings for the Commandant are undeniable, even after their disastrous breaking.

She agrees to try again, but entering into a new contract with a broken heart is a recipe for disaster.

This time, the Alpha is nothing like the Commandant. Violent, jealous, and dominant, he's unsympathetic to Nora's angst, and brooks no rivals. Shackled to him for the next three months, she's running out of time, because if she can't survive his attentions long enough to conceive, the Reunification may never happen. The Source has turned its eyes North, and if there isn't a child ready to lead the South in rebellion before the Harvest, there may not be any free Talents left.

ACKNOWLEDGMENTS

I wrote *Exile* while going through possibly one of the shittiest years I can remember. I won't say *the* shittiest, because that's just asking for the universe to one-up itself, but it was not fantastic. Writing about Flynn's dark night of the soul whilst having one of my own was like balancing on Alice's knife edge.

That said, there were also some nuggets of awesomeness. *Exile* will be my twenty-sixth title published, and I almost feel like I might know what the hell I'm doing. Don't worry, I'm sure it's a temporary development and will pass.

In the meantime, I have to thank my editor, Jonathan Oliver, who didn't even blink when he saw the size of this file, and JJ and my mom who both eagerly read it and then asked where the next one was. It's because of JJ that you got an extra scene in there with Cal, and one less bimbo. Meanwhile, my mom and I just sit around and gossip about Glynfyls like it's real. She's the one who's keen to know what's going on with the Seers.

Guess I'm gonna have to deliver in *Dyad*.

BOOKS BY AK NEVERMORE

THE DAE DIARIES - URBAN FANTASY WITH SPICE

- *One Night in Bliss* — FREE TO READ
- *Flame & Shadow*
- *Air & Darkness*
- *Playing with Fire* — FREE TO READ

THE PRICE OF TALENT - SPICY DYSTOPIAN ROMANCE

- *Breeder* — FREE TO READ
- *Breaker*
- *Destroyer* — FREE TO READ
- *Binder*
- *Conspirator* — *available at the back of Overlord*
- *Split*
- *Overlord*
- *Exile*
- *Dyad* — *(Forthcoming)*

THE MAW OF MAYHEM - PARANORMAL MC EROTICA

- *Bites of Mayhem* — FREE TO READ
- *The Maw of Mayhem* — FREE TO READ
- *Grimdarke*
- *Darker*
- *Kit-Kat*
- *Katherine*
- *Deuce* — *(Forthcoming)*

ANTHOLOGIES & STANDALONES

- *Secrets We Keep*
- *Changeling MC Chapters*
- *Sense, Sensibility, & Shifters*
- *Weres and Witchery*
- *Wards and Warlocks*

ABOUT THE AUTHOR

AK Nevermore is a bestselling author of paranormal, dystopian science fiction, and urban fantasy romance. She enjoys operating heavy machinery, freebases coffee, and gives up sarcasm for Lent every year.

A Jane-of-all-trades, she's a certified chef, restores antiques, and dabbles in beekeeping when she's not reading voraciously or running down the dream in her beat-up camo Chucks.

Unable to ignore the voices in her head, and unwilling to become medicated, she writes full time. Her books explore dark worlds, perversely irreverent and profound, and always entertaining.

Want more Nevermore?
Sign up for her newsletter and never miss a release!

aknevermore.com